PRAISE FOR THESE
New York Times
Bestselling Authors

Barbara Delinsky

"When you care to read the very best, the name of Barbara Delinsky should come immediately to mind."
—*Rave Reviews*

An author "of sensibility and style."
—*Publishers Weekly*

Catherine Coulter

"Catherine Coulter has created some of the most memorable characters in romance."
—*Atlanta Journal-Constitution*

"Coulter is excellent at portraying the romantic tension between her heroes and heroines."
—*Milwaukee Journal*

Linda Howard

"Ms Howard can wring so much emotion and tension out of her characters that no matter how satisfied you are when you finish a book, you still want more."
—*Rendezvous*

"Howard's writing is compelling."
—*Publishers Weekly*

Barbara Delinsky was born and raised in suburban Boston. She worked as a researcher, photographer and reporter before turning to writing full-time in 1980. With more than fifty novels to her credit, she is truly one of the shining stars of contemporary romance fiction! This talented author has received numerous awards and honors, and her books have appeared on many bestseller lists. With over twelve million copies in print worldwide, Barbara's appeal is definitely universal.

Catherine Coulter has enticed millions of readers with her bestselling novels. A versatile and prolific author, she began her writing career penning Regency romances. She has since garnered wide acclaim and earned a large and loyal following for both her historical and contemporary romances, and regularly graces the bestseller lists. Catherine continues to write her stories from the Northern California home she shares with her husband.

Linda Howard claims that whether she's reading or writing them, books have long played a profound role in her life. She cut her teeth on Margaret Mitchell and from then on continued to read widely and eagerly. In recent years her interest has settled on romance fiction, because she's "easily bored by murder, mayhem and politics." After twenty-one years of penning stories for her own enjoyment, Linda finally worked up the courage to submit a novel for publication—and has since met with great success! This Alabama author has been steadily publishing ever since.

Forever Yours

BARBARA DELINSKY

CATHERINE COULTER

LINDA HOWARD

Harlequin Books

TORONTO • NEW YORK • LONDON
AMSTERDAM • PARIS • SYDNEY • HAMBURG
STOCKHOLM • ATHENS • TOKYO • MILAN
MADRID • WARSAW • BUDAPEST • AUCKLAND

HARLEQUIN BOOKS
225 Duncan Mill Road, Don Mills,
Ontario, Canada M3B 3K9

ISBN 0-373-83353-9

FOREVER YOURS

The publisher acknowledges the copyright holders
of the individual works as follows:

THREATS AND PROMISES
Copyright © 1986 by Barbara Delinsky

THE ARISTOCRAT
Copyright © 1986 by Catherine Coulter

MACKENZIE'S MOUNTAIN
Copyright © 1989 by Linda Howington

This edition published by arrangement with Harlequin Books S.A.

® and TM are trademarks of the publisher. Trademarks indicated with ® are registered in the United States Patent and Trademark Office, the Canadian Trade Marks Office and in other countries.

Printed in U.S.A.

Threats and Promises

Prologue

The dark of night lay thick in the garden of the lavish Hollywood Hills estate where two shadowed figures conversed in low tones. Both were men. One was tall, broad and physical; the other was smooth, arrogant and cerebral.

"Are you sure? Absolutely sure?" the smooth one demanded, sounding less smooth than usual as his eyes pierced the darkness to bead mercilessly at his companion.

"She wasn't in that car," the tall one insisted quietly.

"You said she was. I buried her."

"You buried ashes of what we thought was her. We were wrong."

The smooth one's nostrils flared, but he kept his voice low. "And how can you be sure it wasn't her?"

"One of our men heard talk around the coroner's office. There was no evidence of a body, charred or otherwise. A burned purse and shoes, but no body. Unofficially, of course. Officially, at least as far as the heat's concerned, she's dead."

The arrogant one cursed under his breath. He pulled a pack of cigarettes from his pocket and barely had time to raise one to his mouth when the underling snapped a match with his thumbnail and lit it.

"No body," he muttered, squaring his shoulders. "So she got away."

The physical one had enough sense to keep still. He knew what was to come, knew he had his work cut out for him.

"I want her found," the smooth one growled. "I want her found *now*."

Still the physical one remained silent.

"She didn't have any family, at least none she ever told me about. She wasn't in touch with anyone else, and her friends were mine." A long drag on the cigarette momentarily brightened its glowing red tip. "She must have had help." Smoke curled out with the words and dissipated into the air. "New identity, new location, money…. Damn it," he gritted out as the wheels of his mind turned, "she sold the jewels. There wasn't any burglary. The bitch took the jewels herself and sold them!"

"I'll find her."

"Damn right you will. Half a million in diamonds and rubies, not to mention another hundred thou in furs—no woman can steal like that from me!''

"Do you want me to bring her back?''

The tall man's boss pondered that as he stroked the closely shaved skin above his lip. When he spoke, his voice was low once more and as dark as the night. "She's a thief. And a traitor. I've given her a funeral fit for a queen. I won't suffer the embarrassment of having her materialize from the grave.'' He paused for a moment before continuing smoothly, arrogantly, cerebrally, in his own perverted way. "She's dead. That's how I want her. Make her squirm first. Let her know that I know what she's done. Get the jewels and whatever else you can from her. Then see that she's buried, this time with an unmarked stone.''

Tossing the cigarette to the grass, he ground it out beneath the sole of his imported leather shoe. Then he straightened his silk evening jacket, thrust out his chin and walked calmly, coolly, back toward the house.

Chapter One

Lauren Stevenson looked at herself in the mirror. And looked. And looked. "It doesn't matter how long I stand here," she said breathlessly. "I still can't believe it's me!"

Richard Bowen grinned at her reflection. "It's you, and if I do say so myself, it's smashing."

She slanted him a shy glance. In the weeks during which she'd come to know this man, she'd grown perfectly comfortable with him as her doctor. But she couldn't ignore the fact that he was attractive; hence his compliment was that much more weighty. "I'll bet you say that to all the women you've worked on."

"Not necessarily. Some only look good. Some only look better than they did before. For that matter," he added with a wink, "some looked better before the surgery."

"You don't tell them that, do you?" she chided.

"Are you kidding? If it's vanity that's brought them down here, I'm not about to make an enemy for life. But it wasn't vanity that brought you here, Lauren Stevenson, was it?"

She shook her head. "It was sheer necessity." Once again she eyed herself in the mirror. "I'm amazed, though. I knew there'd be an improvement..." She faltered. Narcissism was foreign to her nature. Her cheeks grew red, her voice humble. "I didn't expect half this."

Richard's laugh was filled with intense satisfaction. "Cases like yours are the most gratifying. You had the makings of a real beauty when you walked in here. All it took was a little rearranging."

Very lightly, she ran her fingertips down her straight nose, then along her newly reformed jawline. "More than a little." Her hand fell to graze her hip as she turned back to Richard. "And I've put on ten pounds in as many weeks. Funny, but I would have thought that having my jaws banded together and drinking through a straw would make me lose weight."

"You couldn't afford to have that happen, which was why I put you on a high-calorie liquid diet. And now that you can take in solids, I want you to follow the regimen I gave you to the letter. You could still use another five pounds on that slender frame of yours, which means you'll have to work at eating. Remember, you'll be able to chew just a little at a time until the muscles of your jaws regain their strength. How's it been since we removed the bands?''

"A little sore, but okay."

"It's only been three days. The soreness will ease off. You're talking well. In some cases we have to bring in a speech therapist, but I don't think you have to worry about that." He rose from where he'd been perched on the corner of his desk. A soft breeze wafted from the open window behind him, bringing with it the gentle rustle of palms and the fragile essence of frangipani blossoms. "So what do you think? Are you ready to go home?"

Her sigh was a teasing one, and her eyes twinkled. "I don't know. Ten weeks in the Bahamas...body wraps, massages, manicures...sun and sand and sipping all kinds of goodies through straws.... It's not a bad life."

"But the best is ahead. When does your plane leave?"

"In two hours."

"Nervous?"

"About my debut?" She sent him a helpless look of apology. "A little."

"Will someone be meeting you when you land in Boston?"

"Uh-huh. Beth."

He squinted and raised a finger, trying to keep names straight. "Your business partner, right?"

Lauren smiled. "Right. She's dying to show me everything she's done since I've been gone. She rented the spot we wanted in the Marketplace, and from what she writes, the renovations are nearly done. We've got prints and frames on order and have been in close contact with the artists we'll be representing, so it's just a question of getting everything framed and on display."

"For what it's worth, Lauren, you strike me as a patient but determined woman. I'm sure you'll be successful." He threw a gentle arm over her shoulders as she started for the door. "You'll drop me a line and let me know how things are going?"

"Uh-huh."

"And you've got the name I gave you of the specialist in Boston in case you have a problem?"

"Uh-huh."

"And you'll be sure to eat—and eat well?"

"I'll try."

Releasing her shoulder, he turned to study her face a final time. His gaze took in the symmetry of her nose, the graceful line of her jaw and the now-perfect alignment of her chin before coming to rest with warmth on her pale gray eyes. "Smashing, Lauren. I'm telling you, you look smashing."

"Thank you. Thank you for everything, Richard."

"My pleasure, sweet lady." He gave her hand a tight go-get-'em squeeze, then turned back to his office. The last thing Lauren heard him say was a smug but thoroughly endearing "Good work, Richard. You done us proud this time."

Laughing softly, she retrieved her suitcase from the reception area and headed for the airport.

"YOU...LOOK...*smashing!*" was the first thing Beth Lavin could manage to say through her astonishment when, after Lauren had grinned at her for a full minute, she finally realized that it was indeed Lauren Stevenson who stood before her.

The two women hugged each other, and Lauren laughed. "You sound like my doctor."

"Well, he's right!" Beth's eyes were wide. Hands on Lauren's shoulders, she shifted her friend first to one side, then the next. "I don't believe it! Your profile is gorgeous, and you've filled out, and your eyes look huge and wide-set, and you had your hair cut...."

In a self-conscious gesture, one of pure habit, Lauren threaded her fingers into the hair above her ear to draw the thick chestnut fall forward. Then she caught herself. With a concerted effort, she completed the backward swing, letting her hair swirl gently around her ears so that her face was free of the cover she'd hid behind for years. "I really look okay?" There was honest anxiety in her voice.

"You have to ask?"

Lauren gave an awkward half shrug. "I look at myself in the mirror and see a new person, but in my mind I'm the way I've always been."

"I'm no psychologist, but I'd say that's normal." Beth's expression brimmed with excitement and the touch of mischief Lauren knew so well. "A different person—think of the possibilities! What if you were to bump into someone you'd known before, someone like Rafe Johnson—"

"Macho Rafe?"

"Macho Rafe, who would never have thought to look at either of us, but all of a sudden he sees this gorgeous woman and makes his play. You could string him along, then reveal your true identity and cut him off dead. Ah, the satisfaction!"

"You're awful, Beth."

But Beth was staring at her again, this time with a touch of awe. "Maybe.... God, you look marvelous," she said, moments before her face twisted in mock horror. "And *I'm* going to look positively plain next to you!"

"Fat chance, Beth Lavin." Lauren hooked her elbow through her friend's and started them both toward the baggage pickup. She knew that Beth was attractive; she also knew that Beth had worn her dark brown hair in the same long, straight hairstyle for fifteen years and that her clothes—the round-collared blouse, wraparound skirt and flat leather sandals she wore now being a case in point—were as down-country as Lauren's own had always been. "Neither one of us is going to look plain by the time we're ready to open that shop. I learned a lot down there, Beth. There were seminars on hairstyling and makeup and dressing for success. I took tons of notes—"

"You would."

"So would you, so don't give me that," Lauren teased gently. "Tell me, what's the latest with the shop?"

Beth took a deep breath. "I finally got the ad to look the way I wanted it. It'll appear in the next issue of *Boston*. The workmen should be done in another day or two—which is good, because the prints have started arriving. Not to mention the order forms, sales slips and stationery. And the frames and hooks, wire and labels. I've got everything stashed in my apartment."

"How *is* the apartment?"

"I like it. It's compact and within easy walking distance of the shop. Beacon Hill is exciting." Beth paused to ogle her friend again. "I can't believe you!"

"In another minute I'm going to put a bag over my head."

"Don't you dare. I'm thoroughly enjoying riding on your coattails. For that matter, I still wish you'd let me take a bigger apartment so we could room together."

"Rooming together *and* working together, we'd get on each other's nerves in no time. Besides, you want the city, while I want the country. Lots of room, wide-open spaces, trees, peace and quiet."

"You're thinking of that farmhouse."

"Uh-huh."

"You'll be isolated!"

"In Lincoln?" Lauren crinkled her nose. "Nah. I'll only have three acres. When the trees are bare, I'll be able to see neighbors on either side. And the commute will be little more than half an hour."

"But that farmhouse is a wreck!"

"It's simply in need of loving."

"Tell me you've already put in an offer."

Lauren grinned. "I've already put in an offer." At Beth's moan, Lauren delivered an affectionate nudge to her ribs. "When I couldn't get the place out of my mind, I called the realtor. The purchase agreement is ready and waiting to be signed."

"Lauren, Lauren, Lauren, what am I going to do with you?"

Lauren's eyes twinkled. "You're going to put me up at your place tonight. Then, tomorrow morning, you're going to take me on a grand tour of our pride and joy. After that we are both going shopping on Newbury Street.''

''Oh?''

''Uh-huh.''

''Could be expensive.''

''That's right,'' Lauren agreed remorselessly.

Beth hunched up her shoulders and gave a naughty chuckle. ''I love it, I love it.'' Then she abruptly narrowed her eyes and flattened her voice to a newspaper-headline drone. ''Country bumpkins take city by storm. Effect transformation reminiscent of Clark Kent.''

''Clark Kent?'' was Lauren's wincing echo.

''Or Wonder Woman, or whomever. Of course, you know we're both a little crazy, don't you?''

''We're twenty-nine. We deserve it.''

''I'll tell that to the creditors when they come calling.''

Lauren Stevenson wasn't worried about the creditors. She wasn't a spendthrift, but she'd finally come to the realization that life was too short to be lived in a cocoon of timidity. Thanks to her saving prudently and the legacy she'd received when her brother had died nearly a year ago, Lauren had enough money to buy and renovate the farmhouse, pay what little wasn't covered by insurance for the corrective surgery she'd had, get a wardrobe befitting the new Lauren and establish the business.

''Here we go,'' she said as her luggage appeared on the revolving carousel. ''Did you drive over or take a cab?''

''I drove. Your poor car was so glad to see me, I swear it got all choked up.''

Lauren grunted. ''Must need an oil change. On second thought, it needs to get out of the city. See, *it* wants to live in the country, too.''

They left the enclosure of the terminal and headed for the parking lot. ''Will you be driving north this weekend?'' Beth ventured.

''To see my parents? I guess I'd better.''

''I'd think you'd be excited—the new you and all.''

Lauren grimaced. ''You know my parents. For ultraliberals, they're as narrow as a pair of shoelaces. They didn't see the need for facial reconstruction. They thought I was just fine before.''

''But medically, you were suffering!''

''I know that and you know that, and one part of them must know it, too. They're both brilliant, albeit locked in their ivory towers. I think they associate plastic surgery with vanity alone, and vanity isn't high on their list of admired traits. They said they loved me the way I was, and I'm sure they did, because that's what being a parent is all about. But let me tell you, I feel so much better now, even aside from the medical issue, I'm not sure they'd understand.''

"Of course they would."

Lauren didn't argue further. Her trepidation about seeing her parents went far beyond the reconstructive surgery she'd had. She was starting a new life, and much of that life was being underwritten by her brother's bequest. Her parents resented that. Brad had been estranged from the family for eleven years preceding his death. Colin and Nadine Stevenson had neither forgotten nor forgiven what they'd considered to be their only son's abdication from the throne of the literati.

Lauren sighed. "Well, whatever the case may be, I'll see them this weekend. It may be the last time I'll be able to in a while." Lips toying with a smile, she darted a knowing glance at Beth. "I have a feeling that the next few weeks are going to be hectic."

"HECTIC" WAS PUTTING IT mildly, though the pace was interlaced with such excitement that Lauren wouldn't have dreamed of complaining. With the completion of the redecoration of the shop, she and Beth began transferring things from Beth's apartment. Prints were framed and hung on the walls. Large art folders, filled with a myriad of additional prints and silk screens, were set in open cases on the floor for easy browsing. Vees of mat board in an endless assortment of colors were placed on Plexiglas stands atop the large butcher-block checkout counter, behind which were systematically arranged frame-corner samples, each attached to the wall with Velcro to facilitate their removal and replacement. Bolts of hand-screened fabric were attractively displayed beside bins containing unstained-wood frame kits; matching pillows were suspended from the ceiling like bananas from a tree.

Lauren signed the agreement on the farmhouse in Lincoln and, since it was already vacant, moved in a short week later. Her enthusiasm wasn't the slightest bit dampened when she saw at firsthand the amount of renovation the place would need. She had only to stand on her front porch and look across the lush yard to the forested growth surrounding her, or to smell the roses that climbed the porch-side trellis, or to listen to the birds as they whistled their spring mating ritual, to know that she'd made the right decision.

And, more than anything, she had only to look in the mirror to realize that she'd truly begun a new life.

In keeping with that new life, she and Beth did go shopping. They bought chic slacks, skirts, bright summer sweaters and lightweight dresses. They bought shoes and costume jewelry to coordinate with the outfits, all the while feeling slightly irresponsible yet enjoying every minute of it. Neither of them had been irresponsible before in their lives, but now they had earned the luxury.

Three weeks after Lauren returned from the Bahamas, the print-and-frame shop opened. It was the second week of June, and the fair-weather influx of visitors to the Marketplace kept a steady stream of shoppers circulating. With sales brisk, Lauren and Beth were ecstatic, so much so that on the first Friday night after closing, they took themselves to nearby Houlihan's to celebrate.

"If business continues this way, we'll have to hire someone to help," Lauren suggested. They were sitting at the crowded bar nursing cool drinks while they waited for their table.

"Tell me about it," Beth complained, but in delight. "There isn't enough time during the day to do bookkeeping, so I've been taking care of it at night. And you're going to need time to work with printmakers and the framer."

"I'll call the museum. Maybe they'll know of someone who'd be interested. If not, we can advertise in the newspaper."

In slow amazement, Beth shook her head. "I can't believe how good things were this week. We really lucked out with the location. There are people all over the place."

"Summer's always a busy season, what with tourists in the city. The Fanueil Hall is one of *the* spots to see."

"Wintertime's supposedly as good. At least, that's what Tom next door—you know, at the sports shop—told me."

Lauren's lips twitched mischievously. "So you've befriended Tom, have you? See what a new hairdo and clothes can do?"

Raking a hand through wavy black hair that had newly been cut to shoulder length, Beth wiggled her brows. "Look who's talking. That guy over there hasn't taken his eyes off you since we walked in."

"He's probably in a drunken stupor and I just happened into his line of vision."

"That's a crazy thing to say. You don't believe how good you look!"

Beth was right. Lauren had been accustomed to being practically invisible where men were concerned, and old habits die hard. Now she dared a quick glance in the mirror behind the bar to remind herself of the woman she'd become. Even her smart cotton sundress of crimson and cream was an eye-catcher.

With a conspiratorial glimmer in her eyes, she turned again to Beth. "Tell me about him. I don't want to be obvious and stare."

Beth had no such qualms, but she spoke in little more than a whisper. "He's of medium height and build and is wearing a brown suit. His hair's dark, a little too short. He's got aviator-style glasses—must be an affectation, since they don't go with the rest of him." Her voice suddenly frosted. "Oops, there's a wedding band." She instantly swiveled in her seat and stared straight ahead. "Forget him. He'd only be trouble."

Lauren grinned. "Forgotten."

"Doesn't it bother you? I mean, I'm sure he'd make a play for you if you flirted a little, and the bum's married."

Shrugging with her eyebrows alone, Lauren took a sip of her drink. "I think you're making too much of it. I was probably right the first time. He's probably in a fog."

Beth grew more thoughtful. "We're going to have to do something about this situation."

"What situation?"

"Our love lives."

"What love lives?"

"That's the point. They're nonexistent. We have to meet guys."

"We have. There's Tom from the sports shop, and Anthony from the music store across the way, and Peter, who sells those super hand-painted sweatshirts, and your neighbors, those three bachelors... We could always reconsider and go to one of their parties."

Beth snorted. "We'd probably get high just walking into the room. I'm sure they're on something. Whenever I run into them, they seem off the wall. I'm telling you, we were smart to chicken out last time. We're so naive that the place could be raided and everyone would run out through the back and leave us holding the bag."

"Hmm. Maybe we'd meet a cute cop."

"I don't know, Lauren. I still think you should have gone out with that guy who came in on Wednesday."

"He was a total stranger, just browsing around."

"He was nice enough. And he did ask you out for drinks. For that matter, the fellow who came in this morning was even nicer and better-looking."

"He was a pest—trying to be so nonchalant about asking where I come from and where I live and, by the way, what my astrological sign is. I don't know what my astrological sign is. I've never been into that."

"You're scared."

Lauren hesitated for only a minute. "Yup."

"But why? You've dated before."

"That was different."

"You're right. This is supposed to be a new life you're leading!"

"On the outside it is. On the inside, well, I guess it'll take me a little longer to catch up. I don't know, Beth. Those guys seemed so...fast. So slick and sophisticated."

"You look slick and sophisticated."

"*Look*, not *am*. You know me as well as anyone does. I've lived a pretty sedate life. What dates I had were with quiet men, more serious, bookish types."

"Bo-ring."

"Maybe. But I'm not a swinger."

"Maybe you're gonna have to learn."

The hostess called their table then, but Beth picked up the conversation the instant they were seated in the glass-domed room just below street level. "Maybe we should try a singles bar, or a dating service."

"If we didn't have the guts to go to your neighbors' party, we'd never have the guts to go to a singles bar. And blind dates give me the willies."

"Blind dates gave the 'old' you the willies. The 'new' you doesn't have anything to worry about. Besides, it's not really a blind date if you go through a dating service. You get to express your preferences and pick through the possibilities."

"Just like they get to pick through us. Uh-uh, Beth. I don't really think I'm up for that."

"Well, we have to do something. Here we are, two wonderful women who are bright and available, and we should be having dinner with two equally as captivating men."

"Maybe we should put an ad in the paper," Lauren joked, then promptly scowled. "Only problem is that we're cowards. All talk, no action." Her eyes grew dreamy. "They say that good things come to those who wait. I'm more than willing to wait if one day some gorgeous guy who is bright and available and gentle and easygoing will walk up to me and introduce himself."

"According to women's lib," Beth offered tongue-in-cheek, "we shouldn't have to sit back and wait. We can take the bull by the horns."

Lauren glanced over Beth's shoulder toward the table at which a lone man sat, just finishing his dinner. He wasn't gorgeous, but he was certainly pleasant-looking. When he looked up and caught her eye, he smiled. Curious, Beth turned also; he shared his smile with her.

"There's your chance," Lauren coaxed in a stage whisper filled with good-humored challenge. "I don't want him, so he's all yours. Go ahead. Take the bull by the horns."

Turning back to their own table, Beth opened her menu and concentrated on its contents. Lauren followed suit. Neither woman noticed when the lone man took his check from the waitress and headed for the cash register.

Chapter Two

The second week of the shop's existence was as promising as the first had been. Just as Lauren was wondering how she and Beth would be able to cope with the continued pace on their own, a free-lance photographer came in, peddling his wares. He was a young man—Lauren guessed him to be no more than twenty-five—and his pictures were good. He was also looking for part-time work to pay for the increasing costs of his materials and equipment. She hired him instantly, and neither she nor Beth regretted the decision. Now they could take an hour off here or there—albeit separately—to do paperwork, go out for lunch or shop through downtown Boston.

On one such occasion, a week after Jamie had signed on, Lauren returned to the shop with a new sweater in a bag under her arm and a faint pallor on her face. Beth quickly joined her in the back room. "Are you okay?"

Setting the bag on the desk, Lauren sank into a chair. "I think so. You wouldn't believe what just happened to me, Beth. I'd bought this sweater and was walking back along Newbury Street when a car lost control and veered onto the sidewalk. I was daydreaming, feeling on top of the world, looking at my reflection as I passed store windows. I mean, I was so caught up in being happy that I wasn't paying attention to what was going on around me. If it hadn't been for some stranger who grabbed me out of the way in the nick of time, God only knows what would have happened!"

"Don't think about that. You're safe, and that's all that matters. Was the driver drunk?"

"Who knows? He regained control of the car and went on his merry way again. Didn't even bother to stop and make sure no one was hurt."

"Bastard."

"Mmm."

"The stranger who saved you...was he cute?"

"He was a she," Lauren snapped, but her annoyance was contrived. "And what kind of question is that to ask at a time like this?"

"Have to restore a little humor here. Just think how romantic it would have been if you'd been snatched from the hands of death by a tall, dark and handsome stranger. You could have fainted away in his arms, and he'd have lifted you, holding you ever so gently against his rock-hard chest while he gazed, smitten, upon your lovely face.''

Lauren rolled her eyes. "Oh, God."

Beth wagged a finger at her. "Someday it might happen. Miracles are like that, y'know."

"Is this the same woman who was putting in a plug for women's lib not so long ago?" Lauren asked the calendar on the wall, looking back at Beth only when she felt a hand on her arm.

"Are you okay now?" The question was soft and filled with concern. "Want a cold drink or something?"

Taking a deep breath, Lauren shook her head. "I'm fine. It was after the fact, while I was walking, that the shakes set in. But I'm better now. I'd really like to get back to work. That'll keep my mind occupied."

It did, and by the time Lauren arrived in Lincoln that evening, she'd pretty much forgotten the incident. By the next day, it was lost amid more important and immediate activities relating to the shop.

That night she went home, changed into a T-shirt and jeans and made herself dinner, dutifully following the guidelines Richard Bowen had given her. It was an effort at times, since she seemed to be eating so much, but she'd gained three of the five pounds Richard had prescribed, and she had to agree that they looked good on her.

What with the time demands that the shop had made since her return from the Bahamas, she'd had precious little opportunity to organize her thoughts with regard to renovating the farmhouse. Now, pen and paper in hand, she walked from room to room, making lists of what she wanted to have done. The realtor who'd sold her the house had given her the names of a local contractor, a carpenter, an electrician and a plumber. Though she wasn't about to hire any one of them without checking them out further, she wanted to have her thoughts together before arranging preliminary meetings.

After more than an hour of taking detailed notes, she put down the pen and paper and went out to the front porch. The night was clear, the moon a silver crescent in the star-studded sky. On an impulse, she wandered across the yard and stopped at its center, then tipped her head back and singled out a star to wish on.

But what did one wish for when life was already so good? She was totally healthy for the first time in many years. She had a new look, which she adored. She had a new business, and it was well on its way to becoming a success. She had a home of her own, with potential enough to keep her happy for a long, long time.

What did one wish for? Perhaps a man. Perhaps children. In time.

Lowering her head, she started slowly back toward the house. A sound caught her ear. She stopped and frowned. It was a sound of nature, yet odd. It had been distinctly unfriendly.

When it came again, she whirled around. A low growl. She cocked her head toward the nearby trees, then narrowed her eyes on the creature that slowly advanced on her. A dog. She breathed a sigh of relief. Probably one of the neighbors' pets.

Pressing a hand to her racing heart, she spoke aloud. "You frightened me, dog. Is that any way to greet a new neighbor?" As she took a step forward to befriend the animal, it bared its teeth and issued another growl, this one clearly in warning. Lauren held her hands out, palms up, and said softly, "I won't hurt you, boy." She lowered one hand. "Here. Sniff."

Rather than approaching her, the dog growled again, accompanying the hostile sound with a crouch that suggested an imminent attack.

"Hey, don't get upset—" She barely had time to manage the tremulous words when the dog was on her, knocking her to the ground, snarling viciously. Struggling to fend off the beast, she put her arms up to protect herself and kicked out. But as quickly as it had lunged, the dog retreated, galloping toward the trees and disappearing into the dense growth.

Trembling wildly, Lauren pushed herself up to a seated position. Then, not willing to take a chance that the dog might return, she stumbled to her feet and made a frantic beeline for the house.

Once inside, she leaned back against the firmly shut door, closed her eyes and dragged in a shaky breath. When the worst of the shock had subsided, anger set in. Had it not been so late at night, she would have called the Youngs, her neighbors on the side from which the dog had come. Then again, she realized, perhaps it was lucky it was too late to make a call. Furious as she was that anyone would let such a savage animal loose in even as rural an area as this, she was apt to say something she might later regret. She'd met Carol Young only once. She didn't want to alienate the woman, or her husband, or one of their teenaged boys. Better to let herself calm down. She'd call tomorrow.

Hence, from work the next morning, she dialed the Youngs' number and was relieved to hear Carol herself answer the phone. "Carol, this is Lauren Stevenson. We met several weeks ago when I moved in next door."

"Sure, Lauren. It's good to hear from you. How's it going?"

"Really well.... I hope I'm not dragging you away from anything."

"Don't be silly. One of the luxuries of working at a computer terminal out of my house is that I can take a break whenever I want. The boys have gone to visit their grandparents in Maryland for a week, so I've got more than enough time for a phone call or two. How's the house?"

"Pretty raw still. I've been so busy here at the shop that I haven't had much of a chance to look into hiring workers to fix things up. But that's not why I called." Lauren chose her words carefully, striving to be as diplomatic as possible. "I had an awful scare last night. I was walking out in the yard sometime around eleven when I was attacked by a dog."

"*Attacked?* Are you all right?"

"I'm fine. The dog jumped me, bared its teeth and made ugly noises, but it ran off before it did any harm."

"My God! I didn't think there were any wild dogs around here!"

"Then...it's not yours?"

"God, no. Is that what you thought?"

"It came from the trees on your side.... I'm sorry, I just assumed..."

"You should have called us last night. We might have been able to help you track it down. What did it look like?"

"It was big and dark. Short-haired. Maybe a Doberman, but it was too dark out for me to see the dog's exact coloration, and besides, I was too terrified to notice much of anything."

"You poor girl. I'd have been terrified, too." Carol paused, thinking. "To my knowledge, no one in the neighborhood has a dog like that, certainly not one that would attack a person. Sometimes strange animals do wander into the area, though. Maybe you should call the local police."

Lauren was lukewarm to that idea. As a new resident, she hated to make a stir. "I—I don't think that's necessary. As long as I know the dog wasn't from the immediate vicinity, I feel better. It's probably a watchdog that escaped and got lost. And it didn't hurt me, much as it looked like it could have."

"Listen, we'll keep an eye out for it, and I'll mention it to some of the other neighbors. But if you catch sight of it again, you really should file a complaint. There's no reason why you should be frightened to walk on your own property."

Lauren sighed. "I'll be on guard in the future. Thanks, Carol. You've been a help."

"I wish I could do more. Let me know if something comes up, okay?"

"Okay."

As Lauren hung up the phone, Beth straightened up from where she'd been leaning unnoticed against the door. "A dog? First a car, now a dog. Lord, the new you is attracting some pretty weird elements."

"Go ahead," Lauren teased, "have a good laugh at my expense."

"I'm not laughing." Beth rubbed her hands together in anticipation of high drama. "Maybe someone's out to get you...someone who lived in that old farmhouse a century ago and whose ghost will never be laid to rest until the rightful owner of the place returns."

"Beth..."

Beth held up a hand. "No, listen. Suppose, just suppose, the ghost is determined to run you out of town, so it plots all kinds of little 'accidents' designed to scare you to death—"

"Beth!"

"And then some gorgeous hunk arrives and just happens to have a secret weapon that can zap even a ghost and reduce it to—to a shredded sheet...."

Lauren sat back in her chair, helpless to contain the beginnings of a grin. "Are you done?"

"Oh, no. The best part comes after the ghost is shredded and you and the gorgeous hunk fall madly in love and live happily ever after."

"Why aren't you working?"

"Because Jamie's working."

"I think *you* should be working." Lauren pushed herself out of her seat. "I think *I* should be working." With a fond squeeze to Beth's arm as she passed, she returned to the front of the shop.

SEVERAL DAYS LATER, Lauren knew that she had to do something about starting the renovation work on her house. The garage door had unexpectedly slammed to the ground when she'd been within mere inches of it. Ironically, if the garage had been nearly as old as the farmhouse itself, its doors would have swung open from the center to the sides, and she would never have been in danger of a skull fracture. But the garage had been added twenty-five years before. Apparently, she mused in frustration, it had been as neglected by recent owners as the house.

She made several calls, setting up appointments to discuss repairs with the men whose names she'd been given. None of them had impressed her on the phone, though she reasoned that there was no harm in meeting with them before she sought out additional contacts. She wanted her home to be perfect, and she was willing to pay to make it so.

With that settled in her mind, she sat down on the living room floor, using the low coffee table as a desk, to write up orders for the framer. But she was distracted. Repeatedly her pen grew still and her gaze wandered to the window. It was dark as pitch outside. She was alone. Anyone could see in, watch her, study her.

Cursing both Beth for her fanciful imaginings and herself for her own surprising susceptibility, she returned to her work. But that night, to her chagrin, she fell asleep wondering if one-hundred-year-old ghosts were capable of sabotaging twenty-five-year-old garage doors.

SHORTLY AFTER NOON on the following day, Lauren saw him for the first time. She was working in the front window of the shop, replacing a framed picture that had been bought that morning, when she happened to glance toward the bench just outside. He was sitting there, quietly and intently. And he was staring at her.

With a tight smile, she looked quickly away, finished hanging the new print, then took refuge in the inner sanctum of the shop.

Fifteen minutes later, during a brief lull in business, she glanced out to find that he hadn't moved. One arm slung over the back of the bench, one knee crossed casually over the other, he appeared to be innocently people-watching—until his gaze penetrated the front window once more.

Again Lauren looked away, this time wondering why she had. There was nothing unusual about a man sitting on a bench in the Marketplace; people did it all the time. And this man, wearing a short-sleeved plaid shirt, jeans and sneakers, looked like a typical passerby. Though he wasn't munching on fried dough or licking an ice cream cone, as so many of the others did, she assumed he was enjoying the pleasant atmosphere. Or waiting for someone. Or simply resting his legs. The fact that he kept looking into the shop was understandable, since it was smack in front of him.

A telephone call came through from one of the printmakers she'd been trying to reach; then customers occupied her time for the next hour and a half. She'd nearly forgotten about the man outside until she left the shop to buy stamps, and even then she was perplexed that she should think of him at all.

He was nowhere to be seen.

AT HOME THAT NIGHT, Lauren was strangely on edge. She didn't know why, and for lack of anything better, she blamed it on the two cups of coffee she'd had that afternoon.

With a critical eye, she looked around the kitchen as she waited for the bouillabaisse she'd bought at a gourmet take-out shop to heat. She intended to do this room in white—white cabinets with white ash trim, white stove and refrigerator, white ceramic tile on the floor. The accent would be pale blue, as in enamel cookware, patterned wallpaper, prints on the wall. Perhaps she'd order a pale blue pleated miniblind—not that she'd originally planned to put anything on the windows, but it occurred to her that she might like the option of privacy for moments like these when the night seemed mysterious.

She was edgy. Too much coffee. That was all.

THE FOLLOWING MORNING, the man was back. Wearing a crisp white polo shirt with his jeans, he was sitting on the bench again, this time with his legs sprawled before him.

"Remarkable, isn't he?" Beth quipped, coming up beside Lauren.

"Who?"

"That guy you're looking at. Have you ever seen such gorgeous hair?" It was light brown with a sun-streaked sheen and was neatly brushed, but thick and on the long side.

"No."

"Or such long legs?"

"No."

"Wonder who he is."

"I don't know."

"Probably just another tourist. Why is it the good ones are here today, gone tomorrow?"

"This one was here yesterday."

"What?"

Lauren blinked once, dragging her gaze from the man to her friend. Absently she wiped damp palms on her slim-cut green linen skirt. "I saw him here yesterday."

Beth's eyes widened. "You're kidding! Do you think he's waiting for...us?"

"Come on, Beth. Why in the world would he be waiting for us?"

"Maybe he heard about these two terrific ladies who own the print-and-frame shop, and he's come to investigate."

"If he had any guts, he'd come in."

"If we had any guts, we'd go out."

"Well, we don't, and apparently he doesn't, either, so that's that." As the two watched, the man got to his feet and ambled off. "That's that," Lauren repeated, not quite sure whether to be relieved or disappointed. There had been something fascinating about the man, not only his legs and his hair but also a certain sturdiness. She wondered if he'd ever owned a black dog that snarled. Then she promptly pushed that thought from her mind, along with all other thoughts of the man—until she caught sight of him again that afternoon.

At first he walked slowly past the shop without sparing it a glance. A few minutes later he returned from the opposite direction, this time pausing near the door before heading for the bench. When Lauren saw him sink onto it, leaning forward with his knees spread and his hands clasped between them, she couldn't help but grow apprehensive. There was something definitely suspicious about the way he glanced toward the shop, then away, then back again.

"Who *is* that man?" she whispered to Beth, who promptly looked up from the VISA charge form she was filling out to follow Lauren's worried gaze.

"So he's back, is he?" Beth resumed writing but spoke under her breath. "He's a little too rugged for my tastes. You can have him."

"I don't want him," Lauren grumbled from the corner of her mouth, "but I would like to know why he's been loitering around here for two days straight."

"Why don't you go and ask him?" Beth murmured, then, smiling, handed the charge slip and a pen to her customer. "If you'll just sign this and put your address and phone number at the bottom..."

Lauren whispered back in a miffed tone of voice. "I can't just walk out there and *ask* him! He's probably got a very good reason for being there, and I'd feel like a fool.''

"Then stop worrying. I'm sure he's harmless.''

Lauren wasn't so sure. The man was too intent in his scrutiny of the shop, and she felt the touch of his gaze too strongly to forget him.

When a customer approached her to buy a piece of fabric and have it stretched onto a frame, Lauren welcomed the diversion. When another customer selected a print and needed advice on its framing, she was more than happy to oblige. When a third customer entered the shop in search of several prints to coordinate with swatches of fabric and wallpaper, she immersed herself in the project.

By the time the closing hour drew near, Lauren was tired. She was in the back room, dutifully updating inventory cards and looking forward to a leisurely drive home, a quiet dinner and what was left of the evening with a good book.

"Lauren?'' The low urgency in Beth's voice brought Lauren's head up quickly. "He's here, asking for *you*.''

"Who—''

"Him.'' Beth's eyes darted back over her shoulder. "The guy from the bench.''

Lauren put down the cards. "He's asking for *me*?''

"By name.''

"How did he...he must have...where is he?''

"Right here,'' Beth mouthed in a way that would have been comical had Lauren been feeling particularly confident.

But she wasn't. This man was different. Not boring-looking. Not slick and sophisticated-looking. Very...different.

Beth made an urgent gesture with her hand.

"I'm coming. I'm coming,'' Lauren murmured unsteadily. She stood up, smoothing the hip-length ivory cotton sweater over her skirt and squared her shoulders. Then, praying that she looked more composed than she felt, she slowly and reluctantly left her refuge.

Chapter Three

He was much taller close up than he'd appeared through the shop window. And broader in the shoulders. And more tanned. What was most surprising, though, was that he seemed just a little unsure of himself.

"Lauren Stevenson?" he asked cautiously.

She'd come to a stop several feet away and rested her hand on the butcher-block table. "Yes?"

As he studied her more closely, his puzzlement grew. "It's really strange. You're not at all as I expected you to be."

Lauren held her breath for a minute, then asked with a caution of her own, "What had you expected?"

"Someone...well, someone different."

If he had some connection to her past, she realized, not only was his puzzlement understandable but his tact was commendable. Still, she couldn't deny her wariness. The man had been staking her out for two days. "Do you know me? Should I know you?"

For the first time, he smiled. It was a self-conscious smile, endearing in its way. "My name's Matthew Kruger. Matt." He hestitated for a split second. "I was a friend of your brother's."

Lauren wasn't sure what *she* had expected, but it hadn't been this. "Brad's friend?" She was unable to hide either her surprise or her skepticism.

"That's right. I was with him just after the accident. I'm...sorry about his death."

"I am, too," she returned honestly, her brow lightly furrowed as she studied Matthew Kruger. He didn't quite fit into the mold she'd constructed of Brad and his friends. Strange that she'd never heard of him. Then again, perhaps not so strange. She hadn't been any closer to Brad before his death than her parents had been. "But...it's been a year since he died." Silently she asked herself why this so-called friend of Brad's had waited this long to contact her.

"I know you weren't close, but Brad did mention you to me several times, and since I had to come east on business, I thought I'd look you up."

"What kind of business are you in?"

Another split second's hesitation. "I'm a builder. The development firm I work for has just contracted to do some work in western Massachusetts. I'm here to set things up—to get the ball rolling, so to speak."

She nodded. A builder. Given the pale crow's feet at the corners of his eyes, he was not a builder who directed things from his desk. He was a builder who got his hands dirty. And whose body was well-toned through hard physical labor. *That* she could associate with the image she'd formed of her brother's new life and friends, though if her parents' opinion had been valid, she would have expected someone far coarser. On the surface, at least, Matthew Kruger didn't appear to be coarse. "Clean and all-American" was a more apt description. Could the surface appearance be deceptive?

"I see," she said. Then, feeling uncomfortable, she averted her gaze. In truth, she'd known little about her brother and his way of life...and then there was the matter of this man's physical presence. He intimidated her. "Have you, uh, have you been in Boston very long?"

"A week."

She nodded.

"I'm staying at the Long Wharf Marriott."

"If your work is in the western part of the state, wouldn't it be easier to stay out there?"

"I have been, but our investors are here and there's some paperwork to do, so I decided to take a few days to sightsee." When he suddenly looked beyond her, Lauren swung her head around.

"I'm going to lock up," Beth whispered, darting a curious glance at Matt as she started to pass.

Lauren reached out and caught her arm. "Uh, Beth, this is Matthew Kruger. He is—was—a friend of Brad's." Lauren still had her doubts about that, but saying it simplified the introduction. "Matt, Beth Lavin."

Beth had known Brad Stevenson before he'd struck out on his own, and since she wasn't a member of his immediate family, she'd been more objective about his departure. Hands clasped tightly before her, she smiled shyly at Matt. "I'm pleased to meet you."

"The pleasure's mine," Matt said, returning her smile. His gaze quickly grew apologetic when it sought Lauren's again. "I don't want to hold you up if there's something you should be doing now."

Lauren opened her mouth to say that she really did have work to finish, but Beth spoke first. "Oh, you're not holding her up. We were pretty much done for the day when you came in. I finished the inventory cards, Lauren. Why don't you and Matt take off? I'll close up."

The last thing Lauren wanted to do was to take off with Matt. She wasn't convinced he was who he said he was, and even if it was so, they were on opposite sides of a rift. Besides, he hadn't asked her to "take off" with him.

As though on cue, he did. "How about it, Lauren?" He paused, then took a quick breath. "I heard there was a sunset cruise around the harbor. If we hurry, we can make it."

"Uh, I really shouldn't...."

"Go on, Lauren," Beth coaxed. Subtlety had never been her forte. "You haven't been out much. It's a beautiful night. The fresh air will do you good."

"I'd really like the company," Matt urged softly.

His last words trapped Lauren. If he'd come on strong, she might have easily refused. But he sounded sincere, and she caught a drift of the same unsureness she'd seen when she'd first faced him. Though large and rugged-looking, he had an odd gentleness to him. His eyes were brown, warm and soft. At that moment they hinted at vulnerability; above all, Lauren Stevenson was a sucker for vulnerability.

Releasing the breath she'd subconsciously been holding, Lauren acknowledged an internal truce. "I'll get my things," she whispered.

Soon after, she and Matt were walking side by side toward the waterfront. He was as quiet as she, casting intermittent glances her way, and she wondered if he felt as strange as she did.

In an attempt to break the silence, she asked the first thing that came to mind. "How did you know I was in Boston?"

"Your parents told me."

"My *parents*!"

He sent her a sidelong glance. "Shouldn't they have?"

"No—yes—I mean, I'm just surprised. That's all."

They walked a little farther before he spoke again. "You're thinking that they wouldn't have willingly given your address to any friend of Brad's."

"I...guess that says it."

A muscle in his jaw flexed. "At least you're honest."

She shrugged. "How much do you know about Brad's reasons for leaving?"

"Only what Brad told me—that your parents couldn't accept his wanting to work with his hands rather than with his mind, that they flipped out when he left college and pretty much washed their hands of him."

Perhaps Matt had known Brad after all. "Spoken that way, it sounds cruel."

"It was, in a way. Brad was badly hurt by the split."

"So were my parents, yet none of the three tried to mend it."

"And you, Lauren? Did you do anything?"

Her gaze shot sharply to his, then softened and fell. "No," she admitted quietly. "I think I might have in time. Then time ran out."

"You regretted the distance?"

"Brad was my only brother. We had no other siblings. He was four years older than I, and his interests were always different. We weren't close as kids, but I like to think that we might have found common ground as we'd gotten older."

They had reached Atlantic Avenue. Matt put a light hand on her elbow as they trotted across to avoid an onrushing car. He dropped it when they reached the median strip, where they waited for a minute before finishing the crossing.

"Then you were seventeen when Brad left."

Lauren blew out a breath. "You really *do* know about Brad, don't you?"

"He told me he was twenty-one when he dropped out. If you were four years his junior..." Matt's voice trailed off and his features tensed. "Did you think I was lying about being his friend?"

"No. Well, maybe. I have to take your word for it that you knew him, since he can't verify it, can he?"

"Are you always distrustful?"

She looked him in the eye. "Only when I see someone lurking outside my shop for two days before coming in."

"Oh. You saw me."

"Yes." Was that a sudden rush of color to his cheeks? She wondered if it was guilt, or embarrassment. In case it was the latter, she softened her tone. "I assume you weren't trying to hide."

"Actually," he confessed, "I was trying to get up the nerve to come in."

That was a new one in her experience. "Why ever would you have to get up the nerve to approach *me*?"

"Several reasons. First, I knew there were hard feelings where Brad was concerned and I wasn't sure how I'd be received. Second, I wasn't sure if it was really you." His gaze slid from one to another of her features. Again that puzzled look crossed his face. "You look so different. Very...very pretty."

Lauren clutched the shoulder strap of her bag more tightly. "Brad had a picture."

"An old one. You were sixteen at the time."

For reasons she wasn't about to analyze, she didn't want to go into the matter of her reconstructive surgery. "It was a long time ago," she said quietly. "People change."

"I'll say," Matt drawled. "Still, it's amazing..." He seemed about to go on, and for an instant Lauren wondered just how much Brad had told him about her. She was saved when he looked up and announced tentatively, "I think this is it."

She followed his gaze toward where the wharf and its cruise boats loomed. "Looks like it. This is really the blind leading the blind. I went to college in Boston, but that was a while ago. I haven't been back for very long."

"Are you living here in the city?"

The glance she sent him held subtle accusation, but there was a whisper of amusement underlying her words. "What did my parents tell you?"

Reading her loud and clear, he fought back a grin. "Just the name of the shop. I assume they wanted to keep things on a strictly business level."

"I'm sure they did."

"And you?"

"And me what?"

He was suddenly serious. "Would you put me down because I don't have a Ph.D. in some esoteric subject?"

"I don't have a Ph.D. in *any* subject."

"You have a master's degree in art. I never went to college."

"But you're successful in what you do. At least, if you're traveling across the country, the firm you work for must be doing well...you must be valued." Having doubted his story such a short time ago, she amazed herself by coming to his defense. Suckers for vulnerability weren't always the most prudent. She took a deep breath. "No, Matt. I'm not like my parents. Brad wasn't the only one who had differences with them. It's just taken me a little longer to act on those differences."

Their conversation was cut short when they arrived at the ticket booth. Matt paid their fare, and they boarded the boat. Wending their way through the other groups that had gathered, they climbed to the top deck and found an empty place by the rail to look back at the city skyline.

"I love Boston," Lauren mused after several minutes of silent appreciation.

"Explain."

"It's bigger than Bennington and that much more exciting, yet smaller than New York and that much more manageable. You can understand it, get to know it. It's livable."

"You have an apartment?"

"A farmhouse."

"In the *city*?"

"In Lincoln—" She caught herself and scowled at him. "That was sneaky. You took advantage of me when my defenses were down."

He grinned amiably. "Sorry about that. Do you really own a farmhouse?"

Somehow further prevarication seemed silly. "Uh-huh. It's old and needs a whole load of work before its potential can be realized, but it's on a great piece of land and has charm, real charm."

"Old places are like that. History adds character. That's one of the reasons *I* like Boston. Wandering around, seeing where the Boston Massacre took place or where the Declaration of Independence was first read—it gives you goose bumps." He paused, staring at Lauren. "Why are you grinning?"

"You and goose bumps. You're so big and solid. It seems a contradiction."

"No," he said gently. "The goose bumps I'm talking about have an emotional cause. Big and solid don't necessarily mean unfeeling."

"I didn't mean—"

"I know." His point made, he left it at that.

They lapsed into silence, watching as the gangplank was drawn up and the boat inched away from the dock. Soon the engines growled louder. The boat made a laborious turn, then picked up speed and entered the main body of the harbor, moving at a steady, if chugging, pace.

"Would you like a drink?" Matt asked.

Lauren drew herself back from her immersion in the scenery. "No—uh, make that yes. A wine spritzer, if they can handle it, or lemonade. Something cool."

With a nod, he made his way back across the deck and disappeared down the stairs leading to the lower level. Following his progress, Lauren had to admit that he was as attractive as any other man in sight. It wasn't that he was beautiful in the classic sense; his chin was too square, his nose a shade crooked, his skin too weathered. But he exuded good health and strength and competence. He'd crossed the shimmying deck without faltering.

The wind whipped through her hair as she turned to face the sea once more. She concentrated on the sights—the Aquarium, the Harbor Towers, the piers with their assortment of fishing boats and tankers, the waterfront restaurants. Only when Matt returned and she smiled did she realize how much nicer the setting seemed with him by her side.

"Two lemonades." He handed her one. "The spritzer was beyond the bartender, and the other drinks were heavier. There were some hot dogs down there, but they looked pretty sad." He took a bag of potato chips from under his arm, opened it and held it out. She munched one, then washed it down with a drink.

"Tell me about Brad," she surprised herself by saying.

Somber-eyed, he studied her expression. "I'm not sure you really want to know."

She attributed his hesitancy to her own obvious ambivalence. "You may be right. But...I guess I really am curious. I've never met anyone who knew him after he left. I'm not sure I should pass the opportunity by."

Matt tossed several chips into his mouth. "What do you want to know?" he asked between stilted bites.

"Did he work for your company?"

"No."

"Had he always been in San Francisco?" She knew that was where he'd died.

"He started out in Sacramento."

"As a carpenter."

"That's right. By the time he came to San Francisco, though, he was doing a lot of designing."

"Designing what?"

Matt hesitated for an instant. "Houses, mostly. Some office parks. As an architect, he was a natural."

"Is that how he was viewed—as an architect?"

"No. He didn't have the credentials. He was like a ghost-writer, presenting rough sketches to the company's architect, who then embellished and formalized the sketches."

"Were you familiar with his company?"

"We were competitors."

The words were simple and straightforward, yet something about the way they'd been offered gave Lauren the impression that Matt hadn't particularly cared for Brad's outfit. "But still, you were friends. How did that work?"

Matt seemed to relax somewhat. "Very comfortably. Our respective superiors held the patent on rivalry. Brad and I rather enjoyed fraternizing with the enemy."

"How did you meet?"

"In a bowling league."

Her expression grew distant. "Funny, I can't picture Brad bowling. But then, I can't picture him sweating on the roof of a house, either." She tore herself from her musings. "What else did you do together?"

"Ate out. Sometimes double-dated. We vacationed together—there were six of us, actually. We rafted down the Colorado, went on horseback through parts of Montana. It was fun."

"Very macho," she teased and was rewarded by a sheepish grin from Matt.

"I suppose."

Her smile lingered for a minute before fading. "Brad never married." She'd learned that when she'd been informed by the lawyer that she was the sole beneficiary of her brother's estate. "I wonder why."

"Maybe he never met the right girl, one who could accept him as he was."

"Have you ever married?" she asked on impulse. Matt stared at her for a minute, then shook his head. "Why not?"

"Same reason."

She pondered his answer quietly. "I can understand it in Brad's case.

He grew up in an atmosphere in which intellectual excellence was the only valid goal. He struggled to keep up for a while, then simply threw in the towel. Neither my parents nor their circle of friends could accept his behavior. Long before he left, he was labeled a misfit. I'm sure he was sensitive about it.''

"We all have our sensitivities.''

"What are yours, Matt? Why would a woman have trouble accepting you as you are?''

He chomped several more potato chips and would have seemed perfectly nonchalant had it not been for the ominous darkening of his eyes. "I'm blue-collar all the way. I don't have a pedigree, or a series of fancy qualifying initials to put after my name. Over the years I've done well in my work, but that doesn't mean I aspire to own my own company, or that one day I won't decide to chuck it all and go back to building log cabins. If a woman thinks she's getting a future real-estate tycoon in me, she'd better think again.''

Lauren couldn't miss the bitterness in his words. "You've been burned.''

"Several times.'' He looked out over the water and his tone gentled, growing apologetic enough to defy arrogance. "I've always attracted women pretty easily. But physical attraction isn't enough. Not by a long shot.''

"The grass is always greener...'' she said softly. "There are those of us who'd *love* to have looks that would attract.''

Matt eyed her as if she were crazy. "But you *do*! I can't believe there isn't a line of men waiting to take you out!''

It took Lauren a minute to realize what she'd said and why Matt had answered as forcefully as he had. She'd forgotten. That happened a lot. A slow warmth crept up her neck. Compliments were still new to her, and from as physically superb a man as Matthew Kruger... "I don't know about a line,'' she said simply.

"Then there's one man?''

She shook her head.

"You're a beautiful woman, Lauren. Surely you've had offers.''

Again she shook her head, this time with a self-conscious half smile. "Why not?''

At his bluntness, she burst out laughing. "You're almost as undiplomatic as Beth.''

"I'm sorry. I was just curious.'' He held up a large, well-formed hand. "Not that I'm saying you should be married. You're only, what, twenty-nine, and you're obviously building a career for yourself.'' A new thought hit him, and he frowned. "You said you haven't been in Boston for very long. Then the shop is a recent thing?''

"We've been open barely a month.''

"And before that?"

"I worked in a museum back home."

He rubbed his forefinger along the rim of his paper cup. "Back home. That could explain it. Brad told me about back home."

"What did he say?"

"That it was stifling. One-dimensional. You were either an artist or an academician affiliated with the college."

"He was being unfair. Bennington's a beautiful place. Some fascinating people chose to live there. Brad just didn't."

"Nor did you, apparently. Why did you leave, Lauren?"

"Because I wanted to open the shop."

"But you could have opened a shop in Bennington."

She shook her head. "Too small a market."

"So you're going for the big time."

"I want the shop to be a success, yes," she said on a defensive note. "I may not aspire to put out one profound treatise after another the way Mom and Dad have, but that doesn't mean I can't aim to do what I do well."

There was a wistfulness to Matt's smile. "Now you *do* sound like Brad. He was so determined...." A flicker of uncertainty crossed his brow.

"So determined...?"

It was a while before Matt finished his sentence, and then it was with care. "To be successful. Recognized. I'm not sure he realized it, or realized what was driving him, but as often as he claimed that he was doing his own thing and didn't care what his family thought, I think he was kidding himself."

"Was he happy, Matt?"

Matt had to consider that. "In a way, yes."

Peering down at the bits of lemon pulp clinging to the sides of her cup, Lauren spoke more slowly. "All we were told about the accident was that he was supervising some blasting and got caught in the mess. Was there...anything more to it?"

"That was it."

He'd answered quickly and with finality. Not knowing why, Lauren was taken aback. "You saw him right after?"

"At the hospital." His tone was clipped. As he went on, its harshness eased. "Brad was lucid for a time, but between the internal injuries and everything else—well, maybe it was for the best. If he'd lived—and the chances of that were slim from the start—he would have been a quadraplegic. I don't think he would have been able to bear that."

"No," she whispered, and when she looked up, her eyes were moist. "I feel guilty about it sometimes."

"Guilty?"

"Everything I have now—the shop, the farmhouse, this—" she gestured broadly toward herself "—has come from the money he left me. Did you know that?"

Matt put his hand on her shoulder and massaged it gently. His voice was much, much softer, his focus shifted. "That was Brad's wish. I was the one who passed it on to the lawyer. Given the circumstances, Brad gained a measure of peace from it."

Lauren nodded, then somehow couldn't stop the overflow of words. "If it hadn't been for Brad, I'd probably still be back in Bennington. Even aside from the money, his death was a turning point for me. For the first time in my life, I stopped to think of my own mortality, of what I'd have to my credit when the time came, of what I'd be leaving behind. That was when I decided to move to Boston and open the shop. I only wish Brad could know how much better I feel about myself now."

"It's enough that you know, Lauren. If Brad were here to see you, I'm sure he'd be proud."

She looked timidly at Matt, then away, and took a long, shuddering breath. "It's too bad we can't have it both ways—too bad I can't have what I do and have Brad alive to see it."

Slipping his arm across her back, Matt drew her to his side. His warmth was the comfort she needed. "Life is cruel that way, filled with choice and compromise. Even those who reach the heights make sacrifices along the way. The best we can do is to decide exactly how much we're prepared to give up and move on from there."

As she raised her gaze to his, her cheek brushed his shoulder. It seemed a perfectly natural gesture. "But that's a negative view."

"It's realistic."

"Maybe I'm more of a romantic, then. I want to focus on the goals and face the hurdles as I come to them."

He shrugged. "And I want to be prepared for the hurdles. It's just a different approach. Who's to say which one is better?"

She didn't answer. Her gaze was suddenly locked with his, lost in his, and she struggled to cope with the intensity. He was a virtual stranger, yet she'd told him things she'd never told another soul. Was it the fact that he was a link to her brother, or that he was a good listener, or that he'd shared his own thoughts with her? She'd been wary of him at first; she still was, in some respects. And yet...and yet she was drawn to him....

The sudden blast of the boat's horn made them both jump. They looked around to find the bulk of the passengers crowded on the other side of the deck, waving to a passing tall ship. Without releasing her, Matt moved to join them.

"Impressive," he breathed, taking in the towering masts and ancient fittings of the proud vessel. "Too bad she's not under sail."

"Mmm. It's almost disillusioning. There weren't any motors in the old days."

"Or Sony Walkmans." He pointed to the sailor perched on the rigging, headset firmly in place. Lauren smiled at the sight, then shifted her gaze to the airport.

"If I had a downtown office with a view of all this, I doubt I'd ever get any work done. I could sit for hours watching the planes take off and land."

"Not me. Even watching gives me the willies. I'm a white-knuckle flier."

Lauren stared at him in disbelief. "A big guy like you?"

"Big guys crash harder."

She suppressed a smile. "I suppose you've got a point. But you do fly."

His expression was priceless, a blend of revulsion and resignation. "When necessary."

"Which is far too often for your tastes."

"You got it."

Her eyes took on an extra glow. "I don't think I could ever fly too often for my tastes. Not that I've flown that much, but I've always been so excited about getting where I'm going that I just sit back and relax. That's about all you can do, y'know. Once you're in the air, you're in fate's hands. It's not as if you have control over anything that might happen to the plane."

His grunt was eloquent. "That's what bothers me. I *like* to be in control. Just like measuring hurdles...."

Lauren narrowed her eyes playfully. "I'll bet you're the type who checks over every blessed inch of a new car before you venture to slide behind the wheel."

"I also sample the whipped cream, then the nuts, then the hot fudge, then the ice cream before I take a complete spoonful of a sundae."

"But where's the surprise, then?"

"The surprise is in the perfect blend of ingredients. The way I do it, y'see, I minimize the chance of disappointment. If something's not quite right, I can get it fixed, and if I can't do that, at least I'm prepared, so my expectations are on a par with reality."

"You're a man of caution."

"Quite."

"Another reason why you sat outside my shop for two days." She tipped her head. "Tell me, what would have happened if I'd looked exactly like that picture you'd seen?"

"I'd have come in the first day."

Lauren had wondered if he would ever have come in. "I don't understand. My looks made you *cautious*?"

"That's right."

"But...I look better than I did in the picture, don't I?"

"You look gorgeous."

"Then?" Mired in confusion, she made no protest when he turned her into him and crossed his wrists on the small of her back.

"Gorgeous women intimidate me. I've been burned, remember?"

His smile didn't ease her this time. Her eyes widened. "Do you think I'm after your *body*?"

He winced and shot an embarrassed glance to either side. "Shh."

She grasped his arms to push him away. When he held her steady, she whispered, but vehemently, "Is that what you think? Well, let me tell you, *I* didn't ask you to walk into my shop. I didn't ask you to take me on a cruise. I don't want any part of your body! And even if I did, that wouldn't be all I'd want. Before I ever got around to your body, I'd make sure that I wanted the rest." She snorted in disgust and turned her face away. "Of all the self-centered, arrogant—"

"That wasn't what I meant, Lauren. You're jumping to conclusions. Has it ever occurred to you that you can intimidate a man?"

"Me?"

"Yes, you. I'd expected to find a quiet—" he hesitated, then cleared his throat "—rather thin and plain-looking young woman living an equally quiet life in the country. At least, that was what Brad had implied. If he could only see you now! You own your own shop—in the city, no less. You're beautiful. You dress smartly. You're bright as all get-out. And you're sure as hell not falling at *my* feet." He took a begrudging breath. "Yes, I'm intimidated."

Lauren had felt suspended during his short speech. Now she realized how absurd her own attack must have sounded. "Funny," she managed to say in a small voice, "you don't look intimidated."

He squeezed his eyes together. Even before they relaxed and opened, a smile had begun to form on his lips. "I guess I'm not now, at least not as much as I was before. For someone who is beautiful and chic and super-intelligent, you're really pretty normal."

She smiled self-consciously, averting her gaze. "I think we're missing the sunset."

"I think you're right."

They returned to their own side of the boat, then switched when the vessel made a slow turn and headed back to the docks. Neither of them said very much. Lauren, for one, was lost in her own thoughts.

In spite of Matt's explanation, she still felt stunned that her looks had put him off. Initially her pride had been hurt. The thought that she'd drastically improved her appearance only to find that it kept men away was unsettling; hence she'd lashed out.

Or had she simply been searching for a wedge to put between Matt and her?

He was too attractive, too easy to be with, too firmly aligned with Brad and a way of life that she'd been indoctrinated to frown on. No, she wasn't exactly frowning now, but neither could she turn her back on the disappointment of Brad's long-ago desertion. And then came the guilt. She'd acceded to her parents' view of Brad as a failure, yet she'd accepted his money—lots of it. Did an architect masquerading as a carpenter earn that much money? Had he banked every spare cent for some eleven years?

She realized that there were many more questions she wanted to ask Matt about Brad. In hindsight, she wondered if he'd been evasive when talking about her brother's work. His answers had been short, his expression solemn. He'd opened up more about Brad's personal life, yet she couldn't help but wonder if there were some things he hadn't said.

The boat pulled alongside the dock, its lines were secured, and the gangplank was lowered.

"You must be starving," Matt said. "Want to catch a bite at my hotel?" The Marriott was only a short distance from where they stood, but Lauren quickly shook her head.

"I'd better be getting home. It's been a long day."

"Are you sure?"

This time she steeled herself against the cocoa softness of his gaze. She needed time to acclimate herself to his appearance in her life. He was a figure from Brad's past, yet the immediacy of him unbalanced her. What she craved was the solid footing of her own home.

"I'm sure," she said with a gentle smile. "But…thank you, Matt. This has been lovely."

"At least let me walk you to your car. It's pretty dark."

"And the path to my car is well lighted all the way. Really, I'll be fine."

Matt straightened his shoulders and nodded. "Well, take care, then."

She started off, half turning as she walked. "Good luck with your work. I hope it goes well."

He nodded again and waved, then turned and headed for his hotel. Lauren didn't look back until she'd crossed Atlantic Avenue, and by then he was gone.

THE LATE-AFTERNOON SUN glanced brilliantly over the Hollywood Hills, but the shades in the study were drawn as its proprietor entered, strode across the tiled floor to the desk and picked up the telephone.

"Yes?"

"We're on our way."

"It's about time. I'd assumed I would have heard from you sooner."

"She's a clever girl. Covered her tracks like a pro—almost. I still don't know who helped her out of L.A., but you were right about the Bahamas.

She went back to the same clinic she visited when the two of you were vacationing on the islands last fall. That was her only slipup.''

"Then you've found her?"

"She had plastic surgery, just like you thought she would. Not much. Subtle changes. There was a phony 'before' shot stuck into the doctor's files and a bunch of misleading medical reports, but the 'after' shot had just enough similarity to the real thing to give her away. Her hair's different now, darker and shorter. And she's taken a different name.''

"We knew she would. Where is she?"

"Boston. She just opened a little print-and-frame shop."

"With the money from the gifts *I* gave her. A print-and-frame shop. That's priceless."

"You'd be amazed if you saw her. She's the image of innocence. Dresses just so—stylish but understated, nothing flashy like before. Drives a Saab she must have picked up secondhand. Has this woman working with her who looks nearly as snowy-pure as she does, and a young guy who's probably eating out of—''

"What about the jewels? Have you located the fence?"

"No. No sign of the jewels at all. She may have started with the furs. They'd be easy to sell and nearly impossible to trace."

"Have you made contact with her?"

"Got a good man on it. She's already had a couple of little 'accidents'—nothing to hurt her actually, just set her to wondering."

"Is she?"

"Yeah. She's looking nervously around her front yard each time she leaves the house."

"The house?"

"An old farmhouse she picked up outside the city."

"With my money!"

"It'll all come back to you. Between the shop and the house, she's made investments that'll come back with interest."

"I want you to find the jewels."

"We're looking. She doesn't have them at home. I went through the place myself today."

"Ransacked it?"

"Nothing that obvious. Just moved little things here and there. She'll suspect someone's been snooping, but she won't be sure enough to call the cops."

"She wouldn't *dare* call the cops. She knows how long my arm is, and she wouldn't do anything to risk blowing her cover. So where do we go from here?"

"I've got a few more mishaps up my sleeve. You want her to squirm. I want her to squirm. She's gonna squirm."

"You're having fun, aren't you?"

"You could say that. I feel like I let you down before, and it was her fault. This is my revenge."

"It's *my* revenge, and don't you forget it."

"No way, boss. No way."

Chapter Four

Beth was lying in wait for Lauren when she arrived at work the next morning. "Well? How did it go? What happened? Your parents would *die* if they knew you were dating him, but I think it's great! A sunset cruise... I've never heard of anything so romantic in my life. He may be rugged, but he's got style. Was he nice? Did you invite him back to Lincoln after the cruise? I almost called you, but I didn't dare. *Tell* me, Lauren. Tell me *everything*!"

Closely shadowed by her friend, Lauren continued through to the back room and plunked her purse in the bottom drawer of the file cabinet. "How can I tell you anything if I can't get a word in edgewise?"

"Okay. I'll shush. Give."

Lauren only wished she could. She'd spent a good part of the night thinking about Matthew Kruger, and she still didn't know what to make of him. "Yes, he was nice. Yes, the cruise was nice. Romantic? Well, I don't know about that. And no, I did not invite him back to Lincoln."

"Why not?"

"Because it wasn't called for. And we weren't on a *date*. He was my brother's friend. That's all. We talked a little about Brad and a little about other things. Period."

"Did he explain why he'd been hanging around outside for so long?"

For the first time that morning, Lauren smiled. Dryly. "If you can believe it, he was trying to get up his nerve to come in. Brad had shown him a picture of me. I wasn't quite what he'd expected."

"That's marvelous!" Beth's eyes grew rounder. "The handsome prince was so taken with your beauty that he was actually awestruck. I love it!"

Lauren screwed up her face and carefully enunciated her words. "Handsome prince? Taken with my beauty? Awestruck? What *have* you been reading, Beth?"

"Come on. I think this is great. Are you seeing him again?"

"I don't know."

"What do you mean, you don't know?"

"Just that. He didn't say anything about seeing me again, and I wasn't

about to put him on the spot." Lauren reached for a can and began to
spoon fresh coffee into a filter.

"'Put him on the spot.'" Beth snorted. "Straight from the mouth of
the old you. The new you is sought-after. You'd be doing him a favor to
consider seeing him again.... Well?"

"Well, what?"

"Are you?"

"What?" Lauren measured out water and poured it into the top of the
coffee maker.

Beth sighed in frustration. "Considering seeing him again."

"I don't know."

As coffee began to trickle slowly into the carafe, Beth rolled her eyes
and muttered, "This is absurd. We're going in circles. Do you or do you
not want to see the man again?"

Lauren turned toward her friend. "I don't know! Damn it, Beth, how
can I give you a better answer if I don't have one myself? Yes, I liked
him, and under normal circumstances I'd be glad to see him again. But
these aren't exactly normal circumstances. In the first place, the man lives
on the West Coast. He's only here doing business, most of which keeps
him in the western part of the state. He'll be going back to San Francisco
and he hates to fly. I don't exactly have the time to zip out to see him
every weekend—not to mention the money, when there are so many other
things I have it earmarked for." She sucked in a breath. "And in the
second place, he was Brad's friend. You're right. My parents would go
bonkers."

"You're an adult. They didn't want you to go to the Bahamas, but you
did it. They didn't want you to leave Bennington or open this shop, but
you did both. You don't need their permission. You can do whatever you
want and see whomever you want."

Lauren sighed loudly. "I know that, Beth. I'm not asking their permission for anything. I have qualms of my own about seeing Matt again.
He was a friend of Brad's. He sees me and my parents through Brad's
eyes. And he's a confirmed bachelor who loves taking off with the guys
and shooting the rapids for a week. So what's the point?"

"The point," Beth murmured, wiggling her brows, "is that he's single
and gorgeous."

"I thought he was too rugged for you."

"For me, yes. For you, no. The two of you looked great walking out
of here together last night. I'm telling you, see where it leads."

"You have a one-track mind," Lauren grumbled, brushing a wisp of
hair from her low-belted, apricot jersey dress.

"And you're in a lousy mood. Where's your sense of humor? Hey,
I'll bet Matthew Kruger would be the *perfect* one to ward off the ghost
that's hanging out at your farm."

"Humph. I'm beginning to think I need something. That ghost was at work again."

Beth blinked once, then again. The coffee continued to trickle in the background, its rich aroma wafting from the carafe and spreading through the small room. "Excuse me?"

"That ghost. I swear it went through my things yesterday."

"Wait a minute, Lauren. There are no such things as ghosts."

"You're the one who's been touting them."

"I was teasing."

"Then I guess you've teased once too often. I'm almost becoming a believer."

"You're not serious!"

"Well, maybe not. But still...it was weird." She made a face accordingly. "I could have sworn I'd put certain things in certain places at home, and they were still there, just...shifted somehow."

Beth leaned back against the desk and crossed her arms over her chest. She might have been a psychiatrist for the indulgent tone of her voice. "I think you're going to have to be more specific. In what ways were they 'shifted'?"

"Small ways. A bottle of perfume turned around so that the sculpted bird faced the wall. A pair of shoes neatly set in the closet, with the right shoe on the left and the left one on the right. A pair of underpants perfectly folded, but inside out. I always turn them the right way before I fold them. *Underpants*." She shuddered, then whispered in dismay, "Can you believe it?"

"Maybe you should call the police."

"I thought about that, but I feel like a fool! I mean, it's not as if anything were taken. The locks on the doors were intact, and as far as I could tell, none of the windows had been jimmied open. Ruling out a breaking and entering, I'd say someone might have just walked in, except that I'm the only one with a key."

"How about the realtor who sold you the place?"

"I had the locks changed right after I moved in." Lauren gave a guttural laugh. "That's about all I've done, but it does preclude a human visitor." She took a deep breath. "So either it *was* a ghost, or I'm simply not as meticulous about things as I used to be. Maybe that's it. I mean, I suppose I have been preoccupied with the shop. It's very possible that I wasn't paying attention when I put the perfume bottle back or took the shoes off or folded the laundry." She looked beseechingly at Beth. "So what are the police going to say?"

"Mmm. I see your point. Maybe you should get a dog."

"One encounter with a dog on my property was enough."

"Then a burglar alarm system."

"A burglar alarm isn't going to stop a ghost. And it sure isn't going to improve my own absentmindedness, if that's what it was.'' She reached for a clean mug and poured herself some coffee. When she looked up to find a smug smile spreading over Beth's face, she scowled. "Now what are you thinking?"

"That I was right all along. Matthew Kruger may be just the one to protect you. All you have to do is to coax him along. Before you know it, he'll be thinking of that farmhouse as his second home."

"Matt is going back to San Francisco. How many times must I tell you that? And even if he wasn't, I can't use the man that way."

"Seems to me he'd get something out of the arrangement."

"Humph. When—and if—I take a live-in lover, it'll be because I truly adore whoever he is, not because I need him as a bodyguard."

"You could truly adore your bodyguard."

Lauren sank into a chair and raised her mug. She spoke slowly and distinctly, as though her friend might not understand her otherwise. "I am going to drink my coffee now and gather my thoughts. Then I am going to face this new day with a bright smile and a free mind." She closed her eyes, brought the mug to her lips, sipped the coffee, then sighed.

Somewhere between the sip and sigh, Beth gave up on her and left the room.

THE SHOP GREW BUSIER as the noon hour approached, and Jamie's arrival at one was a relief. Beth ran out to pick up sandwiches, returning shortly thereafter with news far more interesting than that the rye bread had caraway seeds.

"Have you looked outside lately?" she murmured excitedly to Lauren as she passed on her way to the back room.

Lauren had been helping a customer decide which of two silk-screen prints to buy. She glanced toward the front window.

Matt. Sitting on the bench she was coming to think of as his. Reading a book.

Reading a book? That was a novel approach! Not that she doubted he was a reader; he looked more than comfortable with the paperback in his hand. But reading a book in the middle of the bustling Marketplace and on that particular bench? What was he thinking? What did he want?

She returned her attention to her customer, pleased that in the minute she'd been distracted he'd decided on the print she'd originally recommended. Decisions on its framing proved to be more difficult, what with so many different mat boards and frames to choose from, but Lauren didn't mind. This was the part of the job she really enjoyed, and the shop made far more money on matting and framing than on the sale of the prints themselves.

It was only after she'd written up the customer's order, taken a deposit and let her gaze follow him to the door that she glanced again at the bench outside.

Matt was still reading.

Beth, who'd finished her lunch and come to relieve Lauren, was perplexed. "What's he doing out there?"

"Reading, obviously."

"But what's he *really* doing?"

"Beats me."

"Aren't you curious?"

"Sure."

"Aren't you going to satisfy your curiosity?"

"I'm going to have lunch. I'm famished."

"You're hopeless, is what you are," Beth declared. Lauren merely shrugged as she headed for the back room.

"Hopeless" wasn't exactly the word for it. She was flattered. Matt couldn't have chosen that bench by chance. But she was also puzzled. If he wanted to see her, wouldn't he simply come into the shop?

Did she want to see him? She still wasn't sure. There was something intimidating about him, and she couldn't quite pinpoint its cause.

Unwrapping her sandwich, she ate it slowly, sipping occasionally from a can of Coke. By the time she was finished, her curiosity had risen right along with her energy level. She *did* want to know what Matthew Kruger was up to. What right did he have to monopolize that bench? What right did he have to distract her? What right did he have to make her feel *guilty* for not acknowledging his presence?

Without further thought, she crossed through the shop, breezed out the door and approached the bench. Matt didn't look up. She stood there for a minute, then quietly eased herself down on the bench several feet away from him, far enough to preclude any implication of intimacy.

While he continued to read, she studied him closely. Other than his eyes, which moved rhythmically from one line to the next, his features were at rest. His lean cheeks were freshly shaved. His tawny hair was clean and vaguely windblown, haphazardly brushing his forehead and collar. He wore his usual jeans and sneakers, but today he'd put on a pink oxford cloth shirt. If she'd ever thought pink was feminine, she quickly revised that opinion. With his sleeves rolled to just beneath the elbow, and with the bronzed hue of his forearms, neck and chin contrasting handsomely with the shirt, he looked thoroughly male. Almost rawly so.

Reaching out, Lauren removed the book from his hands. She caught a brief glimpse of his startled expression before she turned the book over, carefully holding his place with her fingers, and examined the cover.

"*A Savage Place*," she read aloud. "It's a good one. But some of

Parker's other books are set more in Boston. His descriptions of the city are priceless. You really should read them.''

"I have,'' Matt answered. His liquid brown eyes caught hers when she lifted her head. "I've been a Parker fan for years.''

Any indignance Lauren might have felt when she'd marched out of the shop had vanished. For that matter, she couldn't remember what doubts she'd had about Matt yesterday, last night, this morning. She couldn't seem to think of anything except the fact that his eyes were the warmest she'd ever seen and that his smile did something strange to her insides.

With a determined effort, she refocused on the book. "Like mystery and a little bit of violence, do you? Or is it Spenser's machismo that intrigues you?'' The softness of her tone kept any sting from her words.

"Actually, it's Parker's writing style I enjoy. It's clean and crisp. Fast-paced. Filled with wit and dry humor.''

She nodded. So it hadn't been an act, Matt's immersion in the book. He obviously knew his Parker and appreciated him.

"Why this bench?'' Lauren asked suddenly. Her eyes had narrowed and were teasing in their way.

Matt stared at her, opened his mouth, then promptly shut it again. As she watched, his expression grew sheepish, filled with a boyish guilt that tugged at her heartstrings. When he finally did explain, she knew she was lost.

"I like this bench because it's close to your shop. I guess I was hoping you'd come out. What I was *really* hoping was that you'd take off with me for the afternoon and we'd rent a sailboat and join the others on the Charles. I got a view of the Basin from the thirty-second floor this morning. It looked so inviting.'' His voice fell, along with the expression on his face. "But you have to work. I know. It's not fair for me to come along and expect you to drop everything you're doing. You have responsibilities. I accept that, and respect it.''

Lauren didn't know whether to hug him in consolation or hit him over the head with his book. "How can you *do* this to me, Matt? It's not fair!'' That he should be a lovable little boy in a virile man's body. That he should be a stranger, yet so very familiar. That he should offer excitement in such a gentle and undemanding way. None of it was fair.

"Then you'll come sailing with me?''

"You were right the first time. I can't.''

"But you would if you could.''

"Yes.''

He smiled and relaxed against the bench. "I guess I can live with that.'' Almost as soon as he'd sat back, he came forward again. "How about tonight? There's a Boston Pops concert on the Esplanade. We could pick up something to take out and eat while we listen.''

Lauren knew that an hour later, or two or three, she'd find all kinds of reasons why she shouldn't go. At the moment, however, she couldn't think of a one. "That'd be fun. I'd like it."

"Great! What time can you get off?"

"What time does the concert start?"

Matt's eyes widened. "I hadn't thought that far." He jumped up, staying her with his hand. "Don't move. I'll be right back."

She watched him sprint toward Bostix, the ticket and information booth adjacent to Fanueil Hall, where he managed to wedge himself through the crowd at the window. Within minutes, he had trotted back to her.

"Eight o'clock. They suggested we get there early for the best spots on the grass, but the music carries pretty far, so if you can't get away from the shop until later—"

"I think I can convince Jamie to give Beth a hand until the shop closes. If we want to allow time to walk over the hill... How about your coming by at, say, seven? I'll call in an order for dinner—"

"Let me take care of that. I'm on a quasi vacation, remember? My work is done for the day, while you've still got more to do."

With a shy smile, she stood up. "Okay, then. I'll see you later?"

"Sure thing."

She nodded and had started for the shop when Matt called out to stop her. "Uh, Lauren?" Brows raised in question, she looked back. His gaze dropped from hers to the book she still held in her hand. She blushed, hurried back and gave it to him.

"Sorry. I'd forgotten I was holding it."

"I hadn't. If I can't go sailing this afternoon, I'll have to keep myself occupied somehow. Even aside from Parker's style, I suppose there is something to be said for mystery and a little bit of violence. And as for machismo—"

"Don't say it," she interrupted with a teasing glint in her eyes. "I don't think I want to hear it. A girl can take only so much, y'know." She'd pretty much reached her limit already. Another minute or two, and she'd chuck the shop and run off to the Charles with Matt. And that she would certainly regret. The shop was lasting. Matt wasn't. She'd have to remember that.

It was hard for her to remember much of anything that afternoon— other than the fact that Matt would be coming by for her at seven, of course. Beth teased her mercilessly when she rang something up wrong on the cash register, then again when she began to stretch fabric on a frame backside-to.

She thought seven o'clock would never arrive, but it did, bringing Matt, a blanket "compliments of the Marriott" and a large brown bag filled with all kinds of promising goodies. They walked over Beacon Hill, past the State House, the Common and the Public Garden, then across to Storrow Drive and the Hatch Shell.

They weren't the first to arrive, but they found a patch of grass within easy viewing of the raised stage. In truth, Lauren could have sat half a mile off under a tree by the water. The fact of the concert was secondary to that of the pleasure she felt being with Matt. She didn't analyze it, didn't stop to wonder why she was letting herself get so carried away about a man who'd be gone before she knew it. She simply wanted to enjoy, and enjoy she did.

Matt doubled up the blanket and spread it on the grass; then, after they had both sat down, he pulled out one container of food after another. He'd brought spinach turnovers, chicken salad with grapes and walnuts, Brie and crackers, fruit and a tumbler of frothy raspberry cooler. Lauren wondered where they'd ever put such a feast and told him so. He merely laughed, then laughed again when they'd eaten nearly everything. The concert was well under way by that time. He stuffed the remains of their picnic back into the bag, then sat close to Lauren with one arm propped straight on the grass behind him.

The assembled crowd was far from quiet; esplanade concerts were that way, informal evenings geared toward lighthearted company and relaxation. Families with children, young couples, middle-aged couples, elderly couples, mixed groups—all shared the pleasure of an evening along the Charles with the sweet smell of the outdoors, the gentle breeze, the exquisite blend of strings, horns and percussion.

As the evening progressed, Lauren and Matt sat closer and closer together. Lauren couldn't remember ever having felt so replete, and the dinner was only partly responsible. Matt was with *her*. Not with the pretty blonde to their right or the adorable redhead to their left. He was with *her*. She had only to drop her eyes from the stage to see his strong legs stretching endlessly before him. He'd changed into a white shirt and a pair of tan slacks that were more tailored than the jeans but no less sexy. His thighs were solid beneath the lightweight cloth, his hips proportionally lean. She felt the warmth of his shoulder as it gently supported her back; felt the goodness of its fit and its strength. His arm cut a diagonal swath to her hip, beside which his hand was flattened. His hand...long, tanned fingers, fine golden hairs, a well-formed wrist...

One song ended on a round of enthusiastic applause. When another began, the applause never quite stopped, for this song was a popular one with a heady beat, and the temptation to clap along was too great to resist. Too great, at least, for everyone but Lauren and Matt. They grinned along with the others, but neither seemed to want to disturb the physical closeness they'd captured. It seemed natural, and right, and very, very special.

Bidden by a silent call, Lauren turned her head to look up at Matt, and what she saw made her breath catch. His eyes were dark, drawing hers with a magnetic warmth, and his expression was one of gentle but insistent hunger. She might have been frightened by it, had her own body not been as insistently hungry. A glowing sun seemed to have risen inside her, radiating sparkles that speeded up the beat of her heart and her pulse and gave the faintest quiver to her limbs.

Lowering his head just the fraction that was necessary, he shadow-kissed her, openmouthed, not quite touching her lips. He drew back for an instant, dazed, then tipped his head and kissed her the same way, but from a different angle. The first kiss had been tantalizing enough for Lauren, but the second one was devastating. Acting purely on instinct, driven by the ache of desire, she opened her mouth in the invitation he'd been waiting for.

When he lowered his head this time, there was nothing shadowy about his kiss. It was full and binding, caressing her with a passion she'd never have believed mere lips to be capable of. She smelled the faint musk of his skin, tasted the fresh, fruity tang of his mouth, felt the sensual abrasion of his tongue as it swept through the moist recesses she offered.

She was about to turn into him, wrap her arms around his neck and draw him closer, when he dragged his mouth from hers and pressed it to her forehead. Though he didn't speak, the harsh rasp of his breath was eloquent and comforting, since Lauren was working equally hard to suck in the air she needed. Eyes closed, she gradually regained control.

Matt shifted and drew her back against his chest, fully this time, with her head resting on his opposite shoulder and his arms wrapped tightly around her waist. They stayed very much that way until the last encore was over. Then, with reluctance, they got up, gathered their things together and let the leisurely movement of the crowd carry them back the way they'd come.

Matt held the folded blanket under one arm. His other arm was draped over Lauren's shoulder. She held tightly to the hand that dangled by her collarbone.

They were nearly at the State House before he spoke. "I've got to be heading back to Leominster."

"When?"

"Tomorrow morning. Early. I have a nine o'clock appointment and probably should have driven out tonight, but I wanted to be with you."

She nodded, not knowing what else to say.

"I'll have to be there through Sunday. I'm sorry. It would have been nice to do something together on the weekend."

"That's okay. The shop's open seven days a week. I've forgotten what a weekend is."

"You have to have *some* time off each week."

"I will, once things get more settled. We weren't sure how soon we'd be able to hire extra help, but business has been going so well that we're trying to convince Jamie to work full-time so Beth and I can stagger days off for ourselves.''

"That'd be nice. There must be things you need to do."

"At least a million. Sundays are a help—we're only open from one till six—but I'd really like a day off in the middle of the week once in a while. If I don't start hiring people to fix up my farmhouse, it's apt to give a final groan and crumble at my feet."

"Maybe I could help with that."

"With the farmhouse? But you're leaving."

"I've got some good contacts, and while I'm in Leominster I can check around for more. What do you need?"

"You name it. Plumber, electrician, roofer, carpenter. Actually, I was exaggerating before. The structure of the house is sound. I had that checked out before I bought the place. But I want to do extensive modernizing inside, and I need good people I can trust, since I won't be able to stand around and supervise."

He gave her hand a squeeze. "Got it. I'll see what I can do."

They walked on in silence for a time. Lauren felt simultaneously content and unsettled, if that were possible. Finally she couldn't help but ask, "When will you be flying back to San Francisco?"

"Not for another week or two. I'll be here in the city early next week, then back in Leominster.... Where are you parked?"

She pointed in the direction of the garage. "You don't need to—"

"I insist."

"But it's out of your way."

"What else do I have to do?" he teased.

"Sleep. You'll have to be on the road very early to get to Leominster by nine."

"It's okay. I'll sleep tomorrow night."

All too soon, they had reached the garage, climbed to the third level and found her car. Reluctantly, she unlocked the door and opened it, only then turning to Matt. "Can I give you a lift back to the hotel?"

He shook his head. "It's out of your way."

"But this was out of yours."

"I'm on foot. It's ten times harder by car, what with one-way streets and all."

"I don't mind. Really—"

Any further words she might have said were stopped at her lips by the single finger he placed there. The dim light of the garage couldn't disguise the way his eyes slowly covered her face. They were hypnotic, those mellow brown eyes, and they conspired with the unmistakable vibrations from his body to suspend Lauren's thought processes once more.

His finger slid to her chin, where it collaborated with his thumb to tip her face up. He kissed her once, then again, then brushed his lips over her cheeks, eyes and nose. Lauren was entranced. Her own lips parted, then waited, waited until he'd completed the erotic journey and returned home.

But if she'd thought what he'd already done was erotic, she was in for an awakening. The tip of his tongue flicked out to paint her lips in the rosy hue of passion, and if she hadn't been clutching the top of the car door, she might have collapsed. She'd never experienced anything as electric, and the hardest part to believe was that the only points where their bodies touched were his tongue and her lips.

When he severed that connection, she stood still, eyes closed, mesmerized by the lingering flicker of a sweet, sweet longing. With regret, she finally opened her eyes.

"Can I come out to see you when I get back to town?" he asked. There was a trace of hoarseness in his voice.

Clearly implied was that he wanted to see her in Lincoln. Without a second thought, she nodded. "I'd like that."

He smiled, then cocked his head toward the car. "Get in. I might not let you leave if you wait much longer."

"Is that a threat or a promise?" she quipped softly, but she was already sliding behind the wheel. One part of her was tempted to wait much, much longer. The other part knew that things were happening quickly and that there were too many considerations to be made before she dared Matt to follow through.

After he had shut the door, she locked it, then started the car and backed out of the space. Matt stood to the side, watching. He gave a short wave as she began the slow, twisting descent. Soon he was lost to her view.

Lauren smiled all the way down Cambridge Street. She was still smiling when she curved into Storrow Drive and was ebullient enough to ignore the harsh beam of headlights from a car following too close on her tail. When she crossed the Eliot Bridge onto Route 2 and the same car remained behind her, she indulgently assured herself that if she was patient, the car would turn off soon.

It didn't.

She passed through Fresh Pond, circled the far rotary and moved into the right lane of what was now a comfortable superhighway. The car stayed with her. She tossed frequent glances in the rearview mirror and frowned. The traffic wasn't heavy. Surely whoever it was could move to the left and pass her, rather than tail her at forty-five miles per hour.

The highway was well lighted. She could see that the car was a late-model compact and that the driver was alone. Some kid having fun? There was no weaving to suggest he was drunk. Neither was there any hint that he was trying to tell her something, such as that her car had a flat tire or was on fire. He was simply following her and succeeding in making her extremely nervous.

Lauren pressed her foot on the gas pedal, pulled into the middle lane and held steady. The other car accelerated, pulled into the middle lane and held steady. She moved back into the right lane. The compact followed suit. She pumped her brakes lightly in an attempt to signal the driver to pass her, but he only slowed accordingly, then resumed speed when she did. In a last-ditch attempt to free herself of the tail, she flicked on the signal lights, moved into the breakdown lane and came to a cautious stop, prepared to floor the gas pedal if the other car stopped.

It swung to the left and passed her.

Breathing a shaky sigh of relief, Lauren sat for several minutes to recompose herself. Since she'd realized she was actively being followed, her imagination had taken her to frightening places. Too many little things had happened to her lately—the near accident on Newbury Street, the vicious dog in her yard, the garage door's fall, the subtle suggestion that someone had been in her home—for her to dismiss summarily this instance as a prank.

Yet as she entered the driving lane once more, that was exactly what she forced herself to do. A prank. A dangerous prank.

Then she crested a hill and saw taillights in the breakdown lane. She passed them by, instinctively speeding up, but within minutes the same car was behind her once more.

She swore softly, but that did no good. The car remained in pursuit. Five minutes went by. She searched the road for a sign of a police cruiser she might hail, but there was none. Another five minutes elapsed, and her knuckles were white on the steering wheel.

She approached her exit and held her breath, praying that when she turned off, the driver of the compact car would consider the game not worth any further effort.

He exited directly behind her and proceeded to follow her along the suddenly darker, narrower road.

Praying now that her car wouldn't break down and leave her at the mercy of the nameless, faceless lunatic, she drove along the road as fast as she dared, heading directly for the center of town.

For the first time she blessed every chase movie she'd suffered through in which the dumb innocent was pursued up and down hills, around corners and through dark alleys without grasping at the simplest solution. Lauren Stevenson was no dummy. She had no intention of heading off into a side street, much less leading someone to her farmhouse, where she would be totally unprotected.

She headed for the police station.

What she hadn't expected when she pulled up in front was that the car that had been on her tail all the way home would swing smoothly—with no qualms or hesitation—into a space in the parking lot. Between two police cruisers.

Lauren quickly shifted into drive and headed home.

She was mortified. Apparently she'd imagined the worst for nothing. Yes, she was angry. For an officer of the law, plainclothes or otherwise, to have behaved in such an irresponsible fashion was inexcusable!

But what could she do? If she marched into the police station and complained, she'd be making a certain enemy. Policemen protected their own, and if what she'd read so often in the newspapers was correct, they weren't beyond administering their own subtle forms of punishment. Someday she might need them, really need them. Could she risk turning them off to her now?

Moreover, what could she say? That she'd been terrified because so many strange things had happened to her of late? They'd think she was nuts. A wild dog. A garage door that went bump. A ghost in her underwear. Maybe she *was* nuts.

No one was following her now, but then, she hadn't expected that anyone would be. Some cop had been playing his own perverse game, perhaps simply practicing up on the technique of the chase. It must be boring being a cop in as peaceful a town as Lincoln. No doubt he'd enjoyed the excitement of his little escapade. At that moment he was probably sitting in the back room with his police buddies, having a good laugh.

Lauren put the car in the garage, then all but ran for the side door of the farmhouse. No doubt about it, she was spooked. She'd left her pursuer at the police station. She'd reasoned away all of her other little nearmishaps. Still, she was spooked.

Coincidence and imagination were a combustible combination.

Turning on every available light, she walked from room to room before satisfying herself that everything was the same as when she'd left that morning. That morning seemed so very far away. And that evening had been so very special, but somehow tarnished by the terrifying experience she'd just been through.

After leaving a single bright light on downstairs, she went up to bed, thinking about the outside floodlights she would have put in when she finally found an electrician. Perhaps she *should* consider a burglar alarm. God, she hated that thought. One of the reasons she'd bought a home in the country was to avoid the stereotypical city fears.

She was making something out of nothing, she reminded herself for the umpteenth time as she lay in the dark of her bedroom, afraid to move. She was letting Beth's wild imagination get to her. She was letting her own wild imagination get to her. Maybe Beth was right. Maybe she did need a bodyguard. The thought of Matt Kruger—strong, capable of protecting her, capable of thrilling her with a kiss—brought some measure of relaxation, so that at last she was able to fall asleep.

THAT WEEKEND, working around the hours when the shop was open, Lauren met with three different general contractors to discuss what she wanted to do with the farmhouse. None of the three impressed her.

The first was too traditional in his orientation. What she wanted wasn't exactly restoration, she tried to explain. Yes, she wanted the outside of the farmhouse to look much the way it always had. But she wanted the inside to be a modern surprise of sorts.

Unfortunately, number one didn't have much imagination when it came to modern surprises.

Number two was both patronizing and condescending. "I know exactly what you want," he informed her, then proceeded to tell her what he'd do to the farmhouse. It was exactly what she didn't want.

Number three was not only late for the appointment, but both he and his truck were filthy. That said a lot in her book. She could just picture hiring the man and having him show up for work when the mood suited him. He'd probably leave a mess behind every day for her to trip over, and then she'd have to hire a team of workers to clean up after him.

She'd gone to the contractors first in the hope of finding someone who would then issue subcontracts for things like plumbing and electricity. Now, having struck out, she debated calling the plumbers and electricians herself. Lord only knew she desperately needed to get the job done.

She decided to wait for Matt to return. He'd help her. And she trusted him. She'd never seen his work, but she somehow knew that any recommendations he made would be solid.

By Sunday night, she was thinking of Matt more and more, wondering when he'd be returning and what would happen then. She liked him—very, very much. She wanted to believe that his finest qualities—his gentleness, honesty and spontaneity—were indicative of the way Brad had been, too. She still wondered about Brad, still had questions for Matt to answer. But when she was with Matt she wasn't thinking brotherly thoughts. Matt intrigued her. He excited her. He seemed to take the best of both worlds—brain and brawn—and emerge superior. He wasn't quite like anyone she'd ever known before.

Nor did he kiss like anyone she'd ever known before. Not that she was anywhere near to being an expert on kissing. But she'd dreamed of feeling things in a kiss, and Matt had taken her far, far beyond those dreams—so much so that the restlessness she felt was no mystery.

Knowledge of the cause of a problem was not, however, a solution in itself. And since the solution was for the present out of reach, Lauren did the next best thing. Leaving a light burning in the living room, which had become a habit, she headed upstairs to treat herself to a long, soothing shower.

"Treat" was the operative word. As with most everything else pertaining to the farmhouse, the hot-water heater was small and outmoded. Even with its thermostat set on high, the "hot" was negligible. She'd quickly learned that she couldn't take a shower and then expect there to be enough hot water for the laundry. But she wasn't doing laundry that night, and she fully intended to indulge herself until the water ran cold.

Tossing her clothes into the hamper, she took a fresh nightgown from her drawer and went into the bathroom. The shower was little more than a head rigged high in the bathtub, but it served the purpose. She turned on the water, drew the curtain, waited until steam rose above it, then stepped inside.

Heaven. Just what the doctor ordered. Eyes closed, she tipped back her head and let the warmth flow over her hair, shoulders, back and legs. Soap in hand, she lathered her body, then turned, inch by inch, to rinse off. Relaxation seeped through her. She rocked slowly to the pulse of the water.

Then she heard a noise. Her head shot up and her eyes flew open. The slam of a door? Or was it her imagination? She lingered beneath the spray, listening closely. She thought she felt vibrations.

Without pausing to decide whether the vibrations were footsteps or her own thudding heart, she reached back and quickly turned off the water. Then she grabbed her towel and, with jerky movements, began to dry off. Under the circumstances, she did a commendable job, though her nightgown didn't realize that. It stuck so perversely to the damp spots she'd left that she was all but screaming in frustration by the time she finally managed to get it on properly.

Holding her breath, she peered around the bathroom door into the bedroom. When she didn't see anyone there, she dashed out to her closet and grabbed the first weapon she could find. The heavy, workhorse of a Nikon camera, which she hadn't used in years, would certainly serve as a makeshift club, particularly when heaved from its strap.

She tiptoed to the wall by the open bedroom door, flattened herself against it and listened. And listened. Nothing.

She took a deep breath, then yelled as forcefully as she could, "I've already connected with the police department and they're on their way! Better get out while you can!"

Silence.

Of course, she hadn't connected with the police department. They'd think she was a fool. Old houses made noises all the time, and she wasn't sure she'd lived long enough in this one to be able to identify all its characteristic moans and groans. No, she wasn't convinced there was an intruder.

On the other hand, she wasn't convinced there wasn't one, either.

Figuring that she'd need every precious moment if someone should storm in, she reached for the light switch and threw the room into a darkness that was broken only by a faint glow from the bathroom. Then, moving as silently as she could, given that she was more than a little unsteady on her feet, she wedged herself behind the bedroom door and peered through the crack, waiting for someone to creep up the stairs or emerge from one of the other two bedrooms.

No one did.

Noiselessly, Lauren sank to the floor, her gaze never once leaving the narrow slit of a peephole. She waited and watched and listened, growing stiff with tension but not daring to move. Five minutes passed, and there was nothing. Ten minutes passed, and she continued to wait, her temple now pressed wearily to the wall. By the time fifteen minutes had elapsed, she had to admit that she'd very possibly jumped to conclusions.

She wasn't convinced enough to leave herself unprotected, though. To that measure, she carefully closed the bedroom door, carried over a chair and propped it beneath the knob. Then, with the strap of the camera still wound around her hand, she climbed into bed and lay stiffly, listening, waiting. The only thing she was sure about as the hours crept by was that she very definitely would have a burglar alarm system installed when the house was sufficiently readied for it. Nights like this she didn't need.

Unless, of course, she had that bodyguard.

Chapter Five

When the phone rang early the next morning, Lauren jumped. She was in the kitchen, trying to force down a breakfast she didn't really want, and the unexpected sound jarred her already taut nerves. Snatching up the receiver after the first ring, she gasped a breathless "Hello?"

"Lauren? It's Matt."

Hand over her heart, she let out a sigh of relief. It wasn't that she'd actually expected someone menacing to be on the other end of the line but, rather, that the sound of Matt's voice was an instant and incredible comfort. "Matt," she murmured. "I'm so glad...."

There was a slight pause. "Is something wrong?"

"No, no. Just me and my imagination." She put her hand on the top of her head and found herself spilling it all. "I had the worst time last night. I was in the shower and thought I heard a noise. It turned out to be nothing, but the weirdest things have been happening lately, Matt. You wouldn't believe it. After I left you the night of the concert, some car tailed me all the way home. Well, not all the way, but almost. And before that the garage door had missed me by inches, and the dog had attacked me, and the car had swerved into the sidewalk—"

"Whoa, sweetheart. Slow up a bit. It doesn't sound like it's all been your imagination."

"No, but my imagination has been connecting all these little things that have nothing to do with one another and could really have happened to anyone—"

"But they happened to you." His voice was low and distinctly grim. "When did this all start?"

"I don't know...maybe a week and a half ago. It's like every few days something happens. I never thought I was accident-prone, but I'm beginning to wonder. Beth thought it was a ghost—"

"A ghost? Come on!"

"I know, I know, but if someone's trying to scare me out of this farmhouse, he's doing one hell of a job."

Matt was silent for several long seconds. "Listen, I'm still in Leominster, but I'll be driving back later this afternoon. Why don't I meet you at home? If I get there before you do, I can take a look around."

Lauren was without pride at that moment, and self-sufficiency was a luxury she couldn't afford. "Would you? I'd be so grateful, Matt! I've never been one to be spooked, but I'm as spooked as they come right about now. I don't think I slept more than two or three hours last night, and that was with a chair propped against the bedroom door and a camera nearby."

"You were going to take pictures?" he asked in meek disbelief.

"I was going to hit whoever it was over the head! My camera was the closest thing to a weapon I had. And then this morning I crept around the house looking for signs of an intruder. Crept around my own house in broad daylight—I must be getting paranoid!"

"Shh. Don't say things like that, Lauren. I'm sure there are perfectly logical explanations for everything that's happened."

"That's what I've been telling myself, but it's getting harder to believe. I mean, I can't deny that a car nearly ran me down, or that a dog attacked me, or that the garage door fell…but someone going through my lingerie?"

Matt cleared his throat. "Someone going through your lingerie?"

"See? You think I'm crazy, too!"

"I do not think you're crazy. Never that. You strike me as one of the most together women I've ever known."

"But you don't know me. Not really."

"Well, we'll have to do something about that, then. Tonight?"

"Promise you'll come?"

"I promise."

Lauren gave him directions; then, for the first time that morning, she smiled. "Thanks, Matt. I feel better already."

"So do I, sweetheart. See ya later."

LAUREN ARRIVED HOME from work that night to find a car in the drive. It was a brown Topaz and had local license plates. She assumed it was Matt's rental, but, seeing no sign of him, she felt a momentary tension. The car that had tailed her the Thursday before had been of a similar size, and though she'd had only glimpses of it when it passed beneath lights, she'd guessed it was either maroon or brown.

Staying where she was, safely locked inside her car with the motor running just in case, she leaned heavily on the horn. Then she waited. She seemed to be doing a lot of that lately.

This time she didn't have long to wait. Within a minute, Matt opened the front door of the house and loped out to greet her. The relief and sheer pleasure she felt upon seeing him eclipsed the fact that he'd somehow entered her house without a key.

Killing the motor, she scrambled from the car and threw herself into his arms. It seemed the most natural thing to do and, given the way Matt's arms wound tightly around her, he appeared to have no objections.

When at last he set her down, they exchanged silly grins.

"You look wonderful," he said. "A little tired, maybe, but a sight for sore eyes."

"I could say the same." Her hands were looped around his neck, her lower body flush with his. He looked positively gorgeous, sun-baked skin, slightly crooked nose, too-square chin and all. "Thanks for coming, Matt. I really needed you here. Did you have any trouble finding the place?"

"Nope. Your directions were perfect. I got here a couple of hours ago. It's a nice place, Lauren. I can see why you bought it. It does have charm."

"But does it have ghosts? That's what I *really* need to know."

Taking her hand, he started with her toward the house. "No ghosts. Just lots of things that need repairing." He cleared his throat. "For starters, the lock on one of the back windows is broken. I had no trouble climbing inside."

So that was how he'd done it. Simple enough. "But I tested all the locks. I was sure they worked!"

"Oh, this one works, all right. Until you raise the window. The wood around the screws has rotted. The entire lock simply slides up with the window. Close the window and the lock is in place again." He paused. "Which means that there's good news and bad news."

"Mmm." She dropped her purse on the chair just inside the front door. "The good news is that there's no ghost. The bad news is that the moving around of things inside the house was caused by a human intruder."

"Right. Hey, don't look so down. Every other lock in the house is solid, so it's just a matter of fixing this one. I've already been to the hardware store and picked up larger screws and packing. That'll hold the lock until the wood can be replaced."

"Oh, Matt, you didn't have to."

"I did it for my own peace of mind, if nothing else. Besides, fixing things is my speciality." He eyed her apologetically as they entered the kitchen. "I'm not sure I did as well with dinner. I picked up some things in town, but I'm afraid I'm not all that good a cook."

"I could have taken care of that."

"You'll still have to. I made a salad and husked some sweet corn, but I didn't know what in the hell to do with the chicken. At home I douse it in barbecue sauce and throw it on the grill, but you don't have a grill, and for the life of me I couldn't figure out how the broiler in that stove of yours works." His eyes shot daggers at the appliance in question.

She laughed. "It doesn't. The stove has to be replaced along with the refrigerator, the hot-water heater, the furnace—I could go on and on."

"So what do we do with the chicken?" Opening the refrigerator, he removed the plastic-wrapped package.

"We bake it. And I've got a super sauce. You'll think you're eating the best of barbecue." She looked toward the single cabinet on the wall beside the sink, then down at her sleeveless beige jump suit. "I'd better change first. By the way, was that a bottle of wine I saw in the refrigerator?"

He nodded. "California's finest, already chilled. I'll pour while you change. Then we can talk."

Talk. For a minute she'd forgotten what they needed to discuss. She felt so good, so safe, with Matt that the last thing on her mind had been her series of recent misadventures. But she wanted to tell him. Matt was levelheaded and straightforward. She trusted that he'd be honest with her and let her know if she was making a mountain out of a molehill.

She trotted upstairs to her bedroom, changed into a pair of jeans and an oversize gray shirt that she knotted at the waist, then returned to the kitchen in record time.

Matt stood at the kitchen window, looking out at the field beyond. He spun around in surprise when she breezed into the room, then stared at her and swallowed hard.

"I...is something wrong?" She glanced down at herself.

"No. Not at all. It's just that I've never seen you in play clothes."

Lauren could have kicked herself for not having taken the time to touch up her makeup and brush out her hair. In the past those things had never mattered. She'd looked as good—or as bad—with or without the primping. She'd forgotten that she had something to work with now. But it was too late.

Self-consciously, she reached up to finger-comb her hair toward her cheek, but Matt crossed the room in two long strides and stayed her hand. "Don't. Don't do that." Releasing her hand, he used his own fingers as a comb to smooth the hair back. "You look so pretty. I want to see your face."

You look so pretty. I want to see your face. So hard to believe. So... strange. "I look tired. I should have done something."

"You look beautiful—and with only two or three hours' sleep." Dipping his head, he brushed a kiss on her cheek, another closer to her mouth, then another closer still. His hand was curved around her jaw by the time he reached her lips, though Lauren wouldn't have pulled away even if he hadn't held her. His nearness was drugging, his kiss intoxicating. His breath mingled with hers, seeming to bring her to life as she'd never lived it before. She forgot all else but the sweet sensation of closeness, of awareness, of longing that the caress of his mouth inspired.

"Ahh," he breathed against her lips at last, "your kiss takes me..."

"You have it...the wrong way around."

"Then it's reciprocal, which is why it happens to begin with."

"This is getting confusing."

"Mmm." He smacked his mouth to hers, then set her back and put his wineglass in her hand. She sipped the wine, perfectly content to drink from his glass while he laid claim to the second he'd poured. "Now, let me watch you make this super sauce of yours. I want to see what you put in it."

She grinned. "Cautious, Matthew. Hungry but cautious."

"Quite" was all he said, but the grin he gave her stole her breath almost as completely as his kiss had. Fearing for the state of her health, she quickly set to work mixing the ingredients of her super sauce, then indulged Matt by offering him the spoon for a taste.

"Mmm." He licked his lips. "Not bad. Not bad at all."

"Don't give me 'not bad.' It's *super*. At least," she added in a demure undertone, "that's what it was called in the cookbook I took it from."

"Ah, a cookbook reader." He glanced around. "But I don't see any cookbooks."

She flipped open the cabinet and pointed.

"Two cookbooks? That's all? A cookbook reader is supposed to have a huge collection."

"I'm, uh, I'm a little new at it." She unwrapped the chicken and rinsed it under the faucet.

"You didn't used to cook?"

"I didn't used to eat."

Matt chuckled and scratched his forehead. "That picture. I'd forgotten. You were pretty skinny back then—no offense intended."

"None taken. You're right, I was pretty skinny. It's just recently that I've been forcing myself to eat. I don't dare tell that to many people, mind you," she added, patting the chicken dry with a paper towel. "Most of them get annoyed."

"Jealousy, plain and simple."

She sent him a mischievous grin, then knelt down to remove a baking dish from the lone lower cabinet. That took some doing on her part. Pots were piled on top of pots, which were piled on top of pans, which were piled on top of the baking dish. "Top priority in this kitchen," she announced, rising at last, "is new cabinets, and plenty of them."

"Cabinets—easily done. What else?"

As Lauren dipped the pieces of chicken, one by one, into the sauce and placed them in the baking dish, she outlined her concept of the perfect kitchen, only to find that Matt's suggestions and additions made her plans more perfect than before.

"Why didn't *I* think of a center island?" she asked as she shoved the baking dish into the oven.

"Because you're not a builder."

"And you do this kind of thing?"

His shrug was one of modesty. "The development we're planning in Leominster is a cluster-home type of complex, a planned-community thing. Modern and elegant but also practical. Island counters in the kitchens are an option. They can be used for storage underneath and eating above, or for a sink and a stovetop. Lord only knows, this kitchen's big enough to handle an island."

"And you know people who can do this for me?"

He patted the breast pocket of his shirt. "Names and numbers, already checked out."

With exaggerated greed, she put out her hand. "Gimme. I'll make the calls tomorrow." She proceeded to tell him of the contractors she'd interviewed herself; well before she had finished, he'd closed her fingers around his list. She promptly secured the piece of paper with a decorative magnet on the refrigerator door, then reached for the foil-wrapped loaf of French bread Matt had brought.

He clasped her wrist. "Set the timer for twenty-five minutes. That'll be plenty early to put the bread in the oven." While she did so and then put a pot of water on to heat for the corn, he refilled their wineglasses. "Come on. Let's go out back. I want to hear more about your... escapades."

With vague reluctance, since she'd enjoyed talking with Matt about lighter subjects, Lauren led the way through the back door to the yard. A weathered bench under the canopy of an apple tree provided them with seats. Sunset approached; shards of orange and gold sliced through the trees and threw elongated shadows on the grass.

"Okay," he said. "Start from the top. I want to hear about each thing as it happened."

Encouraged that at least he was taking her seriously, she turned her thoughts to the days that had passed. "The first incident took place more than a week and a half ago, I guess." She related the Newbury Street story. "I don't know if the driver was drunk. I don't even know if it was a man or a woman."

"How about the car? Size? Color?"

She shook her head. "It came from behind. I don't think it was red or yellow. Nothing bright—that would have stuck with me. It must have been some nondescript color. As for the size, God only knows."

"Did you go to the police?"

"What could the police do? The car was gone."

"Maybe there was a witness who caught the license number."

"If there was one, he or she certainly didn't come forward. I just assumed I'd had a close call with a freak accident and left it at that."

He nodded. "Okay. What next?"

"Next was the dog. My run-in with him was...I don't know, maybe two days after the incident with the car." She described what had happened. "As soon as I was down on the ground and thoroughly frightened, he took off. Like he'd simply lost interest."

"You said it was a Doberman?"

"I said it *might* have been a Doberman. It's the same with the car. You're so stunned when it happens that the details slip by you. And anyway, it was dark."

"Was the dog wearing a collar?"

"That's the last detail I'd have noticed."

"Not if your hand had hit something when you tried to push him away."

"My hands were busy protecting my face. I kicked out with my legs—pretty ineffectively, I'd guess. If that dog hadn't wanted to leave, he wouldn't have."

Matt seemed about to say something, then stopped and took a breath. "Did you call the police?"

Lauren shook her head. "The dog was gone. It hasn't been back since."

Even in the fading light, the tension on Matt's face was marked. "Then what?"

She took a drink of wine for fortification. On the one hand, Matt's grim concern was reassuring. On the other, it seemed to make the situation all the more real and, therefore, ominous. "Then the garage door crashed down. It's an old garage, an old door. I'd simply assumed it would hold."

"I checked it out. There's no apparent reason why it didn't. The chains are strong. So are the coils."

"Then what could explain it?"

He looked off toward the shadowed trees and didn't speak for several minutes. "There are ways to rig a door like that."

"But it worked perfectly the next day, and every day since!"

"There's rigging—and unrigging."

Apprehension made her gray eyes larger. "You're suggesting that whoever might have tampered with it before it crashed down went back and fixed it again? But why would anyone *do* that?"

"What happened next?"

Lauren stared at him. He hadn't attempted to answer her question. Not that he ought to have an answer when she didn't, but at least he could have tried to soothe her. Brows lowered, she looked away. What had happened next? "I'm not sure about the next thing. It wasn't as obvious as the others...I mean, it could have been me."

"What was it, Lauren?"

She took a short breath. "After we'd gone on the cruise that night, I came home and noticed that some things were out of place in my bedroom. At least, they seemed out of place to me, but it might have been my own carelessness.'' When his silence demanded further explanation, she told him about the perfume, the shoes and the underwear.

"Nothing was taken? Money? Jewelry?"

"I don't have much of either lying around, but no, nothing was taken."

"And it was only the bedroom that was touched?"

"As far as I could tell."

"Did you go through the other rooms?"

"Of course I did! And nothing was touched—*as far as I could tell.* Honestly, Matt! I mean, it's possible that the spoons in the kitchen drawer were rearranged, but I don't set them up in any special pattern, so how would I know?"

He held up a hand. "Okay, okay. Take it easy."

Even the softening of his tone did little to calm her. "How can I take it easy? I feel like I'm at an inquisition, and the implication is that you think I've been irresponsible. Well, I haven't! Taken separately, not one of these incidents is particularly unusual. People on the streets have close calls with cars all the time. Wild dogs get loose; they attack innocent victims. Garage doors malfunction. And as for my personal effects, that could just as well have been my own fault. I'm not perfect! I might have been distracted! And *don't* ask me if I called the police, because I didn't!"

"I didn't ask," he said. His words were gently spoken; his gaze was solicitous. "And I'm sorry if I sounded critical. It's just that I'm concerned...and I'm a stickler for details. I like to know exactly what I'm facing." He slanted her a lopsided smile. "You were supposed to know that already."

Immediately ashamed of her outburst, Lauren sent him a look of apology. "I forgot."

"Well, don't," Matt went on in the same soft voice. "I'm looking for any possible detail that would give us some clue to whether the things that have happened are unrelated or not."

She shivered at the latter thought. "I know. And I appreciate your listening to all this. But I don't know in which direction to turn at this point."

"Which is why you should tell me everything." He paused. "All set?" When she nodded, he released a breath. "Okay. Some things were amiss in your bedroom. Possibly your own fault. What was the next thing that happened?"

"The car followed me home."

"Did you see where it picked you up?"

She shook her head. "It could have been anywhere. I was on Storrow Drive when I first noticed the headlights in my rearview mirror."

"Make of the car?"

She shrugged and shook her head.

"Color?"

"Dark. At the time I thought it was maroon or brown, but it was hard to tell." Her eyes widened. "Do you think it could have been the same car that nearly hit me on Newbury Street?"

"I don't know. There are a hell of a lot of maroon and brown cars on the road. Without a make and model, we're clutching at straws."

"I'm sorry," she murmured. "Cars aren't my thing. I'm no good at identifying them."

"That's okay, Lauren. Do you remember when it finally dropped away?"

"It didn't, in a sense." She explained how she'd headed straight for the police station, where the car had nonchalantly pulled into a parking space. When Matt remained silent, she feared that he would chide her for not entering the station and complaining; she still wondered if she should have done that. "Well?"

"It's odd," he said at last. "Could have been a policeman having a little fun on his way to work, but all the way from Boston? And he stopped, then picked you up again."

"But he had to be harmless if he was a policeman."

"If, and that's a big if."

"Matt, he pulled into that space as if he knew just where he was going!"

"He may have pulled out just as smoothly once you drove on."

"And if I'd gone in to file a complaint?"

"He could have driven off anyway. You would have led the officer on duty to the parking lot, only to find that there wasn't any car there."

"Mmm. And the officer would have thought I'd dreamed the whole thing up."

"Possibly. Okay, the only thing left, then, is the matter of strange noises last night. Tell me exactly what you heard."

She did. "By the time I came out of the shower, there was nothing. Maybe I imagined it all."

"Maybe."

Then again, maybe not. "If someone had gotten *in* the house, wouldn't he have had to get *out*? I was so spooked that even the tiniest creak in the floorboards would have sounded like thunder to me. But there was nothing. I'm sure of it."

"And when you got up in the morning, there was no sign of an intruder?"

"Nothing."

"No window partway open? No dirt tracked onto the floor?"

"Nothing."

"And is that it? No other suspicious incidents in the past few weeks? Anything that, with a twist of the imagination, might seem odd?"

She thought about it, going back over the days with a fine-tooth comb. Eventually she shook her head. "Nothing."

Matt sat back on the bench, deep in thought. Sandy brows shaded his eyes. His mouth was drawn into a tight line. Lauren studied him, waiting to hear what he had to say. When he stood up abruptly and began to walk back toward the house, she was mystified.

"Matt?" She bolted to her feet, jogging to catch up. He looked at her almost in surprise, and she wondered where his thoughts had been.

"Oh. Sorry. I thought I'd put the bread in the oven now."

"But the timer—"

"We wouldn't have heard it." Sure enough, as they mounted the back steps they caught the insistent buzz.

Biding her time with some effort, she watched him open the oven door, flip over each piece of chicken, then slip the prebuttered loaf onto the lower shelf. Without missing a beat, he carefully dropped the husked ears of corn into the now-boiling water.

Finally she couldn't wait any longer. "Well? What do you think?"

"Mmm. Chicken smells good."

"Not the chicken. My *predicament. Is* someone after me?"

Straightening, he leaned back against the chipped counter and studied her. "Is there a *reason* that someone should be after you?"

She couldn't believe the question. "Of course not! I haven't done anything. I haven't hurt anyone. To my knowledge, I don't have any enemies. I'm amazed you'd even ask that!"

"Just ruling it out. It's as good a place as any to start."

"Well, we've started. A more probable possibility is that these incidents have something to do with the farmhouse. Everything began after I moved in."

"When, exactly, did you move in?"

"The first week in June."

"And the car incident took place, what, at the end of the month?" He thrust out his jaw. "The delay doesn't make sense. If someone legitimately didn't want you living here, the incidents would have started while you were first looking over the place, or certainly as soon as you'd moved in. Besides, not all of the things have happened here. Nah, I don't think they have anything to do with the farmhouse."

"That'd be the most plausible explanation," she pointed out. "And it'd be the easiest one to follow up. I've considered the possibility that one of the neighbors doesn't want me here, but the few I've met have been pleasant enough, and I can't think of any reason that my presence would be objectionable. I know nothing about the former owners, though. I could speak with the realtor and go through the records of who has lived here in the past. If necessary, I could call in a private investigator, or even the police—"

"Don't do that," Matt interrupted, then quickly gentled his voice. "Not yet, at least."

Though Lauren herself hadn't been anxious to call the police, she was surprised by his vehemence. It occurred to her that he might be indulging her in her fancy while not quite taking it to heart. "What do you suggest?" she asked more cautiously.

"Let's consider the possibilities." He squinted with one eye. "Are you sure you can't think of someone who might get his jollies by scaring you?"

"Like who?"

He shrugged. "An old boyfriend?"

"An old boyfriend who'd come all the way from Bennington in search of a little mischief?"

"Then maybe someone you might have met since you've been here. Someone who asked you out. Or followed you around. Or just…looked at you for hours on end."

"You're the only one who's done that," she replied with a smirk. "Maybe you've got a Jekyll and Hyde thing going."

The twitch of his nose told her what he thought of that idea.

"Well," she went on, thinking aloud, "it could always be a random lunatic."

He shook his head. "Too persistent. Your average random lunatic may hit once, even twice, but not six times. Your average random lunatic wouldn't have access to a trained attack dog—"

Horrified, Lauren interrupted him. "Trained? Do you think that dog was trained?"

Matt gnawed on his lower lip, as though regretting what he'd said, but the damage had been done. "It's possible. If it was trained to respond to a high-pitched whistle that our ears can't detect, that would explain why it retreated so abruptly."

"Just enough to frighten me…not enough to harm me. What kind of insanity are we dealing with?" Her voice had reached its own high pitch.

He gave her shoulder a reassuring squeeze. "We don't know anything for sure, except that so far you haven't been hurt."

"But I *could* have been. If I'd been a little slower in leaving my garage that night…if there'd been no Good Samaritan near me on Newbury Street that day…"

Responding to the sudden pallor of her skin, Matt drew her against him and slowly rubbed her back. "Don't think about what might have been," he murmured. "Nothing's happened, and if I have any say in the matter, nothing will."

With her head pressed to his heart, Lauren believed every word he said. She didn't stop to ask him how he intended to protect her. She didn't stop to ask herself why she, who valued her independence highly, welcomed the protection. She only knew that Matthew Kruger filled a spot that, at this particular point in her life, was open and waiting for him.

He drew back from her to ask, "Think that chicken's almost ready?"

"The chicken!" Pushing herself away from him, Lauren flung open the oven door, reached for a pair of mitts and pulled out first the chicken, then the bread. "Thank goodness it's not burned! I'd forgotten all about it!" She teased him with a punishing glance. "And it's *your* fault."

"My fault?" He was the image of innocence. "You said *you* were the cook around here."

"But you've kept me preoccupied. I haven't even set the table!" The item in question was of the card-table variety, albeit inlaid with cane, and there were folding chairs to match. She'd picked them up to use until she bought regular furniture.

"Then you do that while I toss the salad," Matt suggested. He was already draining the sweet corn. "I picked up a creamy cucumber dressing—unless you've got a super dressing of your own."

The twinkle in his eye brought fresh color to her cheeks and a momentary curl of warmth to the pit of her stomach. "Creamy cucumber's fine. Super sauce I can handle; super dressing is still a way down the road." As she reached for the dishes, she said, "It's amazing..."

"What is?" Matt asked, removing the salad from the refrigerator.

"That you can take my mind off things. Not only dinner, but everything else. One minute I can be worried sick about what's been happening; the next, I forget all about it."

"Maybe you've been worrying for nothing," he ventured quietly. "Maybe all that's happened really *is* a coincidence."

"Maybe...but it's crazy. Everything's been so wonderful. I left Bennington. I have a new job, new home, new look—" The last had slipped out. She rushed on. "Maybe it's all too good to be true."

Matt poured dressing on the salad and began to toss it. "I'm sure that whatever's been going on can be taken care of."

"But how can it be taken care of if I don't know what it is?"

"In time, Lauren. In time. Let's get back to the random-lunatic theory. Lunatic, perhaps. Random, unlikely." He held the salad tongs in the air for a minute before resuming his tossing. "Are you absolutely sure you can't think of anyone who might be behind it?"

Lauren set the silverware on the table with far greater force than necessary. "Yes, I'm sure. I've told you that, Matt. I don't know anyone who'd be capable of doing what has been done. Why do you keep harping on it?"

He hesitated. "Because the only other possibility is that we're facing someone who is neither lunatic nor random, but who has a very specific ax to grind. Maybe someone who has a grudge against your family.''

Her jaw fell open, then snapped back into place. ''If you knew my parents, you'd never even suggest that. They are utterly harmless. They live in an insulated little world. There may be competition within the academic community, but my parents have been so well accepted for so long that I can't begin to imagine anyone's acting out of jealousy, much less trying to seek revenge. And if someone did, he or she sure as hell wouldn't do it through me. I've declared my independence in ways that have my parents climbing those ivy-covered walls of theirs—'' Her voice broke abruptly, and for a minute she wished she could retract what she'd said. Then she realized that there was no point in being coy. Matt, more than anyone, would understand.

He brooded for a minute as he placed the salad on the table, then reached for the wine. ''What do you mean?''

Lauren opened the foil-wrapped bread with care. It was hot. ''What I'm doing with my life isn't exactly what my parents had wanted me to do.''

''In what sense?''

''Oh,'' she began, juggling the steaming loaf into a bread basket, ''they would have preferred that I stay in Bennington and work at the museum. I'd be surrounded by culture, attend plays and lectures, take part in a weekly reading-and-discussion group. Then I'd marry some nice, pale-faced fellow whose interests lay in Babylonian astronomy or medieval art or comparative linguistics. I'd go on to have sweet little children who would take up the cello at age four, read Dostoyevsky at age eight, write a novel at age twelve and beg for college admittance at age fourteen.''

''And you? What would you prefer?''

''Me?'' She set the bread basket on the table and looked up at him pleadingly. ''I want to be happy. I want to do well at whatever I choose to do. I want to feel good about myself.''

''And a husband and children?''

Shrugging, she brought the plates to the stove. ''I haven't thought that far yet.''

''Sure you have. Every woman dreams.''

''Every man does, too,'' she countered.

''But I asked you first. What do you want in a husband? What do you want for your children?''

She put two pieces of chicken on Matt's plate, a single piece on her own. ''The same thing I want for myself, I suppose. If a person is happy, and feels good about himself, everything else falls into place.'' She added an ear of corn to each plate before bringing both to the table.

''How can your parents argue with that?''

"They believe that certain things make a person happy. We just disagree on what those things are."

Matt was standing with one hand on his hip as he watched her. Straightening suddenly, he tilted a chair out and gestured for her to sit. "Brad's philosophy was similar. It's amazing how alike you are in so many ways. Then again, there are differences."

"Tell me more about him, Matt. Did he really feel the same way I do?"

Matt slowly seated himself and didn't speak until he'd pulled his chair in and spread a napkin on his lap. His expression was pensive. "He felt that what your parents wanted was different from what he wanted. But you already know that. I think he would have been surprised that you agree with him. He saw himself as the black sheep of the family."

"So much so that, regardless of what he did, it didn't seem to measure up?" she asked.

Matt frowned, then shifted in his seat. He drew the salad bowl toward him and prodded the lettuce with the tongs. In a sudden spurt of movement, he began to pile salad on Lauren's plate. "Is that the way *you* feel? That nothing you do can measure up?"

"Hey." She put her hand on his and pushed the tongs toward his own plate. "That's enough."

He served himself. "Do you feel that way, Lauren?"

"No. I'm pleased with what I'm doing. Brad tried to meet my parents' expectations, failed, then took off. I went along with their wishes and was fairly successful at it before realizing that it wasn't what I wanted. I left because I chose to. Brad left because he had to. I could have gone on forever up there, I suppose. Brad couldn't have survived." She took a breath. Her fork dangled over the chicken. "It wasn't that he didn't have the brains for it, but his temperament was totally different. He was more impulsive, more restless. Hyperactive, my parents always said, but I think they were wrong. He just wanted to use his brains for things other than scholarly pursuits."

"He did that," Matt drawled under his breath, but there was no humor in his expression. When he saw Lauren staring at him, puzzled, he spoke quickly. "Designing houses, interesting houses, takes brains, although it's not considered a scholarly occupation. It's too bad your parents couldn't have seen some of the work Brad did."

"They never even knew about it" was her sad reply. "They didn't know who he worked for or what he did. They were shocked at the amount of money that came to me when he died." She rolled her eyes. "For that matter, so was I."

Matt's hesitation was a weighty one. "They didn't begrudge it to you, did they?"

"No." She snorted. "The only thing they begrudged was what I *did* with it." Spearing a tomato wedge, she waved it for an instant. "Family interrelationships are weird things. Expectations are often so unrealistic. It's as if we have blinkers on. I suppose I'm not that much more understanding of my parents than they are of me, but it's a shame. I'm an adult now. They're adults. Wouldn't it be nice if we *liked* one another?"

"It's not that simple. You're right. Unrealistic expectations can stand in the way. Or ego needs. It must be difficult in a situation like yours, where it would be impossible for you to rise above what your parents have done. They've been so successful in their fields. Maybe that's why both you and Brad felt the need to strike out on your own."

"Maybe. I hadn't thought about it that way." Lauren mulled over the prospect for several minutes, but what lingered with her was how insightful Matt was. "What about you? Are you close to your family?"

"Very."

"Are they in San Francisco, too?"

He shook his head. "L.A. I guess I needed a little distance, just as you do. The pressure coming from my parents was a more traditional one. They're retired now, but for years they both worked in a factory. They wanted my sister and me to rise higher, to advance socially. Unfortunately, there wasn't much money for college. I suppose I could have tried for a scholarship, but I wanted to work. Once I got going, I discovered that I could get the education I needed on the job. I've taken business courses here and there, and I've advanced, so I can't complain."

"How about your sister?"

Matt warmed Lauren with a grin. "Maggie's a speech therapist. She *did* go for a scholarship, won it and wowed 'em all at UCLA. I'm really proud of her. We all are."

"I can see that," Lauren said. His grin was contagious, or was it the way his cheeks bunched up and his eyes crinkled? Whatever, she was grinning back at him, wondering how a man could be so gentle and giving, yet so wickedly attractive. "Tell me more," she urged. "About when you were a kid, what you were like, what you did."

He made a face and tilted his head to the side. "It's really not all that exciting."

"Tell me anyway." She perched her chin in her palm and waited expectantly.

"Only if you eat while I talk. You haven't had more than a bite, and the chicken is fantastic."

Listening to Matt and watching him drove all thought of food from her mind. But if eating was his precondition, well...

He talked and she ate. She made observations and asked questions while he ate, then resumed her own meal when he talked more. By the time they'd had seconds of just about everything, including wine, she'd learned that, though a mischievous Matt had received his share of spankings as a boy, he'd grown up in a house filled with love. She'd also learned, but between the lines, that what Matt craved most was his own house filled with love.

When he offered to help her clean up, she accepted. It wasn't that she needed the help or that she was liberated enough to demand it. She'd thoroughly enjoyed the way they'd worked together getting the dinner ready, and she wanted to draw out the evening as long as possible.

Apparently Matt had the same idea. When the kitchen was as spotless as one that age could be, he suggested they relax for a few minutes before he left. They settled in the living room, which, aside from Lauren's bedroom, was the only room with furnishings. There was one sofa and two side chairs. They shared the sofa.

Lauren felt peaceful and happy and tremendously drawn to the man beside her. His arm was slung across the back of the sofa, his fingers tangling in her hair. The clean, manly scent that clung to his skin heightened her senses, while his warmth bridged the small space between them with its invisible touch.

"This has been nice," she told him, slanting a shy glance his way. "I'm glad you came."

His voice was like a velvet mist. "So am I." Sliding his arm around her shoulders, he drew her closer even as he met her halfway. His lips touched one corner of her mouth, then the other, then her cupid's bow, then her lower lip. He'd opened his mouth to kiss her fully when, unable to help herself, she laughed.

He drew back and stared at her for a minute, then cried in mock dismay, "Lauren! What kind of behavior is that? Didn't anyone ever tell you not to laugh in a man's face when he's about to kiss you?"

"I'm sorry... It's just that...you were tasting me one little bit at a time.... You really *are* cautious!"

His eyes danced mischievously. "Caution's gone" was all he said before he covered her mouth with his and proceeded to deliver the most thorough kiss she'd ever received. No part of her mouth was left untouched by any part of his, and by the time he buried his face in her hair, she felt totally devoured. She might have told him so had she been able to speak, but her breath was caught somewhere between her lungs and her throat, for his hand was sliding over her waist, over and up, ever higher, and anticipation had become as tangible as those long, bronzed fingers. When at last they reached her breast, she let out a soft moan and succumbed to the exquisite sensations shooting through her.

Lauren had never been touched this way, yet there was nothing demure in her response. Both mind and body said that what she was experiencing was right and natural; instinct, goaded by desire, set her fingers to combing through his thick hair, running over his broad shoulders, splaying eagerly across his sinewed back.

"Lauren." His voice was hoarse. "Lauren...I have to...we have to stop...."

"No," she whispered. She held his head with one hand, pressing it to her neck. Her other hand covered his at her breast. "Don't stop."

A groan came from deep in his chest. "Do you know what you're saying, sweetheart? What it does to me?" His voice was thicker now, foreign to her ears yet exciting. She held her breath when he transferred her hand to his own chest and slowly slid it lower.

Lauren could feel the strength beneath her palm, the tautness of his stomach, then the stunning rigidity beneath the fly of his jeans. She wanted to hold him, explore him, let him satisfy the ache that had taken hold deep in her belly, but the newness of it all brought a measure of sanity. With a shuddering breath, she sagged against him.

"Yes. Do stop," she whispered. She was shocked by her own abandon, not quite sure what to make of it. "Everything...everything's happened so fast...and there's still the other matter." Of her own accord, she retreated from him, taking refuge in her corner of the sofa and clasping her hands tightly in her lap. The aura of arousal, a telltale quiver, lingered in her body, but thought of that "other matter" gradually put it to rest.

Matt, too, retreated to his corner of the sofa. He shifted in an attempt to get comfortable, finally hunching forward with his elbows on his knees. His fingers were interlaced, not quite at ease. He cleared his throat. "Yes...that other matter."

"We didn't reach any conclusions."

A pause. "No."

"What do you think?"

Another pause. "I don't know."

"Should I call the police?"

"No." Emphatically.

"Why not?"

He didn't answer, but studied his hands and frowned. "I have to ask you this, Lauren. I know it may sound terrible...but you did mention that your parents were against your coming here—"

"My parents? You think my *parents* could have been behind what's happened?" Vehemently she shook her head. "No. Absolutely not. They may disagree with me, but they'd never try to harm me."

"Maybe just scare you into going back—"

"No." She was still shaking her head. "Not possible! They wouldn't be capable of conceiving of violence."

"Maybe not violence, but if they've already lost one of their children—"

"Forget it, Matt. It's simply not possible.... I think I should call the police."

"*No.*"

"You've been very firm about that. Why, Matt?"

He offered the longest pause yet. "Maybe it's... premature."

"Premature? Then you don't think there's a connection between the things that have happened?"

"I didn't say that. I just think we ought to give it a little time. Let me see what I can do."

"What can you possibly do? Neither of us knows where to begin!"

He didn't argue with her; neither did he agree. Instead, he scowled at his hands.

"Matt, I'm frightened." As much by the strangeness of his response as by everything else, she told herself. "I haven't been hurt so far, but maybe I've just been lucky. What if the next time—"

"You won't be hurt," he gritted out, raising his dark brown eyes to hers. She tried to read his feelings, but they were shuttered. "I'll stay here. If something happens, I can take care of it."

Lauren stared at him. "You can't stay here! My bed's the only one— and—and anyway, you can't be with me every single minute of the day. You have to work. So do I. How can you anticipate when something will happen?"

"*If* something happens."

She bolted from the sofa and began to prowl the room. She was confused and upset. "You think I'm paranoid. I know you do. You think I'm making something out of nothing." Whirling to face him, she stuck her fists on her hips and glared. "The little lady with the rampant imagination. The fanciful little woman to be indulged—that's the macho attitude isn't it? That's where *you're* coming from!"

Matt's face paled. He sat up straight, then rose and began to walk stiffly toward the front door. His voice was flat. "I think I'd better leave. If that's the way you feel..."

Lauren watched him open the door, then close it behind him. What had she said? Had *she* put that look of hurt in his eyes? Had she been responsible for draining the emotion from his voice, that very same voice that had always been so wonderfully expressive?

Her gaze flew to the window. It was dark outside. Once Matt left, she'd be alone. Unable to take back the ugly words she'd said. Open prey to her own impulsiveness and...

The growl of his engine hit her ears as she wrenched open the front door. "Wait!" she cried, arms waving as she tore down the walk. "Matt, wait!" The car was halfway down the drive. Thinking only that she needed him with her, she flew in pursuit. "Don't go, Matt! I'm sorry! Please...don't...go!"

The taillights went on at the end of the drive, and the car slowed, about to turn onto the street. Lauren's steps faltered. She came to a tapering halt. She'd lost him. He was gone.

The car began to turn, then stopped.

She held her breath, then started running again. "Matt! Please! Wait!"

His tall figure emerged from the car but didn't move farther. Again she faltered and stopped. But the hesitation was only momentary. She knew what she wanted, knew what she needed. With a tiny cry of thanks that she'd been given a second chance, she raced forward.

Chapter Six

Flinging her arms around him, Lauren hung on for dear life. "I'm sorry—so sorry, Matt!" She pressed her cheek to the warm column of his neck. "I didn't mean what I said. I was nervous and frustrated. I took it out on you." Slowly she eased her grip on him and met his gaze. Her voice grew softer. "Don't go. Please?"

"I don't disbelieve you, Lauren," he stated quietly.

"I know that. I accused you unfairly. I expected you to have answers where I didn't. It was wrong of me."

"Nothing's changed. I still don't have answers."

"I know that."

"And you still have only one bed." His hands came to rest lightly on her hips, fingers splayed. "If I were a saint, I'd offer to sleep on the couch, but I'm not a saint."

His words and the look in his eyes sent ripples of excitement through her. "I know that," she whispered.

"Then you know what I want?" he asked as softly.

Unable to speak, she nodded.

His gaze held hers captive for a minute longer; then he grabbed her hand. "Get into the car."

"What—?"

He was urging her into the driver's seat, his hands on her shoulders. "Slide in. Over a little. That's it." He was mere inches behind her, then flush to her side. "I'm not taking the chance that you'll change your mind." Tucking her arm through his, he put the car in reverse and sped backward up the drive. Then he all but swung her from the car, fitted one strong arm over her shoulder and half ran to the house.

"Matt?" She was laughing, breathless.

"Shhh."

Once inside, he continued up the stairs, straight to her bedroom. The light was off. He made no attempt to alter the darkness, and Lauren was relieved. She knew that she wanted what was about to happen. She also knew that the darkness added to its dreamlike quality. That a man like

Matt wanted *her* was mind-boggling. Surely if he turned on the light, he'd have second thoughts; she'd have second thoughts....

He took her in his arms and kissed her until the only thoughts she had were how wonderful he was, how unbelievably desirable he made her feel, how lucky she was to have found him. She gave herself up to his kiss, to his hands as they unbuttoned her shirt and unclasped her bra, to his fingers as they charted her flesh, branding her woman with fire and grace.

A soft moan came from deep in her throat, and she arched her back to offer herself more fully. Acceding to her wordless plea, he stroked her with gentle expertise. His fingers made firm swells of her breasts; his thumbs, tight buds of her nipples. And all the while his tongue correspondingly familiarized itself with every nook and cranny of her mouth.

His hands left her only to free himself of his shirt, and then he was back, crushing her close. His chest was warm and lightly furred. Its texture exhilarated her, though she wondered if it was simply the closeness, male to female, that pleased her so. There was something very, very right about what she felt. There was something very, very right about Matt. At that moment she didn't know how she'd ever doubted him.

While he held her lips captive, he reached for the snap of her jeans, released it, lowered the zipper. She gasped for breath when he knelt and eased the denim from her legs, then did the same with her panties. She clutched his shoulders for support and shivered, though her blood was hot, her body aching for completion. Modesty was nonexistent; she wanted him too badly.

"Please," she whispered shakily, "I need you, Matt."

For an instant, he buried his face in her stomach while he caressed the backs of her legs and her bottom. His breath was ragged, his hair damp against her hot flesh. She drove her fingers into the thick, sun-streaked pelt and held him closer, then urged him upward.

He didn't need much urging. Standing, he shed the rest of his clothes, then came to her naked, pressing her to him, graphically showing her that the need wasn't hers alone. She thrilled to the knowledge, unable to be afraid when Matt was all she'd ever wanted, all she'd ever dreamed about. The fact that she could arouse him to the state he was in was as heady as the state of arousal he'd himself brought her to.

He moved from her only to tug back the spread before lowering her gently to the sheets. "Lauren...God, Lauren..." he murmured, then kissed her again. He caressed and teased with his hands, his lips, his tongue, but the play took its toll. His body seemed on fire, trembling under the strain of the heat, finally unable to withstand it. Threading his fingers through hers, he anchored them by her shoulders and positioned himself between her thighs. With one powerful thrust, he surged forward.

Lauren arched her back against the sudden invasion, and a tiny cry escaped her lips. When he stiffened, she wrapped her arms around him to draw him close to her. He resisted.

"Lauren?" His voice was little more than a throaty whisper.

"It's okay…don't stop…don't stop."

His breathing grew all the more labored and he pressed his forehead to her shoulder. "I couldn't if…I wanted to," he finally managed, "but I can be more…gentle."

"Don't be!" she cried, for the instant of pain was gone, leaving only that swelling knot of need low in her belly.

But he was gentle and caring, moving slowly at first, letting her body adjust to his presence before he adopted the rhythm designed to drive her insane. What he didn't realize was that even his initial, cautious movements were delicious. His fullness inside her gave Lauren an incredible sense of satisfaction; the idea of receiving a man, of receiving Matt in this way, was the sweetest delight.

By the time he moved faster, Lauren was right with him. She adored the way his thighs brushed hers, the way their stomachs rubbed. When he bent his head, she strained higher. His mouth closed over her breast and began a sucking that pulled at her womb from one direction while the smooth stroking of his manhood pulled at it from another. Her hands roamed over and around his firm body, but even had she not touched him, she would have been intimately aware of every hard plane and sinewed swell he possessed. Their bodies were that close, working in tandem.

He murmured soft words of encouragement and praise. "That's it, sweetheart…ahhh…your legs…yes, there…so good…"

They moved as one then, each complementing and completing the other. Lauren experienced a beauty she'd never imagined. She was drawn beyond herself into Matt, sharing, collaborating, merging with him into a greater being for those precious moments of emotional and physical bliss.

After the climax had passed, it was a long time before either of them could speak. They gasped for air, alternately panting and moaning, laughing from time to time at their inability to do anything more. At last Matt slid slowly to her side, leaving one leg and an arm over her in a statement of possession she had no wish to deny. His head was beside hers on the pillow, his cheek cushioned in her hair.

"How do you feel?" he asked in a thick whisper.

"Stunned," she whispered back. "I never imagined…"

"*You* never imagined…"

She forced her lids open and looked at him. "Then…it was okay?"

"It was more than okay," he teased in throaty chiding, "but you had to know that."

"No. I didn't."

His grin faded, replaced by a look of tender concern. He brought a shaky hand up to smooth damp strands of hair from her brow. "I'm sorry if I hurt you, Lauren. If I'd known, I might have been able to make it easier."

"It couldn't have been easier. I've never felt so wonderful in my life."

"Even at the start?" His arched brow dared her to deny the moment of pain she'd felt.

"Even then. If I hadn't felt a thing, something would have been lost. I wanted the pain. Does that make any sense?"

He didn't answer. Instead, he traced her eyebrow with his finger. "Why didn't you tell me, sweetheart?"

"I didn't think it mattered." She paused, experiencing a frisson of apprehension. "Did it? I mean, we're both adults. I knew what I was doing."

"Did you?"

"Yes!" She didn't understand what he was getting at.

"Lauren, I didn't do anything to protect you. It's possible I've just made you pregnant."

Her jaw slackened only slightly. Then, unable to control herself, she burst into a smile. "What an exciting thought!"

Matt closed his eyes for a minute. "You're supposed to be worried, sweetheart." He propped himself up on an elbow and looked down at her. "You're supposed to be thinking about this new life you have, the shop, your independence."

"But a baby!" Her eyes were wide. "I could adjust to that. It would be marvelous!"

"I didn't know you wanted a baby so badly."

"Neither did I." She scrunched up her nose. "But it probably won't happen. Just once, Matt. And it's the wrong time of the month." She brushed the strands of hair from his forehead and left her fingers to tangle in the wet thatch. "Are *you* worried?"

"Of course I'm worried. Babies should be planned, the logistics worked out. Everything should be clear from the start."

"There you go again. So cautious." She tugged playfully at his hair. "If I were to become pregnant, I'd manage. One way or another I would, because I'd want the baby enough to make everything fall into place."

"Such a romantic," Matt murmured, but there was a sadness in his eyes.

Her smile faded. "You're thinking that you'll be leaving soon."

"Sooner or later I will."

"It's okay, Matt. There are no strings attached to what happened tonight. I won't ask any more of you than you want to give."

He snorted and flopped back on the pillow. "That's cavalier of you."

"Would you rather I demand marriage?" she asked, confused. "Times have changed. Just because we made love doesn't mean you have to make an 'honest woman' of me. I don't feel dishonest. I feel...lucky.''

He turned his head on the pillow so that he faced her again. "Explain."

"I never expected what happened tonight. What I felt, what I experienced, were so much more than I've ever dared to dream."

"Why not? That's what I don't understand. I don't understand why you were a virgin. You're beautiful, charming and intelligent. And you're right. Times have changed. Women your age are rarely inexperienced."

"Would you have had me throw myself at just any old man for the sake of experience?"

At the sound of hurt in her voice, he rolled over to cover her body. With his large hands cupping her face, he spoke gently. "No, sweetheart. Of course not. I'm the one who's been lucky tonight. To know that you've given me what you've given no other man...that was one of the reasons I couldn't stop when I realized what was happening."

"One of the reasons?"

Even in the dark she caught his sheepish grin. "The others are right here." He dropped a hand to her knee and lifted his body only enough to permit that hand a slow rise. He touched each and every erogenous zone before tapping his finger against her temple. "All of you—mind, body, soul. You turn me on, Lauren."

"Oh, God" was all she could whisper, because his tactile answer had set her body to aching again, and she hadn't believed it could be possible. She didn't know whether to be pleased or embarrassed, but that was her mind talking. Of its own accord, her body shifted beneath his with a story of its own.

As she'd already learned, Matthew Kruger was a good reader.

When the last page of this second chapter had been turned, she fell asleep. Her body was exhausted yet replete, her mind at peace. She was totally unaware that Matt lay awake beside her for long hours before curving his body protectively around hers and at last allowing himself the luxury of escape.

LAUREN AWOKE the next morning to a strange sensation of heat running the entire length of the back of her body. Her lids flew open and she held her breath. Only her eyeballs moved, questioning, seeking, finally alighting on the large, tanned hand flattened on the sheet by her stomach.

Matt.

Shifting her head, she followed a line from that hand, up a lean but powerful arm to an even stronger shoulder.

Matt.

Quietly, almost stealthily, she turned until she faced him, and her heart melted. He was sound asleep, tawny lashes resting above his cheekbones, his mouth slightly parted, lips relaxed. Unable to help herself, she let her gaze fall along his body. Last night she'd savored him with her hands; this morning it was her eyes' turn to feast.

He was magnificent. Soft hair swirled over his chest, tapering toward his navel, below which the sheet was casually bunched. His hips were lean, as she'd known they'd be; the sheet was nearly as erotic a covering as the air alone might have been.

A self-satisfied smile spread over her face. She felt good. Complete. All woman. Giving in to temptation, she leaned forward and kissed his chest. He smelled of man, earthy but wonderful. Eyes closed, she drank in that essence as she continued to press the lightest of kisses into the warmest of skin.

When a hand suddenly tightened around her waist, her head flew up. Matt's eyes were still closed, but he wore the roguish shadow of a beard on his cheeks and a faint smile on his lips. "Am I dreaming?" he whispered.

In answer, Lauren shimmied higher, slid her arms around his neck and kissed his smile wider. She was further rewarded when he rolled onto his back and hauled her over him. Only then did he open his eyes.

For long minutes, they simply looked at each other. She wasn't sure what her own eyes were saying, but Matt's quite clearly spoke of pleasure. And affection. They made her feel special.

"Hi," he whispered at last.

She swallowed the lump of emotion in her throat. "Hi."

"How'd you sleep?"

"Fine."

"No ghosts?"

She shook her head.

"No strange noises?"

She shook her head. "Beth was right. She said I needed a bodyguard."

He closed his hands around her bottom and gave her a punishing squeeze. "So that's why you did it? Because you wanted a bodyguard?"

"You know better than that." She sucked in a breath when his hands pressed her intimately closer. "Matt?"

He was grinning. "It's your fault. You started it. In case you didn't know, a man's at his peak in the morning."

"I thought a man was at his peak in his twenties, and you're a mite beyond. You're shocking me."

"You're the one with the bag of surprises. A virgin is supposed to be shy and demure."

She grinned. "I'm not a virgin anymore, so my behavior is excusable."

Rolling over, he set her on her back, then held himself up so that he could look at her. Just as hers had done moments earlier, his eyes touched her body as only his hands had done the night before. "You are beautiful, Lauren. God, I can't believe it." He met her gaze. "No regrets?"

Still basking in his approval, which both stunned and thrilled her, she shook her head. "How about you?"

One long forefinger drew a bisecting line from the hollow of her throat to the apex of her thighs. "No," he answered, but gruffly. "Not about this. About not having the answer to your problem, yes, I have regrets."

"Don't think about that," she whispered, feeling a strange urgency not to let anything intrude on this precious time with Matt. "Not now."

His grin was lopsided, slightly forced, and his eyes lingered on the soft curves of her body. "I think I'd better. It's either that or ravish you again, and I imagine you're going to be a little sore."

"Me? Sore?"

"Yes. You, sore."

"Oh."

With a deep growl, he gathered her into his arms and held her tightly. When his grip loosened, it was with reluctance. "I could use a shower and some breakfast. It's a workday, or had you forgotten?"

"Oh, my god!" She twisted toward the clock on the dresser, then pushed herself from his arms and bolted out of bed. "I'll take the shower first," she called over her shoulder. Remembering her sadly deficient water heater, she added, "Real quick."

Lauren was true to her word, but by the time she had returned to the bedroom, Matt was nowhere in sight. For a split second she panicked. Then she caught sight of his clothes on the floor. "Matt?" Wrapped in her towel, she headed for the stairs. "Matt?"

The aroma of fresh coffee filled the air, but he didn't answer. She was halfway down the staircase when the front door opened and Matt strode through, carrying a large leather suitcase. He was stark naked.

"Matthew Kruger! Where is your sense of decency? If one of my neighbors saw you—"

He'd taken the stairs by twos, and the smack of his lips on hers cut off her teasing tirade. He continued upward. "The trees were my cover. It's a gorgeous day outside."

Lauren couldn't think to argue. He was spectacular. Tall and straight. Broad back, narrow hips, tight buttocks. If it hadn't been for the time, she'd have followed him into the shower just to touch him again. The mere sight of him took her breath away.

But time was of the essence. She blow-dried her hair and put on makeup while Matt showered and shaved; then she dressed quickly and hurried to the kitchen. They were seated side by side, finishing off the last of the scrambled eggs and toast, when Matt laid out his plans for the day.

"I've got meetings set for ten and two. We can take my car into Boston, meet for lunch, then grab something on the way home tonight. Sound okay?"

His words were offered gently, not at all imperiously, yet they brought back to Lauren the crux of Matt's present mission. He intended to protect her as he'd promised, which meant that he was going to stick as close to her side as possible. On one level, she was thrilled with that prospect. On another...

"About my problem, Matt. Are we just going to...wait?"

"Pretty much. It'll be interesting to see if my presence here makes any difference."

"But if nothing happens, we won't know if you've scared someone off for good or simply put him off for a while. And you can't stay here forever."

"I know." He looked away. "I'm going to make some calls today."

"What kind of calls? To whom?"

"People who may have more insight than we do." There was an edge to his voice, but his gaze was soft when he glanced back at her. "Let me do the worrying for now, Lauren. You've done your share."

"But it's my problem! I can't just dump it on your shoulders and wipe my hands of it. That's not fair to you. You don't owe me anything."

For a minute he looked as if he would argue. He gnawed on the inside of his cheek, then lifted his mug and drained the last of his coffee. "Let's just say I owe it to Brad, then. He was my friend and you're his sister. The least I can do is to help you out when you need it."

That wasn't quite the answer she wanted, but she knew she'd have to settle for it.

"Anyway," he added with an endearing grin, "I've got broad shoulders. I can handle it. Maybe it's the Spenser in me coming out, after all."

"Better you than Robert Urich. But are you sure?"

"Very sure. Hey, as far as work on the house goes, are you going to call those names I gave you or would you like me to do it?"

She winced. "Got a cold shower, did you?"

"Well..."

"I'll do it. You're doing enough. I'd love it if you were here when I meet with them, though. I have a feeling some of those guys show more respect when a man's around." The last had been offered on a dry note. She paused, then asked cautiously, "How long will you be here?" She envisioned two or three days, and the thought left her feeling empty.

He rubbed the back of his neck. "I was thinking about that last night. I have to be in Leominster on Thursday and Friday, but I could almost commute from here." He took a fast breath. "Unless you'd rather have the house to yourself again. I'll understand, Lauren. It's okay, really it is—Hey, crumpled napkins in the face I can do without first thing in the morning!"

"Then don't give me that little-boy pout," she chided as she carried their plates to the sink. But when she returned to the table, she gave him a hug from behind. "Of course I want you here," she murmured with her cheek pressed to his. "For as long as you can stay. Besides, you *do* owe it to me."

His hands clasped hers at the open collar of his shirt. "I do?"

"Uh-huh. You've awakened me to some of the finer points in life. Seems to me there's got to be an awful lot I still don't know."

"Then you *are* after my body! I knew it all along!"

"Could be," she answered with a grin. "Could be."

DURING THE NEXT FEW DAYS, Lauren and Matt spent every possible minute with each other. They drove to and from Boston together. They met for lunch each day. When Matt wasn't working but Lauren was, he was parked so frequently on the bench outside the shop that Beth suggested they charge him rent.

"Either that, or hire him part-time."

Lauren wrinkled her nose. "After all we went through to convince Jamie to start full-time next week? No way. Besides, what does Matt know about art?"

"What does he know about *other* things?" Beth drawled suggestively. "That's what *I* want to know."

"Oh, quite a bit" was all Lauren would admit. She knew Beth was fishing. She hadn't made a secret of the fact that Matt was staying with her in Lincoln. But some things were sacred, not to be discussed with even the closest of friends, and for more than the obvious reasons. Lauren felt she was living a fairy tale. By her own admission, Beth was envious. The last thing Lauren wanted to do was to rub it in.

"Well," Beth said with a sigh, "at least he's managed to keep you safe."

"That he has."

Since Matt had been with her, there'd been no accidents, no close calls, no questionable occurrences. Indeed, Lauren felt safe enough almost to forget there was a problem.

Almost, but not quite.

Tuesday evening she asked Matt if he'd made any calls to those "people who may have more insight than we do." He said he had and that the ball was rolling. His tone was light. She hadn't dared ask more.

Wednesday evening, though, she couldn't help herself. As gently as she could, she inquired about it again.

"Have you heard anything yet?"

"No. It takes time."

"Time to do what? I don't understand."

"Questions can be asked, people consulted. Trust me, Lauren. Please?" Put that way, with an eruption of tension dissolving abruptly into beseechfulness, she'd surrendered.

But much as she tried, she couldn't shake the conviction that the things she'd experienced were linked and that, despite Matt's protective shield, they were bound to resume at some point. And she was frightened.

THURSDAY MORNING Matt crawled out of bed at dawn, showered, shaved and dressed, then woke Lauren to say goodbye. She was groggy. It had been another late night of sweet, prolonged loving. Only the realization that Matt was leaving brought her from her self-satisfied stupor.

"You should have wakened me sooner," she whispered, reaching up to touch his freshly shaved cheek. "I'd have made you breakfast."

"No time. They'll have coffee and doughnuts there."

"I wish you didn't have to go."

"I'll be back tonight."

"I know, but I've been spoiled. Leominster seems so far away."

He sighed. "I agree." He pressed his lips together, then forced a smile. "You take care of yourself, sweetheart, you hear? Drive carefully, and be sure to lock the doors."

"I will."

Lifting her in his arms, he hugged her before setting her back with a kiss on the tip of her nose. She knew not to ask for more. Where temptation was concerned, they were both decidedly weak.

"Good luck, Matt. I hope everything goes well."

He waved as he left the room. Climbing from the bed, she crossed to the window and watched him slide into his car, start the engine and drive off. In an attempt to parry the unease that settled over her, she took a shower and dressed, then forced herself to make breakfast for one and eat every last bit.

Only when she'd finished did she permit herself to sit back and think. She missed Matt. Already. After only two full days together, she'd gotten used to his presence. More than used to it. Addicted to it. Breakfast wasn't the same without him. Neither would lunch be. For that matter, she'd miss being able to look up at odd times and find him on the bench outside the shop.

She wished he could stay forever, but that was an unrealistically romantic thought if ever there was one. Today he was off to Leominster. Next week, or soon after, he'd be back in California. What then? Would they talk on the phone? Visit each other from time to time?

She knew it wouldn't be enough for her. She wanted him in Lincoln with her. Whatever initial reservations she'd had about his background, his occupation or his character were nonexistent now. His background was blue-collar and strong, his occupation solid, his character sterling. She'd never once glimpsed anything coarse in him. Rather, he'd proved to be unfailingly gentle and giving. Even his reticence about discussing

Brad had ceased to matter. He was simply protective, skirting around what he knew to be a sensitive subject.

And he'd brought out a new side of her. Since she'd met him, she'd matured as a woman. He made her believe in both her looks and her sexuality. Whereas her confidence had come from looking in the mirror when she'd first returned from the Bahamas, now it came from the reflection of admiration in Matt's eyes. She didn't care what anyone else thought of her. Only Matt mattered.

So where was she to go from here? Sighing, she rose from the table. She'd clean up the kitchen, go to work and come home. Soon after that, Matt would return. She wasn't even going to think about tomorrow.

One day at a time. All she could do was take one day at a time.

Cleaning up the kitchen was no problem at all. Going to work was another matter. When she tried to start her car, the engine refused to turn over. Not one to beat a dead horse, she returned to the house, called AAA, then sat waiting for half an hour until the tow truck arrived.

"Battery's dead" was the mechanic's laconic diagnosis.

"But that's impossible. This battery's barely four months old!"

"It's dead."

"How can a four-month-old battery die?"

Taking jumper cables from his truck, the man set to work recharging the battery. "Maybe you left the headlights on."

"I never do that."

"Anyone else drive this car? A kid? Maybe he forgot and left 'em on."

"There's no kid, and I'm the only one who drives the car. It's been sitting in the garage since Tuesday morning—" that was when Matt, in fact, had put it away, but he wouldn't have left the lights on "—but it's sat for longer than that without any trouble."

"No sweat, lady. The battery looks okay otherwise. I'll have it working in no time."

He did, and Lauren was only fifteen minutes late for work, but she was bothered by the incident. It occurred to her that the same person who'd sabotaged her garage door might have entered the garage during those days when the car was idle, switched the lights on for a good, long time, then switched them off without her being any the wiser. She decided to discuss it with Matt that night, but the sense of solace in that resolution wasn't enough to prevent a certain nervousness when she returned to the car after work. She found herself glancing around the large parking garage and into the back seat of the car before she dared climb into the front.

She held her breath. The car started. She drove to Lincoln without any trouble.

Matt wasn't due back until nine at the earliest, so she took the time to stop for groceries before arriving at the farmhouse. It was still light out, and she was grateful. She imagined herself being watched and knew that, had it been dark, she would have been terrified.

Relief came in small measure after she was locked safely inside the house. Focusing determinedly on Matt's return, she stowed the groceries, prepared all the fixings for dinner, then poured herself a glass of wine and took refuge in the living room. While lights were burning in the rest of the house, she chose to sit in the dark. Hiding. Brooding. Wondering. Worrying. She knew that her imagination was getting the best of her, but that didn't stop it from happening.

Minutes seemed to stretch into an eternity, though it was barely after nine when finally she heard a car whip up the drive. Hurrying to the window, she peered cautiously out. Her relief was immediate and considerable when Matt climbed from the car. Even before he'd stepped over the threshold, her arms were around his neck.

"Matt, it's wonderful to have you back!"

He had one hand at the back of her head, the other arm around her waist. "Mmm. You're good for my ego. Such a welcome, and I haven't even been gone fourteen hours."

"Close. Thirteen and a half." She lifted her face for a kiss that was instantly comforting and thoroughly satisfying. "How did it go?"

"Very well. I think we've finally worked out the last of the bugs with the locals, so we can get the permit we need, which is great, since we've got everyone else lined up and ready to go."

"Good deal!"

"And I spoke with Thomas." Thomas Gehling was the general contractor whom Lauren had called on Tuesday. "He's looking forward to meeting with us Sunday morning."

"But if he's going to be involved with your project, will he have time to do mine?"

Matt threw an arm around her shoulder and drew her into the house with him. "You have to understand construction lingo. When I say that everyone is lined up and ready to go, it means that if we're lucky, we'll have broken ground within six weeks. And then there's the heavy work that has to be done first—blasting, digging, pouring foundations. The plumbers and electricians and carpenters you'll need won't be required at our site for three months minimum. Thomas will have more than enough time to oversee work here—that is, if you find that you like him and what he has to say. You're under no obligation to use him. There are other names on that list."

"Of the ones I spoke with, I liked him the best. Call it instinct, or whatever, but something meshed even on the phone." She was well aware of the fact that Matt's using Thomas Gehling for his own work might have slanted her view. She trusted Matt's judgment. But she had liked

Thomas. He spoke intelligently and seemed perfectly comfortable dealing with a woman.

"I think you'll be impressed when you meet him." Having reached the kitchen, Matt went directly to the sink, turned on the water and squirted a liberal amount of liquid soap on his hands. "So how was your day, sweetheart?"

"Fine—I mean, okay. God, I can't believe it happened again."

"What?"

"I've been a nervous wreck all day, counting the minutes until you got back so I could tell you what happened. Then you walk in here, bringing a sense of security, and I forget all about it."

He stared at her over his shoulder. "What happened?"

"My car wouldn't start this morning. The battery was dead. I had to get a truck here to jump-start it."

"The battery was dead? Didn't you say you'd gotten a new one just before you left Bennington?"

"I did. That's what's so weird. The man from the garage suggested that I'd left my lights on by mistake. I'm sure I'd never do that."

A thick cloud of suds coated Matt's hands, but he paid it little heed. His brows knitted low over his eyes. "I was the last one to drive your car. I put it in the garage Tuesday morning before we left for Boston in mine. I'm sure the lights were off. There'd have been no reason for me to turn them on to begin with, and the car started perfectly, so they couldn't have been left on the night before."

"That's what I figured." She was standing close by the sink. "The only logical explanation is that someone's been tampering in the garage again."

He shot her a sharp glance. "Was anything else wrong with the car?"

"No, and it started perfectly when I left work tonight."

Bending over the sink, Matt splashed soapy water on his face. Lauren reached into a drawer and had a clean towel waiting by the time he'd rinsed and straightened up. No amount of wiping, though, could remove the concern from his features.

"It may have been a fluke," he suggested quietly.

"Do you believe that?"

He hesitated. "No."

"Matt, don't you think it's time we called the police? I mean, when it was only a couple of incidents, they might have thought I was crazy, but at this stage the situation has to be considered suspicious. At least if the police were aware of the possibilities, they could patrol the area more closely."

Matt's expression grew more troubled than ever. "The police might scare him off, and then he'd only wait for things to die down before starting again. What we need to do is to catch him."

"Come on, Matt," she chided, "I was only kidding about playing Spenser."

"It wouldn't be too hard to rig up some booby traps." His eyes were growing animated; he was obviously warming up to the idea. "I think I could manage it, with a little help from a friend."

"From what friend?"

"One of the guys I met in Leominster. He works at a nearby lumber-yard." Matt gave a mock grimace and scratched the back of his head. "Seems to me that he mentioned something about having done time."

"A convict? You're going to enlist a *convict* to save me?"

"An ex-convict. And he's been straight for ten years."

"Matt, what *is* this?"

"His specialty was breaking and entering, and he was a genius at it."

Lauren narrowed her eyes. "How long did you spend with this guy?"

"Not long. Can I help it if he's proud of what he's done?"

"Not only after, but before." She grunted, then muttered under her breath, "I can't believe I'm standing here listening when I should be on the phone talking to the police."

Matt put his hands on her arms and stroked her coaxingly. "Come on, Lauren. It's worth a try. You know how the police are—"

"I don't know how the police are. I've never had dealings with them before, contrary to *some* of your friends."

He kissed her forehead. "The police ask millions of questions and then get their minds set on an answer that isn't the one you've given or the one you want to hear. These local departments just aren't geared to taking the offensive, and they sure as hell wouldn't call in the state police or the FBI in a situation like this." His voice softened, taking on a hint of teasing that was reflected in his eyes. "If you were worried about contractors being chauvinists, just wait until you've met the police. They'll treat you like a sweet little thing who's slightly soft in the head." He cupped said item in his hand and gently massaged her scalp. "And even if they decided that you just might be on to something, there's the matter of red tape. They could step up their patrols, but that'd be all. They'd have trouble getting authorization for much else. More than anything, they'd be reluctant to do something that might backfire in court."

Lauren was having trouble fighting him when he was so close and touching her so gently. "You're not reluctant," she stated, but the accusation she'd intended came out sounding more like admiration.

"Not one bit." His thumbs traced the delicate curves of her ears. "I want whoever's been harassing you to be caught. I have to believe that once we find out who it is, we'll find a motive as well."

"You're seducing me," she breathed.

"Me?"

"Don't look so innocent. You're seducing me."

"I am not. I'm simply trying to convince you to let me have a go at it."

"At what? That's the issue." Her voice was whisper-soft, not seductive in itself, simply...taken. "Do you want a go at playing cops and robbers, or at making love with me?"

"I'll make you forget, Lauren," he murmured, lowering his head until his lips feathered hers. "I'll make you forget everything else."

She caught her breath when he nipped at her lower lip. He was already making her forget, damn him—bless him. At this moment, she wanted to forget.

"I'll make you forget everything else," he repeated hotly against her neck. "And that's a promise. Word of honor."

MATT MADE GOOD on his promise. Right there, propping Lauren against the kitchen counter, he made love to her with such daring that she forgot everything else but what she felt for him, with him.

He also made good on the promise to call his friend, the breaking-and-entering expert, who showed up at the farmhouse bright and early the very next morning with a carload full of booby-trap makings the likes of which Lauren had never imagined. She had to leave for work before the last of the snares were set, and remarked only half in jest that she'd never make it back into the house alive.

Matt called her from Leominster in the middle of the afternoon to say that he was going to have to attend a dinner meeting and that he wouldn't be back until late. Disappointed but fully appreciative of the demands of his work, she decided to stay in the city after the shop closed to have dinner with Beth and then see a movie.

"Nervous about going home?" Beth teased.

Lauren chuckled—yes, nervously. "It'll be dark, and they've hooked up so many gadgets that it's very possible I'll be the first one caught. You wouldn't believe it, Beth. There's a gizmo on the garage door that has to be deactivated, or else a huge black net descends on an intruder. And once the net falls, *it* sets off a god-awful clanging. The doors to the house have hidden latches that are attached to electrical devices that deliver a shock powerful enough to stun, and the shock in turn sets off an alarm."

"You're right in the middle of a spy novel. I love it!"

"You wouldn't if you had to negotiate everything yourself. There are even hidden snares along the edge of the woods. You'd think we were trapping mink."

"I'm telling you, you've got all the makings of a best-seller. Just think, when this is over, you can write it up. Before you know it, you'll be signing autographs and doing the talk-show circuit."

"Thank you, Beth. I'll settle for catching one man and turning him over to the police."

"But what if it isn't *one* man?" Beth tossed out with imaginative anticipation. "What if there's a whole syndicate that's got some kind of grudge against you? What if you catch one man and another takes over where the first leaves off, so you catch the second? Meanwhile, the first dies mysteriously in jail, so the second decides to sing, and before you know it, there's enough evidence to convict the *entire* syndicate. You'll be a hero!"

"Heroine," Lauren correct dryly. "And I don't believe we're dealing with any syndicate. What would a syndicate have against me?"

"Maybe it was using your vacant farmhouse as its headquarters, and then you came along and, boom, moved in lickety-split, and there's still some very valuable and potentially condemning material stored in the cellar—"

Lauren scowled at her. "What happened to your theory about the ghost of inhabitants past?"

"Too passé. I think I like the syndicate idea better."

"I don't like *either* of them, and if we're going to have dinner together, you'll have to swear you won't go on like this. You're making me nervous."

"I thought you were already nervous."

"You're making me *more* nervous."

Beth patted her arm, then squeezed it. "I'm just teasing, Lauren. You know that. Just teasing."

THAT WAS WHAT LAUREN told herself when, later that night, after the movie had let out and she and Beth had gone their separate ways on the streets of Boston, she had the uncanny sensation of being followed.

Chapter Seven

The sensation was vague at first, and Lauren wondered if her imagination was simply working overtime. She glanced over her shoulder, then faced forward again. There were people around—she wished there were even more—but none appeared to be suspicious. At least, no one had ducked into a doorway when she'd looked back.

She had walked a bit farther and turned a corner when the sensation intensified. A prickling arose at the back of her neck, accompanied by a frisson of fear. Instinctively she quickened her step, mentally charting the course she'd have to take to reach the garage. It consisted of main streets for the most part, with a single alleyway at the end.

She darted another glance behind her and saw the same outwardly innocuous people—several couples, a handful of singles, all staggered at intervals. If someone grabbed her, she'd yell. There were plenty of bodies to help.

She walked on. Fewer people were ahead of her now; some had turned off toward the subway stop. She assumed the same was true for those behind her, and the thought added to her unease.

She turned another corner. There was no one ahead of her now, and she didn't dare look back. Unbidden, she recalled her childhood. There'd been a dog in the neighborhood, a large German shepherd of which she'd been terrified. Her mother had always instructed her to walk calmly past it on the theory that dogs could smell fear. Could people smell fear? Lauren wondered now. She was sure she reeked of it.

Imagination. That was all it was. Imagination getting a little out of hand. The sounds she heard not far behind weren't footsteps. They were the knocking of the air-conditioning unit in the building she passed...or the creaking of heat as it escaped from the engine of a newly parked car alongside the curb...or...

Eyes wide, she shot a frightened glance over her shoulder and gasped. There was a man. He was very tall, large-set, dressed in black, and he was not twenty feet behind and gaining steadily on her.

Uncaring if she was jumping to conclusions, she began to run. She turned another corner and ran even faster. Her heels beat a rapid tattoo on the pavement, merging with the thundering of her heart to drown out all other night sounds of the city.

She passed another long—agonizingly long—building, then reached the alley, in actuality a single-lane driveway. At its end stood her salvation, a guard booth.

She was breathless and shaking, terrified of looking back and losing time, tripping or slamming into the wall. She cursed her side, which ached; cursed the shoes she wore and the heat that seemed to buffet her and slow her progress. By the time she reached the booth, she felt as though she'd run a marathon.

"Thank God," she whispered, panting as she sagged against the thick plastic enclosure. Then, with a burst of energy, she scrambled to the booth's opening. The guard, a young man with a punk hairstyle at odds with his uniform, sat balanced on the back legs of his chair. A dog-eared magazine lay open on his lap. The heavy beat of rock music thrummed from the stereo box by his side. He was chewing gum; the vigorous action of his jaw only enhanced the indolence of his stare.

"Someone was following me," Lauren gasped and darted a frantic glance toward the alley through which she'd run.

Looking thoroughly bored, the guard followed her gaze. There was no one in sight.

"He must have turned away when he saw me heading toward you," she explained, trying to calm herself enough to think clearly. "Listen, I need a big favor."

The young man blew a bubble, popped it and licked the gum back into his mouth. "Depends what it is."

"Could you walk me to my car?"

He gave a one-shouldered shrug. "I'm on duty."

"I know, but there aren't many cars leaving the garage now. With the gate down, they'll wait. It won't take you long—two, maybe three minutes. Just until I lock myself in."

He fingered his earlobe, which sported a crescent of multiple studs. "I'm not supposed to leave this booth."

"But I'm in danger!"

Slowly, his head nodding in time with the music, he looked back toward the street. "Don't see anyone."

"He may have taken the stairs. Please! I need your help!"

After what seemed forever, the front legs of the chair hit the floor. "So. Chivalry calls." The guard stood up, yawned, then pushed his shoulders back.

The show was wasted on Lauren, who saw right through it to the scrawniness of his physique. Not much to protect her with. But he wore a uniform. There was safety in a uniform.

"I'm the new guy on the block," he drawled. "I was given specific instructions—"

She felt sweat trickling down her back. "Look, I'll argue on your behalf if you get into trouble. It seems to me your boss would reward you for helping a regular tenant."

"You're a regular tenant?" His gaze drifted down her body.

"Yes." She sighed in exasperation, feeling suddenly tired. Instinctively she knew she was safe standing at the booth with even as unlikely a guard as this, but there was still the threat of the inner garage to overcome. She wanted nothing more than to be locked in her car and on the road, headed for home. "Please. Just walk me upstairs. You could have been up and back in the time you've spent talking with me."

He grinned. "Yeah, but talking with you beats sitting here by myself." He cocked his head to one side. "Sure. I'll walk you upstairs."

Lauren jerked her eyes toward the thick pipes overhead. "Thank you," she breathed. By the time she looked down, the guard had let himself out of his cage and was swaggering toward her.

She glanced worriedly back toward the exit, but it remained empty.

"Come on, love. Up we go." He took her elbow and she jumped, wondering for an instant if she'd leaped from the frying pan into the fire. Unfortunately, she was the proverbial beggar who couldn't be choosy. So she clamped her mouth shut and let her cocky gallant lead the way to the stairs.

He dropped her elbow to open the door. Her apprehensive gaze examined every nook of the stairwell as they started up.

"Floor?"

"Third." Had the stairwell always been this narrow?

He chewed away at his gum. "Work around here?"

"Yes." Had the stairwell always been this confining?

"Kind of late leaving, aren't you?"

"Yes." He wouldn't try anything. He wouldn't dare. She knew where and for whom he worked.

"Hot date?"

"Yes...he'll be waiting for me on the corner as soon as I leave here."

They climbed the last set of stairs in silence. Though Lauren didn't look, she could feel the smirk on her companion's face. He hadn't believed her. She'd hesitated too long, then spoken too quickly. Damn, but she wasn't good at this.

He swung open the door, then stood aside to let her through. "Always park on the third floor?"

She was looking nervously from side to side, trying to see into corners where a tall, large, dark form might be lurking. "It depends," she offered distractedly. With no assailant in sight, she blindly fumbled in her bag for the keys.

"Where's your car?"

She pointed. They reached it half a minute later.

"There," he announced as she unlocked the door, checked the back seat, then all but threw herself behind the wheel. "Safe and sound."

She locked the door and rolled her window down, just enough to murmur a heartfelt "Thank you. I do appreciate what you've done."

"How about a ride down?"

"Uh..." Dumbly, she looked at the passenger seat, then leaned over and tugged up the button on the opposite door. Already striding around the front of the car, the guard let himself in.

She had her window up tight and the car started before he'd closed the door, and she took the ramps at breakneck speed. Her passenger didn't seem to mind. She suspected he enjoyed the daring ride.

She brought the car to an abrupt halt by the booth, let the guard out and quickly relocked the door. By the time she'd straightened up, he was at her window and making a rolling gesture with his hand. Again she lowered the window several inches.

"Your card?" he asked with an impudent grin.

"Oh." She rummaged in her purse, drew out the card and handed it over. While he studied it, her gaze alternated between the rearview mirror and the windows on either side.

"Looks okay...Lauren." Chomping briskly on his gum, he returned the card, then winked. "Drive carefully now." The last word was muted through her reclosed window. He twisted backward in a move she was sure he practiced regularly on the dance floor, pressed a button and released the gate.

Without another word, Lauren stepped on the gas. She held her breath and didn't expel it until she'd reached the relative safety of Government Center.

With great effort, she forced her rigid fingers to relax on the steering wheel. She took long, deep breaths, feeling safer with each block she put between herself and the parking garage. No one appeared to be following her. To double-check, she swung from one lane to the other, then, a block later to the first lane. She annoyed several drivers, but she didn't care. All that mattered was that the headlights in her rearview mirror were ever varied.

During the drive home, her emotions ran the gamut from fear to confusion to anger. It was the latter that was dominant by the time she pulled up in front of her own garage. She left the engine running and the headlights on; she had a death grip on the wheel again, and her teeth were clenched. She barely had time to debate whether she should sit this way until Matt returned—she didn't expect him for a while yet—when a pair of headlights pierced the darkness behind her.

She sucked in a breath. It was *him*! He'd followed her after all! Frantic, she struggled to decide on the best course of action. The other car neared. She had to think quickly. She could make a mad dash for the safety of the house, but it would take time for her to work around the booby traps.

Too late.

She could run from the car and head for the woods in an attempt to make it to a neighbor's before being overtaken, but the woods, too, were booby-trapped, and that man had been large and ominously physical-looking.

Too risky.

She could lean on the horn in the hope that the noise would either scare him off or arouse someone's attention.

That seemed her only option.

Her hand was on the horn, about to exert force, when the car behind her sounded its own horn in short, repetitive blasts. Her fear-filled gaze snapped to the rearview mirror.

Matt! It was *Matt!*

Lauren had never felt so relieved, or so foolish, or so furious in her entire life. Storming from her car, she met him halfway between the two. "I cannot *take* any more of this!" she screamed, hands clenched by her sides.

"Lauren, what—"

"It's gone on too long! Why *me?* What have *I* ever done to deserve this—this torture?"

"Take it easy, sweetheart—"

"I've *had* it, Matt!" She took a step back, eluding the hands he would have put on her shoulders. "This isn't fair! I'm a nervous wreck. I'm getting a permanent crick in my neck from looking over my shoulder. Someone's following me. Someone isn't. Someone's been in the house. Someone hasn't. Someone's sicced a dog on me. Someone hasn't. I don't know who to trust and who not to. For all I know, *you* were the one who stalked me in Boston!"

"*Me?* I just this minute got back from Leominster!"

"But how do I know that?" she fired at him. She was visibly shaking; the emotional strain was taking its toll. "How do I know *anything?* It's always in the dark. *I'm* always in the dark. I'm afraid to pull into my garage for fear I'll become a sitting duck in a big black net. I'm afraid to go into my house for fear I'll be electrocuted at the front door." Her voice grew as wobbly as her knees. "I can't live this way." She ducked her head and withered into herself, whispering, "Damn it, I can't live this way."

She didn't have the strength to elude Matt this time. He put his arms around her and held her while she cried softly.

"It's okay, sweetheart," he murmured. "Let it out. You'll feel better, and then we'll talk."

"I won't feel...better...."

His arms tightened, hands gently kneading her back. "Sure you will. You're upset now. Sounds like you had a bad day."

"Bad night...."

"Come on. Let's go inside."

A short time later, Lauren was huddled in a corner of the living room sofa, holding the glass of brandy Matt had pressed into her hand. He drew one of the side chairs close and propped his elbows on his knees. "Okay. From the top. What happened tonight?"

"It's not just what happened tonight. It's *everything*."

"But tell me about tonight. I need to know, Lauren."

She studied the rim of the brandy snifter and shrugged. "I panicked." Painstakingly, she explained how she'd walked back to the garage. "Then there was that awful last stretch when only one man was behind me."

"Did you see what he looked like?"

She tipped the snifter until the brandy came perilously close to its rim. "Not really. I glanced back once and got the impression of someone big and tall and dark. Then I started running and didn't look back again."

"He didn't follow you once you ran?"

"I don't know. I didn't look. By the time I reached the garage, I couldn't see him. I conned the guard into walking me up to my car."

"Smart girl."

She snorted. "Fine for you to say. You didn't see the guard."

"It was still smart. A paid guard wouldn't try anything. He'd never get away with it."

"That was what I figured, not that I had much choice at the time."

"But you made it to your car safely. Did you see anyone when you were driving away from the garage?"

"I wasn't looking." She paused to take a healthy swallow of brandy, made a face, recovered, then went on. "I just locked the doors and drove. No one followed me home, at least no one I could see. I was checking for that." Her voice rose. "But when I got here, I didn't know what to do. Everything was dark, and I was sure that if I tried to get into the house, I'd get caught in one of your snares. Then you drove up, and I thought it was *him*—but I really don't know if there *was* a him. The man I saw could have been after me. Then again, he could have been minding his own business."

Matt closed his hand over hers and urged the snifter to her lips again. The brandy was doing its thing; at least she'd stopped shaking.

"I'm sorry I frightened you," he said.

"I thought you'd be later."

"I left Leominster as soon as I could. I was worried."

The eyes Lauren raised brimmed with discouragement. "What am I going to do, Matt?" she whispered. "I can't go on this way."

"I know, sweetheart. I know." His expression was grim. "Do you think someone's keeping tabs on you during the day?"

"While I'm at work, you mean?"

He nodded. "Have you ever gotten the feeling that you're being followed in broad daylight?"

She thought for a minute. "No."

"Ever remember seeing anyone who might fit the description of the man you saw tonight?"

Again she pondered his question, then shrugged in frustration. "There have to be dozens of tall, large-set men who wander through the Marketplace each day. I've never noticed anyone special...other than you." When he glowered at her, she added a sad "That was a compliment," and his glower promptly faded.

"Oh. Thank you."

"What *am* I going to do?"

"I'm thinking. I'm thinking." It was a while before he spoke again, and then it was almost to himself. "You haven't gotten any strange phone calls, heavy-breathing type of thing? And there hasn't been any direct contact, like a note or anything?"

She shook her head, but Matt's attention was on the floor. His brows were knitted together, his lips clamped into a thin line.

"I think," he said at last, "that you should finish your brandy and get to bed. You've had a frightening—"

"Finish my brandy and get to bed? That won't solve anything!"

"There's nothing to be solved tonight. You're safely locked in, and I'm here."

"But tomorrow! I have to go to work tomorrow! You can't be with me every minute, and I don't even want that. I've never been helpless or clinging before, but it seems that lately I'm throwing myself at you the instant you get here."

"I don't mind," he volunteered with a half grin, only to be cut off.

"Well, I do! I don't like what I've become, Matt. I can't continue living this way. I won't!"

What had existed of a grin was wiped clean from his face. "I agree, Lauren. Something has to be done. It's simply a matter of deciding what. Just...just let me sleep on it, okay?"

"I know what should be done. The police should be called in."

He took her hand. "Do you trust me?"

"Of course I trust you. I just think that—"

"Do you *trust* me?"

She knew he was testing her. There was nothing of the little boy about him now. He was all man. Eyes locked with his, she nodded.

"Then let me sleep on it. Give me until morning to figure out what the next step should be."

At that moment, Lauren came out of herself enough to see the lines of fatigue that shadowed Matt's face. He was tired. And worried. "But it's not your responsibility—"

"Till morning?"

She clamped her lower lip between her teeth, then let it slide out. Her nod was slower in coming this time, but when it did, it conveyed the trust he sought.

MORNING ARRIVED, and Lauren awoke to find that Matt was no longer in bed. Tossing her robe on, she hurried off in search of him. He was just replacing the telephone receiver when she entered the kitchen.

"Matt?" She halted abruptly and stood suspended on the threshold. There was something about the tired slump of his shoulders that filled her with dread.

He covered the distance between them and took her in his arms. His words came out in a rush. "I have to go back to California for a couple of days, Lauren. I've just spoken with the airline and made a reservation."

For a minute she couldn't say anything. She'd known that sooner or later he'd be leaving, but... "Now?" she whispered through a tight throat. "Why *now*?"

"It's important. You know I wouldn't leave if it weren't."

"But...what should I do?" The instant she said the words, she hated them, hated herself, hated the situation.

"I think you should consider visiting your parents."

"No."

"What about Beth? You could sleep over at her place."

"No."

"Then take a room at a hotel. Maybe the Bostonian, or the Marriott. Something close to work."

"No!" She freed herself from his grasp and wrapped her arms around her waist. "I'm not running away. I won't be forced out of my own home!"

Matt ran a hand through his hair, which looked as if he'd done that more than once. For that matter, between the creases on his brow and the weary look in his eyes, she wondered if he'd slept at all. He seemed to be exerting a taut control over himself, but then, so was she. She refused to fall apart, to be reduced to a simpering weakling. No strings, she'd told Matt, and no strings there would be.

"It's very important that I go, Lauren."

Her chin was firm. "It's all right. You can go."

"I don't want to."

"But it's all right. I'll be fine." Hadn't she always been before?

"It's just for two or three days."

"I understand."

"No, you don't. You think I'm running out on you."

"I think just what you told me, that it's important for you to fly back." She was feeling distinctly numb. "When does your plane leave?"

He glanced at his watch. "In two hours."

"I can drop you at the airport on my way—"

"You'll be late. I'll drive myself and leave the car at the airport."

She nodded. Without another word, she turned and retraced her steps to the bedroom. She thought of nothing but getting ready for a regular day's work.

Matt showered while she dressed. They said little to each other during breakfast. Only when she had swung her pocketbook to her shoulder did she look at him. Even her self-imposed anesthetization couldn't fully immunize her against the swell of emotion that hit her.

"Have a safe flight," she whispered.

He walked her to the door. "You know how to work the latch for this thing?"

"Yes." He'd reviewed the process in detail when they'd entered the house last night.

"Be sure to reset it once you've let yourself in or out."

"I will."

They passed through and headed for the garage. "And this one?"

"Yes. I've got it now."

"Lauren, I really wish—"

"Shh. Please, Matt. You have to do your thing, and I have to do mine." She pressed the hidden switch that allowed her access to the garage without mishap, but before she could enter the car, Matt stopped her. He put both hands on her shoulders and looked her straight in the eye.

"I know you're angry, Lauren, and hurt. Believe me, I'd never be leaving if I didn't think it was absolutely necessary."

She stared up at him, saying nothing because there was nothing she would permit herself to say. Only when he tugged her close and wrapped his arms tightly around her did she allow herself a moment's softening. Closing her eyes, she leaned into his strength. By the time he'd released her, though, she was on her own again.

"Be cautious, Lauren," he said. His voice was thick, his gaze clouded. "When in doubt, go with your instincts. They're good. Trust them."

For a split second, she wavered. Her instincts told her that Matt shouldn't go, that she needed him here, that whatever it was that drew him back to California wasn't as important as what was happening between them in Massachusetts. Her instincts told her that his trip would bring no good where they were concerned.

But reason ruled. Matt's home and job were in San Francisco. She had no claim on either. She was right in what she'd told him; he had to do his thing and she had to do hers. And hers was to carry on with her life, just as it had been before Matthew Kruger had entered it.

"Take care," she whispered, then slipped into her car. She didn't look back to see Matt by the garage door after she'd backed out and around, or to see him still standing there when she drove down the drive and turned into the street. If she was aware that she'd left part of herself with him, she put that particular ache down to the general upheaval her life had gone through in the past few weeks. Doggedly she kept her sights ahead.

AS THE DAY PASSED, Lauren had less control over her emotional state than she might have liked. Much as she tried not to, she thought of Matt. *He's arriving at the airport now. His plane is taking off now. He's over Pennsylvania, Illinois, Kansas, Utah.* Out of the blue, she'd feel tears in her eyes, and though she cursed her preoccupation, she knew that it was diverting her mind from other thoughts.

Beth, who'd been quick to sense something amiss, tried to get her to talk, but all Lauren would say was that Matt had been called back to his home office for a few days.

"But I thought he was here for another week at least."

"Things come up."

"And he didn't elaborate?" There was an undercurrent of accusation in Beth's words.

Lauren, who was carelessly flipping through the morning's mail, ignored it. "Other than to say it was important that he go." She frowned. "I don't believe it. Another letter for Susan Miles."

"Who's Susan Miles?"

"Beats me. But it's addressed to her, care of this shop. There was one yesterday, too."

"Mark it 'return to sender, addressee unknown' and stick it back in the mail."

"I would if I could, but I can't. There's no return address."

"Postmark?"

"Boston. If whoever sent it doesn't get an answer, he'll just have to show up here to see what's wrong."

"He? How do you know it's a he?"

Lauren held out the letter. "Look at the handwriting. It's heavy. And messy. Has to be a he."

Beth donned her imagination-at-work look. "A he. Hmm, I smell possibilities in this one. You've already got a guy, so forget you. Let's concentrate on me. Suppose, just suppose, some fellow was given the name of a girl he was told worked here. A blind-date kind of thing. Only either he got the girl's name screwed up or the friend who set him up was playing a joke."

"Why would a guy *write* to set up a blind date?"

"Maybe he's too shy to call. Or he's simply taking a new approach. A new approach—that's it." She eyed Lauren through a playful squint. "Not all that different from sitting on a bench for two days, or sitting on it for hours a third day just reading."

"Point taken," Lauren admitted dryly. "I suppose this guy's gorgeous and witty and bright."

"Naturally."

"Then why does his handwriting look like a thug's?"

"It's not like a thug's. It's...creative."

"Ahh. Then whatever is inside this envelope," Lauren said, waving it, "must be equally as creative."

"I'm sure it is." Beth's voice dropped conspiratorially. "Let's open it."

"We can't do that, Beth. It's not addressed to us."

"It's addressed to our shop."

"And what if your gorgeous guy comes in to collect the letters he's incorrectly addressed? He'll be mortified."

"He'll be so taken with me that he won't have time to be mortified. Besides, we can say we threw the letters out. So what harm is there in opening them first? Do you have the other one?"

"Yes, but, Beth, I don't think this is a great idea."

"Don't think." Snatching the gray envelope from Lauren's hand, Beth quickly opened it. She removed a sheet of matching stationery, unfolded it, then turned it over, puzzled. "Blank. There's nothing on it."

Lauren, too, stared at the blank sheet. "Maybe he lost his nerve the second time around."

"Where's the first?"

Lauren fished the envelope from a drawer in the desk and, her own curiosity piqued, opened it. "The same. The paper is blank. What's going on here, Beth?"

"Who knows?" Beth continued the game, but her enthusiasm was waning. "Maybe his tactic is to be mysterious for a while."

"So we have to wait for the next installment to find out who the mad letter writer is?"

Beth shrugged. "Looks that way." She headed for the front of the store, leaving Lauren to dispose of the blank love letters as she saw fit. For some reason Lauren herself didn't understand, she folded both sheets back into their envelopes and tucked the envelopes into the drawer.

This activity had provided only a temporary respite for Lauren, as did most of work that day. Unfortunately, by the time she knew that Matt had landed and been swallowed up in his own life again, she could no longer free herself of those other, more ominous thoughts.

"How'd you like a roommate for a night or two?" she asked Beth when they were getting ready to close the shop. She'd tried to sound nonchalant, but the gesture was lost on Beth, who knew better.

"I'd love it, Lauren. You know that. You're welcome to stay at my place whenever you want."

"I know you have a date—"

"No, I don't."

"Listen, it's okay. I just don't feel like driving back to Lincoln. You can go out. I'll make myself at home—"

"I don't have a date, Lauren."

"But that fellow Joe—"

"Asked me out and I refused. He wanted to go camping. Overnight. I didn't have equipment, and I'm not keen on camping, and I'm even less keen on Joe."

"How do you know? You've just met the guy."

"Exactly. Have you ever heard of camping overnight for a first date?"

Lauren shrugged. "Might have been interesting."

"Maybe for you and Matt. No, chalk that." Beth grunted. "Matt might have left you stranded in the woods while he raced off to scale some nearby peak. How could he simply abandon you this way, Lauren? I still can't believe it."

Lauren kept her voice calm. "He has his own life."

"But he's barged his way into yours—"

"He didn't barge his way in anywhere."

"Okay, then he wormed his way in. He's made himself nearly indispensable—"

"He has *not*. I can do just fine without him."

"Mmm. That's why you can't bear the thought of going home."

Lauren's gaze lowered to the scrap of fabric she was fraying. "It's not that. But after last night I feel...uncomfortable." She'd told Beth earlier about the episode near the garage. "It's still too fresh in my mind."

"Matt wasn't around then, either. Why do men do this, Lauren? Why aren't they around when you need them?"

"It's not a question of need," Lauren rationalized. "I'm independent. I can take care of myself."

"You should go to the police. I think what you're facing is more than even Matt can handle. Why is he so vehement against it?"

"He has good reasons. He may be right."

"Maybe his reasons aren't so noble."

Lauren tensed. "What do you mean?"

"It's occurred to me that much of what's happened to you has been since Matt showed up."

"That's not true! Three of those incidents happened before he ever got here!"

"No," Beth returned, determined to make her point. "If my memory's correct, three of those incidents happened within mere days of his first introducing himself to you. He said he was here in Boston on business. For all you know, he was here in the city that very first time, when the car just missed you on Newbury Street.''

"I'm not sure I like what you're implying.''

"I'm not sure I do, either, but it may be worth considering.''

"Absolutely not! What could Matt possibly have to do with those incidents? What reason could he have to wish me harm?''

"Maybe something to do with Brad?''

"That's impossible. Don't even think it, Beth. It's out of the question.''

No more was said about it, but Beth had accomplished her objective. Lauren fought it. She told herself that Beth was either playing the game she played so well or simply jealous. Lauren closed her mind to it while she and Beth walked over Beacon Hill to Beth's apartment, where they shared a congenial dinner and evening. Later that night, though, while Lauren lay quietly on the sofa bed trying to fall asleep, unwanted thoughts flitted in fragments through her mind.

Ironically, Matt's phone call didn't help. It came at two in the morning, shortly after Lauren had fallen into a restless sleep. The phone was on the table by her head. She nearly jumped out of her skin when it rang.

"Hello?''

"Lauren! I've been worried sick! When there was no answer at the farmhouse, I started calling hotels. You said you *weren't* going to Beth's!'' He sounded angry. That was all Lauren needed.

"Why, Matt, how good of you to call in the middle of the night. I'm fine, thank you. How are you?''

"Lauren, you said you weren't going anywhere!''

"I changed my mind.''

"Damn it, you could have let me know. I was sure something had happened!''

"How could I have let you know? I don't know where you are, much less at what phone number.''

"I'm at home, and I'm the only Matthew Kruger in the San Francisco book!''

"How did I know you'd be trying me? You didn't say anything about calling.''

She heard a deep sigh at the other end of the line. "Right. I'm sorry. It was my fault. Are you okay?''

"I'm tired, Matt.'' *And confused. Very confused.* The sound of Matt's voice, imperious, then gentle, only added to her confusion.

"I'm sorry to be calling so late. I started trying the house an hour and a half ago. When there was no answer, I figured maybe you'd gone to another movie or something, but when you didn't return, I started imagining things and it all began to spiral. You are okay?''

"Yes, I'm okay."

"Nothing happened today?"

"No, nothing happened."

"Thank goodness."

His voice clearly held relief. For that matter, Lauren mused, everything about his voice was clear. He could just as well be calling her from around the corner....

"Well," he went on, less sure of himself now, "I just wanted to hear your voice. And to tell you that I'm going to try to catch an afternoon flight out of here tomorrow. By the time I get into Logan and on the road, it's apt to be pretty late. It may be easier if I go to a hotel—"

"No!" she interrupted. She could hear the fatigue in his voice, and it pulled a string somewhere deep inside her. This was Matt, the man she missed, the man she wanted to see, to be with. "No. Meet me in Lincoln. I'll be there."

"But you may be sleeping. I'll frighten you."

"Just give a honk like you did the other night and I'll know it's you."

"Are you sure?"

"I'm sure."

"Okay, sweetheart." His voice lowered. "I miss you."

"Me, too, Matt."

"See you tomorrow night, then?"

"Uh-huh."

"Take care, sweetheart."

"You, too. Bye-bye, Matt."

She replaced the receiver and sank back to the bed, only then realizing that she hadn't even asked how he was doing. Maybe she hadn't wanted to. Maybe she'd been afraid he'd give her an evasive answer. He hadn't spelled out the reason for his abrupt return to San Francisco—if indeed he was there. Was his business on the West Coast shrouded in mystery, or was her imagination at work again?

After tossing and turning for better than an hour, she finally fell back to sleep. When she awoke on Sunday morning, she felt weary and tense. Even Beth's lighthearted chatter didn't lighten her mood; irrationally, perhaps, she blamed Beth for having planted the seeds of doubt in her mind.

Driving to Lincoln in broad daylight was accomplished comfortably. Lauren arrived there moments before Thomas Gehling pulled up. She liked him instantly, finding him easygoing, intelligent and polite. As they walked through the house, they discussed a wide range of possibilities. She hired him on the spot.

That was the high point of her day. The tension, the confusion, the worry, were back in full swing by the time she'd returned to Boston. Work at the shop was a blessing, but a short-lived one. All too soon she was headed back to Lincoln. This time around, she was a bundle of raw nerves.

A confrontation was imminent. She felt it in every fiber of her being. By nature she was a peaceful, accommodating sort, but the events of the past few weeks had upset her equilibrium. It was one thing to suspect that an unknown lunatic was after her, yet quite another to suspect that it was Matt. He was either with her or against her. She had to know one way or the other.

Arriving home at dusk, she was assailed by every one of the fears she'd been free of that morning. Glancing anxiously from side to side, she inched her way up the drive. Her first thought was to leave the car outside, but she knew that its protection, and hence her own, came from the trap that was set inside. Dashing quickly from the car to the garage, she fumbled to disengage the alarm and raise the door. That done, she quickly brought the car inside, lowered the door and reengaged the snare, then tackled the front door of the house. Beads of sweat were dotting her upper lip by the time she'd finally closed the door behind her and reset the alarm.

Then she made dinner, ate practically none of it and waited. She picked up a book, turned page after page without absorbing a word and waited. She dozed on the living room sofa, awakening with a jolt at the slightest sound—though most were in her dreams—and waited.

Midnight came and went. Then one o'clock. It was nearly one-thirty when she finally heard a car approach. This time she didn't rush to the window. She didn't so much as shift on the sofa. She sat quietly in the dark, waiting.

Chapter Eight

Lauren held her breath when she identified the click and scrape at the front door as the disengagement of the makeshift electrical alarm. Her eyes pierced the darkness, never once leaving the broad oak expanse as, with an aged creak, the door slowly opened. The man who came quietly through was tall, very tall, and large-set. Though he could have doubled for the man she'd seen behind her in Boston on the previous Friday night, there was no doubt in her mind that this time it was Matt.

"You didn't honk," she accused in a voice that shook.

His head twisted. "Lauren!" Setting his suitcase on the floor, he groped for the light switch. The weak glow that subsequently filtered into the living room from the hall was enough to reveal her position on the sofa. "What are you doing up, sweetheart? I thought for sure you'd be in bed."

"You didn't honk."

He paused, turning his head slightly. "The thought of it seemed jarring at this hour. I really didn't want to wake you up." He stood backlighted in the archway of the living room, his face in shadows. "But you weren't sleeping, were you?" Crossing the room, he hunkered down and curled his fingers lightly around her arms. Her skin was cold. "Why aren't you in bed?" he asked softly.

"We have to talk."

"You sound strange. What's wrong?"

She didn't move. "I'm not sure. That's one of the things we have to discuss."

He frowned at his hands, dropped them to the sofa on either side of her hips, then met her gaze. "What is it, Lauren?"

"I've been sitting here thinking. I've spent most of the day thinking. And last night, too."

He sank back on his heels, hands falling to his sides. "About what?"

"You. I want the truth, Matt." It was a struggle to keep her voice steady when so much was at stake, but she managed commendably. "I want all of it. No evasion. No seduction. I want to ask questions and have them answered."

"I don't understand. I've always given you answers—"

"They were never enough, but that may be my fault. Maybe I haven't *asked* enough."

"I don't know what you're getting at."

She tucked her legs more tightly beneath her. "Three weeks ago I was happy. My life was shaping up so beautifully that I had to pinch myself to make sure it was real. Then certain things started happening, and I'm suddenly stuck in the middle of a nightmare. Someone is after me. I don't know who or why."

"What's this got to do with *me*?"

"You showed up right after it all began, Matt. By some coincidence, you appeared out of nowhere. You claim to be a friend of my brother's, but my brother has been dead for a year, so I can't ask him about it. You have biographical facts about Brad, any of which you could have picked up by reading a standard job résumé. You have insight into his character, most of which you could have gained in one night of heavy drinking with him, even if he'd been a total stranger up until then."

"I don't believe this," Matt muttered, but Lauren was just beginning.

"That first night when you introduced yourself to me, you said you'd been in Boston for a week. It was during that very week that I was nearly run down by a car on Newbury Street. Nothing about the car registered with me. It could very easily have been a nondescript rental, just like the one you've been driving."

"Lauren—"

"Then a dog attacked me. You were the one who suggested it might have been trained to pull away when a special whistle was blown. That thought wouldn't even have occurred to me, yet it did to you. Why?"

"It's common knowledge—"

"And then my garage door crashed down." Despite the warmth of the night, her hands were freezing. She tucked them more deeply in the folds of her shirt. "You're a builder. You seemed familiar enough with the workings of that door to be able to rig, and unrig, a malfunction."

"This is absurd, Lauren! Do you know what you're saying?"

"I'm not done," she declared. "Let me finish."

He was on his feet, prowling the room. "I can't wait to hear the rest."

She ignored his sarcasm, knowing only that the time for silence had passed. "There was the matter of an intruder in my house. You found the problem immediately. A lock on one of the windows was broken. In fact, you used that very window to get into the house, supposedly to scout around. How can I be sure it was the first time you'd entered the house that way?" When Matt took a sharp breath to defend himself, she rushed on. "The car that followed me all the way home from Boston was compatible in both size and shade to your rental. And the timing was perfect. You could have left me at my garage, picked up your own car—

even on another floor of the same garage—and tailed me out. Then there was the night when I heard strange noises. You said you were in Leominster. It was a convenient alibi, but I have no proof, do I?''

"I'll give you names and numbers—"

"My car battery went dead; you were the last one to drive the car. Someone followed me late at night in Boston; you conveniently arrived here within minutes after I did.''

"I was in *Leominster*—but I told you that once before, didn't I? I thought we agreed on it.''

"That was what you wanted, for me to agree on it.''

"I wanted you to trust me.''

"So you told me. Many times. And I've been completely taken in, because I thought you were one of the most sincere, straightforward men I've ever met. Maybe I was wrong, Matt. Maybe I've been playing into your hands all along.''

He stood before her then, hands on his hips, his face a mask of steel. The oblique light from the hall did nothing to blunt his obvious irritation. "What brought all this on? That's what I'd like to know. You did trust me. At least, I thought you did. Where did I go wrong?''

Lauren's composure was beginning to slip. If Matt was innocent—and his reaction was far from conclusive on that score—she was going to hate herself for the accusations she'd made. On the other hand, if he was guilty as charged, she was in a lot of trouble.

"You went wrong," she began with a shaky breath, "when you took off for California on Saturday morning.''

"You *were* angry.''

"No. But I was puzzled and maybe a little hurt, because the trip was so sudden and you were so tight-lipped about it. And that got me to thinking, and suddenly there were more questions than ever. I'm an intelligent person, Matt. 'Together,' to quote you. You could have told me anything and I'd have understood. Okay, what happens with your work is your business. But you've shared other things with me, which I realize in hindsight you've been very selective about. Why discuss some things and not others? Unless you're hiding something. Unless there's something you don't want me to know.''

He threw a hand in the air. "It's Beth. You've been listening to Beth. This sounds like one of her harebrained plots.''

Lauren stared him out. "Days ago I wanted to go to the police. Any person in his right mind would do that in a situation like mine. But I didn't go to the police, because you told me not to. You've been adamant about it! *Why?*''

"You want to know why?" Matt raged suddenly. His eyes were narrowed, his head thrust forward. "I'll tell you why! Because your brother, Brad, was up to no good during the last few years of his life, and if I'd gone to the police when I suspected that Brad's boss was behind what was happening to you, it would have all come out. *You'd* have been hurt. I was trying to protect *you!*"

Lauren sat in stunned silence as the warm summer night crowded in on her. One minute she felt smothered, the next chilled. In the third, she was stifling again and began to sweat. Dropping her gaze to the floor, she pressed a finger to her moist upper lip, frowned, then looked back at Matt. "What did you say about Brad?" she asked in a timid whisper.

Matt stood with his feet braced apart, one hand massaging the taut muscles at the back of his neck. At her question, he lowered his head, put two fingers to his forehead and rubbed. "Brad was in trouble." His voice held a blend of sadness and defeat. Lauren knew he'd have to be a consummate actor to produce such a heart-wrenching tone on cue.

"What kind of trouble?" Her stomach had begun to jump. She pressed a hand to it.

"Please. Lauren, you don't want—"

"What kind of trouble?" When he didn't answer, she repeated the question a third time. *"What kind of trouble?"*

Matt sighed in resignation. "He'd been padding invoices and expense vouchers, then pocketing the difference."

"I don't believe you."

"Maybe that's just as well. Brad's dead. Nothing will ever be proved one way or another. Just rumors. Lousy rumors."

"You believe them."

"I knew Brad." He took a quick breath. "Please, don't misunderstand me. Brad and I were close. He was a loyal friend. I respected him in many, many ways."

"But?"

"But all along I knew there was one part of him that was unsettled. It was as if he was looking for an opening, and his boss unwittingly gave him one. Chester Hawkins was a crook. We both knew it. We discussed it many times. Bribes, kickbacks—you name it, Hawkins did it."

"But padding expense vouchers—that's small-time stuff. What could Brad have hoped to gain?"

"It's not small-time when it's done over and over again."

"For how long?"

"Two years, maybe three. It adds up."

"But *why*? Why would he have done it?"

Matt dropped into a side chair. "Maybe he felt it was poetic justice, stealing from a thief. More likely he felt that an accumulation of wealth was the only way he could prove his worth."

Lauren moaned softly. Her head fell back against the sofa and she closed her eyes. When she spoke, her voice was wobbly. "I knew there was too much money. It didn't make sense. Right from the start I wondered, but I took it. I took it and I used it.''

"Which was exactly what you *should* have done!" Matt sat forward and spoke with renewed force. "Brad earned every cent of that money. He was overworked and underpaid for years. What he did might have been punishable in a court of law, but there was still a certain justice to it. He gave Hawkins his life, for God's sake, and there was only a piddling insurance policy on it! Hawkins wasn't big on employee benefits. He gave the bare minimum. Brad earned that money, Lauren. And he wanted you to have it.''

Lauren swallowed hard, trying to ingest all that Matt had told her. "Did he really? Or did you tell me that just to make me feel better?''

"He said it. Believe me—ah, hell." Matt flopped back in the chair. "Believe what you want. The fact is that you've put the money to good use. No one can ever take it away from you.''

They were back to square one. "Someone's trying. Is it this fellow, Hawkins?'' she asked nervously.

"He claims not.''

"You *spoke* to him?''

Matt was out of his seat, pacing again. "What did you think I went to San Francisco for?''

"I didn't know! I assumed it had something to do with your own work. You didn't volunteer any details!''

"I went to confront Hawkins.''

"And?''

"He says he's innocent.''

"Do you believe him?''

"I'm not sure." Matt stopped his pacing and stared at her. "On the one hand, he wouldn't dare try anything. I wasn't the only friend Brad had. If Hawkins tries to pin something on Brad, even posthumously, any number of us will cry foul. Hawkins can't risk that. There's too much that can be pinned right back on him.''

"On the other hand...''

He took a deep breath. "On the other hand, I wouldn't put it past him to try something on the sly. He and Brad had reached a stalemate. Each knew what the other was doing, so it was a form of mutual blackmail. Hawkins didn't dare fire Brad for fear he'd squeal. But Brad's gone now. It's possible that Hawkins thought he'd go after some of that money—''

"By terrorizing *me*?''

"Sick minds work in sick ways. Besides, Hawkins wouldn't do it himself. He'd hire someone. If he's discovered that you've invested the money between the shop and this place, he may be out for his own private form of revenge.''

"So we're back where we started.''

"Not...quite," Matt stated with such quiet thunder that Lauren's pulse skipped a beat before racing on. "There are still certain allegations you've made that have to be resolved. Y'know, you're right." He cocked his head and eyed her insolently. "I may well be the man Hawkins hired, playing you now just as I've played you all along—orchestrating events, then showing up and explaining them away."

"But why *would* you?" she cried.

"You're the one with the answers." He flung himself back into the chair. "You tell me."

"I don't *have* the answers. That's what this—this is all about! I don't have *any* answers. My mind is running in circles!"

"Could be I'm getting paid a pretty penny for this."

"You don't want the money," she protested. "You're not ambitious that way! You told me so the first time we met!"

"Could be I was lying. Could be it was all an act." He jacked forward in the chair. "And since you're hurling accusations, I've got a few of my own. You were a virgin for twenty-nine years. Then you met me, and within a week we became lovers. Strange things were happening to you. You were frightened. You needed protection." He snorted. "Pretty high price to pay for it, I'd say."

She felt as though she'd been slapped. "No! I didn't—"

"Then again, maybe you were truly infatuated. I was different from the men you'd known. More physical. Brawny. But now that you've gotten what you wanted, you're scrabbling for reasons to put me off."

"No, Matt! How can you—"

"I don't meet your high standards. Is that it, Lauren?" His eyes bore into hers. "You're prepared to believe the worst because you just don't think I'm good enough for you?"

Unable to bear another word, Lauren sprang up from the sofa and rounded on him. "That's not true!" she screamed, grabbing his shoulders and shaking him. It was a pitiful gesture, since he was so much larger than she, but her fury was beyond reason. "It's not true! And I wasn't *prepared* to believe the worst!" His face blurred before her eyes. "But I had to know—had to know. I'd never been with another man, because no man had meant anything to me until you came along!" Tears trickled unheeded down her cheeks, and her hands stilled, impotent fingers clutching fistfuls of his shirt. "I've been dying, slowly dying for the past two days, grasping at straws, wondering if it was possible that—that I'd made a big mistake and given you everything and that you were really on the other side."

Her knees gave out then, and she sank to the floor between his legs. Her head was bowed. She wept softly. "It hurt so to...to think that, and I knew I had to get...get it out in the open, but that hurt, too...

and...and..." Her fingers curved around his knee, gently kneading in a silent bid for forgiveness.

Matt put a tentative hand on her hair. "And what, Lauren?" he asked softly.

Her head remained down, her muffled voice punctuated by sniffles. "I love you...and I've hurt you...and somehow this new life that was supposed...supposed to be so wonderful is all messed up!"

With a low groan, he slid to the floor. His thighs flanked hers as he took her into the circle of his arms. "Oh, baby. Sweetheart, shhh." He rocked her tenderly. "You've just said the magic words. Nothing's messed up. Everything's suddenly clear."

She shook her head against his chest, too upset to comprehend.

He spread a large hand over the back of her head, buried his face in her hair and pressed her closer. "It's all right," he whispered between soft kisses. "Everything's going to be all right."

Lauren let her tears flow. They were a purging of sorts. It wasn't that she agreed with Matt or understood things as he seemed to, but being held in his arms this way, absorbing his strength and incredible tenderness, she felt herself slowly emerging from the hell she'd been living for the past few days.

He rubbed her back, caressing her gently. He whispered soft words of endearment and encouragement; with each one the darkness receded and she moved closer to the light. The warmth of his body thawed her inner chill. She fed on his strength like a creature starved for it.

Then he tipped her chin up and kissed her, and the last of her anguish broke and dissipated like a fever at the end of a long illness. She felt suddenly free, lightheaded and very much in love. Shaping her hands to his cheeks, she gave herself up to his kiss; but because she offered as much as she received, Matt was as aroused as she by the time they finally parted, panting.

While she strung slow kisses along the line of his jaw and his chin, she worked at the buttons of first her shirt, then his. His hands were already in full possession of her breasts before she'd finished the latter, and when she came to her knees to press closer, the squeeze of her thighs against the mounting ache between them was a necessity.

From numbness such a short time before to this rich blossoming of the senses, Lauren reeled. Everything about Matt turned her on, from the vitality of the thick, sun-burnished hair through which her fingers wound to the musky scent of the rough, sweat-dampened skin beneath her lips to the virile cords of muscle straining against the rest of her body.

"I love you," she whispered against his mouth. "I love you, Matt." Her hands slid from his head down his chest, savoring the journey. But urgency was quickly mounting. She released the snap of his jeans, then the zipper, and worked her way beneath the waistband of his shorts until her fingers found what they sought. He was thick and hard, needing her in the same way that she needed him.

He gave an openmouthed moan and whispered her name, then set her back and shoved his jeans lower. "Hurry," he rasped as Lauren rocked back on her bottom and tore her own jeans off in jerky movements. He reached for her with urgent fingers, bringing her close until she straddled his thighs.

"Love me, Matt. Please, love me..."

"God, yes..."

His hands covered her buttocks, urging her downward even as she guided him inside her, and there was nothing then but paradise. His hands on her body, stroking...inflaming...lifting. His tongue wet and greedy on her throat, her collarbone, her breasts. Her own hands clutching his bronzed flesh, molding...straining...her mouth rapacious, her hips meeting his every thrust with matching ferocity.

They brought each other to near-peak after near-peak of exquisite sensation, and when the final climax hit, their cries were simultaneous, prolonged and distinctly triumphant.

For long moments, Lauren was aware of nothing but the state of heavenly bliss in which she floated. Then came Matt's ragged breathing. It took her a minute longer to realize that her own throat was contributing to the rasping sound.

Very gradually the gasping eased, then ended, yet neither of them made a move to leave the other's arms. Their bodies remained joined, and Matt defied the limpness of his limbs to hold her even closer.

"I love you, Lauren," he murmured hoarsely. "Please, please don't doubt me again. I think it would—" His voice broke. "It would destroy me."

Her face buried in the warm crook of his neck, she whispered his name over and over again. Her arms, too, had taken on a strength that denied passion's drain, and she held him with no intention of ever letting go. "I'm sorry" came her muffled cry. "I shouldn't have suggested those awful things."

"No, it's good you did. You were right. They had to come out in the open." He tipped her head back and looked into her eyes. "We need the truth, sweetheart. Both of us. There are so many things we can't figure out, but the situation becomes only more complicated if we can't be honest about ourselves and our feelings." With one arm supporting her back, he gently smoothed damp tendrils of hair from her cheeks. "I have insecurities. Lots of them. They hit me like a ton of bricks when I first met you, and they've kept me a little off balance ever since."

"You didn't need to worry about *anything*!"

"But I did. At the start I worried that you'd associate me only with Brad and that you'd transfer the rift between you and him to me. I worried that you'd turn down your nose at my occupation, that you'd categorize me and put me in a slot and wouldn't like the things I suggested we do. Then, when I began to realize how I felt about you, I was afraid you wouldn't feel the same.'' He slid his cheek against her temple. ''And all the time I was worried about what was happening to you. I imagined Hawkins might be behind it, and I was reluctant to tell you the truth. Maybe I wouldn't be able to protect you or catch the bastard before he really hurt you.''

''You'll be dead long before I will if you keep up that worrying,'' Lauren quipped softly, ''and *then* where will I be?''

''Do you love me?''

''I do love you.''

''And you're not bothered by who I am and where I come from?''

''Only that you come from the opposite coast, and that's much too far away.''

A tremor shot through his body and he gave her a bone-crushing squeeze. ''God, you're wonderful. You're beautiful and bright and warm and giving. What did I ever do to deserve you?''

Lauren was thinking the very same thing, but with the pronouns reversed. ''I love you,'' she whispered. She'd never tire of telling him so, and with that knowledge and the intimate closeness of his body, her insides began to quiver. She tightened her lower muscles and was rewarded by the faint catch in Matt's breath; then, as he grew inside her, she began to move.

It was much, much later, after they'd finally sought out her bed, that she turned in his arms. ''Matt?''

His eyes were closed. She was wondering if he was asleep when she heard his low ''Hmm?''

''Do you realize what we did?''

He shifted his hips and smiled smugly. ''Mmm-hmm.''

''But without anything.'' After that first night, Matt had taken the responsibility of protecting her. ''Aren't you worried?''

''You told me to stop worrying.''

''But if we make a baby...''

His eyes opened slowly, but the smugness remained on his face. ''If we make a baby, we'll have it. It'll be beautiful and bright and healthy.''

''But the planning, the logistics...''

The light in his eyes grew brighter. ''I love you, Lauren. If a baby comes out of that love, I think I'd be the happiest man alive.''

With a soft sigh of elation, she nestled more snugly against him. ''Oh, Matt, I love you so.'' Basking in a special glow, lulled by the strong and steady beat of his heart, she fell into a deep and untroubled sleep.

COME MORNING, Lauren and Matt awoke together, showered together, dressed together, cooked and ate breakfast together. Neither seemed to tire of touching the other, or smiling, or whispering those three precious words.

It was only when they were getting ready to drive into Boston that Lauren permitted herself to think beyond the fact of their newly shared love. Matt sat sideways on the sofa, sorting through papers in his briefcase. Curling an arm around his neck, she slid onto his lap.

"We can't go to the police," she began quietly. "You're right. If they start looking into things and somehow come upon Brad's dealings, his memory will be sullied. I'm not sure my parents would care, but I would. So that leaves us back where we began. What should we do?"

Matt finished straightening a pile of letters, set them in the briefcase and snapped it shut. "I think maybe it's time to call in some help. Not the police—someone private." He slipped an arm around her waist. "That way we can control what comes out. Hawkins may be behind this, or it may be someone totally unrelated to him."

"In which case the motive is still a mystery."

"We need a fresh ear, someone who might ask questions we haven't thought of or see things from a new angle." He paused. "Should I get a name and make a call?"

"Yes. We have to do something. I don't want to live with a shadow hanging over me, especially not now."

Matt was in total agreement. Through one of the corporate powers he'd been dealing with in Boston, he contacted a reputable private investigator by the name of Phillip Huber and set up a meeting for the following morning. In the meantime, he stayed as close to Lauren as he could, returning to the shop between business meetings of his own, taking her to lunch, then dinner. When they finally arrived back in Lincoln, it was late. Given the minimum of sleep each had had—not to mention the strain of jet travel on Matt, about which Lauren teased him unmercifully—they were both tired.

Absently she picked up the mail and flipped through it. Gas bill. MasterCard bill. Advertisements. She lifted the next piece of mail, a disconcertingly familiar gray envelope, and stared at it.

Susan Miles. Addressed directly to the farmhouse.

Fingers trembling, she tore open the flap, pulled out the stationery and unfolded it. A separate piece of paper floated to the floor, but once again, the stationery itself was blank. Stooping, she lifted the paper that had been enclosed. Roughly cut at the edges, it was a picture of a gleaming fox fur coat, apparently taken from a magazine. The model had been unceremoniously decapitated.

"Matt?" she called faintly, then louder: "Matt!"

He appeared at the top of the stairs, his shirt unbuttoned, its tails loose. Lauren's anxious expression brought him trotting down immediately.

She spoke quickly. "Last Friday and again on Saturday we received a letter at the shop addressed to a Susan Miles. Neither Beth nor I know anyone by that name. We assumed it was simply a mistake. Now there's a letter addressed to Susan Miles *here*." She held out the piece of stationery and watched him turn it from front to back.

"It's blank."

"So were the other two. The only difference is that this one came with a magazine clipping." She offered it as well. "Just a picture of a fur coat. Nothing else."

Matt studied the clipping, frowned back at the blank sheet of stationery, then took the envelope from her hand and examined the raggedly scrawled address. "There's got to be a message here," he said at last. "We may not be understanding it, but there's got to be one. You say the other two letters were exactly like this one, but without the clipping?"

"That's right. Same gray stationery."

"Same handwriting on the envelope?"

"Yes. And the same Boston postmark. I didn't think much of the first two. They were addressed to the shop. It could have been a simple mistake. Taken with this last one, though, there has to be something more personal in it. Whoever sent them knows my home address. He's got the name wrong, but he knows where I work *and* where I live."

Much as Lauren's stomach was doing, Matt's jaw clenched. "Right." He rubbed his forehead with his finger. "Is it possible that you've been mistaken for someone else? For this Susan Miles, perhaps?"

Lauren didn't say anything. Her heart was hammering, and the knots in her stomach had tightened painfully.

Matt's focus remained on the pieces of paper he held. "Mistaken identity...that would make sense. All along you've had no idea who would have a reason to threaten you. We know there's a chance it could be Hawkins, but if it's not, this might be something to go on. If we could identify and locate this Susan Miles..." He looked up and caught Lauren's stricken expression. "Sweetheart?" When she swayed, he held her arms to steady her. "What is it?"

"I don't believe this is happening," she whispered. Her eyes were wide, dry but filled with the horror of conviction. "I don't believe it. I knew it was too good to be true."

Matt ducked his head, bringing his face level with hers. Every one of his features broadcast love and tenderness, and his voice was filled with hope. "It's okay, sweetheart. It's good, in fact. At least it's another lead to follow, and now that we've contacted an investigator—"

She covered her face with her hands. "My parents were right. I shouldn't have done it. I played with what fate had decreed, and now I'm paying for it."

"Lauren, what—"

"My face, Matt!" she cried. "It didn't always look this way. When I was a very little girl, my bones developed improperly. I was ugly. You saw a picture! You know!"

"My God," he whispered, finally putting the last piece of the puzzle into place. "I thought it was just a bad picture. I never dreamed..." Seizing her wrists, he drew her hands from her face and clutched them to his chest. His eyes slowly toured her features. "You had surgery," he said in amazement.

She nodded. "My chin was practically nonexistent, and my jaw was so badly misaligned that I had trouble eating. That's why I was so skinny."

"And you're so beautiful now. It's incredible!" He took her chin and turned her face first to one side, then the other. "No scars," he announced excitely. "It must have been done from the inside. When, sweetheart?"

"This past spring, right before I came to Boston. I went to a clinic in the Bahamas. The recuperative period was ten weeks. Part of that time I stayed in a rented apartment and returned to the clinic on an outpatient basis."

"Unbelievable." Done with its journey, his gaze coupled with hers. "Just this past spring. So if I'd come six months before, I'd have found you in Bennington looking exactly as I'd expected. It all makes sense now—your inexperience with men, your talk of a new life, a new look..." His eyes lit with pleasure at a new thought. "Part of Brad's money went toward this, didn't it?"

"Some. Insurance paid for most of the surgery, since it had become a legitimate medical problem."

"And you feel better?"

"Physically *and* emotionally." She hesitated. "What about you, Matt? How do you feel?"

"How do I feel?" he echoed, puzzled.

"About what I did. Having plastic surgery and all."

"I think it's marvelous! If you'd looked this gorgeous much earlier, you'd have been snapped up before I could have found you."

"But what do you think about the surgery itself? Does it...bother you?"

"Of course not! Why would it bother me?"

"It bothers my parents. They were against my doing it."

"Hell, it's no different from a kid wearing braces on his teeth to correct a bite problem that would become troublesome in time. Or someone having his nose fixed to correct a deviated septum."

Lauren blushed. "I had that done, too."

"You did!" He grinned. "What did it look like before? The picture I saw was a head-on shot."

"It was crooked," she admitted sheepishly. "And lousy for breathing. I used to snore something awful."

"You sure don't now. I love your nose." He ran a finger down its smooth slope. "It looks so—so natural. The whole thing looks so natural! I'd honestly decided that the picture was just a bad one. Either that, or you'd simply come into your own as you'd grown older."

"Then Brad didn't say anything specific?"

Matt's voice mellowed. "No. It wasn't often that Brad spoke of home, but when he mentioned you, there was always a certain tenderness in his voice. In spite of the rift, you had a special place in his heart. He worried about you. Wow, if he could only see you now!"

"Yeah," Lauren drawled wryly. "I've got a new face that apparently looks so much like someone else's that an enemy of that someone else is out for blood."

"Hey, we don't know that!"

"Well, maybe not blood, but something, that's for sure." She sent a pleading look to the ceiling. "I don't believe this. I just don't believe it. It's like something only Beth could have dreamed up, but she didn't." She arched a brow at Matt. "You do agree that the mistaken-identity theory is the strongest one we've had?"

"Mmm. Not that I'm ruling out Hawkins. But, given the letters for Susan Miles, this theory is more plausible."

"What could the newspaper clipping mean?"

"I don't know. If the letters were real letters with writing and all, it wouldn't be so bad. But three blank sheets of stationery—that's odd."

Lauren sighed. "So, we look for Susan Miles."

"It's the way to go. Seems to me that'd be right down our investigator's alley."

IT SHOULD HAVE BEEN. Lauren and Matt met with the detective at a small coffee shop in Boston early the next morning. They told him everything, from a detailed account of each of Lauren's mysterious incidents to their theories involving, alternately, Brad's boss and Lauren's new face.

Phillip Huber went off in search of Susan Miles. Unfortunately, after a full day of poring through State House and registry records, he could find no evidence of anyone by that name living in the area.

The next day he went through the records of the local and state police, and the day after that he made use of his considerable network of contacts to broaden the search to include the rest of New England and New York.

By Thursday night, Lauren and Matt were no closer to finding Susan Miles than they'd been at the start, and by Friday afternoon, the search was temporarily abandoned.

LAUREN LEFT THE SHOP shortly before four, intent on getting to the bank and back before Matt came for her. He'd been her shadow for most of the week, and she'd loved it. But that day he'd had business to attend to, so she set out on the errand alone.

With the luxury of Jamie's working full-time, Lauren was taking off early. It was a beautiful day. She and Matt planned to return to Lincoln to change, then drive one town over, rent a canoe and explore the Concord River.

She walked at a confident pace, buoyed by the anticipation of the outing, lulled into security by the peaceful week it had been. Since Monday, when the letter for Susan Miles had arrived at the farmhouse, there had been no incidents. Of course, Matt had been close at hand, a visible deterrent to mischief, and Phillip Huber had taken his turn when Matt had been busy.

Lauren had barely turned down the side street on which the bank was located when a car slid smoothly to the curb. Its door opened, and she was jostled inside by a burly hulk that had come from nowhere on her opposite side. Before she knew what had happened, she was seated in the back seat of a car that would have been roomy except for the two giants who crowded her between them.

She tried to squirm, but she was solidly pinned. "What—what is this?" she cried between attempts to free herself.

"Sit still, pretty lady," the man on her left said. "You know what it is."

"I—do—not." She was trying to elbow herself out of the human vise, only to find that the vise had tightened. "Let me out of this car!" she gritted. She began to pound at the thighs flanking hers but succeeded only in having her wrists immobilized by a single beefy paw on either side. "You can't do this!"

"We've just done it," the same man pointed out. His voice was calm, matter-of-fact, infuriating.

"Well—" she kicked out "—I'm not—" she writhed lower in the seat "—having it!" She managed to hike herself forward but was pitched back by the arm of steel that crossed her collarbone and tightened. She bit at the arm and heard a low grunt. Before she could struggle free, she was slapped viciously across the side of her head. Sharp pain radiated through her entire skull, rendering her utterly dazed. She sagged limply against the seat and fought to catch her breath.

"That's better," the man on her left said. "Now sit there and *don't move.*"

She couldn't have moved if she'd tried, and she couldn't even try. The blow had robbed her of what little strength had remained after her futile attempt to escape. Her head lolled against the upholstered seat, and for long moments she could do nothing but hope to regain her equilibrium. Her jaw hurt something fierce, and she felt a momentary flash of hysteria.

If they'd broken her jaw after all she'd gone through to set it right, after all she was going through because she *had* set it right...

"You've got the wrong girl," she managed to mumble through stiff lips.

"Mmm" came a hum from her left. "Somehow we knew you'd say that."

"You do." Gingerly she worked her jaw. It was sore, but at least it functioned. "I don't really look like this...I had repair work done to correct a problem..."

"We know the problem."

The one on the left was apparently the designated speaker. She dared a glance at him. He was dark-haired, dark-eyed, dark-looking in every respect. His eyes were focused straight ahead, following the course the driver was taking.

"If you know the problem," Lauren ventured, "then you know this is all a mistake."

"The problem is that you didn't want to be found." He looked at her then, and she cringed under his scrutiny. "It's subtle, I have to say that much. You're clever. Didn't do anything drastic, thought we'd be off looking for someone *completely* different. Or maybe you just thought what you had was too beautiful to tamper much with. You always were a haughty bitch."

"You've got the wrong woman," Lauren pleaded in a shaky voice. "As God is my witness, I'm telling the truth. The surgery I had was to correct a problem I've had from childhood. You can contact the clinic. My doctor will tell you."

The man was looking forward again, a smug look on his face. "We've already been to the clinic. That was a fancy job you did with the records, and if we were stupid we might have been put off. But we're not stupid, Susan. I think it's about time you realize that."

"I'm not Susan! I know you think I'm Susan Miles, because that's the name on those envelopes, but *my* name is Lauren Stevenson! Lauren Stevenson, from Bennington, Vermont. I have family and friends still there—you can check."

"Lauren Stevenson." He rolled the name around on his tongue in a way that made her want to vomit. "It's as good an alias as any."

"It's *not* an alias!"

Dark eyes glittered dangerously back at her. "Keep your voice down. I have a headache."

"I'll talk as loud as I want—" she fairly shouted, only to have her words cut off by the human mitt that clamped over her mouth. It had come from the right, but the voice, as always, came from the left.

"I'll gag you. Is that what you want?"

"No," Lauren answered the instant the mitt had left her mouth. She had to be able to communicate if she was to get anywhere.

"Then keep your voice down. And talk with respect." The last had been tacked on almost as an afterthought, but the man appeared to find immense satisfaction in it.

She wasn't about to argue. Physically, she was outsized and outnumbered. All three men—one on either side of her, plus the driver—were huge. Their sedate business suits did nothing to disguise the bulk of their physiques. Intellectually, though, she had to believe she was at least on a par with them, if not above. Yes, she was terrified, and terror had a way of fudging the workings of the mind. But if she could stay cool and somehow control her fear, she had a chance.

In keeping with that, she considered her captor's command. If it was a respectful tone he wanted, a respectful tone he'd get. Far more could be accomplished with sugar than with vinegar.

"Who are you?" she asked quietly, directing her efforts solely to the man on the left.

"Now, that is an insult if I ever heard one. You know who I am."

"I don't."

"I sure know you." He tilted his head to the side and studied her lazily. "You're looking good, Susan. Hair's a little shorter. Face looks good. Makeup's different. Easing up on it, are you?"

"Where are you taking me?"

He gave a careless shrug. "I'm not sure."

"What are you going to do with me?"

"I'm not sure."

"You must have a plan."

"Oh, yes."

She waited, but he said nothing more, so she dropped her gaze to her lap. "The plan is to make me nervous. Just as you've been doing for the past two weeks."

He puckered his lips, then relaxed them in acknowledgement of her perception. "Very good."

"But you do have the wrong person," she argued, albeit in a respectful tone. "The first few things you did didn't even make me nervous, because I had no reason to suspect there was anything to them."

"You wised up."

"Not really. It was the mail for Susan Miles that pulled it all together. Up until then I couldn't imagine what anyone would have against me." The issue of Chester Hawkins was irrelevant. "That's when I realized it had to be a case of mistaken identity."

"Sure," he drawled.

Lauren felt a movement in the arm that was pressed against her right side, and she looked sharply toward the hulk connected to it. The man was laughing. Silently, but laughing nonetheless. On the one hand, she was livid; on the other, she was more frightened than ever. They were obviously prepared for her denials, which practically defeated her efforts before they'd begun, but she wouldn't give up. There had to be *some* way out of this mess—if only she could find it!

Chapter Nine

For the first time since her abduction, Lauren looked beyond the confines of the car to the outside world. If she'd expected to see narrow, unfamiliar streets, she was mistaken. The car was on Storrow Drive, taking the very same route out of the city that she traveled every day.

She wished she knew what her wardens were up to, but she hadn't gotten that far yet, so she thought of Matt. Surely he'd have arrived at the shop. Surely he and Beth would be getting nervous when she didn't return from the bank. The bank!

"I have money," she exclaimed in a burst of hope. "If it's money you want, I'll give you all I've got." She fumbled in her purse for the envelope containing the cash and checks she'd been on her way to deposit, but her offer was immediately denied.

"We don't want money. The boss pays us plenty."

"Who's the boss?"

"Come on, Susan. We're not really as dumb as you'd like to think."

"I don't think you're dumb at all," Lauren declared quietly. "You've just made an innocent mistake. I'm not Susan, and I don't know who 'the boss' is. And *because* you're not stupid, you'll realize that I'm telling you the truth before you do anything drastic. If you go ahead with whatever you're planning, sooner or later someone *will* call you stupid—because you'll have done whatever you're planning to do to the wrong person."

He shot her a sidelong glance. "You've gotten quick with words. You never used to talk this much."

"Maybe Susan Miles didn't, but I always have. Look, there are any number of people—people who've known me for years—who can vouch for my identity."

"Like the medical records in that clinic did?" His question dripped of sarcasm.

"If you don't believe the records, that's not my problem."

"But it is. Seems to me it's very much your problem."

He was right. She had to take a different tack. "Okay. So you don't believe the records and you won't believe my friends. You tell me. Who am I supposed to be? Just who *is* this Susan Miles?''

"You want to play games? I'll play games. Susan Miles was the boss's best girl. He gave her everything any woman could want—'' his eyes pierced Lauren's and his voice grew emphatic ''—like a safe full of jewels and a closet full of furs. Where are they, Susan? We haven't been able to find them yet. Did you sell everything to bankroll that little shop you've got, or the house?''

"Jewels?''

"And furs.''

"That clipping,'' she murmured, horrified. "Matt was right. There was a message in the clipping, but we just didn't get it.''

The man on her left said nothing.

"I don't have jewels *or* furs. I bought the shop and the house with a legacy from my brother, who died a year ago.'' In other circumstances she'd never have volunteered that information, but these were unusual circumstances, to say the least.

"A legacy from your brother. Touching, but not terribly original, although I suppose it is different from the dead-uncle or maiden-aunt story, or that of the parents who were tragically killed in an automobile accident.''

"My parents are alive and well and living in Bennington, Vermont. Check it out in a phone book. Colin and Nadine Stevenson.''

The man on her left was silent.

"How *else* would I get money to open that shop? I've never had anything of my own like that before.''

"Oh, please.''

"I did?''

"How quickly you forget.''

"What was it? What did I own?''

"A charming little boutique in Westwood Village. Actually, you were running it into the ground. After you died, the boss put one of his own men in charge, and it's begun to turn a pretty profit.''

"I *died*?'' Lauren felt as if she were in the middle of a slapstick comedy, only nothing was funny. She was totally bewildered. "But if I died, what am I doing here and why are you after me?''

The man on her left seemed to weary of her questions. "You didn't die,'' he growled. "You just made it look like you'd died. You took off with the jewels and furs, changed your face, bought your shop and your house and thought you could get away scot-free.'' His expression grew even darker. "Well, let me tell you, no one does that to the boss and gets away with it. And no one does it to *me*!''

"What did I do to you?'' she whispered fearfully.

"You made a fool of me. I was the one who reported that you burned to death in that car."

"Oh."

"Yes, 'oh.' It's been a sweet pleasure putting you through hell these past couple of weeks. What was it like, Susan, knowing someone was on to you?"

"I *didn't*. I told you—"

"I'll bet you didn't believe it at first. You always were arrogant, with your pretty little nose stuck up in the air."

"It's not my nose—"

"When you finally admitted to yourself that you'd been found out, did you think of running? It wouldn't have done you any good. We'd have been right on your heels." He sniffed loudly. Lauren decided he had a deviated septum of his own. "I've enjoyed it. And the best is yet to come. What I've got planned for today will singe your hair. I mean *really*, this time. Think about *that* while we take our little drive."

Their "little drive" had already taken them to the outskirts of Lincoln. Lauren stared out the window and swallowed hard. *Singe?* She began to shake. What was he planning? Did he intend to kill her? She had to escape. And soon. But how?

They turned off Route 2 and began the drive down the street she took each night. She would have stiffened in her seat, or sat straighter, but she had precious little room to move in and barely more strength. Her arms and legs were beginning to ache from a combination of tension and the steady pressure applied from both sides. Her face hurt. Her stomach was knotting.

"Where are we going?" she asked in a small voice.

"Don't you recognize the streets?"

At that moment they turned down the very road that would lead to her house.

"Thought you might want to take a last look."

"A...last look?"

The man on her left said nothing.

"This is a mistake. It's all a mistake. I really am Lauren Stevenson. *Really*."

"Sure."

She took a quick breath. "Look, you can come inside the house and I'll show you everything. I have identification—a birth certificate, college diplomas, even pictures of my family." Her captor's snort told her what he thought of the validity of that identification. She barely had time to wonder how one could possibly forge family pictures when another thought hit her. "I have a passport! Picture and all!" It didn't take a snort from her left for her to realize she'd struck out again. The passport would do her no good. If there'd been various point-of-entry stamps recorded over a period of time, she might have proved that Lauren Stevenson had existed long before Susan Miles had supposedly died. But Lauren's passport had been issued shortly before her trip to the Bahamas. Ironically, she hadn't needed it; it had never even been stamped. And yes, the picture was of her "before" face, but the files in the clinic had contained a similar picture, which these men had written off.

"So much for identification," she muttered under her breath. Then her head shot up. "My car! The registration!" Her face dropped again. "I reregistered it when I came to Massachusetts."

The man on her left seemed to be enjoying himself. "Keep thinking, pretty lady. See if you can come up with something we haven't already looked over. Don't forget, we've been through most of your belongings."

Lauren's nostrils flared, and for a minute she forgot herself. "You know, it wasn't so bad that you sampled my perfume and fiddled with my shoes. If that's what turns you on, okay. But my *underwear*? I mean, there's kinky and then there's—ahh!" Her arm had been wrenched up sharply against her back. She twisted to ease the pain. "Please," she gasped out in a whisper. "Please—that hurts!"

"I don't have to take your smart mouth. You're not calling the shots around here—*I* am!"

"Please," she begged, then gasped again when her arm was released. She hugged it close and alternately rubbed her elbow and her shoulder.

By this time the car was approaching the farmhouse. Lauren held her breath as she peered out the window, praying that Matt might be there, though she knew he wouldn't be. He was in Boston, waiting for her, maybe out looking for her by now.

The driver slowed in front of the garage, shifted into reverse, backed the car around and headed for the street again.

"Weird place," the man on her left said. "Pretty run-down. I really thought you had more class."

Lauren bit her lip and said nothing. She gazed longingly out of the window, hoping to see a neighbor walking along the side of the road, in which case she'd force some sort of ruckus inside the car that would attract attention. But she saw no one. The road was as quiet and peaceful as it had always been.

To her amazement, they drove on into the center of town. She marveled at the gall of her keepers, until she realized that she couldn't have made a stir if she'd tried. Large hands suddenly manacled both of her arms, just as burly legs had gripped her calves. She might have bucked in the middle, but no one outside the car would have noticed. And if she yelled—

"Don't even think it," the man on her left advised. "Mouse here has a mean right hook. It'll be even meaner the second time around."

"But if you're going to kill me anyway, why would it matter?"

He grinned. "The pain, Susan. The suffering. It'll be bad enough for you as it is. If you want it worse, well, then, go ahead and scream."

Lauren didn't scream. But she did decide that this man's grin had to be the ugliest thing she'd ever seen. And she vowed that if she ever escaped, she'd take great pleasure in personally wiping if from his smug face!

They passed the police station, and she stifled a cry. They passed the market, and she bit her lip. "You won't get away with this. There are two good men who are probably on our trail right now."

"Two good men? Well, I know about the dick you hired. I suppose he's a good man, but he won't find a thing. As for Kruger, haven't you figured that out yet?"

"Figured what out?"

"He's one of ours."

She didn't even blink. "You're lying."

The man on her left shrugged. "Suit yourself. Cling to romantic illusion if you want."

"You can say anything else and it might make me nervous. But Matt—one of *yours*? Not by a long shot."

"What do you think his quickie trip to the coast last weekend was for, if not to check in with the boss?"

"I know what his trip was for, and it wasn't your boss he was checking in with."

"You're awfully sure of yourself."

"Where Matt's concerned, yes."

"Why? What proof do you have that he's not with us?"

She knew she'd be wasting her breath to mention things like love and trust. "He has the proof. Or, if you want to be crude, it was on my sheets the morning after we first made love. I was a virgin. If Matt had been with you, he'd have known something was strange. Unless, of course, your boss is some kind of eunuch."

"A virgin," the man on her left mused. "Kruger didn't mention that to us."

"Of course not. He doesn't know you from Adam."

When he shrugged again and simply repeated, "Suit yourself," Lauren knew she'd scored a point.

That was the last bit of satisfaction she was to have in a while. They left Lincoln behind and drove along backcountry roads with no obvious destination, at least none obvious to Lauren. Her mind jumped ahead, touching on possible stopping places and possible forms of punishment in store for her, then recoiled in fear, seeking refuge in more purposeful thoughts.

"Did she have any birthmarks?" Lauren asked suddenly.

The man on her left frowned at her.

"Susan Miles. Did she have any distinctive birthmarks? There had to be *some* way I can prove I'm not her."

"Birthmarks. That's an interesting thought. I could ask the boss about it. Do *you* have any distinctive birthmarks?"

"No."

"Are you sure?"

"Yes."

"Maybe we should pull over to the side of the road. If you strip, I can check you out."

He was goading her. She looked away. "I don't have any birthmarks," she muttered half to herself as she shriveled into the seat. Her arms and legs had been released once they'd left Lincoln proper, but she might as well have been shackled for the little freedom she'd gained. Shoulders hunched, she tried to minimize contact with the bodies on either side by making herself more narrow. It was a token gesture; the more she narrowed, the more the two men spread.

They drove on and on. She lost track of their direction, and much of the scenery was unfamiliar. With each mile, though, she grew more edgy. They couldn't drive forever. Sooner or later they'd have to stop. And what then?

"Y'know," the man on her left offered, "you really blew it. You had it all. The boss adored you—"

"Who is he?"

"Oh, Lord."

"What's his name? If he's the one who's behind all this, don't I have a right to know his name?"

"You don't have *any* rights, pretty lady. You gave them up when you double-crossed him."

"I didn't double-cross anyone!"

His nonchalance faded. "I'd watch my tone if I were you. It's getting uppity, and if there's one thing Mouse can't stand, it's uppity women. Right, Mouse?"

Mouse grunted.

"I'm sorry," Lauren said as conciliatorily as she could. "I didn't mean to sound uppity. It's just that you assume I know everything, but I don't, and I feel as if this whole thing has to be an awful joke, except no one's laughing, and I'm sitting here trying to figure out a way to prove to you who I am, but my mind is getting all foggy and...and..." She'd begun to shake. Tucking in her chin, she closed her eyes. "I don't feel very well."

"Throw up in this car, lady, and I'll make you lick it up."

She swallowed hard against the rising bile and took several deep breaths through her nose. The strain was getting to her. Her insides continued to shake; she wrapped her arms around her middle as though to hold them still, but it didn't work. She was hot and tired and positively terrified.

"It's amazing," the man on her left said. "You're quite an actress, after all. Funny, you should be such a flop in Hollywood."

"I thought you said Susan had a boutique," Lauren murmured weakly.

"Yeah. But she was like everyone else in that town. Between running the boutique and pleasing the boss, she read for every bit part she could. Had a couple of walk-ons." He sent her a look of ridicule. "She wasn't much of an actress, at least not on the silver screen. What she's doing now is remarkable."

"I have never been, nor had the slightest desire to be, an actress."

"Sure."

Lauren didn't have the strength to argue further, and they didn't stop driving. Dusk fell over the landscape. She thought she'd explode if something didn't happen soon. Once she cast a glance over her shoulder. The man on her left picked up on it instantly.

"Sorry. No one's following."

She grew defensive. "Aren't we stopping for dinner or something?"

He simply laughed.

"Or the bathroom? Don't any of you need one?"

"We're like camels. You'd better be, too. No, we're not stopping. Sorry, but you'll have to think of some other way to escape."

She tried. Oh, Lord, she tried. But, imprisoned in the car between two dark-suited sides of beef, she was hamstrung. There was no hope for escape unless they stopped, and it terrified her to think of where that would be and what they had planned for her then.

Just as she was beginning to bemoan the darkness, she noticed that the car was heading back toward the city. Of course. It made sense. Psychological torture. The purpose of the long ride had been to set her further on edge.

"Look, you've accomplished what you've wanted," she confessed without pride. "I'm thoroughly frightened. You can drop me off anywhere. I'll even take my chances and thumb a ride home."

"Is that what you thought, that we'd just let you go? Susan, Susan, how naive you are."

"What are you planning?"

The man on her left made a ceremony of debating whether or not to tell her. He moistened his lips, scratched the back of his head, then shrugged. "I guess it's time you knew. We're gonna do what we thought had been done months ago."

Lauren's heart was slamming against her breast. "What was that?"

"Your car plunged off the road and burst into flames. There was nothing left but ashes. The ashes were supposed to be you, so the boss gave you a fine burial." He sighed. "In this case, the burial came before the death, so we're kinda doing things ass-backward. But you will burn, Susan. Take that as a promise. You will burn.''

Where Lauren got the breath to speak was a mystery. Perhaps the source was her desperation. ''It's a threat, and you won't get away with it.''

''Oh, we'll get away with it, all right. We're not novices at this type of thing.''

''You're killers, then. Hit men. Is your boss connected with the mob? Well, let me tell you, if the mob kills its own, that's one thing. But I've got nothing to do with the mob or your boss or Susan Miles or you, and that makes me an innocent victim. I swear, you won't get away with it!''

The man on her left laughed. ''Ah, pretty lady, that's priceless. Tell me, what do you intend to do once you're dead? Haunt us?'' He laughed again.

Lauren gritted her teeth, no mean feat since they were chattering. ''You'll get yours. So help me, you'll get yours.''

When his laugh only came louder, she lapsed into silence. She'd save her strength, she decided. At some place, at some time, she'd glimpse a chance to escape. She'd need every resource she had when that time came.

Unfortunately, she couldn't seem to glimpse that chance to escape. After they had arrived back in Boston, the car drove down Atlantic Avenue, parallel to the harbor. It turned into a darkened path, continued to the end and stopped.

''Let's go,'' the man on her left said.

Before he'd even left the car, the man on her right had seized her. His arms were like cords of steel around her legs and shoulders. She was literally crunched into a ball with her face smothered against his chest. As she was carried from the car, she called on those resources she'd saved to try to free herself, but her bonds only tightened. Her scream was a pathetic sound muffled against the man's shirt, and she grew dizzy from the lack of air.

Terror was a driving force, though. Frantically she fought against the arms that held her. Futilely she tried to turn her head and gasp for air. While the doomed battle waged, she was carted up a flight of stairs, then another and another. Her captors' footsteps hammered against the wood planks, each forceful beat driving another nail into her coffin.

Then she was released, dumped unceremoniously onto the floor of a cavernous room. Gasping and trembling, she pushed herself up and looked around. It was dark, but she knew she was in a warehouse—rank and decaying, abandoned warehouse.

The two men loomed over her. Their bodies were straight, their legs planted firmly apart. Their stance was aggressive, but it couldn't have intimidated her any more than she already was.

The man who'd been on her left abruptly hunkered down. She inched back on the floor, but she couldn't escape his hand when he took a strand of her hair between his fingers. He spoke with lethal quiet. "Your final resting place, pretty lady. Take a look around. Try to find a way out. It'll keep your mind busy."

"Where are you going?" she whispered.

"I've got a call to make."

"To whom?"

He let the strand of hair sift through his fingers. "Who do you think?"

"Your boss?" A sudden flare of fury gave her voice greater force. "You tell him for me that he's an idiot! You tell him that he's murdering the wrong woman and that he'll pay—"

When the man raised his hand, palm up, she ducked her head and shrank back. But he didn't hit her. Instead, he slowly lowered his hand until it gently brushed her cheek. "Such a pretty face," he murmured. "Such a shame—"

Her lips moved in a mere whisper. "You know I'm telling the truth. You do."

"I know you'd like to think that. It's okay. Hold on to the hope if you want. It won't be much longer. We'll be back soon."

"And then?" The devil made her ask that. Her eyes were wide with pleading.

"Then," he answered quietly, ever calmly, "we will sprinkle you with gasoline and set you on fire." She gasped and began to shake her head, but he went on. Too late, she realized she'd played into his hands by asking what he planned to do. Clearly, he took pleasure in her horror. "We'll watch you burn, Susan. This time there will be no doubt that you've died."

"Someone...will find me."

"I think not. Y'see, there's a contract out on this building. The man who owns it wants to build condominiums here, like those others along the waterfront, only he's a little strapped for money." The man glanced at his watch. "Roughly two hours from now, one of Boston's best torches will set fire to this place. It'll go up so quick that by the time the fire department gets here, the floor you're on will have long since fallen through. Your ashes will be hopelessly scattered. There's no way anyone will know you've been here, much less be able to prove you died here."

"Please," she cried, feebly grasping the lapels of his jacket, "please don't do this."

"Are you sorry, Susan? Do you finally regret what you've done?"

Lauren was weeping softly. "I haven't done anything...you *have* to believe me...*I'm not Susan Miles!*"

The man threw back his head, took a deep breath and stood up. Together with his sidekick, he made the long walk across the rotting floor. At the door, he looked back.

"You can scream as much as you want. No one will hear you. And Mouse will be right outside this door in case you decide you want to take a walk." He glanced at his buddy. "I think he'd like to get his hands on you again. Right, Mouse?"

Lauren never heard Mouse's answer. She found herself alone, trembling wildly and feeling more frightened than ever. For long moments of mental paralysis, she remained where she was. Then the bottom line came to her. It was do or die. Life or death. Scrambling to her feet, she began to explore her prison, seeking any possible hole or loose plank or trapdoor that might offer escape.

THE BOSS WAS LOUNGING by the pool when his houseboy brought out the cordless phone. He took it, nodded at the boy in dismissal, then put the instrument to his ear. "Yes?"

"We have her. She's safely tucked away. And she's dying just thinking about dying."

"Good. When will you do it?"

"Soon. Uh—did you get the pictures I sent?"

"This morning."

"What do you think?"

"With her hair that way and the clothes, she looks a little younger, more innocent, but it's Susan, all right."

"Are you sure?"

There was a pause. "Aren't you?"

"I thought I was until we picked her up today. Somehow, close up, she seems different."

"That was her intent."

"No. Not just in looks, but in character. The woman we've got does seem more innocent. Susan would have tried a come-on. She'd have promised us all kinds of little favors if we let her go. This one hasn't done that—like it's never occurred to her that she's got a marketable commodity. She's terrified, but half of it seems to be that we won't believe her story. Either Susan has suddenly become one hell of an actress, or we've been tricked."

The boss lit a cigarette and took a long drag. "You think it's someone else?"

A pause. "I'm not sure."

"Is it possible that Susan could have set up someone else to smoke us out?"

"Possible, but not probable. This one claims she had her face fixed to repair a medical problem, just like the clinic records said. If she's telling the truth, it'd be just too convenient that Susan would have happened to

find her, looking so similar and all. And if she knew about Susan, she'd
have squealed by now. She's scared, really scared."

"So it wasn't a setup. It has to be Susan."

"Or someone who looks like her."

Silence dominated the next half minute. Then, "It's not like you to get
cold feet."

"That's what I've been telling myself, but something just doesn't feel
right. If we do have the wrong woman, we'll be in trouble."

"I thought you had it arranged so that no one would know."

"I do. It's foolproof."

"So what's the problem? If it's really Susan, she'll be getting her due.
If it's not Susan, but someone she set up to take the fall for her, let her
take the fall. That'll get Susan to shaking all the more."

"And if it's simply a case of mistaken identity?"

"I can't believe that. The resemblance is too strong."

"But we'll never know. That's the problem. Once this one's dead,
we'll never know for sure whether we've taken care of Susan or not."

"Damn it, what do you suggest?"

"I suggest...that we let this one escape and then continue to follow
her for a while. If she suddenly runs from Boston and tries to change her
looks again and sets herself up somewhere else, we'll know for sure that
she's Susan. She won't have a head start on us this time. We'll be watching her constantly."

"I don't like this. I want Susan dead."

"So do I. But I want to make sure it *is* Susan who's dead."

"I thought this was all clear-cut. You'd found her. You'd been tor-
menting her. You've got her set to fry. It's all very neat. I don't like
waffling."

"It's your decision, Boss."

The silence this time was the lengthiest yet. It ended with a low growl
of frustration. "Ah, hell. Let the girl go. Then follow her. Do you understand? *Follow her.* If you lose her, so help me, you'll die right along
with her!"

"Right."

"And let me know what's happening."

"Right."

LAUREN WAS AMAZED by the simplicity of her escape, although she assumed anything would have seemed simple in comparison to what she'd
been through and the fate she'd so vividly been made to envision. After
a lengthy search of the room, she'd found old planks sealing up a shaft.
She'd pried them off—most had crumbled in her hands—and discovered
a door leading to what was a cross between a dumbwaiter and a freight
elevator. After climbing onto the platform, she'd pulled and tugged on a

fraying cord of rope until she'd lowered the platform to its base. Then she'd shouldered her way through the rotting wood of the door and burst into a run along the street floor of the warehouse. Moments later, she was in the summer night's air.

Smelling vaguely of dead fish and other refuse, the air was the sweetest she'd ever breathed. But she didn't pause to savor it. She continued running out to Atlantic Avenue, veered left around the corner and didn't stop until she'd reached the first of the waterfront restaurants. She barged inside and made her way to the maître d's desk.

"I need a phone," she gasped, hunching her shoulders against the pain in her chest.

The maître d' smiled politely and gestured. "Right over there, in front of the rest rooms."

"No! I don't dare!" She shot a glance at the phone by his hand. "You've got one here. I'm being followed, and if I go back there, they're apt to catch...me again and I can't risk it...because they want to kill me and I...have to make this call. Please?" Her breath was coming in agonizing gulps, but she was beyond caring.

"This phone is reserved for—"

"Please!" she whispered. "It's critical!"

"I could call the police for you."

"Let me...please?"

Whether he acquiesced because, in her disheveled state, she didn't look like a troublemaker, or because he had a hidden streak of protectiveness in him, Lauren would never know. As soon as he reached to turn the phone her way, she snatched up the receiver and began to punch out the number of the shop. It was the closest place Matt might be, unless he was out searching. She had to try three times before her shaking fingers hit the right buttons.

"Lauren! My God, where *are* you?" Beth exclaimed. "We've been looking all over for you! Matt's half out of his mind, and the police won't do anything about a missing person for at least twenty-four—"

"Where is he? I need him, Beth. Where is he?"

"You sound awful!"

"Where's Matt?"

"He's out looking for you. He calls in here every few minutes. We've got Jamie stationed at your house."

Lauren's fingers had a death grip on the ridge of wood running around the top of the maître d's desk. "I'm at Fathoms. The restaurant. On Atlantic Avenue. Tell him to come *right away*."

"Where have you been? Are you all right?"

"Just tell Matt. I have to go." Lauren set the receiver back in its cradle, looked up at the maître d' and said, "You can call the police now." Then her knees buckled and she sank to the floor in a dead faint.

By the time she came to, she was lying on a couch in the manager's office. It took her a minute to get her bearings; then she bolted up, only to be restrained by two firm but gentle pairs of hands.

"It's all right, miss. You're safe. The police are on their way."

She recognized the maître d' but looked warily at his companion.

"I'm the manager, and you're going to be just fine."

"Matt...Matthew Kruger...he'll be looking for me."

"It's all right," the manager assured her. "The police will be here any minute. We won't let him get to you—"

"No! He's my—my—he's okay. He's not one of them. I need him."

The two men exchanged a glance before the manager spoke again. "Then we should let him in?"

"Yes!"

He nodded toward the maître d' who turned and left. When the door opened several minutes later, two uniformed officers entered. By this time, Lauren was sitting upright, sipping shakily from a glass of water. One of the officers sat down beside her on the couch; the other knelt before her and began to ask questions. Lauren barely heard the questions, much less her answers. At the slightest movement or sound, her eyes flew toward the door.

After what seemed forever, but was probably no longer than fifteen minutes, Matt burst in. His eyes were wild, his tanned skin was pale and his entire body was trembling, but that didn't stop him from catching Lauren when she rocketed into his arms or from crushing her tightly to him.

Brokenly, he whispered her name. He took her weight when her legs seemed to dissolve from under her and melded her body to his. She was crying softly, clinging to his neck, unable to say anything for a very long time. At last he lifted her and carried her back to the couch, which the seated officer had vacated for that purpose. Taking her onto his lap, Matt began to stroke her hair, her back, her arms.

"It's all right, sweetheart. Everything's going to be all right. I'm here. Shh." His breath was warm on her forehead, her ear, her cheek.

"Oh, Matt...you have...no idea..."

Framing her head with his hands, Matt examined her closely. "Are you all right?" His gaze focused on the faintly discolored side of her face, and his voice came out in a croak. "What happened to your cheek?"

"He hit me. It was Mouse, but he wasn't the one in charge."

Matt looked up quickly at the manager. "Can we get some ice for this?"

The man nodded and hurried out, but Matt's attention was already back on Lauren. "Can you talk about it, sweetheart? From the beginning?" His thumbs stroked the tears from beneath her eyes. "The officers will listen. You'll have to go through it only once."

Nodding, Lauren slowly launched into her tale. It was interrupted from time to time—when the ice arrived; when she began to cry again; when Phillip, who'd been out searching for her, too, joined them—but she managed to get through it all before she collapsed, emotionally drained, against Matt.

It was Phillip, soft-spoken and dependable, who turned to the officers. "You'll look for the car?"

"You bet," the older of the two answered. "And if the warehouse hasn't already been torched, we'll search it." He grimaced and rubbed his neck. "I'm afraid we don't have much to go on. Dark blue Plymouths are pretty common. But we'll check out the local rental agencies and the hotels. Three oversize men might be remembered, particularly if they've been here for a while. Of course, they could be staying somewhere other than at a hotel."

Matt was cradling Lauren against his chest. "We'd be grateful for anything you can do. And we'd like to be kept informed."

"Can we reach you at—" The officer flipped back several pages in his notebook and read off Lauren's Lincoln address.

Matt caught Phillip's headshake. "No. They know the house. I can't take the chance they won't return. We'll be at the Long Wharf Marriott. You can either call us there or leave a message at the print shop."

With a nod, the policemen left, followed several minutes later by Phillip. Matt studied Lauren with tender concern. "Feel up to moving, sweetheart?"

When she nodded, he helped her to her feet, then wrapped an arm around her waist and guided her out. Less than half an hour later, they were in a spacious hotel room overlooking the harbor. Despite her exhaustion, Lauren insisted on taking a shower. She felt dirty all over. With her eyes closed or open, she could smell the men who'd abducted her.

She scrubbed herself until her skin was pink, while Matt stood immediately outside the shower. He helped her dry off, tucked her in bed, then sat down beside her. If she'd ever doubted his love, she doubted no more; it was indelibly etched on every one of his features.

"Want some aspirin?"

She shook her head and managed a wan smile. "We don't have any, anyway."

"I could call down for some."

"I'm okay." She reached for him and whispered, "Just hold me, Matt. Just hold me."

He did. After a time, he moved back to shed his own clothes, then climbed under the sheets with her and held her for the rest of the night.

Come morning, Lauren had recovered to the point where she could think more clearly. Matt had been at that stage from the moment she'd fallen asleep in his arms.

They were sitting cross-legged on the bed, dressed only in white terry velour robes. She'd begun to gnaw on a strip of bacon when she set it back down. "I've been thinking, Matt. Theoretically, those guys are still after me. But something's odd. I escaped too easily."

Matt wasn't eating, either. "I know."

"It took me a while to find that shaft, but the one who went to make a phone call hadn't returned. No one heard me tearing off the strips of wood. No one heard the elevator. No one chased me down the street. Considering the way they manhandled me earlier and spelled out exactly what they planned to do to me, it just doesn't make sense."

"Maybe the terror they put you through was the end point of the exercise."

She thought about that for a while as she leaned against the headboard and sipped her coffee. "I suggested that to him, and he denied it. Maybe I managed to convince him that I wasn't Susan Miles, or at least plant some doubts—"

"In which case he *let* you escape. If only we knew for sure whether your escape was deliberate or accidental. I have no intention of assuming that you're off the hook until I have proof of it, which means either finding those thugs or—"

"Finding Susan Miles."

"Right. If we could find her and convince her to go to the police, they could question this boss of hers. At least then he'd know he had the wrong woman in you, and we could breathe freely."

Lauren sat forward and reached for the bacon. Matt's presence, his commitment to her cause, the fact of the two of them working together to resolve the problem—all gave her a sense of optimism that, in turn, awakened her appetite. "So," she said between bites, "we have to find Susan Miles, which may be easier said than done. No doubt she's using a different name, and she's probably had plastic surgery to alter her looks, so that's where we'll begin."

He nodded. "The clinic in the Bahamas."

"Right. That's where the boss found out about me, though how he knew to check out that particular clinic is a mystery. I wonder if Susan had been there before, or if she'd mentioned it to him at some point."

"If that was the case," Matt reasoned, "I doubt she'd be stupid enough to go back there when she was trying to flee him. On the other hand, the boss may have had some information we don't. Airline tickets, hotel reservations, something. I think we should fly down and talk with your doctor. Can they spare you at the shop?"

"They'll have to. The shop means a lot to me, but my own health and safety mean more. Between Beth and Jamie, things will run smoothly."

Matt popped a cube of cantaloupe into his mouth. "That Beth is a character. You wouldn't believe some of the stories she came up with to explain your disappearance. She even dared to hint that Brad had come back from the dead and taken you off to some hideaway to heal old wounds!''

"Did she really say *that*?" Lauren grimaced, then sighed. "She's got an unbelievable imagination. I think she's incurable."

"I think she's also incredibly devoted and loyal. She refused to budge from that shop yesterday because she wanted to be there if you called, and when you finally did, she all but sent out the cavalry to find me. She called Jamie to pass on your message in case I contacted the farmhouse first. She got in touch with Phillip—he has a phone in his car—and sent him looking for me. She was ready to tell the police I'd stolen her car so they would go out in pursuit. You're lucky to have her for a friend, Lauren."

Lauren reached out and touched his cheek. There was warmth in her fingers and love in her eyes. "I'm lucky about a lot of things. Very, very lucky."

THE POLICE weren't so lucky. They had nothing to report to Matt except the fact that shortly before they'd arrived to search it the night before, the warehouse had gone up in flames. The fire marshal's office was investigating arson, but that case had little to do with Lauren's, and there was no sign whatsoever of either the dark blue Plymouth or the three oversize thugs.

Accompanied by a pair of officers from the Lincoln police department, Lauren and Matt returned to the farmhouse at noontime on Saturday, packed their bags and headed for the airport. Matt took a few minutes to phone Phillip to keep him abreast of their plans. Then he and Lauren were airborne, en route to the Bahamas.

To the best of their knowledge, they hadn't been followed.

Chapter Ten

Upon landing, Matt took Lauren directly to one of the plush hotels on the island. It had become clear to him in the course of the flight that she was suffering a delayed reaction to what had happened the day before. She'd been shaky and restless, unable to do more than pick at the meal that was served. She'd dozed off, then awakened with a start to a fit of uncontrollable trembling. He'd teased her, saying that *he* was the one who was supposed to be nervous, but his fear of flying took a back seat to her upset. He'd known that what she needed most was a peaceful restorative night.

First thing the next day, though, they went to the clinic. Purposely, they didn't call in advance. They knew that the boss's men had been there, and they weren't sure how they'd be received. Lauren was convinced that the doctor would not have willingly colluded with thugs, but Matt reserved his own judgment until their meeting.

Richard Bowen was in surgery. They insisted on waiting in the room just outside his office and caught him the minute he returned. Richard was surprised and pleased to see Lauren, doubly pleased to find her with Matt. After the brief introductions, he ushered them into his sanctuary. Neither Lauren nor Matt missed the subtle blanching of his face as she explained what had happened.

"They made it very clear that they'd seen your files," Matt concluded for her when he sensed that Lauren wasn't sure exactly how to confront the doctor. She obviously liked and trusted him, and she was loath to toss accusations his way. Matt had no such qualm. "Did you show anyone those files, or know that they'd been seen?"

To Lauren's relief, Richard was not offended and deeply shared their concern. "My files are confidential. The only way I'd have shown them to anyone would have been if Lauren had specifically requested it."

"Then how—" Lauren began, only to be interrupted.

"About a month ago there was a break-in here. My file cabinets were forced open and the files rifled. Records of hundreds of patients were left scattered all over the office. Nothing was taken that I could tell. Until now I've had no idea what the burglars were after."

"And Susan Miles?" Matt prompted. "Have you treated a patient by that name?"

Richard widened his eyes for an exaggerated second. "Treated, no. Spoken with, yes. Oh, yes. She came by to see me last fall, maybe early winter. She wanted to discuss having some minor work done. It never got past the discussion stage, so I don't have a file on her, but I'll never forget her face. She was stunning. A real beauty." He cast an apologetic glance at Lauren. "Yes, Lauren, you do look a lot like her now."

"Did you do it intentionally?" Matt growled. It was obvious that Richard Bowen had been taken with Susan Miles's looks. For him to try to form another woman in her image might have been conceivable, if infuriating and possibly unethical.

Richard chuckled. "I'm a plastic surgeon, not a miracle worker. It's only in the movies that one face can be completely altered to look like another. No, in Lauren's case, it was pure coincidence. The hair's the same in texture and color, and the figure is complementary, now that Lauren's put on weight. The eyes were alike all along. But, if I remember correctly, and I'm sure I do, Susan Miles wore much more makeup. As for the rest—the nose, the cheekbones, the jaw—they all just came together. You have to understand that in cases like Lauren's, the end results are sometimes a mystery even to the doctor until everything's done. Reconstructive work can go this way or that in the healing process." He smiled ruefully at Lauren. "Yours went the way of Susan Miles."

"From what you say, I should be happy about that," Lauren mused, "but given all that's happened..."

"There are differences," Richard pointed out, "but mostly I think they come from within. The woman I spoke with had a harder edge to her. She was very much like so many of the others I treat, women whose inner tension does things to their faces that no amount of plastic surgery can correct."

"Then she didn't really need plastic surgery?" Lauren asked. She looked at Matt. "Maybe she was planning on disappearing even back then."

Richard spoke before Matt could comment on that supposition. "There were a few things that could have been touched up, but basically they could have gone another five or ten years without attention. People would have thought her beautiful if she'd done nothing."

"Did you tell her that?" Matt inquired. Richard gave him a wry, what-do-*you*-think look. "But she didn't come back."

"No. I never saw her again."

Lauren sat forward. "We have to find her. We know she came from the L.A. area and had a boutique there. Did she say anything to you— drop any names—that might give us a clue?"

Richard sat back in his chair and frowned, trying to absorb all that Lauren had told him. "I don't think so."

"She was probably with a man," Matt offered. "A very wealthy and powerful man."

"Wealthy and powerful men are a dime a dozen on the islands. She did say that she was here on a pleasure trip and had heard about the clinic from a friend."

"No name?" Matt asked.

Richard shook his head. "Fully one-third of my patients have been from the West Coast. They like coming here for the ambience, and for the distance. They can go on an extended vacation far from home, then return looking positively marvelous with no one the wiser." His frown deepened, and he chafed one eyebrow with the knuckle of his forefinger. "I can picture her sitting here talking with me. I'm sure I asked her where she way staying—it's standard small talk in a place like this—and I don't think it was one of the large hotels, because I would have formed a mental image of her there. Maybe a smaller—no—" He hesitated, concentrating. "A boat. I think she mentioned something about the marina."

Matt grunted. "There have to be dozens of marinas. She didn't say which one?"

"If she did, I don't remember."

"Then it'll be like finding a needle in a haystack, and we don't even know which haystack to search."

"How about other clinics on the islands?" Lauren asked.

"There are none I'd recommend, and I doubt a woman like that would go to a second-rate place." Richard held up a hand. "No conceit intended."

"None presumed," Matt offered in his first show of faith. "Can you tell us anything else about her—how she wore her hair, any distinctive jewelry or style of dress?"

Richard closed his eyes as he called back the full image from his memory bank. "Her hair was pulled away from her face in a chic kind of knot. She was wearing gold jewelry—large hoops at the ears, a chain around her neck. She had several rings, maybe one with a stone, and she was wearing white silk slacks and a blouse. Oh, and high-heeled sandals. I noticed that because her toenails were polished to match her fingernails, and the pink was the same color as the sash around her waist."

"You were very observant." was Matt's wry comment.

Richard laughed good-naturedly. "It's my business to be observant when it comes to women's looks, and this woman was well worth the look. I remember thinking how elegantly she'd coordinated everything. She was stunning. Truly stunning."

Matt pushed himself from his chair. "The description may prove to be helpful somewhere along the line. I hope." It went without saying that they were still at the very start of that line. He held out a hand for Lauren. "Come on, sweetheart. We'll have to rethink our strategy."

Richard walked them to the door. "I'm really sorry I have no more information. If only—" His brow rippled. "Wait a minute. There is something. I mean, it'd still be a long shot, but—"

Matt and Lauren had turned hopeful faces his way. "What is it?" Lauren asked, holding her breath.

"She smoked. I remembered thinking that in time her face would show it. It does, you know."

"But where does that get us?" Matt prodded.

"She was using a little green box of matches. Not a matchbook, but a little green box. I remembered thinking, 'Ah, she's been to Terrance Cove.' It's one of the more showy restaurants around here. Just the place for the wealthy and powerful."

Matt and Lauren exchanged a look of excitement. "Let's try it, Matt," she said. "We've got nothing to lose."

It was Matt who turned to shake Richard's hand and thank him. Belatedly, and purely on impulse, Lauren gave the doctor a hug. "You've been great, Richard. How can we ever thank you?"

His grin was crooked. "You can find Susan Miles and get both of you out of danger. Her friends don't sound very charitable."

Lauren agreed, then slid her hand into Matt's.

A taxi took them to Terrance Cove, which, fortunately, had just opened for lunch.

"What are you going to say?" Lauren asked. "If Susan Miles was with the boss, who presumably made the reservations, the people at the restaurant would have no way of knowing, much less remembering, her name."

"But the face," Matt cooed. "Ah, the face. Susan Miles had a memorable face. And, sweetheart, you've got that face. *I* always knew it was memorable, but then, I'm slightly biased."

Lauren pinched him in the ribs, but she was buoyed. She held her head high when they entered the restaurant, and tried to look every bit the boss's woman while Matt did the talking. His story sounded conceivable enough.

"My fiancée is looking for her identical twin. They've been separated for two years, and we just got word that she was here last winter. Her name is Susan Miles." He looked at Lauren affectionately. "And this is her face. Does it look at all familiar? Ring any bells? Susan might have had her hair pulled back, and she was probably wearing more makeup and jewelry. But the similarities are marked." He paused. "She might have been with a rather impressive man, and if we can find him, we can get a lead on her."

The maître d' stared at Lauren long and hard. "I'm sorry," he said in crisply accented English. "I don't recognize her. But I only work afternoons. The man who was working evenings last winter was recently retired. He is living in Miami with his daughter and grandchildren."

"It's very important that we reach him," Lauren urged. "We have no other leads. Do you have an address or a phone number?"

The man seemed to waver. His indecision came to an end when Matt pressed a folded bill into his hand. "Wait here, please. I'll see what I can do."

As soon as he had disappeared, Lauren leaned close and whispered to Matt, "Why does that always work?"

He whispered back, "It doesn't, at least not always. I was prepared to give him another. He sold himself cheap."

"That was quite a story. *Identical twin?*"

"Beats the other explanation."

Neither of them commented on the fiancée part of the tale.

Within minutes the man returned with a small index card on which he'd printed the name of the former employee and his Miami address. Matt pocketed the card, and he and Lauren headed back to the hotel.

"To Miami?" Lauren asked.

"To Miami."

"When?"

Matt glanced at his watch. "As soon as we can get a flight."

They both knew that the personal visit was a must. They could easily get the man's phone number and call him, but Lauren's face was the key. So they put back the few things they'd taken out of their suitcases, returned to the airport they'd landed at less than twenty-four hours before, and caught the first plane to Miami.

The flight was short and uneventful. As always, they were watchful, alert to any face that would be familiar, or threatening, or in any way suggestive of a tail. As always, they saw none.

After the plane had landed, they took a taxi straight to the address printed on the index card—a modest house on the outskirts of the city. Various bicycles and toys littered its driveway. Instructing the driver to wait, they approached the door.

It was opened by a gentleman in his early seventies. The children crowding behind him called him "Papa," but his actual name was Henry Frolinette.

Matt repeated the story they'd given the maître d' at Terrance Cove, stressing simultaneously their regret at disturbing him and the urgency of their mission. The man nodded, looked closely at Lauren and nodded again.

"I don't know the name," he admitted, "but I do remember the face. They came to the restaurant more than once."

"They," Matt echoed. "Then she was with the man."

"Oh, yes. A dapper sort, and a generous spender. There were usually eight or ten in his party, though the individuals differed—except for the woman. Miss...Miles, you say?" When Lauren nodded quickly, he went on. "Miss Miles was always with him. And Mr. Prinz always picked up the check for the entire group. He paid in cash, too, I might add."

Lauren's gaze met Matt's. "Prinz," she breathed.

Matt was already looking back at Henry. "Do you know his first name?"

"Oh, yes. He's been quite a presence in the islands over the years. Theodore Prinz, from Los Angeles. Not that everyone speaks highly of him, mind you. There have been rumors about the nature of his work. I never believed them, personally. He is a good-looking man, very well behaved and dignified, and he was always more than gracious to me."

Unfortunately, Henry Frolinette was unable to give them any specific information on Susan Miles. Lauren and Matt discussed it that night over dinner at the beachfront hotel they'd checked into.

"At least we have the boss's name," Lauren mused, "but that's about all. I suppose we could show up on his doorstep and tell him he's made a mistake, but—"

"He wouldn't believe us, and we'd only be putting ourselves right back in his hands. No, if anything's going to stick, we have to find Susan Miles. If Henry had been able to pinpoint a marina, maybe we could have gone back and found someone who might give us a clue to where she went when she left Prinz. But to use Theodore Prinz's name alone would only be asking for trouble. Word is bound to get back to him, and if he's half as powerful as I suspect, we'd be playing with fire."

"So?"

"We call Phillip, who can use his contacts to get the lowdown on Prinz. If Prinz is involved enough with that boutique to have his own man running it, the name of the place will be sandwiched in there with the rest of the information. At least, it will be if Phillip is worth his salt, and from what I've seen, he is."

Lauren didn't understand. "But what good will it do to know the name of the boutique? We can't show up there, any more than we can show up at Prinz's home. If we start asking questions of nearby shopkeepers, they're apt to call Prinz. Besides, I'm sure he had his men question everyone in sight when he started looking for Susan himself."

"True. But what if we go further back? What if Phillip can get hold of the original papers for that shop?"

"What if Prinz bought it for her in the first place?"

"Maybe he did and maybe he didn't. If he didn't, there might just be some information—even data on loan applications—that could lead us to where she came from—or even to a friend or a family member whom she might have contacted when she relocated."

"But wouldn't Prinz have done that?"

Matt's eyes were filled with excitement, and his voice held a kind of restrained glee. "Prinz went forward. He obviously felt he knew Susan well enough to anticipate what she'd do. He must have known of her visit to the clinic when they were in the Bahamas. That's why his men went there right away. They found what they were looking for, so why look further?"

"But you'd go backward," Lauren stated with sudden comprehension. And admiration. "Cautious Matt. Wants to know the ingredients before he takes a taste."

"It makes sense, doesn't it?"

"Sure does. And in spite of the danger, you're enjoying yourself."

"Sure am. I read somewhere—maybe not in a Spenser novel, but somewhere—that private investigators often locate people who've been missing for years by staking out the graves of their parents. Unless this Susan Miles is truly made of ice, she's been in touch with someone from her past, and more likely than not, that someone is a family member." He straightened in his seat and sighed. It was as though he'd suddenly set down the mystery novel he'd been reading and returned to reality with a jolt. "All *we* have to do is find that family member."

"WHAT'S HAPPENING?"

"They flew back to Boston. Looks like she's not trying to disappear. Kruger's with her constantly. They're staying in a hotel in town, but that may be because workmen have started tearing up her farmhouse."

"Tearing it up?"

"Remodeling. At least, that's what it says on the side of the truck parked out front. I don't think she's planning to abandon the place, Boss."

"Then she's not Susan."

"Looks that way. She's still pretty nervous, y'know. Looks all around her whenever she goes out, and, like I said, she doesn't go anywhere alone. More than that, the police are in and out of her shop."

"Susan wouldn't have dared call the police."

"Right."

"So. She's not Susan. Do you think she's given up the search for Susan?"

"I don't know. Word has it that the detective's been doing some research."

"About what?"

"The boutique."

"You have to be kidding! How did they find out about that?"

"I told her."

"Not smart. Not smart at all."

"It was when I had her in the car. I thought she was Susan then."

"They'll get my name."

"They've already got it."

There was a pause, then an arrogant "No problem. The boutique's on the up-and-up. You'll just have to be doubly careful with Susan's demise."

"What about Lauren Stevenson? And Kruger? And the dick, for that matter? If they do manage to find Susan for us and then something happens to her, they'll know who to blame."

"But Susan's death won't be traceable to us. It could be an accident; it could be part of a larger scheme. If it looks like someone else kills her, that's not my worry. And if a whole bunch of people shoot each other to bits, so much the better. I don't care how you do it, but keep us clean. I pay you good money to handle things like this. Do what you have to. Don't bore me with the details. I want Susan dead!"

"WE'VE HIT PAY DIRT!" Matt exclaimed with a broad grin as he set down the telephone. He was seated at the desk in the back room of the shop, and Lauren was propped expectantly at its edge.

"What did he say?" The call had been from Phillip. She'd known that much, but had been unable to follow the conversation, which had been distinctly one-sided in favor of the detective.

"He said," Matt began slowly, savoring the suspense, "that Susan bought the boutique herself and she financed it with a loan from a local bank. The loan application listed two people as references, neither of whom are named Miles, but both of whom are from Kansas City."

"Kansas City. Where she grew up?"

"Either that, or where she was living before she hit L.A. It doesn't really matter. At least we have contacts." He patted the scrap of paper on which he'd jotted the two names.

"But what if these contacts are somehow related to Prinz? What if one or the other of them was the instrument of Susan's introduction to him?"

Matt was shaking his head. "According to Phillip, neither of the names has shown up in any of the information he's gathered on Prinz. There's still that possibility, but I think it's remote. And even if it's not, neither one has any direct association with Prinz now, which means that we'll be safe." He lifted the receiver again and called the airport. Within hours, he and Lauren were headed for Kansas City.

"Poor Matt," Lauren mused when they were airborne again. "For someone who hates flying, you've done your share in the past few days."

He leaned close to her, denying the steel arm between them. "It's worth it. Every hateful minute."

Lauren smiled and whispered. "You are a wonderful man."

"Nah. I'm just along for the ride."

"That's one of the reasons I love you." She kissed his too-square chin. "You didn't ask for any of this."

"But I asked for you," he murmured deeply. "All my life I've been asking for you, and now that I've found you, I'll take any ride, as long as you're along." He sought and captured her lips, kissing her thoroughly. "And when this is all over," he whispered against her mouth, "we are going to take a vacation to beat all vacations. We'll fly somewhere and stay put for two weeks, just the two of us. Sun and sand and moonlit nights…"

"Sounds wonderful, but you'll have used up all your vacation time by then."

"So I'll take more."

"And if your boss objects?"

"I'll quit."

She grinned. "Mmm. I'd like that. San Francisco's too far away."

"My thoughts exactly." He kissed her again, softly, deeply. His mouth was just leaving hers when the flight attendant came by with lunch.

Beneath the lighthearted teasing, Lauren had been very serious. San Francisco *was* too far away. But she couldn't think about the future. Not yet. There was still too much to be done to ensure that she had a future at all.

BRIGHT AND EARLY the next morning, Lauren and Matt showed up in the office of one Timothy Trennis. The office was done in obvious taste and at obvious cost; the man was in his early forties, neatly dressed and pleasant-looking. When he saw them, his mouth dropped open. His eyes were riveted to Lauren's face.

"Susan?" he asked uncertainly.

"Almost," Lauren said gently, "but not quite. I am looking for her, though. We thought maybe you could help us."

Timothy continued to stare at her, then slowly shook his head. "The resemblance is remarkable. It's been a long time since I've seen Susan. I could have sworn—" He seemed to catch himself, and his cheeks reddened. "But you'd know, wouldn't you?"

Lauren nodded. "It's very important that we reach her. Do you have any idea where she might be?"

"Is she in trouble?" he asked with genuine concern.

Lauren looked hesitantly at Matt, who took over. "She may be if we don't find her. Someone else is looking for her. It's critical that we find her first."

"It's that Prinz guy, isn't it?"

"Do you know about him?" Lauren asked.

Belatedly, Timothy gestured for them to sit. When they'd done so, he lowered himself into a chair near his desk. "Susan and I dated for a time.

I always knew she had greater ambitions—ambitions that went beyond Kansas City, I mean. When she decided to move to Los Angeles, I wasn't surprised. We kept in touch for a while, so I knew she was seeing Prinz. I made it my business to find out about him, and when I tried to caution her subtly, she pretty much severed all contact between us."

"When was the last time you heard from her?" Matt asked.

Timothy thought about that for a minute, making rough calculations in his mind. "It had to have been more than three years ago."

"And there's been nothing since then?"

Timothy shook his head.

"Is there someone she *might* have contacted? Someone she's kept in touch with—family, maybe?"

"If there is, I don't know about it. Susan rarely talked about family. There was an older sister, and her mother. The father died when she was a child, and the mother remarried. Susan detested her stepfather. She left as soon as she could."

"Do you know where the mother lives?" Lauren asked.

"Susan grew up in a small town in Indiana. Whether the mother's still there is anyone's guess. I don't even know her married name."

"How about the sister?" Matt queried.

"The sister was older by five or six years, took off after high school and got married. Susan never mentioned her. I simply assumed they'd lost contact, too."

Matt looked at Lauren. "Another strikeout." He fished the scrap of paper from his pocket. "What about, uh, Alexander Fraun? Do you know him?"

Timothy nodded. "Susan worked for him. He owns a pair of dress shops in the area. Nice-enough fellow. You could try him. He may have information I don't." As Lauren and Matt stood up to leave, he added, "I hope you find her. I always wished her happiness."

Lauren smiled warmly. She liked this man and felt he'd given them the first positive picture of Susan Miles to date. "We'll tell her that when we find her," she said. *When*, not *if*. Pessimism had no place here; there was too much at stake for all of them.

"THEY'RE IN KANSAS CITY."

"Kansas City? Clever. Susan was from Kansas City. They *are* looking for her."

"Will they find her?"

"In Kansas City? No. She wouldn't go back there. It's too obvious." There was a pause. "It is possible, though, that she's contacted one of her old friends there." A smug smile. "And if that's the case, Kruger and the girl will find out. They're doing our legwork for us."

"Seems to me I'm doing it anyway, following them around like this."

"You're not stupid enough to let them see you, are you? After that little kidnapping stunt, the girl would recognize you instantly."

"Don't worry. We've got Jimbo tailing them close, and she never saw him, so we're safe."

"But you're not far."

"No, sir."

"Good. I don't trust Jimbo to do the heavy work."

"Neither do I, and I have a personal investment here, too. Susan's kept us running in circles. That kind of thing inspires revenge."

"Mmm. I like that. Very good."

ALEXANDER FRAUN was harder to reach. When Lauren and Matt arrived at the address Phillip had given them, they were told that Fraun was at the other store. When they arrived at that one, they were told that he'd gone to a luncheon meeting and would be back at the first store that afternoon.

They went to lunch themselves, then returned to the first store to await the elusive Mr. Fraun. Shortly before two o'clock, he entered the small outer office in which they sat. He had started to pass through into his own office, after glancing briefly their way, when he did a double take on Lauren and came to an abrupt halt.

"Susan?" he asked uncertainly.

"Almost," she said gently, "but not quite." She felt she was living a broken record and quickly moved to free the needle from its cracked groove. "My name is Lauren Stevenson. And this is Matt Kruger. We're looking for Susan and thought you might have some idea as to her whereabouts."

"Come into my office," the man said with a broad wave of his hand. He was as different from Timothy Trennis as night from day. Not only was his office a disaster area, but the man himself looked as though he'd seen better days. Lauren estimated that he was in his late fifties. His bald pate was scantily covered with strands of gray that had been called to the rescue from somewhere just above his ear. He had chipmunk cheeks and a multitiered chin, both of which coordinated perfectly with his girth. There was something about him, something strangely genuine, that made Lauren like him on the spot.

"Now," he said, scooping a pile of ancient magazines from the torn vinyl sofa so that Lauren and Matt could sit down, "what's this about Susan?" He propped himself on the edge of the desk. The wood groaned.

"We're trying to find her," Matt explained. "We were told she worked for you once."

"What do you want with her?" Fraun shot back with such suspicion that Lauren, for one, wondered if Prinz's men had reached him first.

Matt did the talking, apparently taking the man's suspicion for protectiveness. He explained just why he and Lauren were anxious to find Susan.

Fraun shifted his gaze back to Lauren. "You look just like her. For a minute when I walked in, I thought she'd come back."

"We know that she went to Los Angeles when she left here," Lauren offered, "but we were hoping that you might have heard from her."

"She's not still there?"

Lauren shook her head.

The wrinkles on Fraun's brow echoed higher on his bald head. "I thought she was. Last thing I heard from her, she had her own boutique." He smiled. "Susan was good. She had a way with color and style." He gave his head a little toss. "She was wasted here. I told her so. I mean, my goods are nice enough, but she needed high fashion to make the most of her talents."

"When was the last time you heard from her?" Matt asked.

Fraun suddenly scowled at him. "How do I know you're on the up-and-up? How do I know you two haven't come to do her harm?"

Lauren, too, saw protectiveness this time. As briefly but meaningfully as she could, she told him where she'd come from and where she worked, then did the same for Matt. "We don't wish Susan any harm. We have no reason to do her harm. If Matt and I can locate her, Susan and I stand to benefit—Susan, because she'll be aware of the danger and be able to do something about it; me, because if Susan does something about it, I'll be out of danger, too."

Fraun tugged a slightly warped pad of paper from beneath a haphazard pile of letters. "I'm going to write down your names and addresses. That way, if anything happens to Susan, I'll know who to call."

"Then you know where she is?" Lauren asked in excitement.

"Driver's licenses, please."

Lauren and Matt exchanged a glance and dug into their respective pockets for identification. Only when the man had taken notes to his satisfaction did he put down the pad and face them.

"No, I don't know where Susan is," he admitted. "The last time I heard from her was nearly two years ago. She sounded fine then. Why did she leave L.A.?"

"We're not sure," Matt answered. "But we do know she left. We'd hoped she'd contacted you, or someone else she knew before."

"You could try Tim—"

"We already have. He suggested we try you."

Fraun sighed and gave a shrug that made his belly shake. "I don't know what to tell you. I can't believe Susan's in trouble. She was always honest, and a hard worker."

"She probably still is," Lauren speculated. "It's just that she had the ill fortune to get mixed up with a man who's probably neither of those things. Can you think of anyone she may have contacted? Timothy said she wasn't close to her family, but there's always a chance she could be in touch with one of them.''

Fraun shook his head. This time his jowls shimmied. ''Tim was right. She wasn't big on her family. She did mention the sister from time to time.''

''Do you know her married name,'' Matt asked, ''or where she's living?''

''Nah— Wait just a minute.'' He bounced off the desk and tugged at the drawer of a file cabinet. It resisted his efforts, yielding at last, but with reluctance. Lauren understood why. The drawer was nearly as overstuffed as was the man rummaging through it.

''How can you find anything in there?'' she asked on impulse.

''I find. I find. It just takes a little time.''

It took a good fifteen minutes, during which Lauren and Matt sat by helplessly, glancing from each other's faces to the man at work to the calamity of his office.

''Here we go!'' Fraun exclaimed at last. He held up a sheet of paper that had a permanent press running diagonally through it. ''Susan's original employment application. You see,'' he cried victoriously, ''it sometimes pays not to clean out drawers.'' Holding the paper at arm's length, he ran his eyes down the form. ''Aha! Person to call in case of emergency: Mrs. Peter—Ann—Broszczynski. Relationship: sister.'' Proudly, he offered the form to Lauren. ''St. Louis. Think you can get there?''

Lauren looked from the form to Matt and grinned. ''You bet we can.'' When she returned her gaze to Alexander Fraun, she realized that, with a beard and a little more hair, he would have reminded her of Santa Claus.

ANN BROSZCZYNSKI was not living at the address listed on the employment application, which was understandable, Lauren and Matt told each other, since the application had been filled out seven years before. The people presently living at that address didn't know what had become of the Broszcynskis, but the telephone company did.

A phone booth with its book miraculously attached and intact gave them the information they needed, and a taxi delivered them to the right address. It was another apartment, but a nicer one, more a garden complex. Lauren felt a certain pleasure that Susan's sister had moved up in the world.

The door was answered by a teenage girl who reminded Lauren of the guard at the garage where she parked. Definitely a music fan. If the net of lace banding her curly hair, the penciled mole just above her lip, or the abbreviated top and minuscule straight skirt hadn't given her away, the fingerless lace glove on her hand would have.

"Mmm?" the girl mumbled.

"We're looking for Ann Broszczynski," Lauren explained. "Is she in?"

The girl tilted her head back and hollered to the ceiling, "Mom!" A minute later she stepped aside to make room for the woman who approached.

Ann Broszczynski was a clean and attractive representative of middle America. She wore jeans, a sleeveless blouse and an apron, the latter serving at the moment as a towel for her wet hands. Her hair, a little lighter than Lauren's, was shoulder-length and swept behind her ears. Even devoid of makeup, her face was lovely.

It was also momentarily stricken. Her eyes were huge. She opened her mouth, then closed it and stared at Lauren in puzzlement.

Lauren smiled. "I look a lot like Susan, I know, but my name's Lauren Stevenson. This is Matt Kruger. We wonder if we could talk with you for a few minutes."

"Are you friends of Susan's?" the woman asked, more wary than curious, a fact that Lauren attributed to the distance between the sisters.

"Indirectly, yes," Lauren answered. "May we come in?"

Ann didn't budge. "Susan and I don't see each other," she returned a little too quickly. "We go our own ways."

"I know that. But we need to talk with you. No one else has been able to help us."

"Why do you need help?" Ann shot back.

Matt, who'd been silent up to that point, suddenly understood the problem. "We don't wish Susan any harm, Mrs. Broszczynski. If anything, the contrary is true, which is why we're here. Susan is in danger. Apparently you know that, or at least you know she's living somewhere new under an assumed name and that there's a potential for danger if she is discovered. What you don't know is that Lauren was mistaken for Susan by Theodore Prinz's men. For weeks they've put her through hell, using one scare tactic after another. Last week they abducted her and came very close to killing her. It was during the time she was being held that she learned about Susan." He spoke with soft urgency. "We need to find your sister. She must be told that she's being hunted. We have to convince her to go to the police. Between her testimony and Lauren's, we know that something can be done about Prinz."

Ann was pale. She gnawed at her lower lip and clutched the folds of the apron in her fists.

"May we come in?" Lauren asked again, this time pleadingly.

After another moment's hesitation, the woman nodded. Shooing her daughter away, she led them into a small, modestly furnished living room. None of them sat; the air was too tense for that.

"I'm not sure if I know what you're talking about," Ann burst out. "I'm not involved in Susan's life."

"We realize that," Matt said quietly, intent on convincing her of the legitimacy of their mission. "We've just come from Kansas City, where we spoke with both Timothy Trennis and Alexander Fraun. Do those names ring a bell?"

After a pause, Ann nodded.

"Do you trust them?" he asked. When, after another pause, Ann nodded again, he went on. "Alexander Fraun was the one who found your name on Susan's old employment application. He was obviously fond of Susan and wouldn't have given us your name unless he trusted us." Though he raised a hand to emphasize his point, his voice remained soft. "We wouldn't be bothering you if we had anywhere else to turn, but no one seems to know where Susan is or what she's doing. Prinz doesn't seem to be aware that Susan had any family, which may explain why no one has reached you sooner. But it's simply a matter of time before he gets to you, and then to Susan, because it may well be that you're the only one who knows Susan's new name and address." He paused, gentling his voice all the more. "Will you tell us, Ann? We only want to help."

"I wish my husband were here," Ann wailed softly, hands tightly clenched before her. "I'm no good at things like this."

"You're Susan's sister. It's your decision, more so than your husband's."

"But things are so tenuous between Susan and me," she argued. "For years we had very little contact. She was in one world, I was in another. There was no middle ground between us. I don't want to do something that will anger her, or worse, put her in danger."

"Then you have to tell us where she is," Lauren urged. "*None* of us will be safe until we find her and convince her to go to the police with us. For all we know, Matt and I are just one step ahead of Prinz's men right now."

Ann pondered Lauren's words nervously, her gaze shifting from one spot in the room to another. Then she brightened. "Why don't you let *me* call Susan? I can tell her everything you've told me—"

"Do you think she'll believe you—or that we're legitimate?" Matt cut in. "She'll run, Ann. She's done it before, and she'll do it again if this isn't handled right. She needs to *see* Lauren and the physical similarity between them in order to believe what's happened."

Ann looked from one face to the other. "You're asking an awful lot."

Lauren nodded. "We know."

"If you turn out to be the bad guys—"

"We're not! You can call the police back home, either in Boston or Lincoln. They'll verify everything that's happened to me."

"And Fraun took precautions of his own," Matt added soberly. "He has our names and addresses. He knows where to send the police if anything happens to Susan."

"I'll never forgive myself if she's hurt because of me!"

Matt put every ounce of feeling into a single, last-ditch plea. "*No* one will be hurt if we reach her in time. But time is of the essence, and we can't reach her if we don't know where she is."

Ann worried the issue for several minutes longer, her eyes filled with concern, her lips clamped tightly together. Her gaze slid from Lauren to Matt and back to Lauren, asking questions for which there were, as yet, no answers.

Just as Lauren was about to scream in frustration, Ann straightened her shoulders, took a deep breath, let it out in a sigh and surrendered.

Chapter Eleven

A single long shadow stretched across the grass behind him as Ted Prinz stood in his garden staring out over the hills. Absently he lit a cigarette and dragged deeply on it. Pensive, he narrowed his eyes through the tunnel of smoke.

So Susan was in Washington, D.C. That made sense. He could picture her trying to hook up with a politician who had enough clout to protect her.

He grinned. She'd never make it. His men would make sure of that. At this very moment Kruger and the girl were being staked out at the Hay-Adams House. When they moved, his men would, too.

And Susan would regret the day she'd been born.

"WHADDYA THINK?" Matt asked, looking at his watch. "Should we make a stab at it tonight?"

Lauren pressed a hand to her chest. "My heart is pounding. I can't believe we've found her."

"Don't believe it until you see it. There could be a catch yet."

But Lauren was shaking her head. "Ann said she'd spoken to her just last week. Oh, she's here all right. I can *feel* it."

Slinging an arm around her shoulder, Matt tugged her close. "My eternal optimist." He popped a kiss on her nose. "So. What will it be? Tonight, or tomorrow morning?"

Lauren pondered the choice. "If we go tonight, it'll have to be to her apartment. Ann said it's a nice place, which means there will be security guards—"

"Who call up to announce your arrival and get permission to let you in. Susan doesn't know us. She'll never allow it. No, I think we'll have to take her by surprise. Any advance announcement of our presence will put her on guard and, in turn, put us at an immediate disadvantage."

"On the one hand," Lauren mused, "I hate to wait. The sooner we get to her, the sooner we'll all breathe freely. But another twelve hours, after all this time…it can't hurt."

Matt nodded his agreement. "We know where she works. If we surprise her there tomorrow, she won't have a chance to turn us away sight unseen. And if she gets scared and tries to run, we can stop her."

"But we need time with her, time to explain what we're about." Lauren ran her tongue back and forth over her lower lip, then expressed her thoughts aloud. "She's a beauty consultant, Ann said. That figures. From what we've learned, she has a way with makeup and color and style. What if I call first thing in the morning and make an appointment? If we just drop in, she's apt to be with a client. On the other hand, if I can guarantee us a piece of her time…"

A slow grin spread over Matt's face. "Smart girl. I *knew* there was a reason why I brought you along."

Lauren grabbed his ears, tugged him down and kissed his yelp away. She lingered to savor his returning kiss, her fingers tangling in his sun-kissed hair. At last she dropped her arms to his waist and pressed her cheek to his chest.

They were silent for a time, enjoying the closeness. But Lauren's thoughts of the day to come refused to stay in abeyance for long. "Poor Susan. If she only knew tonight what was in store for her tomorrow."

"Save your sympathy, sweetheart," Matt murmured. "Susan Miles may still put us through an ordeal. Confronting her is one thing, convincing her that we're on the level is another, but selling her on the idea of going to the police may be a different can of worms entirely."

MICHELE SLOANE, as Susan now called herself, had set up her business in fashionable Georgetown. Lauren got the phone number from directory assistance and started calling at eight-thirty in the morning on the chance that the shop opened early for the prework set. It wasn't until nine that she got through.

Luck was with her. Michele had a cancellation and could see her at eleven-thirty.

The minutes ticked by with agonizing slowness as Lauren and Matt pushed their breakfasts around their plates in the hotel dining room. Then, to expend nervous energy, they went out for a walk. But while the White House, the Mall and the Lincoln Memorial should have inspired awe, they were too preoccupied in anticipation of the coming meeting to award these sights their due.

Ten o'clock came and went, then ten-thirty. Back in their hotel room, Lauren began to pace the floor. By eleven she was ready to jump out of her skin, but it wasn't until eleven-ten that she and Matt left the room, rode the elevator in silence, walked calmly through the hotel lobby and climbed into the cab that the doorman had whistled up. They'd calculated well for the traffic. It was eleven-thirty on the dot when the cabbie pulled up at the address they'd given him.

For a minute Matt and Lauren stood before the stately brownstone on the ground floor of which was Susan's shop. The sign on the front window, a contemporary logo in burgundy, read "Elegance, Inc." Smaller letters, far below, advertised fashion advice and salon services.

Taking a collective breath for courage, they crossed the sidewalk, descended three steps to the door and entered the shop. An aura of quiet dignity surrounded them instantly. The reception area was done in shades of a soothing pale gray and peach. Soft pop music hummed in the background, low enough to create a modern mood yet be unobtrusive.

A woman sat in a chair reading a magazine, apparently awaiting her appointment. Lauren and Matt made their way directly to the receptionist.

"May I help you?" she asked politely.

"Yes. My name is Lauren Stevenson. I have an eleven-thirty appointment with Michele Sloane."

The receptionist consulted the large book open before her, put a tiny dot next to Lauren's name, then smiled up at her. "Why don't you have a seat? Michele is just finishing up with another client. She'll be with you in a minute."

Lauren thanked her and settled into one of a pair of chairs farthest from the receptionist. She crossed her legs, folded her hands in her lap and leaned closer to Matt, who'd taken the chair immediately on her left.

"When was the last time you were in a place like this?" she whispered in an attempt at levity.

His soft grunt was the only answer she got, the only thing that betrayed his mood. He looked self-confident and composed. Taking her cue from him, she breathed deeply and straightened her shoulders. They were so close, so close....

Moments later another woman entered the shop, checked in with the receptionist and was sent directly through to one of the back rooms. Lauren stared after her, noting a long hallway sporting two doors on the side she could see. She assumed another two doors were on the opposite side.

Just then, from that blind side came the soft murmur of conversation. It was immediately followed by the appearance of two women, but Lauren's eyes homed in on only one of them.

Susan Miles was everything she'd been built up to be. She was indeed stunning. Very much Lauren's own height and build, she wore a pale yellow dress whose shoulder pads gave a breadth that narrowed, past a hip belt, into a pencil-slim skirt. Chunky beads hung around her neck. A coordinated bracelet ringed her wrist. Whether she wore earrings was not immediately apparent, for her chin-length hair was a mass of thick waves that framed her face in haphazard tumble.

The entire look was chic without being ostentatious. Lauren, who mere moments before had felt sufficiently confident in her own stylish tunic and slacks, was envious.

She was also puzzled. Susan Miles looked very much like her, yet very different. Apparently the receptionist had missed the resemblance. Now, studying Susan, Lauren could understand why.

Susan's hair was far lighter than Lauren's, for one thing. It had obviously been colored, though there was nothing obviously doctored about the blond, sun-streaked tangle. It blended perfectly with Susan's skin tone and makeup and looked completely natural.

Makeup. Yes, another difference. While Lauren wore it lightly and for simple enhancement, Susan's makeup sculpted her face, shading and contouring with a skill that was remarkable. Plastic surgery? Lauren doubted it. Yet there was something about the nose...a small bump...

The woman who'd been with Susan left. Susan bent over the desk to examine the appointment book, then followed the receptionist's finger to Lauren and Matt. She smiled as she straightened and approached them, but her smile wavered as she neared. Lauren thought she saw a faint drain of color from Susan's face. The smile remained but was more forced.

Lauren stood up, finding solace in the warmth of Matt's body by her side. If Susan was playing a part, she herself was doing no less. She held out her hand, willing it not to shake. "Michele?"

Susan met her clasp. "Yes. You're Lauren. And..." Her gaze slid to Matt.

"Matt Kruger," he said with a smile.

Susan nodded, but she was already looking back at Lauren. She folded her hands at her waist, hesitated a minute too long, then cleared her throat. "Well. You're here for a consultation. Why don't you come back to my office?"

They followed her down the hall to the last door on the right. The office they entered was simply decorated and furnished, exuding the same quiet dignity as the front room had. Large semiabstract watercolors—one of a woman's face—hung on the walls. Had it been another time, Lauren would have paused to admire the pictures themselves, if not their matting and framing, but she was too busy trying to organize her words and thoughts to handle anything else.

They were all three seated—Susan behind her desk, Matt and Lauren in comfortable chairs before it—when Susan spoke. "What can I do for you?" she asked. Her tone was thoroughly cordial, even warm. The wariness in her eyes was subtle enough to go unnoticed by any but the most watchful of observers. Lauren and Matt were that.

Lauren went straight for the heart. "You've noticed the resemblance, haven't you?"

Susan frowned. "Resemblance?" Her expression was one of confusion, but it was studied. A second, almost imperceptible drain of color from her face betrayed her.

"I have a problem," Lauren explained softly, her eyes never once leaving Susan's. "I was hoping you could help me. Several months back I had plastic surgery, reconstructive work, actually, to correct a long-standing medical problem. The work was extensive, and when it was done, I looked like a new person. But after I returned to the States—the clinic where I had the surgery was in the Bahamas—I ran into trouble. Things started happening. Odd things. Dangerous things." She gave several examples, then paused, looking for a reaction in Susan. But the latter, aside from her underlying pallor, remained composed, so Lauren went on.

"Matt and I put two and two together when I began to get letters addressed to Susan Miles. We realized that I was being mistaken for someone else, but we couldn't find a Susan Miles in the area and we didn't know what to do next. Then, just about a week ago, I was abducted, forced off the street into a car by two men who firmly believed I was Susan Miles."

Susan blinked. That was all.

"They drove me around for hours, finally brought me to an abandoned warehouse and told me their plan. They meant to set me on fire and watch me burn. They had every intention of seeing me dead, as their boss wanted me to be." Lauren paused again, this time out of necessity. Her voice began to shake, whether from remembered terror or the utterly bland look on Susan Miles's face, she didn't know.

Matt came to her aid. "Lauren managed to escape. But we don't know if they're still out looking for her or if they actually let her go because she managed to convince them she wasn't Susan. The police have nothing to go on, at least nothing that's leading them anywhere, and Lauren can't live under guard indefinitely. We realized then that our only hope was in finding Susan."

For the first time, Susan stirred. She propped her elbow on the arm of her chair and rested her chin on her knuckles. Her fingernails were beautifully shaped and painted a sheer pink noncolor. "I'm not sure I understand. I'm a beauty consultant, not a detective. Why have you come to me?"

Lauren resumed speaking, more calmly, now, and briefly sketched the course of their search. She concluded with a soft "Ann Broszczynski sent us here."

Susan's eyes were blank and she was shaking her head, but her knuckles had curved into a fist. "None of those names mean anything to me. Ann—whoever she is—must have been wrong. I have no idea why she sent you here."

"I think you do," Matt challenged. "You saw the resemblance to your old self the minute you looked at Lauren, and we saw the resemblance the minute we looked at you."

A hoarse laugh tripped from Susan's throat. "This is ludicrous! I don't know why I'm even sitting here listening to you." But she didn't move. "Do you really expect me to swallow the story you've told? I'm sorry. Even if I believed it, which I don't, I don't know why someone would have sent you to *me*. And as far as the resemblance is concerned, you're mistaken—"

"No." Matt spoke softly, trying his best to understand her fear as he tamped down his own impatience. "We're not here to hurt you. You have a problem, and because of that, Lauren has a problem. I, for one, don't think it's fair that she's been saddled with it. She did nothing but try to correct a medical deficiency, and now she's being punished. We know that Theodore Prinz is at the root of the problem. We also know that unless you agree to go to the police and testify along with Lauren, he'll snake his way free." Susan's telephone chirped melodically. Matt ignored it. "It's only a matter of time before he finds you—Ann realized that—and he may well kill Lauren along the way."

When the phone on the desk chimed a second time, Susan picked it up. Her every movement was carefully controlled. "Yes?... She's back?... No, no, don't let her go. I'll be there in a second." Replacing the receiver, she rose from her seat and headed for the door. Matt was instantly on his feet, but she held him off with a hand. "There's a problem at the front desk. I have to see to it, but I'll be back. Please don't go anywhere. I'd like to hear more about this Theodore Prinz."

With that, she left the office. The door had no sooner closed behind her than the phone rang again, that same soft tinkle. Matt stared at it and frowned. When he made a move toward it, Lauren was one step ahead. Their lines of sight merged on the keyboard. A red dot flashed beside the bottommost number, one that was separate from the others, one totally apart from that marked "X" that would connect the interoffice line.

"Damn it," Matt barked, heading for the door, "she's gone! That wasn't the receptionist. It was someone on her personal line, someone who's calling back now to find out what in the hell she was talking about." He was in the hall, looking first one way, then the other, with Lauren by his side. "I'll take the back, sweetheart. It probably leads to an alley. No, you take the back. I'll circle around and head her off." He burst into a run toward the front of the shop.

Brushing past the white curtain at the end of the hall, Lauren raced through the back room, threw open the door and dashed up the steps. Yes, there was an alley, a long, long alley strewn with trash cans and miscellaneous other debris. Susan Miles was about halfway down its length and running.

"Michele!" Lauren screamed as she, too, broke into a run. "Wait!"

Susan wasn't waiting. She was running as if the devil himself were at her heels, and would have long since made it to the end of the alley had it not been for the dodging the obstacle course demanded.

"Michele! Wait! It's dangerous!"

But Susan had no intention of stopping. Had it not been for Matt's timely appearance at the end of the alley, she'd have escaped. As it was, when she saw him, she whirled around, saw Lauren, whirled again and made for the nearest doorway. Matt reached her before she made it.

Capturing her bodily, he swung her up and wrestled her back until he'd pinned her to the nearest brick wall. "I am *not* going to hurt you, Susan," he gritted out between breaths, "but neither...neither am I going to let you get away. Not...after all we've been through to find you, not after all Lauren's been through *because* of you."

Lauren came to a breathless halt just as Susan sagged lower against the wall. Matt simply shifted his grip, veeing his hands under her arms and propping her right back up. She'd tricked him once. Lauren agreed with his caution.

"It wasn't my fault," Susan gasped. Her composure had vanished. There was near panic in the eyes that skipped from Matt's face to Lauren's and back. "I'd been with Ted for two years before I discovered who he really was. I wanted to leave him then, but he wouldn't hear of it. For a year, a whole year, I tried, but he threatened awful things and I kept giving in until I hated myself nearly as much as I hated him. I was desperate...so desperate that I tried to kill myself."

"A suicide attempt?" Matt drawled. "We knew about the accident, but that's a new twist to the story."

"Why else would I drive over a cliff? You thought I wasn't in the car when it went over the edge? I was. *I was.* But I was thrown free when the car began to roll." Trembling, she shoved the hair from her forehead. Just below her hairline was a three-inch scar. "I broke an arm and several ribs, but I could breathe and think and feel, and it was then that I realized I'd been given a second chance. So I let them think that I'd died, and I ran. Don't ask me what hospital I went to—it was in some godforsaken town in northern Arizona."

"How did you get there?"

"I hitchhiked."

"Talk of ludicrous stories!"

"It's the truth. At the time, nothing was more dangerous than staying where I was."

"Why didn't you go to the police? If Prinz threatened you—"

"Ted *owns* the police, or half of them, and what he doesn't own he has connections to. I know what I'm talking about. I've seen him buy his way out of serious investigations. That was what tipped me off in the first place!"

Lauren entered the conversation at that point. She was beginning to feel sorry for Susan. While she understood Matt's anger, she wanted to put the other woman at ease. They still needed her cooperation. "Okay," she said gently. "You felt you couldn't go to the police. Where did you go? What did you use for money? The two men who kidnapped me mentioned furs and jewels."

"I had both. Ted had given them to me. As far as I was concerned, I'd earned them."

"But how did you get them? You'd have to have gone back to Los Angeles."

"A friend did it." Susan's voice softened. "He was a little old man who used to sell flowers on a street corner not far from the boutique. I liked him. He reminded me of my father—or what my father would have been like if he'd lived beyond forty," she added in a whisper. "Sam was kind and gentle. I knew he'd do anything for me." She averted her gaze. "Maybe it was wrong of me, or arrogant. I knew Sam was dying. He'd told me that he'd been given six months to live. I figured that he wouldn't mind the risk, that he'd take pleasure in helping me out." Her eyes met Lauren's. "And he did. He told me so in a note he stuck inside the pocket of one of the coats."

"An old man, breaking into your apartment and stealing your things?" Matt was clearly skeptical.

"He didn't steal them," Susan shot back. "He simply returned to me what was mine. As for breaking into my apartment—he had friends who would have done anything for him, just as I would have."

"But you never got the chance," Matt concluded sarcastically, only to be instantly corrected.

"I did. After I sold the very first ring, I sent him a large chunk of the money. I know he received it, because I called him to make sure." Susan took a ragged breath. "Whether he lived long enough to enjoy it, I'll never know. I've tried to call him again, but there's been no answer. He may be using the money to travel, or he may be...well, I'll never know."

Matt stared at her. "Prinz's men may have had him killed."

"Do you think I don't know that?" Susan cried. "I've *seen* Ted in action—"

"Isn't it about time you did something about it?"

The air between the two sizzled. Lauren set about diffusing it. "We're getting ahead of ourselves. Did you come directly to Washington from Arizona?"

Susan was leaning against the brick on her own now, Matt having released her and stepped back. She took several calming breaths. "I made a few stops. I wasn't sure where I wanted to settle. But each time I stopped, I felt I was still too close to Ted, so I kept going. When I reached Washington, it was either stay or swim. So I stayed."

"What about your nose?" Lauren frowned as she leaned to the side for a profile view. "We assumed you'd have plastic surgery to change your looks. Prinz's men assumed the same, which was how they got onto me.''

"I figured they'd think that, so I avoided it." Susan gave a self-conscious half shrug. "My nose had been broken in the accident, and I didn't trust the doctors in that hospital to do more than tape it up. When the bandages came off, I saw the bump. It was subtle enough to change my profile just that little bit. I told myself it'd give my face character." She snorted. "Obviously it didn't fool you."

"We started with an advantage." It was Matt speaking, more gently now. "We had your name and knew where to find you. Even before you walked into that reception area, we were primed to see Susan Miles."

With an air of helplessness, Susan raised her eyes to the sliver of sky above. "Well, you saw her. And you have her cornered. I suppose I knew that someday someone would find me. In some ways, it's a relief that it's you."

"Then you do trust us?" he asked.

Her gaze met his. "Trust? Maybe that's going a little too far."

Lauren grasped her arm. "But you do believe that what we've told you is the truth."

Susan studied her for a long time. "The resemblance...it's amazing. What did you look like before?"

Dropping Susan's arm, Lauren glanced awkwardly at Matt, who nodded. "I was awful." Lauren proceeded to paint a brief, if blunt, picture of her former self. "Richard took care of it all, bless him." She winced. "Then again..."

Matt curved his hand around her neck. "No, no, sweetheart. From a purely medical standpoint, it is a blessing, what he did. And as for this other, we'll work it all out. Susan will go to the police with us—"

"Whoa. I never said that."

"But you have to!" Lauren cried. "It's your only chance. Sooner or later those guys will find you—"

A deep voice cut her off with an ominously sarcastic "Hel-lo, hel-lo."

All three heads jerked around. Lauren and Susan gasped in tandem. Matt grew rigid.

"What have we here?" drawled the man whose face and voice Lauren would never in a million years forget. He stood several yards away, a human wall with a gleaming gun in his hand. "Matthew Kruger, Lauren Stevenson...and if it isn't the elusive Miss Susan Miles."

"What do you want, Leo?" Susan demanded. Her eyes were hard, glittering more with disgust than with fear.

Leo grinned, that ugly grin Lauren remembered so well, and looked first at Mouse on his left, then at another thug on his right. The eyes he refocused on Susan were nearly black. "You know what I want. I want you."

"I'm not available."

"Seems to me you are." He cocked his head toward Lauren and Matt. "These two don't want you, that's for sure. You've been a thorn in their sides."

"I'd pick her any day—" Lauren began, only to be silenced by the restraining hand Matt put on her arm, and by his own retort.

"You've got the three of us, and you know damn well that if you so much as touch Susan, we'll go straight to the police. Do you plan a triple murder?"

"Wouldn't bother the boss any. I have his okay."

"Think, Leo, think," Susan urged. "There are too many people involved now. If you do something to Matt and Lauren, someone *else* will go to the police. This isn't another one of your little in-house jobs. If you kill one of your own, you're doing us all a favor. But to kill me—and these two, who are totally innocent... The police will get you one day, Leo. And if you think Ted will come forward on your behalf, you're crazy."

Leo laughed. "The police won't get me. I'm good at what I do. We'll have it arranged so it looks like you shot the others, then killed yourself. Very clean."

"Very simpleminded," Susan retorted. When Leo made a move toward her, she slipped into a half crouch, arms raised. "I think it's only fair to warn you that I've learned karate."

Lauren and Matt glanced at each other, then at Susan. Leo threw back his head and laughed louder. "Talk of simpleminded. That threat's the oldest in the book, and in your case it's empty. You haven't had the time to learn enough karate to protect yourself."

"I'm a quick study."

"Against a gun?"

Susan had no answer for that, and Matt and Lauren said nothing. They were concentrating on the gun, measuring the distance between Leo and his accomplices, peripherally evaluating the potential weaponry within reach.

"Gotcha there, don't I?" Leo said. He took a step back. "Okay, I want the three of you to start moving. Straight to the car at the head of the alley." He gestured at Susan with the gun. "You first."

Lauren swallowed hard. She had no desire to be in a car with Leo and company. She knew the helplessness of that. No, if a move was to be made, it had to be now.

Matt's hand remained on her arm, but it was steadily tightening. He agreed with her. She waited for his signal.

Slowly Susan moved forward. She hadn't taken two steps, though, when her ankle turned and she buckled over.

"Ah, hell," Leo moaned. "That's the corniest move I've ever seen. It won't get you anywhere, Susan, and if you think I'm going to carry you, you're nuts.''

"These heels," Susan gasped. "They're too high."

Matt's hand tightened all the more on Lauren's arm. They both knew from personal experience how well Susan could maneuver, high heels or no. Internally coiled and ready, they watched her unstrap the thin buckles and remove the shoes.

"Come on, come on. We haven't all day—" Leo's words were abruptly cut off by a totally unexpected, lightning-quick move. As Susan straightened, she hiked her slim skirt high on her thighs, spun around and delivered a kick that would have made her instructor proud.

The gun went flying, as did Matt, who barreled into Leo's midsection, knocking the burly man to the ground. Susan, meanwhile, turned her attention to the other men, throwing strategically placed kicks with such speed that they barely knew what hit them. When Mouse doubled over in pain, she whirled around and into his pal, and by the time she was done with him, she was aiming lethal chops at Mouse again.

Lauren came to her aid. Grabbing a heavy shovel from its resting place beside a nearby trash bin, she slammed it repeatedly against the back of whichever man Susan wasn't battering. Each slam vented a little more of her anger, and she might have actually enjoyed herself if she hadn't shot a glance at Matt.

He and Leo were fighting hand to hand, tumbling on the filthy pavement, each landing his share of punches.

Dropping the shovel, Lauren scrambled along the alley, returning seconds later to put an end to the fray. *"That's it!"* she screamed. *"Enough!"* She stood a safe distance back with her feet planted firmly, both hands curved around Leo's gun. The fact that she didn't know how to use it was secondary to the proprietary air with which she held it. Her chest was heaving, the only part of her that betrayed any weakness.

Later she realized that if she'd had to shoot, she'd never have been able to separate Matt from Leo, so fast were they shifting. But her strident yell brought all heads up in surprise. Matt took advantage of the precious seconds to free himself and stumble to her side. He grabbed the gun and turned it on the trio.

"Susan! That's enough!" he ordered. She'd been poised to deliver another side-handed slice to Mouse's head, and only with reluctance did she lower her arm and move back.

Matt motioned with the gun toward the three. "Okay, up! And if you think I don't know how to use this, think again. I'm an avid hunter." His knees were bent; both hands were on the gun, holding it aimed and steady. Not once did his eyes leave the men. "Lauren, go back inside the shop and call the police—"

The sound of shoes clattering on the pavement interrupted him, and seconds later the police themselves rounded the corner and entered the alley with their guns drawn. Slowly Matt straightened. He didn't lower his arm until each of Prinz's men had been handcuffed.

"Mr. Kruger?" one of the officers asked. He was the only one not in uniform and was obviously the man in command. "I'm Detective Walker. Phil Huber gave me a call and told me to keep an eye out. He sensed there might be some trouble."

"How did you know where to come?" Matt wondered. His voice shook. He shot a glance behind him to make sure Lauren was safe.

Walker smiled and cocked his head toward Susan, who stood warily at the side. "Miss Miles's receptionist gave us a call when she found out that something had gone awry with your, uh, beauty consultation. Sorry we didn't get here sooner." He studied Matt's face. "We might have spared you a little of that."

Gingerly Matt fingered his cheek, then his mouth. In the next instant, he reached out for Lauren and hauled her close. She was eager to support him; he'd fought valiantly and had to be uncomfortable.

"Those three thugs intended to kill us," he said.

Lauren pointed. "Those *two* were the ones who kidnapped me back in Boston."

"No doubt," Matt added, his eyes filled with venom, "the third is another of Prinz's men."

"His name is Hank Ober, but he's called Rat," Susan stated stiffly. "The one with the ugly nose is Leo Charney, and the other, Mouse, is Malcolm Donnia." She watched as the three men were hustled off. "What will you do with them?"

The detective faced her. "Book them for attempted murder."

"Then what?"

"They'll be arraigned, and if they can post bond, they'll be released until their trial."

"*Released!* Do you know what they'll do once they hit the streets? They'll disappear. But before they do that, they'll finish off one or another of us, if not all three!"

"Susan..." Matt took her shoulder with his free hand. "That won't happen. The police won't *let* it—"

"The police! If they're not already in Ted's pocket, they will be soon!"

"Just a minute now," Walker growled. He took a menacing step closer. "I have never been, and will never be, in anyone's pocket, and I can safely vouch for three-quarters of my men."

"And the other quarter?"

"They won't be allowed anywhere *near* this case. The Ted Prinzes of the world would like to believe they can buy their way out of trouble, but it won't work here."

"You know of Ted?" Susan asked, wavering.

"Every major law-enforcement officer in the country knows of him. It will be one of the greatest thrills of my career to nail him, but I can do that only if you're willing to testify."

"You have to, Susan," Lauren begged. "Once and for all, it has to be put to rest."

Matt echoed her sentiment. "Lauren's right. If the three of us work together, we can do it. Lauren and I alone...well, it'll be tougher."

"He'll still come after me. It won't matter if he's in prison."

Walker spoke up. "He won't *dare* come after you. Nor will he send anyone else. He knows we'll be watching his every step. I've seen how these men work, Susan. Revenge may eat them alive, but in the end they opt for survival. Prinz will be signing his own death warrant if he comes near you again. He'll know that. Believe me, he'll know it."

Susan swallowed and looked from the detective to Matt and Lauren. "I want to believe. Really I do."

"Trust him," Matt urged. "Trust *us*. But then, you already do, don't you?"

"What makes you think that?" she returned, but there was a softness in her tone.

Matt smiled, then winced when his bruised lip protested. He soothed the spot with his finger. "You really do know karate, but you don't try it on me. One kick, and you'd have escaped. The fact that you didn't try it had to mean something." He ventured a second smile, this one more carefully. "How *did* you learn it so quickly?"

Susan shrugged and gave a tentative grin of her own. "Like I told Leo, I'm a quick study."

Matt chuckled softly. Reaching out, he drew Susan to his side at the same time that his arm tightened around Lauren. "You'll work with us, Susan, won't you?"

Susan moistened her lips, but it was Lauren she was looking at. "After all you've gone through for me, I guess I'll have to." She jerked her head toward Matt. "Where did you even find this big lummox, Lauren? Do you think maybe he has an identical twin stashed away somewhere?"

Lauren grinned up at Matt. "I don't think there's another man like him on the face of the earth. He's pretty special, isn't he?"

Purpled cheek, bruised lip, battered ribs and all, Matt sucked in a deep breath and threw back his head. "Ahhhh. Paradise. One pretty lady on the left, one pretty lady on the right...if only my buddies at the beer hall could see me now!"

"THE BEER HALL? You never talked about a beer hall. For that matter," Lauren said, scowling, "you never said you were an avid hunter." They were back in the hotel room after spending the afternoon at the police station. Lauren had insisted that Matt take a long, hot bath to soothe his aching body, but now she had him in bed, exactly where she wanted him.

Matt looked up at her through one half-lidded eye. "Where did you think construction workers went for fun?" He steeled himself against an attack that never came.

"Did you get drunk?" Lauren asked.

"On occasion."

"What were you like…drunk?"

He shrugged the shoulder she wasn't leaning against. "I don't know. I was too far out of it to tell."

She grinned. "And the hunting?"

"Wooden ducks at an amusement park. We should go sometime. I'll win you a huge stuffed teddy bear."

Lauren settled onto him, gently and with a sigh. "Thanks, but I've already got one." She rubbed her ear against the tawny hair on his chest and stilled only when he began to stroke her back.

"You're pretty special yourself," he murmured. "The way you thought to go for that gun, and then the way you held it…I thought for a minute that *you* were the one with experience."

"All a bluff. I've never held a gun in my life."

"Not even a water gun?"

"Nope. My parents were pacifists. Dead set against weapons of any kind. That's one of the things that drove them crazy about Brad. He used to make guns out of whatever toys he had handy. Some of them were pretty creative."

"Lauren?"

She took a deep breath, inhaling the clean, male scent of his skin. "Mmm?"

"What will your parents say about me?"

"That depends," she said softly and raised her head. "It depends on what I tell them first."

"How about you tell them that I love you and want to marry you?"

"How about I tell them that you're fearless and strong, or that you've got brains as well as brawn, or that you saved my life?"

"I didn't save your life. You escaped from the warehouse on your own. Then, today, you were the one who saved all of our lives."

"You saved my life."

"How did I save your life?"

"You gave it deep, deep, lasting meaning. A good job is fine. So's a good house, even a pretty face. But the thing that really pulled it all together was you. I love you, Matt. Love is what counts. Always has been, always will be."

Matt cleared his throat, but his voice still came out hoarse. "How about you tell them that I love you and want to marry you?"

"They'll hit the roof, but you know something?" Lauren asked, pushing her chin out. "I don't care! If they love me—and I'm sure they do—they'll come around in time. So. Any other questions?"

"Just one. Aren't you worried about where we'll live?"

She turned the tables on him. "Are you?"

"No."

"Why not?"

"Because I've already decided that if my boss won't open a permanent Boston office, I'm quitting. I've made enough contacts here to get another job. And I love the farmhouse in Lincoln." He paused, narrowing his eyes. "But you knew that. You've known all along. You're too smart, that's what you are. You've got me wrapped around your little finger. Y'know, maybe I ought to rethink this. If I'm going to be led around by the nose for another fifty or sixty years—"

Lauren's lips silenced him, and within seconds he was fully involved in the nonverbal give-and-take of love. Belying the punishment he had taken that day, he rolled over to cover her with his body. Hands buried deep in her hair, hips poised above hers, he whispered thickly, "...for another fifty or sixty years, I'll love it...every...sweet...minute."

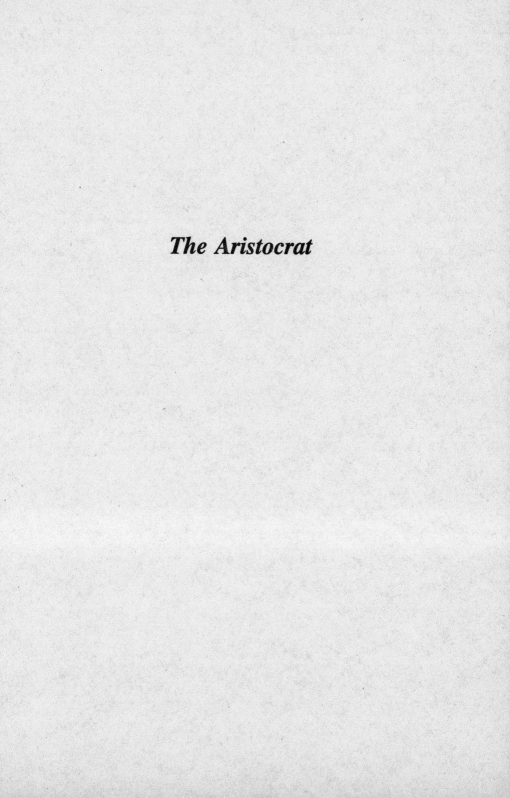

The Aristocrat

Prologue

The New York Astros' offense stood helplessly on the sidelines, gripping their helmets, their eyes glued on the players on the field as the Steelers' field goal kicker, Karpatian, sent a high, slicing kick from the forty-third yard line toward the uprights. Brant Asher watched the ball sail inside the right goalpost by no more than inches and watched tensely for the signals.

The kick was good.

Guy Richardson, the Astros' kicker, threw his helmet to the ground and stomped his feet in disbelieving frustration. *"Damnation!* I don't believe it, for God's sake! He couldn't get the other two up in the air! Fifty-three yards!"

Karpatian jumped a good three feet in the air and disappeared into a mob of teammates.

"The fans here in Three Rivers Stadium are going bananas!" screamed the excited field announcer. It felt, Brant thought blankly, as if the stands were trembling.

Brant heard some vivid cursing from his teammates, but most of them stood quietly, their heads lowered. He looked over at the final score flashing on the electronic scoreboard: 24 to 21. This play-off game was over; it was history. Their chance at the Superbowl was down the tubes. He shut out the noise from the crowd, clutched his helmet tightly in his hands and made his way to Sam Carverelli, the Astros' coach. He looked as rotten as Brant felt. His bushy gray eyebrows nearly met over his forehead, his shoulders were slumped, and his lips were a thin white line.

"Jesus," Brant heard him whisper. "Now I've got to go congratulate that polecat Howard! A damned fluke! Karpatian is the biggest mistake he ever made!"

Brant wrapped a muscled arm around his coach's shoulders. "Luck's the next best thing," he said, for want of anything better.

Sam Carverelli pulled himself together by a thread and blinked up at his prized quarterback's face. "Hell, Brant, it isn't fair. Our second winning season—oh, what's the use? Let's get over there before this crowd goes ape."

Most of the Astros were already on the field, congratulating the Steelers. The tension was over. The Steeler fans would soon forget this football game, for they had another game to think about in only a week. The Astros would be home watching the rest of the play-offs and the Superbowl on TV.

They'd played well today, for the most part, Brant thought as he jogged toward the center of the field to congratulate Joe Marks, the Steelers' quarterback. If Eddie Riggs hadn't fumbled in the second quarter on the Steelers' thirty-eight yard line, if he hadn't thrown that one interception in the first quarter. Too many damned ifs. He'd had twenty-four completions today, including two for touchdowns to Lloyd Nolan, and Washington Taylor had rushed for over a hundred yards. But it hadn't been enough. He was deaf to the incredible noise as he trod over the football field, unwary now of the uprooted clumps of turf that could easily trip up a quarterback. There would be no more football until next summer.

Joe Marks was so euphoric that he didn't at first recognize Brant. "Lordie, Lordie," he shouted over and over again, clapping Brant on the back until he realized who he was. He doused his elation and clamped down on his competitiveness. He was the winner. "We lucked out, Brant, didn't we?"

"Sure did. Good game, Joe." *How sweet it is.* He almost grinned at Jackie Gleason's famous quote. Sweet for Joe and the Steelers.

The two longtime competitors shook hands, and Brant stepped back, letting Joe return to his moment of glory. The locker room scene with champagne soaking sweaty uniforms, plastering everyone's hair to their heads with booze, would be his today.

Brant fell in with a group of his silent teammates on their trek to the Astros' locker room. He was thirty-one, at the height of his career. He thought for one depressed moment that maybe it was time to retire from football, retire with dignity. Then he thought of Kenny Stabler, the Snake, still out there, taking on all comers. He wondered how the Snake felt, seeing those huge young men on the field, eager to stomp all over him. Age, he'd begun to realize once he reached thirty, wasn't a relative thing in football. Even at thirty-one, he faced men eight years his junior. He grinned for a brief moment. He imagined that Joe Marks, over thirty himself, wasn't thinking about being at all old right now.

The locker room was subdued. Suddenly Brant wanted to yell at all his glum teammates that losing in the play-offs wasn't the end of the world, for God's sake. They'd had their second winning season in a row. The owner might be crying now, but he'd made a lot of money with the Astros the past two years.

Brant Asher, all-pro quarterback, jumped on one of the benches and shouted, "All right, you turkeys! Before the press breaks down the doors, I want you to stop acting like I've just screwed your wife!" At least I'm getting their attention, he thought, willing the bummed-out athletes to respond to him.

"There wasn't a damned thing we could do about Karpatian's kick. At least the man still has a job—next year, anyway."

A laugh came from Nolan Lloyd.

"He can't even speak English," growled Guy Richardson, "and he's got a beer gut."

"And a lucky foot," Brant said. "Listen up, you guys, we're going out winners. George, give a towel to Lance. I saw a *person* of the press out there, and we don't want Lance to scare her. Give the lady something to wonder about."

Good, Brant thought as he stepped off the bench, seeing a few grins. He briefly turned an eye toward the horde of reporters filing into the locker room. He watched Lance Carver, a huge lineman, quickly wrap his towel around his waist.

Because he'd won and lost countless games since high school, and been on the receiving end of endless pushy questions during his first three years in pro ball with a consistently losing team, Brant fielded the press's questions with aplomb. He saw from the corner of his eye that one of the media people had managed to get Tiny Phipps, only twenty-two and a rookie, in a lather of emotion. He quickly answered several more questions, then made his way to the young linebacker, clapped the two-hundred-seventy pound player on the back and said to the reporter, whose microphone was inches from his nose, "You'll be seeing Tiny next year, folks. This guy's got a helluva future." In Tiny's ear he whispered, "Don't give them what they want, Tiny. Just give 'em a victory sign and send it to your mother."

It was a good forty-five minutes before the press left the team in peace. Brant stood under the shower, letting the hot needles of water soak into his sore muscles. His right arm was in agony. Maybe he'd need an operation next season, maybe he'd lose his famous snap... *Stop it, you fool! Why don't you listen to your own speech!*

It was close to another hour before he was free of his teammates and out of the Astros' locker room. They were flying back to New York tonight, and he wanted the quiet of his hotel room for a couple of hours.

But he wasn't going to get it. The press *person* he had spotted earlier was waiting for him. She was a forceful, no-nonsense woman, and her eyes fastened on him like a vulture's who'd just trapped her prey. She was elegant-looking, of course. All the female press corps who covered sports were.

"Mr. Asher," JoAnn Marrow said, her pencil poised over an open notebook. "I wanted to speak to you just a moment." She gave him a wide smile, and he noticed that her front teeth were so perfect they defied nature. She gave a high, grating laugh. "I guess you'll want to be called Viscount Asherwood now!"

He blinked at her. It was a moment before he saw her TV crew stealthily ease up behind her. Before the microphone was hooked up, he said, "What did you say? Viscount?"

Her artificial laughter floated upward, picked up by the microphones. "You didn't know? It just came over the wire service. Your great uncle has just died in England and left you an estate and a title."

"Hey, Brant," one of the crew called out, "you're an English aristocrat!"

There was good-natured laughter.

"Make that the top of the line: 'Brant the Dancer—Aristocrat!'"

"Brant the Dancer runs for ten yards in the House of Lords."

"What do the English call that book of theirs? Oh yeah, DeBretts. You're a star, Dancer, and not in the Football Hall of Fame!"

"I can just hear them on the tube next season: 'Now, folks, our star quarterback, my lord Asherwood'!"

Brant stared vacantly at the lot of them, faded memories flooding his mind. Asherwood. Lord Asherwood, an ancient old relic who'd more or less commanded his appearance in England last year. He hadn't gone, put off by the obnoxiousness of the old man's letter to his heir. Now he was dead. He'd never had a whit of interest in England, or his father's unobtrusive relatives, unobtrusive at least until a year ago. Brant's grandfather, Arthur, had come to the United States in the early twenties and shortened his name to Asher, and Brant had never thought of himself as anything but an Asher and an American. Good God, he thought blankly, who the hell cares if I'm Lord Asherwood or Count Dracula?

There was a microphone in front of his face. JoAnn Marrow was waiting for his comment. He pulled himself together and said pleasantly, "I haven't heard a word about this. But," he managed a thin smile, "I am not surprised that you are way ahead of me. The press always has the jump on everyone else. I'll have a statement when I find out exactly what has happened."

"But you knew, didn't you, Brant, that you were heir to an English title?"

He gave JoAnn as big a white-toothed smile as she was bestowing on him. "Yeah, I knew. I'll be certain to invite all of you to a big bash when I get everything straightened out."

He wasn't allowed to get away that easily, but finally, by dint of simply shutting himself in his rented Corvette and revving the powerful engine, he blocked them out. He knew he couldn't go back to the hotel. They'd be waiting for him. He drove around Pittsburgh, not really seeing the sights, until he had to return to his hotel and pack for the return flight.

He managed to sneak in the back way. On the way out of the hotel, buried in a group of his teammates, he saw the six o'clock news blaring loudly on a color TV in the lobby. He shook his head in disbelief as he watched himself and JoAnn Marrow. Lord Asherwood had upstaged the game! He felt the nudge of an elbow in his ribs and gave Nolan Lloyd a bemused shake of his head.

Brant was feeling closer to sixty than thirty-one when he finally drove into the underground parking garage of his west-side New York condominium. His muscles were stiff, and a bruise on his ribs from a crunching tackle throbbed. He focused his thoughts on his Jacuzzi as he retrieved his suitcase from the trunk of his Porsche. And then bed, to sleep for a good twelve hours. He would turn on his answering machine and bolt the front door. No press, no questions until he could call his mother and sort out what had happened. Who, he wondered, had spilled the news to the press?

His two-bedroom condo was on the thirty-fifth floor, and the elevator had never seemed slower. Two residents were in the elevator with him, and they were solicitous about the loss to the Steelers. They said nothing, bless them, about his newly acquired dignities.

He unlocked the front door, stepped inside and firmly closed it behind him. Home, he thought as he fastened the extra chain-lock in place. He strode through the living room, not bothering to turn on the lights as he flipped on the answering machine and went straight to the immense bathroom. He'd stripped off his clothes and lowered his grateful body into the hot swirling water of his Jacuzzi when he heard a noise. He cocked one eye open and turned toward the open door of the bathroom.

Marcie Ellis stood there, her tall, charmingly formed body silhouetted in the bathroom light. He started to smile, but didn't have the chance, because she said abruptly, "I can't believe you didn't tell me, Brant! I look like an utter fool with that bitch JoAnn Marrow getting the jump on me!"

"Marcie, I was kind of busy with the game, just like everyone else. Who cares who interviews the loser, anyway?"

"I'm not talking about the ridiculous game. You an English lord and I knew nothing about it!" Her dark brown eyes flashed magnificently, and she tossed back her thick auburn hair with an impatient hand.

"Ridiculous, Marcie? I promise my body doesn't agree with you, at least at the moment. It is how I make my living, you know."

Marcie flushed and lowered her eyes. She knew Brant well enough to realize that when he spoke very quietly, his voice nearly emotionless, he was angry. "I—I'm sorry, darling. I was dreadfully disappointed that the Astros lost. I know how much it meant to you and the team." She shrugged slightly, one thin strap of her nightgown falling down her arm. "You'll make it next year; I know you will."

"Yeah, it's possible," he agreed. "What are you doing here, Marcie? You know that I'm half-dead after a game."

She rarely considered deception, particularly with Brant, because he had an uncanny ability to see through it. "I hadn't intended to come," she said truthfully, "but after I saw the news, I wanted to know why the hell you hadn't told me yourself."

That was one thing he liked about Marcie, other than her exquisite sensitivity in bed. If suitably encouraged, she could be frighteningly blunt. It was a quality that made her an excellent reporter. "I really never thought about it," he said with equal honesty. "I knew the old bird was getting older, but I don't care about English titles. Good God, I'm as American as the stadium hot dogs. In fact, I can't believe the media are making such a fuss about it."

"Don't be stupid," Marcie said sharply. "It's not like you're Joe Schmuck from Kansas!"

"I'm not Joe Montana from California, either."

"You're still famous, and people eat up a story like this. I can just see JoAnn's headline now: *Athletic Aristocrat.* It isn't fair. If only I'd known!"

A lot of things weren't fair today. "I think I'd prefer something less cutesy, like nothing at all."

"You can take your preferences and flush them, Brant. It'll take a good week for all this to cool down."

The other strap fell, and the gown slithered down a good three inches. He felt his muscles ease miraculously. Lord, he loved her breasts. "Tell you what," he said, rising from the tub and reaching for a towel, "I'll give you an exclusive interview when I find out what the hell is going on. Okay?"

Marcie forgot her snit for a moment as her eyes traveled down his body. "There's an ugly bruise on your ribs," she said.

"Yeah," he said, giving her a wide grin. "Do you think you can limit yourself to the north and south?"

"Primarily south," she said on a slow smile.

Chapter One

Daphne Claire Asherwood sat cross-legged on her blue flowered beach towel, watching the tourists, mainly German, board the small motorboat tied to the dock of the Elounda Beach Hotel. They were off for a day of fishing and swimming on one of the many deserted islands off the north-eastern coast of Crete.

As usual, the Greek sun was so hot she could feel her knee caps beginning to burn after only thirty minutes. Blast her fair complexion, she thought, reaching for her bottle of sunscreen. As she rubbed the thick cream into her warm flesh, she smiled ruefully at the two brief strips of bright orange nylon that covered her. Uncle Clarence would have had a seizure if he'd seen her in something so very revealing.

Uncle Clarence, dead now, and with no more control over her life. She felt little grief at his passing at ninety years of age, only an occasional expectation of hearing his voice, commanding in his querulous way for her to fetch something for him. He's a lonely old man, she'd told herself when she'd felt the familiar spurt of resentment. He really can't help that he's hateful and treats me like a housekeeper, nurse and servant, a possession to be at his beck and call at any time, day or night. I owe him because he took me in when my parents died. It was a litany that had become more difficult over the years. Now she was free of him. She sighed and carefully fastened the cap on the sunscreen. Aunt Cloe would tell her roundly to stop dwelling on those long, empty years at Asherwood. "Life," Aunt Cloe would say grandly, "life, my dear little egg, awaits you!"

Well, Daphne thought, thrusting her chin upward, I'm ready for it...I think. But how did one go about grasping life if one had no notion of what to grasp at? What was she going to do when she returned to England? I am an adult, twenty-three years old, she told herself yet again, a new litany in response to the thorny question. An adult always thinks of something. She looked down her body at the bikini and shook her head, bemused. She would never forget the look on Aunt Cloe's face when she'd emerged from the posh dressing room in an Athens department store, slinking forward, her hands furtively trying to cover herself.

"Merciful heavens!" Aunt Cloe had exclaimed. "And here I thought you a skinny little twit! Goodness, love, what a bosom! Now that I think of it, your dear mama was marvelously endowed. I shan't despair, no indeed, I shan't despair."

Despair about what? Daphne had wondered. It was true about the bosom, hidden for so many years beneath her loose jumpers and oversized windcheaters. She personally thought she looked lopsided, particularly since the rest of her was so skinny.

"No, love, not skinny," Aunt Cloe had said sharply, demolishing Daphne's tentative observation. "Fashionably svelte! Like a model, at least from the seventh or eighth rib down."

And now here she was in Greece, on the island of Crete, a place she'd dreamed for years of visiting, sitting on a beach and looking like a model, from the ribs down. Eighth rib.

Why, she groaned silently, running one hand distractedly through her long hair, did I let Aunt Cloe talk me into this? Not that Crete wasn't one of the most beautiful places Daphne had ever seen, for it was. Aunt Cloe had known for years that Daphne had spun dreams of visiting the Acropolis and the Greek isles, and particularly King Minos' palace, now partially restored, on the outskirts of the capitol of Crete, Herakleion. And, of course, Aunt Cloe knew she would simply adore the exquisite small village of St. Nicholas with all its colorful fishing boats and quaint canals. "Well, little egg," Aunt Cloe had said to her in mild exasperation when she'd dithered, "do you intend to rot here by yourself at Asherwood until you're booted out by the new viscount? It's time, my girl, to do something for yourself!" Daphne had let Aunt Cloe sweep her away from England after Uncle Clarence's funeral. I'm like a limp noodle, she told herself in silent disgust. Always bending to the stronger will. But at least Aunt Cloe wanted her to have fun.

Suddenly aware that a man was looking her way, his dark eyes resting with a good deal of interest on her bosom, she eased herself quickly into a robe and skittered from the beach. Men, she thought, another problem. What did one *do* with them?

Where the dickens was Aunt Cloe?

Cloe Sparks was busy making an appointment with the French hairdresser in St. Nicholas, Monsieur Etienne.

"She has looked the *jeune fille* for all her life, *monsieur*," she was explaining. "Now she is twenty-three and still looks fourteen. You know, too gamine. We must have something dramatic, scintillating, oh, something *je ne sais quoi*!''

"I understand, *madame*," Monsieur Etienne said, the veil of boredom glazing his dark eyes. These pushy Englishwomen and their deplorable, heavy-handed French! Undoubtedly this gamine was a squat, depressingly plain girl who was probably better off just as she was. "When would you like to bring the young lady to me?" He picked up his appointment book and gave her one of his special intimate smiles.

"Tomorrow at nine o'clock," Cloe said firmly. On the taxi ride back to the Elounda Beach Hotel, Cloe chewed her lower lip, painfully chapped from the relentless Greek sun. She'd forced Daphne into this trip, whirling her willy-nilly away after the old curmudgeon's funeral to Athens, then on to Crete. She'd taken advantage of the girl's sweet biddable nature, just as the old curmudgeon had always done. But, dammit, it was for her own good. Yes, she thought, resolutely, Daphne had to have her chance. She wasn't plain, not by any means. She still had to get Daphne out of those ridiculous glasses of hers and into contacts. She drew a deep breath. One thing at a time, Cloe, she told herself. Everything was right on schedule. She had to remember, she reminded herself, to send a cable to Reggie Hucksley in London. She needed another week, at least.

Brant hugged his mother tightly. "Peace and quiet at last, lots of tender loving care, and no hassles. It's so good to be home. You look beautiful as ever, Mom." She usually teased him when he told her that, because he was her masculine counterpart in looks.

Alice Asher said nothing for a few moments, feeling an equal surge of affection for her splendid son. Thank heaven he wasn't like his father, embarrassed to show his feelings, as if that would make him less than a man. "Welcome home, Brant. It's so good to see you again. In addition to tender loving care, I've made you your favorite dinner—stuffed pork chops and homemade noodles."

"My body will think it's died and gone to heaven with a home-cooked meal, Mom." He gave her another hug and released her.

"There's lots to talk about."

Her eyes searched his face for a moment. He looked tired and, oddly enough, wary and uncertain. "Yes, I imagine there is. But first, honey, why don't you just relax for a while?"

Brant sat down and leaned back against the soft cushions of his mother's infinitely old and comfortable velvet sofa. He grabbed one of the cushions, shoved it behind his head and closed his eyes.

"It's been a hard several days I would imagine," Alice Asher said, her eyes, as brilliant a blue as her only son's, resting sympathetically on on his tired face. "I'm glad you managed to get here in secret. The press has been hounding me, too. Luckily, they haven't managed to track Lily down."

"She's cruising the Aegean, right?" Brant asked, cocking an eye open.

"Yes, this time with her husband," came the tart response.

"It is her honeymoon, Mom," Brant said, grinning at her.

"Her third! And of all things, Danny, Patricia and Keith are staying with *his* mother."

"Don't fret," Brant said. "I like Crusty Dusty, and so do the kids. Lord knows he's rich enough to give her whatever she wants."

"He's closer to my age than Lily's!"

"You know as well as I do that Lily needed someone like Dusty, someone older to keep her in line."

"You should hear his Texas accent!"

"I have. You're not turning into a snob, are you, Mom, just because you're now a dowager viscountess, or something? The way the nobility address each other is craziness."

Alice Asher smiled ruefully. "You're right. I'm a regular old fool, and I sound like an obnoxious mother-in-law." She sighed deeply, clasping her hands in her lap. "I wonder what your father would say to all this."

"He'd laugh, a big belly laugh, and tell them to go shove it. The ridiculous title and the moldering estate."

"Moldering?" Her fair left eyebrow shot up. "What do you know that I don't, Brant?"

He felt a surge of restlessness and bolted up from the sofa. He said over his shoulder as he strode to the bow window that looked into the beautifully landscaped front lawn of his mother's Connecticut home, "I spent several hours yesterday with my lawyer, Tom Bradan, and a *solicitor*—as they say—who'd come all the way from London to 'inform me of my good fortune,' which is exactly what he said in that affected accent. Fellow's name is Harlow Hucksley, of all things! About my age, I'd guess, acts like a pompous nerd, and covers himself with tweed. And skinny as your azalea stems, not a muscle on him."

Alice Asher laughed, picturing Harlow Hucksley with no difficulty. Her splendid athletic son didn't think much of men who were "soft as mulch." She imagined that with his teammates he would be far more specific and excessively graphic.

"He was the jerk who spilled the beans to the press, dam—*darn* him."

"You gave him a tongue-lashing, I suppose."

Brant turned and gave her a crooked grin. "Well, Tom did run a bit of interference for the guy. I tried to outflank him, but it didn't work. He expected me—no, he really *demanded*—that I fly to London and get everything squared away."

"You will go, of course," Alice said calmly.

"Why the...heck should I?" Brant said sharply. "It makes no difference to me what happens to any of it."

Alice Asher gave her son a long, thoughtful look. "I know your father never spoke much about his English relations, and neither did your grandfather, for that matter, but England is a part of your heritage, honey. You are more than half-English, you know, because I've got a drop or two in there somewhere. Remember that letter he wrote you last year? The old man knew a lot about you."

"Obnoxious," Brant said.

"Perhaps. I reread the letter, you know, after you phoned me. It was really rather pathetic."

"Mom, listen. Harlow told me very little, but I gather there are no estates, and no money. Just this moldering old house in a place called Surrey, and maybe some worthless acres surrounding it."

"The house is called Asherwood Hall, and its located in a quaint village, East Grinstead."

"And don't forget that the title had to come to me, so Harlow Hucksley says. The old coot had no choice about that. The rest of it he probably willed to me because it's worthless, and he realized that the American branch had some money and would pour it back into his tomb of a house."

"Well, son," Alice said logically, "you do have money. It really wouldn't hurt for you to at least go see the place. The season's over, after all. You are at loose ends for a while, aren't you?"

Brant shrugged. "I'm supposed to do a commercial for a sporting goods company, but not right away."

"At least it's not shaving cream!"

Brant laughed. "True. Lily told me she'd never speak to me again if I bared my face to the world covered with white sh—stuff." He shot his mother a guilty look from the corner of his eye.

"Don't feel guilty about your...lapses, dear," Alice said, rising. "I expect it'll take you a while to get yourself under control. Last year, if I remember correctly, it took about two months. As for your sister's language—" She shrugged, slanting her right shoulder just as her son did.

"Look, Mom," Brant said, fighting what he knew was now a losing battle, "maybe you should go. You could take charge of things and tell me what you think."

"Brant," she said, her blue eyes sparkling with mischief. "I already have culture. It's time you acquired some. Roots, Brant. They are important. As a personal favor to me, honey."

"Damn," he muttered. "It's not as if I didn't have any culture, for God's sake! I have been to Europe, and I did go to college."

"Yes, dear, I know."

"I didn't have to be tutored like a lot of the athletes!"

"Yes, dear, of course."

"My degree isn't totally worthless. Communications. Maybe I'll go into announcing when I retire from football."

"Yes, dear, an admirable choice."

"Duke isn't a second-rate college."

"Of course not. You exhibited tremendous foresight. I am quite proud of you, as was your father, of course. Now, why don't you think about it for a while? I'm going to go stuff the pork chops."

He gave up the battle and said, mimicking her, "Yes, dear, an excellent idea."

Brant was feeling full and mellow when he answered the phone after dinner. Lily, exuberant from a distance of five thousand miles, yelled over the phone, "Lord Asherwood! As I live and breathe! Lordie, does that make me a countess or something, brother dear?"

"Hello, Lily," Brant said. "How are Athens and Dusty?"

"Both unbelievably warm, darling," Lily said, laughing deeply.

"Yeah, I bet. When are you coming home?"

"To Connecticut or to London, darling?"

"Texas. That is where your husband lives?"

"Houston, Brant. It's hot there, even this time of year. I don't know if I could take it." She giggled. "All right, stop screwing up your mouth. I can just see you now! How can you be so disapproving, and you a jock? Of course, it's only because I'm your sister, I know. Maybe an English lord should be straitlaced, but—"

"Lily," Brant broke in, "as a personal favor to Mom, I'm going to London, all right? The end of next week. Do you want me to buy you anything?"

Brant had to hold the phone away from his ear at her crow of delight. He could hear her yelling to Crusty Dusty in the background. "I've talked him around, lovey! All he needed was some good reasons for—" Thankfully, he couldn't hear the rest of what she said, because Dusty Montgomery grabbed the phone away from his bride.

"Good, Brant," he said in his slow, measured drawl. "Hey, boy, sorry about the play-off game. It'd be a lot easier for you if you played for the Dallas Cowboys. But I'll tell you, that pass to Nolan in the second quarter was mighty impressive. And that draw play, what a call!"

"Thanks, Dusty. It was a good game, despite the outcome."

"Damned foreigner and his toe," Dusty said, and Brant could picture him shaking his head in mournful disgust.

"Yeah. Well, you guys having a good time?"

"There ain't no other kind around your sister, Brant. Place is old, though. Not an oil well around. Maybe we'll see something on the cruise. These ruins are getting to me."

Speaking of ruins... No, I can't say that, even as a joke, Brant thought, and quickly asked about the islands they were going to visit.

"Thank you, honey," Alice Asher said to Brant after she'd spent some ten minutes more talking to her daughter.

"No reason to thank me," Brant said.

"Yes, of course there is. I know you're going for me, and I appreciate it." She paused a moment, wiping her hands on her apron. "Will you take Marcie with you?"

Marcie, beautiful Marcie, who'd decided only a week ago that it would suit her just fine to marry a somewhat famous jock who was also an English viscount. "No," he said, surprised, "of course not."

"She's called twice today."

Brant ran his hand through his thick dark hair, the color of his mother's mahogany piano, she'd always told him. "I was hoping she'd cool down a bit."

"You're thirty-one, Brant. Marcie is serious, isn't she?"

"You hoping for another grandchild, Mom? I promise you, Marcie isn't into children. After all, she does have a dynamite career, to be fair about it."

"Yes, that's true enough," Alice said with the utmost composure. "But that really isn't the point. I've never been particularly blind, Brant. So many years now you've gadded about like the gay bachelor. So many women."

"Yeah, most of them out to have their names and faces in the paper with a famous jock."

"And a very handsome and kind man. It's too bad, you know, both for those women and for you. I think you've gotten the least bit cynical. It's understandable, I suppose. I'm glad you're going to England. Come here a moment. I want to show you a family album that you haven't seen in years. I dug it out of the attic just before you arrived."

"You didn't need to drag out the album, Mom. You knew you'd convince me without it."

"It never hurts to have reinforcements, just in case."

Brant sat beside his mother on the sofa, balancing a cup of coffee on his knee.

"So many people that we never even met."

There were faded photographs of great uncle Asherwood, looking irascible and formidable, even in those old pictures from the twenties. He looked as unremittingly stern as any hellfire minister, but no more stern-faced than the flock of females surrounding him, whoever they all were.

"This is your poor Uncle Henry, who died in World War II when he was only twenty-one years old. And your Aunt Loretta, who passed away in 1976, I believe it was. She never married. So, you see, your great uncle had no one left in his direct line. And this is Asherwood."

Brant was surprised that it was so impressive looking. But it looked dark and uninviting with all the tangled ivy covering it. There was an unpaved circular drive, and an old 1940's car parked in front of the house. He felt absolutely no sense of his touted roots as he stared at the house.

"Here's your grandfather, Edward Charles, as a little boy."

Brant laughed. "He certainly improved with age!"

"Indeed he did. Incidentally, you were the picture of him at the same age."

"You know that's not true!" Brant laughed. "You've always told me I'm the spitting image of you. You can't have it both ways, Mom."

There were more pictures of children, dressed in styles suited to the twenties. There were no pictures of Brant's grandfather as a young man.

"Why?" he asked his mother.

"Well, he came to the United States in 1919, just after the war, with his English bride, Melanie. I think there was some sort of falling out between the two brothers shortly after your great grandfather died. He never talked about it."

"Asherwood must have been furious that his title would pass to an unwashed American, particularly if he and my grandfather weren't speaking to each other."

"Yes, I imagine he was somewhat disappointed."

"I suppose all that damned ivy has roots, anyway," Brant said slowly, his forefinger tracing over the photo of Asherwood Hall. "Are you sure you don't want to come with me, Mom?"

"No, Brant. They're not my roots, just yours. I'm almost pure Bostonian, remember? A provincial colonist of no worth at all."

Chapter Two

"I can't believe it's really me!" Daphne Asherwood stared at herself, openmouthed, in the mirror. Her contacts had been tinted according to Aunt Cloe's instructions, and her eyes shone back at her a vivid green. A fake green, she thought rebelliously, but only for a moment. She'd never known a moment's vanity in her entire twenty-three years, until now. She rather liked it.

"It's you, my pet," Cloe said, quite pleased with the results. Cloe, in fact, couldn't believe it was the same young woman. "Your green eyes are lovely with your tan and your blond hair."

"Streaked blond hair, Aunt," Daphne said. "Monsieur Etienne, well, he was most thorough, wasn't he?"

"Oh, indeed, my pet, most thorough, but look at the result! I'm glad he left your hair long; it's so lovely. Are the contacts comfortable?"

"I don't even feel them," Daphne said, rolling her eyes about and blinking rapidly. "And the doctor says I can wear them for a full week or so without even taking them out."

"I won't remind you of all the witless arguments you gave me, my pet. Now that you see I'm right, we're off to pick up your clothes from Mademoiselle Fournier."

"I haven't been to Paris since I was fifteen," Daphne said. "Then it was only for three days. Uncle Clarence let me come over one summer with the rector and his family. It's so very lovely, isn't it, Aunt?"

Actually, Cloe thought, gazing for a moment at the heavy dark clouds, Paris in February was a rather dreadful, dank place, and bloody cold to boot. "Yes, indeed, love," she said. She efficiently flagged down a taxi outside the eye doctor's ornate office on the Champs Elysee and directed the driver to the Place Opera. *"Numéro quatorze,"* she said in ringing tones.

"Bien," said the French taxi driver, not looking up.

As he zipped them through the snarled traffic in a most intoxicating fashion, Cloe listened to Daphne's expressions of delight at everything in sight. Poor child! Three days with the rector! Good lord, how utterly like Clarence, her impossible father. How dare that old man keep Daphne in that damned tomb of a house, denying her everything! Friends, school, fun. She'd pleaded with him to let her take Daphne to Scotland to live with her, but he'd refused.

"Impossible!" her father had roared more than once. "She'd come back to me one of those insufferable modern chits! I won't have it!" She thought of the terms of his will and stilled her niggling guilt. Only she and Reggie knew what was afoot. She pictured the photos she'd studied of the new viscount as she'd sorted through everything Reggie had found out about him. Utterly handsome fellow. Lord, think of the things he could teach Daphne! She flushed at her thoughts, but only slightly. After all, she wasn't that old. She'd decided irrevocably on her present course after Reggie had told her the terms of the will and asked her advice on how to proceed with Daphne. "The girl's not up to snuff, Cloe. I haven't the foggiest notion of how to carry on."

But Cloe did. In a flash of inspiration she had realized exactly what she must do. Then Reggie had given her the report old Clarence had prepared on young Brant Asher. "Here you are, Cloe, all the information old Lord Asherwood gathered on Brant, including newspaper articles and photos of him. He's no brainless fellow, as one might expect from an athlete, particularly one from America. Quite the virile bachelor, I'd say. Look at the women he's with in this picture. He's got money, though, and that might prove to be a problem."

"There's no such thing as having too much money," Cloe had said firmly. "He'll come through. And don't you dare get cold feet, Reggie! I'm going to have enough problems with Daphne!"

But what about Lucilla? Damn Clarence anyway! Why Lucilla? Obviously he wanted the same thing I want. Why couldn't he just let me handle everything? No, she thought, I won't worry about Lucilla; there's no need. Maybe. And she turned to smile complacently at Daphne.

To Cloe's utter delight, when she handed the surly taxi driver the requisite francs for the fare he didn't even count them, his eyes fastened like a dazed famine victim's on a succulent Daphne.

Hoorah! She'd always thought of French cab drivers as the most blasé men in the world.

There can be no more dismal a place than London in February, Brant thought, trying to make out details of the landscape below as the 747 circled Heathrow. It looked cold, foggy and depressing. He didn't think about the blackened snow that had made Boston look equally depressing when he'd left. It had been a smart move, leaving from Logan. The press had expected him to take off from Kennedy.

The man seated next to him was still dozing peacefully when the plane swooped down at Heathrow. One of the flight attendants, ever-smiling Laurie, was more observant, and Brant caught her eye on him, studying him closely. He quickly put his sunglasses back on.

At least in London, he thought, he could lose himself in the crowd. He grinned, thinking he'd have to buy himself a tweed sports coat to ensure that he'd blend right in.

He was met as he left customs by none other than Harlow Hucksley himself. He wondered briefly if all Englishmen were so tweedy and twirpy. The designer glasses he wore were the final touch.

"Ah, Lord Asherwood, such a pleasure to see you again!"

"Mr. Asher is just fine, or Brant."

"Then call me Harlow. I fancy we're going to become quite chummy before all of this is settled." He laughed, and his protuberant adam's apple bobbed.

"Fine, Harlow."

An underling appeared at an unobtrusive nod from Harlow, and Brant's luggage was taken away. Brant arched a thick brow.

"Old Frank will see to it, nothing to get uprooted about," Harlow said.

Brant was greeted outside the airport by a blast of Arctic air and swirling snowflakes.

"Bloody awful weather we're having," Harlow said, unconcerned.

"Yes, bloody dreadful," Brant said.

"London's knee deep in muck, but it won't bother you. The limousine is at your service, of course."

"First class treatment," Brant said, eyeing the gas-guzzling black car that pulled up alongside the curb.

"Certainly," Harlow said over his shoulder as he climbed into the back seat and unfolded his long, skinny legs.

"Compliments of the firm, Harlow? Didn't you tell me there was no money involved in my inheritance?"

"Scarce a sou, old chum," Harlow said. "Even so, my father insisted that you be treated appropriately."

"Very nice of him," Brant said.

"Not really, just good business. At least, that's what he told me. The Old Man's always alert. By the by, Brant, I had thought this car monstrous, but with you in it, it looks like one of those little German boxes. Most impressive, your size."

"I'd have been in trouble if I weren't this size."

"Are all American rugby chaps as big as you?"

"Football, Harlow, football it's called. Actually, I'm something of a shrimp compared to the men on the line. A mere one hundred ninety-five pounds."

Harlow fell into intense thought. "That's a goodly number of stone."

"Probably a whole bagful. What's a stone?"

"A stone is around fourteen of your American pounds," Harlow said. "Equates to the size of Jonah's whale, in your case. Odd business, this." Before Brant could seek clarification, Harlow continued blandly, "Yes, indeed. Who would have imagined an American athlete claiming an English title? You'll be in for some raised brows, old boy. Talk's already around, you know. But don't worry, no one knew exactly when you were to arrive. The Old Man insisted that mum's the word!"

"Good for the Old Man," Brant said. "I assume he's your father?"

"Indeed. Reginald Darwin Hucksley. Very proper sort, and no relation to *the* Darwin," he added.

Brant stared out the limousine window at the cramped, boxlike rows of houses they were passing. The light, swirling snow made them look quite quaint, but he imagined that when the snow melted the black smoke that belched from the pot-shaped chimneys, their charm dwindled fast.

"The Old Man's been trying to round up your relatives."

"Relatives," Brant said sharply, turning to face Harlow. "You said nothing about relatives in New York."

"Well, no, actually. We weren't quite certain how many there were, or where they were. The Old Man doesn't like to spring things without being certain of his facts. I told him they'd be dribbling out of the lamp shades if there was any money involved, which of course there isn't, at least not enough to fill a hat, so my father told me."

"My mother didn't mention any relatives," Brant said. "Who are they?"

"You Yanks do spread yourselves out so, don't you? Lose track of people, and all that. Well, let me see. There's an aunt legging about somewhere in Scotland. Glasgow, we think."

"An aunt," Brant repeated blankly, beginning to feel like a damned parrot.

"Righto. An adopted daughter of old Lord Asherwood, married a chap named Sparks, Carl Sparks, a Scot. Dashed ridiculous name I told the Old Man, but there you have it. Sparks, Cloe Sparks, widow. She was an Asherwood, of course, until she married this bloke, Sparks."

"Any more relatives hanging about in the wings?" Brant asked.

"Quite. There's a young female in there, your father's younger brother's wife's first cousin's offspring."

Brant was silent, weaving his way through this morass of genealogy. Uncle Damon, whom he'd never met. He'd died when Brant was a young boy. His wife's first cousin's kid. "And what, may I ask, is her name now?"

"Ah, she was a Bradberry, but after her parents were killed in an auto accident in 1974, old Lord Asherwood took her in and had her name legally changed to Asherwood. Can't remember what her first name is. The Old Man will know. She grew up at Asherwood. Then, when your great uncle cocked up his toes, she popped out—to Greece, we believe."

"I can't believe the old coot forced her to change her name to Asherwood!"

"Well," Harlow said reasonably, "it certainly gave the girl a leg up, you know. Asherwood's a much more cushy name than Bradberry."

"Still, it seems to me that people are entitled to keep their true names."

"I don't know, old chum, look at your name. Asher, not Asherwood. Incidentally, there's one other female, a *femme fatale*, if you get my meaning."

"Yes, I get it," Brant said. He was startled that Harlow could manage a leer. Did Englishmen poke you in the ribs when they made a dirty joke?

"She comes off one of the old bird aunts. Loretta, I think, or maybe not. I'm really not certain. Named Lucilla. Dashed goer from what I hear."

"Does she have a confounding last name?"

"Oh no, changes her names like her jumpers. She's married to a rich German industrialist by the name of Meitter and lives in Bonn. That's the lot of them. Doubt you'll have to worry about them barging in and queering your lay. No money and all that, just the bloody house."

"Hall," Brant corrected blandly. "Asherwood Hall, I believe."

"Quite, old boy, quite!"

"Where are we now?" Brant asked.

"Coming up to Westminster Bridge. The Old Man said I should show you some of the sights. He wants you to feel at home. That gray matter swishing down below is the Thames."

Brant perked up to take in Big Ben and all the government buildings. The driver gave them a quick spin along Downing Street, then turned back onto Horse Guards Road.

"St. James Park, old chum. Thought you'd like to see it. Soon we'll be coming up to Buckingham. The queen's in residence now."

Traffic was incredible. Much like New York, Brant thought, except all the cabs were black and on the wrong side of the road.

"Here, Brant, is Hyde Park. See over there..."

Brant closed him out. He was tired, beginning to feel wrung out from jet lag, and wanted nothing more than to sack out for a while, without any "quites" or "indeeds" sounding in his head.

"Your hotel, old chum. The Stanhope. Quiet, and quite private. No

nosey blokes hanging about here. You can walk in Hyde Park and sort
out your mind and all that.''

Curzon Street, Brant read silently. It was a beautiful tree-lined street,
calm and restful. The snow fell like a lacy white curtain, obscuring anything that might dilute the serenity. The Stanhope was small, old and
reeked of Victorian atmosphere. The lobby was empty, which was just
as well, because Brant couldn't imagine very many guests managing to
weave their way through the dark, heavy stuffed sofas and chairs. A thin,
tweedy clerk was at the desk. He eyed Brant with a good deal of interest.

"They don't get many foreigners here," Harlow said kindly. "Particularly blokes your size. Here now," Harlow continued to the clerk, taking
charge, "this is Lord Asherwood. Reservations for your best room."

Brant handed over his passport and signed his name to an ornate old-
fashioned register. From the corner of his eye he saw a hunched old man
struggling with his luggage.

"Let me help you with the elevator," Brant said, striding over to the
old trouper.

"Eh?" the grizzled old man asked.

"The lift, old chum," Harlow said. "I had the same trouble in America. I kept asking for the loo! Wouldn't believe the tooty looks I got.''

Brant closed his eyes for a moment, wishing he'd never come to England. He turned and stuck out his hand to Harlow. "I think I'll tuck up
for a bit, Harlow." He grinned, liking his choice of words. If it wasn't
English slang, it should be.

"Righto, Brant. Follow the fellow upstairs. I'll send the limousine for
you tomorrow, say about ten o'clock?"

"To see the Old Man?"

"Quite," said Harlow.

"Welcome to London, my boy! Sit down, sit down! Betty, fetch a cup
of tea for Lord Asherwood."

Brant felt as though he'd stepped into the last century. The law offices
of Hucksley, Hucksley and Maplethorpe on Salisbury Court, were som-
ber, dark and, Brant guessed, admitted only male solicitors through their
staunch portals. As for the Old Man, he was heavily jowled, nearly bald,
and wore stiff wire-rimmed glasses. They were anything but designer
frames. He wore a very conservative dark suit, the jacket buttoned and
stretched over his ample stomach. Brant had no difficulty picturing him
with one of those curled white wigs on.

"Mr. Hucksley," Brant said, shaking the older man's hand. "A pleasure to meet you, sir."

Brant was aware that he was being scrutinized closely and bore up
without shifting a muscle.

Mr. Hucksley said to his son, "You didn't tell me Lord Asherwood was such a demmed good-looking sort. The girls will be swarming all over him, starting with pop-eyed Betty.''

Pop-eyed Betty did gape at him a bit, but nothing more obtrusive than that as she handed him his tea. Thank God, Brant thought, staring at the repulsive brown liquid, he'd drunk two cups of black coffee for breakfast.

There were amenities to be sorted through and Brant stilled his impatience. Oddly enough, by the time Mr. Hucksley sat back in his huge leather chair, Brant felt relaxed.

"Now, my boy," the Old Man said, his voice shifting gears to a businesslike tone, "it's time to discuss what's to be done with you.''

Brant cocked a thick dark brow. "Done with me, sir? I'm afraid I don't quite understand. Harlow has told me that there's only the house and nothing to go along with it, except, of course, the title.''

Reginald Hucksley picked up a gold pen and began to tap the side of his impressive nose with it. "That's correct, to a point." He sent a bland look toward his son.

"Point, sir?" Harlow asked, popping forward in his chair like an eager schoolboy.

Brant had the sudden feeling that this scene had been played through many times between them in the past. Obviously the Old Man kept some things, probably some very important things, to himself. Poor Harlow looked for all the world like an eager puppy waiting for a meaty bone from his master.

"Well, you see, there are some stipulations in the late Lord Asherwood's will.''

"Stipulations?" Harlow asked, as if on cue.

Brant said nothing. What the hell is going on, he wondered. He felt himself tensing.

The Old Man's gold pen moved more slowly over his nose. "I assume, my lord, that Harlow here told you about the three women?''

"Yes," Brant said. If Hucksley senior wanted to make a drama out of this, he didn't feel like helping him.

"Humph," said Reginald Hucksley, the only sign that he was at all disappointed by Brant's cool reaction. "Actually, only the two young ones are of any concern. Daphne Claire Asherwood and Lucilla Meitter. Both distant cousins of yours, my lord. More disparate females I've yet to see. Rather than read you your great uncle's will, which I must admit is a bit difficult to grasp, I'll explain it to you.''

"I understood from Harlow," Brant said slowly, "that there was really nothing to be concerned about. And I will be frank with you, sir, the only reason I came to England was as a favor to my mother.''

"Perhaps I should begin with an apology, my lord. I must admit that I have held some things back, as per the late Lord Asherwood's instructions. You see, your great Uncle Clarence most seriously desired that you come to England, and I was to use any means at my disposal to get you here.''

"Then I suggest, sir,'' Brant said very quietly, "that you get on with your explanations. I expect I'll be leaving London soon, quite soon.''

"Well, yes, indeed, my lord,'' the senior Hucksley said. "First, dear, sweet Daphne Claire, a very properly brought up young lady. Lucilla Meitter, on the other hand, well, she's a bird of very different plumage! Just received word yesterday that she's indeed free and clear of her German husband—indeed, she was back in business before the old lord passed on—and is wending her way back to London after getting over her, ah, disappointment in the South of France.''

"You didn't tell me!'' Harlow said, looking much aggrieved. "I told Brant she was still married!''

"Ah, didn't I? Well, now you know, my boy.''

"What,'' Brant asked, his voice ominously quiet, "do they have to do with me? And with these stipulations?''

The gold pen slowly descended from the Old Man's nose, and he sat forward in his chair. His shrewd eyes glittered from behind his glasses.

"The long and short of it is, my lord, that old Lord Asherwood did leave a bit of money. After all the taxes, it comes to about 400,000 pounds. That would be about half a million dollars.''

"Sir!'' Harlow nearly shouted, jumping up from his chair. "You didn't tell me!''

"Well, my boy, now you know. Do sit down. Now, my lord, you will inherit all the money and Asherwood Hall, if—''

"If?'' Brant wanted to leap over the Old Man's desk and throttle him. Of all the ridiculous charades!

"If you marry Daphne Claire Asherwood, the dear, sweet young lady.''

Brant stared at him, one incredulous brow raised a good inch.

"Isn't that clear, my lord?''

That's ludicrous! He nodded, tight-lipped.

"Very good. Now, listen carefully, sir. This is, ah, rather detailed and quite specific. If, my lord, you refuse to marry Daphne, you will get nothing, Daphne will inherit a mere five hundred pounds, Lucilla gets half the money and the Hall, and the other half of the inheritance goes to the old lord's favorite charity, the Foundation for Abandoned Foreign Children.''

Brant wished at that moment that old Lord Asherwood was there. That old fool!

"Is that clear, my lord?''

That's even more ludicrous! "Oh, yes,'' Brant said, "quite clear.'' He sat back and crossed his arms over his chest. "I can't wait to hear the rest of it.''

Hucksley Senior ignored his sarcasm. "Now then, if, on the other hand, the impossible happens, and Daphne refuses to marry *you*, then you get nothing, Daphne receives only one hundred pounds, and Lucilla inherits everything."

Brant's stare became more pronounced. Suddenly he threw back his head and burst into laughter.

"I say," the Old Man said, looking shocked, "surely you understand! Really, my lord, you must realize that the estate isn't entailed. Old Lord Asherwood could do anything he wished with it."

So, Brant thought, sorting through this maze of insane information, if he married Daphne the Dog—Daphne, the dear sweet young lady—he got the money, the Hall and a wife. If he refused to marry her, he got nothing and Daphne got practically nothing. Ah, Lucilla! If Daphne refused him, he still got nothing and she was out on her ear with one hundred pounds in her pocket. "Jesus," he muttered, "my great uncle must have been insane!" He raised his eyes to the Old Man and asked, "What does entailed mean?"

"Ah, you Americans!"

"It means, Brant," Harlow said, eager to be able to contribute to the unfolding drama at long last, "that old Lord Asherwood didn't have to bequeath anything except the title to the next male in line. By law, he could do whatever he pleased with his money and the Hall."

"Perhaps you know why my great uncle made such a ridic—ah, unusual stipulation?"

"He didn't want the future viscountess of Asherwood to be an American. He wanted his bloodline to continue."

"But a viscount who's an American is all right?"

"In that, he had no choice," Hucksley Senior said primly. "But after all, your blood isn't entirely diluted."

"Quite good," Harlow said. "All the pitter-pattering little feet should have British blood."

Pitter-pattering little *what*? Jesus, I've got to wake up soon! But nothing occurred to end the scene, and Brant asked, "And what happens to the money if both I and my far-removed cousin refuse to marry each other simultaneously?"

"Everything goes to Lucilla. Understand, my lord, that old Lord Asherwood wanted Daphne cared for."

Is she incompetent? A half-wit? "That, sir, is quite obvious. It's also blackmail of the lowest sort." He felt another surge of anger at his great uncle well up in him. Not for himself, but for his whatever-degree cousin, Daphne. He didn't give a damn about the wretched house or the money. But to leave the poor girl stranded if either of them didn't cooperate with the insane will...! He said with furious irony, "It is obvious that my great uncle was truly fond of this Daphne. So fond of her, in fact, that he's trying to condemn both of us, with me the villain if I don't marry her! This is unbelievable!''

"Now, now, my boy," Hucksley Senior said, adopting his most placating tone, "I must admit that old Clarence did go a bit far. As for Daphne, my lord, I can't frankly consider her refusing to marry you. And, as you say, if you do the refusing, well, as you know, both of you lose everything. And Daphne, I'm afraid, would be left penniless and homeless.''

"But what if we find each other equally repellent?"

'"Not possible," Harlow said firmly. "It isn't as though you parade about looking like a gnome.''

Brant bit back a wild surge of sarcastic laughter. "Another question, sir. What if I had already been married? What would have happened to all these stipulations then?''

"Old Lord Asherwood knew you weren't married. It never came up."

"What if I were to tell you that I'm already engaged to be married— to an American?''

There was a moment of stunned silence. "Surely you are jesting, my lord," the Old Man said, his eyes narrowing in disapproval. "Of course the old lord had you thoroughly, er, investigated, as I believe you Americans put it. We know that you're seen with a lot of women, but no one woman in particular.''

Brant rose from his chair. "I think, sir, Harlow, that I'm going to pay a visit to the Tower of London. Check out all the torture devices and see if the block is still there. Good day, Harlow, Mr. Hucksley.''

"But—"

"I say, old chum—"

"I'll talk to you later," Brant said over his shoulder.

"Don't miss the royal jewels!" Harlow called after him.

Brant turned suddenly in the doorway. "It sounds to me like my great uncle wasn't playing with a full deck. That means queer in the attic,'' he added at the blank expressions. "Loony, off his rocker, ready for Bedlam.''

"Ridiculous!''

"Not to be thought of. Really, my boy, four hundred thousand pounds isn't to be sniffed at!''

Brant sniffed, wheeled about and strode from the room.

"The boy's a bit upset," said the Old Man.

Chapter Three

"Harlow, you're pushing me, you know."

"Now, old chum, it's but another hour and we'll be there!"

"That's not what I mean, and you and the Old Man know it! I've given this entire...mess a good deal of thought. I am quite willing to settle some money on Daphne. She won't be destitute then, and she can go on with her life without—"

"Good God, Brant! You can't do that! I mean, it's not what the Old Man, that is—"

I'm getting tired of arching my eyebrows, Brant thought.

"Ah, Brant, you can't think of legging it now! You'll love the old place, you'll see. You've got to see it before you decide anything, and Daphne—"

"Have you ever seen it, Harlow?"

"Well, actually, old boy, that is..."

"I thought not. I, on the other hand, have seen a photo of the place, and it didn't turn me on."

"Turn you on?"

"I was indifferent to it, Harlow. I could probably shine it on without a second thought."

"Shine it on?"

"Dismiss it, ignore it, send it to hell."

"Ah, well, just another forty-eight minutes."

Brant sat back in the comfortable limousine and closed his eyes. The scenery was beautiful, but he didn't want to gaze at another perfect quilt-like field or another perfectly trimmed hedgerow. Hucksley Senior, the old devil, had held him in London for a full week before insisting that he come to Surrey to see his *ancestral home*. Every damned play he'd sat through in Drury Lane he'd already seen in New York. You're being a jerk and an ugly American, he told himself, and not honest. Westminster Abbey had moved him deeply, as had, oddly enough, the British Museum. Who wouldn't be moved at seeing an original of the Magna Carta? Whenever he could shake the ubiquitous Harlow, he'd roved all over London, enjoying Great Russell Street just as much as Piccadilly. Even Madame Tussaud's on Marylebone Road had fascinated him.

Asherwood Hall. Old, bringing back the dim past. Hucksley Senior had duly filled him in on the history of the place over a formal black-tie dinner at the Savoy. Unlike Harlow, the Old Man had visited Asherwood Hall on many occasions.

"Old red brick, my boy, mellowed in tone, contrasting so well with the green things that clothe or neighbor it. What charm! The River Wey winds all about the place in the most romantic fashion. As to particulars, Brant, Sir Richard Worton was granted the land by that old demon, Henry VIII. There was an immense brangle with the king and Anne Boleyn, but the family survived, even prospered under Elizabeth. The Wortons died out in the direct line in 1782, and a gentleman of Herefordshire, John Gebbe, took over the name. Ah, the transoms and the mullions. Some of the best examples of Tudor architecture in all of England. There are even some painted glass windows with the rose *en soleil*, don't you know, from Edward IV."

"*En soleil?* Why, how unusual! You're certain it's not a fake?"

"Really, old chum," Harlow had said, frowning at Brant's sarcasm, "there's nothing like it, believe me!"

"How many rooms are there?" Brant had asked when the Old Man paused in his monologue to eat his mushroom soup.

"It's not large at all, actually. Not more than twenty rooms."

"Hardly enough room for pets," Brant had agreed.

After that night at the Savoy, Brant simply couldn't contemplate leaving, for there was to be a formal reception for him, given by the Earl and Countess of Rutherford.

"I say, old chum," Harlow said, tugging at his suede jacket. "That's the Wey. Dashed lovely, eh?"

"Utterly dashed," Brant said, eyeing the sluggishly winding river, its water brown from the winter mud.

"We're now driving through Guildford. Be there in just a sec!"

Guildford was another sleepy little village with lots of sturdy, leafy trees and quaint pubs set around a common green. There were even ducks strolling about the brackish pond in the center of the green.

Brant felt restless. He wanted to go home. He didn't even want to meet the dog, Daphne.

He asked suddenly, "You said that Daphne is in Greece?"

"That's what the Old Man told me."

In that case, Brant thought, the girl could be anywhere!

"And she doesn't know the terms of the will?"

"That's what the Old—"

"Yes, what the Old Man told you."

"Ah, we're here! I think."

The limousine turned into a drive between two high stone pillars. Overhead on a rusting circular iron grill were the scrolled words, Asherwood Hall. The wide graveled drive was surrounded on either side with more sturdy, leafy trees. Oaks, he thought, or maybe beeches. Suddenly, out of nowhere, he felt a very odd sensation, as if he'd been smashed by a lineman in the stomach. It was something of a déjà vu, an inescapable feeling that he'd been tied to this place, somehow, in the distant past.

He stared at the huge house. Slowly he climbed out of the limousine, his eyes never leaving the graceful old structure before him. It was three stories high, not quite square, with ivy climbing up to the chimney pots on the sloped roof and twining about the many steep gables. A surge of pride, of possession, washed through him. He wanted suddenly to scrub the dirty panes of glass in the mullioned windows until they sparkled. He wanted to cut away the ivy and bring light into the rooms. He wanted to lovingly replace each of the torn slates on the roof.

I'm turning into a senile fool.

He wanted to run his hands over the huge oak double doors and peel away the rot, then stain them to their former splendor. He wanted to polish the huge brass griffen-head door-knockers.

I'm losing my damned mind.

He drew a deep breath. Suddenly the doors were pulled open, and he heard them creak on their hinges. They have become warped through the years, he thought. How will I fix that?

A scrappy-looking old woman emerged, wiping her hands on her apron. She looked for all the world like an over-the-hill wood sprite. "Eyuh?" she said, staring at Brant and Harlow warily, as if they were there to collect on an overdue grocery bill.

"Mrs. Mulroy, I believe," Harlow said. "This is Lord Asherwood."

"Eyuh," Mrs. Mulroy said. To Brant's surprise, she dropped him a curtsey. "Welcome, my lord." Her voice sounded as creaky as her old bones likely were. Brant heard himself mutter something.

"You were expecting us, weren't you, Mrs. Mulroy?" Harlow asked.

"Oh, uh," said Mrs. Mulroy. "'Tain't much of a homecoming for his lordship, but me and two girls from the village been cleaning out the muck, just as Mr. Reggie instructed. As for Mr. Winterspoon, he's still on holiday. Old Maddy agreed to cook for a bit until his lordship could find someone permanent. It'll taste like fly paper, but ain't nothing for me to say about it. My, but you're a grand fellow, my lord! I ain't never seen a lord as big as you, if you don't mind my saying so."

"No, I don't mind." The front stone steps were chipped. He supposed there were masons in England. He hoped they'd know what to do about that, and where to find the right kind of stone.

"Well, righto! Do you want to see the inside, Brant?"

"Yes."

He was aware that Harlow was looking at him somewhat oddly, but he didn't care. Indeed, Harlow barely impinged on his conscious thoughts.

The old wood sprite scratched her thin gray bun and led the way into the huge, black-and-white marbled entryway. Were there special cleaners to shine up the marble squares? Brant wondered. The ceiling was simply the underside of the roof, some forty feet above. Directly ahead was a beautiful old oak staircase, winding to the second-floor landing. He drew closer and ran his fingers over the smooth old wood. He swore for a moment that he could feel the warmth from hundreds of years of hands that had touched the bannister.

"This here's the Armor Hall," Mrs. Mulroy said, not a hint of awe in her voice as she creaked toward the open doors to the left.

Brant turned reluctantly and followed her, Harlow behind him. He stepped through the twenty-foot-high double doors and sucked in his breath. He'd never before imagined that a room like this could exist. It appeared to be at least forty feet long and some twenty-five feet wide. It had thick beamed ceilings, a huge fireplace against the far wall, tall narrow windows that gave onto the front drive, and a very odd mix of furnishings. Suits of armor, many of them missing parts, were both standing and sitting along the walls like an array of drunken soldiers. Maces, lances, long bows, battle-axes and other pieces of assorted medieval fighting equipment whose names he didn't know were affixed to the paint-peeling walls above the drunken soldiers. One battle-ax had obviously fallen at some time, conking a suit of armor on the head, and had been fixed back on the wall with a crooked knot. Brant moved forward to examine a medieval-type chair, caught the toe of his shoe in the threadbare carpet, and went flying.

"Yoicks!" Harlow shouted. "Careful there, Brant. The place isn't quite all up to snuff!"

Brant picked himself up and grinned at the wizened guffaw that erupted from the old sprite. He shook off Harlow's hand and began a closer examination. Lord, the work he'd need to do in here! How did one replace armor parts? He couldn't imagine wandering into London's equivalent of Macy's and asking for a steel arm, circa 1500. The fireplace was huge enough to roast a whole cow, and so blackened that it looked like an immense dark cavern. The heavy, hewn-oak furniture looked as if it hadn't been polished for at least two centuries.

"Eyuh, my lord," Mrs. Mulroy said in a commanding voice, "'tis time to see the rest of the place. Can't be spending an afternoon in each room. Those lazy girls are in the kitchen, likely drinking tea without me to tell them what to do.''

He was tempted to give the old sprite a salute.

There were ten odd more rooms on the ground floor: a long, narrow dining room that would be a perfect setting for candles and ghost stories; a large ballroom that boasted haphazard groupings of heavy Victorian sofas and chairs; and the Golden Salon. Again Brant felt that odd, unsettling feeling when he walked into the room. He knew next to nothing about architecture, but in this room he felt generations of loving care. There was no decay here, no musty smell or peeling paint. It was light, spacious and, he noted, would be wonderfully airy if the damned ivy were cleared away from the wide windows. There were cherubs and other such things along the molding in the ceiling, and an exquisite light marble fireplace that some fool had painted gold! The furniture was grouped in small conversational arrangements, each grouping from a different bygone era. Delicate white and gold pieces by the windows; heavy dark mahogany pieces he suspected were Victorian; and even some light-wood sofas and chairs from this century. There was bric-a-brac everywhere, and a line of photographs on the mantle. His feet drew him forward, and he studied the faded black-and-white pictures. So many people he'd never known! There were several more recent photos: one of an older woman who had fascinating eyes that seemed to mock the world, and another of a young woman who was squinting at the camera through ugly thick glasses, had her hair scraped back from her face in a fat bun, and wore a shapeless, dowdy jumper. Suddenly he smiled. The signature at the bottom of the photo was ''Daphne Asherwood.'' The dog! Then he stiffened. He was supposed to marry *that*? His hands felt clammy and he thrust them into the pockets of his corduroy trousers. As he followed Harlow and the old sprite from the room, he noticed that the floors were in awful shape. How, he wondered, would he be able to bring them to their former beauty?

''Eyuh, my lord,'' Commander Wood Sprite said, ''time for the upstairs.''

The next thirty minutes passed in rather a daze. The half-dozen rooms on the second floor were in depressing shape, but each one of them fascinated Brant. There were endless little nooks and cupboards, even a priest's hole that the old wood sprite pointed out proudly. There was a long, narrow portrait gallery, filled with centuries of paintings, many of them so dark that the faces were difficult to make out. Brant gulped. It would cost a fortune, he guessed, to bring in an expert to clean them up. *It would eat well into the 400,000 pounds.*

There was only one bathroom on the entire floor and it was a shrine to the inefficient opulence of the last century. He was still fretting about how to modernize the bathroom when Mrs. Mulroy led the way into old Lord Asherwood's suite.

My God, Brant thought, still somewhat dazed, this is my room! It was as rich and splendid as the Golden Salon downstairs, a strange combination of styles that fascinated rather than repelled. He immediately strode to the heavy burgundy draperies along the west wall and jerked them open.

I've got to paint the walls a light color, and get rid of that ridiculous dark wall paper.

"Aubusson, they call it," Mrs. Mulroy said, pointing at the beautiful red carpet that stretched a good twenty feet in each direction. The bed was canopied, a monstrosity that was raised, of all things. Brant suddenly pictured himself climbing into the thing, and smiled. The crimson spread would have to go. Moths had taken their yearly meals here for two generations at least.

"I hope you're not too disappointed, Brant," Harlow said as they wended their way back downstairs. "The place is in dreadful shape, something the Old Man didn't mention to me. But it's filled with tradition—"

"Yes, roots."

"I hope you're not too disappointed."

Disappointed! Brant stared at him as if he were crazy. "It is perfect," he said simply, and turned away, his mind buzzing with plans.

Chapter Four

"I don't see a photo of my cousin, Lucilla Meitter."

Mrs. Mulroy sniffed loudly. "She ain't here often," she offered by way of an answer. "Two years ago it was Outrake, and before that, Vargas."

Brant grinned. "A woman of international tastes. No photo of her?"

"If it 'tain't there, 'tain't one, I don't imagine. His old lordship was vastly amused by Miss Lucilla, used to tell her without a husband, she was like a cup of tea without the lemon. Why, look ye here! It's Mr. Winterspoon, my lord."

Winterspoon?

"My lord!"

Brant stared at the short, very chubby little man whose bald head came even with his chin.

"I'm Winterspoon, my lord, Oscar Winterspoon. I was the old lord's valet." His bright blue eyes took in every inch of Brant. "I'm here, my lord, to take care of you." Goodness, his look said clearly, do you ever need it! "I do apologize for not being here when you arrived yesterday, but I was on holiday. Bath, you know."

"Stuffy sod," Mrs. Mulroy sniffed under her breath.

Winterspoon drew himself up to his full height, looking so dignified that Brant had the momentary urge to salute. "Are all your things upstairs, sir? If so, I'll see to your unpacking."

A valet, Brant thought blankly. Then he smiled, remembering one of his favorite authors, Wodehouse, and the inimitable valet, Jeeves. I hope this vintage dapper doesn't think I'm mentally incompetent. He stuffed the hand that wanted to salute into his jeans pocket and said, "I'm not certain actually, er, Winterspoon, that I'll be here at Asherwood Hall all that long." His eyes fell on the peeling paint around the floorboard, a detail he hadn't noticed on the first tour he'd taken the previous afternoon. *I've got to scrape that and stain it.*

"Certainly, sir, but doubtless you'll remain until Miss Daphne arrives?"

"And Mrs. Cloe, don't forget," Mrs. Mulroy snapped.

"Indeed, Mrs. Sparks. And Mrs. Meitter also, I understand."

"I say, what's all this?" said Harlow, stifling a yawn as he strolled into the Golden Salon. "Just who, my good man," he asked, staring hard at Winterspoon, "are you?"

"Winterspoon, sir."

"My valet," Brant added smoothly.

"My father didn't tell me about the valet," Harlow said.

"Well, Winterspoon," Brant said, turning to the dignified little gentleman, "let us say that you stay on as long as I'm in England. All right with you?"

"Yes, sir. Most proper. In my last position, with Lord Culpepper, I also acted in the position of butler, sir, when his lordship's finances took something of a downturn." He cast a deprecating eye toward Mrs. Mulroy. "Since Mr. Hume, his late lordship's butler, won't be returning, perhaps you would like me to assume his responsibilities now?"

"Eyuh!" Mrs. Mulroy said. "As if I can't answer the door!"

"Perhaps," Brant said to both his retainers, "it would be best, Mrs. Mulroy, if you spent your time getting the house to rights. I imagine it will be up to Mrs. Meitter to decide about the future disposition of Asherwood Hall."

"Mrs. Meitter!" Mrs. Mulroy exclaimed. "What about poor Miss Daphne?"

Brant didn't wish for the moment to strangle himself in explanations, and said only, "We'll speak of it later. If you would both see to your responsibilities for the moment..."

The vintage dapper and the wood sprite left the room, Mrs. Mulroy calling over her shoulder that breakfast was ready in the breakfast room.

"We'll be right there," Brant said.

"Where," Winterspoon asked with awful calm, "is Mr. O'Reilly?"

"Who is Mr. O'Reilly?" Brant asked as he entered the breakfast room.

"His old lordship's cook, my lord."

Brant bent an eye toward Mrs. Mulroy. "He bagged it," she said. "Took a case of his old lordship's best brandy with him. Bloody blighter!"

"He is Irish, my lord," Winterspoon said by way of explanation. "I trust, Mrs. Mulroy, that the kitchen is in competent hands?"

Mrs. Mulroy drew herself up, looking like a bantam-weight fighter.

"I'm certain that all hands are competent enough," Brant said quickly.

"Did you sleep well, Brant?" Harlow asked once they were alone.

"Yes, I slept very well."

"No ghosts or strange noises?"

"No..." *It was like coming home and sleeping in my own bed. Only better.* "It was a noble experience sleeping in a huge bed three feet off the floor."

Over a rather uninspired breakfast of one egg, too well-done, soggy toast and weak coffee, Harlow said, "The Old Man wanted me to tell you that expenses for the staff would be picked up by the estate, until...everything was finally settled."

"Too bad O'Reilly bagged it," Brant said, wincing as he gingerly took another sip of coffee.

"If you like, Brant, I can call up an agency and see about getting you a proper cook."

Brant's attention was on the stained and faded wallpaper in the breakfast room, and the hideously dark wainscotting. Lord, he was thinking, this room could be flooded with light. *I must do something with it soon, since I'll be eating three meals a day in here.*

"I say, old boy, is that all right with you?"

"What? Oh, certainly, Harlow. Tell you what, drive me back to London this morning and I'll rent a car for myself."

"You don't mean you're leaving Asherwood today!"

"I'm coming back. There's so much to be done, you see. Oh, one thing you can do for me, Harlow. I want you to contact an agency or whatever, and find me a cook."

Harlow chewed thoughtfully on his toast, wondering if it were an American trait to be witless in the morning. He said only, "For what period of time, Brant?"

"Make it two weeks, why don't you?" He glanced at the wallpaper, smiled to himself, and said, "No, a month."

My God, what has happened! Daphne stared openmouthed as the cab drove through the gates of Asherwood. The drive was cleared; there were two men trimming bushes; and another was mowing the dead winter grass. The thick ivy was gone, all of it, and the windows sparkled in the bright February afternoon sun. She saw another man, wearing old, faded jeans, a wool shirt and sneakers, high on a ladder, doing something to the roof.

"This is the place, Miss?" the cab driver asked, turning to see the young lady staring fixedly at the house.

"What? Oh yes, thank you! Please, just put my suitcases on the drive."

None of the men turned, and she realized they couldn't hear the taxi over the low roar of a buzz saw. She stood in the drive a moment, staring about her, wondering yet again why Aunt Cloe had insisted that she had things to do in London and had sent her on ahead.

Brant didn't know what made him turn on the ladder, but when he did he saw a taxi leaving through the front gate, and a gorgeous young woman standing in front of the house, looking blankly about her.

Lucilla Meitter, he thought. Lucilla the Vamp, he added to himself. Lord, what a face and figure! He climbed slowly down the ladder, jumping the remaining few feet to the soggy ground. He stared at her a moment, taking in the waving streaked blond hair that fell softly to her shoulders, the incredible wide green eyes, and her endless stretch of legs. She was wearing a soft blue wool coat that was belted at her narrow waist.

"What," Daphne asked, eyeing the staring man, "are you doing?"

Brant gave her a crooked grin, knowing he was gaping at her like a horny goat. "The gutter was filled with leaves and other things. I was cleaning it out."

"It appears that the new viscount has taken control. The house looks so different, quite lovely, really, without all that tangled, depressing ivy."

"Thank you, ma'am. I—we are all doing our best."

Daphne studied the man more closely, suddenly aware of his strange accent. He was a lovely looking man, too, and it pleased her that he was smiling at her. "Are you a friend of Lord Asherwood's? You sound American, I think."

"Oh yes, we're quite close." Brant thrust out his hand. "Actually, we're one and the same person."

Daphne blinked at him, and gave him her hand without thinking. His grip was warm and firm. "Oh, I'm sorry! I suppose I hadn't expected you to be clambering about on the roof. You're the football player."

"That's right." He paused a moment, clasping her hand a bit tighter, and said, "I don't think I have to ask your name. You're my cousin, Lucilla Meitter, right?"

Lucilla!

She gave him a thin smile and removed her hand. "Why do you think that?"

Brant thrust his hands in his jeans pockets, and Daphne's eyes followed his movements. She gulped. He was a beautiful man, and so well put together! *But he thinks you're Lucilla.* He gave her another lovely smile, and she just looked at him, waiting.

"Well, actually, it didn't require a great deal of intelligence on my part. I was informed that my cousin Lucilla was the beauty, and, of course, I've seen a photo of my other cousin, Daphne."

Daphne thought of the single picture of her in the Golden Salon and winced. Ugly, ugly, ugly! Still, he didn't have to be so...

"I understand that Daphne has changed a good deal," she said, clutching her purse tightly, and wishing her newfound self-confidence weren't plummeting to her toes.

"Has she? Well, like this house, I imagine that any change would improve matters. Do you know her well?"

"Oh yes, quite well, as a matter of fact."

"Then you also know the terms of the infamous will?"

Daphne shook her head. "No, I didn't stop in London to see Mr. Hucksley. Aunt Cl—that is, I imagine I'll find out soon enough."

"Good grief!" Brant said. He began to laugh. "Well, since Asherwood Hall will doubtless be yours quite soon, may I recommend that we adjourn to the Golden Salon? Unfortunately, the old spr—er, Mrs. Mulroy is in the village right now, so I can't offer you any refreshment."

Brant picked up her suitcases and strode to the open front doors saying over his shoulder, "I'm expecting a cook shortly. I was informed by Mrs. Mulroy that O'Reilly bagged it with a case of his old lordship's brandy."

For a moment Daphne simply stared after him, not attending to his words. What did he mean that Asherwood would shortly be Lucilla's? Impossible! It was his; it had to be.

She followed him numbly into the house, at first not noticing the shining marble floor. Then she did, and blinked.

"Come on in here, Lucilla," Brant said. "I just finished the Golden Salon two days ago. I started there first, since there wasn't too much to be done. I've also been working on the breakfast room. Hopefully, you'll approve my changes. If you don't..." He shrugged.

She couldn't think of a word to say. If the house was Lucilla's, why was he doing all this work? She paused in the doorway and looked around. The large room was filled with clear winter sunlight. The walls had been repainted a cream color, and the furniture had been reduced to the Regency settings. All the heavy mahogany pieces that she'd hated were gone, as were the piles of ugly bric-a-brac.

"It's beautiful," she said. "And the carpets are so clean! I never realized they were so lovely."

"Thank you. I'm glad you approve. I was surprised myself that they came out so well. I was certain they'd have to be replaced. Here, let me help you off with your coat."

He slipped it off her shoulders and placed it on a chair back. "Won't you sit down?"

Daphne sat in her favorite chair, a small, high-backed blue satin-covered affair that had been relegated, before Uncle Clarence's death, to the far corner.

She crossed her legs, unaware that Brant was studying each exposed inch.

"So," he said, forcing his eyes to her lovely face, "you don't know about your good fortune?"

"No," she said, "I don't. Perhaps you'd be good enough to tell me about the will."

She didn't have the look of a swinger, he thought. Nor did she look old enough to have gone through three husbands. She looked fresh as sunshine, and...

"The will?"

"Forgive me," Brant said. "It's just that you're something of a surprise. I knew, of course, that you were...lovely, but I thought you'd be older."

"I take good care of myself," she said, trying to keep her voice light. *Tell him who you are, you fool!* But she said nothing more.

"Ah, the will. Shouldn't we wait for Hucksley Senior?"

"I don't see why we should."

"It's quite complicated, actually, and in my opinion, odd in the extreme. Basically, it all boils down to this: I inherit all the money and Asherwood Hall if I marry my cousin, Daphne Asherwood."

"Marry Daphne! Why, that's ridiculous!"

"My feelings exactly," Brant agreed in a dry voice. "Evidently old Lord Asherwood wanted her taken care of. Why he didn't leave her the money to take care of herself is quite beyond me! From what I've heard, though, it's likely the girl doesn't have a notion of what to do."

"But what if you don't wish to marry Daphne?"

"Ah, then the fun begins! If I refuse, then you, Cousin Lucilla, and a charity, split everything, and poor little Daphne is out with only five hundred pounds in her purse. If she refuses to marry me, then we're both out, and this time it's all yours."

Everything fell into place. The scales have fallen from my eyes, she thought, utterly distracted. Uncle Clarence muttered something about taking care of me, but this! Oh no, it can't be true! Aunt Cloe must have known; she must have! Why else would she have insisted that I needed to be redone, top to toe? "How much money is there?" she asked.

"If you're not a rich woman now, Lucilla, you soon will be. The estate amounts to four hundred thousand pounds."

"Four hundred thousand pounds! But why didn't Uncle Clarence spend some of that precious money on the Hall? I begged him and begged him not to let it fall into ruin! Oh, that impossible old man! I'd like to strangle him!"

"You're a bit late," Brant said.

"Daphne is supposed to marry you," she repeated blankly. "But I...she doesn't even know you! And you don't know her!"

"I can't say I'm particularly looking forward to our meeting," Brant said.

"Why is that?"

Brant shrugged. "I think that is rather obvious. The will, my great uncle's ridiculous stipulations, Daphne herself..."

"What," she heard herself asking in a shrill voice, "about Daphne herself?"

"I've seen a photo of her, as I told you," Brant said with disarming frankness. "She is not what I ever envisioned my wife to look like, nor do I expect her personality to be particularly invigorating. I've heard her referred as 'that poor, sweet young lady.'"

Conceited, arrogant beast! Jerk! Cad! Her mental list of insults came to a grinding halt. Ah ha, bastard!

And true, all of it!

"Why, if you have no intention of marrying Daphne, are you spending your time here, doing all this work?"

Brant clasped his hands together between his thighs. "I don't know," he said, honest puzzlement in his voice. He raised his eyes to hers. "I didn't even want to come to England. I didn't want to see this house, but when I did..." He shrugged. "It's like I've been here before, long ago, perhaps. I have these pictures in my mind of how it should look. Sounds dumb, doesn't it?"

"No," she said. "No, it doesn't, not at all. I'm delighted that you kept the Regency furniture in here. It is my favorite. Many times I've pictured myself reclining gracefully on that sofa, pretending to be a rich, beautiful lady of 1810, dressed perhaps in a soft muslin gown—oh! You must think I'm bonkers!"

He was smiling at her, open approval and liking lighting his blue eyes. "I don't think either of us is dumb or bonkers." He rose and paced across the room, Daphne's eyes following his progress. "Then you feel the draw of the house, too?" he asked.

"Draw? Oh, do you mean that I feel an affinity toward it? Why, yes, I suppose that I have always felt that way. That's why it always made me so angry that Uncle Clarence was letting it fall down around his ears." She added, without pause, "You don't look like a viscount."

He thrust his hands into his jeans pockets, drawing the pants down further, which made her mouth feel strangely dry. "Wait until you meet my valet, Winterspoon. Likely he's hiding in a closet right now, bemoaning the fact that I'm such an ugly, informal American, but just wait until evening. He turns me out in fine fashion, whether I want it or not."

"Winterspoon is here? How marvelous. I've missed him."

Brant sent her a quizzical look. "I wasn't under the impression that you'd visited Asherwood Hall all that often."

Daphne forced herself to shrug. She couldn't believe that she was actually carrying on a conversation with a man. It's what Lucilla would do, she told herself. Daphne would sit huddled up, looking and acting like a tongue-tied fool.

"Perhaps you'll like Daphne," she heard herself say.

"Fat chance!"

"What?"

"Very unlikely. I suppose I'm not being very kind, but I've thought of her as a double bagger."

"A double what?"

"American slang. Forgive me. To be blunt, then, a dog. Probably a very sweet dog, but a dog nonetheless."

She was trembling. It's all your own fault, she was repeating silently to herself. It's like eavesdropping. You never hear anything good about yourself. But a *dog*! "Just maybe," she said viciously, "she'll think *you're* a double bottle."

"No, double *bagger*. You could be right. I shouldn't be saying things like that to you, her cousin. It's just that I'm damned mad about the whole situation." He raked his fingers through his thick hair. "Are you here to stay? Since you will be the owner, I should stop with all my plans. They should be your plans."

The bitterness in his voice made her blink. He had indeed fallen in love with the Hall. Well, to hell with him! Lucilla would get the "dump," as she'd always stigmatized Asherwood Hall. She rose jerkily to her feet.

"No," she said, "it's not up to me, I can assure you of that!"

"I tell you, I won't be marrying Daphne! I'll be returning to the United States shortly, and it'll be all yours."

"None of it will be mine, since I'm not—"

There came a gasp from the open doorway. "Miss! Lawks, you're home! And just look at you—what a stunner!"

"Mrs. Mulroy," Daphne said, smiling at the beaming old woman. "How good it is to see you again. His lordship has been telling me that Winterspoon is here, also."

Brant was seized by a very funny feeling. Something was wrong here, quite wrong. He looked from Lucilla to Mrs. Mulroy and back again.

"You're not Lucilla Meitter?" he said in a very low and controlled voice.

"No, I'm not, my lord!" She swept him an insulting bow.

"Mrs. Meitter!" Mrs. Mulroy gasped. "Certainly not, my lord. This is Miss Daphne!"

"Yes," Daphne said with furious calm, "the double bagging dog."

Brant flushed deeply, and cursed very softly and very fluently under his breath.

Chapter Five

They faced each other across the dining table in the formal dining room. Brant was dressed according to Winterspoon's notions, in a dark suit and white dress shirt. Daphne wore a dark gray wool dress that Aunt Cloe had insisted upon in Paris. It hugged her body like a York glove, and gave additional oomph to her magnificent bosom with its small pleats splaying downward like an opened fan from a circular neckline. She wore no jewelry; she had none. For once Daphne didn't feel like hunching her shoulders forward. She sent Brant a studied, insolent look, one that she'd been practicing, and sipped from her wineglass.

She'd walked out on him that afternoon, and this was the first time he'd seen her since their debacle. He'd managed to whip himself into a fine state, and her nasty silence egged him on.

He said, his voice as cold as her stare, "You should have told me immediately who you really were. Your behavior was infantile, like a schoolgirl wanting to write her own Shakespearian scenes, with all the silly mix-ups and people at cross-purposes."

Daphne's fingers tightened on her glass. Oddly enough, for the first time in her twenty-three years she didn't feel at all embarrassed or intimidated by being in a man's company, alone. She was too furious. She pulled back her shoulders, with the result that her breasts could not help but draw his attention. "I," she said finally, in an equally cold voice, "have never thought much of Lucilla's looks." *Lord, what a lie! I've been jealous of her since I was ten!* "On the other hand, my lord, you were just as I knew you'd be: brash, rude, insulting, arrogant, conceited—"

"Well, that certainly must cover it!"

"—and you were wearing disgusting American clothes!"

"So you liked my jeans, huh?"

"I don't know how you could bend over! What's more—"

"Don't strain your brain for more charming adjectives!"

"I never *strain my brain.*"

"Perhaps you should consider straining it a bit more in this particular instance. I repeat, Miss Asherwood, your behavior was every bit as ridiculous as mine, no, more so. And yes, I admit that I was out of line."

"Is that to be construed as an apology?" she asked sweetly.

"Construe it as you like," he said, and forked down a bit of leathery roast beef. "Surely you can't take exception to my clothes this evening. Winterspoon assures me that this is what the well-dressed English lord wears to dinner."

"Clothes," she said, "do not make the lord."

"But clothes," he said, eyeing her bosom with lecherous interest, "do tell me a lot about what a woman has to offer."

She choked on her roast beef, too angry to think of a retort, and frowned at the taste. "Oh, how I wish O'Reilly were here!" she exclaimed. "This is terrible. How have you managed to survive?"

"I keep asking for hamburgers. They're hard to screw up."

"Who would want to screw a hamburger?"

"I've never wanted to screw a hamburger. What I mean is that hamburgers are hard to ruin, to mess up."

"Oh."

"Now I suppose you'll tell me that I can't speak proper English."

"Oh no. It appears that you already recognize your...lacks, at least in that area."

Brant dropped his fork and leaned against the high-backed chair, folding his arms over his chest. "Why don't you tell me why the hell you don't even remotely resemble that *double bagger* in the photo? Was it all some elaborate joke? Who is that girl?"

Daphne toyed a moment with a slice of bread. "I'm not certain to which photograph you are referring."

"The one of the girl who looks frumpy, dowdy, unappetizing, completely without style, with a face that could sink a thousand ships—"

"Now, I believe *you* can cease with *your* sterling adjectives! Actually, that photo is of Lucilla, taken when she was much younger. Her first husband saw to it that she was done over. I haven't seen her for quite a while, but I've heard that she looks much different now."

"Just why is the photo signed Daphne Asherwood?"

She looked at him with wide, innocent eyes, and stared limpidly into his suspicious, narrowed ones. "Is it? Well, perhaps it was added as a joke, you understand."

"And why are you referred to by everyone as 'poor, sweet, little Daphne'?"

She surprised herself by giving him a saucy grin. "Well, it does appear as if I now am poor. What is it, five hundred pounds?"

"Only if I refuse to marry you!"

"And I'm certainly sweet."

He stared at her breasts. "But not little!"

I will not let him embarrass me! "I'm not all that tall," she said blandly, surprising herself even more.

"Perhaps," he said, with a wolfish gleam in his eyes, "we'll see just how you size up."

"Size up?"

"How you fit against me."

Her eyes widened; she couldn't help it. She felt a flush rising from her neck to her cheeks. "Are all Americans so abominably conceited and rude?"

"Do all English women turn into little red roses when they can't stand the heat?"

"Little red roses! What heat?"

"You're blushing, and you haven't retorted with much aplomb," he said. "Thus, I applied the heat, and you couldn't handle it."

"Have I mentioned how very muscular your chest looks with the shirt buttons straining so...so provocatively?"

He threw back his head and laughed deeply. "Bravo! My little English rose is getting into the swing of things!"

Where is Daphne? she wondered for a brief moment, marveling at herself. She should be under the table by now. "I very much enjoyed watching you thrusting your hands in your jeans pockets." She rolled her eyes. "What a treat!"

"I'm glad you thought so. I think I'd prefer *your* hands thrusting in my pockets, though."

Her eyes fell from his face as fairly specific images flitted through her mind.

"Gotcha!" he said. "Now, if you're through fencing about with me, a poor mortal man, perhaps we can get serious."

"Serious about what?" she asked, relieved that he'd changed the subject. But then again, she felt so alive, so sparkling...

"Serious about why my Great Uncle Clarence produced such an outrageous will."

She set to crumbling her bread into small bits. "I believe he thought me incapable of doing anything on my own."

Brant shook his head. "Was he blind? You're beautiful, you're witty, and I can see you being capable at anything you tried."

The string of compliments, said quite seriously, stunned her for a moment. Am I really beautiful and witty, she wanted to ask him. "You don't understand," she said, sighing a bit. "I came to live at Asherwood when

I was very young. I grew up here, alone, except for Uncle Clarence and the servants, of course.''

"Surely you went to school.''

She looked stricken for a brief moment, a look not lost on Brant. "Uncle brought in a tutor, an obnoxious little man who treated me like a half-wit. He left when I turned seventeen. Uncle had other uses for me then.''

"Like what?''

She swallowed and forced her voice to indifferent calm. "Oh, I sort of ran things here at the Hall. You know, housekeeper, fetcher, bill-payer, gardener, and anything else he wanted of me.''

"General all-purpose slave, in fact.''

"Nothing quite so…degrading. And, of course, he let Aunt Cloe come to see me on occasion. I even went once to Scotland to visit her.''

"You must have died of excitement,'' Brant said. Miserable old codger!

"Aunt Cloe loves me. In fact, she took me to Greece just after the funeral.''

"Where is Aunt Cloe?''

"In London, I think. She sent me on ahead. She said something about business with Mr. Hucksley.''

"Ah.''

"Ah, what?''

He didn't reply for a long moment. Instead he gazed at her, a thoughtful expression on his face. "That is your photo, isn't it?''

"Yes,'' she said, "it is. I lied about Lucilla; she's been beautiful since she was born. I was the one who needed doing over, and Aunt Cloe saw to it, I guess you'd say.''

"She couldn't have achieved this result if all the ingredients hadn't been lurking about, ready to come together.''

"My eyes aren't really such a vivid green. They're kind of a washed out hazel. These are colored contacts. Aunt Cloe insisted.''

"Confession time? Your lovely hair…is that a wig?''

"No, it's mine. Monsieur Etienne streaked it.''

"And your clothes?''

"Aunt Cloe took me to Paris.''

"This transformation began just after the funeral?'' At her nod, he continued. "Look, Daphne, I'm delighted someone cared enough about you to do something. Obviously, all you needed was a bit of a boost.''

"You are kind to say so.''

"No, on the contrary, I'm being honest.'' Suddenly he grinned. "Obviously your Aunt Cloe knew what she was about, as did Reginald Hucksley, I'll bet.''

Daphne's eyes drew together. "I don't understand.''

"Don't you, yet? I would imagine that she and the Old Man—Hucksley Senior—plotted this together. You see, Aunt Cloe wanted you to have your chance, to present you in all your glorious new plumage to the new Lord Asherwood."

"That's...ridiculous! I don't know you! You're an American!"

"I wondered why Hucksley kept insisting that I remain in England," Brant continued, ignoring her spate of words. "He ran me all over the place, then insisted that I come here, to Asherwood Hall."

Daphne didn't reply. She was thinking about what he'd said, and she knew he was right. They'd planned to truss her up like a Christmas goose and present her on the new viscount's platter! Her hands flew up to her face, and she pressed her palms against her cheeks.

"This is awful! Why, you don't even like me!"

"I don't?" he asked blandly.

"No! And I think you're...well, I won't insult you! But what about me and my feelings?"

It was a wail of fury and chagrin.

"Eyuh! You all finished, my lord?"

Brant cast a distracted, impatient eye towards Mrs. Mulroy. "Yes," he said shortly, "we're finished. Coffee in the Golden Salon, if you please."

Daphne pulled herself together with an effort. "It was quite fine, Mrs. Mulroy. Thank you."

"Well, little Miss, you didn't eat much," said Mrs. Mulroy, judiciously eyeing Daphne's plate.

"It must be all the...excitement," Brant said. "Will you come along now, Daphne?"

"But I made some singin' hinnies for you, Miss Daphne!"

"Singin' what?" Brant asked, bending a fascinated eye on the old wood sprite.

Daphne said smoothly, "They're scones. Very fattening, indigestible, and really quite delicious. Just wrap them up, Mrs. Mulroy, and we'll enjoy them tomorrow."

"Eyuh," said Mrs. Mulroy, and left them, shaking her head.

Daphne rose and took Brant's proffered arm. "Perhaps you can tell me what 'eyuh' means," Brant said, smiling down at her.

"It's an all-purpose word that can convey anything from dire chagrin to immense joy. I meant to tell you," she continued after a brief pause, all too aware of the strength of his arm beneath her hand, "the entrance-way looks marvelous."

"Yes, it does, doesn't it?" he said smoothly. "Stop a moment, Daphne."

She did, looking up at him, a question in her eyes.

He drew her toward him, very slowly, very gently. "You aren't too tall, even with your heels on. A nice fit, though, a very nice fit. Probably perfect in your bare feet.''

He saw the surprise in her widened eyes, then the uncertainty. "Come along," he said. "Let's continue our discussion over coffee, such as it will be.''

Once Brant managed to remove the old wood sprite from the room, he sat back on the sofa and said, "Won't you sit down? You're prowling about like a caged tiger. Tigress, rather. Not that I'm not enjoying the view, of course.''

"No, I don't want to sit," she snapped at him. "I'm too mad.''

"Oh? You didn't seem at all mad in the entrance hall.''

"Stop drawing me! You have realized their...plot! But what about me? Am I supposed to fall into your arms and beg you to marry me? I don't even like you!''

"As I recall," Brant said, eyeing her closely, "I believe you were even referred to as being dreadfully shy. Odd, I haven't noticed any shyness in you at all." *Except when I brought you against me.*

Daphne drew up short, her hands on her hips, her head cocked to one side. "You're right," she said, her voice puzzled. "I am shy, dreadfully so, as you said. At least, I always thought I was. Uncle Clarence always called me his bashful little peahen. I don't understand...''

"I imagine that starting out our relationship as Lucilla the Vamp helped you get over it. And then you were so angry with me, you forgot to act like the old Daphne. Incidentally, Uncle Clarence was a complete and utter idiot and fool.''

She frowned and waved a dismissing hand toward him. "But why did he write his will in such a way? I guess he knew you weren't married, but you must have friends, women friends.''

"Yes," he said, "I do, but no one terminally serious. Undoubtedly Uncle Clarence did something of a work-up on me. As Harlow told me, he must have believed this the ideal way to have pitter-pattering little British feet running about Asherwood Hall. You, I take it, are all British?''

"Yes," she said absently. She flopped down into a chair and crossed her legs. "What," she said, raising her eyes to his face, "are we going to do?''

I think I should get the hell out of Asherwood Hall and out of England as soon as I can, he thought, pulling his eyes away from those glorious long legs. Instead he said coolly, "Let's not worry about it now. You've just arrived. Perhaps I can draft you into helping me with the house. There's a great deal to be done.''

"Lucilla's house? Why bother? As soon as she takes ownership she'll turn it over to the National Trust. That or sell it.''

"Perhaps you're right," Brant said. "Still, I don't have to be back in the U.S. for another month. It amuses me to work on the house. Besides, I'll bet you've got some great ideas."

"Why would you bet that?"

"You love it," he said simply. "It must have made you furious to see it go to rack and ruin."

"I planted the rose garden in the back. It's not impressive now, but wait until spring."

"Roots," Brant said.

"Yes, of course rose bushes have roots."

"No," he said smiling as he rose, "I meant roots as in where a person hails from, belongs."

"You're rooted in the United States, aren't you?"

"I'm not quite certain. Actually, I'm really not certain about a whole bunch of things right now. Are you ready to sack out?"

"Sack what?"

"Go to bed, sleep."

"Yes," she said without guile or wiles, "I would like to go to bed. It's been a terribly enlightening day, hasn't it?"

"Frighteningly so," he agreed. "Incidentally, do you have any idea where I can find replacement parts for the armor?"

She burst into merry laughter. "I worried about that for the longest time! I told Uncle Clarence that I wanted to reassemble them, taking parts from one knight to make another one whole." She paused a moment, a sad glint in her eyes. "He didn't let me."

"Screw Uncle Clarence," Brant said.

"As in screwing hamburger?"

"As in damn and blast Uncle Clarence, and let's forget him."

"You Yanks have the oddest way of talking," she said, grinning up at him. "Screwing this and screwing that, all with different meanings! How do you keep it all straight?"

"That particular expression," he said, appearing much struck, "does have many different meanings. There's one special one, though, that tops them all."

"And what is that?"

"Perhaps," he said slowly, "I'll tell you, someday."

Chapter Six

"You had the *nerve* to criticize my jeans?"

Daphne skittered to an abrupt halt in the doorway of the Armor Room at the sound of Brant's teasing voice. "Oh dear," she said, feeling suddenly as if she were on display, "I shouldn't have used that as an insult." She wanted to cover herself somehow, but she didn't know where to put her hands.

"No," he agreed, gracefully coming to his feet. "You shouldn't have." His eyes traveled from her bulky cream wool sweater to the very new designer jeans she was wearing. Not wearing, he thought, dazzled by the sight. Poured into was more like it. Endless long legs, lovely shape, no bulges, no... He shook his head and said abruptly, "You ready for some breakfast?"

She nodded, saying impishly, "Maybe Mrs. Mulroy has put out the singin' hinnies!"

"Lord save us!"

She fell into step beside him. "Or maybe some kedgeree, or some bangers, or—"

"How 'bout some plain eggs and bacon?"

"Impossible! Too provincial. I think I'd prefer some angels on horseback."

"You got me on that one," he said, grinning into her twinkling eyes. "All right, what are angels on horseback?"

"Oysters wrapped in bacon. But, if you substitute prunes and chutney for the oysters, you have devils instead of angels."

"How about a combination of the two? Too much of one or the other would be boring."

"I have this odd feeling that you're no longer talking about oysters."

"No, and you're not boring. Not at all."

She gave him a sudden, dazzling smile, revealing small white teeth. "Nor am I shy," she said proudly, and blinked.

He wanted to kiss her, run his hands over her bottom and up under her sweater. He wanted... "Oh no," he said, "more soggy toast."

"Shush," Daphne giggled. "Mrs. Mulroy will hear you. Old Maddy does try, Brant, truly she does."

"The new cook is arriving today, hopefully. Winterspoon agreed to pick her up at the train station. Then we can pig out."

"Pig what?"

"Make gluttons of ourselves, eat until we're stuffed."

"We can't. We wouldn't be able to get into our respective jeans. Aunt Cloe told me I shouldn't do anything but drink tea when I wear these."

I'd just as soon see you out of them anyway. "Good point."

"It's raining," Daphne said, looking toward the fogged up windows.

"We've got plenty to do in the Armor Room. You up for fitting armor puzzles together?"

"I'd adore it." She fell silent, dipping pieces of her toast into a cup of tea, tea laced with milk, for God's sake, he observed, wincing at the sight.

"What's the matter?" he asked after a moment. "Your jeans hugging a bit too close?"

She smiled, but only briefly. "Lucilla. Perhaps we shouldn't be changing things, since Asherwood Hall will be hers."

"There is that," he agreed. "I like your hair," he added abruptly.

She smiled tentatively, as if surprised by the compliment.

"And your scrubbed face."

Her scrubbed face fell. "You mean I look like a prim schoolgirl."

"No, that isn't at all what I meant. I don't like much makeup on women. And you're lucky. You don't need it."

"I am wearing eyebrow pencil," she said, thrusting up her chin. "My eyebrows are too light without it. Aunt Cloe told me so."

"I'll have to take a closer look to see if I approve."

She remembered in very specific detail how he'd been quite close for those few moments the night before. Her breathing quickened. She said, her voice full of reproach, "You're making sport of me."

"I? Surely not. I'm merely trying to keep your self-confidence up." *Just as I'd like to pull your jeans down.* How, he wondered silently, surprised at himself, could he be so horny? Daphne—ridiculous name— was lovely, no doubt about it, but take Marcie, for instance. Now, she was beautiful, perfect body...and full of herself.

"Brant, what is football?"

He grinned, waving his fork at her. "Football and baseball are the two most popular American sports. It's similar to rugby, I guess, though I don't know too much about rugby.''

"I don't either, so we're even. But what do you do in football?''

"I'm a quarterback,'' Lord, where to begin? "Tell you what, Daph, I'll call up my mom and have her send over a couple of films of my games. We can rent a projector somewhere around here, can't we?''

"Certainly. You're not in the wilds, Brant. Are you famous? Like a cinema star?''

"I'm not exactly a household word, but I'm fairly good at what I do.''

"And you love it.''

"Yes, I do. Immensely. But I'm getting old.''

"Old! What a silly thing to say. What are you? Thirty?''

"Thirty-one. In football, that's getting up there. It's a very rough contact sport. And every year I get older and my competitors get younger. I've probably got four or five more years, barring any serious injuries.''

"Oh no! You get hurt?''

He grinned wryly. "The opposing team loves nothing more than to cream the quarterback. That is,'' he added, quickly translating, "their objective is keep me from gaining yardage. If they can bury me under a pile, they succeed. Pile of bodies, that is.''

"Have you ever been hurt?''

He unconsciously flexed his throwing arm. "On occasion. My teammates are good about protecting me.''

"It sounds like the Romans and the Christians.''

"It does a bit, doesn't it? In my early professional days I was quarterback for a consistently losing team. I was usually sore all season. No big deal, really,'' he added, seeing her eyes darken with concern. "I realize it's difficult for you to understand until you see the game. I'll explain everything to you then. Okay?''

She sighed, sitting back in her chair. "While you were playing this game and making money, I was rotting here, wondering what was going to happen to me when Uncle Clarence died.''

"And you still wonder?''

"Of course, wouldn't you? Five hundred pounds won't last long, after all. I don't have any skills.''

Her voice was matter-of-fact, not an ounce of bitterness or self-pity, which he would have expected. He said lightly, "You'll probably marry a nice young Englishman.''

"I'll miss my rose garden,'' she said, ignoring his words.

"I'd like to see it.''

"Not today. I don't have a brolly big enough to keep us from drowning.''

"Brolly?''

She looked startled. "You know, Brant, one of those things you raise over your head when it's raining."

"Ah, an umbrella."

"Exactly," she said, giving him an approving look. Like I'm a bright schoolboy, he thought.

"You finished?" he asked, rising. "Ready to attack the knights?"

"Onward!"

They worked throughout the morning, assembling matching arms and legs to form a half-dozen proper suits of armor. Their laughter floated out of the room, reaching Mrs. Mulroy's ears as she dusted in the entrance hall. She smiled benignly.

"Oh, you've a spot of smut on your face." Daphne raised her hand and rubbed his cheek with her fingertips.

Brant felt an alarming jolt of desire at her touch. She was so close he could see her contact lenses. Slowly he raised his own hand and stroked it through her hair. Silky smooth, he thought, and so thick.

Daphne's hand dropped. She looked at him, confusion written all over her face.

"I was just checking to see if you had any spots of smut," he said smoothly, leaning away from her. He had no intention of seducing the castle maiden.

"In my hair?"

"One never knows." He jumped gracefully to his feet and stretched. "I'm ready for some exercise. How 'bout you, Daph?"

"Daph? Is that a common nickname in America?"

Her voice sounded a bit breathless, for she was watching the play of muscles as he stretched his arms over his head.

"No, it's my own. I've never known a woman named Daphne before. It's nearly stopped raining. Why don't you get the um...brolly and let's take a look at your rose garden."

"Righto," she said. "I'll be back in a moment."

He watched her walk gracefully from the room; he couldn't seem to take his eyes off her swaying hips.

Daphne found him a few minutes later in the Golden Salon, standing in front of the fireplace.

"I'm ready," she said.

He turned, and she saw that he was holding the god-awful photo of her in his hand. "I think we can burn this," he said quietly.

"But she still exists, I'm afraid."

"Does she?" He handed Daphne the photo. To his delight, after staring at it for a moment, she giggled. "Goodness," she said, raising eyes brimful of laughter to his face, "what a double bagger!"

* * *

They spent the evening seated on a carpet in front of the fireplace. It was cosy, intimate and utterly enjoyable.

"I talked to my mother. She's sending a couple of films express. You want a bit more brandy?"

"I'm already tipsy. I'd better not."

"I like your dress. I know, Aunt Cloe insisted that the English Rose should wear peach silk."

"It is silk, my very first silk anything. And yes, conceited man, she did insist. At the time I thought it a bit..."

"Sexy? Too revealing?"

"I'm not in the habit of exhibiting myself to such an extent," she said tartly. Her hand moved to cover the deep V of the neckline.

"No, don't," he said, and grasped her hand, drawing it down to her lap. "I'm a simple man, and the sight gives me pleasure."

She flushed, embarrassed, pleased and confused by his manner and his words.

As for Brant, he thought, I'm acting like an idiot. I won't seduce her. Nothing could be more stupid than that. She's not the seducible type. She's revoltingly innocent. I'm leaving England shortly. I'll never see her again. Not those beautiful breasts, not those gorgeous legs...

"Do you have any brothers or sisters?" she asked, turning slightly, so her breasts weren't directly in his line of vision.

"One sister," he said easily, leaning back against the chair. "Her name's Lily, and she's a character. I also have two nephews and a niece. They all live in Texas with Lily's new husband. He's an oilman."

"Just like on the telly? Is he another J.R. Ewing?"

"I'd heard *Dallas* was popular over here." At her excited nod, he continued. "I call him Crusty Dusty. I imagine he's ruthless enough if the situation calls for it. But he loves my sister, and that's good enough for me. I told him before they married that Lily needed a keeper more than a husband, and Dusty drawled that as long as she was housebroken, it was fine with him."

"Housebroken? You mean like a burglar?"

Brant groaned. He clasped her hand and drew it to his mouth, kissing it lightly. "No, not like a burglar. Have you ever had a puppy?"

"Yes, when I was a little girl."

"Well, housebroken means that you train the puppy not to relieve himself on the floor or on the carpet or anywhere in the house. Like breaking a horse, I guess. Get him tamed and under control."

"I'm beginning to get quite fond of American. How long do you think it would take me to speak it fluently?"

"It would all depend on your teacher, I expect."

"You said that you're going home in a month. Will you play football?"

"No, it's the off-season. Practice starts in the summer. No, when I go back, I'm making a commercial for TV."

"For the telly! Oh, I am impressed. Whatever will you be selling?"

"I'll be pushing sports equipment."

Daphne came up on her knees, resting her hands on her thighs. "Do you want to know a secret, Brant?"

He arched a thick brow at her, forcing himself to keep his eyes on her face.

"It's about my Aunt Cloe. Well, you mustn't tell her I told you, but she adores young men. I remember her nearly choking when she saw a poster of one of your American athletes wearing nothing but sexy undershorts."

"Ah, and did you nearly choke, Daph?"

"I was too busy watching her reaction. When she noticed that I'd noticed, she hauled me away." She grinned at him, shaking her head. "I can't wait to see what she does when she lays eyes on you!"

"Shall I greet her in my underwear?"

"She'd love it, but perhaps you'd better not."

Would you love it? "I can see it now," he said lightly. "English Viscount Arrested for Indecent Exposure. Aunt Cloe in Hospital for Severe Palpitations."

Daphne was still laughing when she rose to her feet. "Well, we'll soon know what she thinks about you. She should be coming here soon. Now, my lord, I'm off for bed. My weak head is spinning from that wicked brandy."

"I'll walk up with you," Brant said. He laid his hand lightly on her shoulder when they reached the bedroom. "Do you ride?"

"Of course. Every Englishwoman who lives in the country rides, I'll have you know."

"Fine. If this blasted rain stops and it's not too cold, shall we go out tomorrow morning?"

"I'd love to. I'll even wear my new riding togs."

"I know, Aunt Cloe insisted."

"No, I did. I can't imagine getting on my mare, Julia, in my new jeans."

"I can," Brant said, patted her on her cheek, and walked down the corridor to his room.

The morning was cold, but not overly so, and the sky was overcast, but there was no rain. Brant's mount, borrowed from a neighbor, was strong and fast, and Daphne, astride her Julia, looked good enough to eat in her tailored tan riding pants and jacket. An Englishwoman to the tips of her riding boots.

They galloped and cantered, and he saw her life through her eyes. A circumspect life, he thought. A limited world. She took him into East Grinstead, and he saw the fondness of the locals for her, and their surprise at her appearance. They dismounted and walked along the River Wey, talking about nothing in particular.

"Daphne," he said abruptly as they readied to return to Asherwood, "have you ever dated?"

"Me?" He saw a fleeting glint of anger in her eyes, but it was so quickly gone that he might have imagined it. And there was light amusement in her voice as she replied, "Well, there was the rector, Mr. Theodore Haverleigh. Uncle Clarence let him into the house a couple of times and allowed him to take me to a church picnic."

"Did you like him?"

"Theo? Goodness no! He had no shoulders and no chin, and he was terribly puffed up with himself. I'm sure at the time he honestly believed he was doing me a favor, and perhaps he was...."

"At the time. Now, he'd probably start slobbering at the sight of you."

She gave him a pert salute. "Very true," she said, and lightly dug her heels into Julia's fat sides.

She felt marvelous. Full of humor, full of life. Until they reined in in front of the Hall.

"Oh dear," Daphne said. "That's Lucilla."

Brant gazed toward the woman standing on the front steps looking toward them. She was tall, with raven-black hair, immense blue eyes, and a figure that would stop a train.

"Indeed," he said. "Shall we take the horses to the stable?"

Daphne nodded numbly. She'd seen the admiration in Brant's eyes. Life as she'd known it for the past two days was over. She wanted to howl her disappointment. Instead, she followed Brant to the stables.

Chapter Seven

"Darling! How good to see you again! My, don't you look the smart bird! Whatever happened?"

Daphne suffered herself to be hugged and pecked on her cheek. "Hello, Lucilla. You're looking well. This is Brant Asher, the new Viscount Asherwood."

She's responding to him just as I would if I only knew how, Daphne thought with a stab of resentment.

Lord he's handsome, Lucilla thought as she calmly shook his hand, but her eyes were wide with admiration as she took in every inch of him. "Welcome, my lord, to England and to Asherwood."

She's already acting like the queen of the castle!

"Thank you, Lucilla. May I call you that?"

"Certainly, Brant. Has our little Daphne been showing you around?"

"We've been out riding, if that's what you mean, Lucilla," Daphne said. *Condescending bitch! Why do I feel as if I've just gained weight in my thighs, got greasy hair, and my contact lenses have turned red?*

"Why yes, dear, that's exactly what I meant. I hope," she continued, her eyes on Brant, "that you don't mind my dropping in unannounced?"

"Since Asherwood Hall will belong to you, Lucilla, how can we mind?"

"Oh yes," Lucilla said slowly. "The will."

"As you say," Brant said. "Shall we go in, ladies?"

It would all be extremely amusing, Brant thought, as the three of them sat over tea in the Golden Salon, if Daphne weren't losing her self-confidence by the second. It wasn't that Lucilla was obviously unkind to her. On the contrary, she was all that was gracious, as if she were addressing a sweet, but simple child.

Lucilla said over her tea cup, "The changes you've made, the improvements, Brant, are remarkable. The old tomb looks marvelous. Daphne, would you please hand me a biscuit? Thank you, dear. The entranceway is so very tip-top sparkling. And what you did to the suits of armor— why I would have tossed the lot out!"

"His lordship is quite creative," Daphne said dryly.

"What a lovely thought," Lucilla said, giving him a long, intimate look.

"I expect you saw Mr. Hucksley in London?" Brant asked.

"Oh yes. It's all too remarkable, isn't it? You mustn't worry, dear," she continued to Daphne, gently patting her hand. "I'll see that things are put right. I thought about it all the way up here. Perhaps a trade school, or a try at interior decorating, now that you've got yourself together. You'd enjoy that, wouldn't you, Daphne? Why, there's even business. You'd make an adorable secretary."

"Actually," Daphne said, getting a firm grip on her insecurities, "I think I might try my hand at modeling."

"Why, my dear girl, what a remarkable idea!"

If she says remarkable one more time, I'll yank off her panty hose and strangle her with them! Instead Daphne said, drawing herself up a bit straighter, "Not so remarkable. I certainly have the figure for it."

"Do you, dear? Well, I suppose I must wait to see you in a dress. Riding clothes are so...minimizing, aren't they?"

"I believe, ladies, that it's time for lunch," Brant said, rising. He looked toward Daphne, but her eyes were on Lucilla, who was gazing raptly at the zipper on his jeans.

At the sight of an unappetizing lunch of slipshod-looking sandwiches and thin potato soup, Brant said, "A new cook is arriving this afternoon."

"It's just as well," Lucilla said gently. "It will help us girls keep our weight down, won't it, dear?"

"Quite," Daphne said.

There were several minutes of blessed silence. Lucilla asked, "How long will you remain in England, Brant?"

"Another month, perhaps less."

"I understand from Mr. Hucksley that you're an athlete?"

"Yes, I play professional football for the New York Astros."

"How remarkable! You've certainly the...build for it. I thought you'd probably look grand in your title."

Daphne choked on her soup.

"I also understand that you've a *chère amie* waiting for you in New York, a lovely, independent career woman?"

Brant started to tell her that he had several gorgeous women waiting for him in New York, but he was aware of Daphne's eyes searching his face. "I'm fortunate to have many friends, both men and women."

"And all American, too. You must find our ways very strange."

"Not at all," Brant said pleasantly. Lord, is she playing both sides of the fence, he thought. "Though I will admit that Daphne is giving me quite an education."

"Daphne?" Lucilla's beautiful arched brows arched a bit more over incredulous light blue eyes.

"Yes," Daphne said, goaded. "I think Brant looks charming in his title too."

Lucilla laughed merrily. "My little peahen—as Uncle Clarence so sweetly called her—is changing before my very eyes! How utterly remarkable. Haven't you done something with your eyes, dear?"

"Yes," Daphne said, "I've finally learned to see with them."

"Well, I'm very proud of you, dear." She turned to Brant. "I talked of Daphne to my husband, you know, and he wanted to meet her, take her in hand and all that."

"You're too late, Lucilla," Daphne said. "Aunt Cloe already did."

"Dear Mrs. Sparks. I imagine that she'll be arriving here soon. To keep an eye on her investment, so to speak?"

Why do I feel like the sacrificial goat? "The more the merrier," said Brant. "Now, if you ladies will excuse me, I want to do some planing on the front doors. They're a bit warped."

Daphne's eyes followed his progress from the room. She stiffened when Lucilla said in a pitying voice, "Such a temptation, Daphne, but surely you have some pride?"

"What do you mean, Lucilla?"

"Surely, dear, you wouldn't consider marrying a man who only wanted you for money and Asherwood Hall? A good deal of money, I might add."

"Why not?" Daphne said, angry color staining her cheeks. "After all, it's either that or...trade school! I'll call Mrs. Mulroy to show you to your room, Lucilla."

"A marriage of convenience, dear. Really, what an appalling thought."

"Haven't you done it three times?"

"Why no, dear, not entirely. All three husbands were remarkably virile, you know. Just like Brant. I imagine that he knows every trick to make a woman swoon for him. Don't you agree?"

"Excuse me, Lucilla."

"Remember, Daphne," Lucilla called after her, "Brant is quite experienced with women. I do hope you won't make a fool of yourself over him. Seriously, dear, have a care. Hasn't he already turned your little head, just a bit?"

No, he's just made me feel very good about myself.

Daphne left the breakfast room and went immediately upstairs to change into her jeans and a sweater. Afterward she found Brant working on the front doors.

"Hi," he said, glancing up at her briefly. "Did you survive the first salvo?"

"What's a salvo?"

"A burst of rapidly firing artillery."

Daphne worried her lower lip for a moment, then burst out, "Do you need money, Brant?"

"Ah, that's very stiff cannon fire. No, as a matter of fact, I've got quite enough money."

"But I've heard that Americans view money as a sort of god, that they can never get enough of it."

"I wasn't aware that view was confined to the United States," he said. "As you well know, Daph, this estate runs about four hundred thousand pounds. Nearly a half million dollars. That's not chicken feed. Hand me that piece of sandpaper, will you?"

"This thing? Lucilla's so beautiful."

"Yes, she is. How old is she, anyway?"

"About thirty, I'd say."

"Listen to me, Daph. She's got a tremendous potential investment, all of it riding on what you and I decide to do. Don't let her rile you. If you were in her shoes, you'd likely do the same thing." He grinned at her. "Only not as well."

Daphne sighed. "Why do I feel as if I'm thirteen again, and fat and plain and dowdy?"

"She's quite good. Why don't you just sit back and enjoy her machinations? You might learn something useful."

"You're cynical, aren't you?"

"A bit, I guess. I just want you to use your wits and not get all sullen and defensive. You have got wits, you know, plenty of them."

"So, in other words," Daphne said slowly, "you want to keep her in...suspense?"

"I hadn't thought of that in particular. But it just might be fun. And, Daph, don't worry about your future. I won't let you starve. I'll see that you're set up in whatever you want to do."

"Marvelous," she muttered under her breath. "No, thank you, Brant. It's time, I think, that I looked after myself."

She walked away. She heard the grating sound of the sandpaper against wood cease, and knew he was looking after her.

If Brant felt like the main meal with Lucilla, he definitely felt like a very fattening dessert with Aunt Cloe. She'd examined every inch of him in great, interested detail, a dreamy look in her eyes. He noticed, gazing at her across the dining table over a delicious meal prepared by Mrs.

Woolsey, that she was a tall, big-boned woman, with a strong nose and chin, and penetrating light blue eyes. When they looked at him, they both sparkled and looked speculating. She wore her thick salt-and-pepper hair the way his mother did, in a classic chignon. Her humor was dry, her smile charming. She has a lovely voice, he thought, listening to her speak of her trip.

"Ah, what a delight Paris was. All that gray sky and muzzling rain, but no matter. Such a relief to be home again. In the bosom of my family so to speak. I must say, Brant, you're everything I expected."

"I hope your expectations weren't set too high, Aunt Cloe," he said dryly, grinning at her. She'd arrived but three hours after Lucilla. He wondered if she'd hotfooted it here, knowing that Lucilla would be doing her best to making things unpleasant for her little chick, Daphne.

"Dear boy," Cloe said, wishing she were thirty years younger, "when you've lived as long as I have, you learn to be wary in what you expect. Photos help, of course. I must say, I like to see a man togged up for dinner. Very elegant."

"How long will you be staying, Aunt Cloe?" Lucilla asked, her voice as flat as her enthusiasm. "You must have so much waiting for your attention in Glasgow."

"What an excellent gunner you would have been in the war, Lucilla. Such marksmanship, such precise...yes, well, you know, I've been thinking that I will visit America. I will wait, of course, until Daphne gets settled in."

Brant blinked at her double-edged words. Lucilla gritted her teeth.

Daphne said, "That shouldn't take long, Auntie."

"Yes," Lucilla said. "We will all move her into a nice flat in London. Not long at all."

"Perhaps I'll study to be a carpenter," Daphne said. "I learned today how to plane a door."

"Or," Brant added, "you could work for the British Museum, keeping their armor exhibit in good shape."

"I thought that was probably your idea, Daphne," Lucilla said. "As I said, I should have tossed the lot."

"Oh, I don't know," Brant said. "I suspect the new owner of Asherwood might be delighted at such antiquity."

Cloe gave him a bland smile. "Indeed, my dear boy."

"But then again," he added, shooting her down, "one never knows, does one?"

He wished he'd kept his mouth shut, for Lucilla gave him another one of her patented intimate smiles. He wondered if he should lock his bedroom door tonight. He forked down another bite of the delicious Yorkshire pudding, listening to the well-bred backbiting going on between Aunt Cloe and Lucilla.

"How did you leave your dear third husband, Lucilla?"

"I left him, period, Aunt Cloe. I would have sworn you knew that."

"German men are so fierce and dominating, don't you agree?"

"Basically, Carl was a dear. But," Lucilla added, shooting Brant a honey-coated smile, "he was too old for me. Why, his daughter was Daphne's age, and his son, Dieter, well, such a possessive young man." She gave a little shudder.

"And Brant's age?"

"A bit older, actually. I just hope he doesn't follow me here."

Brant studied Daphne from beneath half-closed lids. She was toying with the fresh peas on her plate, eating little, saying even less. She'd reverted to the old Daphne, he suspected. Withdrawn, shy, all self-confidence obliterated. He wanted to shake her, to draw her into his arms and comfort her. No! If he had half a brain, he knew he'd leave in the morning, early.

"I say, a jolly good dinner," Aunt Cloe said. "Shall we have coffee in the sitting room?"

I've got to get Daphne alone, Cloe thought, as she watched her rise from her chair and walk from the dining room, like a prisoner going to the gallows. I've got to knock some sense into the girl!

To her utter delight Brant said, "Unfortunately, Daphne and I haven't time for coffee. We're going into the village to see a movie. Are you ready, Daphne?"

Daphne stopped dead in her tracks, wondering if she'd heard right. He was rescuing her! She turned and gave him a dazzling smile. "I just have to get my coat." She was off like a shot, nearly running up the stairs.

"I hope you'll forgive us, ladies, for leaving you on your first night here."

"Not at all," Cloe said. "Not at all."

Lucilla was frowning, but just for a moment. She said with just an exquisite touch of wistful disappointment, "I suppose one must keep one's promises. It's very nice of you, Brant, to see to Daphne."

Daphne was looking at herself in the mirror. I don't look like a frump, she said under her breath. I won't let Lucilla make me feel like a refugee from a turnip patch. I won't! However, when she returned to the entrance hall, there was Lucilla, her hand on Brant's arm, laughing up at him. And he, damn him, was smiling down at her.

"Ah, here you are, dear," Lucilla said, turning to give her an approving look. "How lovely your coat is. I've always thought brown such an enduring color, and wool so very wearing. Now, Brant, don't keep her out too late, will you?"

As if I'm some sort of backward adolescent!

Aunt Cloe gave her a quick hug, whispering in her ear, "Don't you dare regard anything she says, love! You look charming, make no mistake about it.''

"You ready, Daph?"

"Yes. Good night, Lucilla, Auntie."

The evening was clear and cold, a quarter moon lighting the drive. "I've always liked enduring things," Brant said, grinning down at her. "Would you drive, Daphne? I still don't trust myself on the wrong side of the road."

She nodded and slipped behind the wheel. "It's a lovely evening," she said inanely.

In response Brant sighed deeply and leaned his head back against the leather seat.

"What's the matter, Brant? Too many salvos?"

"For sure," he said, his eyes closed. "I've never before felt like a duck in hunting season."

And I'm one of the hunters, she thought, suddenly depressed. He must despise the lot of us. "What movie do you want to see?" she asked, forgetting there was just one cinema house.

"Turn on the heater and let's go parking."

"Parking? You mean, stop the car?"

He gave her a long, lazy look. "Yes, find a nice spot with something of a view to liven things up and pull over."

She drove on in silence.

"I told you that you shouldn't let Lucilla get to you."

Her hands gripped the steering wheel. "You invited me out because you didn't want me to continue making a fool of myself. You were feeling sorry for me," she said flatly.

"No, I was feeling sorry for myself. And you're a cute fool."

"Ha! I thought men just loved so much female attention!"

"At least you've got your sharp tongue back."

She shot him a look of pure dislike.

"Also, I invited you out because I'd like to beat some sense into you. Good, I've got your attention. Watch out for that ditch! This looks like a good spot. Pull over here."

She obeyed him and turned off the engine. Daphne had stopped on a slight rise overlooking the Wey. Naked-branched beech trees surrounded them.

"Now, turn around and look at me. I've got lots of things to say to you."

"You sound just like Uncle Clarence," she said, her voice as nasty as she could manage it.

"Do I? Unlike Uncle Clarence, I won't ask you to do anything you don't want to do. Well, maybe that's not totally the case. Why the hell did you regress again? I thought we'd straightened all that out after our memorable lunch.''

She stared at him, unable to find the words to explain her feelings.

"How do you expect to get along if you can't handle all different kinds of people, and that includes women who patronize you?''

"I'll get along," she said. "Why do you care, anyway?''

"Sometimes I think you need a keeper.''

He sounded mildly angry, and that surprised her. "Things are different with Lucilla here," she said slowly, trying to explain it both to him and to herself. "Before, with just the two of us—''

"Daphne," he interrupted, his voice impatient, "Lucilla's really a great deal of fun if you'd just forget all your old stored up envy of her. There's a whole world of people out there that you have to deal with.''

"Just stop it!" she hissed at him. "Just leave me alone, okay? I don't need you to tell me what's wrong with me. And I'm not envious of Lucilla!''

She twisted the ignition key, and the engine turned over. Suddenly his hand was over hers, and the engine died. "Damn you," he said, and pulled her into his arms.

Daphne was too surprised to resist. She opened her mouth to say something—what, she didn't know—and felt his lips cover hers. She stiffened at the attack, and immediately he gentled the pressure. His tongue glided lightly over her lips; his hands stroked up and down her back.

"You taste like Yorkshire pudding," he said against her cheek. He returned to her mouth, gently nibbling, tasting, and slowly she began to relax, and respond.

"That's it," he said softly. "You're a beautiful, intelligent woman, Daphne, and I don't want you to forget it again." *And you're such an innocent I feel like I'm being unfair even kissing you.*

He released her and smiled at the dazed, uncertain look in her eyes. He gently rubbed his thumb over her jaw. "This," he said, "is what we Americans call parking.''

"It's…different.''

"You sound a little out of breath. Let's try again. Trust me and relax.''

She did, without a second thought. He was careful, very careful, well knowing she didn't have a bit of experience. He didn't want to frighten her or put her off. He kept his hands on her back and his kisses light, undemanding. He broke off and gently pressed her face against his shoulder. He thought her breathing was a bit faster.

He stroked his fingers through her soft hair. *I've wanted to do that since I've met her,* he thought. He leaned his cheek against her temple and breathed in her sweet womanly scent. He heard himself say, "I want to make love to you, Daphne.''

She raised her face and gave him a puzzled but glowing look. "You mean, you want to go to bed with me...and..."

He grasped her upper arms, cursing himself silently. "No, that isn't what I meant to say." He dashed his fingers through his hair. "I want you to realize that you're a marvelous person who can do anything she wants."

"Then why did you kiss me?"

Because I'm horny and any port in a storm!

But that wasn't true. He wanted her, only her. He had no idea why. His idea of a good time had never been the company of a repressed female with the experience of a Victorian maiden.

"Did you kiss me because you thought that would give me self-confidence?"

"Yes," he said without thinking.

Slowly she pulled away from him. "Lucilla's right," she said. "And I'm a fool."

"We're both fools," he said in a distracted attempt at humor. "And Lucilla's been right about only one thing I can think of."

"What is that?"

"She's afraid of you," he said slowly, studying her face in the dim shadows. "And she has a right to be."

Daphne shook her head, an abrupt, angry movement. "I just don't believe this. Everything revolves around you; at least, that's the way you see it. All of us are like hens bowing and scraping in front of the cock! Well, I don't care! I intend to see to myself, do you hear? I don't want your help, or Lucilla's help, or Aunt Cloe's! What I would like from you, my lord, is your refusal to marry me. That way I'll get five hundred pounds rather than just one hundred."

Brant clenched his jaws together. How dare she fly off the handle at him like that! Damn her! Accusing him of being some kind of a conceited sheik with a harem! He wanted to help her; he wanted to make her realize how much she had to offer, to... He said quietly, very quietly, "I doubt you'd even know what to do with fifty pounds. I doubt you would even know a checkbook if it bit you. You'd probably last no longer than one week on your own. You want five hundred pounds, lady? Fine, you've got it!"

Chapter Eight

Brant opened his bedroom door quietly, not bothering to turn on the ancient overhead light. He was still angry with Daphne—ridiculous Victorian name—and her dumb accusations. Why should he care, anyway? What she did with her life had nothing whatsoever to do with him. Hell, he'd be home soon, and good riddance to all of them!

Cock, indeed!

He turned on a Victorian lamp with a red velvet shade that sported thick red fringe, and methodically began to strip off his clothes. At least Winterspoon wasn't waiting for him. The thought of his valet helping him out of his pants was unnerving.

"I knew you'd look marvelous in your title."

His fingers stilled over the zipper. He turned slowly to see Lucilla wearing a tight silky thing, lounging pajamas, he supposed, a saucy smile on her lips.

"How 'bout title and trousers?"

"Sounds like the name of a painting," she said. "Perhaps we could frame you and put you up for the Royal Academy."

He grinned at her. "What are you doing in here, Lucilla?"

She shrugged, and one of the straps slipped off her lovely shoulder. He suddenly had the image of Marcie in his mind, standing in his bathroom doorway, wearing finally, after both straps had fallen, nothing but her enticing smile.

"It occurred to me, after seeing you in person, of course, that there were more options, shall we say, than the simple ones presented."

"I think," he said, "that you'd better explain that."

She shrugged again, but fortunately for his peace of mind and body, the other strap stayed put.

"You love this house," she said simply.

"Yes," he agreed, "I do. I'm not certain why, but I do. It's as if," he continued thoughtfully, trying yet again to put his feelings into words, "the house has been waiting for me, as if the house needs me, just as I need it." *Roots,* his mother would have said.

"The house also needs quite a bit of money to reinstate it to whatever its former glory was," she said dryly, giving him an odd look, one he was certain he deserved. It did, he admitted to himself, sound a bit crazy that he'd feel so strongly about what, after all, was only a pile of brick, windows and stone. He mustn't forget the chimney pots that were in dire need of scrubbing down.

"That's true, too."

"I will inherit the house and more than enough money."

Only if I don't marry Daphne.

"I see," he said only.

She chewed on her lower lip a moment, as if uncertain how to proceed. "I think perhaps," she said finally, "that you and I could join forces."

"In what way, Lucilla?"

"I think a nice start might be a vacation to, say, the South of France. St. Tropez, perhaps, or Nice."

"To get to know each other better?"

"Much better. We might just discover that we could do quite well together, Brant. Yes, quite well indeed. You are, I think, a man who appreciates a woman who knows her way about, a woman who would please you and appreciate you also. You are a very nice-looking man, Brant."

And I'd look just dandy on your arm, huh?

"Thank you," he said aloud.

Lucilla walked nearer—glided was more like it, he thought, watching her warily as she came to a halt a half inch from him. She placed her hands on his bare chest. "Very nice," she murmured, stroking him lightly. One hand dipped down, her fingers slipping beneath his shorts.

"Lucilla," he said, grabbing her hand and pulling it away, "I don't think this would be such a good idea."

"Why not?"

He watched her tongue glide over her lower lip. *Because Daphne's in the house and she would find out and she would be hurt.*

"I have a headache," he said.

She burst into merry laughter, but didn't move away from him. "Well, why don't you think about it, Brant? We could, I think, make very nice music together."

He said nothing, and her forehead furrowed into a slight frown. "Daphne, you know," she continued in a sincere voice, "is a very English sort of girl. I do think it a pity that Uncle Clarence kept her so tied up, but what can one do? In fact, I can't imagine taking Daphne to the South of France. And in America she would be lost as a lamb, and desperately unhappy. You know how shy she is."

"Daphne seemed to do okay in Greece," he said in a neutral tone.

"With Aunt Cloe telling her what to do and when and how to do it, she should have done all right. But in your society, Brant? In your particular group of friends? No, it wouldn't do at all, you know. Not at all."

But Daphne wasn't at all shy, he thought, not until you came. He wanted to tell her that Daphne wasn't retarded but she was sliding her hands up his arms to lightly clasp his shoulders. "I fully intend to take care of little Daphne. You mustn't feel guilty about it."

She stood on her tiptoes and kissed him. He felt her darting tongue probe at his closed lips, felt the length of her pressed against his body, and he responded. But just for a moment. His breathing was a bit heavy when he grasped her arms and set her away from him.

"I don't have to leave you tonight, Brant," she said softly, her eyes luminous in the dim light.

He got a hold on himself. This was ridiculous, damn it! He didn't want to make love to Lucilla; he wanted to make love to... Oh no, you don't, he nearly shouted at himself. Oh no.

"I don't think so," he said finally. "I think you should leave now, Lucilla."

"Ah, I was forgetting about your headache. Will you think about things, Brant?"

"You can be certain of it," he said. He didn't move until she had quietly closed the bedroom door behind her.

"Here is your coffee, my lord."

Brant cocked open an eye to see Winterspoon standing patiently by his bed, a tray on his outstretched arms.

"You don't sound too approving," he said, yawning mightily.

"You are an American, my lord."

"I agree. In that case, it should be black and thick and grow hair on my chest."

"The hair is there, my lord—on your chest, that is—so I assume it is all of those things."

"You don't have to wait on me, Winterspoon," Brant said as he sat up and leaned against the thick pillows. "I could have gone down to the breakfast room."

"I don't think that would be such a good idea, my lord."

"Do you know something I don't?"

"Doubtless there are many things, my lord, but it is my job to...protect you from unpleasantness."

"Unpleasantness, huh? Is there a cat fight going on over the scrambled eggs? Delicious coffee. I needed it."

"Cat fight?" Winterspoon shuddered delicately. He looks just like Jeeves must have looked, Brant thought, when Bertie said something gross. But so tolerant.

"I shouldn't have phrased it exactly like that, my lord. But if you're referring to the ladies, I suggest you keep to your room for a bit longer."

"That bad? Well, what can they be doing?"

"I believe, my lord," Winterspoon said very carefully, his eyes trained on the spot above Brant's left shoulder, "that Mrs. Sparks was accusing Mrs. Meitter of trying to—" He cleared his throat and looked heavenward.

"Trying to what, Winterspoon?"

The amusement in his voice earned him a reproachful look. "Mrs. Sparks saw Mrs. Meitter go into your room last night, my lord."

"Ah." His amusement suddenly died, and he stiffened. "Was Miss Daphne there?"

"Yes, my lord."

"Oh no. Damn it!" He pulled back the covers, spilling the remains of his coffee. Winterspoon quickly handed him a robe, his eyes on Brant's adam's apple. "I set out pajamas for you, my lord," he said.

"I can't stand them," Brant said shortly, shrugging into the robe and belting it.

"I noticed, my lord. His old lordship was very fond of that pair. He never wore them, in fact. Saving them for a special occasion, I suppose. I've drawn your bath, my lord."

"I'd give a bundle for a shower," Brant grumbled. "Who wants to sit in their own dirt?"

"I couldn't say, my lord. What will you be requiring by way of dress?"

"Just jeans, shirt and my sneakers. I've got a lot of work to do, and I don't need to wear a tux."

"Very good, my lord."

Thirty minutes later Brant walked with a rather lagging step into the breakfast room. Only Aunt Cloe was there, waiting for him, he quickly realized.

"Good morning," he said.

She gave him a long look. "Handsome is as handsome does," she said.

"I didn't sleep with Lucilla."

"Didn't you? Lucilla didn't give that impression."

"I told her I had a headache."

Cloe wanted to be furious with him, but that calm, rueful string of bluntness made her break out in laughter. "You didn't!" she gasped. "How marvelous! That's called turning the tables, I'd say!"

"Am I forgiven?"

Cloe was shaking her head. "If only Mr. Sparks—my late husband, you know—if only he'd had your sense of humor! When he didn't want to make...well, that is...Yes, my boy, you're quite forgiven. Sit down. Mrs. Mulroy left your breakfast on the sideboard. I," she added handsomely, "will be delighted to serve you."

She was still chuckling when she handed him a plate loaded with scrambled eggs, several strips of crispy bacon and something else he couldn't identify. "What is this?"

"Oh, those are bloaters. Smoked herring, you know."

Brant gingerly tried one and nodded in approval. "Tell me about Mr. Sparks," he said, giving Cloe a boyish, teasing grin.

"Don't be impertinent, laddie. Now, tell me, Brant, what are you going to do?"

"I'm going to hang new wallpaper in this room today. I selected it myself."

"That," she said, frowning, "isn't what I meant! What color wallpaper? Something light, I hope. I always hated this grimy stuff. So depressing, but father wouldn't ever listen to me. Wouldn't listen to Daphne, either."

"It's light yellow, with white and pale blues in it. I hope it will make the room look nice and airy, a perfect setting for bloaters. Where's Daphne?"

Cloe didn't miss a beat. "Out riding. And it should make the room look very livable."

"She couldn't stand the heat, huh?"

"If you mean by that nonsensical American slang, was she upset, yes, she was. She's used to going off by herself when she's upset. She must be broken of that habit."

"And, of course," Brant said blandly, crunching down on a bite of bacon, "you want me to do the breaking."

"Certainly, my boy. You aren't stupid; at least, you don't give me the impression of stupidity. Of course, I could be wrong, I suppose. I remember what I thought of Mr. Sparks when he was courting me. Well, I changed my mind on our wedding night. Do you know what he did...? No, you aren't stupid. I want you to marry her. She'll make you a grand wife. And she loves this house. It was only her Uncle Clarence she detested, and with excellent reason."

Brant said very slowly and calmly, "Cloe, I don't even know Daphne, nor she me. What's more, she's very English and I'm very American. She's also—"

"Opposites attract, I always say," Cloe interrupted serenely. "You'd be good for each other. You would help her grow, and she would do you proud. She's quite the lady, gentle, kind, and she does have a sense of fun. Most pronounced, really, when she's not...what do you Yanks say? Oh yes, not...in heat.''

Brant choked on his eggs and quickly downed half a glass of orange juice. ''No, not quite that, Cloe. It's called can't stand the heat. Incidentally, Daphne informed me quite plainly last night that she thought I was a conceited jerk and she wanted nothing to do with me. I think if she could, she would have punched me out. She wants me to refuse to marry her so she can get five hundred pounds rather than just one hundred.''

''Such passion from my little egg. I'm very pleased.''

Brant could only stare at her. ''Where,'' he asked, ''is that place you Britishers call Bedlam?''

The wallpaper was hung and the breakfast room looked fantastic, at least it did in Brant's modest opinion. He'd been left alone all morning to do the job, and he supposed he'd been pleased about it. Where was Daphne? he wondered for the dozenth time.

She wasn't present at lunch. Lucilla and Cloe complimented him at least as many times as he wondered where Daphne was. He finally made his escape and went to the stables. Her horse was back in its stall.

There was a chill wind, and he zipped his sheepskin jacket all the way up. He called her name. She wasn't in or around the stables.

He wandered to the back of the Hall to her garden. She was there, on her hands and knees, digging furiously in the hard ground. She was wearing a brown knit stocking cap pulled down nearly to her eyebrows, an old pair of slacks and a thick short coat.

''Coward,'' he said, standing over her, his legs spread.

She spun about and tumbled back on her bottom. Brant dropped to his haunches in front of her. ''Coward,'' he repeated.

''Go to hell,'' Daphne said.

''Good grief!'' He slapped his hand over his head. ''The Victorian maiden has uttered a profanity. What is the world coming to?''

''Go to hell in a handbasket.''

''I didn't know you Britishers had that phrase.''

''We don't. I heard it in an American movie.''

''Really? Which one?''

''I don't remember. Would you please leave?''

''No. And you are a coward.''

''I had no intention of watching you and Lucilla making obscene faces at each other!''

''Obscene? Goodness, I've never tried that.''

''It isn't funny! I had it up to here—'' She poked at her eyebrows and dislodged her knit cap. ''Well, anyway, you can do just as you please. I don't care.''

''Thank you for your permission. It means everything to me. And I didn't sleep with Lucilla." At her incredulous look, he continued blandly, "Cloe believed me. Isn't your bottom wet from the cold?" He rose and stretched out his hand to her.

She took it, and he pulled her to her feet. "If Cloe believed you, it's because she likes men, young men. She'll believe anything they say, if they're slick enough."

"I guess I was slick enough, then." He studied her closely for several silent moments. "How bad are your eyes without your contacts?" he asked finally.

"Without them you'd be a pleasant blur, which, I might add, wouldn't be at all a bad thing!"

"Can you sleep in them?"

"Yes. I can wear them an entire week. Why?"

Because when I make love to you I want you to see my face very clearly.

"Just wondered, that's all. Would you help me sand down some of the molding in the library?"

"Why not?" She sighed, swiped off her bottom and fell easily into step beside him.

"I promise you a reward for your help."

"What kind of a reward?"

He grinned at her suspicious tone. "Here's a down payment." He leaned down and quickly kissed her. He gave her no time to react, merely began walking again. "First we need to drive into the village. I need a special fine sort of sandpaper."

Chapter Nine

Brant and Daphne worked in companionable harmony for several hours in the library.

"You're quite good at this," he said. "Just be careful that you don't scratch up your hands."

"Aunt Cloe isn't going to be pleased about my fingernails," Daphne said. "I can't seem to keep them as long as she would like. Maybe it's a lack of calcium or something."

"Let me see," Brant said, sitting on the floor and holding out his hand.

She shot him another one of her patented suspicious looks and tentatively placed her hand in his.

"No ridges on the nails. They look good to me." He gave her a wicked grin. "Personally, I prefer short nails on a woman; it's safer."

"It's true," she said on a sigh. "I'm always scratching myself."

"My point exactly."

"It probably isn't, but I dread to know just what your point is."

"Perhaps you'll find out. Oh, the film of one of my better football games came this morning. You wanna watch it with me?"

Her eyes sparkled. "Oh yes, that would be great sport."

"Let's do it now. We'll finish up in here tomorrow."

The rented projector and screen were in Brant's bedroom. "Safe from interruption, I hope," he said when she gave him another suspicious look. He got the film threaded and turned up the volume. Soon the big screen was filled with his teammates.

"My God! They're so big! Is that you, Brant? You look so different!"

"Yes, now pay attention. You see me calling the toss? I won and chose to receive the football. That means that we're on the offense. You can only score when you have the ball."

"Like ping pong," Daphne said.

"Exactly, but not really."

To Brant's surprise and delight, Daphne's eyes were glued to the set. Suddenly she jumped and clapped her hands. "That was great! So graceful. How can you throw the ball so far?"

"That's not so far," he said modestly. "Only about thirty yards. My prime receiver—a player whose main job is to run down the field to receive or catch a pass—is Lloyd Nolan. You'd like him, I think."

There was a touchdown pass a few plays later, and Daphne clapped her hands, as excited as any Astro fan. "Marvelous! Such precision. I never imagined—wait a second, Brant. They knocked you down. Are you all right?"

"Sure. I didn't get creamed too many times in this game. The Patriots' defense couldn't get to me. Just once or twice. Now you see the score is 6-0. Watch Guy Richardson kick the extra point. It's good. That is, it goes between the goalposts. That gives us another point. We're winning now, 7 to 0."

They got through nearly to halftime.

"Well, hello. What is this?"

Daphne's hands curled into fists. She was shocked at the degree of disappointment and downright jealousy she felt.

"It's a film, Lucilla, of one of Brant's football games."

"How delightful! Do you mind if I join you?"

She did, but Lucilla stayed anyway, and the third quarter passed in stiff discomfort. Brant's explanations grew shorter and shorter, and Daphne's questions fewer and fewer.

"Goodness," Lucilla said, "it's time for tea. Can we watch the rest of the game some other time, Brant?"

"Daph?" Brant asked.

"Sure. I'll join you downstairs soon. I have to wash off my dirt."

"Yes, please do, dear."

Daphne left them to go to her room. "How is your headache, Brant?" Lucilla inquired, shooting him a smile.

"It's under control. How do you like the new wallpaper in the breakfast room?"

"It's lovely." She slanted him a questioning look. "But didn't I tell you I like it? Well, never mind. I was thinking, how would you like to drive down to London? We could take in a play and have a superb dinner. We could even stay the night, if it got too late."

Brant's first thought was why not? It just might make Daphne jealous. He drew up short, appalled at his devious reasoning.

"I don't think it would be a good idea, Lucilla," he said.

"Why not?" she asked, taking the bull by the horns.

"Lucilla," he said, drawing her to a halt beside him on the stairs, "how well off are you financially?"

"Very well," she said; then, realizing the import of her words, she quickly added, "That is, I doubt I'll starve. But taxes in England, you know. They're dreadful. I try very hard to live off my limited income, of course, but—"

"But you were offering to bankroll Daphne."

"Bankroll? Oh, you mean loan her money?"

"No, give her money."

"I could afford it, of course, and I will when I receive my inheritance."

"I see," he said. "Ah, Cloe. Have you been in the library?"

"Yes, Brant. A marvelous job you and Daphne are doing. Where is she?"

"Washing off her dirt," Lucilla said, in such a tone as to imply that Daphne was covered with muck.

"Well, she'll be here in just a moment, then. Cook has made some marvelous scones. They're biscuits, Brant, flaky and not too sweet. You spread them with butter and jam."

He knew well enough what scones were, but he said nothing. Thank God for Cloe, he was thinking, and her timely appearance. Of course, he realized, she had probably been on the lookout for him and Lucilla.

After an appallingly stiff tea time, with honeyed salvos flying back and forth between Lucilla and Cloe, Brant set down his tea cup and rose. "Daphne and I are going for a ride. Come along."

She hesitated, and he added, "I need to discuss our plan of action for the library tomorrow."

"All right," she said, the first two words she'd uttered since tea had begun.

Lucilla looked as if she'd object, but Cloe said quickly, placing a hand on Lucilla's arm, "Did I ever tell you about the lovely Greek hairdresser I met in Crete? Let me tell you, Lucilla, he was utterly magnificent! And those dark, snapping eyes!"

Brant escaped. "Where are you going?" he barked when Daphne turned to go up the stairs.

"To rub on some dirt."

He grinned. "Why is it you only find your acid tongue for me?"

She smiled back, unable to help herself. "You," she said, suppressing a giggle, "are a wretched man!"

"And you," he said softly, the words coming out before his mind approved, "are an adorable woman."

"But my fingernails are too long."

"I'll make sure they're trimmed when the time comes."

"And I'm stupid."

"Only around Lucilla."

"Aunt Cloe calls me her little egg."

He considered that for a moment, stroking his fingertips over his jaw. "I'll have to ask her what she means by that. I don't think she can mean you're hard boiled. Now, come along."

It was very cold, and the wind was blowing strong from the east. There wasn't an ounce of sun to provide any warmth.

Brant knew it was too cold, but he didn't want to return to the house. Their jackets were no match for the wind. He remembered an abandoned, tiny house toward the back of the property, and smiled to himself.

Daphne said nothing as he guided his horse directly toward the house. When it was in sight, he said, shivering dramatically, "Lord, it's cold. I think I'm coming down with pneumonia. Hey, Daph, see that house over there? Do you think the people would mind if we came in for a moment and warmed up?"

"No one lives there. We could stop there, I suppose, and warm up." Ah, he thought, such innocence.

They tethered their horses outside, and Brant pushed open the wobbling front door. There were only two rooms, a small kitchen of ancient vintage, and a living/sleeping room. "How long has the place been abandoned?" he asked.

"For as long as I can remember," Daphne said, moving to the center of the living room. "I guess we could light a fire if you're really cold."

"Let's."

Daphne proved more adept then he, and soon there was a blaze in the fireplace, and a goodly amount of smoke puffing out into the room.

"You know, we could have gone back to the Hall. It was just as close as this place."

"I didn't want to see you turn into a defensive madonna again," Brant said smoothly. "Come on, let's sit down."

They sat cross-legged on the floor in front of the fire.

"Are you still angry at me for last night?" he asked after a few moments.

"No, not really," she said, keeping her profile toward him.

"I didn't mean to sound like a conceited jerk."

"Probably not. It just comes naturally?"

He grinned. "Maybe. Would you have been upset if I'd slept with Lucilla?"

She slewed her head around and blinked at him. "No! It has nothing to do with me!"

"Not even a little bit upset?"

"Well, maybe a little bit."

"But not more than just a tad?"

"If a tad is an American thimble, then you've got it about right! Oh damn. Lucilla's so lovely, I don't know how you could resist, particularly when she turns on that sexy look of hers."

"You ain't so bad yourself, lady. And I was noble as hell."

"And profane as well."

"Lord, are your ears going to turn red when you meet all the jocks on my team. It isn't really cursing, you know. It's just part of the general idiom."

She gave him a long, thoughtful stare, then said very quietly, "I don't know how I'd ever meet your jock teammates, Brant."

Brant jumped to his feet, thrust his hands into his jacket pockets, scowled at her and said, "Oh, hell, Daph, let's get married."

He took a step back, but his eyes remained on her face. She'd flushed a deep red.

"I don't appreciate your notion of a joke, Brant," she said in a voice so cold it could have rivaled the outdoors.

"It isn't a joke, damn it! How can you think that? You're blushing."

Daphne pressed her palms to her cheeks. "Why?" she asked in a bewildered tone.

"Why not?" he snapped.

"But I can't *do* anything!"

"You can be my wife." He removed his hands from his pockets, his body as well as his mind beginning to warm to the idea. Why not indeed? he thought. She was beautiful, witty, not at all shy with him, and he wanted to take her to bed. "I think you could do that quite well."

"Do you really think so? Despite everything?"

He dropped to his knees in front of her and cupped her face between his hands. "Yes," he said, smiling into her eyes. "Despite everything. I think it would benefit both of us equally."

"A marriage of convenience," she said slowly, pursing her lips, and he swooped down and kissed her.

He pulled her up to her knees and enfolded her in his arms. "Part your lips," he said, and she did.

Brant felt her arms tentatively clutch at his shoulders. He deepened his kiss, but kept a firm control on himself. She tasted so sweet; and so surprised. He raised his head and smiled gently down at her. "You've got to breathe through your nose. Then you can kiss until the cows come home."

"Show me," she said.

He did.

"Are the cows here yet?" Her voice was shaky, her eyes somewhat dazed.

"I thought I heard a moo just a second ago. I'm very fond of you, Daph. Do you think you could become a bit fond of me?"

"As in a tad?"

"As in whole bunches. As in let's get married. We'll spend the greater part of the year in the U.S., and the remainder here, at Asherwood. There's so much we can do together."

She scooted away from him, for his nearness made her mind shift into reverse. She said more to herself than to him, "I guess what I feel about Lucilla is jealousy, at least when she monopolizes you. And I do like for you to kiss me. That's very nice."

She paused a moment, and he said, "Continue thinking out loud. That way, there won't be any unanswered questions between us."

"We've not known each other very long. And I'm not entirely a dolt. Your proposal just now, it popped out, didn't it? You didn't mean to ask me to marry you."

"That's true. I do know that I wanted to bring you here so we could be assured of being alone. I also know that I want to make love to you so badly I hurt. I've never felt that way about a woman before."

"You don't love me. You're talking only about sex."

"I don't think fondness and sex are a bad start, do you?"

She rubbed the end of her nose, her expression a combination of bewilderment and confusion. "I might not be any good at sex, Brant. Then you'd be stuck with me."

"I'm willing to take my chances. You're looking ferocious. What are you thinking now?"

"I'm thinking that if Uncle Clarence hadn't written his will the way he did, you wouldn't look at me twice."

Brant looked away from her into the leaping flames, clasping his arms around his knees. "I thought you were gorgeous when you stepped out of that taxi and I looked at every inch of you I could manage before I knew who you really were. But that's not really the point, is it? I think, Daph, that it's impossible to answer that objectively. In any case, I can't. The will does exist, and I wouldn't be honest if I assured you that I didn't give a damn about it, because I do. I love Asherwood, and the money that comes with it will enable me—us—to fix it up exactly as we wish." He sighed. "I just don't know about that. But I do know that we have a good shot at making it work. What do you say?"

He'd said he thought she was gorgeous, Daphne thought, gazing into his eyes. She couldn't imagine a man more lovely than Brant. "Would you teach me how to use a checkbook?" she asked.

"I'll teach you everything you want to know."

But it all sounded so wretchedly lopsided, she thought. She supposed that her dowry of the house and money was something of worth, but it wasn't from her, it was from Uncle Clarence.

"If Lucilla were me, would you have proposed to her instead?"

"No," he said emphatically, with no hesitation. "That I can be quite certain about. I think I would have taken to my heels and been on the first plane back to the U.S.''

She chewed over his words, and believed him. She'd always thought of herself as plain and dowdy. It was difficult to adjust to his image of her. She said slowly, "I've never been to America. I realize we'd live there—"

"And you feel like you'd be traveling to another planet?"

"Something like that. What if your friends don't...like me? What if your mother thinks I'm an adventuress?"

Brant leaned toward her and cupped her face between his hands. "I love it when you talk nineteenth-century to me. An adventuress. I like the sound of that, but everyone will think I'm an adventurer. My friends will love you. And I'll tell you something else, Daph. We're going to take a nice long honeymoon. By the time we return to New York, you're not going to have an unself-confident bone left in your body."

"Just how do you imagine you'll achieve that?"

"You'll see, sweetheart. You'll see. Now, say yes, then we can neck for a while."

She pursed her lips and tilted up her face. "Yes."

Chapter Ten

Brant pulled Daphne into a close embrace behind a thick yew hedge that bordered the drive. He kissed her quickly and said, "I want you to wear something gorgeous tonight. I want you to smile, look at me like I'm the living hunk of your life, and not fall apart when Lucilla blows a fit. Okay?"

She gave him a smart salute and a forced smile.

He patted her bottom. "Good girl. Go get 'em, tiger."

But I'm a woman, not a girl, she thought briefly, then quickly forgot it, trying to match his stride to the house. He left her at her bedroom door with another quick kiss.

"I want you to look gorgeous, too," she called after him.

"Winterspoon will see to it, I promise."

Forty-five minutes later Winterspoon was admiring his handiwork. "Excellent, my lord. Just excellent." He lightly brushed a speck of lint from Brant's tuxedoed shoulder.

"Miss Daphne and I are going to get married," Brant said.

Winterspoon didn't look even remotely surprised. "Congratulations, my lord. His old lordship would be so pleased, indeed he would. Miss Daphne is a most charming young lady."

Brant gave him a wide grin. "My sentiments exactly."

"When is the happy occasion, my lord?"

"As soon as I can manage it. You'll have to tell me how I go about things."

"It will be my pleasure, my lord."

Brant added on a rueful note at the door, "Wish me luck, Winterspoon. I have the distinct feeling that this evening won't be entirely pleasant."

"You will do just fine, my lord. As my father used to say, 'keep your back to the wall'."

I've just been advised by a pro, Brant thought as he strode down the stairs. Winterspoon had probably seen just about everything. He paused a moment before entering the Golden Salon, squared his shoulders, and walked in. His eyes immediately met Daphne's. She looked remarkably beautiful in a gown of obvious French design. It was floor length, of a pale green silky looking material, and accentuated her narrow waist and beautiful full breasts. She'd piled her hair on top of her head, and several tendrils curled about her face. He felt very proud of her, and assured himself again that he was doing the right thing. Yes, everything would work out just fine.

"Good evening," he said. "Cloe, Lucilla, you're both looking great. Shall we go in to dinner?" He took Cloe's arm and winked at Daphne.

When Mrs. Mulroy had finished serving the soup, he called her over a moment and requested a bottle of champagne.

"Eyuh," she said, "so that be how it is."

"That be how it is, yes," Brant said.

When Mrs. Mulroy left the room, Aunt Cloe asked brightly, "Where did you and Daphne ride this afternoon?"

"It got a bit chilly, so we warmed up at that abandoned house at the north end of the property."

"Oh?" Lucilla asked, her soup spoon pausing in mid air.

"Daphne makes a great fire," Brant added blandly.

As for Daphne, she was studying the contents of her soup bowl with intense concentration. Little coward, Brant thought.

"My little egg has so many talents," Cloe said.

"Aunt," Daphne asked suddenly, "why do you call me your little egg?"

"I say, love, I'm not entirely certain. Mr. Sparks used to call me that when we were...well, in moments of fondness."

"I'm going to London tomorrow," Lucilla said. "Would you like to come with me, Brant?"

"First, here's the champagne. Thank you, Mrs. Mulroy." Brant rose and filled everyone's glass. He was aware that Cloe was regarding him with fascinated eyes, that Daphne still had her eyes trained on her plate, and that Lucilla was clutching her fork.

"I have an announcement to make," he said, holding up his glass. "Daphne has agreed to marry me."

"Oh, how marvelous! Congratulations, Brant, Daphne."

The silence that followed Aunt Cloe's excitement was deafening.

"Well," Lucilla said, sitting back in her chair and folding her arms over her breasts, "you're willing to marry a man who doesn't love you, Daphne. I'd thought you'd have more pride."

"Thank you, Lucilla, for your kindness." Daphne's chin was up, and her eyes gleamed bright lime green.

"And as for you, Brant, I would have thought that if you'd wanted money, you could have found a woman who was a bit more—"

"In addition to everything else," Brant interrupted her smoothly, "Daphne and I have discovered that we are quite fond of each other. I trust both of you ladies will come to the wedding. It will be as soon as possible."

Lucilla wanted to howl in fury and disappointment. How the hell could he want Daphne, for God's sake! I will not make a spectacle of myself, she thought. She rose from her chair, carefully placing her napkin beside her plate. "I hope everything works out for both of you as I think it will." With that obscure parting shot, she left the room.

"That wasn't so terrible, was it?" Brant asked Daphne quietly.

"No, it wasn't. It's odd, but I feel bad for her."

"Lucilla won't starve, sweetheart. Cloe, you'll stand up with us?"

"With the greatest pleasure, my boy. We should go to London and see Reggie. Mr. Hucksley, that is. He'll want to get everything in order."

Daphne had the funniest feeling that she'd just been filed away under All Went According to Plan. She heard Aunt Cloe ask Brant if he intended to have a civil service and wondered why she wasn't the one being asked. Because you're a stupid twit and nobody cares what you have to say. She said aloud, her voice shrill, "I want to be married again in the United States. It's not fair to Brant's mother not to be at her son's wedding."

Brant shot her a surprised look. "That would be fine," he said slowly. "My mom would appreciate that, I'm sure."

"And your sister and her husband and children."

"Okay. We should be able to work that out."

"Where are you planning to honeymoon, Brant?" Aunt Cloe asked.

"Hawaii...if that's okay with Daphne," he added.

Her eyes sparkled. "Hawaii!"

"Yes, the island of Kauai, to be exact. I own a condo there. I think you'll enjoy it, sweetheart."

"Goodness!" Cloe exclaimed, rising from her chair. "There's so much to be done! I must make a list. Come along, Daphne."

Every last item on Cloe's list was marked through by the time Brant and Daphne were married in the office of the Registrar General. The ceremony lasted only five minutes.

Daphne was in a daze.

Brant was quite pleased with himself.

Cloe wanted to shout her triumph, and did, to Reggie Hucksley.

Lucilla had left for Italy three days earlier.

Both the Old Man and Harlow rode in the limousine with Daphne, Brant and Cloe to Heathrow airport.

"Yes, indeed, my lord," the Old Man said for the third time, "everything is in order. There are funds in the bank for the work on Asherwood Hall to continue on schedule."

Harlow, who had never seen Daphne before, continued to stare at her in unabashed admiration. "Lovely wedding ring, Mrs. Asher," he said.

"Yes, thank you," Daphne said, staring for a moment at the huge diamond surrounded with sparkling emeralds.

"Hawaii," Aunt Cloe said. "That's an awfully long trip, isn't it, Brant?"

"We'll fly to New York, take a connecting flight to Los Angeles, then fly to Honolulu." He didn't add that there was another connecting flight of forty minutes to be made to Kauai. He hadn't thought about stopping; he always slept on airplanes. Now he realized that he hadn't asked Daphne her opinion. Well, it was too late now. All the arrangements were made. He wanted his wedding night to be in Hawaii. It satisfied his imagination. The balmy weather, the sound of the waves washing onto the beach, Daphne wearing a see-through something.

My God, Daphne was thinking, staring out the window, what have I done? I'm leaving my home. I'm married to a man I scarcely know. She was nearly incoherent with anxiety when Aunt Cloe kissed her goodbye. "I'll come see you in New York, little egg," she assured Daphne. "But I'll give you two time to yourselves first."

"Yes, that's marvelous. Please, Aunt Cloe...yes, do come."

Brant shot a look of indulgent surprise at his bride. He shook hands with the Hucksleys, kissed and hugged Aunt Cloe, clasped his bride around her waist and led her through the tunnel to the plane.

They were flying first class. Suddenly, Daphne paled and said, "I forgot my Dramamine!"

"You get airsick?" Brant asked with awful foreboding. At her mute nod, he jumped from his seat and collared a flight attendant. He had ten minutes until the plane took off. He made it back with three minutes to spare. He watched Daphne swallow the pill, and prayed that it would be effective so close to take-off.

His prayer was answered. She was in a drugged sleep within thirty minutes.

Nearly twenty hours later, they landed at the Lihue airport on Kauai, the time change making it not too many hours after they'd left London. Daphne was in a state of numb exhaustion, and so doped up from all the Dramamine Brant had forced down her that she could barely put one foot in front of the other. As for Brant, he'd gotten his second wind and was raring to go. He breathed in the sweet, clean air, then directed Daphne to a seat inside the small terminal. Thirty minutes later he helped her into a rental car. He loved Kauai and kept up a nonstop monologue about everything they would see and do as he drove down Highway 50 to the southern end of the island. Daphne was asleep when they finally arrived at the Kiahuna Planation on Poipu Beach.

He pulled the Datsun into the space in front of the condo and turned to look at his wife. She was slouched down in the seat, her eyes closed, her face pale with exhaustion. He felt a pang of guilt. Damn, he should have stopped over in New York, or Los Angeles.

So much for your romantic wedding night, old buddy.

"Daphne." He gently shook her shoulder. "Come on, sweetheart, wake up."

"No," she said quite clearly, her eyes remaining tightly closed.

He looked bemused for a moment, then shrugged. He took their luggage upstairs, unlocked the door and turned on the overhead fans. He shot a wistful look at the big queen-size bed in the single bedroom. Forget it, old man, he told himself.

He carried Daphne upstairs and gently eased her down on the bed. Her hair was tangled, her lovely cream-colored dress wrinkled to death. He tried again to wake her, but she didn't budge. He took a quick shower, changed into shorts and a golf shirt, and went out to forage for some dinner.

When he returned nearly an hour later with some carryout Chinese, the first thing he heard was the shower. Her clothes lay in a trail from the bedroom to the bathroom. He looked at her panties and bra, and felt a flood of desire. She was in the shower, naked, and she was his wife.

The bathroom was divided into two small rooms. The door to the shower and toilet was closed. "Daphne," he called, lightly tapping on the door. "Are you all right?"

Daphne raised her head at the sound of his voice and stared dumbly through the glass shower door. She'd come suddenly awake thirty minutes before, aware that something was wrong. It took her a good five minutes to discover it was the sound of the ocean and an overhead fan. She felt dirty, rumpled, and her head ached. She had stared around the bedroom at the rattan furniture and looked up at the whirling fan overhead. I'm in Hawaii, she thought, bemused, and I'm married.

She'd called Brant's name, but there had been no answer, which was an enormous relief. She had dragged herself out of bed and begun to strip off her clothes, her only thought of drowning herself in the shower.

She heard him call her name again and forced herself to call out, "Yes, I'm fine. I'll be out in just a bit."

"I've brought us some dinner."

"Okay."

She sounded as if he'd said he'd brought worms, he thought, staring at the closed bathroom door a few minutes longer. It was dark, but the third floor condo faced the ocean, and the half-moon cast a romantic light, making the ocean waves silvery. He carried the food, plates and forks to the small table on the deck. He opened a beer, sat down, and let the warm air and the sweet smell from all the flowers flood his senses.

"Hi. Here I am."

He slewed his head about and smiled at his wife. Her thick hair was damp from her shower, falling about her shoulders. She wore a sexless cotton robe.

"How do you feel, Daph?"

"More alive now, thank you."

She still looked awfully pale, her movements sluggish. He said, as he served her some sweet and sour pork, "We'll hit the sack after we eat. A good twelve hours will put you to rights again."

Daphne found she was starving. She consumed at least half the three Chinese dishes nonstop, and a half-dozen fortune cookies. "Life in this body still exists," she said, and sat back in her deck chair. "I love Chinese food. This place must be heaven, Brant. I never imagined anything so beautiful." She stretched, drawing his eyes to her breasts, then rose to lean over the balcony.

Doesn't she know that I want to rip her clothes off and make love to her until she... Stop it, you fool! Brant drew a deep breath, and said, "Do you like the condo? I bought it about two years ago. Most of the year it's rented out to tourists. We really lucked out. We've got it for two uninterrupted weeks."

She mumbled something, and Brant continued, "The kitchen's fully stocked; we've got color TV; and the beach is at our back door. Do you snorkel, Daph?"

"Yes," she said, turning. "I learned in Greece."

The soft moonlight behind her made her look like a fairy princess, Brant thought, somewhat dazed. Her hair was dry now, and looked like spun silk. "That's good," he said. "Why don't you come here a moment, Daph? Then we'll go to bed."

She cocked her head at him, watched him lightly pat his bare thighs, and said, "When you told me to bring all my summer things, I really couldn't imagine wearing them. You look nice in those shorts, Brant."

"Thank you. Come here, just for a minute."

"Yes, it's so warm," she mumbled and took several slow steps, coming to a halt in front of him. He gently pulled her down on his lap.

"Just relax, sweetheart." He pressed her head against his shoulder, then settled his hands around her waist. "Listen, I'm not going to make love to you tonight. You're too tired, and jet lag is beginning to hit me, too. We'll start our official honeymoon tomorrow, okay?"

She nodded her head, her soft hair sliding over his chin. She felt enormous relief and, she admitted to herself, just a hint of disappointment. Brant didn't seem at all crazed with desire for her.

"I'm going to take very good care of you, sweetheart. Will you trust me?"

He held her quietly for some minutes, the only sound the lapping waves beneath them, splashing against the shore. He smiled, realizing that she was fast asleep. Just as well, he thought. Less temptation. He rose, clutching her in his arms, and took her into the bedroom. He gently slipped off her robe and pulled the sheet over her.

My wife, he thought again, staring down at her. He took off his own clothes and got into bed beside her. His last thought before he fell asleep was that he'd never before just *slept* with a woman.

Chapter Eleven

Daphne awoke at dawn, a bemused smile on her lips and smooth male skin under her palm. She became even more bemused when she realized that she was pressed tightly against Brant, facing him, one of his legs between hers, one of his arms thrown over her back. Her nightgown was up around her waist, and she could feel his belly pressed against hers.

She didn't budge. He felt so different from her, and very nice. Oh dear, she thought, jerking slightly, did he make love to me and I don't remember? Was I too sleepy to know what was happening? She frowned against his shoulder and lightly stroked her fingers down his back. He moved in his sleep, and his hairy leg moved upward between her thighs.

How dreadful! She hadn't lived through her wedding night, so to speak. But she didn't feel any change in herself. Surely she should feel *different*.

She thought about this for a while as she listened to her husband's even breathing and the steady thudding of his heart. From the books she'd read, the films she'd seen, she knew that she couldn't possibly be lying naked against him and he not have done anything. No, that was impossible. She'd been made love to, but she'd been too drugged to be aware of it. She groaned softly. I must look different, she thought. Slowly she eased herself away from him and came up on her knees on her side of the bed. He mumbled something in his sleep, flung one arm above his head and fell onto his back. The single sheet was around his knees. Daphne gulped. She'd never before seen a naked man. She'd seen a couple of pictures in a racy magazine once, but not *everything*.

Well, I'm seeing everything now. Lord, was he gorgeous. He wasn't covered with hair like many of the men she'd seen on the beach. Just enough, she thought, her hand tingling to touch him. Her inquisitive eyes followed the lovely line of hair down his belly to his... She pressed her palms against her cheeks in pleased embarrassment. She even loved the tuft of hair under his raised arm.

It must have happened, she thought again, and quietly scooted off the bed. She trailed to the bathroom and stared at herself in the mirror. Her hair looked like a bird's nest, her nightgown rumpled and ratty. But she looked like that most mornings, she thought. She touched her breasts, wondering if he'd felt her there.

She remembered the feel of his muscled leg between hers and gave a delicious shudder. It had certainly felt nice when she'd awakened.

She turned and looked back toward the bed. There was no door to the bedroom. In fact, the only door in the entire condo was the one to the shower. He'd moved slightly again, spreading his legs. She gulped, turned quickly away and pulled off her nightgown.

After a quick shower and shampoo, she crept out of the bathroom and looked at him again. He hadn't moved. Maybe, she thought, smiling slightly, she'd exhausted him. Weren't men supposed to be exhausted after making passionate love? That made her feel pleased.

Why don't I feel exhausted? But she didn't; she felt marvelous. Completely rested and full of her usual morning energy. She dried her hair and quickly dressed in a pair of shorts and a matching top. She wandered onto the deck and sucked in her breath at the sight of the rising sun over the ocean. It was every bit as beautiful as Crete. A balmy breeze caressed her cheek and ruffled her hair. And all the flowers! Plumeria, bird of paradise, bougainvillae in whites, bright reds and pinks. She wondered if she'd be able to grow these beautiful flowers in her new home. Brant had told her he lived primarily in New York City. She wondered if he had a good-sized garden. She hoped so.

"Good morning."

She whirled around. Her husband gave her a sleepy smile and ran his hand through his rumpled hair. He'd put on a pair of running shorts.

"Hi," she said, her breathing quickening a bit.

"You're a morning person?"

"Yes, disgusting, isn't it?" Was he looking at her intimately? She hunched her shoulders just a bit.

Brant yawned. Nothing intimate about that, she thought, somewhat disappointed. She straightened again.

"Do you like Kauai so far?"

"It's beautiful. I like it; truly. It's still awfully early. Would you like to go back to bed?"

He gave her a slow, wicked smile. "I can't think of a better way to wake up."

"Oh!"

He watched her turn various shades of red. She jerked her head up from looking down at her bare feet and blurted out, "I don't remember anything!"

He cocked his head at her, wondering what the devil she was talking about. He wasn't at his best in the mornings.

"I'm sorry," she said, flushing more deeply. "I was hoping I would remember something, but I don't. I even thought I'd look different, but I can't see any changes."

He scratched his hand over his stomach. Finally he understood. At least, he thought he did. He grinned at her. "You were great," he said, his voice a deep caress. "You cried out and held onto me and told me you loved it."

She heard only the intimacy, missing the teasing in his voice. "It isn't fair," she said. "Why didn't you pour coffee down me or something?"

"I didn't think about it. You seemed to be having such fun. Did you enjoy the...view this morning?"

"Yes," she said. She suddenly felt inordinately relieved that it was over and she'd responded so well. "You looked very nice."

"Sprawled on my back with my legs apart?"

"That, too. But you see, Brant, I wasn't sure anything had happened, so I didn't look at you all that long. That would have been like invading your privacy."

It was on the tip of his tongue to tell her that nothing at all had happened, but he laughed instead. "Tell you what, sweetheart, why don't we have some coffee and go back to bed? Now that you know everything, it will be even more fun for you. And you can look at me as long as you like. I'd definitely love to invade your privacy. Will you make me some coffee while I shower? I bought some stuff last night for breakfast."

She gazed at him somewhat somberly for a long moment. She said slowly, thoughtfully, "I won't be embarrassed now, will I? There's no need to, is there?"

"None at all," he said. He hugged her briefly; and kissed her lightly against her temple. "No, none at all."

"Well, that's a relief," she said, and smiled up at him.

In between arias in the shower, Brant found himself grinning inanely and wondering if he should tell her the truth. No, he decided. Now he wouldn't have to fight her inherent modesty. He felt a leap of desire and quickly soaped himself, then turned on the cold water for a moment.

After drying his hair, he wrapped the towel around his waist and joined Daphne on the deck. She smiled at him and handed him a cup of coffee. "It's thick and black and very American," she said. "Winterspoon told me that was the way you liked it."

"Did Winterspoon tell you anything else about me?"

She sipped her own very blond coffee. "Just that you were, in his opinion, a nice man, despite your being American. He even admitted that you had some wit.''

"Quite an accolade.'' His gaze flitted from her soft hair downward. "You have a very nice figure, Daph. Yes, very nice.''

"Did you tell me that last night?''

"I must have. Now, why don't we go back to bed and I'll tell you again?''

He looped his arm around her shoulders, leaning down to nibble her ear. "I'll kiss every inch of you...just like I did last night. You loved that, Daph. Every inch.''

She turned in his embrace, wrapping her arms about his back. "I must have,'' she said against his shoulder. "It sure sounds nice right now.''

He grinned over her head and said lightly, "Have I created a monster? A sex fiend?''

"Well, I do have some of Aunt Cloe's blood, and she, I think, adores sex, or at least she must have when Mr. Sparks was alive.''

Brant found that the few steps to the bed had made him so taut with downright lust that he was breathing hard. His wife, he thought. She was his wife. For life, not just a brief fling. He realized how important it was to make everything nice for her. He couldn't imagine his life without sexual satisfaction, both for himself and for his partner. Go slowly, old man, he told himself.

He tumbled her onto her back and came down over her, balancing himself on one elbow. "Hi, wife,'' he said, and leaned down to kiss her. "Open your mouth. How could you forget so soon?''

"You must have short-circuited me,'' she said, and parted her lips.

He didn't touch her below her shoulders for a good ten minutes. It felt strange to be so methodical and, in a sense, Machiavellian, but he held himself in check and continued his slow assault. He felt her ease, then respond to him. "That's it, sweetheart,'' he whispered into her mouth. "Just relax with me. Nothing new, you know.''

Daphne wriggled beneath him. She wanted him to touch her, but she was embarrassed to ask him. What had she done the previous night? "Brant,'' she said finally, her voice ragged, "please.'' She thrust her hips upward; and gasped at the hard feel of him.

Brant eased off her and quickly pulled off her top. "Good God,'' he said, staring down at her. "You are so bloody beautiful.'' Tentatively, he touched her full breasts. So white they were, her breasts appearing almost too large for her slender torso. Her nipples were already taut and darkened to a dusky peach. He began kissing her again as he gently stroked and caressed her breasts. He laid his palm flat for a moment and felt her heart pounding. Slowly he kissed his way down her throat to her shoulders, then took her nipple into his mouth. She cried out, arching her back upward.

He felt her hands frantically kneading his back. Her breasts were very sensitive, and it delighted him. So much more of her to go, so much to anticipate, to appreciate.

"What do you want me to do?" she gasped.

He was gently stroking his tongue over her. "Just lie still and enjoy. This is what a man likes best to do."

He covered her belly with his leg and gently pressed. Daphne was beginning to feel frantic. She wanted to feel him, all of him, and began to wriggle to face him so she could jerk down his shorts.

"Slow down, sweetheart. You first." He pulled off her shorts and panties, then raised himself up on his elbow. She was very fair complexioned. Her waist was narrow, her belly flat. His eyes locked on the tuft of dark blond hair, and he felt himself begin to tremble with need. Slowly he stroked his hand from her breasts downward until he was lightly cupping his palm over her. He looked into her eyes, watching every expression, as his fingers gently probed. He sucked in his breath. She was damp, her delicate woman's flesh swelled and beautifully warm.

He began to rhythmically stroke her. "You like that," he said softly. "Remember?"

"I—I feel urgent. It almost hurts, Brant."

He eased his fingers away and stroked them down her slender thighs.

He eased himself up and pulled off his shorts. Daphne stared at him, her eyes growing wider. "Oh dear," she managed. "I liked *that*?"

It took him a moment to gather his wits. He looked briefly down at himself. Asleep this morning, he imagined he'd looked nothing like this. "Yes," he said, "you did. Very much." He slid his hands between her legs and eased them apart. Slowly he eased down on top of her. He made no move to enter her, though he felt himself straining against her. Hey down there, you've got no brain and no sense! Cool it!

He pressed against her, and she responded. He felt a rippling shudder go through her body. He covered her and began to kiss her, his tongue thrusting into her mouth. He felt her arms tighten almost painfully around his back. All the way, he thought. Yes, all the way. He eased himself down her body, pausing to enjoy her breasts, then her belly. She stiffened, and he raised his head.

"Listen, sweetheart. You wanted to know what you could do for me. I want to kiss you and love you, and I want you to relax and enjoy it. You did...last night."

When his mouth closed over her, Daphne lurched upward. She felt no embarrassment now, assuming that all her embarrassment had happened last night. It felt so good. "I like that," she gasped, tangling her fingers in his thick hair.

Brant did too. She tasted fresh and sweet and... Suddenly she gave a deep shudder, crying out. He felt the tension in her legs, and her release.

Her breathing was ragged, and he felt her uncontrollable trembling. He loved the convulsive little shudders, the soft sounds from her throat. He eased his rhythm, then began again.

Daphne felt dazed. She felt as though she'd been on a roller coaster. It came down, finally. Then it started upward again. She was stunned, but eager. Brant felt it and used every ounce of his expertise to bring her up again. He felt her tense, heard her moaning softly. He quickly reared over her, and with one single thrust, entered her. There was no maidenhead, thank God, but she was very small. He felt her stiffen and press her hands against his shoulders. "Easy, sweetheart," he said. He buried himself deeply within her, then eased down over her, his eyes on her face. "It's okay, Daph. Just a little while longer and any discomfort will be gone. I won't move. Get used to me."

"All right," she whispered. She buried her face against his shoulder. Slowly he felt the tension drain from her, and he began to move within her. He bit down on his lower lip, hoping the brief pain he'd given her would tighten his control. He'd never made love to a virgin before, and it was a heady experience. He could feel her muscles clutching him, and he groaned. "Daphne," he gasped, "no!"

She didn't know what he was talking about. "Brant, please," she said, her voice high and urgent. He slipped his fingers between them and found her.

To his delight and near insanity, she arched upward, drawing him deeper. She yelled his name and nearly bucked him off in her frenzy.

He gritted his teeth and gave her release before he allowed himself to let go. He felt swamped with feeling, feeling so strong that he shook with it.

He collapsed on top of her, his face next to hers on the pillows.

"I'm going to die," she moaned.

He managed to gather enough energy to raise himself on his elbows and look into her dazed eyes. He stroked her hair off her forehead. "You were marvelous," he said. "And you aren't going to die, although I can just see the headline: Sex-Starved Bride Succumbs."

"How about: Bride Buried Smiling?"

She closed her arms about his back and squeezed. "I'm glad we got married. This is such fun."

"You think so, huh? Not bad, I'd say, for your first..."

Her eyes flew open and narrowed on his face. "My first what, Brant?"

He kissed her very seductively, but she was sated and tenacious. "What, Brant?"

He gave her a lopsided grin. "We didn't make love last night, Daph. I'm not into unconscious women."

"You...you crook!"

"Why did you think we had?"

"I woke up all tangled together with you and my nightgown...well, it was up, and not down where it should have been. And you are a crook, and dishonest, and a dreadful tease—"

"Yes, but you weren't embarrassed, were you?"

She chewed a moment on her lower lip, and he quickly kissed her again.

"Still..." she began.

He kissed her once more. "The very pleasurable result," he said with a disarming grin, "justified the means, as the Prince is supposed to have been taught."

She lowered her thick lashes. "Well," she said finally, "maybe. Just maybe. Brant, did I react normally? I mean, I didn't disappoint you, did I?"

"If you'd reacted any more, I'd be dead." He paused a moment, enjoying the feel of her soft body beneath his, "I don't think you could ever disappoint me, sweetheart, not in a thousand and one nights."

"What about a thousand and one days?"

He moaned loudly and collapsed on his back.

Chapter Twelve

"Do you remember the song, 'Puff the Magic Dragon'?"

"Oh yes, it was quite popular in England."

"Well, old Puff was from Hanalei, and that's a town on the northern shore of Kauai. We'll go swimming up there and do some snorkeling."

Daphne sat back, sated from a delicious bacon cheeseburger, and patted her stomach. "Is the drive long enough so I won't sink like a fat whale when I hit the water?"

"Finish your planter's punch and you'll go down happy."

Brant leaned back in his chair and looked out over the Kiahuna Golf Club course. The back part of the restaurant was a roofed patio, and the air was redolent with the sweet scent of flowers and freshly cut grass. He felt good. He'd discovered that he enjoyed the freedom of being married, enjoyed the growing intimacy between him and Daphne. He sent her a sleepy glance, watching her slurp up the final bit of planter's punch. He'd made sure she was well-coated with sunscreen and in the past two days she'd just gotten a bit red, but no sunburn. She'd french-braided her hair this morning, and the plait lay heavy and lustrous between her shoulder blades. She looked fresh, sweet, and so inviting that he felt his body react yet again. He closed his eyes a moment, picturing her in that outrageous orange bikini Cloe had bought her. It was a wonder, he thought, that she hadn't been attacked on the beach in Crete. His presence was the only thing that saved her here.

"When do we take the helicopter ride? You did tell me that a lot of the *Thorn Birds* was filmed here. I want to see the beach where Father Ralph made love to Meggie."

"Inspiration?"

"That," she said, "I don't need"

"I like being married to you," he said, stretching lazily.

"Me too."

"I guess it's time we did something. That is, I guess it's time to show you the island." His eyes fell to her breasts, and his gaze was so intent that Daphne quivered.

"I'll never see it if you keep doing that," she said, her voice shaky. "You, Brant, are very addictive."

"So are you. Maybe I'll leave you alone in fifty years or so."

"So soon? I can just picture you, a little old man, placing your cane carefully by the bed, then creaking in between the sheets."

"And drooling all over you." He looked up to see the waitress grinning down at him. "Our check, please," he said. Out of habit, he watched her walk away and cataloged her finer points.

"You are a dirty young man!"

"Old habits are hard to break."

They left the golf club and walked the quarter of a mile back to the Kiahuna Plantation. "Do you want to learn how to play golf?" he asked.

"It seems rather a silly game, but I'll give it a try. What are we doing this afternoon?"

He gave her a long look. "Why don't we discuss it in bed?"

But they didn't. Her back was arched, the thick braid hanging over her shoulder. Brant let her control the depth of his penetration, let her determine the pace. It drove him wild to see the lightly tanned parts of her and the utter white of her breasts and belly. He felt her thighs hug him, and he gasped. He pulled her down on top of him. "Lie still," he said, gritting his teeth.

Daphne couldn't hold still. She cupped his face between her hands and kissed him deeply. "I love the way you feel inside me," she said between gasping breaths into his mouth. She felt him tighten his grip on her hips, holding her still.

"Sweetheart, I—"

She straddled him again, drawing him deep, and it drove him crazy. He closed his fingers over her and watched the surprised look in her eyes when the building sensations swamped her. Her muscles tightened convulsively, and he let himself go.

He drew her down against him and stroked her nape and back, reveling in the sheet of perspiration on her smooth flesh. "You're so bloody sexy," he whispered in her ear. "And I love the way you look so incredulous just before you start making all those cute little noises."

She was incapable of answering him for several minutes. Slowly she came back to life as she used to know it. It seemed the past two days that she'd been in a kind of dazed fog. "If," she said finally, arching up a bit so she could see his face, "you ever get a headache, I'll never forgive you. It just keeps getting wilder and wilder." She lowered her lashes a moment. "I like being on top. You were so deep."

He felt himself swelling again and groaned. "Let's eat some Macadamia nuts; they're supposed to help."

She giggled and kissed his chin. "They've got such a sweet taste, and such a crisp bite...roasted to perfection, dipped in rich creamy...ouch!"

He rubbed the hip he'd just smacked. "You, Daphne Asher, are a smart-mouthed...creamy..."

She moved over him, and he couldn't have found another word if his life depended on it.

At four o'clock they finally strolled to the beach and fell asleep in the sun.

"Below are the Wailua Falls. If they look familiar it's because they're in the opening scene of *Fantasy Island*."

Daphne snapped three pictures as the helicopter swooped down over the double waterfalls.

"Below is the Huleia National Wildlife Refuge. It's gotta look familiar; it's where part of *Raiders of the Lost Ark* was filmed. Everyone, even you mainlanders, has seen that."

"Damn," Daphne muttered. "I'm out of film."

Brant patted her knee in commiseration, the sound of the helicopter blades made it hard to talk and be heard.

"We'll go up again if you like," Brant said when they'd landed. "Did you like seeing the nurses' beach from *South Pacific*?"

She bubbled with excitement. She skipped beside Brant. "Oh yes. And I can't get over Waimea Canyon. Just like the pictures I've seen of the Grand Canyon! And all the waterfalls, Brant! And the wettest spot in the entire world!"

He smiled down at her, enjoying her enthusiasm. When she'd finally completed giving him a rundown on what they'd seen, he said, "Tonight, Daph, we're going to the Sheraton for a luau. Are you into pig?"

"Just as long as I don't have to watch it being roasted."

"You don't. The entertainment isn't bad, either. And, I swear, there's plenty of planter's punch to keep you afloat."

Brant stopped in Koloa on their way back to Poipu Beach and parked in front of a line of shops. They picked her out several muumuus, not the shapeless ones, but exquisitely fashioned fitted ones. He left her to pay while he went to another shop, and for the first time since their arrival in Kauai she felt an unwelcome jolt of reality.

"I'm sorry, ma'am, but I'll need your husband's signature on those traveler's checks.

Daphne realized that she didn't have a cent. And all the checks were in Brant's name. "But I have the same name," she said

"I'm sorry, ma'am," the sales person repeated, "but I can't break the rules."

"I understand," Daphne said. She left her packages on the counter and wandered outside to sit on the steps to the store. It wasn't that she was used to having her own money, because she wasn't. It just felt odd and somehow embarrassing that she, a married woman, was utterly dependent on her husband for everything.

"Hi, gorgeous," Brant said, sporting a new straw hat. "What's up, sweetheart? Where are your clothes?"

She looked up at his handsome face, so deeply tanned that his eyes looked even bluer. "I couldn't sign your traveler's checks," she said evenly.

"Oh, that, I'll be back in a minute."

He pulled off his straw hat and flipped it to her, frisbee style.

Daphne didn't go back into the store. She was looking at postcards of Spouting Horn when Brant came out carrying several big shopping bags. "You're going to look gorgeous, lady. I like the gold one that's got the thin straps best."

It's not his fault, she thought, forcing a smile. She said formally, "Thank you, Brant. The dresses are lovely. I appreciate them."

He cocked a dark eyebrow at her. "That sounded like a recording. What's up, sweetheart? You change your mind about the dresses?"

She didn't reply until they were seated in the car. She turned slightly and asked, "Brant, there's something I don't understand. The inheritance from Uncle Clarence, is it yours or mine?"

He sent her a startled look. "It's ours, of course. We're married, you know."

"That isn't quite true. Did you inherit the money, or did I?"

"I did. But what difference does it make? What's mine is yours, Daph."

"And what's mine is yours, only I don't have anything to share with you. Nothing."

Brant pulled the car off the road and switched off the motor. "Okay, what's the matter? And don't give me any runaround bull."

She gnawed on her lower lip and shook her head.

"Daph, were you bothered because the traveler's checks were all in my name? If you were, I'm sorry. I just didn't think. Tomorrow I'll flip over to the Waiohai and have some made in your name."

"Thank you."

"Your enthusiasm is deadening," he said, his eyes narrowing on her face. He shrugged. "Look, I guess I'm just used to being on my own, and," he added on a wicked grin, "even when I wasn't on my own, no one ever complained when I picked up the tab. When we get home to New York, I'll set up a checking account for you, in your name, okay?"

"It's still your money, not mine. It's like an allowance that you'd give to a child."

His hands clutched the steering wheel, and he said acidly, "Don't be an ass. You're my wife, my responsibility—"

"An encumbrance, a parasite, a—a dependent."

He cursed softly, started the engine and screeched back onto the narrow highway.

Brant parked the car in their parking space, and they walked up to the third floor in silence. Brant unlocked the door, then stepped back for her to enter first.

"Come here and sit down," he said. "I want to get a few things straight."

She wanted to tell him to go to hell, but the habit of obedience was strong, the habit of bending her will to the stronger. And, after all, what had he done wrong? Nothing, she thought, her shoulders slumping in depression. She sat down.

"I thought," Brant said, standing in front of her, crossing his arms over his chest, "that we understood and agreed on our respective roles. That is, I would bring home the proverbial bacon and you would be responsible for our home. However, if not having your own money bothers you, I'll sign over half the money from the inheritance. Is that what you want? It will make you independent. You can have all the bloody traveler's checks you want in your name."

"I didn't earn that money," she said, thrusting up her chin just a bit.

"Like hell you didn't! You were the old man's slave for how many years? Did he pay you a salary for all the work you did? Let's consider your half of the inheritance as back pay. You can spend it; you can invest it; you can stuff it under your mattress."

"You're very...kind."

He shot her an exasperated frown. "Daph, for God's sake, I want you to be happy. You're my wife. You will have our children."

She stared at him, her face paling under her tan. "Children?"

"I haven't been using any birth control. Have you?"

She paled even more. "I didn't think about it." She rose jerkily to her feet, clasping and unclasping her hands in front of her.

Every bit of irritation disappeared in an instant. He grasped her shoulders and gently drew her against him. "I'm sorry, sweetheart. I was making decisions for you. I just assumed...well, I'll be responsible for birth control. When we get home, we can discuss what you'd like to do. All right?"

She wished for just a brief instant that he would yell and holler and call her an idiot, just like Uncle Clarence had with great regularity. But he was so reasonable, so kind. He was really trying to be nice to her. It was almost depressing. She felt like a fool, an overreactive ass. She felt in the wrong. "All right," she whispered against his shoulder. "I'm sorry. Please forgive me."

"It's not for you to apologize, turkey. It appears that our conversations haven't hit on some very important issues. And that's your fault, of course, for being so delectable that my mouth is kissing you all the time and not talking." He kissed the tip of her nose. "Is that a band of freckles I see?"

She smiled and wrinkled her nose. "I don't know about a band. I think I'd prefer a sprinkle."

"Or a gaggle or a herd?"

She punched him in the stomach, and he obligingly grunted. He cupped her hips and lifted her against him. "We've got a couple of hours before we need to go to our luau," he said, nuzzling her neck. "You got any ideas on how to spend them?"

"How about the beach? Maybe I can get a herd of freckles."

"Forget it," Brant said.

The luau was a major production, Daphne realized as they pulled into the special parking lot at the Sheraton. There were a good one hundred people, much laughter and high spirits. There were no individual tables, so they sat with two other couples. One older man from Ohio recognized Brant, and Daphne sat back and watched her husband wrap everyone at the table in his own special brand of charm.

"Are you newlyweds, dear?" the older man's wife asked Daphne while the men were discussing the Astros' chances for the Superbowl in the upcoming season.

"Yes, we are."

"You're English, aren't you?"

"Yes, ma'am, I am."

"Call me Agnes. Is this your first trip to Hawaii?"

The other woman, a stunning brunette from Seattle, soon joined in, and Daphne forgot her shyness.

"What a wonderful evening," Daphne said later to Brant, her voice just a bit fuzzy from the mai tais.

"I was proud of you, Daph," he said, hugging her against his side. He'd been a bit concerned that she'd clam up meeting strangers, but she hadn't, much to his delight.

"Brant," she said when they were sitting out on the deck a few minutes later, "have you called your mother?"

He was glad it was dark and she couldn't see the flush on his face. "Yes," he said. "I called her a couple of days ago when I was over at the Waiohai."

She felt herself stiffen a bit, wondering why he hadn't called her from the condo. "What did she say?"

He caressed the nape of her neck. "After she got over the shock she started singing hallelujahs." It wasn't precisely the truth, but close enough. Actually, he had been able to see her mind working, wondering just why he'd married an English girl so quickly. He'd ended up telling her the terms of the will. "She can't wait to meet you, sweetheart, and is delighted that you want another ceremony for her and the family. You wanna marry me next month?"

She gave him such a sweet, radiant smile that he froze for a moment, taken aback at the odd, twisting emotions that smile evoked. "Yes," she said, "I think I've compromised you enough without a minister's blessing."

"Are you certain that you weren't a Victorian maiden in your past life? Compromised? I love it."

There were no more snakes in the garden for the remainder of their stay in Kauai. Brant told her about every one of his teammates, his intention being to ease her shyness when she met them. They discussed Asherwood Hall, coming to agreement on all the renovations. Three days before they left Daphne discovered she had no worries about being pregnant, and Brant, groaning, told her he was going to have to live in the shower, under a steady stream of icy water. His joking eased her embarrassment, as he intended it to.

It started as a joke on their return flight to Los Angeles. "Why not have Winterspoon come to New York and be our majordomo?" And it ended up as a plan. "I can't wait for Marcie to get hold of that item," Brant said. "An English valet in residence with a football player!"

"Who's Marcie?" Daphne asked, latching immediately on this heretofore unmentioned name.

"Marcie?" Brant repeated carefully. "Just a friend, sweetheart. She's a reporter for a newspaper in New York."

Ah, Daphne thought, a woman who's done something with her life other than live it at the orders of someone else. But that wasn't true, she chided herself. She would do something. She wouldn't sit around Brant's house doing nothing.

Their arrival in New York's Kennedy Airport was a nightmare. Brant's mother was there, along with a group from the press. A flashbulb went off in Daphne's face, and she shrank against him. "Damn," he muttered, then forced a smile to his lips. He knew she was practically insensible from all the Dramamine. How the hell had the press found out when he was returning?

The afternoon paper turned her into a silent ghost.

"Football Pro Gains Title and Rich Bride." The byline was Marcie's.

Chapter Thirteen

"How is she, Brant?" asked Alice Asher when her son came back into the living room.

"Asleep. She was so doped up to begin with and this—" he flung a disgusted arm toward the newspaper "—this didn't help. How did the press find out, Mom? Do you know?"

"Marcie called me last week and, fool that I am, I told her you'd gotten married in England and were in Hawaii. That's all."

"Of course all she had to do was call the airlines and find out which flight we were coming back on." Brant sat back, pulling a thick sofa cushion behind his head. "And, of course, she called some of her buddies in England. Well, it's done. I'll call Marcie later; you can be sure of that."

"I like Daphne, Brant," said Alice. "She seems unlike all the other women in your life, so—"

"Sweet? Guileless? Innocent as a lamb?"

"Perhaps. We'll get her over this...this nastiness."

Alice went into the kitchen and made some coffee. When she returned to Brant's very modern living room, she saw him standing in front of the large glass window, staring down on Central Park. "May I ask you something personal, honey?"

"Sure, Mom, everyone else does without even asking my permission." He turned to face her, and she saw the weariness on his handsome face.

"Did you marry her because of the will?"

"In part," he said honestly. "As she did me. But I'm fond of her, as she is of me. We both love Asherwood. We both want it restored to what it was years ago. By marrying, we got the house and ensured there'd be enough money to fix it up. She's guileless as hell, it's true. And young and inexperienced.'' He gave her a lopsided grin. ''Well, maybe not so inexperienced about some things now.''

''I gather,'' Alice said dryly, ''that you handled that quite well.''

''I guess there's something to be said about raising a girl in the bowels of the country. She'd had no chance to learn everything she shouldn't like or shouldn't do.''

''Is that your oblique way of telling me that Daphne enjoys the physical side of marriage?''

''Yeah.'' He grinned. ''She's very natural and loving.''

Alice was silently relieved about that. She said, ''Incidentally, Lily and Dusty are ready to fly up from Houston whenever you give them the word.''

''Good. Give me some time to get Daph back in shape, then we can arrange everything. Just family and a few friends, okay, Mom?''

''No problem, honey. I've already talked to Reverend Oakes.''

''Mom, I don't want you ever to think that I would marry just for money. But you know that's what the press is going to continue pushing.''

''I know you would never do such a thing. I was thinking, Brant, once Daphne gets out and meets people, everyone will see what a lovely person she is. And, of course, she's very beautiful.''

Brant drank some of his coffee, but didn't sit down. He began pacing and Alice watched him, a question in her eyes.

''Mom,'' he said abruptly, ''I don't know much about birth control. That is, I know about it, and Lord knows I've been very careful in the past. I just don't want Daphne taking anything that could possibly hurt her. What do you think?''

''I would suggest that you call the medical society and ask for a woman gynecologist.''

''Woman?''

''I think it would make Daphne feel more comfortable, don't you?''

''Yeah, probably. Thanks for coming, Mom. It's late. Are you ready to turn in?''

''Yes.'' She rose and hugged Brant. ''Everything will work out, honey, don't worry.''

''I'll try not to.'' He grinned down at her. ''Would you be willing to make breakfast tomorrow morning? I'll help you. Daphne isn't too much of a marvel in the kitchen.''

''Sure thing. After all, I spoiled you rotten for thirty-one years. Why stop now?''

Brant didn't turn on the bedroom light. He could see Daphne's outline in his large brass bed, and it gave him a warm feeling. He'd sleep next to her every night and wake up next to her every morning. It added a completeness that he'd never really realized wasn't there until he had it.

She murmured softly in her sleep when he eased in beside her. He kissed her lightly on her ear and pulled her into his arms.

"Brant?" Her voice was fuzzy and blurred.

"Shush, sweetheart. Go back to sleep."

"Can we go see the Spouting Horn again tomorrow?"

She was still in Kauai. "Sure thing." He stroked her hair lightly and pressed her cheek against his shoulder. "We'll do whatever you want."

Daphne was a morning person, awake and alert the moment she opened her eyes. But this morning she woke up slowly. She was aware that she was in a strange place, and she reached for Brant. He wasn't there. Slowly she sat up and stared at the expanse of bed. Brant's bedroom, she thought, shaking her head clear of confusion. Brant's home, no, she corrected herself, his condo. What a strange word! She remembered the events of the previous evening and cringed. She'd acted like Daphne the shy, insecure, dowdy, double bagger, and fallen apart in front of Brant's mother.

"You're full of rubbish," she said aloud to the empty room. "How odd," she added softly. Unlike the living room, which was a study in modern glass, chrome and stark furnishings, the bedroom was a study in elegant antiques. She quickly recognized an original eighteenth-century French armoire, and several heavy Spanish chairs. There was a scroll-armed sofa that reminded her of the Regency period, but she wasn't sure. The rug was a thick rich coffee color and covered the center of the polished hardwood floor. She climbed out of bed, pausing a moment to touch the beautiful brass headboard. She found herself wondering how many women had slept in that bed with Brant.

She giggled. With the lights off, it would take two people a good deal of time to find each other in that huge bed. She trooped into the bathroom and stood a moment, gaping at the incredible, utterly decadent tub. It was circular and deep, and there was some kind of a motor settled against one side. She hadn't the foggiest notion of what to do with that, and was thankful there was a separate shower stall. She quickly showered, then set about drying her hair and putting her face to rights.

Forty-five minutes later, dressed in wool slacks and a fitted long sweater with a gold belt at the waist, Daphne opened the bedroom door and peered out. She heard voices and laughter. Brant's mother was there, she thought, squaring her shoulders. She stepped into the small dining room.

"Hi," she said. "Forgive me for being so late. It took me quite a while to get my engine started."

Brant rose and came to her, smiling. "Morning, sweetheart. We've kept breakfast warm for you. You hungry?"

She nodded, flushing when he lightly kissed her in front of his mother.

"Sit down and get acquainted with your dragon mother-in-law, and I'll get you some eggs and bacon."

"Good morning, Daphne," Alice said. "Just ignore the Son of the Dragon and his big mouth. Are you feeling better today?"

"Yes, ma'am. Oh! I hadn't realized it yesterday, but Brant looks so much like you!"

"I'll take that as a compliment if it doesn't include huge shoulders and five-o'clock shadow. Now, tell me how you liked Kauai."

Brant stayed a bit longer in the kitchen than necessary, giving the two women time alone together. He heard the tension ease in Daphne's voice, heard her laugh. Such a sweet, clear sound. It made him feel good.

"Service from the chef," he said, setting her plate in front of her. "There's even tea, Daph."

She grinned up at him. "You the chef? I have this terrible feeling that we're going to starve."

Under Alice's skillful handling Daphne found herself talking about her life in England, Aunt Cloe, Lucilla and the minions at Asherwood. "Did Brant tell you we're going to invite Winterspoon to come over?" she asked, shyly smiling at her husband.

"Talk about culture, honey," his mother said, laughing at him. "I remember reading that all English valets were born with taste and snobbery."

"True enough," Brant said. "Even though you're a dowager something, he'll probably politely turn up his nose at you."

Alice encouraged Daphne to talk more about Hawaii, listening to her guileless enthusiasm and watching her closely when she referred something to Brant. They'll be quite good for each other, she thought. If Daphne wasn't yet in love with her husband, it would be just a matter of time. As for Brant, he seemed so...indulgent, gentle, protective.

Oddly enough, Alice felt herself wanting to protect this charming girl. No, Alice, she told herself sternly. She can't remain a girl. To live in Brant's world, she's going to have to be a woman and stand on her own two feet.

"Now," she said, when there was a lapse in the conversation, "let's talk about your Connecticut wedding."

Later Brant escorted the two women on a brief tour of New York. To avoid any vulturous press, they ate dinner at one of Brant's favorite Spanish restaurants down in the Village. Unfortunately, when they returned home, there were two men waiting for them in the underground garage. There was no way they could escape them.

"Glad you're home, Brant," one of the men said good-naturedly, easing his way carefully forward. "Is this the heiress? Hey, Mrs. Asher, give us a big smile!"

Daphne froze as a flashing light went off in her face. Suddenly she felt

Alice Asher squeeze her hand. I am not Daphne the double bagger, she told herself fiercely, but somehow she couldn't make her muscles move into a smile. Alice said quickly, "My new daughter is very much enjoy-ing New York and her new home. Everyone has been so, so...kind, haven't they, dear?"

Daphne nodded mutely. Why did her hair all of a sudden feel so stringy?

Brant tucked Daphne's hand through the crook of his arm. "Anything else, gentlemen?"

"Yeah. Mrs. Asher, Brant here got a real good deal when he married you, right? Would you like to comment on that, ma'am?"

Brant wanted to smash the man's face in, but he said calmly enough, "We both got a great deal, boys, but you're right. I don't think I've ever seen a prettier lady, have you?"

"Sure, Brant," one of the men said. He said in a carrying voice as he and his partner walked off. "If you like rich girls who are mutes."

Daphne felt tears sting her eyes. She'd let Brant down. Again. She'd acted like a stupid parrot who couldn't talk. I might not look like a double bagger, she thought, her shoulders slumped, but I still act like one.

"It's all right, dear," Alice said, patting her shoulder. "It will just take a bit more time for you to get used to things."

"She's right, Daph. Don't worry about the grubby bastards."

"I'm sorry," she mumbled.

"Don't be an ass," Brant said, ignoring his mother's gasp. "You're shy, Daph. I'll protect you. Just don't get depressed about it. Okay?"

She blinked back tears and nodded. Damn, she wasn't shy around Brant. Why did she have to be such a fool with strangers?

The ride up the elevator was a silent one. When they entered the condo Brant said in a too-hearty voice, "You haven't told me how much you like my house, Daph."

"I like your house a lot," she said.

"What I meant was our house, Daph. If you'd like to change anything, just let me know."

"I just wish there was a garden," she said, walking over to the huge picture window that looked out over Central Park. She gave a self-conscious laugh. "I'd been picturing acres of land. I didn't realize that New York was all buildings. Stupid of me, after all the pictures I've seen."

He frowned at the back of her head. "I suppose we could get a house in the country," he said.

It was a generous offer, but Daphne quickly shook her head. They already had a house in the country, in England.

"Well, my dears," Alice said, smiling at them. "I think I'm ready for bed. I'll see you both in the morning."

Brant kissed his mother good night, then turned toward his wife, who was still standing, staring out the window.

"The lights are beautiful, aren't they?" he said.

She nodded. He pulled her against him, gently kneading her shoulders. "Are you ready for bed, sweetheart?" He leaned down and began nibbling at her ear lobe.

She felt a surge of desire, but it was quickly dashed by her own feelings of inferiority. Was he just humoring her in bed? Was she as much of a failure making love as she was dealing with people? Angry at herself, and anxious to prove to herself that she could do something right, she turned in his arms and crushed herself against him. She stood on her tiptoes, cupped his face between her hands and kissed him.

Good Lord, Brant thought, a bit dazed by her enthusiastic attack. He locked his arms around her, cupping her hips in his hands to draw her closer. He felt her move her hips against him, and moaned into her mouth. "I want you now," he said. He picked her up in his arms and carried her into the bedroom, casting one eye toward his mother's room, thankful that the door was shut.

When he set her on her feet, she didn't let him go, but pulled him down on top of her on the bed. He didn't understand her urgency, but he was feeling near desperation himself, so it didn't matter. He pulled up her skirt, jerked off her panty hose and panties, and gave her what she needed. When she was trembling in the aftershock of pleasure, he jerked down his zipper and entered her warm body.

He lay heavily on top of her, rather stunned at his own violent reaction. He nuzzled her throat and said, "Will you let me go long enough to take my clothes off now?"

"All right," she said. Suddenly she hugged him tightly to her. "I was so afraid."

He eased up on his elbows so he could see her face. "Don't be afraid of those stupid media people. They're not worth it."

"No, not them," she said, biting down on her lower lip.

"Of what, sweetheart?"

"I was afraid that I would fail at everything. I did give you pleasure, didn't I?"

He felt a wave of pity for her, but forced himself to grin at her. "You wanna feel my heart? It's still galloping fast enough to be in the Kentucky Derby."

"So is mine," she said. "You are so nice, Brant."

"Don't forget it, Mrs. Asher. Now, how about taking a shower with me?"

"I think I'd prefer the tub with that engine in it."

Alice Asher left for Connecticut the following day to set the wedding plans into motion. Brant and Daphne would come the following weekend, as would Lily and Dusty. "To do the Deed," Brant said. "Again."

That evening, Brant and Daphne went to a formal dinner party given by a vice president of the ad agency doing Brant's sporting goods commercial. Daphne was wearing a new long gown of soft white chiffon and an emerald pendant Brant had bought her at Tiffany's. Mr. Morrison's house was on Long Island, and as Brant drove his Porsche out of Manhattan, he told Daphne about the people they would meet.

"Morrison's a short, balding, very nice man," he said. "The president of the sporting goods company is named Dicks, and the man's a shark. I just met him once, but not, thank God, in an alley or at the Stock Exchange. Speaking of the Stock Exchange," he continued nonstop, looking briefly toward his silent wife, "we'll go to the bank tomorrow and get your checking account set up. And you'll need credit cards in your name. Then we'll talk to my lawyer about transferring half the inheritance to you. Did I tell you how gorgeous you look tonight?"

"Yes," she said, turning slightly to give him a tentative smile. Like a damned puppy who's just wet on the carpet, he thought.

"Look, Daph, I know Max the doorman showed you the damned paper. Would you please just forget those toads? You'll like most of the people you'll meet tonight, I promise. Just be yourself, but don't treat any of the men like you do me, okay?"

That made her smile real. "None of them could look nearly as lovely as you do. In fact, I sometimes have fantasies that you're starkers under your coat."

"Sometimes..." He laughed. "I like that. You're going to be changing the New York idiom, sweetheart. Will you promise me one thing?"

I'd promise you anything you wanted, she thought. "What?"

No, he thought quickly, don't caution her any more. He gave her a leering smile. "Don't fall out of your gown. Your beautiful breasts are only for me."

She flushed, laughed, and moved closer, sliding her hand up his thigh. She felt his muscles tighten under her fingers.

"Watch what you're doing lady, or we might find ourselves arrested for doing indecent things on the freeway."

Forty-five minutes later they pulled into the large circular drive of the Morrisons' East Hampton home. They stepped through the front door and were inundated with noise from close to fifty guests. "Just remember," Brant whispered in her ear, as their host and hostess approached them, "you're the most beautiful woman here, and you're my wife."

Daphne was reserved, but Mrs. Morrison decided that quality was typically English, and she smiled her approval. All that garbage in the newspapers was just that, she thought. Brant stuck to Daphne through all the introductions, and was relieved when she smiled up at him, completely at ease, and told him she was going to the loo.

Brant patted her arm and watched her walk gracefully to a maid and speak to her. She was doing so well. Her natural sense of humor was coming out, and the women as well as the men were warming to her. He began to look around for Marcie. He'd seen her earlier, and he wanted to talk to her. He couldn't find her.

Daphne was repairing her makeup in the large bathroom off the master suite when she heard a woman's cold voice say, "Well, if it isn't the little English flower. Alone at last."

Her hand jerked, and the lipstick ended up on her cheek. She turned slowly to face a gorgeous redheaded woman, gowned in silver lamé that accentuated every beautiful curve of her body.

"Hello," Daphne said as she wiped off the lipstick.

She's so damned young and pretty, Marcie thought, feeling a stab of jealousy, disappointment and fury. But what had she expected? A troll? "My name is Marcie Ellis. I'm a very close friend of Brant's."

"A pleasure, ma'am. My name is Daphne."

"Ma'am? I'm not that much older than you are. Daphne. What a... clever name, so unused nowadays." Marcie tossed her hair, a studied movement that showed off her long, graceful neck. "Oh yes, I know who you are. You're the stud's little bride."

Daphne felt every muscle in her body stiffen alarmingly. Marcie must be one of Brant's lovers. No, ex-lovers.

"So odd," Marcie continued, wishing she could toss a bottle of pink paint on Daphne's hair. "Brant marrying you so quickly. But then again, he always moves quickly when he wants something, whether it's a new car, a new woman or a good financial deal."

"If you'll excuse me, Miss Ellis," Daphne said, clutching her purse and inching toward the door.

"Tell me, Mrs. Asher, what do you do...profes- sionally?"

"Nothing," Daphne said flatly.

"Ah, the little house *frau*." She laughed. Her lower teeth weren't very straight, and it made Daphne feel better. There was a flaw. "I'll give Brant three months, and then, my dear, you'll be just like any of Brant's other possessions, and you can sit around with his silly antiques and gather dust."

"His antiques are lovely!"

"His lovely brass bed as well? Have you played in his Jacuzzi yet? He enjoys that."

She's treating me like Lucilla does, Daphne thought; she's nasty and condescending. She wanted to rage at the woman, but she could easily picture her in that awesome tub with Brant, frolicking about, and that wiped out any smart retort she could have made. How could he possibly want anything from her except the money? She felt flat-chested, dumpy and stupid. "I don't think you're very nice," she said, and fled from the bathroom, Marcie's laughter ringing in her ears.

Brant was in close conversation with two men, and she didn't consider interrupting him. She slipped onto the lighted patio and cursed herself silently. It was frigidly cold, but she didn't notice.

"Here now, Mrs. Asher. Don't want you to take a cold."

Mr. Morrison gently drew her back inside. "Someone has upset you," he said, eyeing her pale face. He caught a glimpse of Marcie Ellis and heaved a deep sigh. He wanted to comfort Daphne and tell her everything would be all right, but he wasn't stupid, and knew that was the last thing she needed. He said matter-of-factly, "You know, Mrs. Asher, your husband is in a high visibility position. And you, Brant told me, have lived all your life in the country. Most people, you know, are kind, and those who aren't usually have a reason. For example, take Marcie Ellis." She gave a start, but he continued blandly. "She is really a nice woman, but Brant's marriage gave her a nasty start. She and your husband were close, I suppose, but that has nothing to do with anything now. You have two choices, ma'am. Either you turn the other cheek and let her exhaust her venom, or you make a fist and punch her out. If you choose the latter, I hope you won't do it here," he added, giving her a wide grin. "I have high blood pressure, and such a sight just might topple me into the hereafter."

Daphne laughed, unable to keep it in. "Brant told me how kind you were, Mr. Morrison, but he didn't tell me how funny you were!"

"Call me Dan."

"I think you're safe tonight, Dan. I shan't punch her over."

"Out, Mrs. Asher. American slang."

"I'll remember that. You're very kind, sir. The habits of a lifetime are difficult to break, I think." She drew a deep breath and straightened her shoulders. "It's time I stopped hiding behind Brant. I am, after all, a grown woman."

"Quite grown, I'd say," Dan Morrison agreed.

Brant looked up to see his wife in close conversation with Dan Morrison.

"Well, Brant, is your wife that desperate?"

"Hello, Marcie. I tried to get you yesterday, but you were out. How's the news business?"

"All right, I suppose. You haven't given me that exclusive you promised, Brant."

"How badly do you want it?"

She looked at him closely. He was tense, and his eyes glittered brightly.

"A knight in football armor, Brant? My, how ferocious you are! I gather you want to make a deal?"

"Yes, you could say that. No more crap, Marcie, and no more ridiculous attacks on my wife, or innuendos about the circumstances of our marriage. The straightforward, unvarnished truth. That's my deal."

Marcie flinched when he said wife. "I'll think about it," she said finally. "You sure you want the unvarnished truth? As I understand it, unvarnished, it makes little green eyes a gold digger, and you, well..." She turned to go, but couldn't resist saying over her shoulder, "I personally found your *wife* about as interesting as a head of cabbage."

Brant didn't ask Daphne about her conversation with Dan Morrison, and she didn't mention her scene with Marcie Ellis.

The next afternoon Brant was busily showing Daphne how to write a check and maintain a checkbook. He looked up at the sound of the doorbell, and frowned. "Who the hell—" he began.

When he opened the door, he took a step back at the sight of most of the Astros football team, complete with wives and champagne.

"Surprise!"

Chapter Fourteen

"Have another glass of champagne, Daph."

She smiled up at Tiny Phipps and thrust out her glass.

"I've always thought Brant's condo was huge," she said in some bewilderment. "Now, with all of you, it looks like a Liliputian's house bursting with Gulliver's."

"Yeah," said Lloyd Nolan, "we can't even run plays in here. You should see the place when all the players drop in."

"There are more of you?"

"Oh sure. It's the off-season now, and we couldn't round everybody up. So, Daph, what do you think of New York?"

"And football?"

"Yeah, you gotta see Dancer strut his stuff. We brought some tapes over for you"

She nodded enthusiastically. "I'd love it. Brant showed me just one back home."

"Lloyd wants you to admire *him*, too," said a lovely black woman, as she poked Lloyd in the ribs. "I'm Beatrice, his better half, but you don't have to remember it this time. You've got name overload, right?"

"Oh yes," Daphne said happily. "He's really called Dancer? He never told me that, although he was quite graceful when we danced a bit in Kauai—"

There was a hoot of laughter. Daphne felt a huge arm go around her shoulders and hug. "Ignore the fools, Daph," said "Choosy" Williams, a defensive lineman. "Your old man is called Dancer because he can scramble out of the pocket as well as Fran Tarkington. He doesn't want to get his beautiful body wrecked."

"I see," said Daphne with wide-eyed seriousness. "He does have a splendid body."

This guileless observation brought on fresh gales of laughter. Brant, in conversation with his coach, Sam Carverelli, looked over at the group surrounding his wife.

"You look like a fatuous bull," said Sam. "Lovely girl, Brant. And so at ease with everyone. I think Tiny is smitten."

She was at ease, completely at ease, Brant thought, and with a bunch of football players. And their wives, he added to himself, as he watched Cindy Williams lean over to whisper something in Daphne's ear. He couldn't believe it. He heard more champagne corks popping.

He blinked when his wife and a dozen or so players and wives left the living room.

"We're going to show her one of your famous plays, Brant!" Guy Richardson shouted across the room. "You know, the one where you tried a quarterback sneak and got creamed."

When Brant entered the den nearly a half an hour later he saw his wife sitting cross-legged on the floor in front of the TV, surrounded by the women. The men were draped over every piece of furniture in the room.

"Watch this pass, Daph," Lloyd was saying. "Sixty yards and right into my arms."

There was loud cheering when Lloyd trotted across into the end zone for a score, with Daphne's voice one of the loudest.

"How does he keep the ball from wobbling when he throws it so far?" she asked.

"Technique, darlin', technique," Lloyd said.

"He's got lots of that!"

"He sure seems to," said Daphne.

"Come on now, Nolan," Sam Carverelli scolded. "Look, Daphne," he said, showing her a football he'd pulled from the closet. "You have to handle the ball like this. See the seam? Look how I'm holding it. Here, you try it."

"Right over here, Daph," called Lloyd, backing to the far corner of the den.

She flung the ball at him, and he caught it against his chest. He gave a mighty "Ummph," and staggered backward.

"If he hadn't caught it, it would have ended up in Central Park," said Tiny, the self-appointed champagne pourer.

"Talented lady," Beatrice said to Brant.

He grinned. "Small hands, but yes, very talented."

"I love it when you talk dirty, Brant," Tiffy Richardson giggled.

Brant looked over her very pregnant stomach and said blandly, "Talk is cheap, by the looks of it."

"Look at that sweep around the right end!"

Brant blinked. The words had come from his English wife's mouth, and her eyes were glued to the TV screen.

"Oh, Brant, watch out!"

"Sorry, old buddy," Ted Hartland, the center, said, wincing as Brant was tackled by three of the Patriots' players.

"What a mess that play was," said Sam. "You nearly got a cracked rib out of that one, Brant."

Daphne turned to stare up at him. Brant dropped to his haunches. "I wasn't hurt, love. Just a bit black and blue. It's all part of the game, particularly when these idiots turn blind and clumsy on me."

"She doesn't want you to hurt your splendid body, Brant," said Nolan.

"All of you have splendid bodies," Daphne said. "You must be more careful, every one of you. Don't you agree, Beatrice?"

"I sure do. I can't count the times Lloyd comes home looking like a reject from a bruise factory."

"I bet he moans a lot to get sympathy," said Sam.

A good-natured argument between the men and women ensued about machoness and how it lasted only until the players got home. "Then he dissolves like a little boy," said Tiffy. "And Guy hardly ever gets tackled, 'cause he's the kicker."

"But the pain, watching the rest of the guys taking blows," Guy said, rubbing his ribs.

Brant sat on the floor beside Daphne, but he let the other guys tell her about the plays. She's like a sponge, he thought, seeing first confusion in her eyes at an explanation, then understanding. And if she didn't understand, she asked. This is my family, he thought, and she fits right in.

"Hey, Brant, you got a chalkboard?"

He looked up at Lloyd Nolan. "Sorry," he said. "Why?"

"Daph wants to see a double reverse."

"We'll wait for a nice day, then show her everything she wants to see in the park. Would you like to learn touch football, Daph?"

Tiny beamed at her when she nodded enthusiastically.

"You really lucked out," Tiffy Richardson said in a lowered voice to Brant. "We were all so worried."

Brant cocked an eyebrow at her. "Show of support? Or did all of you want to see if I'd married a cretin for money?"

"Well, the most obnoxious innuendoes were from Marcie, of course, and everybody figured she would slant things in the worst possible light. Daphne is…" Tiffy paused, then continued thoughtfully. "She brings out the protective instincts in one, doesn't she? I've never seen the guys so, well…careful. She seems like a lovely girl, Brant."

"Yes," he said, "she is."

"I love listening to her talk. I guess most Americans get off on an English accent."

"Particularly when she talks about a sweep around the right end?" He tried to mimic her accent, and they burst into laughter.

"Oh, Sam," they heard her call out to the coach, "you shouldn't pull your hair like that! It's just one play that went awry."

Guy Richardson showed her the final few minutes of the play-off game they'd lost to the Steelers, all the while explaining to her how their... darned kicker had missed two field goals before this.

She was indignant, hissing with the rest of them at the loss. "That's disgusting! You're the much better kicker, Guy. I'm so sorry." She turned to her husband and hugged him fiercely, surprising him. "Next season you'll demolish them. I promise."

The Astros didn't leave until nearly midnight. Tiny ordered in a dozen pizzas, and Brant watched with the fondness of a proud parent as Daphne laughed when they teased her mercilessly about the anchovies.

Nor did they leave until the wreckage was cleaned up. Daphne was hugged until her ribs ached. When the door closed for the last time she turned to Brant and flung her arms around his waist. "I'm so happy! I've never met so many nice people."

"You're tipsy," he said, running his hands up and down her back.

"Not that tipsy," she said, raising her face, her lips parting.

He kissed the tip of her nose and led her into the bedroom. When she was naked, her turned her onto her stomach, smiling when she looked at him questioningly over her shoulder. "Trust me," he said, leaning down to nip the nape of her neck. He moved deeply into her, and she moaned softly, wriggling beneath him as his hands stroked her breasts and belly. He realized vaguely that she didn't have her doctor's appointment until the following day, but when he tried to pull out of her, she twisted onto her back and held him deep within her.

"Sweetheart," he said desperately, "don't move." But his fingers found her, caressed her, and she jerked upward. "I can't stop," he said, his voice ragged.

"I can feel it," she gasped. "I'm filled with you."

Rippling, wild feelings surged through him, making him oblivious of everything except the warmth of her and the mindless depth of his pleasure.

"Only with you," he said. "Only with you."

In the next instant he was asleep.

What, Daphne wondered, dazed by her own passion, had he meant by that? She curled against him, listened to her galloping heart slow to normal, and fell asleep, replete with happiness.

"I would like to write you a check," Daphne said to the clerk in Lord and Taylor. She and Brant had just come from her doctor, and he had told her they should celebrate. The diaphragm would be ready in two days. The boots on sale in the display window drew them both in. Daphne's were a wreck.

"Certainly, ma'am," the saleswoman said. "Wouldn't you like to have a Lord and Taylor credit card? It's much easier, you know."

Daphne wondered where Brant was. He'd quickly approved her selection of the new leather boots, then wandered off.

"A credit card," she repeated. She'd never owned a credit card in her life. Suddenly it seemed the most important thing in the world. "Yes," she said, "I would like one."

"Excellent. Ah, Mrs. Asher, I'm certain your credit will be approved." She directed Daphne to the sixth floor. That was where Brant found her some twenty minutes later.

She was sitting very straight in the chair opposite a rather tired-looking man whose glasses kept slipping down his nose. He heard the man say, "You will need your husband's approval, Mrs. Asher, and, as I said, his signature."

"But all you have to do is speak to Mr. Edward Caufield, the broker. The card is for me, as I told you, not for my husband."

"Mrs. Asher..." The man was beginning to sound out of patience. "Ma'am, it's policy. You have no income of your own."

"Is there a problem?" Brant asked, stepping into Daphne's line of vision.

The man looked ready to embrace Brant with relief. "Mr. Asher? You're the football player, aren't you? A pleasure, sir." He quickly rose and shook Brant's hand. "We just need your signature, and some information for the application form."

Brant had two major credit cards, and had no wish for another one, but he saw the strained look in Daphne's eyes and quickly succumbed. "Of course," he said, seating himself beside his wife.

He realized that he'd totally misunderstood the situation when she said abruptly, "I want the credit card in my name, not his."

Mr. Reeves sighed and tried again. "Mrs. Asher, I can't imagine that credit is handled that differently in England. Of course you can have a card in your name; it is just that the major account will be in your husband's name. It is his responsibility—"

"No, Mr. Asher doesn't want a Lord and Taylor card. Only I do! *I* will be writing you checks to pay for purchases, not him."

"Ma'am, you have no major, steady source of income." He sent a pleading look at Brant. "You have no job and no credit record."

Damnation, Brant thought, what the hell was he supposed to do now? Daphne looked ready to spit nails. He said as calmly as he could, "My wife does have an income of her own. A thousand dollars a month is deposited into her account. Now, let's get this bloody application filled out."

She was back to an allowance. Although she had over two hundred thousand dollars in investments, arranged two days previously by Brant's broker, all she could prove was that she had quarterly incoming interest from the investments. She bit her tongue, rage flowing through her. Rage at herself for being so utterly worthless. She rose jerkily to her feet, clutching her purse in front of her like a weapon. "I don't want your credit card, Mr. Reeves. I am going to go downstairs and write a check for my purchase."

"Daphne, wait," Brant began, but she was marching out of the office, her shoulders squared like a militant...whatever.

He looked back at Mr. Reeves. "Maybe some other time," he said, and left. The man's commiserating look made Brant want to strangle Daphne.

Daphne wished she had never even seen the damned boots, but she wrote out the check, her very first with elaborate care, and thumped it next to the saleswoman's cash register.

"May I please see your driver's license and a major credit card, Mrs. Asher?"

Daphne looked at her blankly. "What?"

"Since you don't have an account with us, ma'am, I need to see ID with your check. It's store policy."

Brant arrived in time for this exchange. He closed his eyes a moment, wishing he were playing football in California. Hell, he'd even settle for Alaska. It was his own fault. It hadn't occurred to him that she would need ID to write checks.

"I don't have any ID," Daphne said through gritted teeth.

The saleswoman looked at her helplessly. "I understand, ma'am, that you're new in this country. Let me speak to the manager, unless, of course, your husband could provide—" She broke off at Daphne's furious glare and fled.

She was smart enough to escape the impending eruption, Brant thought. He gently laid his hand on Daphne's arm. He could feel her trembling through her coat sleeve. "I forgot," he said. "I'm sorry. We'll get you ID this week."

Her contacts itched with the wretched tears welling up, and she dashed her hand across her eyes, inevitably dislodging a contact. A lime green dot of plastic fell on the counter. She cursed, and Brant was so surprised that he laughed.

"I hate you," she said, her voice low and trembling. "I don't want these damned boots. I don't want anything, do you hear?" She managed to pick up the contact, then left him standing at the counter, feeling like an utter fool. He was aware of pitying glances from other customers.

"I'm sorry, Mr. Asher," the saleswoman said, "but I will have to have your check instead. Or a credit card?"

Brant silently wrote out a check. When the boots were packaged, he went to stand outside the women's room. His wait was a long one, and he was beginning to think that Daphne had left before he'd gotten there. Five minutes later she emerged, her head down, her knitted hat pulled low over her forehead.

"Let's go ice-skating," he said, taking her arm in a firm grasp.

"You have an appointment, don't you?" she asked, not looking up at him.

"The appointment can wait. I'll make a phone call."

They went ice-skating at Rockefeller Center, and Brant watched her take all her frustration out on the ice. She was a very good skater, very graceful, and he was thankful. On the taxi ride back to their building he said calmly, "Tomorrow we're going to get you a New York driver's license."

"I'm sure you won't mind my taking the test in your Porsche?" she said sarcastically.

The thought of anyone but himself driving the Porsche in New York traffic chilled him, but he said nothing.

"What if I wreck your bloody car? I don't have any ID. I don't have any auto insurance. And they won't even accept my check!"

Thank heaven the cab pulled up in front of their building at that moment, and he was saved by having to search for the cab fare.

He said nothing until they were safely inside the condo. He tossed the package containing the infamous boots on the sofa. "All right, we're going to talk, Daph. No more snide remarks from you, no more infantile behavior."

She had the utter nerve to walk away from him into the kitchen. How anticlimactic to argue in front of the sink, he thought, glaring at the back of her head. He watched her drink a glass of water.

"Are you quite through now?" he asked.

"No. I want to go to the bathroom."

"Convenient cause and effect," he muttered. He followed her through the bedroom and stopped abruptly when the bathroom door was slammed in his face.

A wife, he thought, striding back into the living room, is a pain in the butt. He was trying to smooth things out for her, and all he got in return was childish anger and scenes. He was well lathered up when she came into the living room some ten minutes later.

"I'm fed up with you," he said, erupting. "I should have married a woman, not some naive, silly girl whose only claim to anything is her performance in bed." Unfair, he raged at himself once the words were out, but he wouldn't take them back. He'd finally gotten her attention.

Daphne stared at him, her eyes darkening with anger.

"If you start on me again, I'm leaving. Now, do you want to talk like two reasoning adults or continue to carry on? And don't you shake your head at me!'' He grasped her shoulders and shook her slightly. ''Well?'' he demanded.

''I should go get dinner started,'' she said.

''Oh? Burned tuna casserole? Cold scrambled eggs?'' He plowed distracted fingers through his hair. ''Damn it, I'm sorry, I didn't mean that. Come here and sit down. Now.''

She curled up at one end of the long sofa and looked straight ahead at a pink marble sculpture of a naked woman on a side table.

''Daph,'' he said, drawing on his patience, ''what happened today was unfortunate. There was no reason for you to freak out like that. It's no big deal. We'll get your ID, and you'll be free to shop anywhere you want to and write a zillion checks. What else do you want?''

''I want to go home,'' she said, then realized how stupid it all was, and gave a nervous laugh. ''No, that's not true. I just feel so...useless.''

''Useless! You're my wife! Or are you beginning to regret marrying me now?''

''No, it's not that,'' she said unhappily, feeling stupid and inarticulate, and guilty. It wasn't his fault, after all, that she couldn't do what any normal adult person could. How could he ever think that she'd regret having married him? He was the one with the cross to bear. She licked her dry lips. ''It's just—'' Just what? she wanted to yell at herself.

''Please spare me any psychological crap about not knowing who you are and wanting to search out your identity in the scheme of life.''

''All right, but it's not psychological! I'll spare you everything. Don't you have an appointment soon?''

''Yes,'' he said, rising abruptly. ''I do. When I get back, we'll go out to dinner.''

She watched him helplessly as he shrugged into his beautiful leather coat and slammed out the front door.

She wandered around the house before settling in the den. She turned on the VCR and put in a video of one of Brant's football games. She felt pleasure begin to flow through her at the excitement of the plays. ''That,'' she said to the empty room, ''was a draw play. It didn't work, but it was a good call.''

Chapter Fifteen

"Welcome, my dears," said Alice Asher, embracing first Daphne, then Brant. "The house is filled to bursting! Come in quickly, it's so cold outside. Isn't the snow lovely? Here, let me take your coats. And, Daphne, I have quite a surprise for you."

Surprise wasn't the word for it. Daphne stared first at Winterspoon, then at Aunt Cloe, and burst into tears.

"Little egg!" Cloe exclaimed. "What is all this nonsense? Come here and let me give you a big hug. I brought you a reminder of England, that's all. Hush now." She held the slender body tightly against her, meeting Brant's eyes over Daphne's head. He shrugged and said, "Welcome, Aunt Cloe, and you, Winterspoon. I hope your trip wasn't too tiring?"

"Very tolerable, my lord," Winterspoon said.

"Actually, Brant," Cloe said, a pronounced twinkle in her eyes, "Mr. Winterspoon and I inbibed freely across the Atlantic and arrived with vacuous smiles on our faces! Thank you so much for sending the tickets."

Daphne turned in Cloe's arms to look at her husband. "You arranged for them to come?"

"Yes," he said, his eyes intent on her face. "I thought it would please you."

All she could do for the moment was gape at him. In the next instant she hurled herself against him, burying her face against his throat. "That's more like it," he whispered against her temple. The past three days had been tense and strained, except when they were in bed, and Brant had decided the more time in bed, the better. He'd held off since they were married, giving her time to adjust to him sexually. But not during the past three days. To his delight and relief, she'd responded enthusiastically, even though he knew she must be sore. When he'd pointed out that fact she'd moaned softly, telling him she didn't care.

"I don't hate you anymore," she whispered back. "I think you are a very nice man."

"Thank you, love. You've ravished my poor body at least ten times during the past few days. Maybe you should continue hating me. I like the result."

"I'll ravish you even more now, I promise."

"All right, you two love birds," Alice Asher said. "In an hour we're going to have Lily, Dusty and the kids invading us from Houston."

"How are they getting here from New York, Mom?"

Alice laughed. "Silly question, Brant. By limo, of course. Now, I would suggest that you and Daphne get unpacked and prepare yourselves. Cloe, Mr. Winterspoon, why don't we have a cup of tea?"

"Oscar, ma'am."

"Good heavens, Mr. Winterspoon," Cloe said exuberantly, "what a bloody noble name!"

"Thank you, Mrs. Sparks."

"Cloe, sir. After all, we are in America now."

Brant nibbled Daphne's ear as they walked upstairs to his old bedroom. "You didn't forget your diaphragm, did you?"

She slanted him a look that made him instantly horny. "I think," she said primly, "that it's going to be worn out by next week."

"Lord, wouldn't that be a trip! Just think of the look on your doctor's face. I'd have to fight her off with a two-by-four."

"She's fifty-five, Brant."

"With a stick, then?"

"Conceited jerk."

"Just think of it—I'd probably be written up in medical journals. How's this for a title of the article?" He leaned over and whispered in her ear.

"Ten hard what?" she said.

Alice, downstairs in the living room, smiled at the sound of her son's hearty laughter.

The dining room was crammed with food and laughter, adults and boisterous children.

"You're much more beautiful than Brant led me to believe," Lily said after she'd spooned a good helping of green beans on her daughter's plate.

"What a thing to say, darlin'," Dusty said. "I think the good ole boys in Houston would go stark raving mad at the sight of her."

"Well, I didn't mean it the way it came out," Lily said.

"You never do," said Brant. "Lily's got an uncensored brain," he added to Daphne.

But Daphne was gazing at Dusty, fascinated by his accent. "Could you say something else, please, Dusty?"

"After dinner I'll sing y'all a western song, how's that, ma'am?"

"His favorite is 'Flushed Down the Toilet of her Heart' or something exquisitely literate like that."

"This gal ain't got no taste," Dusty said, drawling even more to please his English audience.

"I'd love to hear you sing anything," Daphne said.

"Have some more chicken, dear," Alice said. "You've scarcely touched your dinner."

"I agree," Brant said. "You've got to keep up your strength, sweetheart."

She smiled at him happily, but turned to Cloe. "You must go to Hawaii, to Kauai! It's so beautiful, and everyone is so nice!"

"I bet you wrung their withers in that orange bikini," Cloe said.

"Lord," Brant said, "I had to hire an armed guard to keep the men away."

"Did you really, Uncle Brant?" eight-year-old Keith asked, his fork suspended between plate and mouth.

"Sure I did. All women."

"Brant, don't lie to him," Lily said. "Only half the guard were women, Keith."

"I say, madam," Winterspoon said politely, "this is a very tasty dish. I trust you will give me your recipe."

"Certainly, Oscar," said Alice Asher. "You plan to cook for Brant and Daphne?"

"Of course. Her ladyship was rarely allowed near the kitchen at Asherwood."

"Now, Winterspoon," Brant said firmly, "no more lordships or ladyships. This is America. Plus, it's damned embarrassing."

"I love it," said Lily. "Oh dear, I forgot to curtsey!"

"When does training begin, Brant?" Dusty asked.

"Too soon, I'm afraid. In about four months. We'll be training in upstate New York, and the humidity is enough to knock your socks off."

"How 'bout that commercial, brother?"

"You'll be seeing my handsome puss on TV next week, I think. And, Lily, it's sporting goods, not underwear or shaving cream."

"Well, underwear might be okay. What do you think, Daphne? Would you mind millions of women seeing Brant in his European boxers?"

"Oh no," Daphne burst out. "He's so beautiful—" She skidded to a stop, color flooding her cheeks.

Brant leaned over and whispered in her ear, "But, love, you've rarely seen me in underwear."

"What are you saying, Uncle Brant?" asked Patricia.

"I was just telling your Aunt Daphne that she's got great taste."

"Daphne sure is a funny name," said Danny.

"You can call me Daph. Your uncle does."

"That sounds like Daffy Duck," said Keith.

"Who's Daffy Duck?" asked Daphne.

The English contingent listened with great interest to Keith's convoluted description before Dusty interrupted, chuckling, "Let's keep your new aunt out of cartoons, okay son?"

"Are you and Uncle Brant going to have kids soon?" Patricia asked.

The green beans suddenly lodged in Daphne's throat, and she grabbed at her glass of water. Brant lightly thumped her on the back.

"Yeah," Keith said, adding his two cents. "We'd like some cousins."

"You all right, sweetheart?" Brant asked. At her strangled nod, he turned to his nephew and nieces. "Hey, you guys, it's hard work. What do you think, Daph?"

The ball's in your court, his wicked look told her. He loved her scarlet flush, the curse of all blondes. To his surprise she said, "Actually, I'd love some kids. But your uncle is a very busy man, you know. You'll have to be patient with him."

Brant was so surprised, he blurted out, "But I didn't think that you wanted...that is, you seem to..."

"He did the same thing on the first ten takes for the commercial," Daphne said, lying fluently as she patted his arm. "When he gets nervous, or excited, or surprised, he can't cope with words."

"Good grief, boy," Dusty said. "I never knew that. Always thought you were as slick as a pair of wet boots."

"I did, too," said Brant. His voice held humor, but there was none in his eyes as they searched his wife's face.

Alice cleared her throat. "Tell me, Cloe, how long do you plan to stay with us?"

"Well, I simply must meet all those lovely football players. If they all look like your son..." She gave a delighted shudder, her eyes sparkling.

"They are all marvelous, Aunt Cloe," Daphne said.

"As in huge with great...physiques?"

"Yes, ma'am. But I'm not sure you should meet them all at once."

"Yeah, we don't want you to have cardiac arrest, Cloe," Brant said.

"Dead right, sir," said Oscar.

Reverend Oakes's wedding ceremoney, held in the ultramodern presbyterian church in Stamford the following morning, was simple, elegant and blessedly short. Daphne wore a pale yellow wool dress, and Brant a dark suit. "Do you feel doubly married now?" he asked as he lightly brushed her lips at the close of the service.

"I feel scared to death," Daphne said.

"Why? You know what I'm going to do to that gorgeous body of yours." She didn't laugh as he'd expected her to, but he didn't have time to ask her what was going on in her lovely head.

The children, on their best behavior up to this point, could no longer contain themselves, and clutched at their uncle's arms.

"Mom said you'd never get married, Uncle Brant," Keith said. "Now you've done it twice."

"And to the same lady," said Patricia.

"Yeah, Mom said you like to play the field, but I told her you had to 'cause you're a football player."

"Out of the mouths of little heathens," said Lily. "Congratulations, Daphne," she said, hugging her sister-in-law. "Are you going to drag Brant back to Hawaii?"

"Actually," Brant said, "I'm going to drag her back to England. We've got lots of work to do on Asherwood. What do you think, sweetheart?"

"Yes," she said quietly, not meeting his eyes.

"You and I are going to have a nice, long talk," Brant said firmly. He turned away to speak to Reverend Oakes.

Because they weren't, strictly speaking, newlyweds, Brant spent the afternoon showing Cloe and Winterspoon over Stamford and the surrounding area. He and his bride had no time alone until late that evening.

"No," he said, watching her from the bed, "no nightgown. You won't need it. I'll keep you warm." He patted the bed beside him. "Come here, Daph."

She started to slip off her bra, then leaned over to flip off the bedroom lamp. "No," Brant said, "leave it on. I want to see you."

She hesitated perceptibly, and he frowned. "Daph, I know your body almost as well as my own. What's the matter, sweetheart?"

She shook her head, and turned her back to slip out of her underwear.

"Nice view," he said. "I love those long legs of yours and that cute little—"

"Brant!" She quickly moved into the bed and pulled the covers to her chin.

He was balanced on his elbow, studying her profile. "All right," he said seriously, "enough. No more jokes. Tell me what's wrong."

She shook her head, not looking at him.

"Daph, I'm not going to ravish you until you tell me what's in that mind of yours."

Without warning she threw herself against him, burying her face in his shoulder. He felt her trembling, felt her hands clutching at his back.

"Sweetheart," he said quietly against her hair. "What's all this? Please, talk to me."

She whispered against his throat, "You went through the ceremony today like...like you really wanted to."

He became very still, his hands halting their stroking down her back. "Of course," he said. "What did you expect? That I'd take one look at you and call a screeching halt? We're already married, Daph. This was for my mother."

"You're making the best of a bad bargain."

His hands cupped her buttocks, drawing her closer. "If this is a bad bargain, then certainly pigs will fly, quite soon."

"You'd enjoy sex with any woman, and you know it. You'll be bored with me soon enough."

"Why?"

She raised her head at his bald question. His eyes were resting intently on her face, his eyebrow arched upward. "Because I'm stupid, and make you furious and you're stuck with me."

"You're anything but stupid, yes, and like glue."

"You want to go back to Asherwood because I embarrass you here."

He whistled softly. "So that's what's going on. You're such an idiot, Daphne. Sexy, sweet, but an idiot. I want to go back to Asherwood because I love the place, and I thought you did, too. It's our other home now, and I don't want to neglect it. I never did get to refinish the wainscotting in the library."

"But I'm useless! You don't want to have children with me because that would mean you'd have to stay married to me!"

He didn't say anything. She felt his fingers stroking down her belly to between her thighs.

"What are you doing?" she gasped.

She felt his finger easing inside her, and she tried to jerk away, confused.

"Hold still," he said sharply. "Ah, just a bit further. Here we go. A pity, now we won't have the chance to wear out your diaphragm. I was kinda looking forward to being a new entry in the *Guinness Book of Records*."

She heard it thump onto the floor.

"I don't understand! Why did you do that?"

"We're going to make a baby so I'll be stuck with you forever."

"But you don't want to! You're just doing this because...you're honorable!"

"God, you're warm and soft." She squirmed as his fingers moved downward again, gently probing, stroking, driving her crazy. "Brant!"

"Stop bleating and kiss me. I love to feel you, and in just a few minutes, after you calm down, I'm going to kiss every inch of you."

"You make me sound like a goat," she giggled.

"I'm definitely the goat. I've wanted you all day, Mrs. Asher."

She felt him hard and velvet soft against her thighs. "What was it you said about ten hard—"

He kissed her deeply, easing between her legs and pressing upward.

"You," she gasped, feeling the swamping sensations build in her belly, "are an oversexed man."

"Lord yes," he said. "Aren't you glad?"

Her soft moan was her answer, and he smiled, loving the glazed look in her eyes. "There's quite a bit to be said about awakening a sleeping beauty."

He moved inside her, and felt her muscles tighten convulsively around him. He cursed softly and withdrew from her, his breathing ragged. She tried to bring him into her again, but he whispered, "No, love, not yet. You've blasted my control. I'll leave you if I'm inside you."

"But—"

"Hush, let me make you feel as I do." She opened to him as he caressed her with his mouth, knowing that the marvelous feelings would build and build until she wanted to die with the force of them. When her whimpers became cries, she felt his hand gently covering her mouth. Then his mouth replaced his hand as he eased over her, and she was frantic with the feel of him deep inside her. She moaned into his mouth, whispering brokenly.

Daphne thought the world a most perfect place when she stared up into her husband's face as his own pleasure overtook him. He moaned through his gritted teeth, his head thrown back, his body arched upward.

Brent knew his weight was too much for her, but he didn't have the strength to move. "You are my wife," he said, the simple words mirroring the warm, incredibly tender feelings welling up within him. "My wife."

"Yes," she said, pulling him down to kiss him again.

They listened to each other's breathing slow and even out. Brant said, "I've never made love to another woman in this bedroom."

"I trust not," she said dryly.

He rolled off her onto his back, and turned off the light. When he felt her head on his shoulder, he said, aloud, "No."

"No what?" she asked on a satisfied yawn, snuggling closer against him.

"No, we can't leave for England right away. Aunt Cloe's got to meet the Astros."

"Do you think they'll survive her?"

"I can't wait to find out."

Chapter Sixteen

Tiny Phipps looked shell shocked. He grabbed a beer and threw back his head. Daphne stared at his massive neck, fascinated by the play of muscles as he downed the entire can.

After he lowered the bottle and swiped his mouth with the back of his hand, Daphne asked, her expression deadpan, "Did you enjoy meeting my Aunt Cloe, Tiny?"

"Daph, she patted my butt and told me I was really a cute hunk!" He looked like a little boy who couldn't quite grasp the complexities of the adult world.

Daphne laughed heartily. "Well, you are, Tiny. My aunt has excellent taste. She just learned the word 'hunk' and is simply practicing it on all appropriate males."

"But she's old enough to be my mother. My grandmother!"

"The term 'dirty old man' applying here, guys?" Brant asked.

"With a change in gender," Daphne said. She looked over at her aunt, who was now in avid conversation with Lloyd Nolan and Sam Carverelli. "They'll all survive," she said. "In fact, Sam is giving her the same look he gave Gus Colima after you guys beat the Rams."

"What a game that was," Tiny said. "Brant passed for over three hundred yards."

"I know," Daphne said. "And a seventy-two yarder for a touchdown."

"How 'bout another drink, Daph?" Beatrice asked.

"Not for me or I'll fall asleep before everyone even gets here. Wonderful party, Beatrice. I love your house. It's so rustic and homey and huge."

"Thank you. Lloyd has always had this thing for rocks and glass. It was close, but I managed to talk him out of a rock bathtub.'' She rolled her eyes. "But the glass, well, have you seen the bedroom?''

"I thought I'd haul Daphne in there in a little while and give her a demonstration," Brant said.

"What kind of demonstration would you do with glass?'' Daphne asked. "You mean glass blowing?''

There was a spate of laughter, and Brant moaned.

"Little egg," Cloe said, "what's all this about mirrors in bedrooms?''

"Well," Daphne said, "I'm not really sure. I'm being laughed at; that's the only thing I'm really certain of.''

Cloe said to Tiny, "Why don't you show me? Come, my boy, let's do it now.'' She thrust her arm through Tiny's and dragged him away. "What lovely, monstrous muscles, my dear,'' Daphne heard her say fondly to her captive.

The doorbell rang. "More folk," Beatrice said. "Excuse me, guys.''

Daphne was admiring the beautiful view through the French doors when she felt Brant stiffen beside her.

"What the hell!'' he said softly. She turned to see Marcie Ellis come into the living room on the arm of a man she'd never seen before.

"Who is he?'' she asked, but her eyes were on the beautiful woman at his side, who looked both flamboyant and elegant in a moss-green jump suit. She felt her hair begin to turn stringy, and her front teeth turn crooked.

"Matt Orson, the defensive coach. It looks like Marcie is really doing a number this time. Oh...damn! They've brought along a photographer.''

He shot Daphne a worried look, and she knew he was concerned that she'd shatter again under pressure. And make him look like a fool. And make her look like a moron.

"Well, it looks like old home week," she heard Marcie say to Beatrice.

"We've got a couple of new faces," said Lloyd. "Have you met Daphne? And her aunt, Mrs. Sparks, here from England to visit?''

"Immigration seems to be getting out of hand," Marcie said in a carrying voice as her eyes met Daphne's. "I suspect all things foreign will return home soon enough. Perhaps I'd best do my interview with Brant here, before he's turned loose on New York's women again.''

Oh God, Lloyd thought, so that's the lay of the land, is it? Spare me a cat fight. He shot a look at Matt Orson, who merely shrugged. Lloyd wondered if Matt knew he was being used. Probably so, he wasn't a fool.

"Little egg, how very fascinating, to be sure," said Cloe, coming up behind Daphne. "She's quite lovely, of course, but nothing compared to you," she added, not missing a beat.

"I agree," said Brant easily, but he looked as tense as a man facing a firing squad.

"I can't wait to talk to her," Cloe remarked. "Perhaps she'll be more of a challenge than Lucilla. More wit, I think. Buck up, Daphne! It's about time you realized you had my outrageous blood in your veins.''

"She was Brant's lover before he came to England," Daphne said in a low voice to Cloe.

"So! Dear boy, please fetch me a glass of white wine. Thank you.'' After Brant moved away reluctantly, Cloe continued, "I never thought Brant would bed a woman who wasn't a looker. If you'd but realize it, little egg, this could be most amusing. You are the wife, you know.''

"Yes," Daphne said slowly, her eyes widening, "I am, aren't I? And I can also write checks and balance a checkbook. I'll have my driver's license soon. And a Lord and Taylor credit card.''

"Sounds like the top of the heap to me," said Cloe.

"Well, well, so the wolf left the little shepherd unprotected.''

"Hello, Marcie," Daphne said. "This is my Aunt Cloe, from England.''

"Scotland, actually," said Cloe. "You're a journalist, aren't you, Marcie?''

How did Aunt Cloe know that? Daphne wondered.

Fluttering old lady, Marcie thought. She smiled. "Yes, and I hope to get the true story from Brant today. His being suddenly a lord, a husband, and a castle owner.''

"I dare say Daphne here can tell you all about it," said Cloe, her voice utterly complacent. "I can't say exactly what Brant thinks of being a lord, but he adores being a husband and a castle owner." Cloe shook her head and patted Marcie's hand in a fond, maternal gesture. "I've never before seen a man so smitten. Of course, he had to cut out all her admirers first.''

Daphne did her best not to drop her jaw in surprise at her aunt's words.

"I suppose it's natural enough for an heiress to have many men around," Marcie said. She didn't want to revise her opinion of the old lady, but...

Daphne laughed. "An heiress! That's one thing Brant should have corrected immediately. I'm surprised, Marcie, that Brant didn't tell *you*, of all people. I didn't have a *sou*, a dime even.''

Marcie, who had pulled a pencil and pad out of her purse, looked as if she'd just swallowed the eraser. "What do you mean?''

"Why, just what I said, of course." Daphne gave her what she hoped was an evil smile. Her pulse was racing, but not with fear.

"But Brant told me before he left for England that he'd inherited only the title and a moldering old house.''

Maybe a bit of fear, then. She shrugged. "English solicitors are notorious for keeping little tidbits of information back until they meet their clients face to face. Brant didn't know about me, either.''

"I see," said Marcie, who didn't see at all. She watched Brant approach, a glass of wine in his hand.

Cloe laughed indulgently. "It took him little time to rectify that situation. Ah, my boy, thank you for the wine. Daphne here was just telling the journalist lady that she was poor as a beggar, and not the heiress everyone thought. Love at first sight it was when Brant laid eyes on her. I really didn't believe such a thing existed. Of course, when I met Mr. Sparks, and he took me for a drive in the moonlight, well..."

"Very nearly," Brant said easily. "Remember, Daph? I was working on the roof and turned to see your gorgeous legs coming out of a cab? I nearly expired in the gutter."

Marcie, who was endowed with a pair of the nicest legs in New York, said tightly, "But you always were a leg man, weren't you, darling?"

Brant grinned. "That and other things." He wrapped his arm around Daphne's shoulders. "All of which my beautiful wife has, in abundance."

Marcie was aware of the old lady's eyes resting on her face and started. The old bird was looking at her with pity! Marcie wanted to spit. "What do you intend doing now that you're in America?" she asked Daphne.

"Get a driver's license and run Brant's Porsche into the ground."

There was a crack of laughter behind Marcie. Matt Orson said, "What's this, Brant? You never let anyone drive the Porsche."

Brant, who had no great enthusiasm for Daphne's plans, merely shrugged. "You should see her behind the wheel. She stops traffic." He looked thoughtfully at his wife. "Perhaps I should get you your own car."

"A station wagon to cart around all the kiddies?" Marcie said, wishing that she could leave this wretched party and forget that she ever decided to marry Brant herself. Could he really have fallen in love with this vacuous girl? Well, she had seemed vacuous, she amended to herself. Now she seemed to sparkle with confidence. Was one born with those unbelievable green eyes?

"No," Daphne said with great decisiveness, "that will be the third car."

"Come along, love," Brant said. "It's time I showed you all that glass in the bedroom, particularly since I'm beginning to envision myself in the country, surrounded with infants and autos."

Matt took himself off to the bar, and Marcie was left with Mrs. Sparks, the devious old lady.

"My dear Daphne is getting quite good at launching smart retorts, don't you think? Brant calls them salvos. I'd hoped you'd be a bit more up to snuff, Marcie. Your insults dwindled into catty nothings."

Marcie said ruefully, "She didn't have a word to say for herself when I saw her the first time. Damn it, she was a dolt, and I couldn't imagine Brant putting up with that."

"Things change, I've always found." Cloe patted Marcie's shoulder. "Buck up, my dear. Forget and forgive. You're a bright girl; don't continue swimming upstream with the salmon."

Marcie uttered an obscenity under her breath.

"I know. Did that help?"

"You're a wicked woman, do you know that, Aunt Cloe?"

"Me? Ah, I remember how Mr. Sparks used to say that...well, that's neither here nor there, is it? There's that gorgeous boy, Tiny. What an odd name, to be sure. Excuse me, Marcie. And remember, you're too smart a girl to keep plowing in a field that's no longer fallow."

Brant watched his wife lying on her back, staring up at the mirrored ceiling. "Getting any lascivious ideas, sweetheart?"

"Oh yes," Daphne said enthusiastically. "I could see all of you while you—" She broke off and gave him a come hither smile.

He shuddered slightly, easily picturing himself covering her, her white legs wrapped around him, her arms clutching his back. To distract himself he said, "You handled Marcie quite nicely."

"Yes," she said, her voice surprised. "Yes, I did."

"You didn't need me at all."

Daphne cocked an eyebrow at him. "I thought you were tired of playing knight errant to my damsel in tongue-tied distress?"

Brant ran his fingers through his hair. "I'm crazy. Ignore what I say."

Daphne came up on her knees on the bed. "I think I hear Lloyd shouting about a videotape of one of your games. Let's go see it, okay?"

He cocked his head at her. "You really like football, don't you?"

"I can't wait until August for the exhibition games. I'll be cheering myself hoarse for you. But there's still so much to learn. I've got to talk to Matt Orson. There's lots I need to understand about the defense, particularly how they know what to do when the quarterback does an audible." She continued talking as she walked out of the bedroom, assuming that he was following her.

Brant shook his head. She was changing so quickly that he was having trouble keeping up. He remembered the girl he'd met not two months ago and shook his head again, bemused. Who the hell had told her about audibles? He pictured her driving his Porsche and shuddered.

The following evening, as they left a French restaurant on the east side, a flashbulb went off in their faces. Brant's arm immediately went around his wife's waist, to bring her protectively close. It was the same two men who had trapped them in the garage some time before.

"Hey, Mrs. Asher, you got anything to say this time?" one of them called out.

Brant felt a surge of anger, and his hand clenched. He had no time to do or say anything. Daphne, a snide smile on her face, said, "Hi, guys. Nice to see you again. You've stopped lurking in garages?"

The man ignored that. "Everyone's gotta eat," he said. "I suppose you heiresses are used to dining in the best spots?"

"Tomorrow night Brant is going to take me to a Mexican restaurant. I love tacos. What's your favorite food?"

Ah ha, she thought when he had no answer, satisfied that she'd taken him totally aback. The man's partner snapped another picture.

"What do you think of all your husband's women, Mrs. Asher?"

"He has excellent taste," she said blandly. "I've been meaning to send out letters of condolence."

"Gentlemen," Brant broke in, "I think you've shot your wad. Daph, let's go home."

"All one has to do is feel good about oneself," Daphne said, trying to snuggle closer to Brant, but unable to in the Porsche.

He revved the engine, saying nothing as the Porsche screeched around a corner in Central Park. She'd handled the men like a pro. You want her to fit in, not to be afraid and tongue-tied around people, he chided himself. But somehow he felt as though he'd lost control. Stop it, you're acting like a dog who's lost his own private bone.

When they finally got home they found that Winterspoon and Aunt Cloe were still out. Brant turned to his wife, "Let's go to bed."

"All right," she said, her eyes twinkling up at him.

Brant didn't wait for her to undress. He stripped her, tossed her onto the bed and turned every bit of his uncertainty into wild passion and, he realized vaguely as he thrust into her, a show of complete control and dominance. His savage moan of release filled the silent bedroom.

"Damn," he muttered as his breathing eased. He hadn't given a damn about her feelings, and now he felt like a complete and utter bastard. Her eyes were closed. "Daph," he said softly. "Sweetheart, forgive me." He pulled away from her and yanked off the rest of his clothes. Gently he eased her under the covers and pulled her against him. "I won't let you retreat from me," he said, anger at himself in his voice.

"I don't understand," she said finally against his shoulder.

"I don't either," he admitted. "But I'm going to try my damndest to see that you forget what a jerk I just was. Did I hurt you?"

"No, but it wasn't fun, either."

That's certainly the unvarnished truth, he thought. He called on every ounce of expertise he possessed to bring her to pleasure, and when he succeeded, he again felt that odd combination of power and control. He loved the way she shuddered in her climax, the way her eyes blurred over, the way she burrowed against him as if she wanted to get inside him.

As for Daphne, she was in a daze. She felt like a limp dishcloth, wrung out and used up. She hadn't understood his wildman performance, or the gleam of satisfaction in his eyes when she'd arched and whimpered in her release.

"Are you all right, sweetheart?" she heard him whisper softly against her temple. His hand, big and warm, was still cupped over her, lightly pressing and stroking, as if he wanted more from her. She could feel the wetness from both of them on his fingers.

But she didn't have anything more to give him. She wondered if she'd ever understand men, this one man in particular. She managed to nod against his shoulder before she fell into an exhausted sleep.

Chapter Seventeen

"**D**amnation! Hold it! I want the tree thinned, not denuded!"

The tree man turned off his electric saw and stared down at Lord Asherwood. "What did you say, sir?"

Brant lowered his voice. "I'll point to the branches I want you to take off, okay?"

Daphne, who was coming around from her now-budding rose garden, stopped and grinned. The tree man, Tommy Orville, had a wounded look on his round face. She stood quietly, watching Brant point patiently to a particular dried up branch. He looked so bloody handsome, she thought, her eyes roving over his body. He was wearing a red-and-white Astros sweatshirt, and a pair of very well worn and tight jeans. His thick dark hair shone in the bright afternoon sunlight. Passion was such a nice thing, she reflected, glad she'd discovered it before she'd gotten too much older. She'd asked Brant once after recovering from what she termed bouts of marriage, if it was always like this, and if it was, why people ever got divorced. He'd given her a long, lazy look and assured her that she was the luckiest woman he knew.

"Because you're the world greatest lover?" she'd said with laughing sarcasm.

"You'd give me your vote, wouldn't you?"

When she'd paused, trying to come up with a retort, he had gently begun to caress her breast and nibble on that very sensitive spot just below her right ear. "I give up," she'd giggled. "You're the world's greatest everything!"

"You ain't so bad yourself, cookie," he'd said.

She wondered, though, gazing at him now, if he were as pleased with her as she was with him. Shut away at Asherwood as they had been for three months now, he certainly seemed to be contented. The restoration of the Hall took up a great deal of their time, but they had taken off days at a time to travel, once to Glasgow to visit Aunt Cloe, another up to York, another to the Lake District to stay on Lake Widemere. He seemed fascinated with Daphne's historical tales of all the sites they visited. Stonehenge had been his favorite. "Like huge football players in a huddle," he'd announced. It was like the continuation of their honeymoon.

The electric saw died once again, for the last time. Tommy climbed carefully down and cocked a faded brown eyebrow at Brant.

"That'll be all, thank you," Brant said. "Great job. Hey, Daph, what do you think?"

"Magnificent. Say hello to your sister for me, Tommy."

"Sure thing, Daphne," Tommy said.

"I'm so glad you're using local talent," Daphne said to her husband.

"It was a close thing. I'm glad I came out in time to save the tree from getting a flat top. How's your rose garden coming?"

"Come and see." She tucked her hand in his and lengthened her stride to match his. "Can we afford a gardener to keep things in shape after we go home?"

Home, he thought, smiling down at her. So New York was now home to her, was it? "Yes," he said, "I think we can manage it. I'll probably have to sell the condo and the Porsche, but roses are important, I know, and I wouldn't—"

She poked him in the ribs. "I'll pay for it once I liquidate some of my investments. Hmmm," she added, running her hands over his ribs, "nice."

In the next instant she was squealing. Brant's hand was under her loose top, inching around to cup her breast. "Brant, stop it! What if someone—"

"Just returning the favor, ma'am. You're not bad yourself, and no bra." He felt her quicken and grinned wickedly down at her. "You sure you want to show me the roses now? There's that other lovely garden you just might invite me to play in."

"You're terrible! So you did read some Greek plays in college. All right, I've decided it's time to have my way with you."

She did, to Brant's exhausted delight.

Daphne eased out of bed, leaving Brant sprawled on his back, beautifully naked and asleep. Just like in Hawaii, she thought, studying him in the dying afternoon light. I sure know a lot more about things than I did then, she thought, smiling. Well, she was no longer a naive twit, she thought as she climbed back onto the bed, leaned down on her hands and knees, and rained light kisses over his belly. He mumbled something in his sleep, and she kept kissing, lower. She was totally absorbed in her explorations when she heard him say softly, "Lovely view," and felt his hand lightly stroke over her bottom. He moaned suddenly, his body jerking, and she forgot her temporary embarrassment at him gazing at her backside, her legs slightly parted.

"Daph, sweetheart, you'd better stop before it's too late." He tangled his fingers in the veil of hair that covered her face, and tugged, but she wouldn't release him. "Daph," he managed once again, then gave up, expelling a sigh of pure pleasure.

"What's Winterspoon making for dinner?" he asked her sometime later. He'd wondered for a while if he'd ever be able to talk again.

"I haven't the vaguest idea," Daphne said, burrowing closer. "Sex and food. Is that all you jocks think about?"

"Just food, for the moment. I'll eat anything that doesn't bounce around on my plate. Woman, you wore me out."

"You deserved it," she said, her voice complacent. "I didn't want you to get the idea that only you could initiate...things."

"I swear that's the kind of idea men hate. Anytime you want to ravish my poor body, you go right ahead." She ran her palm down his chest to his belly. "But not right at this moment," he added. "The spirit is willing, but nothing else, I'm afraid."

"I love your spirit," she giggled. "And everything else."

"Good. We're leaving for Paris tomorrow. Say for a week?"

"Brant!" She threw herself on top of him and planted a wet kiss on his mouth.

His hand gently cupped her. "There are so many beautiful gardens in Paris, after all."

"Jerk."

Daphne's feelings were mixed when they returned to New York in mid-June. It was the real world, and she wasn't at all sure that she was ready for it. They flew back on the Concord, a special treat for both of them, and arrived shortly after they'd left London.

"Sir, ma'am," Winterspoon greeted them, flourishing a silver tray of canapés for their welcome home. He'd flown back a week earlier to "set everything to rights," he'd told Brant.

"And champagne, Winterspoon?" Brant asked.

"Champagne!" Daphne exclaimed. "Is this going to be an orgy or something?"

"Well, almost," Brant said, smiling down at her. "One glass and I've got a something to show you."

"Oh?" she asked, slanting him a provocative look.

The something was a new Mercedes 380 SL, silver body with black leather interior. Daphne stared at it, then at her husband. "So that's what your mysterious phone calls were all about."

"Yep."

"And all your ever-so-subtle questions about my preferences about this and that?"

"Yep. If you'll remember, I always asked after we'd made love. I knew your mind would be well beyond suspicious thoughts."

"Very low, Brant, very low."

"That too. You've got to name her and take me for a ride."

By the time Brant left for training camp in upstate New York, nearly every member of the Astros and their spouses had ridden in Gwendolyn, and the car and Daphne were a well-known sight to the doorman, Max.

"I wish," Daphne said on a small sigh to Tiffy Richardson one afternoon as she was cruising Gwendolyn toward Tiffy's home in Westchester, "that we could go up to the training camp."

"I used to wish the same thing," said Tiffy, patting Daphne's knee, "but Guy assured me, as I'm sure Brant did you, that there's absolutely nothing to do, since they're stuck out in the middle of nowhere, and after practice they're all dead."

"Still..." Daphne began.

"You miss him, I know. But it won't be much longer now. The first exhibition game is August 14, against the Lions."

"We'll butcher them," Daphne said with relish. "Their offense relies primarily on the running game, and their defense stinks against the pass. Tiny was telling me—"

"Good grief, Daph! You've really gotten into football, haven't you?"

"I love the game, it's true, and I bought lots of books on football at Barnes and Noble, and Brant's got a huge video collection of games. I'm talking too much, aren't I?"

Tiffy laughed. "No, not at all. I love to hear your starchy English accent when you talk about football. Tell me," she continued without a pause, "how do you like marriage to Brant Asher?"

"Former playboy of the western world?"

"I believe former is the operative world," said Tiffy.

Daphne looked straight ahead at the highway and chewed a moment on her lower lip. "I think the question should be how does he like marriage to me? He's a gentleman, you know. Always says and does the right thing, sticks to his bargain and all that."

"No," Tiffy repeated, "how do you like marriage to him?" Bargain? she wondered silently. What bargain?

"I guess," Daphne said on a long sigh, "that I love him dearly."

"I'm glad to hear it. Brant deserves the best, and I think you're it, Daph."

"The best? Me? I'm really not sure of that, Tiffy. As I said, Brant's a gentleman." And he's never told me he loves me. She thought of all his love words, sometimes slurred when his need for her was great, but never a simple declaration over dinner, say, with Winterspoon in the kitchen. *Well, you haven't said anything either, idiot!* But she'd wanted to. Coward, that's what she was. He was such a gentleman that he'd probably say it back to her out of politeness and concern for her feelings.

"You're not still worried about Marcie, are you?"

"Oh no. I saw her last week at the theatre—I was with Brant's mother—and she was really quite nice. She's been a real brick. Brant's mother, that is."

"You're lucky. My mother-in-law is the martyr type. Drives me nuts. And, of course, whenever she visits us, she treats Guy like he's God's gift to the universe. He's impossible for a good two weeks after she leaves."

They spoke of Tiffy's two children and her interior decorating business, a growing concern in the past year.

"Will you be flying to Detroit for the game?" Daphne asked.

"Oh no. It's just an exhibition game. Guy shouldn't play more than two quarters at most. Sam'll want to give the new guys a chance to perform. Even Brant shouldn't play all that much. Evan Murphy has got to have some practice quarterbacking."

"Yes, I know." *In case Brant ever gets injured.* "But I'm going. I think even Winterspoon wants to give it a try. 'Bloody barbaric,' he calls it, but I've seen him reading some of my books."

"An English butler!" Tiffy laughed.

"It does boggle the mind, doesn't it?"

Daphne spent the final week before Brant's return from training camp with Alice Asher in Connecticut. And on a side street in Stamford one hot afternoon she nearly met her Waterloo, as she later told Alice in the hospital.

"Broadsided by a truck carrying Miller beer as I tried to avoid that boy on his bike. There must be some irony in there somewhere. It's not fair. What will Brant say?" She turned alarmed eyes to her mother-in-law. "I'm okay, Alice, really. You won't call Brant, will you?"

"Hush now, honey. You're very lucky, only a couple of bruised ribs and a mild concussion. And of course I called Brant. You were dead to the world for quite a long time."

"Oh, I wish you hadn't. This is the last thing he needs. He's got to concentrate on football, not get sidetracked by me and Gwen."

"If Gwen looks as good as you do, sweetheart, I won't say a single word."

"Brant!"

He walked over to her bed, leaned down and carefully studied her face. "You all right, woman driver?"

"It wasn't my fault," she said indignantly. "I did everything right, and if it hadn't been for that stupid beer—'' He kissed her pursed lips. "And Alice said that Gwen is an awful mess."

"I'll have a look at her later. Not to worry." He picked up her hand and absently began to stroke her fingers. "What's all this nonsense about sidetracking me from football? Don't be an idiot. You're my wife."

"But the game plan for the Lions!" she wailed. "Watching their tapes, strategy…"

"Shush. I left Evan Murphy chomping at the bit. I like that little bruise over your right eye. Gives you a rakish look." His voice was light, because he'd spoken to her doctor briefly before coming into her room and knew she was all right. "You scared the hell out of me, you know."

Daphne gave Alice a reproachful look. "You shouldn't have worried him," she said.

"That's what husbands are for, honey," Alice said. "Now, I'm going to leave you two alone for a little while. Not too long, Brant; she still has the remains of a concussion."

"You make it sound like the leftovers from a meal," Daphne said.

Brant waited until his mother had closed the hospital door behind her, then seated himself on the bed beside his wife. He pulled back the covers and eased up her hospital gown.

"Whatever are you doing?" Daphne asked, wondering crazily if he wanted to make love to her, here in the hospital, with the nurses clustered not ten feet away at their station.

"Your ribs," he said, and bared them. "Pretty impressive," he said finally, staring at the dark purple and yellow streaks below her left breast. Actually, he tried to keep from swallowing convulsively, even though he knew they weren't broken. His mother's telephone call had done more than scare the hell out of him. He'd felt cold, clammy and seared with fear until she'd finally managed to convince him that Daphne was all right.

"I'll be able to make the exhibition game, I promise," she said. "I won't let you down again, Brant."

He looked briefly at her flat stomach before he carefully eased her hospital gown down over her ribs and pulled the starchy sheet and light blanket back up.

"We'll see about the game," he said, briefly closing his eyes. He wondered if he should tell her that she'd miscarried. No, it wouldn't make any difference, and it would likely make her feel guilty. Early days, the doctor had told him. Barely seven weeks, if that. He shook his head, reaffirming his silent decision.

He felt her fingers tighten over his. "What's the matter, Brant? I'll bet you're very tired from your trip."

"I wish you'd think only about yourself for once. Who the hell cares if I'm tired or not?"

She started at his harsh tone, but her head had begun to ache with a vengeance. "I care," she said quietly. "I care very much."

He saw the brief look of pain in her eyes and rose. "Is it time for a pain pill?"

"Probably," she said, turning her head very slowly to look at him. "I'm feeling completely sober, and they don't seem to like that."

"I'll talk to the nurse. You rest now, love, and I'll see you this evening."

"Will you go look at Gwen?"

"I'll even make sure she gets a pain pill."

Daph had been lucky, very lucky, he thought later as he eyed her Mercedes. The beer truck had hit the passenger side. He started to sweat again, and the humid Connecticut weather had nothing to do with it. He rubbed his hand over his forehead, and the ignoble thought occurred to him that he wouldn't be able to make love to her for a good three weeks. How to convince her not to, he wondered. He shook his head to clear it when he saw the bodyshop owner walking toward him.

Brant flew back to training camp three days later with Daphne's promise that she would remain with his mother and take it easy.

"You can't do anything else anyway," he told her. "Gwendolyn won't be ready to hit the road again for another week."

She hugged him exuberantly and promptly winced from the pain in her ribs. He stroked his fingertips over her smooth cheek. "I'll call you tonight, sweetheart, okay?"

Winterspoon closed up the condo and arrived in Connecticut that afternoon. "You will take care of Miss Daphne," he told Alice Asher, "and I'll see to the meals."

"It beats me how he only had to say that and I folded my tent and retired from the field," Alice said later to Daphne.

"Winterspoon is an autocrat, but a benign one," Daphne said, smiling. She knew not to laugh; it still hurt.

During the next week Alice was to shake her head several times. Daphne had been so unsure of herself, but the constant stream of visitors, all wives of the football players, made Alice realize soon enough that her daughter-in-law was very well-liked indeed.

On August 13, she blinked in surprise upon entering Daphne's bedroom. Daphne was packing.

"I'm going to Detroit to see Brant play," Daphne said firmly.

"Shouldn't you talk to the doctor—"

"Winterstoon is driving me over in about thirty minutes for a final checkup. I'm fine, Alice, really."

"But what will Brant say?"

Daphne twinkled at her. "He doesn't know. It's a surprise."

Chapter Eighteen

Dr. Lowery was running late, and Daphne fidgeted in the waiting room, thumbing through one magazine, then another. Not one sports magazine, she thought, disgruntled.

"Mrs. Asher?"

"Yes," Daphne said, rising to face the nurse.

"Dr. Lowery will be with you in just a few minutes. Why don't you come with me to the examining room?"

Daphne dutifully followed the nurse into a small, sterile room and sat down on the single chair. The nurse handed her a paper gown and fiddled with instruments while Daphne stripped.

"Why do I have to change into this thing?" Daphne asked, looking askance at the paper gown. "It's just my ribs and head."

"Dr. Lowery will want to do a quick internal exam," said the nurse.

"Why?" Daphne asked, frowning. "I had a complete exam just about six months ago."

"I'm sure she'll want to check that you're all right after the miscarriage."

Daphne stared at her. "Miscarriage?" Her voice was thin and high.

The nurse turned and smiled at her. "Not to worry, Mrs. Asher. It's standard procedure, you know, and you were only about seven weeks along. I'm certain you're just fine."

She gave Daphne a reassuring pat on the shoulder and left the small room. Like an automaton, Daphne changed into the ridiculously embarrassing paper gown and perched on the edge of the examining table. *I lost a baby and nobody bothered to tell me about it. Dear God, I didn't even know I was pregnant.* She reviewed the previous weeks before the accident in her mind, realizing that she had missed a period. But she hadn't really thought about it. And she'd never felt ill. She stared at the white walls, her eyes widening. Did Brant know?

"Good afternoon, Mrs. Asher. My, but you're looking lovely and tip-top again."

Daphne said, without preamble, "Why didn't you tell me I'd miscarried, Dr. Lowery?"

Lorraine Lowery knew it had been a mistake to keep that information from Daphne. She should never have let Brant Asher talk her into it. And Jane Coggins, her talkative nurse, must have inadvertently spilled the beans. She sighed and sat down, gathering words together. "You were out of things for quite a while," she said finally, deciding she'd assume the responsibility for the omission. "We asked your mother-in-law if you were pregnant, and she said no, of course. That's standard procedure before we order any x-rays. The accident caused you to miscarry, but we would have had to abort in any case after the series of x-rays were completed. There was nothing anyone could have done. I'm sorry, Mrs. Asher."

Daphne nodded, mute. *You caused it, you fool, in that damned accident!*

Daphne knew about x-rays and pregnant women. She silently endured the examination, answering Dr. Lowery's questions in terse monosyllables.

"Why don't you get dressed and come into my office?" Dr. Lowery said when she was done. Daphne nodded, waiting until she was alone to scoot off the table and change.

When she was sitting across from the doctor, she wanted desperately to ask if Brant knew of the miscarriage, but she was afraid to hear the answer. Of course he didn't know, or else he would have said something to her.

"Your ribs are just fine. You no longer look like a foreign flag. You said you no longer have any headaches, so we can safely assume everything is back to normal there." She paused a moment, tapping her pen on her desktop. "If you wish to become pregnant again, Mrs. Asher, I would advise that you wait for another three months or so. We want your body to have time to heal itself."

"It will be longer than that," Daphne said. "Football season starts in a couple of weeks. I don't want to be pregnant and traveling all over the country at the same time."

"You had no idea you were pregnant?"

Daphne shook her head, her eyes on her fingernails.

"Well, these things happen. Be thankful you weren't farther along. As to sexual relations with your husband, I suggest you wait another week or so." Dr. Lowery rose and extended her hand. Daphne shook it silently. "Have a visit with Dr. Mason in New York in three months, okay? She'll just doublecheck for you. Good luck to your husband and the Astros, Mrs. Asher.''

Sure, Daphne thought as she left the doctor's office. Easy for her to say. Good luck to the football team. Case closed. Too bad, but it was all for the best. Daphne closed her eyes against the bright sunlight. She wouldn't tell Brant. She couldn't. She didn't know how he would react. Did her mother-in-law know? She wouldn't ask her. She wouldn't mention it to anyone. It was done, over with. She would forget it, in time.

"Are you all right, ma'am?" Winterspoon asked as he opened the passenger door for her.

"What? Oh yes, Winterspoon, I'm fine. Just fine.''

The game wasn't even a contest, Daphne thought in disgust as the final seconds ticked off. The Astros won 35 to 7, the Lions' only score coming on a thirty-yard run in the third quarter. Brant had played magnificently, his body agile, the announcers applauding his talent and throwing arm. She'd yelled herself hoarse. She hadn't sat with the few wives present, most of them rookies' wives, not wanting to chance any of the players looking at their special section and telling Brant she was there.

She walked down the stadium steps and positioned herself outside the Astros' locker room. A smile tugged at her lips as she thought of the look on Brant's face when he saw her. She couldn't wait to tell him that no pro football player could be better than number 12, or more handsome in the white uniform with its red lettering.

A man asked, "Are you a wife of one of the players, ma'am?"

She turned and her radiant smile encompassed him. "Yes. I'm Mrs. Asher.''

"Ah, the English heiress," the man said, enthusiasm over his surprise discovery raising his voice a half octave.

"No, the English *wife*. Wasn't that Lions' fumble crazy? It looked like that game—hot potato—for a few minutes." Her eyes began to shine. "Brant is in excellent shape, isn't he? So graceful. It's as if the ball is an extension of his arm. And he runs as swiftly as any of the backs. Lloyd's three touchdown catches—he must have jumped a good three feet to bring the ball in." She continued speaking to her increasingly appreciative audience of one, recounting points of strategy, the performance of the different players in exquisite detail, the obvious outcome. "We're going to the Superbowl this year. Yes, we are.''

Mac Dreyfus wrote as quickly as he could. The girl was a natural. She knew the game. And she was English. It was amazing. Absolutely amazing. He waved to his partner, Tim Maloney. Neither of them had wanted to cover the exhibition game. Lord, what a great break! When Brant finally emerged from the locker room he was met by a brilliantly smiling wife who threw herself into his arms. He kissed her and heard the flash-bulb go off.

"Great game, Brant," Mac said jovially. "And a great wife. Nice to have met you, ma'am."

Other players gathered around Daphne, and Brant heard her giving them all a rundown on the health, current moods and thoughts of their wives, children and pets. He saw Mac Dreyfus turn in his tracks, an arrested look in his eyes. Brant found himself wondering if she ever forgot anything as he listened to her compliment each player on a specific play in which he had been the key. They basked in her praise.

It was close to thirty minutes before they were alone. Daphne hugged him again. "I love Detroit," she said. "I want to stay a day or two and visit one of the automobile places."

"This is quite a surprise," he said once he could get in a word edge-wise.

"Yes, isn't it?" Her smile was sunny, guileless.

"Are you sure you're all right?"

"Winterspoon gave me his stamp of approval," she said. "You were truly brilliant, Brant. It was such a thrill to watch you play in person. I've already arranged for us to get our own tape of the game in less than a week. You know, though, that new pass interference rule is going to cause some problems for a while, I think. You must remind the guys to be sure to *look* back toward the ball before they cream the receiver. Danny looked so furious when he got called, but it was legitimate."

He stopped a moment and gazed down at her. "You're something else, you know that?"

"Just don't squeeze me too hard for a while, okay?" She grinned, wrapping her arms around his waist and hugging.

To her surprise, his eyes darkened with worry.

"My ribs are fine," she said. "Please, there's nothing more to worry about, Brant."

He wasn't thinking about her ribs, but, of course, she couldn't know that. How, he wondered, am I going to keep her from lovemaking tonight? He was certain he shouldn't touch her for another week or so. She had to have time to heal.

"God, I'm happy to see you," he said, and kissed her deeply. "Now, wife, you're going to get your first dose of after-the-game aches and pains from your husband." He flexed his throwing arm.

"I'll rub you all over, I promise," Daphne said. "You only got sacked once. You hurt from that?"

"Nothing a little wifely tender loving care won't cure. You wanna play in the Jacuzzi, little girl?"

"We don't even have to go to California."

* * *

It was, of course, a mistake, but Brant figured the only obvious part of him was underwater, if Daphne would only keep her hands to herself. She did for a while, gently massaging his shoulders, but when she climbed into the swirling water with him, gorgeously naked, he groaned mentally. Distract her and yourself, you idiot, he thought, aware only of her beautiful breasts pressing against his chest.

"Mom's okay?"

"Humm? Oh yes, she's just fine and sends her love. Cloe called and wished you luck, and Winterspoon watched the game on TV."

I don't feel sore at all, Daphne was thinking. And I haven't for days now. No, not sore at all. Dr. Lowery's instruction had just been a suggestion, at least that was how she now chose to interpret it. She wanted her husband, very much, and made no attempt to stem her rising desire for him. She also had a supply of pills, so there was no danger of her getting pregnant until it was safe to do so. Her palm glided down her husband's chest to his belly, paused just a moment, and found him. Ah, she thought, smiling, he wasn't at all indifferent.

"Daph, don't," Brant said, his teeth gritted.

"Why? Haven't you missed me?"

"I'm tired and sore, and only interested locally. Please, sweetheart, not tonight. I feel like I'm an old man."

"I understand," she said, but he saw the confusion in her eyes.

He cursed fluently in his mind. Deception led to ridiculous problems. Here he was, ready to ravish her, yet he couldn't but she didn't know he couldn't. Damn.

"I'm glad you came," he said, drawing a deep breath. "Mac Dreyfus is probably half in love with you. I saw him staring at you in the most fascinated way."

"He just wanted to talk about the game after he got over that stupid English heiress bit. So we did. I probably bored him silly. Is he a sports writer?"

"Yeah, with the Chicago *Sun*. Let's get out of this thing before we turn into prunes."

She insisted on drying him, trying him to the limit. And she wore no nightgown to bed. He groaned when she wrapped herself around him. He could feel her heartbeat, erratic and fast. At least he could ease her, he thought, smiling into the darkness. He pressed her onto her back, balancing himself on his elbow beside her. "Just hold still," he said, and kissed her mouth at the same time his fingers found her. Her quick, surprised intake of breath delighted him. Lord but she was responsive. He wished the light was on when he felt her body begin to quiver. He wanted to see her face. She clutched at him frantically, her last rational thought being that if he was too tired to make love to her, where was he getting the energy for this?

She cried out, and he covered her, taking her moans into his mouth.

"You are the most perfect husband in the whole world," she murmured vaguely as she nestled against him.

He grinned, a bit painfully, and kissed her temple. "You're right," he said.

He awoke from the most intense erotic dream he'd ever experienced, only to realize that it was all too real. Early morning sunlight was filtering through the shades of their hotel room, but it took a moment for him to focus on his wife, who was covering his lower body with her own, her soft mouth caressing him. He couldn't hold back, and his moan of raw pleasure filled the silent room.

"Now, Brant, aren't I the most perfect wife in the whole world?" she asked, grinning up the length of his body.

"I'll let you know when and if I come back from the dead."

She giggled. "You only have about thirty minutes. I ordered breakfast from room service."

It was closer to fifteen minutes later when they were sitting on the bed, breakfast trays on their laps. Brant drank some of the hot black coffee and absently turned the pages of the Detroit paper to the sports section. He set down his coffee cup, very slowly and very carefully. There was a good-sized picture of Daphne kissing him enthusiastically, the caption beneath: "English Wife All-American."

"Good grief," he said, and handed Daphne the paper.

"That's a pun, isn't it? That All-American bit?" she asked in the most pleased voice he'd ever heard.

"Yes," he said, "it is. Mac likes that sort of thing."

"Listen to this, Brant. 'Daphne Asher is probably giving tips to her quarterback husband as well as all the other Astros players. Her understanding of the game is astounding, given the fact she only heard of football six months ago. Take this in, coaches—'" Daphne paused, quickly scanning the rest of the article. "I don't believe this, Brant, he's practically quoted me! It's crazy."

She handed the paper back. Brant read quickly, feeling somewhat dazed. He laid the paper on the bed and asked, "I knew you were learning at a great rate, but this—"

"I've been doing quite a bit of reading," she interrupted him, her voice demure, "and watching lots of films."

"It looks like the world is changing fast. My world, that is."

"Yes," she said, forking down a bite of scrambled eggs, "you're a married man. It's gotta change."

Gotta he thought. How long before she lost her English accent?

He enjoyed her growing popularity with the press until after the game with the Cowboys.

Chapter Nineteen

Brant, sore, bruised and bone-weary from the hard game with the Cowboys, a game they'd lost, stood staring at Daphne, unable to take in what she was saying. He wondered vaguely if Winterspoon, cooking something very English in the kitchen, was listening.

"...so first I'd be doing straight interviews, then by season, if everything goes well, I'll actually be involved in the halftime talks."

Daphne, so excited she could barely talk straight, continued after a tiny pause, "And you'll not believe this, Brant! Maybe, just maybe, I'll be the first woman to actually do the play-by-play. Actually cover the games while they're happening! Joe Namath. Frank Gifford. O.J.—"

"Good God, Daph, hold it a minute." He shook his head, trying to get his mental bearings. "What the hell are you talking about? A network has offered you a sports job?"

"Yes, and they want me to interview my husband, Brant the Dancer, first! Oh, Brant, can you just imagine it? Interviewing you, and we can talk about all the players and your going to the Superbowl! Mr. Irving said that—"

"I don't believe this," he interrupted her in a stunned, incredulous voice. "Why the hell would they offer you a job like that?"

"A Scotch, neat, sir."

"What? Oh, Winterspoon. Thanks." Thank the Lord he'd made it a double.

"Just the thing, sir, to clear away confusion."

"A start, in any case." Brant downed the Scotch and wiped the back of his hand across his mouth. "I'm going to the Jacuzzi," he said. "To clear away more confusion."

Daphne blinked at his back and opened her mouth, only to be forestalled by Winterspoon's calm reflections. "You know how he is after a game, Miss Daphne, and that sack in the third quarter by that brute probably shook his insides."

"But this is important, Winterspoon!" She rushed toward the bedroom after her husband. She saw a trail of clothes leading to the bathroom and grinned, momentarily diverted. His socks were always the last item to go, the left one specifically. He was standing in front of the mirror, slowly and carefully flexing his throwing arm. Daphne bit down on her enthusiasm.

"I've got to talk to the guys on the line, Brant," she said, pursing her lips. "It was Phil, mainly. He left a hole as wide as the Lincoln Tunnel. That's why they made a sandwich of you."

"Daphne," he said, and she started at the use of her full name. "You won't talk to Phil or anyone. You got that?"

"You're just tired and...cranky," she said, giving him a maternal pat on his shoulder. "Come on into the Jacuzzi."

"I am tired, but I'm not a damned five-year-old! Now, why don't you exit and go flutter around Winterspoon? You can offer to threaten the potatoes for him."

She stiffened, watching him with quickly narrowing eyes as he climbed into the swirling hot water. "You don't have to be nasty," she said, her voice as stiff as her back. "And I wasn't *fluttering*; I was trying to be nice and understanding."

Brant closed his eyes and leaned his head back against the tub. "Well, from the sound of it, I won't have to endure your niceness much longer, will I?"

"Just what is that supposed to mean?"

He cocked an eye open to see her standing, hands on hips, beside the tub. "It means that you'll cease being a wife when and if you accept this TV deal."

"What a stupid, mean thing to say! Of course I'm your wife. If I weren't, I doubt anyone would be interested in anything I had to say, regardless of whether I knew a smidgeon about football or not."

"A smidgeon is about all you do know, and I'm glad you finally realize why anyone would offer you anything!"

"Oh, I see now," she said, fury rising to the boiling point. "If it weren't for the great Brant Asher, shortened from Asherwood—the way you Americans shorten and change and butcher everything—I'd still be counting eggs and pruning roses at the Hall, afraid of my own shadow!"

"You got it, lady. Now, will you please just leave me alone?"

Daphne grabbed a washcloth and flung it at him, striking his face. Brant peeled it off and tossed it to the bathroom floor. "Talk about five-year-olds," he muttered.

"I'm not leaving," Daphne said between gritted teeth. "And I'm beginning to think that it would be just great if I didn't have to put up with your wretched aches and pains after every bloody game!''

"You won't, if you take that job. That kind of thing is demanding as hell. You'd barely have time to send me mailgrams.''

"I'd be earning a lot of money, Brant. I could even afford to call you once in a while.''

"I got it now. How many more credit cards do you want? How many more little pieces of paper that prove you're worth something?''

"I am worth something, you...you cad!''

"Back to the 19th century again.'' He sighed. "Why does it bother you so much that I'm the breadwinner in this family? We have a very comfortable life; Gwen will be back on her wheels in no time—''

"I don't understand why you're not thrilled about all this. And this has nothing to do with you making all the money. What do you want, a—a stick in the dirt?''

"Mud,'' he said. "You've been about as much a stick as I've been a hockey player.''

He rose, reaching for a towel. "You wanna be a good little wife and dry my back for me?''

"I'd rather cut your throat!''

"So much for pleasant married life.''

"I'm leaving,'' Daphne said, her body rigid with anger.

"As I recall, I asked you to several times.'' He continued drying himself, then tossed the towel on the floor and strode back to the bedroom. He eased onto the bed and stretched his arms above his head. "You still here?'' he asked.

"Is this how you treated Marcie and all your other women?'' she asked, her voice trembling with an effort at sarcasm.

"No. If you weren't here and Marcie were, she'd be doing all sorts of marvelous things to make me forget my aches and pains.''

Daphne sucked in her breath. "I can do those things, too.''

"Then why aren't you? Why are you harping on that ludicrous plan of yours to gain fame and fortune off your husband's name?''

It was cruel, and he knew it, but her next words made him forget every conciliatory word he'd ever considered saying.

"Damn you, Brant Asher! I don't need your name! I can and will do it all myself!''

"How can you be so damned stupid?'' He jerked upright, anger and frustration churning in him. "If I hadn't agreed to marry you, you'd be whatever Lucilla told you to be, a wretched little file clerk, probably, in a dingy London office. That, or you'd be buried away in Glasgow with Aunt Cloe while she, poor lady, would be trying to marry you off to some unsuspecting soul with credit cards and a profession you'd try to dominate.''

"I could marry anyone I wanted to! Dominate! God, I just don't believe you. Ha! You begged me to marry you."

"Begged, hell. It did, I'll admit, seem like quite a good idea at the time. Here was poor little Daphne, helpless, insecure, with about as much confidence as a drowned rat—"

"Stop it!"

"Why should I? It's the truth, isn't it?"

"I'm not insecure anymore! I'm competent now, and I can do anything, and—"

"Damn it, you couldn't even manage to drive competently enough to keep from losing the baby!"

She froze, her eyes glazing in shock and pain.

Brant cursed himself royally. He rose quickly from the bed, and, to his shock, she backed away from him. He stretched out his hand toward her. "Daph, I'm sorry. I didn't mean that. I've got a big mouth and—"

"You knew," she said dully, turning away from him, her arms clutched about her chest. "And you didn't tell me. I had to find out from a big-mouthed nurse."

He went after her and pulled her rigid body against him. "It was my decision not to tell you, love. The doctor thought you should know, but I insisted. I didn't want you to feel guilty or anything. I'm sorry, but when I get mad I shoot my mouth off. Please, Daph, forgive me."

"That's why you didn't make love with me in Detroit."

"You had to heal. Besides, I did give you pleasure, and I thought you enjoyed it."

He felt her hands flutter against her chest, but she said nothing.

"We can have kids, love, whenever you want."

"Don't call me *love*," she said, her voice steely. "Ours was an old-fashioned marriage of convenience; you know it as well as I do. You saved me from a wretched life; you don't have to remind me of that fact. And you're right. It's not proper of me to take advantage of you and your profession, to dominate, to stick myself in where I obviously don't belong."

He'd rather have her mad and spitting at him, he realized, listening to her emotionless voice against his shoulder. He felt like a prize jerk, a 19th-century cad, and he wished he had another Scotch, neat. What to say to her, what to do? Why had he flown off the handle at her like that? Dumb bastard! He stroked his hands down her arms.

"Daph, about that offer from the network, forget all that nonsense I spouted, please. It's your decision. Really."

She felt his hands move from her arms to begin gently massaging her shoulders, then rove down her back, hugging her more tightly against him. How stupid she'd been to believe he'd be as excited as she was over the offer. He'd kept to his part of the bargain, treating her well, staying faithful to her even when she'd acted like a total twit and nitwit. Why isn't it nit-twit? she thought crazily. But she'd seen what he really thought of her, despite his reassurances now. She understood. Slowly she eased away from him.

"Thank you," she said, not meeting his eyes. "Would you like to rest before dinner? I'll tell Winterspoon to hold it back for as long as you want. I think it's a pot roast, so it shouldn't be a problem. He's...teaching me how to cook, a bit. I'll call you in an hour?"

He let her go, watched her walk to the bedroom door. He stared after her, feeling utterly helpless. "An hour," he repeated. She didn't slam the bedroom door. He wished she had. No, she just slipped through it like a lifeless ghost. He threw himself back down on the bed and stared at the ceiling. Why don't you just admit the truth, at least to yourself, you idiot? Your overblown reaction was because you're afraid of losing her. You want all of her—her zest, her excitement, her caring, her *presence*—you want to know that she's cheering or booing in the stands while you're playing. You don't want her leaving you. You love her, fool. The admission made his guts churn. He'd believed he was immune, and he'd been more or less content to have that vague emptiness in his life. Until Daphne. He wondered now how long he'd loved her. This love business was sneaky, consuming him before he'd realized he'd been had. Oh yes, he'd loved her a long time, but had just been too blind and insensitive to realize it. He started to jump out of bed, to yell it to her, hell, to yell it to all New York. He stopped cold, falling back. She'd never believe him now.

She probably believed now that he was so small-minded, so much a male chauvinist, that he couldn't bear the thought of his wife having a life apart from him. Dog-in-the-manger syndrome, one of his shrink friends had tagged such behavior. No, he was certain he wasn't guilty of that. It wasn't that he was at all threatened by the notion of her success. He remembered Jayne, a professional model who at the time had earned more money than he had. It hadn't bothered him a bit. And Lisa Cormanth, a computer genius. And Marcie Ellis, a very successful journalist. No, boiled down to a proper pulp, he simply wanted his wife with him. He wanted to wallow in his good fortune. Some good fortune his mouth had provided him with now. She was probably ready to toss him out the door and good riddance to him.

And he'd thrown up her miscarriage at her. It occurred to him to wonder why she hadn't told him about it—unless, of course, she'd already known that he'd known. He saw again the pain in her eyes. She'd been carrying around that damned misery by herself, never letting on to him, not worrying him, protecting him, not wanting him to feel pain. And guilt? No, that was ridiculous. The accident hadn't been her fault.

Maybe she's still insecure enough to think you'd hate her if you knew about the miscarriage. That's why she never discussed it with you.

He groaned. He knew her thinking processes well enough to realize it was a possibility, a definite possibility.

But maybe, just maybe, she wanted to be away from him. After his sterling performance in the bathroom, maybe she couldn't wait to sign a contract with the network. Maybe she didn't feel anything close to what he felt about her.

When he emerged from the bedroom thirty minutes later, his agile tongue was a lead weight in his mouth. There was too much at stake, too much to lose, to go spouting off without careful consideration. He'd never felt so scared, so emptied of confidence, in his life.

What he managed to say over dinner, apart from chirpy comments on the weather, was, "Will you please come to Houston next week for the game with the Oilers? We can see Dusty, Lily and the kids while we're there, maybe stay for Thanksgiving."

Daphne looked up from her boiled potatoes after carefully shoving aside sprigs of parsley. Winterspoon loved greenery on a plate. She felt the tension radiating from him, though he spoke calmly, with no emotion in his voice. She studied the stark lines of his face, the high cheekbones, the rakish slant of his dark eyebrows. She loved him so much it hurt.

"Daphne?"

"Yes," she said finally, "I'll be there." Her voice was as calm and flat as his, but with new eyes he saw the uncertainty, the insecurity, in hers.

What to say? What to do?

He was a very physical man. Every woman he'd known intimately had teased him about being oversexed. He'd show her his love for her in bed. But later. Sex simply postponed problems; it didn't solve them.

He watched the distance stretch between them all evening. Her marvelous vivacity, her delightful laugh, had become tense wariness. They played three-handed Hearts with Winterspoon, and the supposed neophyte trounced both of them. "Well, sir," Winterspoon said, "it's only ten dollars, after all."

Much later, after careful and thorough foreplay, Brant watched her face as her body clenched with convulsive pleasure. "God, you're beautiful," he whispered. Daphne, whose body had unconsciously fought against satisfaction, felt as though she were drowning. When he entered her, gently, fully, she gasped with the wonder of it. "Brant, I—"

"I want you to be happy," he said into her mouth as he moved over her. "I want you to be happy with me."

She moaned softly against his shoulder, arching up, bringing him deeper, making him one with her.

"I want you to be happy," he said again, his words widely spaced as he gritted his teeth on the brink of his own release.

Only an absolute fool could be unhappy with him, she thought, dazed. "I want that, too," she whispered, her voice lost and helpless. She hugged him tight, feeling him explode deep within her.

Chapter Twenty

Houston was warm, too warm, Daphne thought, for the end of November, and so humid that within ten minutes of meeting the climate, she felt as though her hair had turned to damp strings about her face.

"Lily! Dusty! Good grief, the whole brood!"

Daphne smiled as she was engulfed first by Lily, then by Dusty, aware that Danny, Keith and Patricia were dancing around them. She dropped all confusing thoughts and swallowed her unhappiness, giving in to the rambunctious greetings.

"Are you still going to keep this sister of mine, Dusty?" she heard Brant asking her brother-in-law as he poked him in the ribs.

"Brant, this little gal is a dynamo. Houston wouldn't be the same without her. Yep, old boy, I'll keep her."

"Ha! Why don't you ask me, brother dear?"

Brant grinned down at his beautiful sister. "You're so easy, Lily, it never occurred to me. Besides, Dusty is so much of a man, I always knew he'd keep you in line."

While Lily was punching Brant, Dusty turned to Daphne. "And how's my gorgeous little English gal?"

Daphne felt warmed by his good nature and grinned up at him. "How about two out of four?"

"Which two?" Dusty asked.

"I never get specific about a compliment," Daphne said, giggling.

"And I'll never get another word in edgewise, not with all these hellions around. All right, kids, let's get out of here. Brant, you're staying with the team until after the game?"

"Yep, then Daph and I will invade you for a couple of days. Okay?"

"You got it. Lily and I've planned a real Texas barbecue for you right after the game. But I swear it'll be turkey and all the fixings for Thanks-giving.''

After another round of hugs, Brant and Daphne took the team bus to the hotel. In the lobby, fans and reporters alike surrounded the men. Daphne shrank against Brant when a reporter she'd seen at the Dallas game spotted her and yelled out, ''Mrs. Asher! Welcome to Houston! You wanna give me your prediction for the game?''

Brant felt her tension and cursed himself yet again, silently. Very gently he said, ''Go ahead, love. You're loaded with predictions; give them what they want.''

Brant watched her from the corner of his eye as he spoke to another reporter. She seemed at first very shy and tongue-tied; then she came alive, and he smiled to see her gesticulate as she made a point, heard her sweet laughter, her starchy English accent. He felt himself swell with pride. You utter ass, he told himself. She's a natural, and you wanted to mold her into whatever it was you wanted. Hoard was more like it. He'd wanted her only for himself. He felt sick with self-disgust.

It wasn't long before other reporters converged on her, as did team-mates. It was probably the most fun pre-game interviewing he'd ever been witness to. Even Sam Carverelli was grinning like a besotted hen over his little chick.

There was only one fly in the ointment, and his name was Richard Monroe, a big sports writer from Los Angeles. He was a bastion of male chauvinism in sports and became livid when a ''girl'' tried to swish her tail around athletes. Brant found himself inching away from his team-mates, ready to pounce if the man gave Daphne a bad time.

Which he was prepared to do. Rich Monroe had eyed Daphne's per-formance and felt his lips thin. He was willing to agree that she was charming, lovely, but hell, let her model if she wanted to show off. He shoved his way into the group of fools surrounding her and asked, ''Do you miss all your athletes in England, Mrs. Asher? The rugby season in full swing?''

''I don't know any, and I have no idea, sir,'' Daphne said, turning her sunny smile and wary eyes to the tall, gaunt-faced man.

''What?'' he asked, his voice dripping sarcasm. ''You mean you've left all your rugby heroes for our American athletes?''

Oh no, Daphne thought, studying the man with the gleaming blue eyes and ready-to-pounce voice. He thinks I'm some sort of groupie. ''Yes, sir, I did, but I don't think they'll miss me.'' Take that, you ill-bred jerk.

''Are rugby players so much less...inviting than our American football players? Surely you must have *known* some of them in England.''

''Not more than half a dozen,'' Daphne said, praying he wouldn't notice that her hands had clenched at her sides. ''They're not nearly as...inviting as, for example, Lloyd here, or Tiny, or Guy.''

"You're a team player, then," Rich Monroe said, his pencil poised over his pad. "The more the merrier. Perhaps a team playerette."

"Perhaps, sir, you should look more closely at my husband, Brant Asher. Then, I promise you, you won't ask any more ignorant questions like that." She heard Lloyd groan in mock sorrow and tossed him a grin. Brant was at her elbow then, and she said, "My husband, sir."

Brant towered over Rich Monroe, and for a brief moment the sportswriter felt a frisson of fear at the barely veiled murderous look in Asher's eyes. Hell, he should have gotten her away from her brute of a husband.

Daphne willingly withdrew, watching Brant cut up the obnoxious man in his pleasant, utterly terrifying calm way.

"Good show, Daph," Brant said to her later. "Want me to break his neck?"

"Just his mean mouth, which you did quite nicely, thank you, Brant."

She hugged him, giving him her sweet smile, and Brant realized that she would never allow any problems between them to interfere with his game and concentration.

They beat Houston 21 to 14 in a wild and woolly fourth quarter that left Daphne hoarse from yelling, and Brant sore as hell.

"Daphne, we've got to talk."

She turned from the mirror, her pearls fastened. She gave him her special, intimate smile and said, "You are the most insatiable man! Here I am still recovering from terminal pleasure, and you—"

He slashed his hand through the air. "Cut it out, Daph. That's not what I meant, and you know it."

Oh yes, she knew it. She lowered her eyes a moment to her elegant Italian leather heels. "I don't want to be late for the barbecue. Lily was in a tizzy when I spoke to her. Really, Brant, Dusty is sending the limo, and it's probably here by now."

Brant frowned, then sighed. He saw the pleading look in her eyes and held his tongue. Later, he thought. They had to clear the air, get things straightened out between them. She had been all that was charming and supportive, wild in bed—and closed up like a clam. The wall she'd put up between them was as firm and immovable as the best offensive line.

"All right," he said. He started to pick up their suitcases, then changed his mind. No, he thought, he wanted to bring her back to the hotel. They had to talk, to be alone, with no interruptions from his well-meaning sister, equally well-meaning brother-in-law, and three oblivious nieces and nephews.

Lily and Dusty lived in a three-story white colonial house in the exclusive River Oaks section of Houston. The grounds were extensive, the swimming pool opulent, and the circular driveway bumper-to-bumper with cars. Almost immediately Daphne was gone from him, willingly or unwillingly he didn't know. He was, he supposed, afraid to find out.

The mood was festive, the guests in all stages of pleasant inebriation, many of them cavorting in the kidney-shaped pool.

Daphne smiled until she felt her face would crack from the effort. And she kept her distance from Brant. She'd just dipped a tortilla chip into a green substance that a guest told her was guacamole—whatever that was—when Lily said from behind her, "Daphne, why don't you come upstairs with me for a minute? I've got to make repairs to my poor face."

Daphne studied her sister-in-law's exquisite face and blinked. "What kind of repairs?"

"You'll see," Lily said briefly and, taking her arm, firmly steered her away from the crowd.

"You have a beautiful home," Daphne said as she followed in Lily's wake up the vast circular stairway.

"Yes," Lily said absently.

"The dinner was delicious."

"Yes," Lily said again. "In here, Daphne."

It was the spacious master suite, and Daphne's jaw dropped in awe. She was so used to Brant's condo. The entire five rooms could fit into this one huge L-shaped suite.

"I want to know what's going on," Lily said without preamble, waving away what she knew would be more complimentary words from her sister-in-law.

"I don't know what you mean, Lily," Daphne said, resentment clear in her voice.

"Now, don't be like that," Lily pleaded, touching her arm. "I love my brother dearly, and I thought you and he were perfect together. I know he loves you."

Daphne's eyes met hers. "I don't think so," she said quietly.

That was a shocker. "Goodness, how can you be so blind, Daph? I've been watching his eyes following you all afternoon. And you've purposely avoided being with him." Daphne said nothing, and Lily said a bit hesitantly after a few moments, "Mom told me about the miscarriage. It's a shame, but if you want children, you can have them. Is that the problem?"

Daphne raised her chin. "Brant is a very honorable, kind man. And I, well, I fully intend now to keep up my end of the bargain. I'd already decided that, regardless of what he felt or didn't feel about me. I wanted to. He's been upset that I might not...keep to my end, that is. In fact, I just realized that I'm—" She broke off. That news was for Brant first.

"What are you talking about?" Lily's voice was clearly bewildered.

"You'll see soon enough," was all Daphne would say. Lily, frustrated, allowed her to leave. Suddenly Daphne turned to face her sister-in-law again. "Do you really think so, Lily?"

"Think what?"

"That Brant loves me?"

"Don't be an ass, Daphne. I heard him tell Dusty that he was the luckiest man in the world. If I recall correctly, he said, 'And to think I almost didn't go to England. Jesus, I must have been born under a lucky star.' Does that convince you?"

Daphne thought her heart would gallop off into the sunset without her. She laughed, and at the same time a tear trickled down her cheek. She hugged Lily tightly, then skipped down the hall. She'd never been one for the grand gesture, but why not? She found Dusty, and he took her into his study, then left her alone. She picked up the phone without a moment's hesitation. It was Sunday, but why not give it a try?

Brant downed another beer. Why the hell couldn't things at least become a little blurry? All around him people were laughing, drinking, swapping jokes and unbelievable stories. It had cooled down considerably, and the Texas sky, true to legend, was clear and gleaming with stars. He watched a beautiful woman pull herself out of the swimming pool nearly as naked as the sunlit day she was born. He objectively noted her lovely breasts and long legs. They didn't do a bloody thing for him. Where was Daphne?

He saw her talking earnestly to a man Dusty had invited from one of the networks. Hell, *the* network. He watched the man shake his head and lean closer. Brant realized his hand was clutching his empty beer can, bending it out of shape, and that his knuckles were white. They'd work it out, he thought. He'd do anything not to lose her, anything.

It was Dusty who called out some ten minutes later, "Hey, folks, we've got an announcement for all of you. Come on, heads up!"

Brant felt the excitement radiating from his teammates as they shoved forward, bringing him with them. The word had leaked out sometime before. How, Brant didn't know. He hadn't said anything. "Hell," Guy had told him, "I don't mind at all if Daph sees me draped in a towel! Tiffy's accusing me of growing a fat gut, and Daph will tell the world the truth."

"I'd like to thank Mr. Donaldson," he heard Daphne say in her clear, precise voice, "and all the people who wanted to take a chance on me." *Wanted?*

"I've given it a lot of thought and have decided that, as a new American, I still have so much to learn about my new home and about football. Perhaps if anyone is still interested in the next couple of years, I'll be there in the locker room to pour champagne on all your heads." She paused a moment, her eyes locked on her husband's face. "But for now, I realize that I want only to tell people just how great you guys are. Mr.

Donaldson has agreed that a few short, special interviews with the Astros players is the way we'll go this year. After the Superbowl I won't be in any shape to see anyone, so we've got only the next two months.''

There was a babble of comment. "That's great—just us!"

"Lordie, an interview in English English!"

Shape? Brant stared at her, his mind refusing to function.

"Thank you all so much. You're all such good friends, and I'll do my best to see that everyone knows just how great each of you is."

There was applause, the sound of glasses clinking in toast, people crowding around Daphne. Brant forced a smile to his lips, accepted handshakes, and couldn't keep his eyes off his wife.

How the hell could he get her alone? Brant smiled grimly. He eased his way through the crowd to Sam Carverelli, clapped his arms about his coach's waist, hefted him up and, amid curses from Sam and boisterous, surprised laughter from everyone else, lifted him high and tossed him into the pool.

He was at his wife's side in the next minute. "Let's go," he said. "Now."

"But, Brant, what about Lily? And poor Sam—"

"Shut up."

Her eyes sparkled, and she said in a mocking voice, "Will you toss me into the pool if I refuse?"

"No, I'll toss you flat on your back." He dragged her out without another word.

Her laughter rang out, sweet and pure and happy.

Brant didn't say a word until they'd reached their hotel room. He closed the door, locked it, then turned to face his wife.

"Your shape is beautiful. What the hell did you mean?"

"Didn't you see how much I ate? And that guacamole stuff...I really pigged in."

"Out," he said automatically.

"But we just got here! Where do you want to go now?"

"No, damn it, pig *out*. That's how you say it."

"Oh."

Brant studied her for a long moment, his fingers stroking his jaw thoughtfully. "Take off your clothes. Now."

Daphne's fingers went to her strand of pearls.

"You can leave those on."

"But why?"

"They won't interfere with anything. I want to see your shape."

"But you saw my shape last night, this morning—"

He was beside her in an instant, his fingers on the single button at the neck of her gray wool dress. She stood quietly as he pulled the dress over her head. Bra, slip and panty hose quickly followed.

Daphne said very softly, "Are you angry with me about my decision?"

"What decision?" he managed to ask, his eyes on her breasts.

"Just to do a few interviews this season. As for the rest, well, that could be, or then again, wouldn't have to be..."

"You sound breathless, Daph." He raised his eyes to her face. "When?" he asked softly.

"Well, first you, of course—"

"That's it!" He picked her up, but unlike his rough treatment with his coach, he laid her very gently on the bed. "Now, wife, enough B.S."

"But Brant, I don't have a degree and if I did, it would have to be a B.A. I don't—"

"I guess we're going to have to retire Gwen. A station wagon, perhaps? A move to Connecticut? A shaggy dog?"

"Winterspoon isn't allergic to dogs, thank goodness."

"Do you think our baby will call him Uncle Oscar? Uncle Spoon?"

"I love you, Brant."

His eyes gleamed, and he gave her a slow, intimate smile. There was a good deal of satisfied triumph in that smile, and she poked him in the stomach.

He didn't give her the satisfaction of a perfunctory grunt. "It's about time, lady. You've had me hanging over a damned cliff so long, well, my fingers are numb."

"Just so long as that's the only part of you that hasn't any feeling left."

"Lord, would you stop treating me like your straight man?"

"I'm scared."

Brant lay down beside her, drawing her close against him. His fingers tangled in her hair and the pearls. "I feel great," he said, burying his face in a mass of hair.

Daphne felt his hand slip between them and gently rove over her stomach. She no longer questioned her intense response to him, just arched more closely against him, her fingers searching out the buttons of his shirt.

He clasped her hand. "No, love, not until you hear what I've got to say."

Daphne arched back so she could see his face. He saw her tongue nervously glide over her lower lip. "No, it's nothing dreadful, I swear. I want you, sweetheart. Now, tomorrow, in the year two thousand and twenty-five. I think I've loved you forever. It took me a long time because I just didn't know what the hell was wrong with me. I want you to be happy. I want you to keep loving me."

"I don't think I could ever stop that. Brant, I'd made the decision a while ago, but I didn't know what to do, so I didn't say anything to anybody, even the network people. I thought maybe I'd end up being a single parent and would have to earn my own living. Then Lily hauled me upstairs and told me that you said you'd been born under a lucky star.''

"I said that?"

"Yes, you did, you jerk! And I was under that star, too, waiting for you."

"Forget the damned star; just make it me you're under." He lightly kissed the tip of her nose, then continued in a very serious voice, "If you want to take over Joe Namath's job as announcer, I'll be your loudest supporter. What do you say? Will you keep me around as your straight man?"

Her lashes swept down, and he couldn't see her eyes. "How straight?" came her demure question.

He groaned and kissed her.

"I love you," he said into her mouth. "Even though you've become a smart-mouthed broad."

"Bird," she said. "That's how we say it in England."

*   *   *   *   *

Mackenzie's Mountain

Chapter One

He needed a woman. Bad.

Wolf Mackenzie spent a restless night, with the bright full moon throwing its silver light on the empty pillow beside him. His body ached with need, the sexual need of a healthy man, and the passing hours only intensified his frustration. Finally he got out of bed and walked naked to the window, his big body moving with fluid power. The wooden floor was icy beneath his bare feet but he welcomed the discomfort, for it cooled the undirected desire that heated his blood.

The colorless moonlight starkly etched the angles and planes of his face, living testimony to his heritage. Even more than the thick black hair worn long to touch his shoulders, even more than the heavy-lidded black eyes, his face proclaimed him Indian. It was in his high, prominent cheekbones and broad forehead, his thin lips and high-bridged nose. Less obvious, but just as fierce, was the Celtic heritage from his father, only one generation removed from the Scottish Highlands. It had refined the Indian features inherited from his mother into a face like a blade, as clean and sharply cut as it was strong. In his veins ran the blood of two of the most warlike peoples in the history of the world, Comanche and Celt. He had been a natural warrior, a fact soon discovered by the military when he had enlisted.

He was also a sensualist. He knew his own nature well, and though he controlled it, there were times when he needed a woman. He usually visited Julie Oakes at those times. She was a divorced woman, several years older, who lived in a small town fifty miles distant. Their arrangement had lasted five years; neither Wolf nor Julie was interested in marriage, but both had needs, and they liked each other. Wolf tried not to visit Julie too often, and he took care that he was never seen entering her house; he accepted the fact, unemotionally, that her neighbors would be outraged if they knew she slept with an Indian. And not just any Indian; a rape charge stuck to a man forever.

The next day was a Saturday. There would be the normal chores, and he had to pick up a load of fencing materials in Ruth, the small town just at the base of his mountain, but Saturday nights were traditionally for howling. He wouldn't howl, but he'd visit Julie and burn off his sexual tension in her bed.

The night was turning colder, and low heavy clouds were moving in.

He watched until they obscured the moon, knowing they meant new snow. He didn't want to return to his empty bed. His face was impassive, but his loins ached. He needed a woman.

Mary Elizabeth Potter had numerous small chores to occupy her time that Saturday morning, but her conscience wouldn't let her rest until she had talked to Joe Mackenzie. The boy had dropped out of school two months before, a month before she had arrived to take the place of a teacher who had abruptly quit. No one had mentioned the boy to Mary, but she'd run across his school record, and curiosity had led her to read it. In the small town of Ruth, Wyoming, there weren't that many students in school, and she had thought she'd met them all. In fact, there were less than sixty students, but the graduation rate was almost one hundred percent, so any dropout was unusual. When she had read Joe Mackenzie's record, she'd been stunned. The boy had been at the *top* of his class, with straight A's in all subjects. Students who did poorly would get discouraged and drop out, but every teaching instinct she had was outraged that such an outstanding student would just quit. She had to talk to him, try to make him understand how important it was to his future that he continue his education. Sixteen was so young to make a mistake that would haunt him the rest of his life. She wouldn't be able to sleep at night until she had done her best to talk him into returning.

It had snowed again during the night and had turned bitterly cold. The cat meowed plaintively as it wound around her ankles, as if complaining about the weather. "I know, Woodrow," she consoled the animal. "The floor must be cold to your feet." She could sympathize. She didn't think her feet had been warm since she had moved to Wyoming.

Before another winter came, she promised herself, she would own a pair of warm, sturdy boots, fur-lined and waterproof, and she would stomp about in the snow as if she'd been doing it all her life, like a native. Actually she needed the boots now, but the expenses of moving had wiped out her cash reserves, and the teachings of her thrifty aunt prevented her from buying the boots on credit.

Woodrow meowed again as she put on the warmest, most sensible shoes she owned, the ones she privately called her "old maid schoolteacher shoes." Mary paused to scratch behind his ears, and his back arched in ecstasy. She had inherited him with the house, which the school board had arranged for her to live in; the cat, like the house, wasn't much. She had no idea how old Woodrow was, but both he and the house looked a little run-down. Mary had always resisted owning a cat—it seemed the crowning touch to an old maid's life—but finally her fate had caught up with her. She *was* an old maid. Now she owned a cat. And wore old maid shoes. The picture was complete.

"Water seeks its own level," she told the cat, who looked back at her with his unconcerned Egyptian gaze. "But what do you care? It doesn't hurt *you* that my personal water level seems to stop at sensible shoes and cats."

But as she looked in the mirror to make certain her hair was tidy, she sighed. Sensible shoes and cats were just her style, along with being pale, slight and nondescript. "Mousy" was a good word. Mary Elizabeth Potter had been born to be an old maid.

She was dressed as warmly as she could manage, unless she put on socks to wear with her sensible shoes, but she drew the line at that. Dainty white anklets with long ruffled skirts were one thing, but knee socks with a wool dress were something else entirely. She was willing to be dowdy for the sake of warmth; she was not willing to be tacky.

Well, there was no point in putting it off; it wasn't going to get any warmer until spring. Mary braced herself for the shock of cold air on a system that still expected the warmth of Savannah. She had left her tidy little nest in Georgia for the challenge of a tiny school in Wyoming, for the excitement of a different way of life; she even admitted to a small yearning for adventure, though of course she never allowed it to surface. But somehow, she hadn't taken the weather into account. She had been prepared for the snow, but not the bitter temperatures. No wonder there were so few students, she thought as she opened the door and gasped as the wind whipped at her. It was too cold for the adults to undress enough to do anything that might result in children!

She got snow in her sensible shoes when she walked to her car, a sensible two-door, midsize Chevrolet sedan, on which she had sensibly put a new set of snow tires when she had moved to Wyoming. According to the weather report on the radio that morning, the high would be seven degrees below zero. Mary sighed again for the weather she had left behind in Savannah; it was March now, and spring would be in full swing, with flowers blooming in a riot of colors.

But Wyoming was beautiful, in a wild, majestic way. The soaring mountains dwarfed the puny man-made dwellings, and she had been told that, come spring, the meadows would be carpeted in wildflowers, and the crystal-clear creeks would sing their own special song. Wyoming was a different world from Savannah, and she was just a transplanted magnolia who was having trouble getting acclimated.

She had gotten instructions on how to get to the Mackenzie residence, though the information had been reluctantly given. It puzzled her that no one seemed interested in the boy, because the people in the little town had been friendly and helpful to her. The most direct comment she had gotten had been from Mr. Hearst, the grocery-store owner, who had muttered that "the Mackenzies aren't worth your trouble." But Mary considered any child worth her trouble. She was a teacher, and she meant to teach.

As she got into her sensible car, she could see the mountain called Mackenzie's Mountain, as well as the narrow road that wound up its side like a ribbon, and she quailed inside. New snow tires notwithstanding, she wasn't a confident driver in this strange environment. Snow was... well, snow was *alien*, not that she'd let it stop her from doing what she had set her mind on doing.

She was already shivering so hard that she could barely fit the key into the ignition. It was so cold! It actually hurt her nose and lungs to inhale. Perhaps she should wait for better weather before attempting the drive. She looked at the mountain again. Maybe in June all of the snow would have melted...but Joe Mackenzie had already been out of school for two months. Maybe in June the gap would seem insurmountable to him, and he wouldn't make the effort. It might already be too late. She had to try, and she didn't dare let even another week go by.

It was her habit to give herself pep talks whenever she was pushing herself to do something she found difficult, so she muttered under her breath as she began the drive. "It won't seem so steep once I'm actually on the road. All uphill roads look vertical from a distance. It's a perfectly negotiable road, otherwise the Mackenzies wouldn't be able to get up and down, and if they can do it, I can do it." Well, perhaps she could do it. Driving on snow was an acquired skill, one she hadn't as yet mastered.

Determination kept her going. When she finally reached the mountain and the road tilted upward, her hands clenched on the steering wheel as she deliberately refrained from looking over the side at the increasing distance to the valley floor. Knowing how far it was possible for her to fall if she drove off the edge wouldn't help her at all; in Mary's opinion, that would be in the category of useless knowledge, of which she already had quite enough.

"I won't slide," she muttered. "I won't go fast enough to lose control. This is like the Ferris wheel. I was certain I was going to fall out, but I didn't." She had ridden the Ferris wheel once, when she'd been nine years old, and no one had ever been able to talk her into trying it again. Carousels were more her style.

"The Mackenzies won't mind if I talk to Joe," she reassured herself in an attempt to get her mind off the drive. "Maybe he had trouble with a girlfriend, and that's why he doesn't want to go to school. At his age, it's probably all blown over by now."

Actually the drive wasn't as bad as she'd feared. She began to breathe a little easier. The incline was more gradual than it had appeared, and she didn't think she had too much farther to go. The mountain wasn't as enormous as it had looked from the valley.

She was so intent on her driving that she didn't notice the red light appear on the dash. She had no warning of overheating until steam suddenly erupted from beneath the hood, the frigid air instantly converting the mist into ice crystals on the windshield. Mary instinctively hit the brakes, then uttered a discreet oath when the wheels began sliding. Quickly she lifted her foot from the brake pedal, and the tires found traction again, but she couldn't see. Closing her eyes, she prayed that she was still going in the right direction and let the car's weight slow it to a stop.

The engine was hissing and bellowing like a dragon. Shaking in reaction, she turned off the ignition and got out of the car, gasping as the wind lashed her like an icy whip. The hood release mechanism was stiff from the bitter cold, but finally yielded, and she raised the hood to see what had happened, on the grounds that it would be nice to know what was wrong with the car even if she couldn't fix it. It didn't take a mechanic to see the problem: one of the water hoses had split, and hot water was spitting fitfully from the break.

Instantly she recognized the precariousness of her position. She couldn't stay in the car, because she couldn't let the motor run to keep her warm. The road was a private one, and the Mackenzies might not leave their ranch at all that day, or that entire weekend. It was too far, and too cold, for her to walk back to her own house. Her only option was to walk to the Mackenzie ranch and pray it wasn't very far. Her feet were already numb.

She didn't let herself dwell on the thought that she might not make it to the Mackenzie ranch, either. Instead she began to walk steadily up the road and tried to ignore the snow that got inside her shoes with each step.

She rounded a curve and lost sight of her car, but when she looked ahead there was still no sign of a house, or even a barn. She felt alone, as if she had been dropped into the middle of a wilderness. There was only the mountain and the snow, the vast sky and herself. The silence was absolute. It hurt to walk, and she found that she was sliding her feet instead of picking them up. She had gone fewer than two hundred yards.

Her lips trembled as she hugged herself in an effort to retain her body's heat. Painful or not, she would just have to keep walking.

Then she heard the low growl of a powerful engine, and she stopped, relief welling in her so painfully that tears burned her eyes. She had a horror of crying in public and blinked them back. There was no sense in crying; she had been walking less than fifteen minutes and hadn't been in any real danger at all. It was just her overactive imagination, as usual. She shuffled through the snow to the side of the road, to get out of the way, and waited for the approaching vehicle.

It came into view, a big black pickup with enormous tires. She could feel the driver's eyes lock on her, and in spite of herself she ducked her head in embarrassment. Old maid schoolteachers weren't accustomed to being the center of attention, and on top of that she felt a perfect fool. It must look as if she had gone for a stroll in the snow.

The truck slowed to a stop opposite her, and a man got out. He was big, and she instinctively disliked that. She disliked the way big men looked down at her, and she disliked being forced by sheer physical size to look up at them. Well, big or not, he was her rescuer. She wound her gloved fingers together and wondered what she should say. How did a person ask to be rescued? She had never hitched a ride before; it didn't seem proper for a settled, respectable schoolteacher.

Wolf stared at the woman, astounded that anyone would be out in the cold while dressed so stupidly. What in hell was she doing on his mountain, anyway? How had she gotten here?

Suddenly he knew who she was; he'd overheard talk in the feed store about the new schoolteacher from someplace down South. He'd never seen anyone who looked more like a schoolteacher than this woman, and she was definitely dressed wrong for a Wyoming winter. Her blue dress and brown coat were so frumpy that she was almost a cliché; he could see wisps of light brown hair straggling out from under her scarf, and oversize horn-rimmed glasses dwarfed her small face. No makeup, not even lip gloss to protect her lips.

And no boots. Snow was caked almost to her knees.

He had surveyed her completely in two seconds and didn't wait to hear what explanation she had for being on his mountain, if she intended to say anything at all. So far she hadn't uttered a word, but continued to stare at him with a faintly outraged look on her face. He wondered if she considered it beneath her to speak to an Indian, even to ask for help. Mentally he shrugged. What the hell, he couldn't leave her out here.

Since she hadn't spoken, he didn't, either. He simply bent down and passed one arm behind her knees and the other behind her back, and lifted her as he would a child, ignoring her gasp. As he carried her to the truck, he reflected that she didn't weigh much more than a child. He saw a flash of startled blue eyes behind the lenses of her glasses; then her arm passed around his neck and she was holding him in a convulsive grip, as if she were afraid he'd drop her.

He shifted her weight so he could open the passenger door and deposited her on the seat, then briskly wiped the snow from her feet and legs as well as he could. He heard her gasp again, but didn't look up. When he had finished, he dusted the snow from his gloves and went around to climb behind the wheel.

"How long have you been walking?" he muttered reluctantly.

Mary started. She hadn't expected his voice to be so deep that it almost reverberated. Her glasses had fogged from the truck's heat, and she snatched them off, feeling her cold cheeks prickle as blood rushed to them. "I...not long," she stammered. "About fifteen minutes. I blew a water hose. That is, my car did."

Wolf glanced at her in time to see her hastily lower her eyes again and noticed her pinkened cheeks. Good, she was getting warm. She was flustered; he could see it in the way she kept twisting her fingers together. Did she think he was going to throw her down on the seat and rape her? After all, he was a renegade Indian, and capable of anything. Then again, the way she looked, maybe this was the most excitement she'd ever had.

They hadn't been far from the ranch house and reached it in a few minutes. Wolf parked close to the kitchen door and got out; he circled the truck and reached the passenger door just as she opened it and began to slid down. "Forget it," he said, and lifted her again. Her sliding motion had made her skirt ride halfway up her thighs. She hastily pushed the fabric down, but not before his black eyes had examined her slim legs, and the color deepened in her cheeks.

The warmth of the house enfolded her, and she inhaled with relief, hardly noticing as he turned a wooden chair away from the table and placed her on it. Without speaking he turned on the hot water tap and let it run, then filled a dishpan, frequently checking the water and adjusting the temperature.

Well, she had reached her destination, and though she hadn't accomplished her arrival in quite the manner she had intended, she might as well get to the purpose of her visit. "I'm Mary Potter, the new schoolteacher."

"I know," he said briefly.

Her eyes widened as she stared at his broad back. "You know?"

"Not many strangers around."

She realized that he hadn't introduced himself and was suddenly unsure. Was she even at the right place? "Are...are you Mr. Mackenzie?"

He glanced over his shoulder at her, and she noticed that his eyes were as black as night. "I'm Wolf Mackenzie."

She was instantly diverted. "I suppose you know your name is uncommon. It's Old English—"

"No," he said, turning around with the dishpan in his hands. He placed it on the floor beside her feet. "It's Indian."

She blinked. "Indian?" She felt incredibly stupid. She should have guessed, given the blackness of his hair and eyes, and the bronze of his skin, but she hadn't. Most of the men in Ruth had weathered skin, and she had simply thought him darker than the others. Then she frowned at him and said in a positive tone, "Mackenzie isn't an Indian name."

He frowned back at her. "Scottish."

"Oh. Are you a half-breed?"

She asked the question with the same unconsciousness as if she had been asking directions, silky brows lifted inquiringly over her blue eyes.

It set his teeth on edge. "Yeah," he grunted. There was something so irritating about the primness of her expression that he wanted to shock her out of her prissiness. Then he noticed the shivers shaking her body, and he pushed his irritation aside, at least until he could get her warm. The clumsy way she had been walking when he'd first seen her had told him that she was in the first stages of hypothermia. He shrugged out of his heavy coat and tossed it aside, then put on a pot of coffee.

Mary sat silently as he made coffee; he wasn't a very talkative person, though that wasn't going to make her give up. She was truly cold; she would wait until she had a cup of that coffee, then begin again. She looked up at him as he turned back to her, but his expression was unreadable. Without a word he took the scarf from her head and began unbuttoning her coat. Startled, she said, "I can do that," but her fingers were so cold that any movement was agony. He stepped back and let her try for a moment, then brushed her hands aside and finished the job himself.

"Why are you taking my coat off when I'm so cold?" she asked in bewilderment as he peeled the coat down her arms.

"So I can rub your arms and legs." Then he proceeded to remove her shoes.

The idea was as alien to her as snow. She wasn't accustomed to anyone touching her, and didn't intend to become accustomed. She started to tell him so, but the words vanished unsaid when he abruptly thrust his hands under her skirt, all the way to her waist. Mary gave a startled shriek and jerked back, almost oversetting the chair. He glared at her, his eyes like black ice.

"You don't have to worry," he snapped. "This is Saturday. I only rape on Tuesdays and Thursdays." He thought about throwing her back out into the snow, but he couldn't let a woman freeze to death, not even a white woman who obviously thought his touch would contaminate her.

Mary's eyes grew so wide they eclipsed the rest of her face. "What's wrong with Saturdays?" she blurted, then realized that she had almost issued him an invitation, for pity's sake! She clapped her gloved hands to her face as a tide of red surged to her cheeks. Her brain must have frozen; it was the only possible explanation.

Wolf jerked his head up, not believing she had actually said that. Wide, horrified blue eyes stared at him from over black leather gloves, which covered the rest of her face but couldn't quite hide the hot color. It had been so long since he'd seen anyone blush that it took him a minute to realize she was acutely embarrassed. Why, she was a prude! It was the final cliché to add to the dowdy, old maid schoolteacher image she presented. Amusement softened his irritation. This was probably the highlight of her life. "I'm going to pull your panty hose off so you can put your feet in the water," he explained in a gruff voice.

"Oh." The word was muffled because her hands were still over her mouth.

His arms were still under her skirt, his hands clasped on her hips. Almost unconsciously he felt the narrowness of her, and the softness. Dowdy or not, she still had the softness of a woman, the sweet scent of a woman, and his heartbeat increased as his body began to respond to her nearness. Damn, he needed a woman worse than he'd thought if this frumpy little schoolteacher could turn him on.

Mary sat very still as one powerful arm closed around her and lifted her so he could strip the panty hose down her hips and legs; the position put his head close to her breasts and stomach, and she stared down at his thick, shiny black hair. He had only to turn his head and his mouth would brush against her breasts. She had read in books that a man took a woman's nipples into his mouth and sucked them as a nursing infant would, and she had always wondered why. Now the thought made her feel breathless, and her nipples tingled. His roughly callused hands brushed against her bare legs; how would *they* feel on her breasts? She began to feel oddly warm, and a little dizzy.

Wolf didn't glance at her as he tossed the insubstantial panty hose to the floor. He lifted her feet onto his thigh and slid the dishpan into place, then slowly lowered her feet into the water. He had made certain the water was only warm, but he knew her feet were so cold even that would be painful. She sucked in her breath but didn't protest, though he saw the gleam of tears in her eyes when he looked up at her.

"It won't hurt for long," he murmured reassuringly, moving so that his legs were on each side of hers, clasping them warmly. Then he carefully removed her gloves, struck by the delicacy of her white, cold hands. He held them between his warm palms for a moment, then made a decision and unbuttoned his shirt as he crowded closer to her.

"This will get them warm," he said, and tucked her hands into the hollows of his armpits.

Mary was dumbstruck. She couldn't believe that her hands were nestled in his armpits like birds. His warmth seared her cold fingers. She wasn't actually touching skin; he wore a T-shirt, but it was still the most intimate she had ever been with another person. Armpits...well, everyone had them, but she certainly wasn't accustomed to touching them. She had never before been this *surrounded* by anyone, least of all a man. His hard legs were on each side of hers, clasping them; she was bent forward a little, her hands neatly tucked beneath his arms, while he briskly rubbed his hands over her arms and shoulders, then down to her thighs. She made a little sound of surprise; she simply couldn't believe this was happening, not to Mary Elizabeth Potter, old maid schoolteacher *ordinaire.*

Wolf had been concentrating on his task but he looked up at the sound she made, into her wide blue eyes. They were an odd blue, he thought, not cornflower or that pure dark blue. There was just a hint of gray in the shade. Slate blue, that was it. Distantly he noticed that her hair was straggling down from the ungodly knot she'd twisted it into, framing her face in silky, pale brown wisps. She was very close, her face just inches from his. She had the most delicate skin he'd ever seen, as fine-grained as an infant's, so pale and translucent he could see the fragile tracery of blue veins at her temples. Only the very young should have skin like that. As he watched, another blush began to stain her cheeks, and unwillingly he felt himself become entranced by the sight. He wondered if her skin was that silky and delicate all over—her breasts, her stomach, her thighs, between her legs. The thought was like an electrical jolt to his system, overloading his nerves. Damn, she smelled sweet! And she would probably jump straight out of that chair if he lifted her skirt the way he wanted to and buried his face against her silky thighs.

Mary licked her lips, oblivious to the way his eyes followed the movement. She had to say something, but she didn't know what. His physical nearness seemed to have paralyzed her thought processes. My goodness, he was warm! And close. She should remember why she had come here in the first place, instead of acting like a ninny because a very good-looking, in a rough sort of way, very masculine person was too close to her. She licked her lips again, cleared her throat, and said, "Ah...I came to speak to Joe, if I may."

His expression changed very little, yet she had the impression that he was instantly aloof. "Joe isn't here. He's doing chores."

"I see. When will he be back?"

"In an hour, maybe two."

She looked at him a little disbelievingly. "Are you Joe's father?"

"Yes."

"His mother is...?"

"Dead."

The flat, solitary word jarred her, yet at the same time she was aware of a faint, shocking sense of relief. She looked away from him again. "How did you feel about Joe quitting school?"

"It was his decision."

"But he's only sixteen! He's just a boy—"

"He's Indian," Wolf interrupted. "He's a man."

Indignation mingled with exasperation to act as a spur. She jerked her hands from his armpits and planted them on her hips. "What does that have to do with anything? He's sixteen years old and he needs to get an education!"

"He can read, write and do math. He also knows everything there is to know about training horses and running a ranch. He chose to quit school and work here full-time. This is my ranch, and my mountain. One day it will be his. He decided what to do with his life, and it's train horses." He didn't like explaining his and Joe's personal business to anyone, but there was something about this huffy, dowdy little teacher that made him answer. She didn't seem to realize he was Indian; intellectually she knew it, but she obviously had no idea what it *meant* to be Indian, and to be Wolf Mackenzie in particular, to have people turn aside to avoid speaking to him.

"I'd like to talk to him anyway," Mary said stubbornly.

"That's up to him. He may not want to talk to you."

"You won't try to influence him at all?"

"No."

"Why not? You should at least have tried to keep him in school!"

Wolf leaned very close, so close that his nose was almost touching hers. She stared into his black eyes, her own eyes widening. "He's Indian, lady. Maybe you don't know what that means. Hell, how could you? You're an Anglo. Indians aren't welcome. What education he has, he got on his own, without any help from the Anglo teachers. When he wasn't being ignored, he was being insulted. Why would he want to go back?"

She swallowed, alarmed by his aggression. She wasn't accustomed to men getting right in her face and swearing at her. Truthfully, Mary admitted that she wasn't accustomed to men at all. When she had been young, the boys had ignored the mousy, bookish girl, and when she had gotten older the men had done the same. She paled a little, but she felt so strongly about the benefits of a good education that she refused to let him intimidate her. Big people often did that to smaller people, probably without even thinking about it, but she wasn't going to give in simply because he was bigger than she. "He was at the head of his class," she said briskly. "If he managed that on his own, think of what he could accomplish with help!"

He straightened to his full height, towering over her. "Like I said, it's up to him." The coffee had long since finished brewing, so he turned to pour a cup and hand it to her. Silence fell between them. He leaned against the cabinets and watched her sip daintily, like a cat. Dainty, yeah, that was a good word for her. She wasn't *tiny*, maybe five three, but she was slightly built. His eyes dropped to her breasts beneath that dowdy blue dress; they weren't big, but they looked nice and round. He wondered if her nipples would be a delicate shell pink, or rosy beige. He wondered if she would be able to take him comfortably, if she would be so tight he'd go wild—

Sharply he brought his erotic thoughts to a halt. Damn it, that particular lesson should have been etched into his soul! Anglo women might flirt with him and twitch themselves around him, but few of them really wanted to get down and dirty with an Indian. This prissy little frump wasn't even flirting, so why was he getting so turned on? Maybe it was because she *was* a frump. He kept imagining how the dainty body beneath that awful dress would look, stripped bare and stretched out on the sheets.

Mary set the cup aside. "I'm much warmer now. Thank you, the coffee did the trick." That, and the way he'd run his hands all over her, but she wasn't about to tell him that. She looked up at him and hesitated, suddenly uncertain when she saw the look in his black eyes. She didn't know what it was, but there was something about him that made her pulse rate increase, made her feel faintly uneasy. Was he actually looking at her *breasts*?

"I think some of Joe's old clothes will fit you," he said, face and voice expressionless.

"Oh, I don't need any clothes. I mean, what I have on is perfectly—"

"Idiotic," he interrupted. "This is Wyoming, lady, not New Orleans, or wherever you're from."

"Savannah," she supplied.

He grunted, which seemed to be one of his basic means of communication, and took a towel from a drawer. Going down on one knee, he lifted her feet from the water and wrapped them in a towel, rubbing them dry with a touch so gentle it was at odds with the thinly veiled hostility of his manner. Then, standing, he said, "Come with me."

"Where are we going?"

"To the bedroom."

Mary stopped, blinking at him, and a bitter smile twisted his mouth. "Don't worry," he said harshly. "I'll control my savage appetites, and after you get dressed, you can get the hell off my mountain."

Mary drew herself up to her full height and lifted her chin, her mouth setting itself in a prim line. "It isn't necessary to make fun of me, Mr. Mackenzie," she said calmly, but her even tone was hard won. She knew she fell short in the come-hither department; she didn't need sarcasm to remind her. Usually she wasn't disturbed by her mousiness, having accepted it as an unchangeable fact, much like having the sun rise in the east. But Mr. Mackenzie made her feel strangely vulnerable, and it was oddly painful that he should have pointed out how unappealing she was.

Wolf's straight black brows drew together over his high-bridged nose. "I wasn't making fun of you," he snapped. "I was dead serious, lady. I want you off of my mountain."

"Then I'll leave, of course," she replied steadily. "But it was still unnecessary to make fun of me."

He put his hands on his hips. "Make fun of you? How?"

A flush tinged her exquisite skin, but her gray-blue eyes never wavered. "I know I'm not an attractive woman, certainly not the type to stir a man's—er, savage appetites."

She was serious. Ten minutes ago he'd have agreed with her that she was plain, and God knew she was no fashion plate, but what astounded him was that she honestly didn't seem to realize what it meant that he was Indian, or what he'd meant by his sarcasm, or even that he had been strongly aroused by her closeness. A lingering throbbing in his loins reminded him that his reaction hadn't completely subsided. He gave a harsh laugh, the sound devoid of amusement. Why not put a little more excitement in her life? When she heard the flat truth, she wouldn't be able to get off his mountain fast enough.

"I wasn't joking or making fun," he said. His black eyes glittered at her. "Touching you like that, being so close to you that I could smell the sweetness, turned me on."

Astonished, she stared at him. "Turned you on?" she asked blankly.

"Yeah." She still stared at him as if he were speaking a different language, and impatiently he added, "Got me hot, however you want to describe it."

She pushed at a silky strand that had escaped from her hairpins. "You're making fun of me again," she accused. It was impossible. She had never made a man...aroused a man in her life.

He was already irritated, already aroused. He had learned to use iron control when dealing with Anglos, but something about this prim little woman got under his skin. Frustration filled him until he thought he might explode. He hadn't intended to touch her, but suddenly he had his hands on her waist, pulling her toward him. "Maybe you need a demonstration," he said in a rough undertone, and bent to cover her mouth with his.

Mary trembled in profound shock, her eyes enormous as he moved his lips over hers. His eyes were closed. She could see the individual lashes, and for a moment marveled at how thick they were. Then his hands, still clasped on her waist, drew her into firm contact with his muscled body, and she gasped. He took instant advantage of her opened mouth, probing inside with his tongue. She quivered again, and her eyes slowly closed as a strange heat began to warm her inside. The pleasure was unfamiliar, and so intense that it frightened her. A host of new sensations assailed her, making her dizzy. There was the firmness of his lips, his heady taste, the startling intimacy of his tongue stroking hers as if enticing it to play. She felt the heat of his body, smelled the warm muskiness of his skin. Her soft breasts were pressed against the muscular planes of his chest, and her nipples began to tingle in that strange, embarrassing way again.

Suddenly he lifted his mouth from hers, and sharp disappointment made her eyes fly open. His black gaze burned her. "Kiss me back," he muttered.

"I don't know how," Mary blurted, still unable to believe this was happening.

His voice was almost guttural. "Like this." He took her mouth again, and this time she parted her lips immediately, eager to accept his tongue and feel that odd, surging pleasure once more. He moved his mouth over hers, molding her lips with fierce pleasure, teaching her how to return the pressure. His tongue touched hers again, and this time she responded shyly in kind, welcoming his small invasion with gentle touches of her own. She was too inexperienced to realize the symbolism of her acceptance, but he began to breathe harder and faster, and his kiss deepened, demanding even more of her.

A frightening excitement exploded through her body, going beyond mere pleasure and becoming a hungry need. She was no longer cold at all, but burning inside as her heartbeat increased until her heart was banging against her ribs. So this was what he meant when he'd said she got him hot. He got her hot, too, and it stunned her to think he had felt this same restless yearning, this incredible wanting. She made a soft, unconscious sound and moved closer to him, not knowing how to control the sensations his experienced kisses had aroused.

His hands tightened painfully on her waist, and a low, rough sound rumbled in his throat. Then he lifted her, pulled her closer, adjusted her hips against his and graphically demonstrated his response to her.

She hadn't known it could be like that. She hadn't known that desire could burn so hot, could make her forget Aunt Ardith's warnings about men and the nasty things they liked to do to women. Mary had quite sensibly decided that those things couldn't be too nasty, or women wouldn't put up with them, but at the same time she had never flirted or tried to attract a boyfriend. The men she had met at college and on the job had seemed normal, not slavering sex fiends; she was comfortable with men, and even considered some to be friends. It was just that she wasn't sexy herself; no man had ever beaten down doors to go out with her, or even managed to accomplish the dialing of her telephone number, so her exposure to men hadn't prepared her for the tightness of Wolf Mackenzie's arms, the hunger of his kisses, or the hardness of his manhood pushing against the juncture of her thighs. Nor had she known that she could want more.

Unconsciously she locked her arms around his neck and squirmed against him, tormented by increasing frustration. Her body was on fire, empty and aching and wanting all at once, and she didn't have the experience to control it. The new sensations were a tidal wave, swamping her mind beneath the overload from her nerve endings.

Wolf jerked his head back, his teeth locked as he relentlessly brought himself back under control. Black fire burned in his eyes as he looked down at her. His kisses had made her soft lips red and pouty, and delicate pink colored her translucent porcelain skin. Her eyes were heavy-lidded as she opened them and slowly met his gaze. Her pale brown hair had slipped completely out of its knot and tumbled silkily around her face and over her shoulders. Desire was on her face; she already looked tousled, as if he had done more than kiss her, and in his mind he had. She was light and delicate in his arms, but she had twisted against him with a hunger that matched his own.

He could take her to bed now; she was that far gone, and he knew it. But when he did, it would be because she had consciously made the decision, not because she was so hot she didn't know what she was doing. Her inexperience was obvious; he'd even had to teach her how to kiss— the thought stopped as abruptly as if he'd hit a mental wall, as he realized the full extent of her inexperience. Damn it, she was a *virgin*!

The thought staggered him. She was looking at him now with those grayish blue eyes both innocent and questioning, languid with desire, as she waited for him to make the next move. She didn't know what to do. Her arms were locked around his neck, her body pressed tightly to his, her legs opened slightly to allow him to nestle against her, and she was waiting for him because she didn't have a clue how to proceed. She hadn't even been kissed before. No man had touched those soft breasts, or taken her nipples in his mouth. No man had loved her at all before.

He swallowed the lump that threatened to choke him, his eyes still locked with hers. "God Almighty, lady, that nearly got out of hand."

She blinked. "Did it?" Her tone was prim, the words clear, but the dazed, sleepy look was still in her eyes.

Slowly, because he didn't want to let her go, and gently, because he knew he had to, he let her body slip down his until she was standing on her feet again. She was innocent of the ramifications, but he wasn't. He was Wolf Mackenzie, half-breed, and she was the schoolteacher. The good citizens of Ruth wouldn't want her associating with him; she was in charge of their young people, with untold influence on their forming morals. No parents would want their impressionable daughter being taught by a woman who was having a wild fling with an Indian ex-con. Why, she might even entice their sons! His prison record could be accepted, but his Indian blood would never go away.

So he had to let her go, no matter how much he wanted to take her to his bedroom and teach her all the things that went on between a man and a woman.

Her arms were still around his neck, her fingers buried in the hair at his nape. She seemed incapable of movement. He reached up to take her wrists and draw her hands away from him.

"I think I'll come back later."

A new voice intruded in Mary's dreamworld of newly discovered sensuality, and she jerked away, color burning her cheeks as she whirled to face the newcomer. A tall, dark-haired boy stood just inside the kitchen door, his hat in his hand. "Sorry, Dad. I didn't mean to barge in."

Wolf stepped away from her. "Stay. She came to see you, anyway."

The boy looked at her quizzically. "You could have fooled me."

Wolf merely shrugged. "This is Miss Mary Potter, the new schoolteacher. Miss Potter, my son, Joe."

Even through her embarrassment, Mary was jolted that he would call her "Miss Potter" after the intimacy they had just shared. But he seemed so calm and controlled, as if it hadn't affected him at all, while every nerve in her body was still jangling. She wanted to fling herself against him and give herself up to that encompassing fire.

Instead she stood there, her arms stiffly at her sides while her face burned, and forced herself to look at Joe Mackenzie. He was the reason she was here, and she wouldn't allow herself to forget it again. As her embarrassment faded, she saw that he was very like his father. Though he was only sixteen, he was already six feet tall and would likely match his father's height, just as his broad young shoulders showed the promise of being as powerful. His face was a younger version of Wolf's, as strong-boned and proud, the features precisely chiseled. He was calm and con-

trolled, far too controlled for a sixteen-year-old, and his eyes, oddly, were
pale, glittering blue. Those eyes held something in them, something un-
tamed, as well as a sort of bitter acceptance and knowledge that made
him old beyond his years. He was his father's son.

There was no way she could give up on him.

She held out her hand to him. "I'd really like to talk to you, Joe."

His expression remained aloof, but he crossed the kitchen to shake her
hand. "I don't know why."

"You dropped out of school."

The statement hardly needed verification, but he nodded. Mary drew a
deep breath. "May I ask why?"

"There was nothing for me there."

She felt frustrated by the calm, flat statement, because she couldn't
sense any uncertainty in this unusual boy. As Wolf had said, Joe had
made up his own mind and didn't intend to change it. She tried to think
of another way to approach him, but Wolf's quiet, deep voice interrupted.

"Miss Potter, you can finish talking after you get into some sensible
clothes. Joe, don't you have some old jeans that might be small enough
to fit her?"

To her astonishment, the boy looked her over with an experienced eye.
"I think so. Maybe the ones I wore when I was ten." For a moment
amusement sparkled in his blue-diamond eyes, and Mary primmed her
mouth. What did these Mackenzie men get out of needlessly pointing out
her lack of attractiveness?

"Socks, shirt, boots and coat," Wolf added to the list. "The boots will
be too big, but two pairs of socks will hold them on."

"Mr. Mackenzie, I really don't need extra clothes. What I have on will
do until I get home."

"No, it won't. The high temperature today is about ten below zero.
You aren't walking out of this house with bare legs and those stupid
shoes."

Her sensible shoes were suddenly stupid? She felt like flying to their
defense, but suddenly remembered the snow that had gotten inside them
and frozen her toes. What was sensible in Savannah was woefully inad-
equate in a Wyoming winter.

"Very well," she assented, but only because it was, after all, the sensible thing to do. She still felt uncomfortable about taking Joe's clothes,
even temporarily. She had never worn anyone else's clothes before, never
swapped sweaters or blouses with chums as an adolescent. Aunt Ardith
had thought such familiarity ill-bred.

"I'll see about your car while you change." Without even glancing at
her again, he put on his coat and hat and walked out the door.

"This way," Joe said, indicating that she should follow him. She did
so, and he looked over his shoulder. "What happened to your car?"

"A water hose blew."

"Where is it?"

She stopped. "It's on the road. Didn't you see it when you drove up?" An awful thought struck her. Had her car somehow slid off the mountain?

"I came up the front side of the mountain. It's not as steep." He looked amused again. "You actually tried driving up the back road in a car, when you're not used to driving in snow?"

"I didn't know that was the back road. I thought it was the only road. Couldn't I have made it? I have snow tires."

"Maybe."

She noticed that he didn't sound very confident in her ability, but she didn't protest, because she wasn't very confident herself. He led the way through a rustic but comfortable living room and down a short hallway to an open door. "My old clothes are boxed up in the storage room, but it won't take long for me to dig them out. You can change in here. It's my bedroom."

"Thank you," she murmured, stepping inside the room. Like the living room, it was rustic, with exposed beams and thick wooden walls. There was nothing in it to indicate it was inhabited by a teenage boy: no sports apparatus of any kind, no clothes on the floor. The full-size bed was neatly made, a homemade quilt smoothed on top. A straight chair stood in one corner. Next to his bed, bookshelves stretched from floor to ceiling; the shelves were obviously handmade, but weren't crude. They had been finished, sanded and varnished. They were crammed with books, and curiosity led her to examine the titles.

It took her a moment to realize that every book had to do with flight, from da Vinci's experiments through *Kitty Hawk* and space exploration. There were books on bombers, fighters, helicopters, radar planes, jets and prop planes, books on air battles fought in each war since pilots first shot at each other with pistols in World War I. There were books on experimental aircraft, on fighter tactics, on wing design and engine capability.

"Here are the clothes." Joe had entered silently and placed the clothes on the bed. Mary looked at him, but his face was impassive.

"You like planes," she said, then winced at her own banality.

"I like planes," he admitted without inflection.

"Have you thought about taking flying lessons?"

"Yes." He didn't add anything to that stark answer, however; he merely left the room and closed the door behind him.

She was thoughtful as she slowly removed her dress and pulled on the things Joe had brought. The collection of books indicated not merely an interest in flying, but an obsession. Obsessions were funny things; unhealthy ones could ruin lives, but some obsessions lifted people to higher planes of life, made them shine with a brighter light, burn with a hotter fire, and if those obsessions weren't fed, then the person withered, a life blighted by starvation of the soul. If she were right, she had a way to reach Joe and get him back in school.

The jeans fit. Disgusted at this further proof that she had the figure of a ten-year-old boy, she pulled on the too-big flannel shirt and buttoned it, then rolled the sleeves up over her hands. As Wolf had predicted, the worn boots were too big, but the two pairs of thick socks padded her feet enough that the boots didn't slip up and down on her heels too much. The warmth was heavenly, and she decided she would pinch pennies any way she could until she could afford a pair of boots.

Joe was adding wood to the fire in the enormous rock fireplace when she entered, and a little grin tugged at his mouth when he saw her. "You sure don't look like Mrs. Langdale, or any other teacher I've ever seen."

She folded her hands. "Looks have nothing to do with ability. I'm a very good teacher—even if I do look like a ten-year-old boy."

"Twelve. I wore those jeans when I was twelve."

"What a consolation."

He laughed aloud, and she felt pleased, because she had the feeling neither he nor his father laughed much.

"Why did you quit school?"

She had learned that if you kept asking the same question, you would often get different answers, and eventually the evasions would cease and the real answer would emerge. But Joe looked at her steadily and gave the same answer as before. "There was nothing for me there."

"Nothing more for you to learn?"

"I'm Indian, Miss Potter. A mixed-breed. What I learned, I learned on my own."

Mary paused. "Mrs. Langdale didn't—" She stopped, unsure of how to phrase her question.

"I was invisible." His young voice was harsh. "From the time I started school. No one took the time to explain anything to me, ask me questions, or include me in anything. I'm surprised my papers were even graded."

"But you were number one in your class."

He shrugged. "I like books."

"Don't you miss school, miss learning?"

"I can read without going to school, and I can help Dad a lot more if I'm here all day. I know horses, ma'am, maybe better than anyone else around here except for Dad, and I didn't learn about them in school. This ranch will be mine someday. This is my life. Why should I waste time in school?"

Mary took a deep breath and played her ace. "To learn how to fly."

He couldn't prevent the avid gleam that shone briefly in his eyes, but it was quickly extinguished. "I can't learn how to fly in Ruth High School. Maybe someday I'll take lessons."

"I wasn't talking about flying lessons. I was talking about the Air Force Academy."

His bronze skin whitened. This time she didn't see a gleam of eagerness, but a deep, anguished need so powerful it shook her, as if he'd been shown a glimpse of heaven. Then he turned his head, and abruptly he looked older. "Don't try to make a fool of me. There's no way."

"Why isn't there a way? From what I saw in your school records, your grade average will be high enough."

"I dropped out."

"You can go back."

"As far behind as I am? I'd have to repeat this grade, and I won't sit still while those jerks call me a stupid Indian."

"You aren't that far behind. I could tutor you, bring you up fast enough that you could start your senior year in the fall. I'm a licensed teacher, Joe, and for your information, my credentials are very good. I'm qualified to tutor you in the classes you need."

He took a poker and jabbed at a log, sending a shower of sparks flying. "What if I do it?" he muttered. "The Academy isn't a college where you take an entrance exam, pay your money and walk in."

"No. The usual way is to be recommended by your congressman."

"Yeah, well, I don't think my congressman is going to recommend an Indian. We're way down on the list of people it's fashionable to help. Dead last, as a matter of fact."

"I think you're making too much of your heritage," Mary said calmly. "You can keep blaming everything on being Indian, or you can get on with your life. You can't do anything about other people's reactions to you, but you *can* do something about your own. You don't know what your congressman will do, so why give up when you haven't even tried yet? Are you a quitter?"

He straightened, his pale eyes fierce. "I don't reckon."

"Then it's time to find out, isn't it? Do you want to fly bad enough that you'll fight for the privilege? Or do you want to die without ever knowing what it's like to sit in the cockpit of a jet doing Mach 1?"

"You hit hard, lady," he whispered.

"Sometimes it takes a knock on the head to get someone's attention. Do you have the guts to try?"

"What about you? The folks in Ruth won't like it if you spend so much time with me. It would be bad enough if I were alone, but with Dad, it's twice as bad."

"If anyone objects to my tutoring you, I'll certainly set him straight," she said firmly. "It's an honor to be accepted into the Academy, and that's our goal. If you'll agree to being tutored, I'll write to your congressman immediately. I think this time your heritage will work in your favor."

It was amazing how proud that strong young face could be. "I don't want it if they give it to me just because I'm Indian."

"Don't be ridiculous," she scoffed. "Of course you won't be accepted into the Academy just because you're half Indian. But if that fact catches the congressman's interest, I say, good. It would only make him remember your name. It'll be up to you to make the grade."

He raked his hand through his black hair, then restlessly walked to the window to look out at the white landscape. "Do you really think it's possible?"

"Of course it's possible. It isn't guaranteed, but it's possible. Can you live with yourself if you don't try? If *we* don't try?" She didn't know how to go about bringing someone to a congressman's attention for consideration for recommendation to the Academy, but she was certainly willing to write to every senator and representative Wyoming had seated in Congress, a letter a week, until she found out.

"If I agreed, it would have to be at night. I have chores around here that have to be done."

"Night is fine with me. Midnight would be fine with me, if it would get you back in school."

He gave her a quick look. "You really mean it, don't you? You actually care that I dropped out of school."

"Of course I care."

"There's no 'of course' about it. I told you, no other teacher cared if I showed up in class. They probably wished I hadn't."

"Well," she said in her briskest voice, "I care. Teaching is what I do, so if I can't teach and feel I'm doing some good, then I lose part of myself. Isn't that how you feel about flying? That you *have* to, or you'll die?"

"I want it so bad it hurts," he admitted, his voice raw.

"I read somewhere that flying is like throwing your soul into the heavens and racing to catch it as it falls."

"I don't think mine would ever fall," he murmured, looking at the clear cold sky. He stared, entranced, as if paradise beckoned, as if he could see forever. He was probably imagining himself up there, free and wild, with a powerful machine screaming beneath him and taking him higher. Then he shook himself, visibly fighting off the dream, and turned to her. "Okay, Miss Teacher, when do we start?"

"Tonight. You've already wasted enough time."

"How long will it take for me to catch up?"

She gave him a withering look. "Catch up? You're going to leave them in the dust. How long it takes depends on how much work you can do."

"Yes, ma'am," he said, grinning a little.

She thought that already he looked younger, more like a boy, than he had before. He was, in all ways, far more mature than the other boys his age in her classes, but he looked as if a burden had been lifted from him. If flying meant that much to him, how had it felt to set himself a course that would deny him what he wanted most?

"Can you be at my house at six? Or would you rather I come here?" She thought of that drive, in the dark and snow, and wondered if she'd make it if he wanted her to come here.

"I'll come to your house, since you aren't used to driving in snow. Where do you live?"

"Go down the back road and take a left. It's the first house on the left." She thought a minute. "I believe it's the first house, period."

"It is. There isn't another house for five miles. That's the old Witcher house."

"So I've been told. It was kind of the school board to arrange living quarters for me."

Joe looked dubious. "More like it was the only way they had of getting another teacher in the middle of the year."

"Well, I appreciated it anyway," she said firmly. She looked out the window. "Shouldn't your father be back by now?"

"Depends on what he found. If it was something he could fix right then, he'd do it. Look, here he comes now."

The black pickup roared to a stop in front of the house, and Wolf got out. Coming up on the porch, he stomped his feet to rid his boots of the snow caked on them and opened the door. His cool black gaze flickered over his son, then to Mary. His eyes widened fractionally as he examined every slim curve exhibited by Joe's old jeans, but he didn't comment.

"Get your things together," he instructed. "I have a spare hose that will fit your car. We'll put it on, then take you home."

"I can drive," she replied. "But thank you for your trouble. How much is the hose? I'll pay you for that."

"Consider it neighborly assistance to a greenhorn. And we'll still take you home. I'd rather you practiced driving in the snow somewhere other than on this mountain."

His dark face was expressionless, as usual, but she sensed that he'd made up his mind and wouldn't budge. She got her dress from Joe's room and the rest of her things from the kitchen. When she returned to the living room, Wolf held a thick coat for her to wear. She slipped into it; since it reached almost to her knees and the sleeves totally obscured her hands, she knew it had to be his.

Joe had on his coat and hat again. "Ready."

Wolf looked at his son. "Have you two had your talk?"

The boy nodded. "Yes." He met his father's eyes squarely. "She's going to tutor me. I'm going to try to get into the Air Force Academy."

"It's your decision. Just make sure you know what you're getting into."

"I have to try."

Wolf nodded once, and that was the end of the discussion. With her sandwiched between them, they left the warmth of the house, and once again Mary was struck by the bitter, merciless cold. She scrambled gratefully into the truck, which had been left running, and the blast of hot air from the heater vents felt like heaven.

Wolf got behind the wheel, and Joe got in beside her, trapping her between their two much bigger bodies. She sat with her hands primly folded and her booted feet placed neatly side-by-side as they drove down to an enormous barn with long stables extending off each side of it like arms. Wolf got out and entered the barn, then returned thirty seconds later with a length of thick black hose.

When they reached her car, both Mackenzies got out and poked their heads under the raised hood, but Wolf told her, in that tone of voice she already recognized as meaning business, to stay in the truck. He was certainly autocratic, but she liked his relationship with Joe. There was a strong sense of respect between them.

She wondered if the townspeople were truly so hostile simply because the Mackenzies were half Indian. Something Joe had said tugged at her memory, something about it would be bad enough if it were just him involved, but it would be twice as bad because of Wolf. What about Wolf? He'd rescued her from an unpleasant, even dangerous, situation, he'd seen to her comfort, and now he was repairing her car.

He'd also kissed her silly.

She could feel her cheeks heat as she remembered those fierce kisses. No, the kisses, and remembering them, begot a different kind of heat. Her cheeks were hot because her own behavior was so appalling she could barely bring herself to think about it. She had never—never!—been so forward with a man. It was totally out of character for her.

Aunt Ardith would have had a conniption fit at the thought of her mousy, sedate niece letting a strange man put his tongue in her mouth. It had to be unsanitary, though it was also, to be honest, exciting in a primitive way.

Her face still felt hot when Wolf got back into the truck, but he didn't even look at her. "It's fixed. Joe will follow us."

"But doesn't it need more water and antifreeze?"

He cast her a disbelieving look. "I had a can of antifreeze in the back of the truck. Weren't you paying attention when I got it out?"

She blushed again. She hadn't been paying attention; she'd been lost in reliving those kisses he'd given her, her heart thundering and her blood racing. It was an extraordinary reaction, and she wasn't certain how to handle it. Ignoring it seemed the wisest course, but was it possible to ignore something like that?

His powerful leg moved against hers as he shifted gears, and abruptly she realized she was still sitting in the middle of the seat. "I'll get out of your way," she said hastily, and slid over by the window.

Wolf had liked the feel of her sitting next to him, so close that his arm and leg brushed her whenever he changed gears, but he didn't tell her that. Things had gotten way out of hand at the house, but he didn't have to let them go any further. This deal with Joe worried him, and Joe was more important to him than the way a soft woman felt in his arms.

"I don't want Joe hurt because your do-gooder instincts won't leave well enough alone." He spoke in a low, silky tone that made her jump, and he knew she sensed the menace in it. "The Air Force Academy! That's climbing high for an Indian kid, with a lot of people waiting to step on his fingers."

If he'd thought to intimidate her, he'd failed. She turned toward him with fire sparking in her eyes, her chin up. "Mr. Mackenzie, I didn't promise Joe he would be accepted into the Academy. He understands that. His grades were high enough to qualify him for recommendation, but he dropped out of school. He has no chance at all unless he gets back into school and gets the credits he needs. That's what I offered him: a chance."

"And if he doesn't make it?"

"He wants to try. Even if he isn't accepted, at least he'll know he tried, and at least he'll have a diploma."

"So he can do exactly what he would have done without the diploma."

"Perhaps. But I'm going to begin checking into the procedure and qualifications on Monday, and writing to people. The competition to get into the Academy is really fierce."

"The people in town won't like you tutoring him."

"That's what Joe said." Her face took on that prim, obstinate look. "But I'll have something to say to anyone who kicks up about it. Just let me handle them, Mr. Mackenzie."

They were already down the mountain that had taken her so long to drive up. Wolf was silent for the rest of the drive, so Mary was, too. But when he pulled up to the old house where she was living, he rested his gloved hands on the steering wheel and said, "It isn't just Joe. For your sake, don't let on that you're doing it. It's better for you if no one knows you've ever even spoken to me."

"Why ever not?"

His smile was wintry. "I'm an ex-con. I did time for rape."

Afterward, Mary kicked herself for simply getting out of the truck without saying a word in response to his bald statement, but at the time she had been shocked to the core and incapable of a response. Rape! The crime was repulsive. It was unbelievable. She had actually kissed him! She'd been so stunned that she'd merely nodded goodbye to him and told Joe that she'd see him that night, then gone in the house without thanking them for all their help and trouble.

Now reality set in. Standing alone in the old-fashioned kitchen, she watched Woodrow hungrily lapping milk from his saucer while she considered the man and his statement. She abruptly snorted. "Hogwash! If that man's a rapist, I'll boil you for supper, Woodrow."

Woodrow looked remarkably unconcerned, which to Mary indicated that the cat agreed with her judgment, and she had a high opinion of Woodrow's ability to know what was best for himself.

After all, Wolf hadn't said that he'd committed rape. He'd said that he had served time in prison for rape. When Mary thought of the way both Mackenzies automatically and bitterly accepted that they would be shunned because of their Indian blood, she wondered if perhaps the fact that Wolf was part Indian figured in his conviction. But he hadn't done it. She knew that as well as she knew her own face. The man who had helped her out of a bad situation, warmed her cold hands against his own body and kissed her with burning male hunger, simply wasn't the type of man who could hurt a woman like that. *He* was the one who had halted before those kisses had gone too far; she had already been putty in his hands.

It was ridiculous. There was no way he was a rapist.

Oh, perhaps it hadn't been any great hardship for him to stop kissing her; after all, she was mousy and inexperienced and would never be voluptuous, but... Her thoughts trailed off as remembered sensations intruded. She was inexperienced, but she wasn't stupid. He had been—well, hard. She had distinctly felt *it*. Perhaps he hadn't had an outlet for his physical appetites lately and she had been handy, but still he hadn't taken advantage of her. He hadn't treated her with a sailor's attitude that any port in a storm would suffice. What was that awful term she had heard one of her students use once? Oh, yes—horny. She could accept that Wolf Mackenzie had been in that condition and she had accidentally stirred his fire in some way that still remained a mystery to her, but the bottom line was that he hadn't pushed his advantage.

What if he had?

Her heart started a strong, heavy beat, and heat crept through her, while an achy, restless feeling settled low inside. Her breasts tightened and began throbbing, and automatically she pressed her palms over them before she realized what she was doing and jerked her hands down. But what if he had touched them? What if he had put his mouth on her? She felt as if she would melt now, just thinking about him. Fantasizing. She pressed her thighs together, trying to ease the hollow ache, and a whimper escaped her lips. The sound was low, but seemed inordinately loud in the silent house, and the cat looked up from his saucer, gave a questioning meow, then returned to the milk.

Would she have been able to stop him? Would she even have tried to stop him? Or would she now be standing here remembering making love instead of trying to imagine how it would be? Her body tingled, but from barely awakened instincts and needs rather than true knowledge.

She had never before known passion, other than the passion for knowledge and teaching. To find her body capable of such strong sensations was frightening, because she had thought she knew herself well. Suddenly her own flesh was alien to her, and her thoughts and emotions were abruptly unruly. It was almost like a betrayal.

Why, this was lust! She, Mary Elizabeth Potter, actually *lusted* after a man! Not just any man, either. Wolf Mackenzie.

It was both amazing and embarrassing.

Joe proved a quick, able student, as Mary had known he would be. He was prompt, arriving right on time, and thankfully alone. After stewing over the morning's events for the entire afternoon, she didn't think she could ever face Wolf Mackenzie again. What must he think of her? To her mind, she had practically attacked the man.

But Joe was alone, and in the three hours that followed, Mary found herself liking him more and more. He was hungry for knowledge and absorbed it like a dry sponge. While he worked on the assignments she had set out for him, she prepared a set of records in which to keep the time he spent on each subject, the matter covered and his test scores. The goal they had set for themselves was much higher than just a high school diploma. Though she hadn't promised it, she knew she wouldn't be satisfied unless Joe was accepted into the Air Force Academy. There had been something in his eyes that told her he would never be complete unless he could fly; he was like a grounded eagle, his soul yearning for the sky.

At nine o'clock she called a halt and noted the time in her records.

Joe yawned as he rocked the chair onto its back legs. "How often do we do this?"

"Every night, if you can," she replied. "At least until you catch up with the rest of your class."

His pale, blue-diamond eyes glittered at her, and again she was struck by how old those eyes were. "Do I have to go back to regular classrooms next year?"

"It would help if you did. You'd be able to get much more work done, and we could do your advanced studies here."

"I'll think about it. I don't want to leave Dad in the lurch. We're expanding the ranch now, and it means a lot more work. We have more horses now than we've ever had before."

"Do you raise horses?"

"Quarter horses. Good ranch horses, trained to handle cattle. We not only breed them, but people bring their own horses to the ranch for Dad to train. He's not just good, he's the best. Folks don't mind that he's an Indian when it comes to training their horses."

Again the bitterness was apparent. Mary propped her elbows on the table and leaned her chin on her upraised, folded hands. "And you?"

"I'm Indian, too, Miss Potter. Half Indian, and that's more than enough for most people. It wasn't as bad when I was younger, but an Indian kid isn't much of a threat to anyone. It's when that kid grows up and starts looking at the white Anglo daughters that all hell breaks loose."

So a girl had been part of the reason Joe had quit school. Mary raised her eyebrows at him. "I imagine the white Anglo daughters looked back, too," she said mildly. "You're very good-looking."

He almost grinned at her. "Yeah. That and two bits will get me a cup of coffee."

"So they looked back?"

"And flirted. One acted like she really cared something about me. But when I asked her to a dance, the door was slammed in my face right quick. I guess it's okay to flirt with me, sort of like waving a red flag at a bull from a safe distance, but there was no way she was actually going to go out with an Indian."

"I'm sorry." Without thinking, Mary reached out and covered his strong young hand with her own. "Is that when you quit school?"

"There didn't seem to be any point in going. Don't think I was serious about her, or anything like that, because it hadn't gotten that far. I was just interested in her. But the whole thing made it plain that I was never going to fit in, that none of those girls would ever go out with me."

"So what did you plan on doing? Working on the ranch for the rest of your life and never dating, never getting married?"

"I'm sure not thinking of getting married!" he said strongly. "As for the rest of it, there are other towns, bigger towns. The ranch is doing pretty good now, and we have a little extra money.'' He didn't add that he'd lost his virginity two years before, on a trip to one of those bigger towns. He didn't want to shock her, and he was certain she would be shocked if she had any idea of his experience. The new teacher wasn't just prim, she was innocent. It made him feel oddly protective. That, and the fact that she was different from the other teachers he'd known. When she looked at him she saw *him*, Joe Mackenzie, not the bronzed skin and black hair of a half-breed. She had looked into his eyes and seen the dream, the obsession he'd always had with planes and flying.

After Joe had left, Mary locked the house and got ready for bed. It had been a tumultuous day for her, but it was a long time before she slept, and then she overslept the next morning. She deliberately kept herself busy that day, not giving herself time to moon over Wolf Mackenzie, or fantasize about things that hadn't happened. She mopped and waxed until the old house was shiny, then dragged out the boxes of books she had brought from Savannah. Books always gave a house a lived-in look. To her frustration, however, there was no place to put them. What she needed was some of that portable shelving; if all it required for assembly was a screwdriver, she should be able to put it up herself. With her customary decisiveness, she made plans to check at the general store the next afternoon. If they didn't have what she needed, she would buy some lumber and hire someone to build some shelves.

At lunch on Monday she made a call to the state board of education to find out what she had to do to make certain Joe's studies would be accepted toward his diploma. She knew she had the qualifications, but there was also a good deal of paperwork to be done before he could earn the necessary credits by private tutoring. She made the call on the pay phone in the tiny teacher's lounge, which was never used because there were only three teachers, each teaching four grades, and there was never any time for a break. Nevertheless it had three chairs and a table, a tiny, dented refrigerator, an automatic coffee maker and the pay phone. It was so unusual for any of the teachers to use the lounge that Mary was surprised when the door opened and Sharon Wycliffe, who taught grades one through four, poked her head in.

"Mary, are you feeling sick or anything?"

"No, I'm fine." Mary stood and dusted off her hands. The receiver had carried a gray coating, evidence of how often it was used. "I was making a call."

"Oh. I just wondered. You'd been in here a long time, and I thought you might not be feeling well. Who were you calling?"

The question was asked without any hesitancy. Sharon had been born in Ruth, had gone to school here, had married a local boy. Everyone in Ruth knew every one of the other one hundred and eighty inhabitants; they all knew each other's business and saw nothing unusual about it.

Small towns were merely large extended families. Mary wasn't taken aback by Sharon's open curiosity, having already experienced it.

"The state board. I needed some information on teaching requirements."

Sharon looked alarmed. "Do you think you aren't properly certified? If there's any trouble, the school board will likely commit mass suicide. You don't know how hard it is to find a teacher with the proper qualifications willing to come to a town as small as Ruth. They were almost at the panic stage when you were located. The kids were going to have to start going to school over sixty miles away."

"No, it isn't that. I thought I might begin private tutoring, if any of the kids need it." She didn't mention Joe Mackenzie, because she couldn't forget the warnings both he and his father had given her.

"Thank goodness it isn't bad news," Sharon exclaimed. "I'd better get back to the kids before they get into trouble." With a wave and a smile she withdrew her head, her curiosity satisfied.

Mary hoped Sharon didn't mention it to Dottie Lancaster, the teacher who taught grades five through eight, but she knew it was a futile hope. Eventually, everything in Ruth became common knowledge. Sharon was warm and full of good humor with her young charges, and Mary's teaching style was rather relaxed, too, but Dottie was strict and abrupt with the students. It made Mary uncomfortable, because she sensed Dottie regarded her job as merely a job, something that was necessary but not enjoyed. She had even heard that Dottie, who was fifty-five, was thinking about an early retirement. For all Dottie's shortcomings, that would certainly upset the local school board, because as Sharon had pointed out, it was almost impossible to get a teacher to relocate to Ruth. The town was just too small and too far away from everything.

As she taught the last classes of the day, Mary found herself studying the young girls and wondering which one had daringly flirted with Joe Mackenzie, then retreated when he had actually asked her out. Several of the girls were very attractive and flirtatious, and though they had the shallowness typical of teenagers, they all seemed likable. But which one would have attracted Joe, who wasn't shallow, whose eyes were far too old for a sixteen-year-old boy? Natalie Ulrich, who was tall and graceful? Pamela Hearst, who had the sort of blond good looks that belonged on a California beach? Or maybe it was Jackie Baugh, with her dark, sultry eyes. It could be any of the eight girls in her classes, she realized. They were used to being pursued, having had the stupendous good luck to be outnumbered, nine to eight, by the boys. They were all flirts. So which one was it?

She wondered why it mattered, but it did. One of these girls, though she hadn't broken Joe's heart, had nevertheless dealt him what could have been a life-destroying blow. Joe had taken it as the final proof that he'd never have a place in the white man's world, and he'd withdrawn. He still might never re-enter this school, but at least he'd agreed to be tutored. If only he didn't lose hope.

When school was out, she swiftly gathered all the materials she would need that night, as well as the papers she had to grade, and hurried to her car. It was only a short drive to Hearst's General Store, and when she asked, Mr. Hearst kindly directed her to the stacks of shelving in a corner.

A few minutes later the door opened to admit another customer. Mary saw Wolf as soon as he entered the store; she had been examining the shelving, but it was as if her skin was an alarm system, signaling his nearness. Her nerves tingled, the hair at the nape of her neck bristled, she looked up, and there he was. Instantly she shivered, and her nipples tightened. Distress at that uncontrollable response sent blood rushing to her face.

With her peripheral vision she saw Mr. Hearst stiffen, and for the first time she truly believed the things Wolf had told her about the way he was regarded in town. He hadn't done anything, hadn't said anything, but it was obvious Mr. Hearst wasn't happy to have him in the store.

Quickly she turned back to the shelving. She couldn't look him in the eye. Her face heated even more when she thought of the way she'd acted, throwing herself at him like a sex-starved old maid. It didn't help her feelings that he probably thought she *was* a sex-starved old maid; she couldn't argue with the old maid part, but she had never paid much attention to the other until Wolf had taken her in his arms. When she thought of the things she had done...

Her face was on fire. Her body was on fire. There was no way she could talk to him. What must he think of her? With fierce concentration, she read the instructions on the box of shelving and pretended she hadn't seen him enter the store.

She had read the instructions three times before she realized she was acting just like the people he had described: too good to speak to him, disdaining to acknowledge knowing him. Mary was normally even-tempered, but suddenly rage filled her, and it was rage at herself. What sort of person was she?

She jerked the box of shelving toward her and nearly staggered under the unexpected weight. Just as she turned, Wolf laid a box of nails on the checkout counter and reached in his pocket for his wallet.

Mr. Hearst glanced briefly at Wolf; then his eyes cut to where Mary was struggling with the box. "Here, Miss Potter, let me get that," he said, rushing from behind the counter to grab the box. He grunted as he hefted it in his arms. "Can't have you wrestling with something this heavy. Why, you might hurt yourself."

Mary wondered how he thought she would get it from her car into her house if she didn't handle it herself, but refrained from pointing that out. She followed him back to the counter, squared her shoulders, took a deep breath, looked up at Wolf and said clearly, "Hello, Mr. Mackenzie. How are you?"

His night-dark eyes glittered, perhaps in warning. "Miss Potter," he said in brief acknowledgment, touching the brim of his hat with his fingers, but he refused to respond to her polite inquiry.

Mr. Hearst looked sharply at Mary. "You know him, Miss Potter?"

"Indeed I do. He rescued me Saturday when my car broke down and I was stranded in the snow." She kept her voice clear and strong.

Mr. Hearst darted a suspicious look at Wolf. "Hmmph," he said, then reached for the box of shelving to ring it up.

"Excuse me," Mary said. "Mr. Mackenzie was here first."

She heard Wolf mutter a curse under his breath, or at least she thought it was a curse. Mr. Hearst turned red.

"I don't mind waiting," Wolf said tightly.

"I wouldn't dream of cutting in front of you." She folded her hands at her waist and pursed her lips. "I couldn't be that rude."

"Ladies first," Mr. Hearst said, trying for a smile.

Mary gave him a stern look. "Ladies shouldn't take advantage of their gender, Mr. Hearst. This is an age of equal treatment and fairness. Mr. Mackenzie was here first, and he should be waited on first."

Wolf shook his head and gave her a disbelieving look. "Are you one of those women's libbers?"

Mr. Hearst glared at him. "Don't take that tone with her, Indian."

"Now, just a minute." Controlling her outrage, she shook her finger at him. "That was rude and entirely uncalled for. Why, your mother would be ashamed of you, Mr. Hearst. Didn't she teach you better than that?"

He turned even redder. "She taught me just fine," he mumbled, staring at her finger.

There was something about a schoolteacher's finger; it had an amazing, mystical power. It made grown men quail before it. She had noticed the effect before and decided that a schoolteacher's finger was an extension of Mother's finger, and as such it wielded unknown authority. Women grew out of the feeling of guilt and helplessness brought on by that accusing finger, perhaps because most of them became mothers and developed their own powerful finger, but men never did. Mr. Hearst was no exception. He looked as if he wanted to crawl under his own counter.

"Then I'm certain you'll want to make her proud of you," she said in her most austere voice. "After you, Mr. Mackenzie."

Wolf made a sound that was almost a growl, but Mary stared at him until he jerked the money from his wallet and threw it on the counter. Without another word, Mr. Hearst rang up the nails and made change.

Equally silent, Wolf grabbed the box of nails, spun on his heel and left the store.

"Thank you," Mary said, finally relenting and bestowing a forgiving smile on Mr. Hearst. "I knew you would understand how important it is to me that I be treated fairly. I don't wish to take advantage of my position as a teacher here." She made it sound as if being a teacher was at least as important as being queen, but Mr. Hearst only nodded, too relieved to pursue the matter. He took her money and dutifully carried the box of shelving out to her car, where he stored it in the trunk for her.

"Thank you," she said again. "By the way, Pamela—she *is* your daughter, isn't she?"

Mr. Hearst looked worried. "Yes, she is." Pam was his youngest, and the apple of his eye.

"She's a lovely girl and a good student. I just wanted you to know that she's doing well in school."

His face was wreathed in smiles as she drove away.

Wolf pulled over at the corner and watched his rearview mirror, waiting for Mary to exit the store. He was so angry he wanted to shake her until her teeth rattled, and that made him even angrier, because he knew he wouldn't do it.

Damn her! He'd warned her, but she hadn't listened. Not only had she made it plain they were acquainted, she had outlined the circumstances of their meeting and then championed him in a way that wouldn't go unnoticed.

Hadn't she understood when he'd told her he was an ex-con, and why? Did she think he'd been joking?

His hands clenched around the steering wheel. She'd had her hair twisted up in a knot again, and those big glasses perched on her nose, hiding the soft slate-blue of her eyes, but he remembered how she had looked with her hair down, wearing Joe's old jeans that had clung tightly to her slender legs and hips. He remembered the way passion had glazed her eyes when he'd kissed her. He remembered the softness of her lips, though she had had them pressed together in a ridiculously prim expression.

If he had any sense he'd just drive away. If he stayed completely away from her, there wouldn't be anything for people to talk about other than the fact that she was tutoring Joe, and that would be bad enough in their eyes.

But how would she get that box out of the car and into the house when she got home? It probably weighed as much as she did. He would just carry the box in for her, and at the same time peel a strip off her hide for not listening to him.

Oh, hell, who was he fooling? He'd had a taste of her, and he wanted more. She was a frumpy old maid, but her skin was as pale and translucent as a baby's, and her slender body would be soft, gently curving under his hands. He wanted to touch her. After kissing her, holding her, he hadn't gone to see Julie Oakes because he hadn't been able to get the feel of Miss Mary Potter out of his mind, off of his body. He still ached. His physical frustration was painful, and it was going to get worse, because if he'd ever known anything, it was that Miss Mary Potter wasn't for him.

Her car pulled out from in front of the store and passed him. Smothering another curse, he put the truck in gear and slowly followed her. She maintained a sedate pace, following the two-lane highway out of town, then turning off on the narrow secondary road that led to her house. She had to see his truck behind her, but she didn't give any indication that she knew she was being followed. Instead she drove straight to her house, carefully turned in at the snow-packed driveway and guided the car around to her customary parking spot behind the house.

Wolf shook his head as he pulled in behind her and got out of the truck. She was already out of her car, and she smiled at him as she fished the house key out of her purse. Didn't she remember what he'd told her? He couldn't believe that he'd told her he'd served time for rape and still she greeted him as calmly as if he were a priest, though they were the only two people for miles around.

"Damn it all, lady!" he barked at her, his long legs carrying him to her in a few strides. "Didn't you listen to anything I said Saturday?"

"Yes, of course I listened. That doesn't mean I agreed." She unlocked the trunk and smiled at him. "While you're here, would you please carry this box in for me? I'd really appreciate it."

"That's why I stopped," he snapped. "I knew you couldn't handle it."

His ill temper didn't seem to faze her. She merely smiled at him again as he lifted the box onto his shoulder, then led the way to the back door and opened it.

The first thing he noticed was that the house had a fresh, sweet smell to it, instead of the musty smell of an old house that had stood empty for a long time. His head lifted, and against his will he inhaled the faint scent. "What's that smell?"

She stopped and sniffed delicately. "What smell?"

"That sweet smell. Like flowers."

"Flowers? Oh, that must be the lilac sachet I put in all the drawers to freshen them. So many of the sachets are overpowering, but the lilacs are just right, don't you think?"

He didn't know anything about sachets, whatever they were, but if she put them in all the drawers, then her underwear must smell like lilacs, too. Her sheets would smell like lilacs and the warm scent of her body.

His body responded strongly to the thought, and he cursed, then set the box down with a thud. Though the house was chilly, he felt sweat break out on his forehead.

"Let me turn up the heat," she said, ignoring his cursing. "The furnace is old and noisy, but I don't have any wood for the fireplace, so it'll have to do." As she talked, she left the kitchen and turned down a hallway, her voice growing fainter. Then she was back, and she smiled at him again. "It'll be warm in just a minute. Would you like a cup of tea?" After giving him a measuring look she said, "Make that coffee. You don't look like a tea-drinking man."

He was already warm. He was burning up. He pulled off his gloves and tossed them on the kitchen table. "Don't you know everybody in that town will be talking about you now? Lady, I'm Indian, and I'm an ex-con—"

"Mary," she interrupted briskly.

"What?"

"My name is Mary, not 'lady.' Mary Elizabeth." She added the second name out of habit because Aunt Ardith had always called her by both names. "Are you certain you don't want coffee? I need something to warm up my insides."

His hat joined the gloves, and he raked an impatient hand through his hair. "All right. Coffee."

Mary turned to run the water and measure the coffee, using the activity to hide the sudden color in her face. His hair. She felt stupid, but she'd hardly noticed his hair before. Maybe she'd been too upset, then too bemused, or maybe it was just that his midnight-black eyes had taken her attention, but she hadn't noticed before how long his hair was. It was thick and black and shiny, and touched his broad shoulders. He looked magnificently pagan; she had immediately pictured him with his powerful chest and legs bare, his body covered only by a breechclout or loincloth, and her pulse rate had gone wild.

He didn't sit down, but propped his long body against the cabinet beside her. Mary kept her head down, hoping her blush would subside. What was it about the man that the mere sight of him triggered erotic fantasies? She had certainly never had any fantasies before, erotic or otherwise. She had never before looked at a man and wondered what he looked like nude, but the thought of Wolf nude made her ache inside, made her hands itch to touch him.

"What the hell are you doing letting me even come in your house, let alone inviting me to have coffee?" he asked in a low, rough voice.

She blinked at him, her expression startled. "Why shouldn't I?"

He thought he might explode with frustration. "Lady—"

"Mary."

His big fists clenched. "*Mary.* Don't you have any better sense than to let an ex-con into your house?"

"Oh, that." She dismissed it with a wave of her hand. "It would be wise to follow your advice if you were truly a criminal, but since you didn't do it, I don't think that applies in this instance. Besides, if you *were* a criminal, you wouldn't give me that advice."

He couldn't believe the casual way she disregarded any possibility of his guilt. "How do you know I didn't do it?"

"You just didn't."

"Do you have any reason for your deduction, Sherlock, or are you going on good old feminine intuition?"

She jerked around and glared at him. "I don't believe a rapist would have handled a woman as tenderly as you—as you handled me," she said, her voice tapering off into a whisper, and the color surged back into her face. Mortified by the stupid way she continued to blush, she slapped her palms to her face in an effort to hide the betraying color.

Wolf clenched his teeth, partly because she was white and therefore not for him, partly because she was so damned innocent, and partly because he wanted so fiercely to touch her that his entire body ached. "Don't build any dreams because I kissed you Saturday," he said harshly. "I've been too long without a woman, and I'm—"

"Horny?" she supplied.

He was staggered by the incongruity of that word coming from her prim mouth. "What?"

"Horny," she said again. "I've heard some of my students say it. It means—"

"I know what it means!"

"Oh. Well, is that what you were? Still are, for all I know."

He wanted to laugh. The urge almost overpowered him, but he changed the sound into a cough. "Yeah, I still am."

She looked sympathetic. "I understand that can be quite a problem."

"It's hard on a guy."

It took a moment, but then her eyes widened, and before she could stop herself, her gaze had slid down his body. Instantly she jerked her head back up. "Oh. I see. I mean—I understand."

The need to touch her was suddenly so strong that he had to give in to it, had to touch her in even the smallest way. He put his hands on her shoulders, savoring her softness, the delicacy of her joints under his palms. "I don't think you do understand. You can't associate with me and still work in this town. At best, you'd be treated like a leper, or a slut. You would probably lose your job."

At that, she pressed her lips together, and a militant light came into her eyes. "I'd like to see someone try to fire me for associating with a law-abiding, tax-paying citizen. I refuse to pretend I don't know you."

"There's knowing, and there's knowing. It would be bad enough for you to be friends with me. Sleeping with me would make your life here impossible."

He felt her stiffen under his hands. "I don't believe I've asked to sleep with you," she said, but the color rose in her face again. She hadn't actually said the words, but he knew she certainly had thought about what it would be like.

"You asked, all right, but you're so damned innocent you didn't realize what you were doing," he muttered. "I could crawl on top of you right now, sweetheart, and I'd do it if you had any real idea of what you're asking for. But the last thing I want is to have some prissy little Anglo screaming 'rape' at me. Believe me, an Indian doesn't get the benefit of the doubt."

"I wouldn't do anything like that!"

He smiled grimly. "Yeah, I've heard that before. I'm probably the only man who has ever kissed you, and you think you'd like more, don't you? But sex isn't pretty and romantic, it's hot and sweaty, and you probably wouldn't like the first time at all. So do me a favor and find some other guinea pig. I have enough troubles without adding you to the list."

Mary jerked away from him, pressing her lips firmly together and blinking her eyes as fast as she could to keep the tears from falling. Not for anything would she let him make her cry.

"I'm sorry I gave you that impression," she said, her voice stifled but even. "It's true I've never been kissed before, but I'm sure you aren't surprised by that. I'm obviously not Miss America material. If my—my response was out of line, I apologize. It won't happen again." She turned briskly to the cabinet. "The coffee is ready. How do you take yours?"

A muscle jerked in his jaw, and he grabbed his hat. "Forget the coffee," he muttered as he jammed the hat on his head and reached for his gloves.

She didn't look at him. "Very well. Goodbye, Mr. Mackenzie."

Wolf slammed out the door, and Mary stood there with an empty coffee cup in her hand. If it really was goodbye, she didn't know how she would be able to stand it.

Mary wasn't weak-willed, and she refused to give in to the desolation that filled her every time she thought of that horrible day. During the days she prodded, cajoled and enticed her students toward knowledge; at night she watched Joe devour the facts she spread before him. His thirst for knowledge was insatiable, and he not only caught up with the students in her regular classes, he passed them.

She had written her letters to the Wyoming members of Congress, and had also written to a friend for all the information she could find on the Air Force Academy. When the package came, she gave it to Joe and watched his eyes take on that fiercely intent, enthralled look he got whenever he thought of flying. Working with Joe was a joy; her only problem was that he reminded her so strongly of his father.

It wasn't that she missed Wolf; how could she miss someone she had seen only twice? He hadn't imbedded himself in her daily routine so that her life seemed empty without him. But while she had been with him, she had felt more vividly alive than she ever had before. With Wolf, she hadn't been Mary Potter, old maid, she had been Mary Potter, woman. His intense masculinity had reached parts of her that she hadn't known existed, bringing to life dormant yearnings and emotions. She argued with herself that what she felt was plain old garden-variety lust, but that didn't stop the ache she felt whenever she thought of him. Even worse was her humiliation because her inexperience had been so obvious, and now she *knew* he thought of her as a sex-starved old maid.

It was April before the inevitable happened and word got out that Joe Mackenzie was spending a lot of time at the new teacher's house. At first Mary wasn't aware of the rumor flying through the town, though the kids in her classes had been watching her strangely, and there had been a lot of whispering. Sharon Wycliffe and Dottie Lancaster, the other two teachers, also took to giving her odd looks and whispering to each other. It didn't take Mary long to decide that the secret was no longer secret, but she went about her business with a serene smile. She had already received a favorable letter from a senator, signaling his interest in Joe, and despite her own arguments for caution, her spirits were high.

The school board's regular meeting was scheduled for the third week in April. The afternoon of the meeting, Sharon, with elaborate casualness, asked Mary if she planned to attend. Mary looked at her in surprise. "Of course. I thought all of us were expected to attend on a regular basis."

"Well, yes. It's just that—I thought—"

"You thought I would avoid the meeting now that everyone knows I've been teaching Joe Mackenzie?" Mary asked directly.

Sharon's mouth fell open. "What?" Her voice was weak.

"You didn't know? Well, it isn't an earth-shattering secret." She shrugged. "Joe thought people would be upset if I tutored him, so I haven't said anything. From the way everyone has been acting, I thought the cat was out of the bag."

"I think it was the wrong cat," Sharon admitted sheepishly. "His truck was seen at your house at night and people—um—got the wrong idea."

Mary felt blank. "What wrong idea?"

"Well, he's big for his age and all."

Still Mary didn't understand, until Sharon blushed hotly. Then comprehension burst on her brain like a flash, and horror filled her, followed swiftly by anger. "They think I'm having an affair with a *sixteen-year-old boy*?" Her voice rose with each word.

"It was late at night when his truck was seen," Sharon added, looking miserable.

"Joe leaves promptly at nine o'clock. Someone's idea of 'late' differs from mine." Mary stood and began shoving papers into her tote, her nostrils flaring, her cheeks white. The awful thing was that she had to simmer until seven o'clock that night, but she didn't think waiting would cool her temper. If anything, pressure would build. She felt savage, not only because her reputation had been impugned, but because Joe had also been attacked. He was trying desperately to make his dreams come true, and people were trying to tear him down. She wasn't a hen fussing with one chick; she was a tigress with one cub, and that cub had been threatened. It didn't matter that the cub was seven inches taller than she and outweighed her by almost eighty pounds; Joe, for all his unusual maturity, was still young and vulnerable. The father had disdained her protection, but there was no power on earth that could stop her from defending the son.

Evidently word had spread, because the school board meeting was unusually crowded that night. There were six members of the board: Mr. Hearst, who owned the general store; Francie Beecham, an eighty-one-year-old former teacher; Walton Isby, the bank president; Harlon Keschel, who owned the combination drugstore/hamburger joint; Eli Baugh, a local rancher whose daughter, Jackie, was in Mary's class; and Cicely Karr, who owned the service station. All of the board members were solid members of the small community, all of them property owners, and all of them except Francie Beecham had stony faces.

The board meeting was held in Dottie's classroom, and extra desks were brought from Mary's classroom so there would be enough seats for everyone, an indication of how many people felt it necessary to attend. Mary was certain that at least one parent of each of her students was present. As she entered the room, every eye turned toward her. The women looked indignant; the men looked both hostile and speculative, and that made Mary even angrier. What right did they have to look down on her for her supposed sins, while at the same time they were wondering about the details?

Leaning against the wall was a tall man in a khaki deputy sheriff's uniform, watching her with narrowed eyes, and she wondered if they meant to have her arrested for sexual misconduct. It was ridiculous! If she had looked anything other than exactly what she was, a slight, mousy old maid, their suspicions would at least have made more sense. She poked an errant strand of hair back into the knot at the back of her head, sat down and folded her arms, intending to let them make the first move.

Walton Isby cleared his throat and called the meeting to order, no doubt feeling the importance of his position with so many people present to watch the proceedings. Mary drummed her fingers on her arm. The board went through the routine of its normal business, and suddenly she decided she wasn't going to wait. The best defense, she'd read, was an attack.

When the normal business was finished, Mr. Isby cleared his throat again, and Mary took it as a signal that they were about to get down to the real purpose of the meeting. She rose to her feet and said clearly, "Mr. Isby, before you continue, I have an announcement to make."

He looked startled, and his florid face turned even redder. "This is— uh, well, irregular, Miss Potter."

"It's also important." She kept her voice at the level she used when lecturing and turned so she could see the entire room. The deputy straightened from his position against the wall as everyone's attention locked on her like a magnet to a steel bar. "I'm certified to tutor pupils privately, and the credits they earn in private lessons are as legitimate as those earned in a public classroom. For the past month, I've been tutoring Joe Mackenzie in my home—"

"I'll just bet you have," someone muttered, and Mary's eyes flashed.

"Who said that?" she demanded crisply. "It was incredibly vulgar."

The room fell silent.

"When I saw Joe Mackenzie's school records, I was outraged that a student of his intelligence had quit school. Perhaps none of you know it, but he was at the top of his class. I contacted him and persuaded him to take lessons to catch up to his classmates, and in one month he has not only caught them, he has surpassed them. I have also been in contact with Senator Allard, who has expressed an interest in Joe. Joe's strong academic standing has made him a candidate for recommendation to the

Air Force Academy. He's an honor to the community, and I know all of you will give him your support.''

She was gratified to see the stunned looks in the room and sat down with the cool poise Aunt Ardith had tirelessly drummed into her. Only rabble got into brawls, Aunt Ardith had said; a lady could make her point in other ways.

Whispers rustled through the room as people put their heads together, and Mr. Isby shuffled the three sheets of paper in front of him as he searched for something to say. The other members of the board put their heads together, too.

She looked around the room, and a shadow in the hall beyond the open door caught her attention. It was only a slight movement; if she hadn't looked at precisely that second, she would have missed it. As it was, it took her a moment to make out the outline of a tall man, and her skin tingled. Wolf. He was out in the hall, listening. It was the first time she had seen him since the day he'd come to her house, and even though all she could see was a darker outline against the shadows, her heart began to pound.

Mr. Isby cleared his throat, and the murmuring in the room settled down. "That is good news, Miss Potter," he began. "However, we don't think you've given the best appearance as an example to our young people—"

"Speak for yourself, Walton," Francie Beecham said testily, her voice cracking with old age.

Mary stood again. "In precisely what way have I given the wrong appearance?"

"It doesn't look right to have that boy in your house all hours of the night!" Mr. Hearst snapped.

"Joe leaves my home at exactly nine o'clock, after three hours of lessons. What is your definition of 'all hours of the night'? However, if the board doesn't approve of the location, I take it all are agreed that the schoolhouse will be used for night classes? I have no objection to moving the lessons here."

Mr. Isby, who was at heart a good-natured soul, looked harassed. The board members put their heads together again.

After a minute of heated consultation, they looked up again. Harlon Keschel wiped his perspiring face with a handkerchief. Francie Beecham looked outraged. This time it was Cicely Karr who spoke. "Miss Potter, this is a difficult situation. The odds against Joe Mackenzie being accepted into the Air Force Academy are high, I'm sure you'll admit, and the truth is that we don't approve of your spending so much time alone with him."

Mary's chin lifted. "Why is that?"

"Because you're a newcomer to this area, I'm sure you don't understand the way things are around here. The Mackenzies have a bad reputation, and we fear for your safety if you continue to associate with the boy.''

"Mrs. Karr, that's hogwash," Mary replied with inelegant candor. Aunt Ardith wouldn't have approved. She thought of Wolf standing out in the hallway listening to these people slandering both him and his son, and she could almost feel the heat of his temper. He wouldn't let it hurt him, but it hurt her to know he was hearing it.

"Wolf Mackenzie helped me out of a dangerous situation when my car broke down and I was stranded in the snow. He was kind and considerate, and refused payment for repairing my car. Joe Mackenzie is an outstanding student who works hard on their ranch, doesn't drink or carouse—'' she hoped that was true "—and has never been anything but respectful. I consider both of them my friends.''

In the hallway, the man standing in the shadows knotted his fists. Damn the little fool, didn't she know this would probably cost her her job? He knew that if he stepped into that room all the hostility would instantly be focused on him, and he started to move, to draw their attention away from her, when he heard her speaking again. Didn't she know when to shut up?

"I would be as concerned if any of your children dropped out of school. I can't bear to see a young person give up on the future. Ladies and gentlemen, I was hired to teach. I intend to do that to the best of my ability. All of you are good people. Would any of you want me to give up if it were *your* child?''

Several people looked away and cleared their throats. Cicely Karr merely raised her chin. "You're sidestepping the point, Miss Potter. This isn't one of our children. This is Joe Mackenzie. He's...he's—''

"Half Indian?" Mary supplied, lifting her brow in question.

"Well, yes. That's part of it. The other part is his father—''

"What about his father?''

Wolf had to stifle a curse, and he started to step forward again when Mary asked scornfully, "Are you concerned because of his prison sentence?''

"That's cause enough, I should think!''

"Should you? Why?''

"Cicely, sit down and hush," Francie Beecham snapped. "The girl has a point, and I agree. If you start trying to think at this stage of your life, it could bring on hot flashes.''

Just for a moment there was stunned silence in the room; then it exploded in thunderous laughter. Rough ranchers and their hard-working wives held their stomachs as they bent double, tears running down their faces. Mr. Isby turned so red his face was almost purple; then he burst into a great whooping laugh that sounded like a hysterical crane laying eggs, or so Cicely Karr told him. Her face was red, too, from anger. Big Eli Baugh actually rolled out of his chair, he was laughing so hard. Cicely grabbed his hat from the back of his chair and hit him over the head with it. He continued to howl with laughter as he protected his head with his arms.

"You can buy your motor oil from some other place from now on!" Cicely roared at Mr. Baugh, continuing to bash him with his hat. "And your gas! Don't you or any of your hands set foot on my property again!"

"Now, Cicely," Eli choked as he tried to dodge his hat.

"Folks, let's have some order in here," Harlon Keschel pleaded, though he looked as if he were enjoying the spectacle of Cicely bashing Eli with his own hat. Certainly everyone else in the room was. Almost everyone, Mary thought, as she spotted Dottie Lancaster's cold face. Suddenly she realized that the other teacher would have been glad to see her fired, and she wondered why. She'd always tried to be friendly with Dottie, but the older woman had rebuffed all overtures. Had *Dottie* seen Joe's truck at Mary's house and started the gossip? Would Dottie have been out driving around at night? There were no other houses on Mary's road, so no one would have been driving past to visit a neighbor.

The uproar had died down, though there was still an occasional chuckle heard around the room. Mrs. Karr continued to glare at Eli Baugh, having for some reason made him the focal point of her embarrassed anger rather than turning it on Francie Beecham, who had started it all.

Even Mr. Isby was still grinning as he raised his voice. "Let's see if we can get back to business here, folks."

Francie Beecham piped up again. "I think we've handled enough business for the night. Miss Potter is giving the Mackenzie boy private school lessons so he can go to the Air Force Academy, and that's that. I'd do the same thing if I were still teaching."

Mr. Hearst said, "It still don't look right—"

"Then she can use the classroom. Everyone agreed?" Francie looked at the other board members, her wrinkled face triumphant. She winked at Mary.

"It's okay by me," Eli Baugh said as he tried to reshape his hat. "The Air Force Academy—well, that's something. I don't reckon anyone from this county has ever been to any of the academies."

Mr. Hearst and Mrs. Karr disagreed, but Mr. Isby and Harlon Keschel sided with Francie and Eli. Mary stared hard at the shadowed hallway, but couldn't see anything now. Had he left? The deputy turned his head to see what she was looking at, but he didn't see anything, either, because he gave a slight shrug and looked back at her, then winked. Mary was startled. More people had winked at her that night than in the rest of her life total. What was the proper way to handle a wink? Were they ignored?

Should she wink back? Aunt Ardith's lectures on proper behavior hadn't covered winking.

The meeting broke up with a good deal of teasing and laughter, and more than a few of the parents took a moment to shake Mary's hand and tell her she was doing a good job. It was half an hour before she was able to get her coat and make it to the door, and when she did, she found the deputy waiting for her.

"I'll walk you to your car," he said in an easy tone. "I'm Clay Armstrong, the local deputy."

"How do you do? Mary Potter," she replied, holding out her hand.

He took it, and her small hand disappeared in his big one. He set his hat on top of dark brown curly hair, but his blue eyes still twinkled, even in the shadow of the brim. She liked him on sight. He was one of those strong, quiet men who were rock steady, but who had a good sense of humor. He'd been delighted by the uproar.

"Everyone in town knows who you are. We don't often have a stranger move in, especially a young single woman from the South. The first day you were here, the whole county heard about your accent. Haven't you noticed that all the girls in school are trying to drawl?"

"Are they?" she asked in surprise.

"They sure are." He slowed his walk to keep pace with her as they walked to her car. The cold air rushed at her, chilling her legs, but the night sky was crystal clear, and a thousand stars winked overhead in compensation.

They reached her car. "Would you tell me something, Mr. Armstrong?"

"Anything. And call me Clay."

"Why did Mrs. Karr get so angry at Mr. Baugh, instead of at Miss Beecham? It was Miss Beecham who started the whole thing."

"Cicely and Eli are first cousins. Cicely's folks died when she was young, and Eli's parents took her to raise. Well, Cicely and Eli are the same age, so they grew up together and fought like wildcats the whole time. Still do, I guess, but some families are like that. They're still pretty close."

That kind of family was strange to Mary, but it sounded warm and secure, too, to be able to fight with someone and know he still loved you.

"So she hit him for laughing at her?"

"And because he was convenient. No one is going to get too angry with Miss Beecham. She taught all the adults in this county, and we all still think a lot of that old lady."

"That sounds so nice," Mary said, smiling. "I hope I'm still here when I'm that old."

"Are you planning to raise cain at school board meetings, too?"

"I hope so," she repeated.

He leaned down to open the car door for her. "I hope so, too. Be careful driving home." After she got in, he closed the door and touched his fingers to his hat brim, then strode away.

He was a nice man. Most of the people in Ruth were nice. They were blind where Wolf Mackenzie was concerned, but basically they weren't vicious people.

Wolf. Where had he gone?

She hoped Joe wouldn't decide to stop his lessons because of this. Though she knew it was foolish to count her chickens prematurely, she felt a growing certainty that he would be accepted into the Academy and was inordinately proud that she could be part of getting him there. Aunt Ardith would have said that pride goeth before a fall, but Mary had often thought that a person would never fall if he didn't first try to stand. On more than one occasion she had countered Aunt Ardith's cliché of choice with her own "nothing ventured, nothing gained." It had always made Aunt Ardith huffy when her favorite weapon was turned against her. Mary sighed. She missed her acerbic aunt so much. Her supply of clichés might wither from lack of use without Aunt Ardith to sharpen her wits against.

When she turned into her driveway, she was tired, hungry and anxious, afraid that Joe would try to be noble and stop his lessons so she wouldn't have any more trouble because of him. "I'll teach him," she muttered aloud as she stepped out of the car, "if I have to follow him around on horseback."

"Who are you following around?" Wolf demanded irritably, and she jumped so violently that she banged her knee against the car door.

"Where did you come from?" she demanded just as irritably. "Darn it, you scared me!"

"Probably not enough. I parked in the barn, out of sight."

She stared up at him, drinking in the sight of his proud, chiseled face and closed expression. The starlight was colorless, revealing his features in stark angles and shadows, but it was enough for her. She hadn't realized how starved she had been for the sight of him, the heart-pounding nearness of him. She couldn't even feel the cold now, the way blood was racing through her veins. This was probably what "being in heat" meant. It was breathtaking and a little scary, but she decided she liked it.

"Let's go in," he said when she made no effort to move, and Mary silently led the way to the back door. She'd left it unlocked so she wouldn't have to fumble with a key in the dark, and Wolf's black brows drew together when she turned the knob and pushed the door open.

They entered, and Mary closed the door behind them, then turned on the light. Wolf stared down at her, at the silky brown hair escaping from its knot, and he had to clench his fists to keep from grabbing her. "Don't leave your door unlocked again," he ordered.

"I don't think I'll be burgled," she countered, then admitted honestly, "I don't have anything a self-respecting burglar would want."

He'd sworn he wouldn't touch her, but even though he'd known it would be difficult to keep his hands to himself, he hadn't realized quite *how* difficult. He wanted to grab her and shake some sense into her, but he knew if he touched her in any way at all, he wouldn't want to stop. Her female scent teased his nostrils, beckoning him closer; she smelled warm and delicately fragrant, so feminine it made his entire body ache with longing. He moved away from her, knowing it was safer for them both if he put some distance between them.

"I wasn't thinking about a burglar."

"No?" She considered that, then realized what he'd meant and what she'd said in response. She cleared her throat and marched to the stove, hoping he wouldn't see her red face. "If I make a pot of coffee, will you drink a cup this time or storm out like you did before as soon as it's made?"

The tart reproach in her voice amused him, and he wondered how he had ever thought her mousy. Her clothes were dowdy, but her personality was anything but timid. She said exactly what she thought and didn't hesitate to take someone to task. Less than an hour before she had taken on the entire county on his behalf. The memory of it sobered him.

"I'll drink the coffee if you insist on making it, but I'd rather you just sat down and listened to me."

Turning, Mary slid into a chair and primly folded her hands on the table. "I'm listening."

He pulled the chair next to her away from the table and turned it to the side, facing her, before he sat down. She turned an unsmiling gaze on him. "I saw you in the hall tonight."

He looked grim. "Damn. Did anyone else notice me?" He wondered how she had seen him, because he'd been very careful, and he was good at not being seen when he didn't want to be.

"I don't think so." She paused. "I'm sorry they said those things."

"I'm not worried about what the good people of Ruth think about me," he said in a hard tone. "I can handle them, and so can Joe. We don't depend on them for our living, but you do. Don't go to bat for us again, unless you don't like your job very much and you're trying to lose it, because that's damn sure what will happen if you keep on."

"I won't lose my job for teaching Joe."

"Maybe not. Maybe they'll have some tolerance for Joe, especially since you threw the Academy at them, but I'm another story."

"Nor will I lose my job for being friendly with you. I have a contract," she explained serenely. "An ironclad contract. It isn't easy to get a teacher in a place as small and isolated as Ruth, especially in the middle of winter. I can lose my job only if I'm judged incompetent, or break the law, and I defy anyone to prove me incompetent.''

He wondered if that meant she didn't rule out breaking the law, but didn't ask her. The kitchen light was shining directly down on her head, turning her hair to a silvery halo and distracting him with its glitter. He knew her hair was brown, but it was such a pale, ash brown that it had no red tones, and when light struck it the strands actually looked silver. She looked like an angel, with her soft blue eyes and translucent skin, and her silky hair slipping from its confining knot to curl around her face. His insides knotted painfully. He wanted to touch her. He wanted her naked beneath him. He wanted to be inside her, to gently ride her until she was all soft and wet, and her nails were clawing at his back—

Mary reached out and put her slim hand on his much larger one, and just that small touch burned him. ''Tell me what happened,'' she invited softly. ''Why were you sent to prison? I know you didn't do it.''

Wolf was a hard man, by nature as well as necessity, but her simple, unquestioning faith in him shook him to the bone. He had always stood alone, isolated by his Indian blood from Anglos and by his Anglo blood from Indians. Not even his parents had been close to him, though they had loved him and he had loved them in return. They had simply never truly known him, never been admitted into his private thoughts. Nor had he been close to his wife, Joe's mother. They had slept together, he'd been fond of her, but she, too, had been kept at a distance. Only with Joe had his reserve been breached, and Joe knew him as no other person on earth did. They were part of each other, and he fiercely loved the boy. Only the thought of Joe had gotten him through the years in prison alive.

It was more than alarming that this slight Anglo woman had a knack for touching nerves he'd thought completely insulated; he didn't want her close to him, not in any emotional way. He wanted to have sex with her, but he didn't want her to matter to him. Angrily he realized that she already mattered to him, and he didn't like it at all.

He stared at her fragile hand on his, her touch light and soft. She didn't shrink from touching him, as if he were dirty; nor was she grasping at him as some women did, rapaciously, wanting to use him, to see if the savage could satisfy their shallow, greedy appetites. She had simply reached out to touch him because she cared.

Ever so slowly he watched his hand turn and engulf hers, enfolding the pale, slim fingers within his callused palm as if to protect them.

''It was nine years ago.'' His voice was low, harsh; she had to lean forward to hear him. ''No—almost ten years. Ten years this June. Joe and I had just moved here. I was working for the Half Moon Ranch. A girl from the next county was raped and killed, and her body dumped just within the far boundary of Half Moon. I was picked up and questioned, but hell, I'd been expecting it from the minute I heard about the girl. I was new to the area, and Indian. But there was no evidence against me, so they had to let me go.

"Three weeks later, another girl was raped. This one was from the Rocking L Ranch, just to the west of town. She was stabbed, like the other girl, but she lived. She'd seen the rapist." He paused for a minute, the expression in his black eyes shuttered as he looked back at those long-ago years. "She said he looked like an Indian. He was dark, with black hair, and he was tall. Not many tall Indians around. I was picked up again before I even knew another girl had been raped. They put me in a lineup with six dark-haired Anglos. The girl identified me, and I was charged. Joe and I lived on Half Moon, but somehow no one remembered seeing me at home the night that girl was raped, except Joe, and a six-year-old Indian kid's word didn't carry much weight."

Her chest hurt when she thought of how it had been for him, and for Joe, who had been only a small child. How much worse had it been for Wolf because of Joe, worrying what would happen to his son? She didn't know of anything she could say now to lessen that ten-year-old outrage, so she didn't try; she just tightened her fingers around his, letting him know he wasn't alone.

"I was put on trial and found guilty. I'm lucky they weren't able to tie me to the first rape, the girl who'd been murdered, or I'd have been lynched. As it was, everyone thought I'd done it."

"You went to prison." It was so hard to believe, even though she knew it was true. "What happened to Joe?"

"He was made a ward of the state. I survived prison. It wasn't easy. A rapist is considered fair game. I had to be the roughest son of a bitch in there just to live from one night to the next."

She had heard tales about what happened to men in prison, and her pain increased. He had been locked up, away from the sun and the mountains, the clear fresh air, and she knew it had been like caging a wild animal. He was innocent, but his freedom and his son had been taken from him, and he'd been thrown in with the dregs of humanity. Had he slept soundly even once the entire time he'd been in prison, or had he merely dozed, his senses attuned to attack?

Her throat was tight and dry. All she could manage was a whisper. "How long were you in?"

"Two years." His face was hard, his eyes full of menace as he stared at her, but she knew the menace was directed inward, at his bitter memories. "Then a series of rapes and murders from Casper to Cheyenne were tied together and the guy was caught. He confessed, seemed proud of his accomplishments, but a little put out that they hadn't given him complete credit. He admitted to the two rapes in this area, and gave them details no one but the rapist could have known."

"Was he Indian?"

His smile was flinty. "Italian. Olive-skinned, curly haired."

"So you were released?"

"Yeah. My name was cleared, and they said 'Sorry about that,' and turned me loose. I'd lost my son, my job, everything I'd owned. I found out where they'd put Joe and hitched there to get him. Then I rodeoed for a while to get some money and lucked out. I did pretty well. I won enough to come back here with something in my pocket. The old guy who had owned Half Moon had died with no heirs, and the land was about to be sold for taxes. It wiped me out, but I bought the land. Joe and I settled here, and I began training horses and building up the ranch."

"Why did you come back?" She couldn't understand it. Why return to the place where he'd been so mistreated?

"Because I was tired of always moving on, never having a place of my own. Damn tired of being looked down on as a trashy, shiftless Indian. Tired of my son not having a home. And because there was no way in hell I was going to let the bastards get the best of me."

The aching in her intensified. She wished she could ease the anger and bitterness in him, wished she dared take him in her arms and soothe him, wished he could become a part of the community instead of a thorn in its side.

"They're not all illegitimate," she said, and wondered why his mouth suddenly twitched as if he might smile. "Any more than all Indians are trashy or shiftless. People are just people, good and bad."

"You need a keeper," he replied. "That Pollyanna attitude is going to get you in trouble. Teach Joe, do what you can for him, but stay the hell away from me, for your own sake. These people didn't change their minds about me just because I was released."

"You haven't tried to change their minds. You've just kept rubbing their noses in their guilt," she pointed out, her tone acerbic.

"Am I supposed to forget what they did?" he asked just as sharply. "Forget that their 'justice' consisted of putting me in a lineup with six Anglos and telling that girl to 'pick out the Indian'? I spent two years in hell. I still don't know what happened to Joe, but it was almost three months after I got him back before he spoke a word. Forget that? Like hell."

"So, they won't change their minds, you won't change your mind, and I won't change mine. I believe we have a stalemate."

His dark eyes burned with frustration as he glared at her, and suddenly he seemed to realize he was still holding her hand. He released her abruptly and stood. "Look, you can't be my friend. *We* can't be friends."

Now that her hand was free, Mary felt abandoned and cold. She clasped her hands in her lap and looked up at him. "Why? Of course, if you simply don't like me..." Her voice trailed off, and she bent her head to examine her hands as if she'd never seen them before.

Not like her? He couldn't sleep, his temper was frayed, he got hard whenever he thought about her, and he thought about her too damn much. He was so physically frustrated that he thought he might go mad, but he couldn't even ease himself with Julie Oakes or any other woman now, because all he could think about was baby-fine brown hair, slate-blue eyes and skin like translucent rose petals. It was all he could do to keep from taking her, and only the knowledge of how the good townspeople of Ruth would turn on her if he made her his woman kept him from grabbing her. Her stubborn principles hadn't prepared her for the pain and trouble she would face.

Suddenly his frustration boiled over, and he was filled with rage at having to walk away from the one woman he wanted to the point of madness. Before he could stop himself, he reached down and grasped her wrists, hauling her to her feet. "No, damn it, we can't be friends! Do you want to know why? Because I can't be around you without thinking of stripping you naked and taking you, wherever we happen to be. Hell, I don't know if I'd take the time to strip you! I want your breasts in my hands, your nipples in my mouth. I want your legs around my waist, or your ankles on my shoulders, or any position at all if I can just get inside you." He'd pulled her so close that his warm breath brushed her cheeks as he rasped the low, harsh words at her. "So, sweetheart, there's no way we can be *friends*."

Mary shivered as her body responded to his words. Though they'd been spoken in anger, they told her that he felt the same way she did, and described actions she could only half imagine. She was too inexperienced and honest to hide her feelings from him, so she didn't even try. Her eyes were filled with painful longing. "Wolf?"

Just that, but the way she said his name, with an aching little inflection at the end, made his grip on her wrists tighten. "No."

"I—I want you."

Her whispered, trembly confession left her completely vulnerable to him, and he knew it. He groaned inwardly. Damn it, didn't she have any sense of self-protection at all? Didn't she know what it did to a man to have the woman he wanted offer herself like that, with no qualifications or holding back? His control was stretched hair-thin, but he grimly held on to it because the hard truth was that she truly didn't know. She was a virgin. She was old-fashioned, strictly raised, and had only the vaguest idea of what she was inviting.

"Don't say that," he finally muttered. "I've told you before—"

"I know," she interrupted. "I'm too inexperienced to be interesting, and you...you don't want to be used as a guinea pig. I remember." She seldom cried, but she felt the salty wetness burning her eyes, and he winced at the hurt he saw there.

"I lied. God, how I lied."

Then his control broke. He had to hold her, feel her in his arms just for a little while, have her taste on his mouth again. He drew her wrists up and placed her hands around his neck, then bent his head even as he locked his arms around her and drew her up tight against him. His mouth covered hers, and her eager response seared him. She knew what to do now; her lips parted, allowing his tongue entrance, where she met him with soft, welcoming touches from her own tongue. He had taught her that, just as he'd taught her to melt against him, and the knowledge drove him almost as crazy as the feel of her soft breasts flattening against his chest.

Mary drowned in the sheer ecstasy of being in his arms again, and the tears that she'd held back spilled past her lashes. This was too painful, and too wonderful, to be mere lust. If this was love, she didn't know if she could bear it.

His mouth was hungry and hard, taking long, deep kisses that left her clinging to him mindlessly. His hand moved surely up her stomach and closed over her breast, and all she could do was make a soft sound of pleasure low in her throat. Her nipples burned and throbbed; his touch both assuaged the pain and intensified it, making her want more. She wanted it the way he had described it, with his mouth on her breasts, and she twisted feverishly against him. She was empty and needed to be filled. She needed to be his woman.

He jerked his head up and pressed her face against his shoulder. "I have to stop. Now." He groaned the words. He was shaking, as hot as any teenage stud in the back seat of his daddy's car.

Mary briefly weighed all of Aunt Ardith's strictures against the way she felt and accepted that she was in love, because this mingled glory and torment could be nothing else. "I don't want to stop," she said raggedly. "I want you to love me."

"No. I'm Indian. You're white. The people in this town would destroy you. Tonight was just a taste of what you'd have to go through."

"I'm willing to risk it!" she cried desperately.

"I'm not. I can take it, but you—you hang on to your Pollyanna principles, sweetheart. I can't offer you anything in return." If he'd thought there was even a fifty-fifty chance of living here in peace, Wolf would have taken the risk, but he knew there wasn't, not the way things were. Other than Joe, she was the only human being in the world he'd ever wanted to protect, and it was the hardest thing he'd ever done.

Mary lifted her head from his shoulder, revealing her wet cheeks. "All I want is you."

"I'm the one thing you can't have. They'd tear you apart." Very gently he pulled her arms down and turned to leave.

Her voice came behind him, low and strained as she fought against tears. "I'll risk it."

He stopped, his hand on the doorknob. "I won't."

For the second time she watched him walk away, and this time was far worse than the first.

Joe was unusually distracted; he was normally the most attentive of students, applying himself to the subject at hand with almost phenomenal concentration, but tonight he had something else on his mind. He'd accepted without comment their move to the school for lessons and never even hinted that he'd learned the subject of the school board meeting that had resulted in the change of locations. As it was the beginning of May, and the day had been unseasonably warm, Mary was half inclined to put his restlessness down to spring fever. It had been a long winter, and she was restless herself.

Finally she closed the book before her. "Why don't we go home early tonight?" she suggested. "We're not getting much done."

Joe closed his own book and pushed his fingers through his thick black hair, identical to his father's. Mary had to look away. "Sorry," he said on a long exhalation. It was typical that he didn't offer an explanation. Joe didn't often feel the need to justify himself.

But in the weeks she'd been tutoring him, they had had a lot of personal conversations between the prepared lessons, and Mary never hesitated when she thought one of her students might be troubled. If it were only spring fever gnawing at him, then she wanted him to say so. "Is something bothering you?"

He gave her a wry smile, one that was too adult to belong to a sixteen-year-old boy. "You could say that."

"Ah." That smile relieved her, because now she thought she knew the cause of his restlessness. It was indeed spring fever, after a fashion. As Aunt Ardith had often lectured her niece, "When a young man's sap rises, a girl should look out. I declare, they seem to run mad." Evidently Joe's sap was rising. Mary wondered if women had sap, too.

He picked up his pen and fiddled with it for a moment before tossing it aside as he made up his mind to say more. "Pam Hearst asked me to take her to a movie."

"*Pam?*" This was a surprise, and possible trouble. Ralph Hearst was one of the townspeople most adamantly opposed to the Mackenzies.

Joe's ice-blue eyes were hooded as he glanced at her. "Pam is the girl I told you about before."

So, it *was* Pam Hearst. She was pretty and bright, and her slim young body had a form guaranteed to affect a young man's sap. Mary wondered if Pam's father knew she had been flirting with Joe and that was one reason for his hostility.

"Are you going to go?"

"No," he said flatly, surprising her.

"Why?"

"There aren't any movie houses in Ruth."

"So?"

"That's the whole point. We'd have to go to another town. No one we know would be likely to see us. She wanted me to pick her up behind the school, after it got dark." He leaned back in his chair and looped his hands behind his head. "She was too ashamed to go to the dance with me, but I'm good enough for her to sneak around and see. Maybe she thought that even if we were seen, the idea that I might go to the Academy would keep her from getting in too much trouble. Folks seem taken with the idea." His tone was ironic. "I guess it makes a difference when the Indian wears a uniform."

Suddenly her impulsive announcement at the school board meeting didn't seem like such a good idea. "Do you wish I hadn't told them?"

"You had to, considering," he replied, and by that she knew he was aware of the subject of that meeting. "It puts extra pressure on me to get into the Academy, because if I don't they'll all say that the Indian just couldn't cut it, but that's not a bad thing. If it will push me to do more, then I'm that much closer to getting in."

Privately, Mary didn't think Joe needed any added incentive; he wanted it so badly now that the need burned in him. She returned the conversation to Pam. "Does it bother you, that she asked now?"

"It made me mad. And it *really* made me mad having to turn her down, because I sure would like to get my hands on her." He stopped abruptly and gave Mary another of those too-adult looks before a little grin tugged at his lips. "Sorry. I didn't mean to get too personal. Let's just say that I'm attracted to her physically, but that's all it is, and I can't afford to fool with that kind of situation. Pam's a nice girl, but she doesn't figure in my plans."

Mary understood what he meant. No woman figured in his plans, other than to provide physical release, for a long time, if ever. There was something solitary about him, as there was about Wolf, and in addition, Joe was so possessed by the specter of flight that part of him was already gone. Pam Hearst would marry some local boy, settle down in Ruth or nearby, and raise her own family in the same calm setting where she'd grown up; she wasn't meant for the brief attention Joe Mackenzie could give her before he moved on.

"Do you have any idea who started the gossip?" Joe asked, his pale eyes hard. He didn't like the idea of anyone hurting this woman.

"No. I haven't tried to find out. It could have been anyone who drove by and saw your truck at my house. But most people seemed to have forgotten about it now, except for—'' She stopped, her eyes troubled.

"Who?" Joe demanded flatly.

"I don't mean that I think she started the gossip," Mary said hastily. "I just feel uneasy around her. She dislikes me, and I don't know why. Maybe she's this way with everyone. Has Dottie Lancaster—"

"Dottie Lancaster!" He gave a harsh laugh. "Now there's a thought. Yeah, she could have started the gossip. She's had a rough life, and I kind of feel sorry for her, but she did her best to make my life hell when I was in her classes."

"Rough? How?"

"Her husband was a truck driver, and he was killed years ago when her son was just a baby. He was on a run in Colorado, and a drunk driver ran him off the side of a cliff. The drunk was an Indian. She never got over it and blames all Indians, I guess."

"That's irrational."

He shrugged, as if to say a lot of things were irrational. "Anyway, she was left alone with her kid, and she had a hard time. Not much money. She started teaching, but she had to pay someone to take care of the kid, and he needed special training when he was old enough to start school, which took even more money."

"I didn't know Dottie had any children," Mary said, surprised.

"Just Robert—Bobby. He's about twenty-three or four, I guess. He still lives with Mrs. Lancaster, but he doesn't go around other people much."

"What's wrong with him? Does he have Down's syndrome, or a learning disability?"

"He's not retarded. Bobby's just different. He likes people, but not in groups. A lot of people together make him nervous, so he pretty much stays to himself. He reads a lot, and listens to music. But once he had a summer job at the building supply store, and Mr. Watkins told Bobby to fill a wheelbarrow full of sand. Instead of pushing the wheelbarrow to the sandpile and shoveling the sand in, Bobby would get a shovelful of sand and carry it back to the wheelbarrow. It's things like that. He'd have trouble getting dressed, because he'd put his shoes on first, and then he couldn't get his jeans on."

Mary had seen people like Bobby, who had trouble with practical problem-solving. It was a learning disability, and took a lot of patient, specialized training to handle. She felt sorry for him, and for Dottie, who couldn't have had a happy life.

Joe pushed his chair back and stood up, stretching his cramped muscles. "Do you ride?" he asked suddenly.

"No. I've never even been on a horse." Mary chuckled. "Will that get me thrown out of Wyoming?"

His tone was grave. "It could. Why don't you come up on the mountain some Saturday and I'll give you riding lessons? School will be out for the summer soon, and you'll have a lot of time to practice."

He couldn't know how appealing the idea was, not only to ride but to see Wolf again. The only thing was, it would hurt just as much to see him as it did not to see him, because he was still out of her reach. "I'll think about it," she promised, but she doubted she would ever take him up on the offer.

Joe didn't push it, but he didn't intend to let it drop, either. He'd get Mary up on the mountain one way or another. He figured Wolf had about reached the limits of his restraint. Parading her right under his nose would be like leading a mare in heat in front of a stallion. His pretty, tart-tongued little teacher would be lucky if his dad didn't have her flat on her back before she had the hello out of her mouth. Joe had to hide his smile. He'd never seen anyone get to Wolf the way Miss Mary Elizabeth Potter had. She had Wolf so tied in knots he was as dangerous as a wounded cougar.

He mentally hummed a few bars of "Matchmaker."

When Mary got home the next Friday afternoon, there was a letter in the mailbox from Senator Allard, and her fingers trembled as she tore it open. If it was bad news for Joe, if Senator Allard had declined to recommend him to the Academy, she didn't know what she would do. Senator Allard wasn't their only possibility, but he had seemed the most receptive, and a turndown from him would really be discouraging.

The senator's letter to her was brief, thanking her for her efforts in bringing Joe to his attention. He had decided to recommend Joe for admittance to the Academy, for the freshman class beginning after Joe's graduation from high school. From there on, it would be up to Joe to pass the rigorous academic and physical examinations.

Enclosed was a private letter of congratulations to Joe.

Mary hugged the letters to her breast, and tears welled in her eyes. They had done it, and it hadn't even been that difficult! She had been prepared to petition every congressman every week until Joe was given his chance, but it hadn't been necessary. Joe's grades and credits had done it for him.

It was news too good to wait, so she got back into her car and drove up Mackenzie's Mountain. The drive was much different now; the snow had melted, and wildflowers bloomed beside the road. After the harsh winter cold, the spring warmth felt like a blessing on her skin, though it still wasn't nearly as warm as the springs she had known in Savannah. She was so excited and happy that she didn't even notice the steep drop on the side of the road as it wound higher, but she did notice the wild grandeur of the mountains, stretching magnificently toward the dark blue heavens. She drew a deep breath and realized that the spring did make up for the winter. It felt like home, a new home, a place dear and familiar.

The tires threw out a spray of gravel as she slid to a stop at the kitchen door of Wolf's one-story frame house, and before the vehicle had rocked back on its springs she was bounding up the steps to pound on the door. "Wolf! Joe!" She knew she was yelling in a very unladylike manner, but she was too happy to care. Some situations just called for yelling.

"Mary!"

The call came from behind her, and she whirled. Wolf was coming from the barn at a dead run, his powerful body surging fluidly. Mary yelped in excitement and launched herself from the steps, her skirt flying up as she bolted down the graveled drive toward the barn. "He got it!" she screamed, waving the letters. "He got it!"

Wolf skidded to a halt and watched the sedate teacher literally skipping and leaping toward him, her skirt kicking up around her thighs with each step. He just had time to realize there was nothing wrong, that she was laughing, when, three steps away, she went airborne. He braced himself and caught her weight against his chest, his brawny arms wrapping around her.

"He got it!" she shrieked again, and threw her arms around his neck.

Wolf could think of only one thing, and it made his mouth go dry. "He got it?"

She waved the letters under his nose. "He got it! Senator Allard—the letter was in my mailbox—I couldn't wait—where's Joe?" She knew she was almost incoherent and made an effort to compose herself, but she just couldn't stop grinning.

"He's in town picking up a load of fencing. Damn it, are you sure that's what it says? He still has a year of school—"

"Not a year, not at the rate he's going. But he'll have to be seventeen, anyway. The senator has recommended him for the freshman class starting after he graduates. Less than a year and a half!"

Fierce pride filled Wolf's face, the warrior's pride he'd inherited from both Comanche and Celt. His eyes glittered with black fire, and exultantly he lifted her high, his hands under her armpits, and twirled around with her. She threw back her head, shrieking with laughter, and suddenly Wolf felt his entire body clench with desire. It was as powerful as a blow to the gut, knocking the wind out of him. She was soft and warm in his arms, her laughter was as fresh as the spring, and he wanted her out of the prim little shirtwaist she wore.

Slowly his face changed to a harder, more primitive cast. She was still laughing as he lowered her, her hands braced on his shoulders, but he stopped when her breasts were level with his face. The laughter died in Mary's throat as he deliberately brought her closer to him and buried his face between her breasts. His grip shifted, one arm locking around her buttocks and the other around her back, and his hot mouth searched for her nipple. He found it, his mouth clamping down on it through the barriers of her dress and bra, but the sensation was still so exquisite that her breath caught on a moan and her back arched, pushing her breast against him.

It wasn't enough. She burrowed her fingers through his hair, digging into his skull to push him harder against her, but it wasn't enough. She wanted him with sudden, fierce desperation. The layers of cloth that kept him from her drove her mad, and she squirmed against him, low whimpers coming from her throat. "Please," she begged. "Wolf—"

He lifted his head, his eyes savage with need. His blood was thundering through his veins, and he was breathing hard. "Do you want more?" The words were guttural, a normal tone beyond him.

She squirmed against him again, her hands clutching desperately. "Yes."

Very gently he let her slide down his body, deliberately rubbing her over the hardened bulge in his jeans, and both of them shuddered. Wolf was beyond thinking of all his reasons for not becoming involved with her, beyond anything but the urge to mate. To hell with what anyone thought.

He looked around, gauging the distance to both house and barn. The barn was closer. Clamping his hand around her wrist, he strode toward the big open double doors that revealed the dim interior.

Mary could barely get her breath as she was all but dragged in his wake. Her senses bewildered by the sudden cessation of pleasure, she was confused by his actions and wanted to ask what he was doing, but she didn't have enough oxygen in her lungs to form the question. Then they were inside the barn, and she was swamped by the perceptions of dim light, animal warmth and the earthy smells of dust, hay, leather and horses. She heard soft nickers and the muffled stamping of hooves on straw. Wolf led her into an empty stall and dragged her down onto the fresh hay. She sprawled on her back, and he came down on top of her, his muscled weight pressing her even deeper into the hay.

"Kiss me," she whispered, reaching up to thrust her fingers into his long hair and pull him down to her.

"I'll kiss you all over before I'm through with you," he muttered, and bent his head. Her mouth opened under the force of his, and his tongue moved into her in a deep rhythm that she instinctively recognized and accepted, responded to eagerly. He was heavy, but it was so natural that she bear his weight that she rejoiced in the pressure of his body. She wrapped her arms around his thickly muscled shoulders and hugged him even tighter to her; she wanted to be as close as she could to him, and to that end her hips undulated slightly, adjusting to the carnal pressure of his loins.

The slow movements of her hips beneath him made him feel as if his head would explode from the rush of blood through his body. He made a low, rough sound in his throat and reached for the zipper at the back of her dress. He thought he would die if he didn't feel her silky skin under his hands, if he didn't sheathe his throbbing flesh inside her.

It was startlingly new to her, bringing a delicate flush to her cheeks, but it was still so *right* that she didn't even think of protesting. She didn't want to protest. She wanted Wolf. She was female to his male, warm and sexual, intensely aware of being a woman and offering herself to the man she loved. She wanted to be naked for him, so she helped him by pulling her arms free of the sleeves as he tugged the dress from her shoulders and let it fall to her waist. She had felt racy, daring to buy a bra with a single front clasp, but as he looked down at her breasts, barely covered by the thin, flesh-colored material, she was so glad she had done it. He deftly opened the clasp with one hand, a trick she hadn't learned yet, and watched the edges pull back to bare her soft curves, stopping before her nipples were revealed.

He made that rough sound again, almost like a growl, and bent to nuzzle the bra aside. His mouth, warm and wet, slid across her breast and clamped on the tightly beaded nipple. She jumped, her entire body reacting to a pleasure so intense it bordered on pain, as he sucked strongly at her. Mary's eyes closed, and she moaned. She couldn't bear it; it felt *too* good, a hot river of pleasure-pain impulses running from breast to loin, where an empty ache made her press her legs together and arch beneath him, silently begging for the release her body had never known, but sensed with ancient wisdom.

Wolf felt her move beneath him again, and the last shred of control he'd retained, vanished. Roughly he jerked her skirt to her waist and kneed her thighs apart, settling himself between the vulnerable V of her legs. She opened her eyes, a little shocked by what she could feel down there, but eager to know more. "Take off your clothes," she whispered frantically, and tore at the buttons on his shirt.

He reared back on his knees and tore his shirt open, then off. His naked skin glistened with a fine patina of sweat; in the dim light, filled with floating dust motes, the overlay of sleek bronze skin on powerful muscles gave him the look of live art sculpted by a master's hand. Mary's gaze moved hungrily, feverishly, over him. He was perfect, strong and male, the scent of his body hot and faintly musky. She reached out for him, her hands sliding over his broad chest, lightly haired in a diamond pattern stretching from nipple to nipple. She touched those tight little buds, and he froze, a massive shiver of pleasure rippling through his muscles.

He groaned aloud and dropped his hands to his belt. He unbuckled the wide band of leather, then unsnapped his jeans and jerked the zipper down, the hissing of the metal teeth blending with their harsh breathing.

With some last desperate fragment of willpower, he kept himself from lowering his pants. She was a virgin; he couldn't allow himself to forget that, even in his urgency. Damn it, he had to regain some control, or he'd both scare and hurt her, and he would die before he turned her first time into a nightmare.

Mary's slim fingers curled in the hair on his chest and tugged lightly. "Wolf," she said. Just his name, just that one word, but her voice was warm and low and drugged sounding, and it beckoned him more powerfully than anything he'd known before.

"Yes," he said in response. "Now." He leaned forward to cover her again, then froze as a distant sound came to his ears.

He swore quietly and sank back on his heels, battling desperately to control his body and his frustration.

"Wolf?" Now her tone was hesitant, consternation and self-consciousness creeping into it. That inflection made him feel murderous, because she hadn't been self-conscious before. She had been warm and loving, willing to give herself without reserve.

"Joe will be here in a few minutes," he said flatly. "I can hear his truck coming up the mountain."

She was still so far out of it that she merely looked confused. "Joe?"

"Yes, Joe. Remember him? My son, the reason you're up here in the first place."

Her cheeks flooded with color, and she jerked into an upright position, as far as she could, because her thighs were still draped over his. "Oh my God," she said. "Oh my God. I'm naked. You're naked. Oh my God."

"We're not naked," Wolf muttered, wiping his sweaty face. "Damn it."

"Almost!"

"Not enough." Even her breasts were rosy with embarrassment now. He looked at them with regret, remembering her sweet taste and the way her velvety little nipple had bloomed in his mouth. But the sound of the truck was much closer now, and with a low, obscene comment on his son's rotten timing, he got to his feet and effortlessly lifted Mary to hers.

Tears blurred her vision as she turned her back to fumble with that blasted space-age clasp on her bra. What ever had possessed her to buy such a contraption? Aunt Ardith would have been outraged. Aunt Ardith would have fallen on the ground in a hissy fit if she'd even thought of her niece *rolling naked in the hay* with a man. And, darn it, she hadn't even been able to finish her rolling!

"Here, I'll do it," Wolf said in a far gentler tone than she'd ever before heard from him. He turned her around and deftly handled the diabolical clasp. Mary kept her head down, unable to look him in the eye, but the contrast of his sun-bronzed hands against her pale breasts made her feel hot again. She swallowed and looked at his belt buckle. He'd zipped his jeans back up and buckled his belt, but the visible swell of his loins told her he wasn't completely unaffected by this interruption. That made her feel better, and she blinked the tears from her eyes as he helped her back into her dress and turned her around to zip it.

"You have hay in your hair," he teased, and picked the straw from the tangled tresses, then brushed it from her dress.

Mary put up both hands to discern the state of her hair and found it had come completely down. "Leave it," Wolf said. "I like it down. It looks like silk."

Nervously she combed her fingers through the strands and watched as he leaned down to pick up his shirt from the hay. "What will Joe think?" she blurted as the truck pulled to a stop outside the barn.

"That he's lucky he's my son, or I'd have killed him," Wolf muttered grimly, and Mary wasn't certain he was teasing. He put his shirt on but didn't bother buttoning it before stepping into the open door. Taking a deep breath, Mary braced herself to get through the embarrassment and followed him.

Joe had just gotten out of the truck, and now he stood beside the door, his ice-blue eyes moving from his father to Mary and back, taking in Wolf's stone face and open shirt, and Mary's tousled hair. "Damn it!" he swore and slammed the door shut. "If it had just taken me fifteen minutes longer—"

"My feelings exactly," Wolf concurred.

"Hey, I'll leave—"

Wolf sighed. "No. She came to see you anyway."

"That's what you said the first time." Joe grinned hugely.

"And I just said it again." He turned to Mary, and some of the enjoyment of her stunning news returned to his eyes. "Tell him."

She couldn't think. "Tell him?'"

"Yeah. Tell him."

Slowly her dazed mind registered what he was saying. She looked in bewilderment at her empty hands. What had happened to the letters? Had they lost them in the hay? How mortifying it would be to have to search through the hay for them! Not knowing what else to do, she spread her hands and said simply, "You're in. I got the letter today."

Blood drained from Joe's face as he stared at her, and he reached out blindly to rest his hand on the truck as if to steady himself. "I got in? The Academy? I got into the Academy?" he asked hoarsely.

"You got the recommendation. It's up to you to pass the exams."

He threw back his head and screamed, an exultant, spine-chilling sound like that of a hunting panther, then leaped at Wolf. The two of them pounded each other's backs, laughing and yelling, then finally just hugging each other in a way two weaker men couldn't have done. Mary folded her hands and watched them, smiling, so happy her heart swelled to the point of pain. Then suddenly an arm reached out and snagged her, and she found herself sandwiched between the two Mackenzies, almost smashed flat by their celebration.

"You're smothering me!" she protested in a gasping voice, wedging her hands against two broad chests and pushing. One of those chests was bare, exposed by an unbuttoned shirt, and the touch of his warm skin made her go weak in the knees. Both of them laughed at her protest, but both of them immediately gentled their embrace.

Mary patted her hair down and smoothed her dress. "The letters are here somewhere. I must have dropped them."

Wolf gave her a wicked look. "You must have."

His teasing made her happy deep inside, and she smiled at him. It was a quietly intimate smile, the sort that a woman gives the man she loves after she has been in his arms, and it warmed him. To cover his reaction, he turned to look for the dropped letters and spotted one on the drive, while the other had fallen close to the barn door. He retrieved both of them, and gave Joe the one addressed to him.

The boy's hands shook as he read the letter, even though he already knew the contents. He couldn't believe it. It had happened so fast. A dream come true should have been harder to attain; he should have had to sweat blood to get it. Oh, he wasn't driving one of those twenty-million dollar babies yet, but he would. He had to, because he would be only half alive without wings.

Mary was watching him with proud indulgence when she felt Wolf stiffen beside her. She looked at him inquiringly. His head was lifted as if he scented danger, and his face was suddenly as impassive as stone. Then she heard the sound of an engine and turned as a deputy sheriff's car rolled to a stop behind Joe's truck.

Joe turned, and his face took on the same stony look as Wolf's as Clay Armstrong got out of the county car.

"Ma'am." Clay spoke to her first, tipping his hat.

"Deputy Armstrong." Two hundred years of strict training on social behavior were in her voice. Aunt Ardith would have been proud. But she sensed some threat to Wolf, and it was all she could do not to put herself between him and the deputy. Only the knowledge that he wouldn't appreciate the action kept her standing at his side.

Clay's friendly blue eyes weren't friendly at all now. "Why are you up here, Miss Potter?"

"Why are you asking?" she shot back, putting her hands on her hips.

"Just skip to the good part, Armstrong," Wolf snapped.

"Fine," Clay snapped back. "You're wanted for questioning. You can come with me now, the easy way, or I can get a warrant for your arrest."

Joe stood frozen, fury and hell in his eyes. This had happened before, and he'd lost his father for two nightmarish years. It seemed even more terrible this time, because just moments before they had been celebrating, and he'd been on top of the world.

Wolf began buttoning his shirt. In a voice like gravel he asked, "What happened this time?"

"We'll talk about that at the sheriff's office."

"We'll talk about it now."

Black eyes met blue, and abruptly Clay realized this man wouldn't move a foot unless he had some answers. "A girl was raped this morning."

Sulfuric rage burned in those night-dark eyes. "So naturally you thought of the Indian." He spat the words like bullets from between clenched teeth. God, this couldn't be happening again. Not twice in one lifetime. The first time had almost killed him, and he knew he'd never go back to that hellhole, no matter what he had to do.

"We're just questioning some people. If you have an alibi, there's no problem. You'll be free to go."

"I suppose you picked up every rancher in this area? Do you have Eli Baugh at the sheriff's office answering questions?"

Clay's face darkened with anger. "No."

"Just the Indian, huh?"

"You have priors." But Clay looked uncomfortable.

"I don't have...one...single...prior conviction," Wolf snarled. "I was *cleared.*"

"Damn it, man, I know that!" Clay suddenly yelled. "I was told to pick you up, and I'm going to do my job."

"Well, why didn't you just say so? I wouldn't want to stop a man from doing his job." After that sarcastic jab, Wolf strode to his truck. "I'll follow you."

"You can ride in the car. I'll bring you back."

"No, thanks. I'd rather have my own wheels, just in case the sheriff decides a walk would do me good."

Swearing under his breath, Clay went to the car and got in. Dust and gravel flew from his tires as he headed back down the mountain, with Wolf behind him slinging even more dust and gravel.

Mary began shaking. At first it was just a tremor, but it swiftly escalated into shudders that rattled her entire body. Joe was standing as if turned to stone, his fists clenched. Suddenly he whirled and slammed his fist into the hood of his truck. "By God, they won't do it to him again," he whispered. *"Not again."*

"No, they certainly won't." She was still shaking, but she squared her shoulders. "If I have to get every judge and court in this country involved, I will. I'll call newspapers, I'll call television networks, I'll call—oh, they don't have any idea of who all I can call." The network of Old

Family contacts she had left behind in Savannah was still there, and more favors would be called in than the sheriff of this county could count. She'd hang him out to dry!

"Why don't you go home?" Joe suggested in a flat tone.

"I want to stay."

He'd expected her to quietly walk to her car, but at her words he looked at her for the first time. Deep inside, part of him had thought she wouldn't be able to leave fast enough, that he and Wolf would be alone again, as they had always been. They were used to being alone. But Mary stood her ground as if she had no intention of budging off this mountain, her slate-blue eyes full of fire and her fragile chin lifted in the way that he'd learned meant others could just get out of her path.

The boy, forced by circumstance to grow up hard and fast, put his strong arms around the woman and held her, desperately absorbing some of her strength, because he was deathly afraid he'd need it. And Mary held him. He was Wolf's son, and she'd protect him with every ounce of fight she had.

It was after nine when they heard Wolf's truck, and both of them froze with mingled tension and relief: tension because they dreaded to hear what had happened, and relief because he was home instead of locked in jail. Mary couldn't imagine Wolf in jail, even though he'd spent two years in prison. He was too wild, like a lobo that could never be tamed. Imprisoning him had been an act so cruel as to be obscene.

He came in the back door and stood there staring at her, his dark face expressionless. She and Joe sat at the kitchen table, nursing cups of coffee. "Why are you still here? Go home."

She ignored the flatness of his tone. He was so angry she could almost feel the heat from across the room, but she knew it wasn't directed against her. Getting up, she dumped her lukewarm coffee into the sink and got another cup from the cabinet, then poured fresh coffee into both cups. "Sit down, drink your coffee and tell us what happened," she said in her best schoolteacher voice.

He did reach for the coffee, but he didn't sit down. He was too angry to sit. The rage boiled in him, robbing his movements of their usual fluidity. It was starting all over again, and he'd be damned if he'd go to prison again for something he hadn't done. He'd fight any way he could and with any weapon he could, but he'd die before he'd go back to prison.

"They let you go," Joe said.

"They had to. The girl was raped around noon. At noon I was delivering two horses to the Bar W R. Wally Rasco verified it, and the sheriff couldn't figure out a way I could have been in two different places, sixty miles apart, at the same time, so he had to let me go."

"Where did it happen?"

Wolf rubbed his forehead, then pinched his nose between his eyes as if he had a headache, or maybe he was just tired. "She was grabbed from behind when she got in her car, parked in her own driveway. He made her drive almost an hour before telling her to pull off on the side of the road. She never saw his face. He wore a ski mask. But she could tell he was tall, and that was enough of a description for the sheriff."

"The side of the road?" Mary blurted. "That's...weird. It doesn't make sense. I know there's not much traffic, but still, someone could have come by at any time."

"Yeah. Not to mention that he was waiting for her in her driveway. The whole thing is strange."

Joe drummed his fingers on the table. "It could have been someone passing through."

"How many people 'pass through' Ruth?" Wolf asked dryly. "Would a drifter have known whose car it was, or when she was likely to come out of the house? What if the car belonged to a man? That's a big chance to take, especially when rape seems to have been the only thing on his mind, because he didn't rob her, even though she had money."

"Are they keeping her identity secret?" Mary asked.

He looked at her. "It won't stay a secret, because her father was in the sheriff's office waving a rifle and threatening to blow my guts out. He attracted a lot of attention, and people talk."

His face was still expressionless, but Mary sensed the bitter rage that filled him. His fierce pride had been dragged in the dust—again. How had he endured being forced to sit there and listen to insults and threats? Because she knew he'd been insulted, by vile words describing his mixed heritage as well as by the very fact he'd been picked up for questioning. He was holding it all in, controlling it, but the rage was there.

"What happened?"

"Armstrong stopped it. Then Wally Rasco got there and cleared me, and the sheriff let me go with a friendly warning."

"A *warning*?" Mary jumped to her feet, her eyes flashing. "For what?"

He pinched her chin and gave her a coldly ferocious smile. "He warned me to stay away from white women, sweetcake. And that's just what I'm going to do. So you go on home now, and stay there. I don't want you on my mountain again."

"You didn't feel that way in the barn," she shot back, then darted a look at Joe and blushed. Joe just quirked an eyebrow and looked strangely self-satisfied. She decided to ignore him and turned back to Wolf. "I can't believe you're letting that mush-brain sheriff tell you who you can see."

He narrowed his eyes at her. "Maybe it hasn't dawned on you yet, but it's all starting again. It doesn't matter that Wally Rasco cleared me. Everyone is going to remember what happened ten years ago, and the way they felt."

"You were cleared of that, too, or doesn't that count?"

"With some people," he finally admitted. "Not with most. They're already afraid of me, already distrust and dislike me. Until this bastard is caught, I probably won't be able to buy anything in that town, not groceries, gas or feed. And any white woman who has anything to do with me could be in real danger of being tarred and feathered."

So that was it. He was still trying to protect her. She stared at him in exasperation. "Wolf, I refuse to live my life according to someone else's prejudices. I appreciate that you're trying to protect me—"

She could hear an audible click as his teeth snapped together. "Do you?" he asked with heavy sarcasm. "Then go home. Stay home, and I'll stay here."

"For how long?"

Instead of answering her question, he made an oblique statement. "I'll always be a half-breed."

"And I'll always be what *I* am, too. I haven't asked you to change," she pointed out, pain creeping into her voice. She looked at him with longing plain in her eyes, as no woman had ever looked at him before, and the rage in him intensified because he couldn't simply reach out and take her in his arms, proclaim to the world that she was his woman. The sheriff's warning had been clear enough, and Wolf knew well that the hostility toward him would rapidly swell to explosive proportions. It could easily spill over onto Mary, and now he wasn't just worried that she would lose her job. A job was nothing compared to the physical danger she could suffer. She could be terrorized in her own home, her property vandalized; she could be cursed and spat upon; she could be physically attacked. For all her sheer determination, she was still just a rather slight woman, and she would be helpless against anyone who wanted to hurt her.

"I know," he finally said, and despite himself, he reached out to touch her hair. "Go home, Mary. When this is over—" He stopped, because he didn't want to make promises he might not be able to keep, but what he'd said was enough to put a glowing light in her eyes.

"All right," she murmured, putting her hand on his. "By the way, I want you to get a haircut."

He looked startled. "A haircut?"

"Yes. You want me to wear my hair down, and I want you to get a haircut."

"Why?"

She gave him a shrewd look. "You don't wear it long because you're Indian. You wear it long just to upset people, so they'll never forget your Indian blood. So get it cut."

"Short hair won't make me less Indian."

"Long hair won't make you more Indian."

She looked as if she would stand there until doomsday unless he agreed to get a haircut. He gave in abruptly, muttering, "All right, I'll get a haircut."

"Good." She smiled at him and went on tiptoe to kiss the corner of his mouth. "Good night. Good night, Joe."

"Goodnight, Mary."

When she was gone, Wolf wearily ran his hand through his hair, then frowned as he realized he'd just agreed to cut it off. He looked up to find Joe watching him steadily.

"What are we going to do?" the boy asked.

"Whatever we have to," Wolf replied, his expression flinty.

When Mary bought groceries the next morning, she found everyone in the store huddling together in small groups of two or three and whispering about the rape. The girl's identity was quickly revealed; it was Cathy Teele, whose younger sister, Christa, was in Mary's class. The entire Teele family was devastated, according to the whispers Mary heard as she gathered her groceries.

Next to the flour and cornmeal, she encountered Dottie Lancaster, who was flanked by a young man Mary assumed was Dottie's son. "Hello, Dottie." Mary greeted the woman pleasantly, even though it was possible Dottie had started the rumor about her and Joe.

"Hello." Dottie wore a distressed expression, rather than her habitual sour one. "Have you heard about that poor Teele girl?"

"I haven't heard anything else since I entered the store."

"They arrested that Indian, but the sheriff had to let him go. I hope now you'll be more careful about the company you keep."

"Wolf wasn't arrested." Mary managed to keep her voice calm. "He was questioned, but he was at Wally Rasco's ranch when the attack occurred, and Mr. Rasco backed him up. Wolf Mackenzie isn't a rapist."

"A court of law said he was and sentenced him to prison."

"He was also cleared when the true rapist was caught and confessed to the crime for which Wolf had been convicted."

Dottie drew back, her face livid. "That's what that Indian said, but as far as we know, he just got out on parole. It's easy to see whose side you're on, but then, you've been running with those Indians since the day you came to Ruth. Well, miss, there's an old saying that if you sleep with dogs, you're bound to get fleas. The Mackenzies are dirty Indian trash—"

"Don't you say another word," Mary interrupted, color high in her cheeks as she took a step toward Dottie. She was furious; her hand itched to slap the woman's self-righteous face. Aunt Ardith had said that a lady never brawled, but Mary was ready to forever relinquish any claim she had to the title. "Wolf is a decent, hard-working man, and I won't let you or anyone else say he isn't."

Dottie's color was mottled, but something in Mary's eyes made her refrain from saying anything else about Wolf. Instead she leaned closer and hissed, "You'd better watch yourself, Miss Goody-Goody, or you'll find yourself in a lot of trouble."

Mary leaned closer, too, her jaw set. "Are you threatening me?" she demanded fiercely.

"Mama, please," the young man behind her whispered in a frantic tone, and tugged at Dottie's arm.

Dottie looked around at him, and her face changed. She drew back, but told Mary contemptuously, "You just mark my words," and stalked away.

Her son, Bobby, was so distressed he was wringing his hands as he hurried after Dottie. Immediately, Mary was sorry she had let the horrid little scene develop; from what Joe had told her, Bobby had a hard enough time handling everyday problems without adding more.

She took a few deep breaths to regain her composure, but almost lost it again when she turned and found several people standing in the aisle, staring at her. They had all obviously heard every word, and looked both shocked and avid. She had no doubt the tale would be all over town within the hour: two of the schoolteachers brawling over Wolf Mackenzie. She groaned inwardly as she picked up a bag of flour. Another scandal was just what Wolf needed.

In the next aisle, she met Cicely Karr. Remembering the woman's comments during the school board meeting, Mary couldn't stop herself from saying, "I've received a letter from Senator Allard, Mrs. Karr. He's recommending Joe Mackenzie for admission to the Academy." She sounded challenging even to her own ears.

To her surprise, Mrs. Karr looked excited. "He is? Why, I never would've believed it. Until Eli explained it to me, I didn't quite realize what an honor it is." Then she sobered. "But now this terrible thing has happened. It's awful. I—I couldn't help overhearing you and Dottie Lancaster. Miss Potter, you can't imagine what it was like ten years ago. People were frightened and angry, and now the same nightmare has started again."

"It's a nightmare for Wolf Mackenzie, too," Mary said hotly. "He was sent to prison for a rape he didn't commit. His record was cleared, but still he was the first person the sheriff picked up for questioning. How do you think he feels? He'll never get back the two years he spent in prison, and now it looks as if everyone is trying to send him there again."

Mrs. Karr looked troubled. "We were all wrong before. The justice system was wrong, too. But even though Mackenzie proved he didn't rape Cathy Teele, don't you see why the sheriff wanted to question him?"

"No, I don't."

"Because Mackenzie had reason to want revenge."

Mary was aghast. "So you thought he'd take revenge by attacking a young woman who was just a child when he was sent to prison? What sort of man do you think he is?" She was horrified by both the idea and the feeling that everyone in Ruth would agree with Mrs. Karr.

"I think he's a man who hates," Mrs. Karr said firmly. Yes, she believed Wolf capable of such horrible, obscene revenge; it was in her eyes.

Mary felt sick; she began shaking her head. "No," she said. "No. Wolf is bitter about the way he was treated, but he doesn't hate. And he would never hurt a woman like that." If she knew anything in this world, she knew that. She had felt urgency in his touch, but never brutality.

But Mrs. Karr was shaking her head, too. "Don't tell me he doesn't hate! It's in those black-as-hell eyes every time he looks at us, any of us. The sheriff found out he'd been in Vietnam, in some special assassination group, or something. God only knows how it warped him! Maybe he didn't rape Cathy Teele, but this would be a perfect opportunity for him to get revenge and have it blamed on whoever *did* rape her!"

"If Wolf wanted revenge, he wouldn't sneak around to get it," Mary said scornfully. "You don't know anything about the kind of man he is, do you? He's lived here for years, and none of you *know* him."

"And I suppose you do?" Mrs. Karr was getting red in the face. "Maybe we're talking about a different kind of 'knowing.' Maybe that rumor about you carrying on with Joe Mackenzie was half right, after all. You've been carrying on with *Wolf* Mackenzie, haven't you?"

The scorn in the woman's voice enraged Mary. "Yes!" she half shouted, and honesty impelled her to add, "But not as much as I'd like."

A chorus of gasps made her look around, and she stared into the faces of the townspeople who had stopped in the aisle to listen. Well, she'd really done it now; Wolf had wanted her to distance herself from him, and instead she'd all but shouted from the rooftops that she'd been "carrying on" with him. But she couldn't feel even the tiniest bit of shame. She felt proud. With Wolf Mackenzie she was a woman, not a dowdy, old maid schoolteacher who even owned a cat, for heaven's sake. She didn't feel dowdy when she was with Wolf; she felt warm, wanted. If she had any regrets, it was that Joe hadn't been fifteen minutes later returning the day before, or even five minutes, because more than anything she wanted to be Wolf's woman in every way, to lie beneath his thrusting body, eagerly accepting the force of his passion and giving him her own. If for that, for loving him, she was ostracized, then she counted society well lost.

Mrs. Karr said icily, "I believe we'll have to have another school board meeting."

"When you do, consider that I have an ironclad contract," Mary shot back, and turned on her heel. She hadn't gathered all of the groceries she needed, but she was too angry to continue. When she plunked the items down on the counter, the clerk looked as if she wanted to refuse to ring them up, but she changed her mind under Mary's glare.

She stormed home and was gratified when the weather seemed to agree with her, if the gray clouds forming overhead were any indication. After storing her groceries, she checked on the cat, who had been acting strange lately. A horrid thought intruded: surely no one would have poisoned the cat? But Woodrow was sunning himself peacefully on the rug, so she dismissed the idea with relief.

When this is over...

The phrase echoed in her memory, tantalizing her and stirring an ache deep inside. She longed for him so intensely that she felt as if she were somehow incomplete. She loved him, and though she understood why he thought it better for her to stay away from him right now, she didn't agree. After what had happened that morning with Dottie Lancaster and Cicely Karr, there was no point in allowing this exile. She might as well have stood in the middle of the street and shouted it: she was Wolf Mackenzie's woman.

Whatever he wanted from her, she was willing to give. Aunt Ardith had raised her to believe that intimacy belonged only in marriage, if a woman for some reason felt she simply *couldn't* live without a man, though Aunt Ardith had made it plain she couldn't imagine what such a reason would be. While Mary had accepted that people obviously were intimate outside of marriage, she had never been tempted to it herself—until she'd met Wolf. If he wanted her for only a short time, she counted that as better than nothing. Even one day with him would be a bright and shining memory to treasure during the long, dreary years without him, a small bit of warmth to comfort her. Her dream was to spend a lifetime with him, but she didn't allow herself to expect it. He was too bitter, too wary; it was unlikely he would permit an Anglo to get that close to him. He would give her his body, perhaps even his affection, but not his heart or his commitment.

Because she loved him, she knew she wouldn't demand more. She didn't want anger or guilt between them. For as long as she could, in whatever way, she wanted to make Wolf happy.

He had asked her to wear her hair down, and the silky weight of it lay around her shoulders. She had been surprised, looking in the mirror that morning, how the relaxed hairstyle softened her face. Her eyes had glowed, because leaving her hair down was something she could do for him. She looked feminine, the way he made her feel.

There was no point in trying to make people think her neutral now, not after those arguments she'd gotten into. When she told him what had happened, he'd see the uselessness of trying to maintain the sham. She even felt relieved, because her heart hadn't been in it.

She had started to change into one of her shapeless housedresses when she caught sight of herself in the mirror and paused. In her mind she relived that moment the day she'd first met Wolf, when he'd seen her in Joe's old jeans and his eyes had momentarily widened with a look so hot and male it had the power, even now, to make her shake. She wanted him to look at her like that again, but he wasn't likely to as long as she kept wearing these—these *feed sacks!*

Suddenly she was dissatisfied with all her clothing. Her dresses were, without exception, sturdy and modest, but they were also too drab and loose-fitting. Her slight build would be better displayed in delicate cottons and light, cheerful colors, or even hip-hugging jeans. She turned and looked at her bottom in the mirror; it was slim and curvy. She could see no reason why she should be ashamed of it. It was a very nice bottom, as bottoms went.

Muttering to herself, she zipped herself back into her serviceable "good" dress and grabbed her purse. Ruth wouldn't offer much in the way of new clothes, but she could certainly buy some jeans and sassy little tops, as well as some neat skirts and blouses that, above all, actually fit her.

And she never wanted to see another "sensible" shoe in her life.

The gray clouds lived up to their promise, and it began to rain as she made the drive into town. It was a steady rain, just the sort ranchers and farmers everywhere loved, rather than a downpour that simply ran off instead of soaking into the ground. Aunt Ardith wouldn't have set foot out of the house during a rain, but Mary ignored it. She stopped first at the one store in Ruth that dealt exclusively in women's clothing, though by necessity the clothes weren't hot from a fashion show in Paris. She bought three pairs of jeans, size six, two lightweight cotton sweaters, and a blue chambray shirt that made her feel like a pioneer. A snazzy denim skirt, paired with a ruby-red sweater, flattered her so much she spun on her heel in delight, just like a child. She also chose a brown skirt, which fit so well she couldn't turn it down despite the color, and teamed a crisp pink blouse with it. Her final choice was a pale lavender cotton skirt and matching top, which sported a delicate lace collar. Still in a fit of defiance and delight, she picked out a pair of dressy white sandals as well as a pair of track shoes. When the saleswoman rang them up and called out the total, Mary didn't even blink an eye. This had been too long in coming.

Nor was she finished. She locked her packages in the car and dashed through the rain to Hearst's general store, where everyone bought boots. Since Mary planned to be spending most of her time on Wolf's mountain, she figured she'd need a pair.

Mr. Hearst was almost rude to her, but she stared him down and briefly thought of shaking her schoolteacher's finger at him. She discarded the idea because the finger lost its power if used too often, and she might really need it sometime in the future. So she ignored him and tried on boots until she finally found a pair that felt comfortable on her feet.

She couldn't wait to get home and put on her jeans and chambray shirt; she might even wear her boots around the house to get them broken in, she thought. Woodrow wouldn't know her. She thought of that look in Wolf's eyes and began to shiver.

Her car was parked up the street, a block away, and it was raining hard enough now that she made a disgusted noise at herself for not driving from the clothing store to Hearst's. Ruth didn't have sidewalks, and already huge puddles were standing on the pavement. Well, she had on her sensible shoes; let them earn their keep!

Putting her head down and holding the box containing her boots up in an effort to ward off part of the rain, she darted from the sheltering overhang of the roof and immediately got wet to the ankles when she stepped into a puddle. She was still grumbling to herself about that when she passed the small alley that ran between the general store and the next building, which had formerly been a barbershop but now stood empty.

She didn't hear anything or see a flurry of movement; she had no warning at all. A big hand, wet with rain, clamped over her mouth, and an arm wrapped around the front of her body, effectively holding her arms down as her attacker began hauling her down the alley, away from the street. Mary fought instinctively, wriggling and kicking while she made muffled sounds behind the man's palm. His hand was so tight on her face that his fingers dug painfully into her cheek.

The tall, wet weeds in the alley stung her legs, and the pounding rain stung her eyes. Terrified, she kicked harder. This couldn't be happening! He couldn't just carry her off in broad daylight! But he could; he had done it to Cathy Teele.

She got one arm free and reached back, clawing for his face. Her desperate fingers found only wet, woolly cloth. He cursed, his voice low and raspy, and hit her on the side of the head with his fist.

Her senses blurred as her head was rocked with pain, and her struggles grew aimless. Vaguely she was aware when they reached the end of the alley and he dragged her behind the abandoned building.

His breathing was fast and harsh in her ear as he forced her down on her stomach in the gravel and mud. She managed to get her arm free again and put her hand out to break her fall; the gravel scraped her palm, but she barely felt it. His hand was still over her mouth, suffocating her; he ground her face into the wet dirt and held her down with his heavy weight on her back.

He scrabbled with his other hand for her skirt, pulling it up. Wildly she clawed at his hand, trying to pull it free so she could scream, and he hit her again. She was terrified and kept clawing. Cursing, he forced her legs apart and thrust himself against her. She could feel him through his pants and her undergarments, pushing at her, and began gagging. *God, no!*

She heard her clothing tear, and overpowering revulsion gave her strength. She bit savagely at his hand and reached back for his eyes, her nails digging for flesh.

There was a roaring in her ears, but she heard a shout. The man on top of her stiffened, then braced his hand beside her head and used it to balance himself as he leaped to his feet. Her vision blurred by rain and mud, she saw only a blue sleeve and a pale, freckled hand before he was gone. From above and behind her came a loud boom, and vaguely she wondered if now she would be struck by lightning. No, lightning came before the thunder.

Running footsteps pounded the ground, going past her. Mary lay still, her body limp and her eyes closed.

She heard low cursing, and the footsteps returned. "Mary," a commanding voice said. "Are you all right?"

She managed to open her eyes and looked up at Clay Armstrong. He was soaked to the skin, his blue eyes furious, but his hands were gentle as he turned her onto her back and lifted her in his arms.

"Are you all right?" The words were sharper now.

The rain stung her face. "Yes," she managed, and turned her head into his shoulder.

"I'll get him," Clay promised. "I swear to you, I'll get the bastard."

There was no doctor in town, but Bessie Pylant was a registered nurse, and Clay carried Mary to Bessie's house. Bessie called the private practitioner for whom she worked and got him to drive over from the next town. In the meantime she carefully cleaned Mary's scrapes and put ice on the bruises, and began pouring hot, too-sweet tea down her.

Clay had disappeared. Bessie's house was suddenly full of women; Sharon Wycliffe came and assured Mary that she and Dottie could handle things on Monday if Mary didn't feel like working; Francie Beecham told tales of her own teaching days, her purpose obvious, and the other women took their cues from her. Mary sat quietly, clutching so tightly at the blanket Bessie had wrapped around her that her knuckles were white. She knew the women were trying to divert her, and was grateful to them; with rigid control she concentrated on their commonplace chatter. Even Cicely Karr came and patted Mary's hand, despite the argument they'd had only a few hours before.

Then the doctor arrived, and Bessie led Mary into a bedroom for privacy while the doctor examined her. She answered his questions in a subdued voice, though she winced when he probed the sore place on the side of her head where the man had struck her with his fist. He checked her pupil response and her blood pressure, and gave her a mild sedative.

"You'll be all right," he finally said, patting her knee. "There's no concussion, so your headache should go away soon. A good night's sleep will do more for you than anything I can prescribe."

"Thank you for driving out here," Mary said politely.

Desperation was growing in her. Everyone had been wonderful, but she could feel a fine wire inside her being coiled tighter and tighter. She

404   *Linda Howard*

felt dirty and exposed. She needed privacy and a shower, and more than anything she needed Wolf.

She left the bedroom and found that Clay had returned. He came to her immediately and took her hand. "How are you feeling?"

"I'm all right." If she had to say that one more time, she thought she would scream.

"I need a statement from you, if you think you can do it now."

"Yes, all right." The sedative was taking effect; she could feel the spreading sensation of remoteness as the drug numbed her emotions. She let Clay lead her to a chair and pulled the blanket tight around her once more. She felt chilled.

"You don't have to be afraid," Clay soothed. "He's been picked up. He's in custody now."

That aroused her interest, and she stared at him. "Picked up? You know who it is?"

"I saw him." The iron was back in Clay's voice.

"But he was wearing a ski mask." She remembered that, remembered feeling the woolly fabric under her fingers.

"Yeah, but his hair was hanging out from under the mask in back."

Mary stared up at him, the numbness in her changing into a kind of horror. His hair was long enough to hang out from under the mask? Surely Clay didn't think—surely not! She felt sick. "Wolf?" she whispered.

"Don't worry. I told you he's in custody."

She clenched her fists so tightly that her nails dug crescents in her palms. "Then let him go."

Clay looked stunned, then angry. "Let him go! Damn, Mary, can't you get it through your head that he attacked you?"

Slowly she shook her head, her face white. "No, he didn't."

"I saw him," Clay said, spacing out each word. "He was tall and had long black hair. Damn it, who else could it have been?"

"I don't know, but it wasn't Wolf."

The women were silent, sitting frozen as they listened to the argument. Cicely Karr spoke up. "We did try to warn you, Mary."

"Then you warned me about the wrong man!" Her eyes burning, Mary stared around the room, then turned her gaze back to Clay. "I saw his hands! He was a white man, an *Anglo*. He had freckled hands. *It wasn't Wolf Mackenzie!*"

Clay's brow creased in a frown. "Are you certain about that?"

"Positive. He put his hand on the ground right in front of my eyes." She reached out and grabbed his sleeve. "Get Wolf out of jail, right now. Right now, do you hear me! And he'd better not have a bruise on him!"

Clay got up and went to the telephone, and once again Mary looked at the women in the room. They were all pale and worried. Mary could guess why. As long as they had suspected Wolf, they had had a safe target for their fear and anger. Now they had to look at themselves, at someone who was one of them. A lot of men in the area had freckled hands, but Wolf didn't. His hands were lean and dark, bronzed by the sun, callused from years of hard manual work and riding. She had felt them on her bare skin. She wanted to shout that Wolf had no reason to attack her, because he could have her any time he wanted, but she didn't. The numbness was returning. She just wanted to wait for Wolf, if he came at all.

An hour later he walked into Bessie's house as if he owned it, without knocking. An audible gasp rose when he appeared in the doorway, his broad shoulders reaching almost from beam to beam. He didn't even glance at the other people in the room. His eyes were on Mary, huddled in her blanket, her face colorless.

His boots rang on the floor as he crossed to her and hunkered down. His black eyes raked her from head to toe; then he touched her chin, turning her head toward the light so he could see the scrape on her cheek and the bruises where hard fingers had bitten into her soft flesh. He lifted her hands and examined her raw palms. His jaw was like granite.

Mary wanted to cry, but instead she managed a wobbly smile. "You got a haircut," she said softly, and linked her fingers together to keep from running them through the thick, silky strands that lay perfectly against his well-shaped head.

"First thing this morning," he murmured. "Are you all right?"

"Yes. He—he didn't manage to…you know."

"I know." He stood. "I'll be back later. I'm going to get him. I promise you, I'll get him."

Clay said sharply, "That's a matter for the law."

Wolf's eyes were cold black fire. "The law isn't doing a very good job." He walked out without another word, and Mary felt chilled again. While he had been there, life had begun tingling in her numb body, but now it was gone. He had said he would be back, but she thought she should go home. Everyone was very kind, too kind; she felt as if she would scream. She couldn't handle any more.

Though he was stunned by Wolf's changed appearance, it took Clay only a moment to follow him. As he had suspected, Wolf stopped his truck at the alley where Mary had been attacked. By the time Clay parked the county car and entered the alley, Wolf was down on one knee, examining the muddy ground. He didn't even glance up when Clay approached. Instead he continued his concentrated examination of every weed and bit of gravel, every scuff mark, every indentation.

Clay said, "When did you get a haircut?"

"This morning. At the barbershop in Harpston."

"Why?"

"Because Mary asked me to," Wolf said flatly, and returned his attention to the ground.

Slowly he moved down the alley and to the back of the buildings, pausing at the spot where Mary's attacker had thrust her to the ground. Then he moved on, following exactly the path the attacker had taken, and it was in the next alley that he gave a grunt of satisfaction and knelt beside a blurred footprint.

Clay had been over the ground himself, and so had many other people. He said as much to Wolf. "That print could belong to anyone."

"No. It's made by a soft-soled shoe, not a boot." After examining the print awhile longer, he said, "He toes in slightly when he walks. I'd guess he weighs about one seventy-five, maybe one eighty. He isn't in very good shape. He was already tired when he got this far."

Clay felt uneasy. Some people would have simply passed off that kind of tracking ability as part of Wolf's Indian heritage, but they would have been wrong. There were excellent trackers of wildlife who could follow a man's footsteps in the wilderness as easily as if he had wet paint on the bottoms of his boots, but the details Wolf had discerned would have been noted only by someone who had been trained to hunt other men. Nor did he doubt what Wolf had told him, because he had seen other men, though not many, who could track like that.

"You were in Nam." He already knew that, but suddenly it seemed far more significant.

Wolf was still examining the footprint. "Yes. You?"

"Twenty-first Infantry. What outfit were you with?"

Wolf looked up, and a very slight, unholy smile touched his lips. "I was a LRRP."

Clay's uneasy feeling became a chill. The LRRPs, pronounced "lurp," were men on long-range reconnaissance patrol. Unlike the regular grunts, the LRRPs spent weeks in the jungles and hill country, living off the land, hunting and being hunted. They survived only by their wits and ability to fight, or to fade away into the shadows, whichever the situation demanded. Clay had seen them come in from the bush, lean and filthy, smelling like the wild animals they essentially were, with death in their eyes and their nerves so raw, so wary, that it was dangerous to touch them unexpectedly, or walk up to their backs. Sometimes they hadn't been able to bear the touch of another human being until their nerves settled down. A smart man walked lightly around a LRRP fresh in from the field.

What was in Wolf's eyes now was cold and deadly, an anger so great Clay could only guess at its force, though he understood it. Wolf smiled again, and in the calmest tone imaginable, one almost gentle, he said, "He made a mistake."

"What was that?"

"He hurt *my* woman."

"It's not your place to hunt him. It's a matter for the law."

"Then the law had better stay close to my heels," Wolf said, and walked away.

Clay stared after him, not even surprised by the blunt words claiming Mary as his woman. The chill ran down his back again and he shivered. The town of Ruth had made a mistake in judging this man, but the rapist had made an even bigger one, one that might prove fatal.

Mary stoically ignored all the protests and pleas when she announced her intention of driving home. They meant well, and she appreciated their concern, but she couldn't stay another moment. She was physically unharmed, and the doctor had said her headache would fade in the next few hours. She simply had to go home.

So she drove alone in the misting rain, her movements automatic. Afterward, she could never recall a moment of the drive. All she was aware of when she let herself into the creaky old house was a feeling of intense relief, and it so frightened her that she pushed it away. She couldn't afford to let herself relax, not now. Maybe later. Right now she had to hold herself together very tightly.

Woodrow looped around her ankles several times, meowing plaintively. Mary stirred herself to feed him, though he was as fat as a butterball already, then found herself exhausted by that brief effort. She sat down at the table and folded her hands in her lap, holding herself motionless.

That was how Wolf found her half an hour later, just as the gray daylight began to fade. "Why didn't you wait for me?" he asked from the doorway, his tone a low, gentle growl.

"I had to come home," Mary explained.

"I would have brought you."

"I know."

He sat down at the table beside her and took her cold, tightly clasped hands in his. She looked at him steadily, and his heart clenched like a fist in his chest.

He would have given anything never to have seen that look in her eyes.

She had always been so indomitable, with her "damn the torpedoes" spirit. She was slight and delicately made, but in her own eyes she had been invincible. Because the very idea of defeat was foreign to her, she had blithely moved through life arranging it to suit herself and accepted it as only natural that shopkeepers quaked before her wagging finger. That attitude had sometimes irritated, but more often entranced, him. The kitten thought herself a tiger, and because she acted like a tiger, other people had given way.

She was no longer indomitable. A horrible vulnerability was in her eyes, and he knew she would never forget the moments when she had been helpless. That scum had hurt her, humiliated her, literally ground her into the dirt.

"Do you know what really horrified me?" she asked after a long silence.

"What?"

"That I wanted the first time to be with you, and he was going to—" She stopped abruptly, unable to finish.

"But he didn't."

"No. He pulled up my skirt and pushed against me, and he was tearing my clothes when Clay—I think Clay shouted. He might have fired a shot. I remember hearing a roaring sound, but I thought it was thunder."

Her flat little monotone bothered him, and he realized she was still in shock. "I won't let him get near you again. I give you my word."

She nodded, then closed her eyes.

"You're going to take a shower," Wolf said, urging her to her feet. "A long, warm shower, and while you're taking it, I'll fix something for you to eat. What would you like?"

She tried to think of something, but even the thought of food was repugnant. "Just tea."

He walked upstairs with her; she was steady, but the steadiness seemed fragile, as if she were barely holding herself under control. He wished that she would cry, or yell, anything that would break the tension encasing her.

"I'll just get my nightgown. You don't mind if I get my nightgown, do you?" She looked anxious, as if afraid she was being too troublesome.

"No." He started to reach out and touch her, to slide his arm around her waist, but dropped his hand before contact was made. She might not want anyone to touch her. A sick feeling grew in him as he realized she might find his, and any other man's, touch disgusting now.

Mary got her nightgown and stood docilely in the old-fashioned bathroom while Wolf adjusted the water. "I'll be downstairs," he said as he straightened and stepped back. "Leave the door unlocked."

"Why?" Her eyes were big and solemn.

"In case you faint, or need me."

"I won't faint."

He smiled a little. No, Miss Mary Elizabeth Potter wouldn't faint; she wouldn't allow herself to be so weak. Maybe it wasn't tension holding her so straight; it might be the iron in her backbone.

He knew he wouldn't be able to coax her to eat much, if anything, but he heated a can of soup anyway. His timing was perfect; the soup had just boiled and the tea finished steeping when Mary entered the kitchen.

She hadn't thought to put on a robe; she wore only the nightgown, a plain white cotton eyelet garment. Wolf felt himself begin to sweat, because as demure as the nightgown was, he could still see the darkness of her nipples through the fabric. He swore silently as she sat down at the table like an obedient child; now wasn't the time for lust. But telling himself that didn't stop it; he wanted her, under any circumstances.

She ate the soup mechanically, without protest, and drank the tea, then thanked him for making it. Wolf cleared the table and washed up the few dishes; when he turned, Mary was still sitting at the table, her hands folded and her eyes staring at nothing. He froze briefly and muttered a curse. He couldn't bear it another minute. Swiftly he lifted her out of the chair and sat down in it, then settled her on his lap.

She was stiff in his arms for a moment; then a sigh filtered between her lips as she relaxed against his chest. "I was so frightened," she whispered.

"I know, honey."

"How can you know? You're a man." She sounded faintly truculent.

"Yeah, but I was in prison, remember?" He wondered if she would know what he was talking about, and he saw her brow furrow as she thought.

Then she said, "Oh." She began scowling fiercely. "If anyone hurt you—" she began.

"Hold it! No, I wasn't attacked. I'm good at fighting, and everyone knew it." He didn't tell her how he'd established a reputation for himself. "But it happened to other prisoners, and I knew it could happen to me, so I was always on guard." He'd slept only in light naps, with a knife made from a sharpened spoon always in his hand; his cell had hidden a variety of weapons, a lot of which the guards had seen and not recognized for what they were. It would have taken another LRRP to have seen some of the things he'd done and the weapons he'd carried. Yeah, he'd been on guard.

"I'm glad," she said, then suddenly bent her head against his throat and began to cry. Wolf held her tightly, his fingers laced through her hair to press against her skull and hold her to him. Her soft, slender body shook with sobs as she wound her arms around his neck. She didn't say anything else, and neither did he, but they didn't need words.

He cradled her until finally she sniffed and observed dazedly, "I need to blow my nose."

He stretched to reach the napkin holder and plucked a napkin from it to place in her hands. Mary blew her nose in a very ladylike manner, then sat still, searching in her depths for the best way to handle what had happened. She knew it could have been much worse, but it had been bad enough. Only one thought surfaced: she didn't want to be alone tonight. She hadn't been able to tolerate the women fussing around her, but if Wolf would just stay with her, she'd be all right.

She looked up at him. "Will you stay with me tonight?"

Every muscle in his big body tensed, but there was no way he could deny her. "You know I will. I'll sleep on the—"

"No. I mean—if you could sleep with me tonight, and hold me so I won't be alone, just for tonight, I think I'll be all right tomorrow."

He hoped it would be that easy for her, but he doubted it. The memories would linger on, springing out from dark corners to catch her when she least expected it. Until the day she died, she would never entirely forget, and for that he wanted to catch her assailant and break the guy's neck. Literally.

"I'll call Joe and let him know where I am," he said, and lifted her from his lap.

It was still early, but her eyelids were drooping, and after he called Joe he decided there was no point in putting it off. She needed to be in bed.

He turned out the lights and put his arm around her as they climbed the narrow stairs together. Her flesh was warm and resilient beneath the thin cotton, and the feel of her made his heart begin a slow, heavy beat. His jaw clenched as blood throbbed through his body, pooling in his groin. He was in for a miserable night, and he knew it.

Her bedroom was so old-fashioned it looked turn-of-the-century, but he hadn't expected anything else. The delicate lilac smell he associated with Mary was stronger up here. The ache in his loins intensified.

"I hope the bed is big enough for you," she said, worrying as she eyed the double bed.

"It'll do." It wasn't big enough, but it would do. He'd have to spend the night curled around her. Her bottom would be nestled against him, and he would quietly go insane. Suddenly he didn't know if he could do it, if he could lie with her all night and not take her. No matter what his mind said, his body knew exactly what it wanted; he was already so hard it was all he could do to keep from groaning.

"Which side do you want?"

What did it matter? Torment was torment, no matter what side he was on. "The left."

Mary nodded and turned back the covers. Wolf wanted to look away as she climbed into bed, but his eyes wouldn't obey. He saw the curve of her buttocks as the nightgown was momentarily pulled tight. He saw her pale, slim legs and immediately pictured them clasped around his waist. He saw the outline of her pretty breasts with their rosy nipples, and he remembered the feel of her breasts in his hands, her nipples in his mouth, her smell and taste.

Abruptly he bent down and pulled the sheet up over her. "I have to take a shower."

He saw the brief dart of fear at being alone in her eyes, but then she conquered it and said, "The towels are in the closet next to the bathroom door."

He was swearing savagely to himself as he stood in the bathroom, jerking his clothes off. A cold shower wouldn't help; he'd had a lot of them lately, and the effect was remarkably short-lived. He needed Mary—naked, beneath him, sheathing his swollen and throbbing flesh. She would be so tight that he wouldn't last a minute—

Damn. He couldn't leave her, not tonight. No matter what it cost him.

His entire body was aching as he stood under the warm, beating water. He couldn't crawl into bed with her like this. The last thing she needed right now was to have him poking at her all night. She needed comfort, not lust. Not only that, he wasn't entirely certain of his control. He'd been too long without a woman, had wanted *her* for too long.

He couldn't leave her, but he couldn't go to her like this. He knew what he had to do, and his soapy hand slid down his body. At least this would give him some modicum of control, because he would rather slit his own throat than see that fear and vulnerability in Mary's eyes again.

She was lying very still when he rejoined her, and she didn't move as he turned out the light. It wasn't until his weight depressed the mattress that she shifted to lie on her side. He positioned himself on his side, too, and hooked an arm around her waist to pull her firmly back into the cradle of his body. She sighed, and he felt the tension slowly ebb from her body as she relaxed against him.

"This is nice," she whispered.

"You aren't afraid?"

"Of you? No. Never of you." Her tone was liquid with tenderness. She lifted her hand to reach back and cup his jaw in her palm. "I'll be all right in the morning, wait and see. I'm just too tired right now to deal with it. Will you hold me all night?"

"If you want me to."

"Please."

He brushed her hair to one side and pressed a kiss into the nape of her neck, delighting in the delicate little shiver that rippled through her body when he did so. "My pleasure," he said gently. "Good night, sweetheart."

It was the storm that woke her. It was barely dawn, the light still dim, though the black clouds contributed to the grayness. The storm was fierce, reminding her of the ferocious thunderstorms in the South. Lightning ripped the dark sky apart, and the booming thunder made the very air vibrate. She lazily counted the seconds between the lightning flashes and the thunder to see how far away the storm was: seven miles. But it was pouring rain, the sound loud on the old tin roof. It was wonderful.

She felt both acutely alive and deeply calm, as if she were waiting for something. Yesterday was, by its very definition, in the past. It could no longer hurt her. Today was the present, and the present was Wolf.

He wasn't in the bed, but she knew he had been there during the night. Even in sleep she had sensed him, felt his strong arms holding her. Sleeping together was a joy so deep she couldn't express it, as if it had been meant to be. Perhaps it had been. She couldn't stop herself from hoping.

Where was he? She thought she smelled coffee and got out of bed. She visited the bathroom, brushed her hair and teeth, and returned to the bedroom to dress. Oddly she felt suddenly constrained by the bra she put on and discarded it. A subtle pulsating sensation had enveloped her entire body, and the sense of waiting increased. Even underpants were too much. She simply pulled on a loose cotton housedress over her nude body and went downstairs in her bare feet.

He wasn't in the parlor, or the kitchen, though the empty coffeepot and the cup in the sink explained the lingering scent. The kitchen door was open, the screen door no barrier to the cool damp air, and the fresh smell of rain mingled with that of the coffee. His truck was still parked at the back porch steps.

It took only a few minutes to boil water and steep a tea bag, and she drank the tea while sitting at the kitchen table, watching the rain sheet down the window. It was cool enough that she should have been chilled, wearing only the thin dress, but she wasn't, even though she could feel how her nipples had tightened. Once that would have embarrassed her. Now she thought only of Wolf.

She was halfway between the table and the sink, empty cup in hand, when suddenly he was there, standing on the other side of the screen door, watching her through the wire mesh. His clothing was plastered to his skin, rainwater dripping off of his face. Mary froze, her head turned to stare at him.

He looked wild, primitive, his eyes narrow and glittering, his feet braced apart. She could see every breath that swelled his chest, see the pulse that throbbed at the base of his throat. Though he was very still, she could feel his entire body pulsating with tension. In that moment she knew he was going to take her, and she knew that was why she had waited.

"I'll always be a half-breed," he said in a low, harsh voice, barely audible over the drumming rain. "There will always be people who look down on me because of it. Think long and hard before you agree to be my woman, because there's no going back."

Softly, clearly, she said, "I don't want to go back."

He opened the screen door and entered the kitchen, his movements slow and deliberate. Mary's hand shook as she reached out to place her cup on the cabinet; then she turned to face him.

He put his hands on her waist and gently drew her up against him; his clothes were wet, and immediately the front of her dress absorbed the moisture until the damp fabric was molded to her body. Mary slid her hands up his shoulders to join at the back of his neck and lifted her mouth to his. His kiss was slow and deep, making her toes curl as hot excitement began to dart through her. She knew how to kiss now and welcomed his tongue while she teased him with her own. His chest lifted with a deep, sharp intake of breath, and his grip on her tightened. Suddenly the kiss was no longer slow, but hungry and urgent, and the pressure of his mouth was almost painful.

She felt him gathering her skirt in his hand to lift it; then his callused palm was sliding up her thigh. He reached her hip and paused, shuddering with violent arousal as he realized she was naked under the dress; then his hand moved to her bare buttocks and caressed them. It was surprisingly pleasurable, and she moved her bottom against his hand. He had opened up an entire new world for her, the world of sensual pleasure, and he was constantly expanding the limits.

He couldn't wait much longer, and he lifted her in his arms. His face was hard and intent as he looked down at her. "Unless the house catches on fire, I won't stop this time," he said quietly. "I don't care if the phone rings, or if anyone drives up, or even knocks on the bedroom door. This time, we finish it."

She didn't reply, but gave him a slow, sweet smile that made him burn to take her right there. His arms tightened as he carried her up the narrow, creaky stairs and into her bedroom, where he carefully placed her on the bed.

He stood looking down at her for a moment, then walked to the window and raised it. "Let's let the storm in," he said, and then it was with them, filling the half-dark room with sound and vibration. The rain-chilled air washed over her, cool and fresh on her heated skin. She sighed, the small sound drowned out by the din of thunder and rain.

There by the window, with the dim gray light outlining the bulge and plane of powerful muscle, Wolf removed his wet clothing. Mary lay quietly on the bed, her head turned to watch him. The shirt went first, revealing his sleek, heavy shoulders and washboard stomach. She knew from touching him that he was unbelievably hard, with no give beneath his smooth skin. He bent down to tug off his boots and socks, then straightened and unbuckled his belt. The noise of the storm made his movements a pantomime, but she imagined the small pop as he unsnapped his jeans, then the hissing of the zipper as metal teeth pulled apart. Without hesitation he pushed down his jeans and underwear and stepped free of them.

He was naked. Her heart jerked painfully in her chest as she stared at him, for the first time feeling remarkably small and helpless beside him. He was big, he was strong, and he was undeniably male. She couldn't look away from his hard manhood. She was going to take him inside her, accept his heavy weight as they joined in the act of mating, and she was a little frightened.

He saw it in her eyes as he eased down beside her. "Don't be afraid," he whispered, brushing her hair away from her face. His hands were gentle as he reached under her and unzipped her dress.

"I know what's going to happen," she murmured, turning her face against his shoulder. "The mechanics of it, anyway. But I just don't see how it's possible."

"It is. I'll take it slow and easy."

"All right." She whispered her acquiescence and let him lift her so he could pull the dress off of her shoulders. Her breasts were bare, and she could feel them tightening, swelling, her nipples puckering. He bent to kiss both nipples, wetting them with his tongue, and her back arched as heat spread through her. He quickly stripped the dress down her hips and legs, the need to have her bare under his hands too urgent for him to ignore it any longer.

Mary quivered, then lay still. It was the first time since babyhood that anyone but herself had seen her completely nude; her cheeks heated, and she closed her eyes as she struggled with the sensations of embarrassment and painful exposure. He touched her breasts, gently squeezing them; then his rough palm slowly moved down her stomach until his fingers touched her silky triangle of curls. She made a small sound, and her eyes flew open to find him watching her with such a fierce, heated expression that she forgot her embarrassment. She was suddenly proud that he wanted her so intensely, that her body aroused him. Her legs relaxed, and one finger delved between her soft folds, lightly stroking the ultra-sensitive flesh he found. Mary's entire body tensed again, and she moaned. She hadn't known anything could feel like that, but she sensed there was more, and she didn't know if she could survive it. This was pleasure too intense to be borne.

"Do you like that?" Wolf murmured.

She gasped, her slender body beginning to writhe slowly on the sheets in a rhythm as old as the ages. He opened her legs farther with his hand, then returned to his sensual exploration, and at the same time bent to hungrily cover her mouth with his own. Mary's head spun, and her nails dug into his shoulders as she clung to him. She couldn't believe how he was touching her, how it made her feel, but she never wanted it to stop. He was causing a fever inside her, one that spread and intensified until she was aware of nothing but her own body and his. His stroking fingers raised her to delirium while his mouth muffled the small moans she made.

She tore her mouth away from his. "Wolf, please," she begged, frantic with need.

"Just a minute longer, sweetheart. Look at me. Let me see your face when I—ahh."

She whimpered. He was touching her even more intimately, finding her damp and swollen. His black gaze was locked with hers as he slowly slid his finger inside her, and they both shuddered convulsively.

Wolf knew he couldn't wait any longer. His entire body was throbbing. She was soft and wet and incredibly tight, and she was writhing on the verge of ecstasy. Her pale, translucent skin intoxicated him, enthralled him; just touching her made him wild. The textures of her body excited him more than anything he'd ever known before. Everything about her was soft and silky. Her hair was baby-fine, her skin delicate and satiny; even the curls between her legs were soft, rather than springy. He wanted her more than he wanted his next breath.

He moved between her legs, spreading them to make room for his hips to nestle against her. She inhaled sharply as she felt him, hard and burning. Their eyes met again as he reached down between their bodies and guided himself into position, then began entering her.

The storm was right over them now. The lightning cracked, and the almost simultaneous thunder boomed, rattling the old house. The sharply gusting wind blew the curtains straight out into the room, spattering rain on the floor in front of the open window and carrying a fine mist over their bodies. Mary cried, her tears mingling with the mist on her face, as she accepted his slow penetration.

He was braced over her on his forearms, his face just an inch from hers. He licked the tears away, then kissed her mouth, and she tasted salt. She could feel burning pain as her body stretched to admit him, and enormous pressure. More tears seeped from the corners of her eyes. He deepened the kiss as his buttocks flexed, exerting more pressure, and suddenly her body's barrier gave way. He pushed deep into her, burying himself to the hilt with a deep, almost tortured groan of pleasure.

There was pain, but there was also a lot more. He'd told her that making love was hot and sweaty, and that she probably wouldn't like it, and he was both right and wrong. It *was* hot and sweaty, and raw, and primitive. It was so powerful that it swept her along with its rhythms. Despite the pain, she felt exalted by his possession. She could feel the tension and savage excitement in his powerful body as she cradled him with her legs and arms, her soft depths filled with him. She loved him, and he needed her. She had never really lived before, until this moment when she gave herself to the man she loved.

She couldn't keep it back, not that it mattered. He had to know already. Mary had never worn an emotional mask. Her hands moved over his sleek, wet shoulders and into his thick hair. "I love you," she said, her soft voice barely audible over another booming roll of thunder.

If he replied, she didn't hear him. He reached down between their bodies again, but this time his hand was on her, and he began moving. Heat shimmered through her again, making the discomfort fade; her body arched, hips lifting in an effort to take him even deeper, and she told him again that she loved him. Sweat beaded his taut face as he tried to control his thrusts, but the storm was in the room, in their bodies. Her hips undulated, rolling, driving him mad. They strained together, their movements punctuated by the thunder, by the thudding of the headboard against the wall, and by the creaking of the bedsprings beneath them. Low groans and soft cries; wet flesh and trembling muscles; hands clutching frantically; harsh, rapid breathing and urgent thrusts—she knew all of that, felt it, heard it, and felt herself being consumed by the fever.

"Wolf?" Her questioning cry was thin, frantic. Her nails dug into the flexing muscles of his back.

"Don't fight it, baby. Let it go." He was groaning, feeling his own completion approaching, and he had no more control left. He removed his hand from between them and gripped her hips, lifting them, fitting himself more solidly to her and rocking against her loins.

Mary felt the tension and fever increase to unbearable levels, and then her senses exploded. She cried out, her entire body shuddering and clenching. It was the sweetest madness imaginable, a pleasure beyond description, and it continued until she thought she might die of it. He held her until she quietened, then began thrusting hard and fast. His guttural cries blended with the thunder as he crushed her against the mattress, his body convulsing as the powerful jetting of completion emptied him.

They were silent afterward, as if words would be an intrusion between them. Their mating had been so compelling and urgent that nothing else had existed. Even the storm, as violent as it was, had been only an accompaniment. Slowly, reluctantly, Mary felt reality return, but she was content to lie beneath him and do nothing more than stroke his hair.

Their breathing had long since steadied and the storm moved away when he disengaged their bodies and shifted onto his side. He cradled her for a time, but now that their skin had cooled, the mist-dampened bed was distinctly uncomfortable. When she began to shiver, he got out of bed and crossed to the window to close it. She watched as his muscles alternately bunched and relaxed with each movement of his nude body. Then he turned, and she was instantly, helplessly, fascinated. She wished for the nerve to run her hands all over him, especially his loins. She wanted to inspect him, like an exploration, going over uncharted territory.

"Like what you see?" His voice was low and filled with amusement.

Things had gone too far between them for her to be embarrassed now. She looked up at him and smiled. "Very much. I imagined you once in a loincloth, but this is much better."

He reached down and plucked her from the bed as easily as if she were a feather. "We'd better get dressed before you get cold, and before I forget my good intentions."

"What good intentions?"

"Not to keep at you until you're so sore you can't walk."

She looked gravely at him. "You made it wonderful for me. Thank you."

"It was pretty damn wonderful for me, too." One side of his mouth quirked upward, and he slid his hands into her silvery brown hair. "No bad moments?"

She understood what he meant and leaned her head against his chest. "No. That was an entirely different thing."

But she hadn't forgotten, either, and he knew it. She was still shaky and vulnerable inside, though she kept her chin proudly lifted. He intended for someone to pay for the damage done to her indomitable spirit.

He'd spent years living quietly on the fringes, maintaining the sort of armed truce that had existed between him and the citizens of Ruth, but no more. For Mary, he would find the creep who had attacked her, and if the townspeople didn't like it, that was just too bad.

She threw Wolf's wet clothes into the dryer, then prepared a late breakfast. Neither of them talked much. Despite her determination to overcome her shock, she couldn't quite forget those horrifying moments when she had been helpless at the hands of a madman, for he certainly was mad. No matter what she was doing or thinking, a lightning flash of memory would catapult her back to the attack, just for a minute, until she could regain control and put it from her again.

Wolf watched her, knowing what she was experiencing by the way her slight body would tense, then slowly relax. He'd lived through flashbacks, of Vietnam, of prison, and he knew how they worked, as well as the toll they took. He wanted to take her to bed again, to keep the shadows at bay for her, but knew from the occasional gingerness of her movements that she was too new to lovemaking for another bout right now to be anything other than abusive. When she was used to him... A very slight smile curved his lips as he thought of the hours of pleasure and all the different ways he would take her.

But first he had to find the man who had attacked her.

When his clothes were dry, he dressed and pulled Mary out to the back porch with him. The rain had diminished to a drizzle, so he figured they wouldn't get too wet. "Come out to the barn with me," he said, taking her hand.

"Why?"

"I want to show you something."

"I've been in the barn. There's nothing interesting in there."

"There is today. You'll like it."

"All right." They hurried through the drizzle to the old barn, which was dark and musty, without the warmth and rich, animal smells of his barn. Dust tickled her nose. "It's too dark to see anything."

"There's enough light. Come on." Still holding her hand, he led her into a stall where a couple of boards were missing from the wall, letting in the dreary light. After the darkness of the inner barn, she could see fairly well.

"What is it?"

"Look under the feed trough."

She bent down and looked. Curled up, in a nest of dusty straw and an old towel she recognized, was Woodrow. Curled against Woodrow's belly were four little rat-looking things.

She straightened abruptly. "Woodrow's a father!"

"Nope. Woodrow's a mother."

"A mother!" She stared at the cat, who stared back at her enigmatically before beginning to lick the kittens. "I was specifically told that Woodrow is male."

"Well, Woodrow is female. Didn't you look?"

Mary gave him a severe look. "I don't make a habit of looking at an animal's private parts."

"Just mine, right?"

She blushed, but couldn't deny the charge. "Right."

He slipped his arms around her waist and pulled her close for a slow, warm kiss. She sighed and softened against him, reaching up to clasp the back of his neck as his mouth moved over hers. The strength of his big body reassured her, made her feel safe. When his hard arms were around her, nothing could harm her.

"I have to go home," he murmured when he lifted his mouth from hers. "Joe will do as much as he can, but it takes both of us to get everything done."

She had thought she could handle it, but panic seized her at the thought of being alone. Quickly she controlled herself and let her arms drop from around his neck. "Okay." She started to ask if she'd see him later, but kept the words unsaid. Oddly, now that their relationship was so intimate, she felt far less sure of herself than she had before. Letting him get that close, letting him enter her body, had exposed a vulnerability she hadn't known was there. That kind of intimacy was a little scary.

"Get a jacket," he said as they left the barn.

"I already have a jacket."

"I meant, get one now. You're going with me."

She gave him a quick look, then dropped her gaze away from the awareness in his. "I have to be alone sometime," she said quietly.

"But not today. Go on, get that jacket."

She got the jacket and climbed up into his truck, feeling as if she had been reprieved from execution. Maybe by the time night came she would have her fears under control.

Joe came out of the barn as they drove up and walked to the passenger side of the truck. When Mary opened the door, he reached in and lifted her from the truck, then hugged her tightly. "Are you all right?" His young voice was gruff.

She hugged him in return. "He didn't hurt me. I was just scared."

Over her head Joe looked at his father and saw the cold, controlled rage in those black eyes as they lingered on the slight woman in his son's arms. Someone had dared to hurt her, and whoever it was would pay.

Joe felt a deep primitive anger, and knew it was only a fraction of what Wolf felt. Their eyes met, and Wolf gave a slight shake of his head, indicating that he didn't want Joe to pursue the subject. Mary was here to relax, not relive the attack.

Wolf approached and looped his arm over her shoulder, using the pressure to turn her toward the stable. "Feel up to helping with the chores?"

Her eyes lit. "Of course. I've always wanted to see how a ranch works."

He automatically shortened his long stride to match hers as the three of them walked toward the stable. "This isn't a ranch, exactly. I run a small herd, but more for training and our personal beef than any other reason."

"What sort of training?"

"Training the horses to work a herd. That's what I do. I break and train horses. Quarter horses mostly, for ranchers, but sometimes I handle the odd show horse or Thoroughbred, or a fractious pleasure mount."

"Don't Thoroughbred owners have their own trainers?"

He shrugged. "Some horses are harder to train than others. An expensive horse isn't worth a damn if no one can get near him." He didn't elaborate, but Mary knew that he got the horses no one else was able to handle.

The long stable jutted out to the right of the barn. When they entered, Mary inhaled the rich earth scents of horses, leather, manure, grain and hay. Long satiny necks poked over the stall doors, and inquisitive whickers filled the air. She had never been around horses much, but she wasn't afraid of them. She moved down the line, patting and stroking, murmuring to the animals. "Are these all quarter horses?"

"No. That one in the next stall is a Canadian cutting horse—that's a type, not a breed. He belongs to a rancher in the next county north. Down in the last stall is a saddle-bred, for some big rancher's wife in Montana. He's going to give her the horse for her birthday in July. The rest of them are quarter horses."

They were all young horses, and as playful as children. Wolf treated them as such, talking to them in a low, crooning tone, gentling them like overgrown babies. Mary spent the entire afternoon in the stables with Wolf and Joe, watching them attend to the endless chores of cleaning and feeding, checking shoes, grooming. The drizzle finally stopped in the late afternoon, and Wolf worked with a couple of the young quarter horses in the pen behind the stable, slowly and gently getting them accustomed to bits and saddles. He didn't rush them, or lose his patience when a fractious young horse shied away from him whenever Wolf tried to lift a saddle onto his back. He just soothed the colt and reassured him before trying again. Before the afternoon was over, the colt was ambling around the pen as if he'd been wearing a saddle for years.

Mary was enthralled, partly by his low, velvety voice, and partly by the way his strong hands moved over the young animals, teaching and soothing all at once. He had done that with her, but his hands had also excited her. She shivered as memories washed over her, and her breasts tightened.

"I've never seen anyone like him," Joe said beside her, keeping his tone low. "I'm good, but not near as good as he is. I've never seen a horse he couldn't settle down. We had a stallion brought to us a couple of years ago. He'd been put out to stud, but he was so damn vicious the handlers couldn't control him. Dad just put him in a stall and left him alone, but every so often he'd leave sugar cubes, apples or carrots on the top of the stall door and stand there until the stallion got a good look at him. Then he'd walk off, and the stallion would get whatever he'd left on the door.

"The stallion started watching for him and snorting at him if Dad was taking his time about getting the food over there. Then Dad stopped moving away, and the stallion, Ringer, had to come up to the door while Dad was there if he wanted the food. The first few times, he tried to tear the stall apart, but finally he gave in and got the food. Next he had to eat out of Dad's hand if he wanted his treat. Dad switched completely to carrots then, to make sure he didn't lose any fingers. Finally Ringer was hanging his head over the stall, and he'd nuzzle Dad's shirt like a kid hunting candy. Dad petted him and groomed him—Ringer loved being brushed—and gradually broke him to the saddle and started riding him. I worked with him, too, after Dad had him settled down, and I guess he finally decided he didn't have to fight all the time.

"We had a mare come in heat, and Dad called Ringer's owner to ask if he wanted us to try Ringer on our mare. The guy gave his okay, Ringer performed like a real gentleman, and everybody was happy. The owner got his expensive stud civilized, and we got a hefty fee, as well as a hell of a colt out of the mare Ringer covered."

Mary blinked at all this talk of being "in heat" and "covered," and cleared her throat. "He's wonderful," she agreed, and cleared her throat again. Her skin felt hot and sensitive. She couldn't take her eyes off Wolf, tall and lean and broad-shouldered, the weak sunlight glinting off his black hair.

"When we get through here, maybe we could do a few lessons tonight, since I missed Friday night," Joe said, interrupting her thoughts.

She didn't like thinking about why he had missed Friday night, about the long hours spent waiting to hear if Wolf had been jailed. This afternoon had been a small oasis of calm, with the semblance of normality, but it would be a long time before things were back to normal in the county. A young girl had been raped, and Mary had been attacked the very next day. People would be enraged and wary, looking at their neighbors and wondering. God help any stranger who happened to wander through, at least until the man was caught.

Tires crunched on the gravel, and Joe left his post to see who had ventured up on Mackenzie's Mountain. He was back in a moment, with Clay Armstrong behind him. It was a replay of Friday afternoon, and Mary felt her heart lurch; surely Clay wasn't going to arrest Wolf now?

"Mary." Clay nodded at her and touched the brim of his hat. "You doing okay?"

"Yes." She said it firmly.

"I thought I'd find you up here. Do you feel like going over it again with me?"

Wolf pulled off his gloves as he approached. His eyes were flinty. "She went over it with you yesterday."

"Sometimes people remember little things after the shock has passed."

Because she sensed Wolf was about to throw Clay off his property, she turned and put her hand on his arm. "It's okay. *I'm* okay."

She was lying, and he knew it, but her mouth had taken on that stubborn set that meant she wouldn't back down. He felt a tinge of amusement; his kitten was getting back some of her confidence, after all. But no way was he going to let Clay question her alone. He looked at Joe. "Put the horse up. I'm going with Mary."

"That isn't necessary," Clay said.

"It is to me."

Mary felt dwarfed between the two big men as they walked up to the house; she thought she might soon find such protectiveness smothering. A smile touched her lips. Clay probably felt he had to protect her from Wolf as well as from another attack, while Wolf was determined to protect her, period. She wondered what Clay would think if he knew that she didn't want to be protected from Wolf. Aunt Ardith would say Wolf had taken advantage of her, and Mary earnestly hoped he would do so again. Soon.

Wolf caught her sidelong glance and stiffened as he felt her interest and warmth. Damn it, didn't she know how he'd react, and that it could get embarrassing? Already he could feel the tension in his loins. But, no, she didn't know. Despite their early morning lovemaking, she was still too innocent about sex in general, and the effect she had on him in particular, to know what that look did to him. He hurried his step. He needed to sit down.

When they entered the kitchen, Mary moved around making coffee as naturally as she would have in her own house, emphasizing to Clay that she and Wolf were a couple. Folks in the county were just going to have to get used to it.

"Let's go through it from the beginning," Clay said.

Mary paused fractionally, then resumed her steady movements as she measured coffee into the percolator. "I'd just bought new boots at Hearst's store and was walking back to my car—my boots! I dropped them! Did you see them? Did anyone pick them up?"

"I saw them, but I don't know what happened to them. I'll ask around."

"He must have been standing against the side of Hearst's store, because I'd have seen him if he had been on the other side of the alley. He just grabbed me and put his hand over my mouth. He held my head arched back, so I couldn't move it at all, and started dragging me down the alley. I got one hand free and reached back, trying to scratch his face, but he had on a ski mask. He hit me in the head with his fist and I—I really don't remember much after that until he pushed me down. I kept scratching him, and I think I clawed his hand, because he hit me again. Then I bit him on the hand, but I don't know if I drew blood.

"Someone yelled, and he got up and ran. He put his hand on the ground right in front of my face when he got up. His sleeve was blue, and he had freckles on his hand. A lot of freckles. Then...you were there."

She fell silent and moved to look out the kitchen window, her back to the men sitting at the table, so she didn't see the murderous look in Wolf's eyes, or the way his big fists clenched, but Clay did, and it worried him.

"I was the one who yelled. I saw the package lying on the ground and went over to see what it was, and then I heard scuffling from the back of the building. When I saw him, I yelled and pulled my revolver, and fired over his head to try to stop him."

Wolf looked savage. "You should have shot the son of a bitch. That would have stopped him."

In retrospect Clay wished he'd shot the guy, too. At least then they wouldn't be racking their brains trying to put an ID to him, and the townspeople wouldn't be so jittery. Women were carrying an assortment of weapons with them wherever they went, even outside to hang the wash to dry. The mood people were in, it would be dangerous for a stranger to stop in the county.

That was what bothered him, and he said as much. "It looks like someone would have noticed a stranger. Ruth is a small town, and people pretty well know everyone in the county. A stranger would have been noticed right off, especially one with long black hair."

Wolf gave a wintry smile. "Everyone would have thought it was me."

At the window, Mary stiffened. She had been trying not to listen, trying to push away the memories that had been called up by her recounting of what had happened. She didn't turn around, but suddenly all her attention was focused on the conversation behind her. What Wolf had said was true. On seeing her attacker's long black hair, Clay had immediately had Wolf arrested.

But that long black hair, so distinctive, didn't fit with the wealth of rust-colored freckles she'd seen on the man's hand. And his skin had been pale. Fair people freckled. The black hair didn't fit.

Unless it was a disguise. Unless the object had been to frame Wolf.

Her spine prickled, and she felt both hot and cold. Whoever had done it hadn't known that Wolf had had his hair cut. But the choice of victim was puzzling; it didn't make sense. Why attack her? Surely no one would think Wolf would attack the one person in town who'd championed him, and she'd made it plain how she felt. Unless she had been a random choice, *it just didn't make sense.* After all, there was no link between herself and Cathy Teele, no common ground. It could all be chance.

Still without turning around, she asked, "Wolf, do you know Cathy Teele? Have you ever spoken to her?"

"I know her by sight. I don't speak to little Anglo girls." His tone was ironic. "Their parents wouldn't like it."

"You're right about that," Clay said wearily. "A few months back Cathy told her mother you were the best-looking man around, and that she wouldn't mind dating Joe if he weren't younger than she was. The whole town heard about it. Mrs. Teele pitched a fit."

That chill ran down Mary's spine again. There was a link, after all: Wolf. Nor could she dismiss it as coincidence, though something about the whole thing was skewed.

She twisted her hands together, and turned to face them. "What if someone is deliberately trying to frame Wolf?"

Wolf's face went hard and blank, but Clay looked startled. "Damn," he muttered. "Why did you think of that?"

"The long black hair. It could have been a wig. The man had freckles on his hand, a lot of freckles, and his skin was pale."

Wolf got to his feet, and though Mary knew she never had anything to fear from him, she fell back a step at the expression in his eyes. He didn't say anything; he didn't have to. She had seen him angry before, but this was different. He was enraged, but it was an icy rage, and he was in perfect control of himself. Perhaps that was what alarmed her.

Then Clay said, "Sorry, but I don't think it'll wash. Once we had all thought about it, it didn't make sense that Wolf would have attacked you, of all people. You've stood up for him right from the beginning, when the rest of the people in town—"

"Wouldn't spit on me if I were on fire," Wolf finished.

Clay couldn't deny it. "Exactly."

The coffee had finished brewing, and Mary poured three cups. They were silent and thoughtful as they sipped, all of them turning things around in their minds, trying to make the pieces fit. The truth was that no matter how things were arranged, something was always off, unless they went with the idea that a criminal had chosen Mary and Cathy at random, and had perhaps used a long black wig for disguise by pure coincidence.

Everything in Mary rejected the idea of coincidence. So that meant someone was deliberately trying to implicate Wolf. But why choose *her* as a victim?

To punish Wolf by hurting the people who had championed him?

It was all supposition, without a shred of evidence. Wolf had lived here for years without anything like this happening, even though his presence was like salt on the wound of the town's conscience. They didn't like him, and he didn't let them forget. Still, they had all existed under a silent truce.

So what had triggered the violence?

She rubbed her temples as a sudden twinge of pain threatened to become a full-scale headache. Since she seldom had headaches, she supposed the tension was getting to her, and determined not to let it. She'd never been a Nervous Nellie and didn't intend to start now.

Clay sighed and pushed his empty cup back. "Thanks for the coffee. I'll get the report finished tomorrow. I'll bring the papers by the school for you to sign—uh, are you planning to go to work, or stay home?"

"Why, work, of course."

"Of course," Wolf muttered, and scowled at her. Mary lifted her chin at him. She saw no reason why she should suddenly become an invalid.

Clay left soon afterward, and Joe came up from the stables to join in the dinner preparations. It felt right, the three of them together, working together as comfortably as if they had done so for years. Joe winked at her once, and she blushed, because it was fairly easy to read the expression in his young-old eyes. Awareness, amusement and approval were all there. Was he simply assuming she and Wolf had become intimate because Wolf had spent the night at her house, which she supposed was the commonsense thing to assume, or was there something different about her? What if everyone in town could just look at her and know?

Wolf curved his hand around her waist. She had been standing motionless for several minutes, the pan in her hand forgotten, as she both frowned and blushed. The blush told him what she was thinking, and the familiar tension in his body made his fingers tighten until they dug into her ribs. She looked up at him, her gray-blue eyes wide and startled; then awareness shot into them, and her eyelids dropped to half veil the desire she couldn't disguise.

Joe reached to take the pan from her nerveless fingers. "I think I'll go see a movie somewhere," he announced.

Mary jerked her head around, tearing herself from the sensual spell Wolf spun about her so easily. "No! Your lessons, remember?"

"Another night won't hurt."

"Another night will hurt," she insisted. "The Academy isn't something you can take for granted just because Senator Allard is going to recommend you. You can't afford to let up for a minute.''

Wolf released her. "She's right, son. You can't let your grades slip." He could wait. Barely.

It was after nine when Mary closed the books she and Joe had been using and stretched her arms over her head. "Could you take me home now?" she asked Wolf, barely suppressing a yawn. It had been an eventful day.

His face was impassive. "Why don't you stay here." It was more of a command than a suggestion.

"I can't do that!"

"Why not?"

"It isn't proper."

"I stayed with you last night."

"That's different."

"How?"

"I was upset."

"Your bed's too small. Mine's bigger."

"I'm getting out of here," Joe said, and suited the action to the words. Mary got huffy. "Did you have to say that in front of him?"

"He knew anyway. Remember what I said about no going back?"

She stilled and said, "Yes." That warm look entered her eyes again. "I don't want to go back. But I can't stay here tonight. I have to go to work in the morning."

"No one would think any less of you if you didn't."

"*I* would." She had that look again, the stubborn, determined expression of a fierce will.

Wolf got to his feet. "All right. I'll take you home." He went into his bedroom and several minutes later reappeared with a small shaving kit in his hand and a change of clothes slung over his shoulder. He knocked briefly on Joe's door as he passed it. "I'll be home in the morning."

The door opened. Joe was barefoot and shirtless, having been preparing to take a shower. "Okay. Are you going to take her to school, or do you want me to?"

"I don't need anyone to take me to work," Mary interrupted.

"That's tough." Wolf turned back to his son. "Baugh is bringing a couple of horses up in the morning, so I'll have to be here. You take her to school, and I'll get her in the afternoon."

"I'm driving my own car, and you can't stop me!"

"That's okay. You'll just have an escort." Wolf crossed the floor to her and took her arm. "Ready?"

Realizing that he'd made up his mind and there wasn't anything she could do about it, Mary walked with him out to the truck. The night air was growing cold, but his big body radiated heat, and she moved closer to him. As soon as they were in the truck, he roughly took her in his arms and bent his head to hers. She opened her mouth beneath his on-slaught and thrust her fingers into his thick hair. The warm taste of his mouth filled her; the pressure of his arms around her rib cage, of his hard-muscled chest on her breasts, drugged her more surely than any sedative. If he had pulled her down onto the seat and taken her right then, she wouldn't have objected.

As it was, when he put her from him, her entire body was throbbing. She sat silently on the drive down the mountain, thinking of their love-making that morning, aching for it to be repeated. A thought echoed in her mind: so this was what it meant to be a woman.

Woodrow was waiting patiently on the back doorstep. Mary fed him—her!—while Wolf showered and shaved. He didn't have a heavy beard, but two days' growth had darkened his jaw, and her face burned a little from contact with his when they had kissed. She felt that deep, almost painful sense of waiting again as she climbed the stairs to her bedroom.

He silently entered and stood for a moment watching her before she sensed his presence and turned. "The shower's yours."

He was naked, and slightly damp from the humidity in the bathroom. His black hair glistened under the light, and glittering droplets of water were caught in the dark curls of hair on his chest. He was already aroused. The throbbing in her body became acute.

She showered, and afterward, for the first time, sprayed perfume on her pulse points. She had never bought perfume in her life, but luckily one of her students in Savannah had given her the bottle for Christmas. The scent was sweetly exotic.

She opened the bathroom door, then gasped and fell back. Wolf was waiting for her in the doorway, his eyes narrow and fierce as they raked her. She had boldly left off her nightgown, and under his perusal the deep throbbing intensified. He put his big hands on her breasts and lifted them slightly so that they were plumped in his palms. Her nipples tightened even before he began rubbing them with his thumbs. Mary stood very still, her breath quick and shallow, her eyes half closed as she tried to deal with the pleasure his hands brought.

Wolf's own eyes were narrow black slits. "I wanted to do this the day I found you on the road," he murmured. "Such a pretty little body inside that ugly dress. I wanted to take it off of you and see you naked."

The heat in his eyes, in his voice, made her shiver and sway toward him. He pulled her out of the doorway and into the dark hall, then put his hands on her waist and lifted her. She remembered when he had done that before and moaned even before his mouth closed over her nipple. He sucked it so strongly that her back arched, and she cried out as her legs parted and wrapped around his hips for balance. He groaned, unable to wait a minute longer. He had to get inside her or go mad. He shifted her, guided himself and entered her.

Mary shuddered, then went very still as he slowly pushed into her. It was even better than before. Her inner muscles gently clasped and relaxed as she accommodated him, sending waves of pleasure radiating out through her body. She clung to him, gasping. Desire worked its magic on her body, tightening some muscles, loosening others, so that she was both taut and pliable as she lifted herself, then sank back down. The effect of that small movement had both of them gasping, and Wolf shifted to brace his back against the wall. She did it again, then again. He put his hands on her buttocks to take control of the motion and began driving into her. Her skin felt on fire. She radiated heat, making her skin feel tight and smooth and so extraordinarily sensitive that she could feel each of his fingers on her bottom, the rasp of his chest hair on her breasts, the tiny nubs of his nipples, the muscled wall of his belly, the coarse hair at his groin. She could feel him deep inside her.

Her back arched, and her nerves convulsed. Wolf fought his own response, not wanting it to end so quickly, and held her until she quietened. Then he carried her into the bedroom, her legs still locked around him, and eased her down on the bed.

She swallowed and relaxed her hold on him. "You haven't—?"

"Not yet," he murmured, and began moving strongly into her.

She didn't want it to end. She took his thrusts, cradled him when a harsh groan tore from his throat and the powerful shudders of completion shook him, and afterward held him as he rested on her body. She didn't want him to withdraw, to leave her empty again. She had existed in a sort of genteel limbo all her life until she had met him and begun to live. In just a few short months he had so completely taken over the focus of her life that the years before were hazy.

He gathered himself and tried to move off her. Mary tightened her legs around him, and he grunted.

"Let me up, sweetheart. I'm too heavy for you."

"No you aren't," she whispered, and kissed his throat.

"I weigh twice what you do. Do you even weigh a hundred pounds?"

"Yes," she said indignantly. She weighed a hundred and five.

"Not much more than that. I weigh two hundred, and I'm a foot taller than you. If I go to sleep on you, you'll smother."

He did sound drowsy. She ran her hand down the muscled ridges of his side. "I want to stay like this."

He thrust gently against her. "Like this?"

"Yes." She breathed the word.

He settled onto her, but shifted part of his weight to the side. "Is this okay?"

It was wonderful. She could breathe, but he was still close to her, still inside her. He quickly dozed off, as content as she with the position, and Mary smiled in the darkness as she held him.

The dark thoughts slowly intruded. Someone had deliberately tried to frame him, to put him back in prison. The thought of Wolf without his freedom was obscene and scary, because she knew enough about him to know he would never let himself be sent to prison again.

She wanted to keep him safe, to shield him in her arms, putting her own body between him and danger. Dear God, what had started it all? Things had been so quiet! What had been the trigger?

Then she knew, and horror almost stopped her breath. *She* had been the trigger.

While Wolf and Joe had been outcasts, punished for their heritage and Wolf's past, everything had been calm. Then she had come to town, an Anglo woman, but instead of aligning herself with the townspeople, she had championed the Mackenzies. With her help, Joe had achieved an honor offered to very few. Other people had begun saying what a nice thing it was that the Mackenzie boy was going to the Academy. Cathy Teele had said that Wolf was the best-looking man in the county. The boundaries between the town and the Mackenzies had begun blurring. Someone, with a maggot of hate festering deep inside, had been unable to stand it.

And she had been the cause of it all. If anything happened to Wolf, it would be her fault.

She didn't know what to do. The thought that she was the cause of all that had happened tormented her, disturbing her sleep. She moved restlessly, waking Wolf, and he sensed her distress though he attributed it to the wrong cause. He soothed her with whispers and pulled her more completely beneath him. She felt him harden inside her. His lovemaking was gentle this time, and when it was over she slept as effortlessly as a child until he awoke her again in the total darkness before dawn. She turned to him without question.

Joe drove up just as she and Wolf were preparing breakfast, and without a word Wolf broke more eggs into a bowl to be scrambled. Mary smiled at him, even though she was placing more bacon in the frying pan. "How do you know he's hungry?"

"He's awake, isn't he? My kid eats like a horse."

Joe came in the back door and headed for the coffee, which had already finished brewing. "Morning."

"Good morning. Breakfast will be ready in about ten minutes."

He grinned at her, and Mary smiled back. Wolf watched her, his gaze sharp. She looked frail this morning, her skin pale and even more translucent than usual, with faint mauve shadows under her eyes. She smiled readily, but he wondered what had made her look so delicate. Had he tired her with his lovemaking, or were memories of the attack disturbing her? He thought it must be the latter, because she had responded eagerly every time he'd reached for her. Knowing that she was still frightened made him even more determined to find whoever had attacked her. After Eli Baugh had delivered the horses and left, Wolf planned to do some tracking.

Joe was right behind Mary's car on the way to the school, and he didn't leave immediately, as she had expected. It was still too early for the students to begin arriving, so he walked with her into the empty building and even inspected the rooms. Then he leaned against the doorjamb and waited.

Mary sighed. "I'm perfectly safe here."

"I'll just wait until some other people show up."

"Did Wolf tell you to do this?"

"Nope. He knew he didn't have to."

How did they communicate? By telepathy? Each seemed to know what the other was thinking. It was disconcerting. She just hoped they couldn't read her thoughts, because she'd had some decidedly erotic ones lately.

What would everyone think of Joe's presence? He was so obviously a watchdog. She wondered if it would trigger another act of violence, and she felt sick, because she knew it might. Instinct, sharpened by her fierce protectiveness for both Mackenzies, told her that her theory was correct. Just the possibility that they could become accepted had driven someone over the edge. It revealed so much hate that she shivered.

Sharon and Dottie entered the building and halted briefly when Joe turned his head and looked at them as they passed the open door. "Mrs. Wycliffe. Mrs. Lancaster," he said in acknowledgment as he touched his fingertips to the brim of his hat in a brief salute.

"Joe," Sharon murmured. "How are you?"

Dottie gave him a brief, almost frightened look and hurried to her classroom. Joe shrugged. "I've been doing a bit of studying," he allowed.

"Just a bit?" Sharon asked wryly. She stepped past him to greet Mary, then said, "If you don't feel like working today, Dottie and I can handle your classes. I never dreamed you'd be here today, anyway."

"I was merely frightened," Mary said firmly. "Clay prevented anything else from happening. Cathy is the one who needs sympathy, not I."

"The whole town is in an uproar. Anyone who has freckles on his hands is getting the third degree."

Mary didn't want to talk about it. The image of that freckled hand made her feel nauseated, and she swallowed convulsively. Joe frowned and stepped forward. Mary put up her hand to keep him from throwing Sharon out of the classroom, but at that moment several students entered, and their chatter distracted everyone. The kids said, "Hi, Joe, howya been?" as they clustered around him. They all wanted to know about his plans for the Academy and how he'd gotten interested.

Sharon left to attend to her own classes, and Mary watched Joe with the kids. He was only sixteen, but he seemed older than even the seniors. Joe was young, but he wasn't a kid, and that was the difference. She noticed that Pam Hearst was in the group. She wasn't saying much, but she never took her eyes off Joe, looking at him with both longing and pain, though she tried to hide it. Several times Joe gave the girl a long look that made her fidget uncomfortably.

Then he checked his watch and left his former classmates to say to Mary, "Dad will be here to follow you home. Don't go anywhere alone."

She started to protest, then thought of the man out there who hated them enough to do what he'd done. She wasn't the only one at risk. She reached out and caught his arm. "You and Wolf be careful. You could be the next targets."

He frowned, as if that hadn't occurred to him. The attacker was a rapist, so men wouldn't consider themselves in danger. She wouldn't have thought of it, either, if she hadn't been convinced that the whole thing was intended to punish the Mackenzies. What greater punishment could there be than to kill them? At some point the madman might decide to take a rifle and dispense his own twisted brand of justice.

Clay showed up at lunch with the papers for her to read and sign. Aware of the kids watching them with acute interest, she walked with him out to the car. "I'm worried," she admitted.

He propped his arm on top of the open door. "You'd be foolish if you weren't worried."

"Not for myself. I think Wolf and Joe are the real targets."

He gave her a quick, sharp look. "How do you figure that?"

Heartened that he hadn't immediately dismissed the idea, but was watching her with a troubled expression in his eyes, Mary told him her theory. "I think Cathy and I were specifically chosen as targets to punish Wolf. Don't you see the link? She said she thought Wolf was handsome, and that she'd like to date Joe. Everyone knows I've been friends with them from the first. So we were chosen."

"And you think he'll attack again?"

"I'm certain he will, but I'm afraid he'll go after one of them this time. I doubt he'd try to manhandle either of them, but what chance would they have against a bullet? How many men in this county have a rifle?"

"Every last mother's son," Clay replied grimly. "But what set this guy off?"

She paused, her face miserable. "I did."

"What?"

"I did. Before I came here, Wolf was an outcast. Everyone was comfortable with that. Then I made friends with him and worked with Joe to get him into the Academy. A lot of people were a little proud of that and were friendlier. It was a crack in the wall, and whoever is doing this just couldn't stand it."

"You're talking about a lot of hate, and it's hard for me to see. People around here don't get along with Wolf, but a lot of it is fear instead of hate. Fear and guilt. The people in this county sent him to prison for something he didn't do, and his presence constantly reminds them of it. He isn't a very forgiving person, is he?"

"Something like that would be a little hard to forgive," Mary pointed out.

He had to agree with that and sighed wearily. "Still, I can't think of anyone who seems to hate him to the point of attacking two women just because they were friendly to him. Hell, Cathy wasn't even friendly. She just made a chance remark."

"So you agree with me? That all of this is because of Wolf?"

"I don't like it, but I guess I do. Nothing else makes sense, because there may be a few coincidences in life, but none in crime. Everything has a motive.''

"So what can we do?"

"*We* won't do anything," he said pointedly. "*I* will talk to the sheriff about it, but the fact is we can't arrest anyone without evidence, and all we have is a theory. We don't even have a suspect."

Her jaw set in firm lines. "Then you're passing up a marvelous chance."

He looked suspicious. "To do what?"

"Set a trap, of course."

"I don't like this. I don't know what you're thinking, but I don't like it."

"It's common sense. He failed in his—er, objective with me. Perhaps I could—"

"No. And before you get on your high horse, just think of what Wolf would say if you told him you were setting yourself up as bait. You might—*might*—be allowed out of his house by Christmas."

That was true enough, but she saw a way around it. "Then I just won't tell him."

"There's no way to keep it from him, unless it didn't work. If it did work—I sure as hell wouldn't want to be around when he found out, and something like that couldn't be kept quiet."

Mary considered all of Wolf's possible reactions and didn't like any of them. On the other hand, she was terrified that something might happen to him. "I'll take the chance," she said, making her decision.

"Not with my help, you won't."

Her chin lifted. "Then I'll do it without your help."

"If you get in the way of our investigations, I'll put you in the pokey so fast your head will spin," he threatened. When she didn't appear impressed, he swore under his breath. "Hell, I'll just tell Wolf and let him ride herd on you."

She frowned and considered shaking her schoolteacher's finger in his face. "You listen to me, Clay Armstrong. I'm the best chance you have of luring this guy out into the open. You don't have any suspects now. What are you going to do, wait until he attacks some other woman and maybe kills her? Is that how you want to work it?"

"No, that isn't how I want to work it! I want you and every other woman to stay alert and not go anywhere alone. I don't want to risk you or anyone else. Have you thought that sometimes traps don't work, that the animal gets the bait and still gets away? Do you really want to face the possibility of that?"

The thought made her sick to her stomach, and she swallowed to control the sudden rise of nausea. "No, but I'd do it anyway," she said steadily.

"For the last time, no. I understand that you want to help, but I don't like the idea. This guy is too unstable. He grabbed Cathy in her own driveway, and took you off of the town's main street. The chances he took are crazy, and *he* probably is, too."

With a sigh, Mary decided that Clay was simply too protective for him to be able to agree to use a woman as bait; it was totally against his basic nature. That didn't mean, however, that she needed his agreement. All she needed was someone who could act as a guard. She hadn't thought of any real plan yet, but obviously there had to be two people to make even the simplest trap work: the bait, and the one who kept the bait from being harmed.

Clay got in the car and closed the door, then leaned out the open window. "I don't want to hear any more about it," he warned.

"You won't," she promised. Not talking to him about it wasn't the same as not doing it.

He gave her a suspicious look, but started the car and drove away. Mary returned to her classroom, her thoughts darting around as she tried to think of a solid plan for luring a rapist with a minimum of danger to herself.

Wolf arrived at the school ten minutes before classes were over. He propped his shoulder against the wall just outside her classroom door and listened to her clear voice instructing her students on how geography and history had combined to produce the current state of Middle East politics. He was certain that wasn't in any of the textbooks, but Mary had a knack for giving her students a way of relating the present to their studies. It made the subjects both more interesting and more understandable. He had heard her doing the same thing with Joe, not that Joe needed encouragement to read. Her students responded easily to her; in such a small class, there was very little formality. They called her "Miss Potter," but weren't shy about asking questions, offering answers, even teasing.

Then she looked at her watch and released them, just as the doors to the other two classrooms opened. Wolf straightened from the wall and walked into her room, aware of how the kids' chatter halted abruptly when they became aware of his presence. Mary looked up and smiled, a private smile meant only for him, and it made his pulse accelerate that she was so open about how she felt.

He removed his hat and shoved his fingers through his hair. "Your escort service has arrived, ma'am," he said.

One of the girls giggled nervously, and Wolf slowly turned his head to look at the motionless teenagers. "Are you girls going home in pairs? Any of you boys making sure they get home all right?"

Christa Teele, Cathy's younger sister, murmured that she and Pam Hearst were walking together. The other four girls said nothing. Wolf looked at the seven boys. "Go with them." It was an order, one that the boys obeyed instantly. The kids left the room, automatically separating so that each girl had at least one male escort.

Mary nodded. "Very nicely done."

"You'll notice that they all had enough sense not to argue that they didn't need an escort."

She frowned at him, because she felt it hadn't been necessary for him to make that point. "Wolf, really, I'm perfectly safe on the drive from my house to here. How could anything happen to me if I don't stop?"

"What if you had a flat? What if a radiator hose blew again?"

It was obvious there was no way she could set her trap if Wolf or Joe was hovering over her every second. It was also obvious from the narrow look Wolf was giving her that he had no intention of changing his mind. Not that it mattered at the moment, as she hadn't come up with a plan yet. But when she did, she would also have to come up with some scheme for slipping away from her watchdogs.

Wolf draped her sweater over her shoulders and picked up her purse and keys, then ushered her out the door. Dottie looked up from where she was locking her own classroom door and stood transfixed while Wolf locked Mary's door, rattled the knob to make certain the lock held, then put his arm around her waist. He saw Dottie and touched the brim of his hat. "Mrs. Lancaster."

Dottie ducked her head and pretended to be having trouble with her key. Her face was flushed. It was the first time Wolf Mackenzie had ever spoken to her, and her hands shook as she dropped the key into her purse. Almost uncontrollable fear made her break out in a sweat. She didn't know what she was going to do.

Wolf's arm was solid around Mary's waist as they walked to her car. Its weight made her heartbeat quicken. All he had to do was put his hands on her and her body began to ready itself for him. An exquisite shudder began deep inside, spreading outward in a warm tide.

He felt the sudden tension in her slender body as he opened the car door. She was breathing faster, too. He looked down at her, and his entire body tightened, because she was watching him with desire plain in her soft, slate-blue eyes. Her cheeks were flushed, her lips parted.

He stepped back. "I'll be right behind you." The words were guttural.

She drove sedately home, though her blood was thundering through her veins and pounding in her ears. Never had the isolated, bedraggled old house looked better. Woodrow was sunning on the steps, and Mary stepped over her to unlock the back door. Wolf was out of his truck and right behind her, just as he had promised, by the time she had the door open.

Without a word she took off her sweater, deposited her purse on a chair and walked up the stairs, acutely aware of the heavy tread of Wolf's boots as he followed. They stepped into her bedroom.

He had her naked before she could gather her wits, though she wouldn't have wanted to protest even if he'd given her time. He bore her down on the bed, his big body overwhelming her, his brawny arms cradling her. The hair on his chest rasped her sensitive nipples into hardened peaks, and with a low moan of excitement she rubbed her breasts against him to increase the sensation. He opened her thighs and settled himself between them. His voice was low and rough as he murmured in her ear an explicit explanation of what he was going to do.

Mary drew back a little, her blue eyes slightly shocked, feeling slightly excited, and also slightly embarrassed *because* she was excited. How was it possible to feel both scandalized and excited? "Wolf Mackenzie!" she said, her eyes going even larger. "You said...that word!"

His hard face looked both tender and amused. "So I did."

She swallowed. "I've never heard anyone say it before. I mean, not in real life. In movies—but of course that isn't real life, and in movies it almost never means what it really means. They use it as an adjective instead of a verb." She looked perplexed at such an inexplicable grammatical oversight.

He was smiling as he entered her, his black eyes shining. "This," he said, "is the verb."

He loved the way she looked when he made love to her, her eyes languorous, her cheeks flushed. She sucked in her breath and moved beneath him, taking him completely into her and enveloping him in her sweet heat. Her hands moved up to the back of his neck. "Yes," she agreed seriously. "This is the verb."

If their first lovemaking had been fierce, since then he had been teaching her how sweet it was when the pleasure was protracted, when the caresses and kisses lingered while tension slowly coiled within until it was so hot and powerful that it exploded out of control. His hunger for her was so strong that he tried to put off his climax for as long as possible, so he could stay inside her and feed that hunger. It wasn't a hunger for sex, per se, though it had a strong sexual base. He didn't simply want to make love, he wanted—*needed*—to make love to her specifically, to Mary Elizabeth Potter. He had to feel her silky, fragile skin under his hands, feel her soft body sheathing him, smell her unique scent of womanhood, forge ancient bonds with each slow thrust and acceptance of their bodies. He was a half-breed; his spirit was strong and uncomplicated, his instincts close to those of his ancestors of both races. With other women, he had had sex; with Mary, he mated.

He wrapped his arms around her and rolled onto his back. Startled, Mary sat up, accidently assuming the exact position he'd wanted her in. She gasped as the motion forced him deep inside her. "What are you doing?"

"Nothing," he murmured, reaching up to place his hands over her breasts. "I'm letting you do the doing."

He watched her face as she considered the situation and was aware of the exact second that her excitement and arousal overcame her discomfort with the unfamiliar position. Her eyelids dropped again, and she bit her lower lip as she moved gently on him. "Like this?"

He almost groaned aloud. That slow movement was exquisite torture, and she quickly got into the rhythm of it. He had thought to prolong their lovemaking by changing positions, but now he was afraid he'd outsmarted himself. As old-fashioned as she was, she was also astonishingly sensuous. After a few minutes he desperately rolled again and put her under him.

Mary linked her arms behind his neck. "I was having fun."

"So was I." He kissed her briefly, then again, their lips lingering together. "Too much."

She smiled, that secret, womanly little smile she used only with him, and the sight of it made him burn. He forgot about control, forgot about everything but the pleasure that awaited them. Afterward, sated and exhausted, they both dozed.

At the sound of a vehicle, Wolf rolled out of bed, instantly alert. Mary stirred sleepily. "What is it?"

"You have company."

"Company?" She sat up and pushed her hair out of her face. "What time is it?"

"Almost six. We must have gone to sleep."

"Six! It's time for Joe's lesson!"

Wolf swore as he began jerking on his clothes. "This situation's getting out of hand. Damn it, every time I make love to you my own son interrupts us. Once was bad enough, but he's making a habit of it."

Mary was scrambling into her own clothes, wishing that the circumstances weren't so embarrassing. It was hard to face Joe when it was so obvious that she and his father had just been in bed together. Aunt Ardith would have disowned her for so forgetting her morals and sense of proper behavior. Then she looked at Wolf as he stamped his feet into his boots, and her heart felt as if it had expanded until it filled her entire chest. She loved him, and there was nothing more moral than love. As for proper behavior—she shrugged, mentally kissing propriety goodbye. One couldn't have everything.

Joe had deposited his books on the table and was making a pot of coffee when they entered the kitchen. He looked up and frowned. "Look, Dad, this situation is getting out of hand. You're cutting into my lesson time." Only the twinkle in his ice-blue eyes kept Wolf from getting angry; after a moment, he tousled his son's hair.

"Son, I've said it before, but you've got lousy timing."

Joe's lesson time was even more limited because they had to take time to eat. They were all starving, so they decided on sandwiches, which were quick, and had just finished when another car drove up.

"My goodness, this house is getting popular," Mary muttered as she got up to open the door.

Clay took his hat off as he entered. He paused and sniffed. "Is that coffee fresh?"

"Yep." Wolf stretched to reach the pot while Mary got a cup from the cabinet for Clay.

He sprawled in one of the chairs and gave a weary sigh, which turned to one of appreciation as he inhaled the fragrant steam rising from the coffee as Wolf poured it. "Thanks. I thought I'd find you two here."

"Has anything come up?" Wolf drawled.

"Nothing except a few complaints. You made some people a little nervous."

"Doing what?" Mary interjected.

"Just looking around," Wolf said in a casual tone that didn't fool her at all, nor did it fool Clay.

"Leave it alone. You're not a one-man vigilante committee. I'm warning you for the last time."

"I don't reckon I've done anything illegal, just walking around and looking. I haven't interfered with any law officers, I haven't questioned anyone, I haven't destroyed or hidden any evidence. All I've done is look." Wolf's eyes gleamed. "If you're smart, you'll use me. I'm the best tracker you're going to find."

"And if you're smart, you'll spend your time looking out after what's yours." Clay looked at Mary, and she primmed her mouth. Darn him, he was going to tell!

"That's what I'm doing."

"Maybe not as well as you think. Mary told me about a plan she's got to use herself as bait to bring this guy out in the open."

Wolf's head snapped around, and his brows lowered over narrowed black eyes as he pinned her with a gaze so furious it was all she could do to keep her own gaze steady. "I'll be damned," he said softly, and it was an expression of determination rather than surprise.

"Yeah, that's what I said. I heard you and Joe are escorting her to and from the school, but what about the time in between? And school will be out in a couple of weeks. What about then?"

Mary drew her slender shoulders up. "I won't be talked around as if I'm invisible. This is my house, and let me remind all of you that I'm well over twenty-one. I'll go where I want, when I want." Let them make of that what they would! She hadn't lived with Aunt Ardith for nothing;

Aunt Ardith would have died, just on principle, before she would have let a man tell her what to do.

Wolf's eyes hadn't wavered from her. "You'll do what you're damn well told."

"If I were you," Clay suggested, "I'd take her up on the mountain and keep her there. Like I said, school will be out in a couple of weeks, and this old house is pretty isolated. No one has to know where she is. It'll be safer that way."

Enraged, Mary reached out and whisked the cup of coffee away from Clay, then dumped the contents in the sink. "You're not drinking *my* coffee, you tattletale!"

He looked astounded. "I'm just trying to protect you!"

"And I'm just trying to protect him!" she shouted.

"Protect who?" Wolf snapped.

"You!"

"Why do I need protecting?"

"Because whoever is doing this is trying to harm you! First by trying to frame you for the attacks, and second by attacking people who don't hate you as he does!"

Wolf froze. When Mary had first advanced the beginnings of her theory the night before, he and Clay hadn't believed it because it simply hadn't made sense that anyone trying to frame Wolf would try to make anyone believe he would attack Mary. But when Mary put it the way she just had, that the attacks were a sort of twisted punishment, it began to make horrible sense. A rapist was warped, so his logic would be warped.

Mary had been attacked because of him. Because he had been so attracted to her that he hadn't been able to control it, some madman had attacked her, terrified and humiliated her, tried to rape her. His lust had brought attention to her.

His expression was cold and blank as he looked at Clay, who shrugged. "I have to buy it," Clay said. "It's the only thing that even halfway makes sense. When she made friends with you and got Joe into the Academy, folks began to look at you differently. Someone couldn't stand it."

Mary twisted her hands. "Since it's my fault, the least I can do is—"

"No!" Wolf roared, surging to his feet and turning over his chair with a clatter. He lowered his voice with a visible effort. "Go upstairs and get your clothes. You're going with us."

Joe slapped his hand on the table. "About damn time." He got up and began clearing the table. "I'll do this while you pack."

Mary pursed her lips. She was torn between wanting the freedom to put her plan into action—when she thought of it—and the powerful temptation of living with Wolf. It wasn't proper. It was a terrible example to her students. The townspeople would be outraged. *He'd watch her like a hawk!* On the other hand, she loved him to distraction and wasn't the least ashamed of their relationship. Embarrassed, sometimes, because she wasn't accustomed to such intimacy and didn't know how to handle it, but never ashamed.

Also on the other hand, if she dug in her heels and remained here, Wolf would simply stay here with her, where they would be far more visible and far more likely to outrage the town's sensibilities. That was what decided her, because she didn't want even more animosity directed at Wolf because of her. That could be all that was needed to goad the rapist into attacking him directly, or going after Joe.

He put his hands on her shoulders and gave her a little push. "Go," he said gently, and she went.

When she was safely upstairs and out of hearing, Clay looked at Wolf with a troubled, angry expression. "For what it's worth, she thinks you and Joe are in danger, that this maniac may just start shooting at you. I kind of agree with her, damn it."

"Let him try," Wolf said, his face and voice expressionless. "She's most vulnerable on the way to and from school, and I don't think this guy is going to wait patiently. He hit two days in a row, but he got scared when you nearly got him. It'll take a while for him to settle down, then he'll be looking for another hit to make. In the meantime, I'll be looking for him."

Clay didn't want to ask, but the question was burning his tongue. "Did you find anything today?"

"I eliminated some people from my list."

"Scared some of them, too."

Wolf shrugged. "Folks had better get used to seeing me around. If they don't like it, tough."

"I also heard that you made the boys escort the girls home from school. The girls' parents were mighty relieved and grateful."

"They should have taken care of it themselves."

"It's a quiet little town. They aren't used to things like this."

"That's no excuse for being stupid." And it *had* been stupid to overlook their daughters' safety. If he'd been that careless in Nam, he would have been dead.

Clay grunted. "I still want to make my point. I agree with Mary that you and Joe are the primary targets. You may be good, but nobody's better than a bullet, and the same goes for Joe. You don't just have to look after Mary, you have to look after yourselves, too. I'd like it if you could keep her from even finishing out the year at school, so the three of you could stay up on your mountain until we catch this guy."

It went against Wolf's grain to hide from anyone, and that was in the look he gave Clay. Wolf had been trained to hunt; more than that, it was in his nature, in the genes passed down from Comanche and Highland warriors that had mingled in his body, in the formation of his character.

"We'll keep Mary safe," was all he said, and Clay knew he'd failed to convince Wolf to stay out of it.

Joe was leaning against the cabinets, listening. "The people in town are going to raise hell if they find out Mary's staying with us," he put in.

"Yeah, they will." Clay stood up and positioned his hat on his head.

"Let them." Wolf's voice was flat. He'd given Mary the chance to play it safe, but she hadn't taken it. She was his now, by God. Let them squawk.

Clay sauntered to the door. "If anyone asks me, I've arranged for her to live in a safer place until this is over. Don't reckon it's anyone's business where that place is, do you? Though of course, knowing Mary, she'll probably tell everyone right out, just like she did Saturday in Hearst's store."

Wolf groaned. "Hell! What did she do? I haven't heard about it."

"Didn't reckon you would have, what with all that happened that afternoon. Seems she got into it with both Dottie Lancaster and Mrs. Karr, and all but told both of them she was yours for the taking." A slow grin shaped Clay's mouth. "From what I heard, she laced into them good."

When Clay had left, Wolf and Joe looked at each other. "It could get interesting around here."

"It could," Joe agreed.

"Keep an eye out, son. If Mary and Armstrong are right, we're the ones this bastard is really after. Don't go anywhere without your rifle, and stay alert."

Joe nodded. Wolf wasn't worried about hand-to-hand fighting, not even if the other guy was armed with a knife, because he'd taught Joe how to fight the way he'd learned in the military. Not karate, kung fu, tae kwon do, or even judo, but a mixture of many, including good old street fighting. The object of a fight wasn't fairness, but winning, in any way possible, with any weapon handy. It was what had kept him alive and relatively unscathed in prison. A rifle was something else, though. They would have to be doubly alert.

Mary returned and plunked two suitcases on the floor. "I have to have my books, too," she announced. "And someone has to get Woodrow and her kittens."

Mary tried to tell herself that she couldn't sleep because she was in a strange bed, because she was too excited, because she was too worried, because—she ran out of excuses and couldn't think of anything else. Though she was pleasantly tired from Wolf's lovemaking, she felt too uneasy to sleep and finally knew why. She turned in his arms and put her hand on his jaw, loving the feel of his facial structure and the slight rasp of his beard beneath her fingers. "Are you awake?" she whispered.

"I wasn't," he said in a low rumble. "But I am now."

She apologized and lay very still. After a moment he squeezed her and pushed her hair away from her face. "Can't you sleep?"

"No. I just feel—strange, I think."

"In what way?"

"Your wife—Joe's mother. I was thinking of her in this bed."

His arms tightened. "She was never in this bed."

"I know. But Joe's in the other room, and I thought this was how it must have been when he was little, before she died."

"Not usually. We were apart a lot, and she died when Joe was two. That was when I got out of the military."

"Tell me about it," she invited, still in a whisper. She needed to know more about this man she loved. "You must have been very young."

"I was seventeen when I enlisted. Even though I knew I'd probably have to do a tour in Vietnam, it was my only way out. My folks were dead, and my grandfather, Mother's father, never really accepted me because I was half Anglo. All I knew was that I had to get off the reservation. It was almost as bad as prison. It *is* prison, in a different way. There was nothing to do, nothing to hope for.

"I met Billie when I was eighteen. She was a Crow half-breed, and I guess she married me because she knew I'd never go back to the reservation. She wanted more. She wanted bright lights and city life. Maybe she thought a soldier had it good, transferring from base to base, partying when he was off duty. But she didn't look down on me because I was a half-breed, and we decided to get married. A month later I was in Nam. I got her a ticket to Hawaii when I had R and R, and she went back pregnant. Joe was born when I was nineteen, but I was home from my first tour and got to see him being born. God, I was so excited. He was screaming his head off. Then they put him in my hands, and it was like taking a heart punch. I loved him so much I would have died for him.''

He was silent for a moment, thinking. Then he gave a low laugh. "So there I was, with a newborn son and a wife who didn't think she'd gotten such a good deal, and my enlistment was almost up. I had no prospects of a job, no way of supporting my baby. So I re-upped, and things got so bad between Billie and me that I volunteered for another tour. She died right before my third tour ended. I got out and came home to take care of Joe.''

"What did you do?"

"Worked ranches. Rodeoed. It was all I knew. Except for the time I spent in service, I can't remember not working with horses. I was horse crazy when I was a kid, and I guess I still am. Joe and I drifted around until it was time for him to start school, and we landed in Ruth. You know the rest of it.''

She lay quietly in his arms, thinking of his life. He hadn't had it easy. But the life he'd led had shaped him into the man he was, a man of strength and iron determination. He had endured war and hell and come out even stronger than before. The thought that someone would want to harm him made her so angry she could barely contain it. Somehow she had to find some way to protect him.

He escorted her to school the next morning, and again Mary was aware of how everyone stared at him. But it wasn't fear or hatred she saw in the kids' eyes; rather, they watched him with intense curiosity, and even awe. After years of tales, he was a larger-than-life figure to them, someone glimpsed only briefly. Their fathers had dealt with him, the boys had watched him at work, and his expertise with horses only added to tales about him. It was said that he could "whisper" a horse, that even the wildest one would respond to a special crooning tone in his voice.

Now he was hunting the rapist. The story was all over the county.

Dottie wouldn't even talk to Mary that day; she walked away whenever she approached and even ate lunch by herself. Sharon sighed and shrugged. "Don't pay any attention to her. She's always had a burr under her blanket about the Mackenzies.''

Mary shrugged, too. There didn't seem to be any way she could reach Dottie.

Joe drove into town that afternoon to follow her home. As they walked out to their respective vehicles, she told him, "I need to stop at Hearst's for a few things.''

"I'll be right behind you.''

He was on her heels when she entered the store, and everyone turned to look at them. Joe gave them a smile that could have come straight from his father, and several people hastily looked away. Sighing, Mary led her six-foot watchdog down the aisle.

Joe paused fractionally when his gaze met that of Pam Hearst. She was standing as if rooted, staring at him. He tipped his hat and followed Mary.

A moment later he felt a light touch on his arm and turned to see Pam standing behind him. "Could I talk to you?" she asked in a low voice. "I—it's important. Please?"

Mary had moved on. Joe shifted his position so he could keep her in sight and said, "Well?"

Pam drew a deep breath. "I thought…maybe…would you go with me to the town dance this Saturday night?" she finished in a rush.

Joe's head jerked. "What?"

"I said—will you go with me to the dance?"

He thumbed his hat back and gave a low whistle under his breath. "You know you're asking for trouble, don't you? Your dad just might lock you in the cellar for a year."

"We don't have a cellar." She gave him a small smile, one that had an immediate reaction on his sixteen-year-old hormones. "And I don't care, anyway. He's wrong, wrong about you and your dad. I've felt horrible about how I acted before. I—I like you, Joe, and I want to go out with you."

He was cynical enough to say, "Yeah. A lot of people started liking me when they found out I had a shot at the Academy. Sure funny how that worked out, isn't it?"

Hot spots of color appeared on her cheeks. "That's not why I'm asking you out!"

"Are you sure? It seems I wasn't good enough to be seen in public with you before. You didn't want people to say Pam Hearst was going out with a 'breed. It's different when they can say you're going out with a candidate for the Air Force Academy."

"That's not true!" Pam was truly angry now, and her voice rose. Several people glanced their way.

"It looks that way to me."

"Well, you're wrong! You're just as wrong as my dad is!"

As if he'd been cued, Mr. Hearst, alerted by Pam's raised voice, started down the aisle toward them. "What's going on back here? Pam, is this br—boy bothering you?"

Joe noticed how quickly "breed" had been changed to "boy" and lifted his eyebrows at Pam. She flushed even redder and whirled to face her father.

"No, he isn't bothering me! Wait. Yes. Yes, he is! He's bothering me because I asked him to go out with me and he refused!"

Everyone in the store heard her. Joe sighed. The fat was in the fire now.

Ralph Hearst turned purplish red, and he halted in his tracks as abruptly as if he'd hit a wall. "What did you say?" he gasped, evidently not believing his ears.

Pam didn't back down, even though her father looked apoplectic. "I said he refused to go out with me! I asked him to the Saturday night dance."

Mr. Hearst's eyes were bulging out of their sockets. "You get on to the house. We'll talk about this later!"

"I don't want to talk about it later, I want to talk about it right now!"

"I said get on to the house!" Hearst roared. He turned his infuriated gaze on Joe. "And you stay away from my daughter, you—"

"He's *been* staying away from me!" Pam yelled. "It's the other way around! I won't stay away from him! This isn't the first time I've asked him out. You and everyone else in this town are wrong for the way you've treated the Mackenzies, and I'm tired of it. Miss Potter is the only one of us who's had the guts to stand up for what she thinks is right!"

"This is all her fault, that do-gooding—"

"Stop right there." Joe spoke for the first time, but there was something in his cool voice, in his pale blue eyes, that stopped the man. Joe was only sixteen, but he was tall and muscular, and there was a sudden alertness to his stance that made the older man pause.

Pam jumped in. She was bright and cheery-natured, but as headstrong as her father. "Don't start on Miss Potter," she warned. "She's the best teacher we've ever had here in Ruth, and if you do anything to get rid of her, I swear I'll drop out of school."

"You'll do no such thing!"

"I swear I will! I love you, Dad, but you're wrong! All of us talked about it at school today, about how we'd seen the teachers treat Joe over the years, and how wrong it was, because he's obviously the smartest of us all! And we talked about how Wolf Mackenzie was the one who made sure all of us girls got home all right yesterday. No one else thought of it! Or don't you care?"

"Of course he cares," Mary said briskly, having walked up without anyone except Joe noticing. "It's just that Wolf, with his military experience, knew what to do." She'd made that up, but it sounded good. She put her hand on Mr. Hearst's arm. "Why don't you take care of your customers and just let them fight it out? You know how teenagers are."

Somehow Ralph Hearst found himself at the front of the store again before he realized it. He stopped and looked down at Mary. "I don't want my girl dating a half-breed!" he said fiercely.

"She'll be safer with that half-breed than with any other boy around," Mary replied. "For one thing, he's steady as a rock. He won't drink or drive fast, and for another, he has no intention of getting involved with any girl around here. He'll be going away, and he knows it."

"I don't want my daughter dating an Indian!"

"Are you saying that character doesn't mean anything? That you'd rather have Pam go out with a drunk Anglo, who might get her killed in a car accident, than with a sober Indian, who would protect her with his life?"

He looked stricken and rubbed his head in agitation. "No, damn it, that isn't what I mean," he muttered.

Mary sighed. "My Aunt Ardith remembered every old chestnut she ever heard, and one of the ones she brought out most often was 'pretty is as pretty does.' You go by how people act, don't you, Mr. Hearst. You've voted according to how the candidates have stood on issues in the past, haven't you?"

"Of course." He looked uncomfortable.

"And?" she prompted.

"All right, all right! It's just—some things are hard to forget, you know? Not things that Joe has done, but just...things. And that father of his is—"

"As proud as you are," she cut in. "All he ever wanted was a place to raise his motherless son." She was laying it on so thick she expected to hear violins in the background any moment now, but it was about time these people realized some things about Wolf. Maybe he was more controlled than civilized, but his control was very good, and they would never know the difference.

Deciding it was time to give him some breathing room, she said, "Why not talk it over with your wife?"

He looked relieved at the suggestion. "I'll do that."

Joe was walking up the aisle; Pam, who had turned her back, was busily neatening a stack of paint thinner in an obvious effort to act casual. Mary paid for the items she'd gathered, and Joe lifted the sack. Silently they walked out together.

"Well?" she asked as soon as they were outside.

"Well, what?"

"Are you taking her to the dance?"

"It looks like it. She won't take no for an answer, like someone else I know."

She gave him a prim look and didn't respond to his teasing. Then, as he opened the car door for her, a thought struck, and she looked at him in horror. "Oh, no," she said softly. "Joe, that man is attacking women who are friendly to you and Wolf."

His whole body jerked, and his mouth tightened. "Damn," he swore. He thought a minute, then shook his head. "I'll tell her tomorrow that I can't go."

"That won't do any good. How many people heard her say what she did? It will be all over the county by tomorrow, whether you take her to the dance or not."

He didn't reply, merely closed the door after she'd gotten into the car. He looked grim, far too grim for a boy his age.

Joe felt grim, too, but an idea was taking form. He'd watch out for Pam and warn her so she'd be on guard, but maybe this would draw the rapist out. He'd use Mary's plan, but with different bait: himself. He'd make certain Pam was safe, but leave himself open at times when he was alone. Maybe, when the guy realized he couldn't get at a helpless woman, he'd get so frustrated he'd go after one of his real targets. Joe knew the chance he was taking, but unless Wolf could find the track he was looking for, he didn't see any other option.

Mary looked around for Wolf when they got home, but she couldn't find him. She changed into jeans and walked outside. She found Joe in the barn, grooming a horse. "Is Wolf out here?"

He shook his head and continued brushing the horse's gleaming hide. "His horse is gone. He's probably checking fences." Or hunting for a certain track, but he didn't say that to Mary.

She got him to show her how to brush the horse and took over for him until her arm began to hurt. The horse snorted when she stopped, so she went back to brushing. "This is harder than it looks," she panted.

Joe grinned at her over the back of another horse. "It'll give you a few muscles. But you've finished with him, so don't spoil him. He'll stand there all day if someone will keep brushing him."

She stopped and stepped back. "Well, why didn't you say so?" He put the horse in his stall, and Mary walked back to the house. She had almost reached the porch when she heard the rhythmic thudding of a horse's hooves and turned to see Wolf riding up. She caught her breath. Even though she was ignorant about horses, she knew that not many people looked the way he did on a horse. There was no bouncing or jiggling; he sat so easily in the saddle, and moved so fluidly with the animal, that he looked motionless. The Comanche had arguably been the world's best horsemen, better even than the Berber or Bedouin, and Wolf had learned well from his mother's people. His powerful legs controlled the big bay stallion he was riding, so that the reins were lightly held and no harm done to the horse's tender mouth.

He slowed the horse to a walk as he approached her. "Any trouble today?"

She decided not to tell him about Pam Hearst. That was Joe's business, if he wanted it known. She knew he'd tell Wolf, but in his own time. "No. We didn't see anyone suspicious, and no one followed us."

He reined in and leaned down to brace his forearm on the saddle horn. His dark eyes drifted over her slim figure. "Do you know how to ride?"

"No. I've never been on a horse."

"Well, that situation is about to be remedied." He kicked his boot free of the stirrup and held his hand out to her. "Put your left foot in the stirrup and lift yourself as I swing you up."

She was willing. She tried. But the horse was too tall, and she couldn't reach the stirrup with her foot. She was staring at the bay with an aggravated expression when Wolf laughed and shifted back in the saddle. "Here, I'll pick you up."

He leaned out of the saddle and caught her under the arms. Mary gasped and grabbed at his biceps as she felt her feet leave the ground; then he straightened and set her firmly on the saddle in front of him. She grabbed the saddle horn as he lifted the reins, and the horse moved forward.

"This is a long way up," she said, bouncing so hard her teeth rattled.

He chuckled and wrapped his left arm around her, pulling her back against him. "Relax and let yourself go with the horse's rhythm. Feel how I'm moving and move with me."

She did as he said and felt the rhythm as soon as she relaxed. Her body automatically seemed to sink deeper into the saddle, and her torso moved with Wolf's. The bouncing stopped. Unfortunately by that time they had reached the barn and her first ride was over. Wolf lifted her down and dismounted.

"I liked that," she announced.

"You did? Good. We'll start you on riding lessons tomorrow."

Joe's voice came to them from a stall farther down. "I started her on grooming lessons today."

"You'll be as comfortable with horses as if you'd been around them all of your life," Wolf said, and leaned down to kiss her. She went on tiptoe, her lips parting. It was a long moment before he lifted his head, and when he did, his breathing was faster. His eyes were hooded and narrow. Damn, she got to him so fast he reacted like a teenager when he was around her.

When Mary had gone back to the house, Joe came out of the stall and looked at his father. "Find anything today?"

Wolf began unsaddling the bay. "No. I've had a good look around the ranches, but none of the prints match. It has to be someone from town."

Joe frowned. "That makes sense. Both of the attacks were in town. But I can't think of anyone it could be. I guess I've never noticed before if someone has freckled hands."

"I'm not looking for freckles, I'm looking for that print. I know how he walks, toeing in a little and putting his weight on the outside of his feet."

"What if you find him? Do you think the sheriff will arrest him just because he has freckles on his hands and walks a certain way?"

Wolf smiled, a movement of his lips that was totally without mirth. His eyes were cold. "When I find him," he said softly, "if he's smart, he'll confess. I'll give the law a chance, but there's no way he'll walk free. He'll be a lot safer in jail than out on the streets, and I'll make certain he knows it.''

It was an hour before they finished with the horses. Joe lingered to look over his tack, and Wolf walked up to the house alone. Mary was absorbed in cooking, humming as she stirred the big pot of beef stew, and she didn't hear him come in the back door. He walked up behind her and put his hand on her shoulder.

Blind terror shot through her. She screamed and threw herself sideways, to press her back against the wall. She held the dripping spoon in her hand like a knife. Her face was utterly white as she stared at him.

His face was hard. In silence they stared at each other, time stretching out between them. Then she dropped the spoon on the floor with a clatter. "Oh God, I'm sorry," she said in a thin voice, and covered her face with her hands.

He drew her to him, his hand in her hair, holding her head to his chest. "You thought it was him again, didn't you?"

She clung to him, trying to drive away the terror. It had come out of nowhere, taking her by surprise and shattering the control she'd managed to gain over her memory and emotions. When Wolf's hand had touched her shoulder, for a brief, horrifying moment it had been happening all over again. She felt cold; she wanted to sink into his warmth, to let the reality of his touch overcome the hideous memory of another touch.

"You don't have to be afraid," he murmured into her hair. "You're safe here." But he knew her memory was still there, that a touch from behind meant a nightmare to her. Somehow he had to take away that fear, so she could be free of it.

She regained control and eased herself away from him, and he let her, because he knew it was important to her. She appeared almost normal through dinner and Joe's lesson; the only sign of strain was an occasional haunted expression in her eyes, as if she hadn't completely succeeded in pushing the memory away.

But when they went to bed and her silky body was under his hands, she turned to him as eagerly as ever. Wolf's lovemaking left her no room for anything else, no lingering memories or vestiges of terror. Her entire body and mind were occupied with him. Afterward she curled against him and slept undisturbed, at least until the graying dawn, when he woke her and pulled her beneath him again.

Mary was fully aware of the tenuousness of both her relationship with Wolf and her presence in his house. He often told her explicitly how much he wanted her, but in terms of lust, not love. He never spoke a word about loving, not even during lovemaking, when she was unable to keep from telling him over and over that she loved him. When the fever of lust passed, he might well cut her out of his life, and she tried to prepare herself for that possibility even while she absorbed the maximum pleasure from the present situation.

She knew that living with him was for her protection, and only temporary. She also knew that it was nothing short of scandalous for a small-town schoolteacher to shack up with the local black sheep, and that was exactly how the townspeople would view the situation if they knew about it. She knew the risk she was taking with her career, and decided that the days and nights with Wolf were worth it. If she lost her job, there were other jobs, but she knew there would be no other loves for her. She was twenty-nine and had never even felt a twinge of interest or excitement over any other man. Some people loved only once, and it appeared she was one of them.

The only time she allowed herself to worry over the future was on the drives to and from school, when she was alone in the car. When she was with Wolf she didn't want to waste even a single second on regrets. With him, she was totally alive, totally female.

She worried about Wolf and Joe, too. She knew Wolf was actively hunting the man who had attacked her, and she was terrified he would be hurt. She couldn't let herself even think that he might be killed. And Joe was up to something; she knew it. He was too much like Wolf for her not to recognize the signs. He was preoccupied, and far too sober, as if faced with making a choice when neither of the alternatives was very attractive. But she couldn't get him to open up to her, and that alone frightened her, for Joe had talked to her from the beginning.

Joe was on edge. He'd told Pam to be more cautious than usual, and he tried to make certain she never walked home alone, but there was always a chance she'd be careless. He'd also made a point of letting himself be seen alone, and evidently unaware of the need for caution, but nothing happened. The town was quiet, if edgy. He was forced to the same awareness that Wolf already had, that with so few clues, all they could do was stay alert and wait until the man made a mistake.

When Joe told his father that he was going to the dance with Pam, Wolf looked piercingly at the boy. "Do you know what you're doing?"

"I hope so."

"Watch your back."

The terse advice brought a thin smile to Joe's mouth. He knew he could be making a big mistake by going to that dance, that the scene could turn ugly, but he'd told Pam he'd take her, and that was that. He'd have to be doubly alert, but damn, he wanted to hold her in his arms while they shuffled slowly across the sawdust floor. Even though he knew he was going away and they'd never have anything permanent between them, he was strongly attracted to her. He couldn't explain it and knew it wouldn't last, but he felt it *now*, and it was now that he had to deal with it.

Pam was edgy, too, when he picked her up. She tried to hide it by talking too fast and too brightly, until he put his hand over her mouth. "I know," he muttered. "It worries me, too."

She tossed her head, freeing her mouth. "I'm not worried. It'll be all right, you'll see. I told you, all of us have talked about it."

"Then why are you so nervous?"

She looked away from him and cleared her throat. "Well, this *is* the first time I've been out with you. I just felt—I don't know—nervous and scared and excited all at once."

He thought about that for a few minutes, and silence filled the cab of the truck. Then he said, "I guess I can understand being nervous and excited, but why scared?"

Now it was Pam's turn to be silent, and she flushed a little when she finally said, "Because you're not like the rest of us."

That grim look settled around Joe's mouth. "Yeah, I know. I'm a 'breed."

"It isn't that," she snapped. "It's—you're *older* than the rest of us, somehow. I know we're the same age, but inside you're all grown up. We're ordinary people. We'll stay right here and ranch the way our folks have. We'll marry people from the same background and stay in the county, or move to another county just like it, and have kids and be content. But you're not like that. You're going to the Academy, and you won't be back, at least not to stay. You may come back for a visit, but that's all it'll be."

It surprised him that she had it so neatly pegged. He did feel old inside, and always had, especially in comparison to other kids his age. And he knew he wouldn't be back here to ranch. He belonged in the sky doing Mach 2, marking his place in the universe with a vapor trail.

They were quiet the rest of the way to the dance. When Joe parked his truck with the collection of other trucks and a few cars, he braced himself for whatever could happen.

He was prepared for almost anything, but not for what actually took place. When he and Pam walked into the rundown old building used for the dances, for a moment there was a certain stillness, a strange silence; then in the next heartbeat the noise picked back up and everyone returned to his own conversation. Pam put her hand in his and squeezed it.

A few minutes later the live band started up, and couples drifted onto the sawdust-covered planks of the dance floor. Pam led him to the middle of the floor and smiled at him.

He smiled back, wryly admitting and admiring her courage. Then he took her in his arms to enter the slow rhythm of the dance.

They didn't talk. After wanting for so long just to touch her, he was content to hold her and move with her. He could smell her perfume, feel the softness of her hair, the resilient mounds of her breasts, the movement of her legs against his. As young people have done from the beginning of time, they swayed together in their own private world, reality suspended.

Reality intruded, however, when he heard an angry mutter of "dirty Indian" and automatically stiffened as he looked around for the speaker.

Pam said, "Please," and drew him back into the dance.

When the song ended, a boy stood on his chair and yelled, "Hey, Joe! Pam! Over here!"

They looked in the direction of the yell, and Joe couldn't help grinning. Every student in the three classes Mary taught was grouped at the table, with two empty chairs waiting for him and Pam. They were waving and calling.

The kids saved the evening. They enveloped him and Pam in a circle of laughter and dancing. Joe danced with every girl in the group; the boys talked horses, cattle, ranching and rodeoing, and between them made certain none of the girls had a chance to sit down much. The kids also talked to the other people at the dance, and soon everyone knew that the half-breed was going to the Air Force Academy. Ranchers are generally hard-working, conservative and firmly patriotic, and before too long, anyone who had a hard word to say about the half-breed found himself hushed and told to mind his manners.

Joe and Pam left before the dance was over, because he didn't want to keep her out too late. As they walked to his truck, he shook his head. "I never would have believed it," he said softly. "Did you know they would all be here?"

Pam denied it. "But they knew I'd asked you. I guess the whole town knew I'd asked you. It was fun, wasn't it?"

"It was fun," he agreed. "But it could have gotten rough. You know that, don't you? If it hadn't been for the guys—"

"And girls!" she interrupted.

"Them, too. If it hadn't been for them, I'd have been thrown out."

"It didn't happen. And next time it will be even better."

"Is there going to be a next time?"

She looked suddenly unsure of herself. "You—you can still come to the dances, even if you don't want to come with me."

Joe laughed as he opened the truck door. He turned and put his hands on her waist, then lifted her onto the seat. "I like being with you."

About halfway back to Ruth, Pam put her hand on his arm. "Joe?"

"Yeah?"

"Do you want to—uh, that is, do you know any place to stop?" She faltered on the words.

He knew he should resist the temptation, but he couldn't. He turned off on the next side road they came to, then left the road to bounce across a meadow for about a mile before he parked beneath a stand of trees.

The mild May night wrapped around them. The moonlight couldn't penetrate the shelter of the trees, and the dark cab of the truck was a warm, safe cave. Pam was a pale, indistinct figure as he reached for her.

She was pliant and eager, yielding to his hands, pressing against him to take more of his kisses. Her firm young body made him feel as if he would explode. Barely aware of what he was doing, Joe shifted and twisted until they were lying on the seat with Pam half beneath him. Soon her breasts were bare, and he heard her strangled intake of breath as he took a nipple into his mouth. Then her nails were digging into his shoulders, and her hips arched.

It was quickly getting out of control. Clothing was opened and pushed aside. Bare skin touched bare skin. Somehow, Pam's jeans were off. But when he slid his hands inside her panties, she whispered, "I've never done this before. Will it hurt?"

Joe groaned aloud, but forced himself to stillness. It took every ounce of willpower he possessed, but he stopped his hands. His body throbbed painfully, and he savagely controlled it. After a long minute he sat up and pulled Pam to a sitting position astride his lap.

"Joe?"

He leaned his forehead against hers. "We can't do it," he murmured regretfully.

"But why?" She moved against him, her body still empty and aching with a need she didn't understand.

"*Because* it would be your first time."

"But I want you!"

"I want you, too." He managed a wry grin. "I guess it's pretty obvious. But your first time—baby, it should be with someone you love. And you don't love me."

"I could," she whispered. "Oh, Joe, I truly could."

He was so frustrated that he could barely control his voice enough to speak, but he managed. "I hope you don't. I'm leaving. I have a chance waiting for me that I'd die before I'd give up."

"And no girl is going to change your mind?"

Joe knew the truth inside him, and he knew Pam wouldn't like it, but he had to be honest with her. "No girl *could* change my mind. I want to go to the Academy so much that nothing can keep me here."

She caught his hands and shyly brought them up to her breasts. "We could still, you know, do it. No one would know."

"You'd know. And when you fall in love with some guy, you'd regret that your first time wasn't with him. God, Pam, don't make this so hard for me! Slap my face or something." The way her firm young breasts filled his hands made him wonder if he wasn't crazy for passing this up.

She leaned forward and rested her head on his shoulder. He felt the way her body shook as she began to cry, and he folded his arms around her.

"You've always been special to me," she said in a stifled tone. "Do you have to be so darn conscientious?"

"Do you want to take a chance on getting pregnant at sixteen?"

That stopped her tears. She sat up. "Oh. I thought you'd have a—don't all boys carry them?"

"I guess not. And it wouldn't matter if I did have one. I don't want to get involved—not this kind of involved—with you or anyone else, because no matter what, I'm going to the Academy. Besides, you're too young."

She couldn't stop the giggle that burst out. "I'm as old as you are."

"Then *we're* too young."

"You're not." She sobered and cupped his face in her hands. "You're not young at all, and I guess that's why you stopped. Every other boy I know would have had his jeans off so fast he'd have fabric burns on his legs. But let's make a bargain, okay?"

"What kind of bargain?"

"We'll still be friends, won't we?"

"You know it."

"Then we'll go around together and keep things light. No more messing around like this, because it hurts too much when you stop. You go away to Colorado like you've planned, and I'll take things as they come. I may get married. But if I don't, you come on back here one summer and we'll *both* be old enough then. Will you be my first lover?"

"It won't keep me in Ruth," he said steadily.

"I don't expect it to. But is it a bargain?"

He accepted that the years could make a difference, and he knew she'd most likely be married. If not—maybe.

"If you still want to then, yeah, it's a bargain."

She held out her hand, and they solemnly shook to seal the deal. Then she kissed him and began putting on her clothes.

Mary was waiting up for him when he got home, an anxious look in her eyes. She got to her feet and tightened the belt of her robe. "Are you okay?" she asked. "Did anything happen?"

"I'm fine. Everything went okay."

Then he saw that the anxious look was really fear. She touched his arm. "You didn't see anyone who—" She stopped, then started again. "No one shot at your truck, or tried to run you off the road?"

"No, it was quiet." They looked at each other for a moment, and Joe realized that Mary had feared the same thing that had occurred to him. More than that, she knew he had decided to take the chance in an effort to draw the rapist out.

He cleared his throat. "Is Dad in bed?"

"No," Wolf said quietly from the doorway. He wore only a pair of jeans. His black eyes were steady. "I wanted to make certain you were okay. This was like watching Daniel walk into the lion's den."

"Well, Daniel made it out okay, didn't he? So did I. It was even fun. The whole class was there."

Mary smiled, the dread lifting from her mind. She knew now what had happened. Knowing that the situation could get ugly if Joe had gone to the dance without backup, the kids had taken it on themselves to make him a part of their group and let everyone at the dance know he was accepted.

Wolf held out his hand, and Mary went to him. She could sleep now. They were safe for another night, these two men whom she loved.

School was out. Mary was intensely proud of her students. The seniors had all graduated, and all of the undergraduates had passed. All of them intended to finish high school, and a couple of them wanted to go to college. It was a record to thrill any teacher's heart.

Joe didn't get a respite. Mary decided he needed more advanced classes in math than she was qualified to teach and began a search for a teacher who was qualified. She found one in a town seventy miles distant, and three times a week Joe made the trip for a two-hour accelerated course. She continued to teach him at night.

The days passed in a haze of happiness for Mary. She seldom left the mountain, seldom saw anyone except Wolf and Joe. Even when they were both gone, she felt safe. It had been only a little over two weeks since the attack, but it seemed as if it had happened a long time ago. Whenever a sliver of memory surfaced to unsettle her emotions, she scolded herself for letting it bother her. Nothing had happened, except she had been terrified. If anyone needed care and consideration, it was Cathy Teele. So Mary pushed the memories away and concentrated on the present. The present, inevitably, was Wolf.

He dominated her life, waking and sleeping. He began teaching her how to ride and how to help him with the horses, and she suspected he used the same method with her that he used with the young colts and fillies that were brought to him. He was firm and demanding, but utterly clear in his instructions and what he wanted out of both her and the horses. When they obeyed, he rewarded them with approval and affection. In fact, Mary mused, he was easier on the horses than he was on her! When *they* disobeyed, he was unfailingly patient. When *she* didn't do something exactly as he'd told her, he let her know about it in unmistakable terms.

But he was always affectionate. Actually, she decided, "lusty" was a better description. He made love to her every night, sometimes twice. He made love to her in the empty stall where Joe had interrupted them. He made love to her in the shower. She knew she wasn't even close to voluptuous, but he seemed enthralled with her body. When they lay in bed at night he would turn on the lamp and lean on his elbow, watching as he stroked his hand over her from shoulders to knees, seemingly fascinated by the difference between her pale, delicate skin and his dark, powerful, work-callused hand.

Wyoming weather in the summer was generally cool and dry, at least compared to Savannah, but the summer vacation from school had scarcely begun when a heat wave sent the temperatures into the nineties, even edging into the low hundreds by late afternoon. For the first time in her life, Mary wished she had some shorts to wear, but Aunt Ardith had never allowed them. She did find, however, that her plain cotton skirts were cooler than the new jeans she was so proud of, allowing for the circulation of whatever breeze happened to wander by. Not that Aunt Ardith would have approved of Mary's attire even then, for Mary declined to wear a slip or hosiery. Aunt Ardith had donned both articles of clothing every day of her life and would have considered anyone who dared to go without a slip an out-and-out hussy.

One morning just after Joe had left to drive to his class, Mary walked out to the barn and reflected on her state of hussiness. All in all, she was satisfied with it. Being a hussy had its advantages.

She could hear some horses snorting and stamping around in the small corral behind the barn, though Wolf usually used the larger one adjacent to the stables for training. The sound of activity, however, told her where she could find him, and that was all she wanted to know.

But when she rounded the corner of the barn, she stopped in her tracks. Wolf's big bay stallion was mounting the mare she had been riding during her lessons. The mare's front hooves were hobbled, and protective boots covered her rear hooves. The stallion was snorting and grunting, and the mare squealed as he entered her. Wolf moved to her head to steady her, and then she stood quietly. "There, sweetheart," he crooned. "You can handle this big old guy, can't you?"

The mare shivered under the impact of the stallion's thrusts, but she stood still for the service and it was over in only a couple of minutes. The stallion snorted and dropped off her, his head down low as he snuffled and blew.

Wolf continued talking in that low, soothing voice to the mare as he bent down to remove the hobble. As he started to remove the boots, Mary stepped forward and caught his attention. "You—you *tied* her!" she said accusingly.

He grinned as he finished unbuckling the protective boots. Miss Mary Elizabeth Potter stood before him in full form, her back ramrod-straight, chin lifted. "I didn't tie her," he said with amused patience. "I hobbled her."

"So she couldn't get away from him!"

"She didn't want to get away from him."

"How do you know?"

"Because she would have kicked him if she hadn't been ready for him to cover her,'' he explained as he led the mare back into the barn. Mary followed, her face still filled with indignation.

"A lot of good it would have done if she'd kicked him—you put those boots on her so she wouldn't hurt him!''

"Well, I didn't want my stallion damaged. On the other hand, if she had resisted service, I would have gotten her out of there. When a mare resists, it means I've misjudged the time, or something is wrong with her. But she took him nicely, didn't you girl?'' he finished, patting the mare's neck.

Mary watched, fidgeting, as he washed the mare. She still didn't like the idea of the mare being unable to run away from the stallion, even though this particular mare was now standing as placidly as if nothing had happened a few minutes ago. It disturbed her on a deep emotional level that didn't respond to logic, and she felt uneasy.

Wolf led the mare to her stall, fed her and gave her fresh water. Then he squatted in front of the faucet to wash his hands and arms. When he looked up, Mary was still standing there, a troubled, almost frightened look in her eyes. He straightened. "What's wrong?''

Desperately she tried to shrug her uneasiness aside, but it didn't work. It was plain in her face and voice. "It looked—it looked....'' Her voice trailed off, but suddenly he understood.

He moved slowly toward her and wasn't surprised when she backed up a step. "Horses aren't people,'' he said gently. "They're big, and they snort and squeal. It looks rough, but that's just how horses mate. It would be even rougher if they were allowed to run free, because they'd kick and bite.''

She looked at the mare. "I know. It's just—'' She stopped, because she really couldn't say what was bothering her.

Wolf reached her and put his hands on her waist, holding her lightly so she wouldn't be alarmed and wouldn't know that she couldn't break free unless he let her. "It's just that the roughness reminded you of being attacked?'' he finished for her.

She gave him a quick, disturbed look, then just as quickly looked away.

"I know the memory is still there, baby.'' He slowly tightened his hands, bringing her close against him and just holding her. After a moment she began to relax, and her silky head rested against his chest. Only then did he put his arms around her, because he didn't want her to feel restrained.

"I want to kiss you,'' he murmured.

She lifted her head and smiled at him. "That's why I came out here: to tempt you into a kiss. I've become a shameless hussy. Aunt Ardith would have disowned me.''

"Aunt Ardith sounds like a pain in the—''

"She was wonderful,'' Mary said firmly. "It's just that she was very old-fashioned and had strict notions of what was proper and what wasn't. For instance, only shameless hussies would wear a skirt without a proper petticoat underneath.'' She lifted her skirt a little to show him.

"Then let's hear it for shameless hussies.'' He bent his head and kissed her, and felt the familiar hot excitement begin building in his body. Ruthlessly he controlled it, because control was critical right now. He had to show Mary something, and he couldn't do it if his libido overcame his common sense. He had to do something to banish that ever-present fear from the back of her mind.

He raised his head and hugged her for a minute before letting his arms drop. Instead he took her hands and held them, and the expression on his face made the smile leave her eyes. He said slowly, "Are you willing to try something that might get you over being frightened?''

She looked cautious. "Such as?''

"We could reenact parts of the attack.''

Mary stared at him. She was curious, but also wary. Part of her didn't want to do anything that would remind her of that day, but on the other hand, she didn't like being afraid. She said, "Which parts?''

"I could chase you.''

"He didn't chase me. He grabbed me from behind.''

"So will I, when I catch you.''

She considered it. "It won't work. I'll know it's you.''

"We could try.''

She stared at him for a long time, then stiffened as a thought came to her. "He threw me facedown on the ground,'' she whispered. "He was on top of me, rubbing himself against me.''

Wolf's face was strained. "Do you want me to do that, too?''

She shuddered. "Want you to? No. But I think you're going to have to. I don't want to be afraid any longer. Make love to me like that—please.''

"What if you get really scared?''

"Don't—'' She swallowed. "Don't stop.''

He looked at her for a long minute, as if measuring her resolve; then his mouth began to quirk up on one side. "All right. Run.''

She didn't. She stared at him. "What?''

"Run. I can't chase you if you don't run.''

All of a sudden she felt silly at the thought of running about the yard like a child. "Just like that?''

"Yeah, just like that. Think of it this way: when I catch you, I'm going to pull your clothes off and make love to you, so why are you waiting?''

He removed his hat to hook it on a post. Mary took a step backward, then, despite her dignity, whirled and ran. She heard the thudding of his boots as he came after her, and laughed with excitement despite herself. She knew she didn't have a prayer of reaching the house; his legs were much longer than hers. Instead she relied on agility and dodged around his truck, then a tree.

"I'm going to get you," he growled, his voice right behind her, and his hand closed briefly on her shoulder before she sprinted away from him.

She sought refuge behind his truck again, with him on the other side. They feinted, but neither gained an advantage. Panting, her face alight with both excitement and triumph, Mary taunted him, "Can't catch me, can't catch me."

A slow, unholy smile touched his mouth as he looked at her. She was almost glowing with her success, her silky brown hair tumbling around her face, and he wanted her so much it hurt. He wanted to take her in his arms and make love to her, and he swore to himself because he couldn't, not right now. First he had to play this through, and, despite her brave words, he hoped she could bear it.

They had been staring at each other, and suddenly it struck her how savage he looked. He was aroused. She knew that look on his face as well as she knew her own, and her breath caught. He wasn't playing; he was deadly earnest. For the first time, fear began to creep in on her. She tried to tamp it down, because she knew Wolf would never hurt her. It was just—oh, damn, something about it *did* remind her of the attack, no matter how she tried to push the thought away. The playfulness drained out of her, and an unreasonable panic took its place. "Wolf? Let's stop now."

His chest rose and fell with his breathing, and a bleak look entered his eyes, but his voice was guttural. "No. I'm going to catch you."

She ran blindly, leaving the dubious safety of the truck. His running steps behind her sounded like thunder, obscuring every other sound, even that of her rasping breath. It was like being in that alley again, even though a part of her clung to the knowledge that this was Wolf, and she wanted him to do this. She hadn't had a chance to run from her attacker, but he had been behind her; she had heard his breathing just as she now heard Wolf's. She screamed, a high, terrified sound, just before Wolf caught her and bore her down, on her stomach, to the ground, his heavy weight coming down on top of her.

He supported himself on his arms to keep from crushing her, and nuzzled her ear. "Ha, I caught you." He forced himself to say the words lightly, but his chest was tight with pain at what she was going through. He could feel the terror that held her in its grip, and he began trying to loosen its bonds, speaking softly to her, reminding her of the heated, sensuous pleasures they had shared. Tears stung his eyes at the sounds she made, those of a trapped and terrified animal. God, he didn't know if he could do it. The lust had died in him at her first scream.

At first she struggled like a wild thing, kicking and bucking, trying to free her arms, but he held them clamped down. She was maddened with fear, so much so that despite the difference in their sizes and strength, she might have hurt him if not for his training. As it was, all he could do was hold her and try to break through the black mist of fear that enveloped her.

"Calm down, sweetheart, calm down. You know I won't hurt you, and I won't let anyone else hurt you. You know who I am." He repeated it over and over, until exhaustion claimed her, and her struggles became weak and aimless. Only then could she begin to listen; only then could his crooning words penetrate the barrier of fear. Suddenly she collapsed on the ground with her face buried in the hot, sweet grass and began to cry.

Wolf lay on top of her with his arms still locked securely around her and soothed her while she cried. He petted her and kissed her hair, her shoulder, her delicate nape, until at last she lay limply on the grass, both tears and energy exhausted. The endless caresses affected him, too, now that she was calmer; he felt a return of the desire that was never far away from him since he'd met her.

He nuzzled her neck again. "Are you still frightened?" he murmured.

Bruised, swollen eyelids were closed over her eyes. "No," she whispered. "I'm sorry I keep putting you through this. I love you."

"I know, sweetheart. Hold on to that thought." Then he lifted himself back on his knees and pushed her skirt to her waist.

Mary's eyes flared open when she felt him pulling down her underpants, and her voice was sharp. "Wolf! No!"

He stripped the garment down her legs, and Mary trembled in reaction. It was so much like before, in the alley. She was on her stomach on the ground, with a man's weight on top of her, and she couldn't bear it. She tried to scramble forward, but he locked one arm around her waist and held her while he unfastened his jeans with the other hand. He kneed her thighs farther apart and eased himself against her, then let his weight down on her again.

"This reminds you of it, doesn't it?" he asked in a low, gentle voice. "Being on the ground, on your stomach, with me behind you. But you know I won't hurt you, that you don't have to be afraid, don't you?"

"I don't care. I don't like this! Let me up, I want up!"

"I know, baby. Come on now, relax. Think of how many times I've made love to you and how much you've enjoyed it. Trust me."

The smell of the hot earth was in her nostrils. "I don't want you to make love to me now," she managed to say, albeit raggedly. "Not like this."

"Then I won't. Don't be afraid, baby. I won't go any further unless you want me to. Just relax, and let's feel each other. I don't want you to be afraid when I come up behind you. I admit, your pretty little rear end turns me on. I like to look at it and touch it, and when you cuddle it against me in bed it drives me crazy. I guess you've noticed, though, haven't you?''

Dazedly, she tried to gather her scattered senses. He'd never hurt her before, and now that the haze of fear was fading, she knew he never would. This was Wolf, the man she loved, not her attacker. She was in his strong arms, where she was safe.

She relaxed, her tired muscles going limp. Yes, he was definitely aroused. She could feel him, nestled between her spread legs, but true to his word he was making no move to enter her.

He stroked her sides and kissed her neck. "Are you all right now?"

She sighed, a barely audible release of breath. "Yes," she whispered.

He shifted to his knees again and sat back on his heels. Before she could guess what he was about, his steely hands lifted her up and back, so she was sitting astride his thighs, but facing away from him. Their naked loins were pressed together, but still he didn't enter her.

The first twinge of excitement sang along her nerves. The moment was doubly erotic because they were out in the open, crouched on the grass with the hot, bright sun blazing down on them. If anyone happened to drive up, they would be caught. The sudden sense of danger sharply heightened her arousal. Actually, from the front they were covered, because her skirt was draped over his thighs.

Then that protective cover was whisked away as he pulled her skirt up and to the side. He held her to him with one hand on her stomach, and the other hand slid down between her legs. The intimate contact brought a sharp little cry to her lips.

"Do you like that?" he murmured against her ear and gently nipped the lobe.

Mary made some incoherent answer. His rough fingertips were rasping over her most sensitive flesh, creating and building such pleasure that she could barely speak. He knew exactly how to touch her, how to build her to readiness and take her to ecstasy. Mindlessly she arched back against him; the movement brought his manhood more solidly against her, and she groaned aloud.

"Wolf—please!"

He groaned, too, from between clenched teeth. "I'll please you any way you want, baby. Just tell me how."

She could barely speak for the powerful coil of sensation tightening inside her. "I want you."

"Now?"

"Yes."

"Like this?"

She moved against him and this time had to choke back a cry. "Yes!"

He eased her forward until she was on her stomach again and covered her. His entry was slow and gentle, and fever enveloped her. Eagerly she met the impact of his thrusts, her body on fire, all thoughts suspended before such all-consuming need. This wasn't a nightmare; this was another part of the sensual delights he'd been teaching her. She writhed against him and felt the coil tighten unbearably. Then it sprang free, and she convulsed in his arms. He clamped his hands on her hips and loosed his own responses, driving into her hard and fast until his pulsing release freed him.

They lay together on the grass for a long time, half-dozing, too exhausted to move. Only when Mary felt her legs begin to tingle from too much sun did she find the strength to push her skirt down. Wolf murmured a protest and slid his hand up her thigh.

She opened her eyes. The sky was bright blue, cloudless, and the sweet scent of fresh grass filled her lungs, radiated through her body. The earth was hot beneath her, the man she loved dozed beside her, and every inch of her still held the remnants of sensation from their lovemaking. The memory of it, so fresh and powerful, began to warm her body to desire again, and suddenly she realized that his plan had worked. He had recreated the scenario that had so terrified her, but substituted himself for the attacker. Instead of fear, pain and humiliation, he had given her desire and, ultimately, an ecstasy so strong it had taken her out of herself. He had replaced a terrible memory with a wonderful one.

His hand was lying low on her abdomen now, and the simple intimacy of his touch stunned her. She could be carrying his child. She had been aware of the probable consequences of making love without protection, but it was what she wanted, and he had made no mention of birth control. Even if their relationship didn't last, she wanted his baby, a child with his strength and fire. If it could be a duplicate of him, nothing would make her happier.

She stirred, and the pressure of his hand on her abdomen increased. "The sun is too hot," she murmured. "I'm getting burned."

He groaned, but fastened his jeans and sat up. Then he picked up her underpants, put them in his pocket and lifted her in his arms in the same motion he used to get to his feet.

"I can walk," she informed him, though she wound her arms around his neck.

"I know." He grinned down at her. "It's just that it's more romantic to carry you into the house to make love."

"But we just made love."

There was fire in his black eyes. "So?"

Wolf was just about to enter the feed store when a tingle touched the back of his neck like a cool wind. He didn't stop, which would have signaled an alarm to anyone watching, but, using his peripheral vision, he took a quick look around. The sense of danger was like a touch. Someone was watching him. His sixth sense was highly developed from hard training and years of application, and further enhanced by the strong mysticism of his heritage.

It wasn't just that he was being watched; he could feel the hatred directed toward him. He strode into the feed store and immediately stepped to the side, flattening himself against the wall as he looked out the door. Conversation in the store halted as if the words had hit a stone wall, but he ignored the thick silence. Adrenaline pumped through his body; he didn't notice that his gloved hand automatically slid over his chest to touch the knife that had been securely attached to the webbing he'd worn sixteen years before, in a steamy, hauntingly beautiful little country that reeked of blood and death. Only when his hand encountered nothing but his shirt did he realize that old habits had come to the fore.

Suddenly he realized that it was the man he'd been hunting, standing somewhere out there and staring at him with hatred, and rage surged through him. He didn't need a knife. Without a word he removed his hat and boots, the hat because it increased his silhouette, the boots because they were too noisy. In his sock feet he ran lightly past the stunned and silent little knot of men who had been standing around chewing the fat. Only one voiced a hesitant, "What's going on?"

Wolf didn't take time to answer, but slipped out the back door of the feed store. His movements were silent, deliberate, as he used every available bit of cover while moving from building to building, working his way around so he would come out behind where he had estimated the man to be. It was hard to pinpoint his position, but Wolf had automatically picked out the best locations for concealment. If he kept looking long enough, he'd find another of the tracks he'd been searching for; the guy would get careless, and Wolf would get him.

He slid around the back of the drugstore, feeling the heat of the sun-warmed boards against his back. He was more cautious than before, not wanting the wood to rasp against his shirt. It was gravelly here, too, and he placed his feet with care to keep the little rocks from making a telltale grinding.

He heard the heavy, thudding sound of someone running, as if he had bolted in panic. Wolf ran around the front of the building and knelt briefly to inspect a faint print in the dust, only a part of a print, but his blood surged. It was the same print, same shoe, same toeing-in stride. He sprinted like the big timber wolf he'd been named for, no longer caring about noise, racing up the street, looking left and right for anyone in the street.

Nothing. No one. The street was empty. He stopped to listen. He heard birds, the rustle of a fitful breeze in the trees, the far-off sound of an engine climbing the slight rise on the north side of the town. Nothing else. No fast breathing, no running footsteps.

Wolf swore to himself. The guy was worse than an amateur, he was clumsy and made stupid moves, as well as being out of shape. If he'd been anywhere close by, Wolf would have been able to hear his labored breathing. Damn it, somehow his quarry had slipped away.

Wolf looked at the quiet houses nestled under the trees. Ruth didn't have residential and commercial zoning; it was too small. The result was that the houses and few businesses were mixed together without order. The man could have gone into any of the houses; the way he'd disappeared so suddenly left no other possibility. It verified Wolf's conviction that the rapist lived in Ruth; after all, both attacks had happened right in town.

He noted who lived in the houses on the street and tried to think of who inside them matched Mary's description of a heavily freckled man. No one came to mind. But someone would. By God, Wolf vowed, someone would. He was slowly eliminating men from his mental list. Eventually, there would be only one left.

From inside a house, a curtain moved fractionally. The sound of his own raspy breathing as he sucked air into his laboring lungs filled the man's ears. Through the tiny crack he'd made, he could see the Indian still standing in the street, staring at first one house, then another. Murderous black eyes moved across the window where the man stood, and he automatically stepped back out of sight.

His own fear sickened and enraged him. He didn't want to be afraid of the Indian, but he was.

"Damn filthy Indian!" He whispered the words, then echoed them in his head. He liked doing that, saying things out loud the first time, then saying them to himself for his private understanding and enjoyment.

The Indian was a murderer. They said he knew more ways of killing people than normal folks could even imagine. The man believed it, because he knew firsthand how Indians could kill.

He'd like to kill the Indian, *and* that boy of his with the strange, pale eyes that looked through him. But he was afraid, because he didn't know how to kill, and he knew he'd wind up getting killed himself. He was too afraid of getting that close to the Indian to even try it.

He'd thought about it, but he couldn't come up with a plan. He'd like to shoot the Indian, because he wouldn't have to get close to do that, but he didn't have a gun, and he didn't want to draw attention to himself by buying one.

But he liked what he'd done to get back at the Indian. It gave him savage satisfaction to know he was punishing the Indian by hurting those stupid women who had taken up for him. Why couldn't they see him for the filthy, murdering trash he was? That stupid Cathy had said the Indian was good-looking! She'd even said she'd go out with the boy, and he knew that meant she'd let the boy touch her, and kiss her. She'd been willing to let the filthy Mackenzies kiss her, but she'd fought and screamed and gagged when *he'd* touched her.

It didn't make sense, but he didn't care. He'd wanted to punish her and punish the Indian for—for being there, for letting stupid Cathy look at him and think he was good-looking.

And the schoolteacher. He hated her almost as much as he hated the Mackenzies, maybe more. She was so goody-goody, making people think the boy was something special, trying to talk people around so they'd be friendly to the half-breeds. Preaching in the general store!

He'd wanted to spit on her. He'd wanted to hurt her, bad. He'd been so excited he almost hadn't been able to stand it when he'd dragged her down that alley and felt her squirming beneath him. If that stupid deputy hadn't shown up, he'd have done to her what he'd done to Cathy, and he knew he'd have liked it more. He'd wanted to hit her with his fists while he did it to her. That would have shown her. She would never have stuck up for the half-breeds again.

He still wanted to get her, to teach her a lesson, but school was out now, and he'd heard people say that the deputy had made her move to some safe place, and no one knew where she was. He didn't want to wait until school started again, but he thought he might have to.

And that stupid Pam Hearst. She needed a lesson, too. He'd heard that she had gone to a dance with the half-breed boy. He knew what that meant. He'd had his hands on her, and she'd probably let him kiss her and maybe do a lot more, because everyone knew what the Mackenzies were like. As far as he was concerned, that made Pam a slut. She deserved to be taught a lesson just like Cathy, and just like the lesson the schoolteacher still had coming.

He peeked outside again. The Indian was gone. He immediately felt safe, and he began to plan.

When Wolf walked back into the feed store, the same group of men were still there. "We don't much like you tracking folks around like we're criminals," one man snapped.

Wolf grunted and sat down to pull on his boots. He didn't care if they liked it or not.

"Did you hear what I said?"

He looked up. "I heard."

"And?"

"And nothing."

"Now look here, damn it!"

"I'm looking."

The men fidgeted under his cold black stare. Another spoke up. "You're making the women nervous."

"They should be nervous. It might keep them on guard, keep them from getting raped."

"It was some drifter trash who blew in and blew out! Likely the sheriff won't ever find who did it."

"It's trash, all right, but he's still here. I just found his track."

The men fell silent and looked at each other. Stu Kilgore, the foreman on Eli Baugh's spread, cleared his throat. "We're supposed to believe you can tell it was made by the same man?"

"I can tell." Wolf gave them a smile that was closer to a snarl. "Uncle Sam made sure I got the best training available. It's the same man. He lives here. He slipped into one of the houses."

"That's hard to believe. We've lived here all our lives. The only stranger around is the schoolteacher. Why would someone just up and start attacking women?"

"Someone did. That's all I care about, that and catching him."

He left the men murmuring among themselves while he loaded his feed.

Pam was bored. Since the two attacks, she hadn't even stepped outside the house by herself; she'd been pretty scared at first, but the days had passed without any more attacks, and the shock had worn off. Women were beginning to venture out again, even by themselves.

She was going to another dance with Joe, and she wanted a new dress. She knew he was going away, knew she couldn't hold him, but there was still something about him that made her heart race. She refused to let herself love him, even though she knew any other boyfriend would have a hard time replacing Joe. Hard, but not impossible. She wasn't going to mope after he'd left; she'd get on with her life—but right now he was still *here*, and she savored every moment with him.

She really wanted a new dress, but she'd promised Joe she wouldn't go anywhere alone, and she didn't intend to break her promise. When her mother returned from shopping with a neighbor, she'd ask her about going with her to get a new dress. Not in Ruth, of course; she wanted to go to a real town, with a real dress shop.

Finally she picked up a book and walked out onto the back porch, away from the sun. There were neighbors on both sides, and she felt safe. She read for a while, then became sleepy and lay down on the porch swing, arranging her long legs over the back of the swing. She dozed immediately.

The abrupt jolting of the swing awakened her some time later. She opened her eyes and stared at a ski mask, with narrowed, hate-filled eyes glittering through the slits. He was already on her when she screamed.

He hit her with his fist, but she jerked her head back so that the blow landed on her shoulder. She screamed again and tried to kick him, and the unsteady swing toppled them to the porch. She kicked again, catching him in the stomach, and he grunted, sounding oddly surprised.

She couldn't stop screaming, even as she scrabbled away from him. She was more terrified than she'd ever been before in her life, but also oddly detached, watching the scene from some safe distance. The wooden slats of the porch scraped her hands and arms, but she kept moving backward. He suddenly sprang, and she kicked at him again, but he caught her ankle. She didn't stop. She just kicked, using both legs, trying to catch him in the head or the groin, and she screamed.

Someone next door yelled. The man jerked his head up and dropped her ankle. Blood had seeped through the multicolored ski mask; she'd managed to kick him in the mouth. He said "Indian's dirty whore" in a hate-thickened voice, and jumped from the porch, already running.

Pam lay on the porch, sobbing in dry, painful gasps. The neighbor yelled again, and somehow she garnered enough strength to scream "Help me!" before the terror made her curl into a ball and whimper like a child.

_____ *Chapter Twelve*

Wolf wasn't surprised when the deputy's car pulled up and Clay got out. He'd had a tight feeling in his gut since he'd found that footprint in town. Clay's tired face told the story.

Mary saw who their visitor was and automatically got a cup for coffee; Clay always wanted coffee. He took off his hat and sat down, heaving a sigh as he did so.

"Who was it this time?" Wolf asked, his deep voice so rough it was almost a growl.

"Pam Hearst."

Joe's head jerked up, and all the color washed out of his face. He was on his feet before Clay's next words came.

"She fought him off. She isn't hurt, but she's scared. He jumped her on the Hearsts' back porch, for God's sake. Mrs. Winston heard her screaming, and the guy ran. Pam said she kicked him in the mouth. She saw blood on the ski mask he was wearing."

"He lives in town," Wolf said. "I found another print, but it's hard to track in town, with people walking around destroying what few prints there are. I think he ducked into one of the houses along Bay Road, but he might not live there."

"Bay Road." Clay frowned as he mentally reviewed the people living on Bay Road; most of the townspeople lived along it, in close little clusters. There was also another cluster of houses on Broad Street, where the Hearsts lived. "We might have him this time. Any man who has a swollen lip will have to have an airtight alibi."

"If it just split his lip, you won't be able to tell. The swelling will be minimal. She would have to have really done some damage for it to be visible more than a day or so." Wolf had had more than his share of split lips, and delivered his share, too. The mouth healed swiftly. Now if Pam had knocked some teeth out, that would be a different story.

"Any blood on the porch?"

"No."

"Then she didn't do any real damage." There would have been blood sprayed all over the porch if she'd kicked out his teeth.

Clay shoved his hand through his hair. "I don't like to think of the uproar it would cause, but I'm going to talk to the sheriff about making a house-to-house search along Bay Road. Damn it, I just can't think of anyone it could be.''

Joe abruptly left the room, and Wolf stared after his son. He knew Joe wanted to go to Pam, and knew that he wouldn't. Some of the barriers had come down, but most of them were still intact.

Clay had watched Joe leave, and he sighed again. ''The bastard called Pam an 'Indian's dirty whore.''' His gaze shifted to Mary, who had stood silently the whole time. ''You were right.''

She didn't reply, because she'd known all along that she was right. It made her sick to hear the name Pam had been called, because it so starkly revealed the hatred behind the attack.

''I suppose all the tracks at Pam's house have been ruined.'' Wolf said it as a statement, not a question.

''Afraid so.'' Clay was regretful, but practically everyone in town had been at the Hearsts' house before he'd gotten there, standing around the back porch and tromping around the area.

Wolf muttered something uncomplimentary under his breath about damn idiots. ''Do you think the sheriff will go along with a house-to-house search?''

''Depends. You know some folks are going to kick up about it no matter what the reason. They'll take it personally. This is an election year,'' he said, and they took his point.

Mary listened to them talking, but she didn't join in. Now Pam had been hurt; who was next? Would the man work up enough courage to attack Wolf or Joe? That was her real terror, because she didn't know if she could bear it. She loved them with all the fierceness of her soul. She would gladly put herself between them and danger.

Which was exactly what she would have to do.

It made her sick to even think of that man's hands on her again, but she knew in that moment that she was going to give him the opportunity. Somehow, she was going to lure him out. She wouldn't allow herself the luxury of hiding out on Mackenzie's Mountain any longer.

She would begin driving into town by herself. The only problem would be in getting away from Wolf; she knew he'd never agree if he had any idea what she was doing. Not only that, he was capable of preventing her from leaving at all, either by disabling her car or even locking her in the bedroom. She didn't underestimate him.

Since he had moved her up on the mountain with him, he'd been delivering and picking up horses, rather than letting the owners come up to the ranch, where they might see her. Her whereabouts were a well-kept secret, known only to Wolf, Joe and Clay. But that meant she was left alone several times a week while Wolf and Joe ran errands and delivered horses. Joe also left for his math lessons, and they had to ride fences and work the small herd of cattle, just as every rancher did. She really had a lot of opportunities for slipping away, at least the first time. It would be infinitely more difficult to get away after that, because Wolf would be on his guard.

She quietly excused herself and went in search of Joe. She peeked into his bedroom, but he wasn't there, so she went out on the front porch. He was leaning against one of the posts, his thumbs hooked in his front pockets.

"It isn't your fault."

He didn't move. "I knew it could happen."

"You aren't responsible for someone else's hate."

"No, but I am responsible for Pam. I knew it could happen, and I should have stayed away from her."

Mary made an unladylike sound. "I seem to remember it was the other way around. Pam made her choice when she made that scene in her father's store."

"All she wanted was to go to a dance. She didn't ask for this."

"Of course not, but it still isn't your fault, any more than it would have been your fault if she'd been in a car accident. You can say you could have delayed her so she'd have been a minute later getting to that particular section of road, or hurried her up so she'd have been earlier, but that's ridiculous, and you know it."

He couldn't prevent a faint smile at the starchiness of her tone. She should be in Congress, cracking her whip and haranguing those senators and representatives into some sort of fiscal responsibility. Instead she'd taken on Ruth, Wyoming, and none of them had been the same since she'd set foot in town.

"All right, so I'm taking too much on myself," he finally said. "But I knew it wasn't smart to go out with her in the first place. It isn't fair. I'll be leaving here when I finish school, and I won't be back. Pam should be dating someone who's going to be around when she needs him."

"You're still taking too much on yourself. Let Pam make her own decisions about who she wants to date. Do you plan to isolate yourself from women forever?"

"I wouldn't go that far," he drawled, and in that moment he sounded so much like his father that it startled her. "But I don't intend to get involved with anyone."

"It doesn't always work out the way you want. You were involved with Pam even before I came here."

That was true, as far as it went. He sighed and leaned his head against the post. "I don't love her."

"Of course not. I never thought you did."

"I like her; I care for her. But not enough to stay, not enough to give up the Academy." He looked at the Wyoming night, the almost painful clarity of the sky, the brightly winking stars, and thought of jockeying an F-15 over these mountains, with the dark earth below and the glittering stars above. No, he couldn't give that up.

"Did you tell her that?"

"Yes."

"Then it was her decision."

They stood in silence, watching the stars. A few minutes later Clay left, and neither of them thought it strange that he hadn't said goodbye. Wolf came out on the porch and automatically slid his arm around Mary's waist, hugging her to his side even as he put his hand on his son's shoulder. "You okay?"

"Okay enough, I suppose." But he understood now the total rage he'd seen in Wolf's eyes when Mary had been attacked, the same rage that still burned in a rigidly controlled fire inside his father. God help the man if Wolf Mackenzie ever got his hands on him.

Wolf tightened his arm around Mary and led her inside, knowing it was best to leave Joe alone now. His son was tough; he'd handle it.

The next morning Mary listened as they discussed their day. There were no horses to deliver or pick up, but Joe had a math lesson that afternoon, and they intended to use the morning inoculating cattle. She had no idea how long it would take to treat the whole herd, but imagined they would both be tied up the entire morning. They would be riding a couple of the young quarter horses, to teach them how to cut cattle.

Joe had changed overnight; it was a subtle change, but one that made Mary ache inside. In repose, his young face held a grimness that saddened her, as if the last faint vestiges of boyhood had been driven from his soul. He'd always looked older than his age, but now, despite the smoothness of his skin, he no longer looked young.

She was a grown woman, almost thirty years old, and the attack had left scars she hadn't been able to handle alone. Cathy and Pam were just kids, and Cathy had to handle a nightmare that was far worse than what Mary and Pam had undergone. Joe had lost his youth. No matter what, that man had to be stopped before he damaged anyone else.

When Wolf and Joe left the house, Mary gave them plenty of time to get far enough away so they wouldn't hear her car start, then hurried out of the house. She didn't know what she was going to do, other than parade through Ruth on the off chance that her presence might trigger another attack. And then what? She didn't know. Somehow she had to be prepared; she had to get someone to keep watch so the man could be caught. It should have been easy to catch him; he'd been so careless, attacking out in the open and in broad daylight, making stupid moves, as if he attacked on impulse and without a plan. He hadn't even taken the simplest precautions against getting caught. The whole thing was strange. It didn't make sense.

Her hands were shaking as she drove into town; she was acutely aware that this was the first time since the day she'd been attacked that she was without protection. She felt exposed, as if her clothing had been stripped away.

She had to get someone to watch her, someone she trusted. Who? Sharon? The young teacher was her friend, but Sharon wasn't aggressive, and she thought the situation called for aggressiveness. Francie Beecham was too old; Cicely Karr would be too cautious. She discounted the men, because they would get all protective and refuse to help. Men were such victims to their own hormones. Machismo had killed a lot more people than PMS.

Pam Hearst sprang to mind. Pam would be extremely interested in catching the man, and she'd been aggressive enough to kick him in the mouth, to fight him off. She was young, but she had courage. She'd had the courage to go against her father and date a half-breed.

Conversation ceased when she walked into Hearst's store; it was the first time she'd been seen since the end of school. She ignored the thick silence, for she had what she suspected was a highly accurate guess as to the subject of the conversation she'd interrupted, and approached the checkout counter where Mr. Hearst stood.

"Is Pam at home?" she asked quietly, not wanting her question to be heard by the entire store.

He looked as if he'd aged ten years overnight, but there was no animosity in his face.

He nodded. The same thing had happened to Miss Potter, he thought. If she could talk to Pam, maybe she could take that haunted look out of his baby girl's eyes. Miss Potter had a lot of backbone for such a little thing; maybe he didn't always agree with her, but he'd damn sure learned to respect her. And Pam thought the world of her.

"I'd appreciate it if you'd talk to her," he said.

There was an odd, almost militant expression in her soft bluish eyes. "I'll do that," she promised, and turned to leave. She almost bumped into Dottie and was startled into a gasp; the woman had been right behind her.

"Good morning," Mary said pleasantly. Aunt Ardith had drilled the importance of good manners into her.

Strangely, Dottie seemed to have aged, too. Her face was haggard. "How are you doing, Mary?"

Mary hesitated, but she could detect none of the hostility she was accustomed to from Dottie. Had the entire town changed? Had this nightmare brought them to their senses about the Mackenzies? "I'm fine. Are you enjoying the vacation?"

Dottie smiled, but it was merely a movement of her facial muscles, not a response of pleasure. "It's been a relief."

She certainly didn't look relieved; she looked worried to a frazzle. Of course, everyone *should* be worried.

"How is your son?" Mary couldn't remember the boy's name, and she felt faintly embarrassed. It wasn't like her to forget names.

To her surprise, Dottie went white. Even her lips were bloodless. "W—why do you ask?" she stammered.

"He seemed upset the last time I saw him," Mary replied. She could hardly say that only good manners had prompted the question. Southerners always asked after family.

"Oh. He—he's all right. He hardly ever leaves the house. He doesn't like going out." Dottie looked around, then blurted "Excuse me," and left the store before Mary could say anything else.

She looked at Mr. Hearst, and he shrugged. He thought Dottie had acted a bit strange, too.

"I'll go see Pam now," she said.

She started to walk to the Hearst house, but the memory of what had happened the last time she'd walked through town made chills run up her spine, and she went to her car. She checked the back seat and floorboard before opening the door. As she started the engine, she saw Dottie walking swiftly up the street, her head down as if she didn't want anyone to speak to her. She hadn't bought anything, Mary realized. Why had she been in Hearst's store, if not to make a purchase? It couldn't be browsing, because everyone knew what every store in town carried. Why had she left so suddenly?

Dottie turned left down the small street where she lived, and abruptly Mary wondered what Dottie was doing walking around alone. Every woman in town should know better. Surely she had enough sense to be cautious.

Mary drove slowly up the street. She craned her neck when she reached the street where Dottie had turned and saw the woman hurrying up the steps of her house. Her eyes fell on the faded sign: Bay Road.

Bay Road was where Wolf thought the rapist had dodged into a house. It made sense that he wouldn't have entered a house that wasn't his home, unless he was a close friend who came and went just like a family member. That was possible, but even a very close friend would give a yell before just walking into someone else's house, and Wolf would have heard that.

Dottie was certainly acting odd. She'd looked as if she'd been stung by a bee when Mary had asked about her son.... Bobby, that was his name. Mary was pleased that she'd remembered.

Bobby. Bobby wasn't "right." He did things in a skewed way. He was unable to apply logic to the simplest of chores, unable to plan a practical course of action.

Mary broke out in a sweat and had to stop the car. She'd only seen him once, but she could picture him in her mind: big, a little soft-looking, with sandy hair and a fair complexion. A fair, freckled complexion.

Was it *Bobby*? The one person in town who wasn't totally responsible for himself? The one person no one would ever suspect?

Except his mother.

She had to tell Wolf.

As soon as the thought formed, she dismissed it. She couldn't tell Wolf, not yet, because she didn't want to put that burden on him. His instincts would tell him to go after Bobby; his conscience would argue that Bobby wasn't a responsible person. Mary knew him well enough to know that, no matter which decision he made, he would always have regrets. Better for the responsibility to be hers than to push Wolf into such a position.

She'd call Clay. It was his job, after all. He'd be better able to deal with the situation.

Only a few seconds passed as her thoughts rushed through her mind. She was still sitting there staring at Dottie's house when Bobby came out on the porch. It took him a moment, but suddenly he noticed her car and looked straight at her. A distance of less than seventy-five yards separated them, still too far for her to read his expression, but she didn't need a close-up for sheer terror to spurt through her. She stomped on the gas pedal and the car shot forward, slinging gravel, the tires squealing.

It was only a short distance to the Hearst house. Mary ran to the front door and banged her fist on it. Her heart felt as if it would explode. That brief moment when she had been face-to-face with him was almost more than she could stand. God, she had to call Clay.

Mrs. Hearst opened the door a crack, then recognized Mary and swung it all the way open. "Miss Potter! Is something wrong?"

Mary realized that she must look wild. "Could I use your phone? It's an emergency."

"Why—of course." She stepped back, allowing Mary inside.

Pam appeared in the hallway. "Miss Potter?" She looked young and scared.

"The phone's in the kitchen."

Mary followed Mrs. Hearst and grabbed the receiver. "What's the number of the sheriff's department?"

Pam got a small telephone book from the countertop and began flipping through the pages. Too agitated to wait, Mary dialed the number for Information.

"Sheriff's department, please."

"What city?" the disembodied voice asked.

She drew a blank. For the life of her, she couldn't remember the name of the town.

"Here it is," Pam said.

Mary disconnected the call to Information, then dialed as Pam recited the number. The various computer clicks as the connection was made seemed to take forever.

"Sheriff's office."

"Deputy Armstrong, please. Clay Armstrong."

"One moment."

It was longer than one moment. Pam and her mother stood tensely, not knowing what was going on but reacting to her urgency. Both of them had dark circles under their eyes. It had been a bad night for the Hearst family.

"Sheriff's office," a different voice said.

"Clay?"

"You looking for Armstrong?"

"Yes. It's an emergency!" she insisted.

"Well, I don't know where he is right now. You want to tell me what the trouble is—hey, Armstrong! Some lady wants you in a hurry." To Mary, he said, "He'll be right here."

A few seconds later Clay's voice said, "Armstrong."

"It's Mary. I'm in town."

"What the hell are you doing there?"

Her teeth were chattering. "It's Bobby. Bobby Lancaster. I saw him—"

"Hang up the phone!"

It was a scream, and she jumped, dropping the receiver, which dangled from the end of its cord. She flattened against the wall, for Bobby stood there, inside the kitchen, with a huge butcher knife in his hand. His face was twisted with both hate and fear.

"You told!" He sounded like an outraged child.

"Told—told what?"

"You told him! I heard you!"

Mrs. Hearst had shrunk back against the cabinets, her hand at her throat. Pam stood as if rooted in the middle of the floor, her face colorless, her eyes locked on the young man she'd known all her life. She could see the slight swelling of his lower lip.

Bobby shifted his weight from one foot to the other, as if he didn't know what to do next. His face was red, and he looked almost tearful.

Mary strove to steady her voice. "That's right, I told him. He's on his way now. You'd better run." Maybe that wasn't the best suggestion in the world, but more than anything she wanted to get him out of the Hearsts' house before he hurt someone. She desperately wanted him to run.

"It's all your fault!" He looked hunted, as if he didn't know what to do except cast blame. "You—you came here and changed things. Mama said you're a dirty Indian-lover."

"I beg your pardon. I prefer clean people."

He blinked, confused. Then he shook his head and said again, "It's your fault."

"Clay will be here in a few minutes. You'd better go."

His hand tightened on the knife, and suddenly he reached out and grabbed her arm. He was big and soft, but he was faster than he looked. Mary cried out as he twisted her arm up behind her back, nearly wrenching her shoulder joint loose.

"You'll be my hostage, just like on television," he said and pushed her out the back door.

Mrs. Hearst was motionless, frozen in shock. Pam leaped for the phone, heard the buzzing that signaled a broken connection and held the button down for a new line. When she got a dial tone, she dialed the Mackenzies' number. It rang endlessly, and she cursed, using words her mother had no idea she knew. All the while she leaned to the side, trying to see where Bobby was taking Mary.

She was just about to hang up when the receiver was picked up and a deep, angry voice roared, "Mary?"

She was so startled that she almost dropped the phone. "No," she choked. "It's Pam. He has Mary. It's Bobby Lancaster, and he just dragged her out of the house—"

"I'll be right there."

Pam shivered at the deadly intent in Wolf Mackenzie's voice.

Mary stumbled over a large rock hidden by the tall grass and gagged as the sudden intense pain made nausea twist her stomach.

"Stand up!" Bobby yelled, jerking at her.

"I twisted my ankle!" It was a lie, but it would give her an excuse to slow him down.

He'd dragged her across the small meadow behind the Hearsts', through a thick line of trees, over a stream, and now they were climbing a small rise. At least it had looked small, but now she knew it was deceptively large. It was a big open area, not the smartest place for Bobby to head, but he didn't plan well. That was what had thrown everyone off from the beginning, what had never seemed quite *right*. There had been no logic to his actions; Bobby reacted rather than planned.

He didn't know what to do for a twisted ankle, so he didn't worry about it, just pushed her along at the same speed. She stumbled again, but somehow managed to retain her balance. She wouldn't be able to bear it if she fell on her stomach and he came down on top of her again.

"Why did you have to tell?" he groaned.

"You hurt Cathy."

"She deserved it!"

"How? How did she deserve it?"

"She liked him—the Indian."

Mary was panting. She estimated they'd gone over a mile. Not a great distance, but the gradual uphill climb was telling on her. It didn't help that her arm was twisted up between her shoulder blades. How long had it been? When could she expect Clay to arrive? It had been at least twenty minutes.

Wolf made it off his mountain in record time. His eyes were like flint as he leaped from the truck before it had rocked to a complete stop. He and Joe both carried rifles, but Wolf's was a sniper rifle, a Remington with a powerful scope. He'd never had occasion to try a thousand-yard shot with it, but he'd never missed his target at closer range.

People milled around the back of the house. He and Joe shouldered their way through the crowd. "Everybody freeze, before you destroy any more tracks!" Wolf roared, and everyone stopped dead.

Pam darted to them. Her face was streaked with tears. "He took her into the trees. There," she said and pointed.

A siren announced Clay's arrival, but Wolf didn't wait for him. The trail across the meadow was as plain to him as a neon sign would have been, and he set off at a lope, with Joe on his heels.

Dottie Lancaster was terrified, and nearly hysterical. Bobby was her son, and she loved him desperately no matter what he'd done. She'd been sick when she'd realized he was the one who had attacked Cathy Teele and Mary; she'd almost worried herself into an early grave as she wrestled with her conscience and the sure knowledge that she'd lose her son if she turned him in. But that was nothing compared to the horror she'd felt when she discovered he'd slipped from the house. She'd followed the sounds of a disturbance and found all of her nightmares coming true: he'd taken Mary, and he had a knife. Now the Mackenzies were after him, and she knew they would kill him.

She grabbed Clay's arm as he surged past her. "Stop them," she sobbed. "Don't let them kill my boy."

Clay barely glanced at her. He shook her loose and ran after them. Distraught, Dottie ran, too.

By then some of the other men had gotten their rifles and were joining the hunt. They'd always felt sorry for Bobby Lancaster, but he'd hurt their women, and there was no excuse for it.

Wolf's heartbeat settled down, and he pushed the panic away. His senses heightened, as they always did when he was on the hunt. Every sound was magnified in his ears, instantly recognizable. He saw every blade of grass, every broken twig and overturned rock. He could smell every scent nature had left, and the faint acrid, coppery tang of fear. His body was a machine, moving smoothly, silently.

He could read every sign. Here Mary had stumbled, and his muscles tightened. She had to be terrified. If he hurt her—she was so slight, no match at all for a man. The bastard had a knife. Wolf thought of a blade touching her delicate, translucent skin, and rage consumed him. He had to push it away because he couldn't afford the mistakes rage could cause.

He broke out of the tree line and suddenly saw them, high on the side of the rise. Bobby was dragging Mary along, but at least she was still alive.

Wolf examined the terrain. He didn't have a good angle. He moved east, along the base of the rise.

"Stop!"

It was Bobby's voice, only faintly heard at that distance. They had halted, and Bobby was holding Mary in front of him. "Stop or I'll kill her!"

Slowly, Wolf went down on one knee and raised the rifle to his shoulder. He sighted through the scope, not for a shot, but to see how he should set it up. The powerful scope plainly revealed the desperation on Bobby's face and the knife at Mary's throat.

"Bobbeee!" Dottie had reached them, and she screamed his name.

"Mama?"

"Bobby, let her go!"

"I can't! She told!"

The men had clustered around. Several of them measured the distance by eye and shook their heads. They couldn't make the shot, not at that range. They were as likely to hit Mary as Bobby, if they hit anything at all.

Clay looked down at Wolf. "Can you make the shot?"

Wolf smiled, and Clay felt that chill run up his spine again at the look in Wolf's eyes. They were cold and murderous. "Yeah."

"No!" Dottie sobbed the word. "Bobby!" she screamed. "Please, come down!"

"I can't! I've got to kill her! She likes him, and he's a dirty Indian! He killed my father!"

Dottie gasped and covered her mouth with her hands. "No," she moaned, then screamed again. "No! He didn't!" Pure hell was living in her eyes.

"He did! You said—an Indian—" Bobby broke off and began dragging Mary backward.

"Do it," Clay said quietly.

Wolf braced the barrel of the rifle in the notch of a sapling. It was small but sturdy enough to be steady. Without a word he sighted in the cross hairs of the scope.

"Wait," Dottie cried, anguish in her voice.

Wolf looked at her.

"Please," she whispered. "Don't kill him. He's all I have."

His black eyes were flat. "I'll try."

He concentrated on the shot, shutting everything out as he always had. It was maybe three hundred yards, but the air was still. The image in the scope was huge and clear and flattened, the depth perception distorted. Mary's face was plain. She looked angry, and she was tugging at the arm around her shoulder, the one that held the knife to her throat.

God, when he got her back safe and sound, he was going to throttle her.

Because she was so small, he had a larger target than would normally have been presented. His instincts were to go for a head shot, to take Bobby Lancaster completely out of life, but he'd promised. Damn, it was going to be a bitch of a shot. They were moving, and he'd limited his own target area by promising not to go for a kill.

The cross hairs settled, and his hands became rock steady. He drew in a breath, let out half of it and gently squeezed the trigger. Almost simultaneously with the sharp thunder in his ear he saw the red stain blossom on Bobby's shoulder and the knife drop from his suddenly useless hand even as he was thrown back by the bullet's impact. Mary staggered to the side and fell, but was instantly on her feet again.

Dottie sagged to her knees, sobbing, her hands over her face.

The men surged up the hill. Mary ran down it and met Wolf halfway. He still had the rifle in his hand, but he caught her up in his arms and held her locked to him, his eyes closed as he absorbed the miracle of her, warm and alive against him, her silky hair against his face, her sweet scent in his lungs. He didn't care who saw them, or what anyone thought. She was his, and he'd just lived through the worst half hour of his existence knowing that at any moment her life could be ended.

Now that it was over, she was crying.

She'd been dragged up the hill, and now Wolf dragged her down it. He was swearing steadily under his breath, ignoring her gasping protests until she stumbled. Then he snatched her up under his arm like a sack and continued down. People stared after them in astonishment, but no one moved to stop him. After today, they all viewed Wolf Mackenzie differently.

Wolf ignored her car and thrust her into his truck. Mary pushed her hair out of her face and decided not to mention the car; they would pick it up later. Wolf was in a rage, his face set and hard.

They had almost reached the road that wound up his mountain before he spoke. "What in hell were you doing in town?" The even tone didn't fool her. The wolf was dangerously angered.

Perhaps she wasn't as cautious as she should have been, but she still wasn't afraid of him, not of the man she loved. She respected his temper, but she didn't fear him. So she said, just as calmly, "I thought seeing me might trigger him into doing something stupid, so we could identify him."

"You *triggered* him, all right. What he did wasn't nearly as stupid as what you did. What did you do, parade up and down the streets until he grabbed you?"

She let the insult pass. "Actually it never came to that. I intended to talk to Pam first. I stopped at the store to ask Mr. Hearst if she was home and bumped into Dottie. She acted so strange and looked so worried that it made me wonder. She almost ran out of the store. Then, when I saw her turn onto Bay Road, I remembered Bobby, what he looked like. He came out on the porch and looked at me, and I knew he was the one."

"So you made a citizen's arrest?" he asked sarcastically.

Mary got huffy. "No. I'm not stupid, and you'd better not make another smart remark, Wolf Mackenzie. I did what I thought I had to do. I'm sorry if you don't like it, but there it is. Enough was enough. I couldn't take the chance someone else could be hurt, or that he might start taking shots at you or Joe.

"I drove to Pam's house and called Clay. I had no intention of confronting Bobby, but it didn't work out that way. He followed me to Pam's and heard me talking on the phone. So he grabbed me. You know what happened then."

She was so matter-of-fact about it that he tightened his hands on the steering wheel to keep from shaking her. If she hadn't been crying just a few minutes ago, he might have lost his tenuous control on his temper.

"Do you know what might have happened if I hadn't come back to the barn for something and noticed your car was missing? It was just chance I was there when Pam called to tell me Bobby had grabbed you!"

"Yes," she said patiently. "I know what could have happened."

"It doesn't bother you that he came close to cutting your throat?"

"Close doesn't count except in horseshoes and hand grenades."

He slammed on the brakes, so enraged he could barely see. He wasn't aware of shutting off the motor, only of closing his hands on her slender shoulders. He was so close to pulling her across his knees that he was shaking, but she didn't seem to realize that she should be frightened. With a faint sound she dived into his arms, clinging to him with surprising strength.

Wolf held her and felt her trembling. The red haze left his vision, and he realized that she *was* frightened, but not of him. With her normal damn-the-torpedoes attitude, she'd done what she'd thought was right and was probably trying to put up a calm front so he wouldn't be alarmed.

As if anything could ever alarm him more than seeing an unbalanced rapist hold a knife to her throat.

Frantically he started the truck. It wasn't far to his house, but he didn't know if he could make it. He had to make love to her, soon, even if it was in the middle of the road. Only then would the fear of losing her begin to fade, when he felt her beneath him once more and she welcomed him into her delicate body.

Mary brooded. It had been four days since Wolf had shot Bobby; the first two days had been filled with statements and police procedures, as well as newspaper interviews and even a request from a television station, which Wolf had refused. The sheriff, not being a fool, had hailed Wolf as a hero and praised the shot he'd made. Wolf's military service record was dug up, and a lot was written about the "much-decorated Vietnam veteran" who had saved a schoolteacher and captured a rapist.

Bobby was recuperating in a hospital in Casper; the bullet had punctured his right lung, but he was lucky to be alive under the circumstances. He was bewildered by everything that had happened and kept asking to go home. Dottie had resigned. She'd have to live the rest of her life knowing that her hatred had taken seed in her son's mind and caused the entire nightmare. She knew Bobby would be taken away from her, at least for a time, and that they would never be able to live in Ruth again, even if he was ever a free man. But wherever Bobby was sent, she intended to be close by. As she'd told Wolf, he was all she had.

It was over, and Mary knew that Wolf would never be treated as an outcast again. The threat was past, and the town was safe. Just knowing who it was and that he'd been caught made a lot of difference in Cathy Teele's recovery, though what had happened would always mark her life.

So there was no reason why Mary couldn't return to her own house.

That was why she was brooding. In those four days, Wolf hadn't said a word about her remaining with him. He'd never said a word of love, not even during their wild lovemaking after he'd snatched her to safety. He hadn't said anything at all about their personal situation.

It was time to go home. She couldn't stay with him forever, not when there was no fear for her safety now. She knew their affair would probably continue, at least for a while, but still the thought of leaving his house depressed her. She'd loved every minute of her time on Mackenzie's Mountain, loved sharing the little commonplace things with him. Life consisted of the small things, with only scattered moments of intensity.

She calmly packed and refused to let herself cry. She was going to be under control and not make a scene. She loaded her suitcases into her car, then waited for Wolf to return to the house. It would be childish to sneak off, and she wouldn't do it; she'd tell him she was returning to her home, thank him for his protection and leave. It would be immensely civilized.

As it happened, it was late afternoon when Wolf got back. He was sweaty and coated with dust, and limping a little, because a cow had stepped on his foot. He wasn't in a good mood.

Mary smiled at him. "I've decided to get out of your hair, since there's no reason to be afraid of staying by myself now. I've already packed and loaded everything in the car, but I wanted to stay until you got home to thank you for everything you've done."

Wolf paused in the act of gulping cool, fresh water down his parched throat. Joe froze on the step, not wanting them to see him. He couldn't believe Wolf would let her leave.

Slowly, Wolf turned his head to look at her. There was a savage expression in his eyes, but she was concentrating too hard on maintaining control to see it. She gave him another smile, but this one was harder, because he hadn't said a word, not even, "I'll call you."

"Well," she said brightly, "I'll see you around. Tell Joe not to forget his lessons."

She marched out the front door and down the steps. She'd gotten half-way to her car when a hard hand clamped down on her shoulder and spun her around.

"I'll be damned if you're setting foot off this mountain," he said in a harsh tone.

He towered over her. For the first time Mary felt it was a disadvantage that she only reached his shoulder. She had to tilt her head back to talk to him, he was so close. The heat from his body enveloped her like steam. "I can't stay here forever," she replied reasonably, but now she could see the look in his eyes and she shivered. "I'm a small-town schoolteacher. I can't just cohabit with you—"

"Shut up," he said.

"Now see here—"

"I said shut up. You aren't going anywhere, and you're damn well going to cohabit with me for the rest of your life. It's too late today, but first thing in the morning we're going into town for our blood tests and license. We're going to be married within a week, so get your little butt back in that house and stay there. I'll bring your suitcases in."

His expression would have made most men back up a few steps, but Mary crossed her arms. "I'm not marrying someone who doesn't love me."

"Hellfire!" he roared and jerked her up against him. "Not love you? Damn, woman, you've been wrapping me around your little finger since the first time I set eyes on you! I'd have killed Bobby Lancaster in a heartbeat for you, so don't you ever say I don't love you!"

As a declaration of love cum marriage proposal, it wasn't exactly romantic, but it was certainly exciting. Mary smiled up at him and went on tiptoe to loop her arms around his neck. "I love you, too."

He glared down at her, but noticed how pretty she looked with her soft pink sweater bringing out the delicate roses in her cheeks, and her slate-blue eyes twinkling at him. A breeze flirted with her silky, silvery-brown

Linda Howard

hair, and suddenly he buried his face in the baby-fine strands at her temple.

"God, I love you," he whispered. He'd never thought he would love any woman, least of all an Anglo, but that was before this slight, delicate creature had bulldozed her way into his life and completely changed it. He could no more live without her now than he could live without air.

"I want children," she stated.

He smiled against her temple. "I'm willing."

She thought about it some more. "I think I'd like four."

A slight frown creased his brow as he held her tighter. "We'll see." She was too small and delicate for that many pregnancies; two would be better. He lifted her in his arms and started for the house, where she belonged.

Joe watched from the window and turned away with a grin as his father lifted Mary against his chest.

Epilogue

Air Force Academy, Colorado Springs, Colorado

Joe opened the letter from Mary and began grinning as he read. His roommate looked at him with interest. "Good news from home?"

"Yeah," Joe said without looking up. "My stepmother is pregnant again."

"I thought she just had a baby."

"Two years ago. This is their third."

His roommate, Bill Stolsky, watched Joe finish the letter. Privately he was a little awed by the calm, remote half-breed. Even when they'd been doolies, first-year cadets, and normally regarded as lower than the low, there had been something about Joe Mackenzie that had kept the upperclassmen from dealing him too much misery. He'd been at the top of his class from the beginning, and it was already known that he was moving on to flight training after graduation. Mackenzie was on the fast track to the top, and even his instructors knew it.

"How old is your stepmother?" Stolsky asked in curiosity. He knew Mackenzie was twenty-one, a year younger than himself, though they were both seniors in the Academy.

Joe shrugged and reached for a picture he kept in his locker. "Young enough. My dad's pretty young, too. He was just a kid when I was born."

Stolsky took the picture and looked at the four people in it. It wasn't a posed photograph, which made it more intimate. Three adults were playing with a baby. The woman was small and delicate, and was looking up from the baby in her lap to smile at a big, dark, eagle-featured man. The man was one tough-looking dude. Stolsky wouldn't want to meet him in an alley, dark or otherwise. He glanced quickly at Joe and saw the strong resemblance.

But the baby was clinging to the big man's finger with a dimpled fist and laughing while Joe tickled his neck. It was a revealing and strangely disturbing look into Mackenzie's private life, into his tightly knit family.

Stolsky cleared his throat. "Is that the newest baby?"

"No, that picture was made when I was a senior in high school. That's Michael. He's four years old now, and Joshua is two." Joe couldn't help grinning and feeling worried at the same time when he thought of Mary's letter. Both his little brothers had been delivered by cesarean, because Mary was simply too slender to have them. After Joshua's birth, Wolf had said there would be no more babies, because Mary had had such a hard time carrying Josh. But Mary had won, as usual. He'd have to make a point of getting off on leave when this baby was due.

"Your stepmother isn't—uh—"

"Indian? No."

"Do you like her?"

Joe smiled. "I love her. I wouldn't be here without her." He stood and walked to the window. Six years of hard work, and he was on the verge of getting what he'd lived for: fighter jets. First there was flight training, then Fighter Training School. More years of hard work loomed before him, but he was eager for them. Only a small percentage made it to fighters, but he was going to be one of them.

The cadets in his class who were going on to flight training had already been thinking of fighter call signs, picking theirs out even though they knew some of them would wash out of flight training, and an even greater number would never make it to fighters. But they never thought it would be them; it was always the other guy who washed out, the other guy who didn't have the stuff.

They'd had a lot of fun thinking up those signs, and Joe had sat quietly, a little apart as he always was. Then Richards had pointed at him and said, "You'll be Chief."

Joe had looked up, his face calm and remote. "I'm not a chief." His tone had been even, but Richards had felt a chill.

"All right," he'd agreed. "What do you want to be called?"

Joe had shrugged. "Call me 'Breed.' It's what I am."

Already, though they hadn't even graduated yet, people were calling him Breed Mackenzie. The name would be painted on his helmet, and a lot of people would forget his real name.

Mary had given him this. She'd pushed and prodded, fought for him, taught him. She'd given him his life, up in the blue.

Mary turned into Wolf's arms. She was nude, and his big hand kept stroking down her pale body as if searching out signs of her as-yet-invisible pregnancy. She knew he was worried, but she felt wonderful and tried to reassure him. "I've never felt better. Face it, pregnancy agrees with me."

He chuckled and stroked her breasts, lifting each one in turn in his palm. They were fuller now, and more sensitive. He could almost bring her to satisfaction just with his mouth on her nipples.

"But this is the last one," he said.

"What if it's another boy? Wouldn't you like to try for a girl just once more?"

He groaned, because that was the argument she'd used to talk him into getting her pregnant this time. She was determined to have her four children.

"Let's make a deal. If this one is a girl, there won't be any more. If it's a boy, we'll have one more baby, but that's the limit, regardless of its sex."

"It's a deal," she agreed. She paused. "Have you thought that it's possible you could father a hundred children and they'd all be boys? You may not have any female sperm. Look at your track record, three boys in a row—"

He put his hand on her mouth. "No more. Four is the absolute limit."

She laughed at him and arched her slender body against him. His response was immediate, even after five years of marriage. Later, when he slept, Mary smiled into the darkness and stroked his strong back. This baby was a boy, too, she felt. But the next one—ah, the next one would be the daughter he craved. She was certain of it.

Breathtaking romance is predicted in your future with Harlequin's newest collection: Fortune Cookie.

Three of your favorite Harlequin authors, **Janice Kaiser, Margaret St. George and M.J. Rodgers** will regale you with the romantic adventures of three heroines who are promised fame, fortune, danger and intrigue when they crack open their fortune cookies on a fateful night at a Chinese restaurant.

Join in the adventure with your own personalized fortune, inserted in every book!

Don't miss this exciting new collection!

Available in September wherever Harlequin books are sold.

HARLEQUIN®

CATHERINE LANIGAN

the bestselling author of
ROMANCING THE STONE and *DANGEROUS LOVE*

Searching—but (almost) never finding...

Susannah Parker and Michael West were meant for each other. They just didn't know it—or each other—yet.

They knew that someday "the one" would come along and their paths would finally cross. While they waited, they pursued their careers, marriages and experienced passion and heartbreak—always hoping to one day meet that stranger they could recognize as a lover....

The search is over...August 1997
at your favorite retail outlet.

"Catherine Lanigan will make you cheer and cry."
—*Romantic Times*

MIRA The brightest star in women's fiction

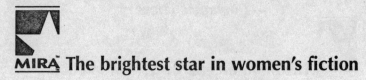

HE SAID

SHE SAID

Explore the mystery of male/female communication in this extraordinary new book from two of your favorite Harlequin authors.

Jasmine Cresswell and Margaret St. George bring you the exciting story of two romantic adversaries—each from their own point of view!

DEV'S STORY. CATHY'S STORY.
As he sees it. As she sees it.
Both sides of the story!

The heat is definitely on, and these two can't stay out of the kitchen!

Don't miss **HE SAID, SHE SAID.**
Available in July wherever Harlequin books are sold.

China's greatest love story...

LOVE IN A CHINESE GARDEN

Available for the first time as a novel in North America

It's been called China's *Romeo and Juliet*. Two young lovers are thwarted by an ambitious mother and an arranged marriage. With the help of a clever confidante, they find opportunities to meet...until, inevitably, their secret is revealed.

Can love prevail against danger and separation? Against the scheming of a determined woman?

Find out how to receive a second book absolutely FREE with the purchase of LOVE IN A CHINESE GARDEN! (details in book)

Available October 1997 at your favorite retail outlet.